BOOK

9

SECRET AGENT "X"

THE COMPLETE SERIES

VOLUME 9

CONTAINING THE LAST FIVE STORIES:

CLAWS OF THE CORPSE CULT
THE CORPSE THAT MURDERED
CURSE OF THE CRIMSON HORDE
CORPSE CONTRABAND
YOKE OF THE CRIMSON COTERIE

PLUS THE CAPTAIN HAZZARD STORY

PYTHON MEN OF LOST CITY

WRITTEN BY

G.T. FLEMING-ROBERTS AND PAUL CHADWICK

BOSTON

ALTUS PRESS

2018

TABLE OF

CONTENTS

BOOK XXXVII

CLAWS OF THE CORPSE CULT

The man of a thousand faces could not
unmask—to save his country's honor.

CHAPTER I

THE MUMMIFIED HAND

HAWAII! RADIANT, SUN-KISSED oasis in the limitless expanse of the Pacific. Pinpoint around which the world of the East and the world of the West revolve. Hawaii! Birthplace of the *hula* and cradle of two worlds' conflicts. Hawaii! Tourists' Paradise and haven for the dregs of five continents! Where the beach comber and the assassin tread the same sands as the socialite, where the fringes of humanity brush the skirts of the anointed. Hawaii! Where spies play with the fate of nations; in whose shadows all men look the same color, and the worth of a man's life is counted in pieces of gold. Hawaii! Refuge of traitors and expatriates; where plots are hatched in incensed drawing rooms; behind whose musty curtains are spawned unknown, unnamed horrors. Hawaii!

Hawaii! Where two worlds mingle in a seething cauldron; where the gentle hand may sheathe a bloody dagger; where the quiet pulse may mask turbulent lusts. Hawaii!

Gilbert Harden belonged to the new world, but his home—the most beautiful mansion in Honolulu—lay in the lap of the old, and across its threshold had passed many strange treasures. From Xanadu to Ceylon, the Orient had opened her vast bosom and into the hands of this wealthy, adventurous American had poured bizarre curios.

Gilbert Marden should never have lived long enough to be confined in a wheel chair. That was the thought that passed through the mind of the slender young man at his right as he studied his host. Those searching, fathomless eyes; the erect, wide-shouldered body; the eloquently powerful hands—wide spaces, strange vistas, violent action were the trumpet that should call Gilbert Marden into the world. Never the imprisoning cage of the wheel chair.

Marden jerked his head at the white-jacketed Filipino servant, indicating that he would wheel himself when they left the dining room. A pleasant smile played across Marden's thick-lipped mouth. Blue eyes glanced up at the slender young man from beneath fiercely jutting white eyebrows.

"Regan," Marden said, "I feel it particularly necessary to justify my present condition in your eyes—you who are a newcomer, a *malahini*—in Hawaii. You, now, who meet me in this state of semi-invalidism, cannot possibly imagine how active a man I have been. Nor how active I will be again, once this cursed leg of mine is on the mend."

The man called Regan, a tall, boyish figure with dark hair and skin, allowed keen eyes to rove about the dining room with

its priceless drapes of China silk, its immense table of uniquely-carved teak, its glittering, crystal-prismed chandelier.

"On the contrary," Regan said, his voice pleasantly low, his words cleanly cut, "I would say that a man must live an active life to amass such treasures as these. Mr. Holme's misfortune in not arriving at the islands in time to attend this dinner party, has been my own fortune. Had Mr. Holme not appointed me as his proxy, I probably would have missed seeing this remarkable mansion. And I would have missed making the acquaintance of a most generous and entertaining host."

GILBERT MARDEN bowed his bald head in acknowledgement of Regan's compliment. A slight shadow fell across his face. "Unless," he confided, "the Sino-Japanese difficulty comes to a speedy conclusion, this house and all within it may fall beneath the auctioneer's hammer. My plants and concessions are in South China and so far have remained outside the battle region. But I can scarcely hope it will always remain so. I would gladly sacrifice my fortune if it would aid America to remain neutral."

"America will remain neutral," Regan said quietly. There was almost a ring of authority in his voice, a ring which brought him a questioning glance from the eyes of the four men at the table.

"You," said Marden to Regan, "are of course in the enviable position to know of what you speak, being secretary to Mr.—ah, Mr. Holme?" Marden made a gesture with his hand as though to indicate that he knew well enough that "Mr. Holme" was but an alias for a certain Washington official who preferred to be known simply as K9.

But under his beetling brows, the piercing eyes of Marden observed more closely the man who made this statement. As if to know better a man who could make so important a statement so authoritatively, so decisively. Regan's eyes, he noticed, had more of the quality of eyes that had seen strange things, that had looked into guns, that had faced death, rather than had spent hours poring over documents. And the hands, he noted in the same fleeting glance, might seem more at home curling around the handle of a *kris,* or around the butt of a gun, than enfolding the proverbial pen of the secretary.

Marden spread a thick-fingered hand. "But let's not talk of war. May I suggest, gentlemen, that we follow the ladies into the drawing room? I have a rare treat for you this evening—the first exhibition of a unique Oriental curio. Something I risked my life to obtain, and no doubt still imperil myself by keeping."

The faces of all the men turned eagerly toward their host. These guests of Gilbert Marden had known the delights of adventure, and the very suggestion of anything that savored of it whetted their interest. There was Don Selwick, whose brilliant achievements in the field of marine engineering had taken him to strange corners of the world. Wine had flushed Selwick's sunken cheeks, but it took the spice of adventure to kindle the fire within his pale, pocketed eyes.

There was Rex Gorham, who had been a submarine navigator during the world war. There was something about the polish of Gorham's hair, the waxy points of his mustache, and the set of his trimly muscled body that lent a uniform nattiness to his conventional dinner clothes.

And there was Barry Lane, whom the man called Regan had met many a time before. Lane, in marked contrast to the sartorially exact Gorham, wore his clothes with a certain slovenliness that Bond Street could not have corrected. His easy-going, unaffected manner served well to mask the grave responsibilities which had often rested upon his young shoulders. Lane was a Secret Service agent of the United States government.

Barry Lane stood up. He stretched contentedly if not politely, "Only curio I consider quaint enough to risk my life in keeping," he said, "is my head."

Gilbert Marden, in his wheel chair, led the way from the dining room into a no less ostentatious drawing room. Two women were there—Myra Silinski, a friend of Marden; and Barry Lane's bride of a few months.

Myra Silinski was tall, sleek-hipped, eye-arresting. Slightly flaring nostrils lent her an air of hauteur. Her gown was black, fitted as though it had been painted on her body. There was music in her movement, sensuous music.

Janet Lane's dark eyes followed Myra Silinski, fully conscious of the fact that Myra had something that she could never possess. For there was nothing sophisticated in the appearance of Barry Lane's bride. Her charm lay in the freshness of youth.

THE MAN called Regan—the man who seemed to observe nothing, yet who saw everything—had watched Barry Lane, Janet, and Myra with more than ordinary interest. There was something odd in Myra's open patronage of Janet Lane. And something unnatural in Barry's coolness toward Myra Silinski. Lane had been almost insolent at times and always nervous when the tall, blonde woman was near. It was patronage and hostility too well staged to deceive the keen eyes of Regan. Perhaps, it did not even deceive the unsophisticated Janet Lane.

"Myra. Mrs. Lane—" began Gilbert Marden.

Myra Silinski rose from her chair. "We are waiting, Gilbert, for that unique surprise you have in store for us. Mrs. Lane and I are really quite eager."

Behind him, Regan heard Don Selwick murmur to Rex Gorham: "The first time Silinski ever included herself and another woman in the same breath."

So Selwick, too, had noticed the little act Myra Silinski was putting on.

"Come into the curio room, my dear," Marden said. "Mine is the misfortune not to be able to offer you my arm. Perhaps you, Barry—"

But Barry Lane had hastily attached himself to his wife and paid no respect to Marden's suggestion. So it was that Rex Gorham escorted Myra into the curio room. Regan and Selwick ambled in side by side.

"Wonder what the old boy has picked up this time." Selwick mused aloud. "Most unusual person, Regan. Most unusual. And this new treasure he is so secretive about ought to be quite a prize. Marden isn't a man to go in for dramatics, yet he has repeatedly warned us that this latest curio is not only a bit horrifying, but possibly dangerous."

Selwick's pocketed eyes rested on Regan's clearly defined features. "Didn't quite catch your occupation when we were introduced. Secretary to someone or something?"

Regan nodded. "Secretary to Mr. Ronald Holme who arrives this evening from San Francisco."

Selwick nodded, though Regan's information had not been enlightening. "Gathered that you were in some branch of government work. You and young Lane seem to be on very good terms."

Regan smiled. "We attended the same college. I am simply Mr. Holme's secretary. Mine is an easy berth, but then I am not as energetic as Barry Lane."

"No," Selwick said, not as if he was entirely sure about that. Regan's eyes, at least, were energetic. They seemed to be always looking at you when you tried to steal an aside glance at him. And his hands—strange, powerful hands for a man whose occupation was sedentary.

They entered the curio room, where in glass-fronted cabinets, reposed a fortune in rarities of the Eastern world. Gilbert Marden had maneuvered his wheel chair about so that he faced them all. There was the light of anticipation in his eyes, and as he spoke, his voice became grave and impressive.

"I must warn you," he said, "that what you are about to see may provoke a sensation of revulsion. I have mentioned this before, but Myra and Mrs. Lane have assured me that they are hardy souls, not subject to feminine qualms. But aside from the disgust this exhibition may awaken, I must also mention that what you are about to see, according to the story, may endanger your very lives. Profane glances, according to those who once guarded this relic, were never to rest upon it and go unpunished. Do you still desire to see this—my latest acquisition?"

"There's no dampening our enthusiasm with threats, Mr. Marden," said Janet Lane with a low laugh.

"We are all eagerness," said Myra Silinski.

Marden bowed his bald head. "Very well then, since you insist." He turned his chair about and rolled it straight for an enameled steel cabinet that looked as strong as a safe. He stopped in front of this cabinet, saw within the shiny surface of its door the reflection of the doorway of the curio room. And standing in that doorway was the figure of a man.

MARDEN turned his head quickly. His mouth dropped open. Marden's guests also turned to look toward the door and beheld a man so tall and thin that he appeared the personification of Famine itself. His skin was nearly black, his features extremely delicate. On his forehead was an odd mark—something like a three-tined fork. A turban of pale-blue cloth brought his height to something above six feet and six inches.

The man called Regan knew immediately that this gaunt intruder was a Hindu of the Brahmin caste.

The Hindu bowed low to Marden and then to the other guests.

"I hope," the Hindu said in meticulous English, "that I am not intruding. Mr. Marden has been so gracious with his hospitality during my stay in Honolulu that I have developed the careless habit of entering unannounced."

"Perfectly all right, Dal Rama," Marden said with a smile. "I believe you've met Selwick, Madam Silinski and Gorham. The other charming lady is Mrs. Lane. Then Mr. Lane and Mr. Regan."

Dal Rama bowed to each in turn. Regan found himself listening as though he half expected to hear joints of this skeleton of a man creak.

"Do not," said Dal Rama, "allow my presence to interfere in any way with the entertainment you had planned for your guests, Mr. Marden. Your servant informed me that you were about to exhibit some curios."

"Of course," said Marden hastily. His hands gripped the wheels of his chair and rolled him quickly away from the steel cabinet to one of the glass-fronted ones. From shelves laden with curios,

Marden took a small, grotesquely carved statue—a squat little figure of clay with a face half man and half Foo-dog.

Regan's eyes narrowed. Gilbert Marden's powerful hands were trembling as he took the statue.

"This little image," said Marden rather hesitantly— And he was interrupted by the sudden appearance of one of his white-jacketed Filipino house boys who bore a small silver tray on which was an envelope.

The house boy bowed. "Message for Mr. Regan."

The man called Regan took the envelope, immediately recognized the handwriting on the outside as that of "Mr. Holme," his immediate superior. Regan excused himself and retired into the drawing room to open the message. It read:

Flew out on the Clipper. At Lane's bungalow.

RONALD HOLME

Regan stepped to the door of the curio room where Marden was telling the story of the hideous image. "Lane," he said quietly.

Barry Lane crossed the room, eyebrows querulously raised above his rimmed glasses.

"He's here," Regan said. "We'd better go to your place."

Lane nodded. "Getting bored anyway. Couldn't see a thing terrifying in Marden's statuette. Shall we leave Janet here?"

Regan nodded. "I think that would be best." He turned, and Lane followed....

Mr. Ronald Holme paced the floor of the living room of Barry Lane's bungalow with such a regular, pounding rhythm that the yellow vase on the center table fairly trembled. Mr. Holme was a small, slight, vigorous man, gray-haired, small-featured, with black, inquiring eyes. His thin lips clenched a dark panatela.

Barry Lane lolled in a rattan chair. The man called Regan stood quietly in a corner, his gray eyes intent upon Lane.

Suddenly Holme stopped his pacing. He pointed at Lane with his cigar.

"You did not send for Regan and me just to discuss the weather on the mainland, did you, Lane? What's this about your assistant, Corby Jones, being killed? And what was that in your code cablegram about imminent threat of war? That's why I'm here, really, not because a secret service man has been killed. You know how firmly determined our government is to maintain peace. War? The subject is taboo. If I did not know you for a fundamentally sober person, I would have said you were drunk when you sent that cablegram. And now that we're here, you're damned uncommunicative."

BARRY LANE stretched his hands above his head. His spectacled eyes were rather uneasy as they rested upon the small, sharp face of Ronald Holme.

"The secret is not entirely my own. Others are involved. When I have succeeded in gathering all available material, I will of course hand it over to you. I cannot endanger the lives of others by telling you what I now only suspect. Honolulu is a hotbed of spies."

"Naturally," said the man called Regan, "because of its proximity to the trouble in the Orient."

"Because of the Sino-Japanese war, rather," Barry Lane said. "Mr. Holme, I must beg you to bear with me a little while, for unless we are all a bit more patient, America may very possibly find herself deeply involved in the trouble in the Orient."

Holme quick-stepped across to Barry Lane's rattan chair. "What do you mean?" he snapped. "America will remain neutral at all costs. The last war taught us enough, I should think. And you have the brass to sit there and tell me to be patient while you take so grave a burden upon your not incapable, but rather inexperienced shoulders!"

Barry Lane raised his hand. "Sorry," he said briefly, "I must still ask you to be patient. Corby Jones' death may be related to this matter of which I speak."

"Of which you don't speak," cracked Holme. "At least, not so that anyone can understand you." He puffed furiously on his cigar, wiped perspiration from his brow. In a softer tone he said: "Tell us about Jones' death."

A slight shudder rippled visibly across Lane's shoulders. "A horrible death," he said. "Jones was found down on the waterfront, his right hand severed at the wrist. Apparently, he had bled to death."

"What does that have to do with this other matter about which you are so reticent?" asked Holme.

"Something," murmured Lane. "I don't know exactly. I can't even guess. It's a hunch, that's all, fortified by this." He took from the pocket of his jacket a small pasteboard box. "In the mail this morning," he said as he opened the box. "Take a look at it."

The man called Regan stepped from his corner and leaned over Barry Lane's chair. Holme reached out and took the open box from Lane's hand. Holme muttered an oath.

Inside the box was a shriveled, blackened, mummified human hand, pierced at the heel of the palm by a half-inch hole.

"Jones' hand?" gasped Holme. He shot a questioning glance at the man called Regan.

Regan shook his head. "I hardly think so. The process through which that mummified hand must have passed must have taken some time."

Barry Lane took the box containing the gruesome hand and slipped it into his pocket. "You tell me what it means. I've thought about it so much today my mind is going around in circles."

The telephone rang. Lane got lazily from his chair and went over to the side of the room where the jingling instrument rested upon a side table. He picked it up, said hello in a guarded voice. He listened in silence a moment, then said: "All right. In a few minutes." He hung up.

Lane took off his glasses and polished them. "I'm sorry, but I'll be forced to leave you for a little while. This concerns the matter we were discussing. I may have some information when I return." He picked up his panama and abruptly left the room. The screen door on the front of the bungalow slammed.

"Secret Agent X," said Holme sharply.

The man called Regan turned. His remarkably intelligent eyes brightened. "Yes, K9?"

Holme's smile came and immediately faded. "What do you think of this man, Barry Lane?"

"A very good man," the man called Regan answered. "But thoroughly normal. Too normal, perhaps."

"What do you mean?"

A SMILE passed over the boyish face of Secret Agent X; rather, the smile illuminated a face that was not his own. For the face he wore was neatly counterfeited from a plastic, volatile material which contributed much to his unequaled ability to impersonate almost anyone. The alias of Regan was but one of many aliases; the face he wore, but one of a thousand faces.

"I happened to note the critical glance Barry Lane gave himself as he passed the mirror in the hall. Barry Lane is going to meet a woman."

"Not his wife, eh?"

"Definitely not his wife," said Secret Agent X. "And, if I am not mistaken, the woman is Myra Silinski."

"Myra Silinski? Who's she? Sounds like a Polish name."

Secret Agent X fingered a cigarette from a package. Lean, graceful fingers had the Agent, fingers that could be as gentle as a woman's and again as hard and cruel as steel hooks. "Myra Silinski, regardless of her nationality, is what the Chinese might call a *t'an fang-ti.*"

"I don't speak Chinese," snapped Holme.

"A superior sort of spy, then," the Secret Agent translated. "What government she represents we can only guess. What government would be highly delighted if America should side with the Chinese in the war?"

Holme scratched a hairless chin. "Oh," he said. "You mean—"

Out of the night an unearthly cry that seemed neither animal nor human severed Holme's sentence cleanly. It mounted to a wavering pinnacle, then drifted off in a horrific echo that must have sounded from Punch Bowl Hill to the waterfront.

Holme, man of steel nerve that he was, was momentarily frozen by that weird cry that was neither of anguish nor of triumph. It seemed, indeed, a vocal offering to some barbaric deity. But scarcely had the sound begun than Agent X pivoted, dashed from the room, from the door of the bungalow and onto the deep, artistically landscaped lawn. His keen eyes darted first one way and then another. Close to a bed of poincianas, he saw a black blotch against the moonlit lawn. His lean legs carried him toward the shrubbery at a run. For the blotch on the lawn was the body of a man, and the flowery fragrance of the night was marred by the sickening odor of new-let blood.

The man was Barry Lane. He lay stretched out on his back, eyes open, glazed. Across his rounded cheeks a sort of bluish shadow was spreading. He was talking, babbling incoherently. And as the Secret Agent bent over him he caught the words: "Above... Golden Lotus... King Street... *Sayo-nara*... Janet." And then he was dead.

The knee of the Agent's trouser leg was warm and sticky with blood that oozed from Barry Lane's right wrist. Several inches apart from the wrist lay Barry's hand, cleanly severed.

The Agent's mind clicked like a telegraph sounder. Barry Lane dead. Lane, who possibly was on the track of something that threatened his country with war. One channel open to Agent X—to impersonate Barry Lane and carry on where the secret service man had been forced to leave off. But first, if his impersonation was to be successful, he must find the man who had killed Lane.

CHAPTER II

STRANGE ASSASSIN

BY THE TIME Holme arrived on the scene, Agent X was moving about the body of Barry Lane, his flashlight pointed at the ground.

"Great hell!" gasped Holme. "Lane! Hand cut off! This is no woman's work, Agent X!"

"But a woman might have been the cause," X said quietly. He stooped, picked up something from the grass.

"Poor boy!" Holme said, and his voice betrayed for a moment the heart beneath the iron exterior he maintained. Then he snapped: "What've you found?"

X opened his hand beneath the light to reveal a viscous, brownish mass of fibers. *"Madjoon,"* he said. "Which fits in nicely with the fact that Lane's right-hand pocket was slashed open by a knife."

"Madjoon? I don't speak Chinese."

"That isn't Chinese, sir," X contradicted quietly. *"Madjoon* is a chewing compound made from *hashish.* It's the favorite drug in the diet of certain Hindu fanatics."

"Hindu? There are no Hindus in Hawaii."

"Not many, but apparently some," X said. "A Hindu murdered Barry Lane, apparently to obtain that box containing the withered hand. Lane didn't bleed to death—died too quickly for that. The knife that was used on him was probably poisoned."

"Yes, yes," Holme said impatiently, "Aconite might have been the poison. Did Lane say anything before he died?"

The photographic mind of Agent X had captured the intelligible words that had crossed Barry Lane's lips. He repeated: "Above... Golden Lotus... King Street... *Sayo-nara...* Janet."

Holme stamped his foot. "I don't speak Chinese! What did he mean?"

"I don't know. *Sayo-nara* is simply Japanese for good-bye. Most of the old-timers in Hawaii use the word. I think he simply meant to say good-bye to Janet, his wife. The rest of it—well, King Street, in Honolulu is a street of doubtful repute. Can you get Barry back to the house? Keep the body concealed until I return. Don't let his wife know. Don't let anyone know. Afterwards, we'll have to smuggle the body to the morgue."

"I see," Holme said. "Up to your old tricks. But you'll have to get the man who killed Lane."

"My intention," said Agent X. "Tracks of a bare foot in the soft earth around the poinciana bed."

Then he was off, moving swiftly across the lawn, his keen eyes jumping from shadow to shadow. He was certain that the man he was hunting was a dacoit, one of the sect of fanatical Hindu assassins, and he well knew how swiftly those kill-crazy men could move and how tireless were their muscles when under the influence of *Madjoon*.

He came to the garden wall, made of flat chunks of lava rock and covered with blossoming creepers. There again he found footprints of the man he pursued. With the aid of a nearby palm tree trunk, Agent X was over the wall in a few seconds to find himself at the edge of a sunken garden belonging to the neighboring cottage. He was running down a natural stairway of dark rock into the garden when his eyes caught sight of a yellow shadow that flickered in and out of a cluster of trees. He watched the shadow—the narrow figure of a man, black, probably naked with the exception of a white loin cloth and turban which marked his every movement—pass through the grove and into the door of a little summer house.

With a quiet swiftness that imitated the movements of the dacoit himself, Agent X crossed the garden, made straight toward the summer house.

At the door of the summer house, he paused, looked between tendrils of vines, saw the Hindu kneeling on earthen floor. Between his angular knees was something that glowed with a soft sheen in the moonlight which sifted through the latticed roof of the building. In the Hindu's hands was a box—the box which had contained the withered hand.

THE SECRET AGENT had made no sound. It was perhaps some super sense, highly keyed by his doped condition, that brought about the Hindu's sudden move. From his squatting position on the floor of the summer house he sprang toward the door. And the thrust of his knife was as unexpected as a bolt of lightning from a clear sky. Only extraordinary agility saved the Agent. But even as he back-stepped, his heel caught on a rock and the weight of the brown-skinned man was enough to throw him to the earth.

Fingers that seemed nothing more than animated bone gouged into the Agent's throat. The dacoits were stranglers first, knife-men second. There was the tenacity of an octopus in the grip of those fingers on X's throat. Red-hot pincers would not have broken it. The Agent's right hand sliced upward, palm and fingers flat. The edge of his hand struck sharply across the Hindu's throat directly above the Adam's apple. It was a blow that would have knocked a white man out, when delivered with the full force of X's perfectly developed muscles behind it. But it served only to temporarily shock the doped nerves of the dacoit—a sort of momentary convulsion which X took immediate advantage of, jerking off the Hindu's stiffened fingers, but not without ripping the flesh of his throat with the man's fingernails.

Then came the knife, a rippling flash of light through the darkness. The agile body of the dacoit arched high to give every ounce of weight to the quick, downward thrust of the blade. The Agent's knees came up. He kicked out with both legs together, spilling the Hindu on his back before the knife thrust was complete.

They were on their feet at exactly the same instant. The Agent's hand blurred upward from his pocket, and in his grasp was his powerful gas pistol, charged with sufficient anesthetizing gas to render a man instantly unconscious. The dacoit paused, knife raised. And then, that weird, unearthly cry that X had heard immediately before he had discovered Barry Lane's body, issued from the Hindu's lips. The dacoit dropped to his knees, turbaned head bowed as though in submission.

The lean, naked body flung out flatly, rolled over on its back. And in the moonlight, X saw the dacoit's two hands clasped on the hilt of the knife. The knife was buried hasp-deep in the dacoit's stomach. Like the scorpion when cornered, this poisonous human devil had preferred suicide to defeat.

Agent X sheathed his gas gun, jerked out his flashlight, turned its beam into the summer house. There on the floor was a square of pale-blue silk, ornamented with diamonds and rubies sewn on with gold thread. In the center of the cloth was the box containing the withered hand. X scooped the box and hand up into the ornamented silk and thrust it into his pocket. Then he hurried back across the garden, over the wall, to return to Barry Lane's house.

Holme met him at the door. "What luck?" he demanded.

"The worst possible for that crazy devil. Killed himself, remorseful over the fact that he couldn't protect the withered hand."

Holme nodded. "I've heard of things like that." He drew a sharp breath. "Well, it's settled. I've spoken to the chief of the Honolulu police. He will take charge of Barry's body personally. You go right ahead. And as always, the same old agreement that has always stood between K9 and Agent X—no holds barred, no expense considered. But if there's anything in what Barry Lane intimated about the danger of plunging America into war, for the love of heaven put an end to it."

"Where's Lane's body?" asked Agent X.

"In the guest room where your luggage is." Holme rubbed his hands together. "You'll impersonate him, of course?"

X nodded, started into the guest room. Holme followed, a look of anticipation on his face. Was it, X wondered, that K9 thought at last he would have the opportunity of seeing the Agent's real face—that face which only one person in the world had seen and lived?

"I found something in a book," Holme said. "About withered hands. Hindus and withered hands. Looked it up in this book in Barry's library. There's a Hindu goddess—blood-thirsty idol, as I understand it. There's a temple devoted to her worship in Upper Burma."

X nodded. "The dacoits are devotees of Kali. That the goddess?"

Holme nodded. "And the great idol of Kali wears no clothing except the human blood that is smeared across her breasts, and a girdle of corpse hands about her loins!"

The Agent raised his eyebrows. "Good. Glad you found that out, sir. It may be helpful." And he slowly closed the door of the guest room. Probably to Holme's disappointment.

THE CORPSE of Barry Lane was not the best possible model after which to fashion the face of a living man. It was, therefore, remarkable that Secret Agent X emerged from the bedroom forty-five minutes later, the living image of the dead man, ruddy cheeks, spectacles, and with his own naturally brown hair stiffened with special chemicals so that it resembled the uncombed shag that had marked Barry Lane. And when he spoke to Holme, his voice might well have been a phonograph record of Lane's own voice.

Holme blanched at the sudden appearance of the Agent. "Man! If I hadn't carried the corpse into that room myself, I'd say Lane lived again!"

"He does," the voice of Barry Lane drawled lazily from the Agent's lips. "And," he added, "his work goes on."

Holme nodded approvingly. "Only try and keep me posted on developments. And by the way, what about Mrs. Lane, your—I mean, his wife? That's going to be awkward. We don't dare tell her the truth. Her attitude would spoil your plan completely."

"I know," X said gravely. "It's unjust not to tell her the truth. It may endanger our country to tell her."

"We won't tell her!" snapped Holme. He stuck out his hand to X. "Good luck. And remember, millions of lives, the fate of America, is in your hands."

"I shall not forget." And it was the Agent's own quiet, unassuming voice that spoke from lips that might have been Barry Lane's....

King Street. Here, scum of East and West met and was churned into a common dish that savored of filth and corruption. Here, architecture intermingled into a curious polyglot that ranged from gaudy pagoda to low, brick slum buildings. Here, vicious pleasures cost few pennies, and the potent *okolehao* liquor flowed like water. Chinese, Japanese, Filipinos and whites nightly turned life into a crazy, kaleidoscopic, intoxicated brawl.

In front of the filthy ornamentation of the Golden Lotus door, Barry Lane's car stopped, and from it stepped Agent X, wearing shoes, clothes, the very body of Barry Lane himself.

He lingered only a moment at the door of the Golden Lotus café, looking through the smoke-choked atmosphere where men and women were like gray ghosts rising through the mist to indulge in macabre dance. Then his eyes spotted a dark doorway at the corner of the building and a flight of steps leading upward. "Above... Golden Lotus," Barry Lane had said. And above the Golden Lotus, a light yellowed a shaded window. Secret Agent X quietly climbed the steps.

A door confronted him at the top of the steps. As he raised his hand to knock, a blaze of light beamed directly in his face.

The Agent's right hand crawled toward the pocket of his coat, sagged by the weight of Barry Lane's automatic. Behind the light, a man grunted. A deep, rumbling voice said grudgingly: "I suppose I must let you in." Was the man's English tainted with a faint Slavic accent?

A huge hand reached out of the darkness behind the light and inserted a key in the lock. The door opened, and a hand dropped upon the Agent's shoulder to thrust him into a small vestibule, lighted by a dingy globe. X saw that the man who had permitted his entrance was a dark-bearded giant with curiously intelligent eyes set in a heavy, contrastingly dull face. And then the door of the vestibule was opened by Myra Silinski.

Surprise rapidly gave place to joy in the lovely blue eyes of the woman. The surprise was genuine enough, since there was hardly any reason to counterfeit it. The joy, X wondered about.

"Barry!" Myra Silinski exclaimed. "How dear of you to come! I simply couldn't endure Gilbert Marden's party a moment longer."

"Weren't you expecting me, then?" X said in Lane's voice.

"No. You said you would not come tonight." And there was something in the emphasis she placed on the final word that gave X his cue.

"Had to see you, Myra," he said, stepping into the room.

Myra Silinski frowned at the bearded giant. "Wait outside, Peter," she ordered. Then, as the bearded man left, she took the Agent's hand in warm, strong fingers and led him to a couch in the corner of the room.

The outer appearance of the apartment was deceiving. The interior of the place was beautifully furnished. Nothing had been omitted that could add to comfort. Even a modern air-conditioner made the room cool and sweetened the unpleasant air of King Street for the haughty nose of Myra Silinski to breathe.

SHE seated herself beside the Agent, still clinging to his fingers. X lolled, as Barry Lane might have lolled, and feasted appreciative eyes on Myra's beauty; found in that beauty something that was damnably dangerous.

"Your guest, what was his name, did not arrive then, Barry?" the woman asked, carelessly. But he knew her to be far more curious than her tone indicated.

"Holme? Awful bore. Oh, he's there, thundering all over the place. Just couldn't stand it. Your call came at just the right time."

Again Myra frowned slightly. "My call? I did not call."

"No? Somebody did." X thought the phone call had been only a ruse to get Barry Lane out of the house.

Myra looked at him earnestly for a second. "Barry," she said finally, laughing a little, "tell me what it is that is bothering you."

"Me? Why, nothing."

Myra raised her shoulder eloquently, leaned forward. "You are so cool, so different tonight from last night." She was leaning farther forward, bending over his head which rested against the back of the couch. Lips slightly parted, almost motionless, she whispered: "Kiss me, Barry."

The Agent's arms encircled her, drew her to him. As their lips met, his mind tocsined: "Danger! Danger!" He told himself that this might be the very reason why Barry Lane was dead. He had met such women before, knew their snares. The odds were very much against Myra's affection for Barry Lane being anything else than a smooth method of extracting information from him. What the woman was after, he didn't know. Perhaps she supported the very thing that Lane had been fighting against—the threat of war.

She drew back from his embrace. Again her eyes were examining him so closely that he wondered his disguise was not penetrated.

"Still troubled, Barry?" she said softly. "Tell me. What is this thing that bothers you?"

X reached into his pocket and brought out the silk cloth and the box containing the withered hand which he had taken from the Hindu. He unfolded the cloth, opened the box, thrust it suddenly beneath Myra's gaze.

"Ever see anything like that before?" he asked.

Horror lighted in her eyes. Revulsion curled her lips. "What is it?" she demanded. "A hand? No, I have never seen anything like it. Put it away, Barry."

Again he wondered if red lips and blue eyes were in accord, and truth-telling. He put the box away. "That's what's worrying me," he said.

The door of the room suddenly opened. The bearded giant stood there, his barrel-shaped chest rising and falling rapidly. "I have known it would happen like this!" he rumbled. "He—" indicating X— "has brought one of his spies with him to this place!"

Myra Silinski was on her feet in a moment. Her palm smoothed the black satin over the sleek lines of her hips. There was a hostile gleam in her eyes as she regarded the Secret Agent.

"So!" she said scornfully. "I should not have trusted you, then. Always I have told you that our meetings must be kept absolutely secret."

The bearded giant tapped his broad chest with his fingers. "I and you, too, Silinski—we maybe lose our lives for this, except that I am watchful and have caught the spy. How many times must I tell you that it is not safe to mix two things like business and love-making."

Myra stamped a tiny slipper. "No chiding from you, Peter—you who are only a watch dog!"

"And a very good thing I am a good watch dog," said Peter gravely. "I have this spy woman outside. The mistake would be easily and noiselessly erased—with a knife, eh?"

"Just a minute," said X lazily. "I had no one follow me. Certainly no woman. What's all this about, anyway?"

PETER moved ponderously into the vestibule and returned gripping the arm of Janet Lane. The small, dark-eyed girl was less frightened than furious, and less furious than hurt. Her full, sweet mouth quivered an instant over the name, "Barry!" Then her lips tightened. Her eyes clashed with the eyes of Myra Silinski. "Intuition, perhaps," she said coolly, "but when I first laid eyes on you, I knew you were that kind of a woman."

Myra laughed, a low, musical laugh. "What kind, my dear Mrs. Lane?" she asked mockingly. "Charming? Charming enough to steal your husband's affection?"

"That—that isn't true," Janet said, not thoroughly convinced by her own denial. "Not Barry. No—"

Myra's lips taunted: "It might interest you to know that Barry and I have planned to leave the islands on the next ship. Isn't that true, Barry?"

X stood up. Here was a situation he had never met before. He had not the slightest idea what sort of a bargain Lane might have made with the blonde woman. To deny all knowledge of it might mean that Myra Silinski would conclude that he was an imposter. And he was particularly anxious to retain the identity of Lane in order to continue his investigation.

Yet he could not bring himself to ruin a man's reputation in the eyes of that man's loving wife by admitting that any such arrangement had been made. After all, Barry Lane's association with Myra Silinski might have been for but one reason—to gain information which the woman spy possessed.

He turned rather stiffly toward Myra. "Sorry, but the excursion you mention is all news to me. Sorry about the scene and all. Damned sorry about everything." He walked over and took the arm of Barry Lane's wife.

In Janet's dark eyes, tear-glistened though they were, was a light of triumph. Agent X wondered just how kind his deception had been.

CHAPTER III

THE HAND AND THE CIPHER

"I SUPPOSE," AGENT X said as he and Janet Lane drove back toward the Lane bungalow, "you know that you messed things up quite a bit, tonight, Janet. You don't really think Myra Silinski meant anything to me, do you?"

"Of course," Janet Lane said. "I've followed you before. I've watched you when around Myra. Oh, Barry, I'll never be able to understand it all." A sob choked the woman.

"Then just try and understand it's a part of the business. Myra Silinski has information which the department must have. She's a spy. Try and look at it as though you were married to an actor, because that's all it is—just acting to try and get Myra's secret. Can't you think of it that way?"

"I—I'll try," Janet said in a small, unhappy voice. "We won't quarrel, Barry. As soon as you get home and get her nasty-colored lip rouge washed off your mouth, maybe we'll kiss and make up." She laughed a little then, rested her head on the Agent's shoulder. "Oh, Barry, I'm silly. I know I am. But I'm simply mad about my husband and I can't bear to see him as much as smile at another woman."

"Okay," X said with a semblance of gaiety, "no more smiles from me without special permission of the copyright owner. Now let's forget it."

X drove the rest of the way in silence, driving slowly with the fervent hope that Holme would have time to remove the body of Barry Lane before their arrival. Holme had evidently accomplished everything, for he met them at the door of the bungalow, smiling and rubbing his hands.

X entered the living room, tossed the box containing the withered hand on the table. Then he and Holme left Janet and went on the screened-in porch for a few moments of confidential talk.

"What did you find?" Holme asked eagerly.

"That Myra Silinski has been trying to pump Lane," X said quietly. "Maybe he thought he was getting information from her, but the chances are she got more from him. And just what that information was about, we've no idea. This Silinski woman lives over a dive on King Street. Why, we don't know, but the dive may be worth investigating. Myra apparently knows nothing about the withered hand. The withered hand is sacred to Hindu dacoits. How it ties up with the puzzle, I've no idea."

A sharp cry from the living room brought both men out of their chairs and into the living room, Janet stood at the side of the center table, one hand clutching her lovely throat, the other unconsciously clenched over the gruesome withered hand which X had dropped on the table. Her large, dark eyes were frozen on the window which looked out upon the garden.

When she could jerk her glance away, she ran to the Agent's arms, sobbing: "There's a man at the window, Barry. A terrible man, standing there watching me. I just *felt* his eyes upon me, looked up, and there he was. I—I'm terrified!"

X stroked her brown curls gently. Above her head, his eyes met Holme's. "A man at the window, eh? What'd he look like?"

"Horrible. Like that Dal Rama who came to Marden's house tonight. Only it wasn't Dal Rama, But there was that same queer mark on his forehead. I'm afraid, Barry."

"No need to be," X whispered. "I'll take care of you. You run on to bed and get some sleep. I've got some work to do." He took her head between both hands, raised it, kissed her lightly on the forehead. "That better?"

She smiled, seemed to notice Holme for the first time, laughed apologetically. "You'll think me very foolish, Mr. Holme, won't you?"

Holme cleared his throat uncomfortably. "Not at all. Not at all. By the way, Mrs. Lane, one of your guests has left. Mr. Regan had to go away on some business of mine. Told me to say good-bye and thanks for the hospitality. Good night, Mrs. Lane."

And when Janet Lane had left the room, X turned to Holme. He made a little helpless gesture with his hands. "Digging in deeper all the time."

"What the devil can we do, Agent X?" Holme whispered. "If we tell her about Barry's death, she'll insist on seeing the body. And we can't let her do that. She'll demand—" Holme shrugged. "And your little scheme goes up in smoke. Damned mess. What's on your mind now?"

"I'll dig through Barry's papers and see if I can find anything to start on. I suggest, sir, that you get a little rest."

Holme nodded. "I intend to. Good night."

ALONE, the Agent's first act was to pick up the withered hand which Janet had dropped when they had entered the room. He turned it over in his fingers. It was perfectly preserved, probably hundreds of years old. It was closely connected with the death of Corby Jones and Barry Lane, but where there was any connection between the hand and the rumored threat of war in the Orient, he could not see.

He carried the hand to the room which he had occupied as Regan, and placed it in a small box of peculiar design. Then he returned to a small alcove off the living room where Barry Lane's desk was.

It was at the hush of midnight that X came across something in Lane's files that awakened his interest. It was a narrow slip of paper upon which was written:

XGYEU ZPG QEYLGM YEZJT HKML ZPG R2F GKQPZ XYEA4T
HBER UGTZ AEBMGB ZPBGG HBER XEZZER.

For a long time he sat, smoking and musing over the cipher. Then he took out pencil and paper. The cipher fitted into no known pattern with which he was familiar. It looked as though it could be solved only by means of the letter frequency method. He laid aside his cigarette, bent over the desk, began making a careful tabulation of the letters. Out of the corner of his eye he caught the sudden movement in the column of cigarette smoke that had been rising straight and narrow in the still air. Now the smoke wavered, and the column of gray was broken into a swirling cloud.

Instantly, he turned in his chair. Directly behind him stood a thin, half-naked dacoit.

The Agent's rapid movement saved his life, for as he turned, the silken loop of the thug's strangling cord brushed his cheek and dropped harmlessly to his shoulder.

X sprang from the chair so swiftly that it crashed over against the desk. The agile Hindu backstepped, traded his silken noose for a knife, and as the Agent came to grips with the brown body, the knife flashed downward across the Agent's left wrist. Nothing but the wrist watch he wore saved him from the possible loss of a hand.

A right to the Hindu's flat belly knocked the man back far enough so that X could yank Barry Lane's automatic from his pocket. He fired once, aiming low, as the dacoit sprang soundlessly as a shadow across the room. The shot missed. The dacoit flashed a snarling smile over one dark, angular shoulder and sprang through the window, shattering the pane with his naked body.

No one but a madman or a drugged fanatic would have thought of such an exit. X ran to the shattered window, peered out into the blackness. Ronald Holme in pajamas and dressing gown broke into the room, his face the same shade of gray as his hair, his eyes popping.

"What was that?" Holme shouted.

X turned, shoved the automatic into his pocket as Janet Lane came running from her bedroom, a silken négligée hastily thrown over her nightgown.

"Barry!" she gasped. "You're all right. Not hurt, darling?"

"Not hurt," X said lazily, taking the girl's small body in his arms. Over the charming disarray of her brown curls, he glanced at the living room table. The silken wrapper and the box which had contained the withered hand were gone. Undoubtedly, the dacoit supposed that he had retrieved the hand itself.

"Get dressed," he said to the girl. "Holme is taking you over to Marden's house at once. It's unsafe for you to stay here."

For the Agent knew that not only were the Hindus determined to recover the withered hand, but also to kill all unbelievers who had touched the sacred relic. And the Hindu whom Janet had seen peering through the window, had watched Janet examining the hand.

"Marden's. Why there?" Janet demanded wide-eyed.

"It'll be safer," X explained. "Marden has about twenty servants, most of them armed, to protect his house and grounds against marauders. He has already offered his hospitality to Holme and he'll certainly be glad to have you around for a day or two until things settle down."

"But you—"

"Now, now, Mrs. Lane," said Holme sharply. "When you marry a Service man you're in the Service, too. You've got to take orders from your captain. Go get ready. We'll leave at once."

When the girl had gone, Holme crossed to the Agent. "What happened?" he asked.

THE AGENT fingered his throat thoughtfully, then glanced at the smashed crystal of the wrist watch he wore. "And her dacoit. Fortunately, he escaped to tell his chief that Barry Lane still lives. We have no quarrel with these Oriental fanatics. We've got to get the man higher up."

"Or the woman higher up," Holme suggested.

"Or the woman," X echoed. Then he went over to Lane's desk and picked up the cipher message. He showed it to Holme. "This may be the key to the mystery. I've got to decipher it. As soon as I make anything comprehensible out of it, I'll let you know."

Hardly had X settled down once more to the solution of the baffling cipher than the lonely silence of the night was shattered by the jangle of the telephone. He reached across the desk, picked up the phone, drawled: "Barry Lane."

"Selwick speaking."

The Agent recalled the hollow-cheeked, pocket-eyed engineer he had met at Marden's party that evening. "Yes?" he said cautiously.

"Have you got the map yet?" Selwick's voice was tense with excitement. It sounded as though his mouth was dry.

Map? What was the man talking about?

"No."

"Then don't get it, for the love of heaven," Selwick pleaded. "They've found out about you and me. It's only a wonder that I'm alive now. You make any further progress, and I'm a dead man. Are you alone now? I've got to see you."

"I'm alone," X said. "What's the excitement?"

"I don't know exactly. I arrived at the hotel after Marden's dinner. A bit later, a special messenger brought a package to me. I want to show it to you."

"A hand?" asked X, "Package contain a mummified human hand?"

"Yes. What does it mean?"

"Means you'd better stick inside your room. I'll be over in a few minutes." The Agent hung up.

It took X approximately five minutes to discover at which hotel Don Selwick was staying. No doubt the real Barry Lane would have had that information, but X had not dared to ask Selwick outright. He had simply resorted to the process of trial and error until he had located a hotel desk-clerk who informed him that Selwick was staying in one of their rooms.

X thrust the cipher into his pocket beside Barry Lane's automatic and left the house.

Ten minutes later, he stopped Lane's car in front of the John Young Hotel. He entered the building, learned that Selwick's room was on the fourth floor. He knocked. And there was no sound within the corridor except the echo of his knock.

Quickly he took a ring of keys from his pocket. They were master keys, made especially for his use and capable of opening any standard lock. He inserted the most promising-looking key into the lock, turned it, and threw open the door.

For a moment, he stood there motionless. He had met horror many times before, but never anything like this. The thing on the door gripped him with a strange fascination that for a moment he could not shake off. It was simply a revolver gripped in the fingers of a human hand. No arm attached to the hand. Only Selwick's hand and the gun with which he had tried to protect himself.

X stepped inside the room. Up against the wall, hidden by the open door, he found Don Selwick's body. The man's irregular-featured face was frozen into a hellishly-contorted mask. His skin had a faintly bluish cast. His right wrist ended his arm—a dark smear of blood.

Selwick's hideously twisted lips were moving. His glazed eyes searched upward toward X's face. X dropped to his knees.

"Barry," Selwick whispered huskily. "Didn't know—what—I was doing. Got to stop it. War—Egg—I—"

The Agent gripped the dying man's shoulder in steely fingers. Selwick's eyes rolled horribly. Inarticulate sounds tumbled from his lips. He raised his right arm slightly, saw, perhaps, the raw, ragged, handless wrist. Breath screamed from his throat. A final convulsion racked his body.

CHAPTER IV

TRAPDOOR TO HELL

X **CLOSED THE** door opening into the corridor of the hotel. Then he crossed the room to the open window and looked out. Three feet from the sill, a large, square copper drain-pipe leading from the eaves would have been ladder enough for a barefoot dacoit. The murderous Hindu had evidently crept up behind Selwick's back while Selwick covered the door of his room with a gun.

X turned around, gazed steadily at the corpse on the floor. What was it that Selwick had been trying to tell him? Selwick hadn't known what he was doing— What had the man meant by that? And something about stopping something. War? And what was that nonsense about an egg?

One thing seemed evident. Selwick, though not associated with the government, had evidently been giving Barry Lane secret information. Lane and Selwick had been working together. Both were dead. Because of withered hands that had been sent to each of them, or because they had knowledge dangerous to someone.

X dropped into a chair in front of Selwick's desk. He let his gaze wander out the window and toward the dark harbor where scurrying lights on the wharfs were like sparks from a distant bonfire. His gray eyes brightened. He took from his pocket the strip of paper bearing the cipher message. Then he rummaged in the pigeonholes of Selwick's desk, found a large piece of paper which was covered with a large and complicated free-hand drawing of some sort of mechanism unfamiliar to X. Beneath the drawing were notes and figures presumably in Selwick's handwriting. He compared the writing on the drawing with that on the cipher message. They were identical.

On the phone, when speaking to X whom he supposed to be Lane, Selwick had asked something about "the map." Was there a chance that the cipher message referred to this mysterious map?

X scanned the cipher message, found two three-letter words together and jotted them down on a separate piece of paper:

ZPG R2F

Directly beneath them he wrote:

THE MAP

He then wrote the cipher out completely:

XGYEU ZPG QEYLGM YEZJT HKML ZPG R2F GKQPZ XYEA4T HBER UGTZ AEBMGB ZPBGG HBER XEZZER.

For every "Z" in the cipher he wrote a "T," for every "P" an "H," and for every "G" an "E." In the same way "R"s became "M"s, the "2" became an "A," and the "F" a "P." The last word in the cipher next claimed his attention. If he was so far correct, he had three of its six letters. And he made the following note:

XEZZER

TT M

The only English word of six letters ending in "M" and having two "T"s in the middle, that he could think of, was "bottom." So XEZZER became BOTTOM. This gave him new letters to work with, and the cipher word HBER, which was repeated, quickly became FROM, and another letter was gained.

Twenty minutes' concentrated effort in this manner and he had translated the cipher as follows:

XGYEU ZPG QEYLGM YEZJT HKML

BELOW THE GOLDEN LOTUS FIND

ZPG R2F GKQPZ XYEA4T HBER UGTZ

THE MAP EIGHT BLOCKS FROM WEST

AEBMGB ZPBGG HBER XEZZER.

CORNER THREE FROM BOTTOM.

THE AGENT scooped his notes into the large piece of paper which was covered with Selwick's drawings, rolled them up into a compact cylinder, and looped a rubber band around them. Then he hurried from the hotel and drove to Marden's mansion. He turned the Lane car into the drive, got out, climbed the long flight of stone steps to the porch, and knocked at the door. One of Marden's Filipino servants admitted him, and he was taken into the drawing room where Holme and Marden were sitting.

Ronald Holme sprang to his feet, rubbing his hands. "Any news, Lane?" he demanded.

Gilbert Marden waved a big hand. "Won't you sit down, Lane?" he invited, large lips smiling pleasantly.

"Thank you, no," X said. "Just a word with Mr. Holme; then I'll have to be off."

Gilbert Marden bowed his head. "Certainly." His powerful fingers gripped the wheels of his chair and he started to push himself from the room.

Holme held up a checking hand. "Don't think of moving, Mr. Marden. We're really nothing but intruders, sir, intruders who have taken advantage of your generously offered hospitality. If you'll excuse Lane and me a moment, please." And Holme ushered X into a small, book-walled library. The Agent closed the door, unrolled his cylinder of paper, and showed Holme the cipher.

"I'm going to the Golden Lotus immediately," he whispered. "Where's Janet?"

"I insisted that she go to bed as soon as we arrived," Holme said. "What's that?" He pointed abruptly at the drawing which X had found in Selwick's room.

X shrugged. "I haven't any idea. It looks like some sort of a mechanical drawing. Looks something like the details of a pump of some sort."

"Pump? So it does. Very well, Agent X. On your way. And if you can hook Hindus, withered hands, a map, murder, and a drawing of a pump together to make sense, I'll take off my hat to you. As if I hadn't been taking off my hat to you for a long time." Holme smiled happily.

"One thing more to fit into the puzzle," X said. "Thought perhaps you could suggest a manner to do it. Selwick was murdered, you understand, and evidently by one of these Hindu devils. About the last thing he said was something about an egg."

Holme frowned. "Now you're joking."

X shook his head. "Not at all."

"Of course not," Holme snapped. "This isn't a joking matter. Egg. Let me see—egg. Afraid I don't see any connection."

"And," X said quietly, "Barry Lane was not the only one who smelled the smoke of war just around the corner. Selwick said something about war, too."

Holme slammed his right fist into his left palm. "Can't be. Simply *can't* be! Yet I've known it to happen before—known wars to be precipitated by some damn fool plot that set off the spark. Got to stop it, I tell you. There's no motive, no occasion for America to plunge into this Oriental hell of bombs and bloodshed. Yet a motive can be made. That's what you've got to stop, Agent X."

"I'll do my best, sir," said X gravely.

They left the library. Gilbert Marden, still seated in his chair, held his big head in his hands. He raised his eyes as they entered, smiled as X hurried toward the door. "What I wouldn't give to join you, Barry Lane," he said. "If it were not for this cursed leg of mine, I would, by damn. I'd like to be up to my neck in trouble right now."

X shook his head. "Not me," he said in the drawl of Barry Lane. "Like I said once this evening, the only curio I'd risk my life to keep would be my own head." And he left the Marden mansion.

AT TWO A.M. the Golden Lotus was in full bloom. A ship had docked that afternoon, and a large portion of the crew was there, dancing with powdered and painted Chinese and half-caste girls to the tin-pan tunes ground out by a nickel phonograph. Seamen and shoremen draped over the red-and-gold ornate bar and shouted for glasses of "oke."

The odors of smoke, cheap liquor, perfume and perspiration reminded X of just how foul a creature man could be, as he elbowed his way unnoticed through the crowd in the stuffy room. Within the blaring beam of jazz from the electric phonograph grill, a man could have been shot and the sound wouldn't have been heard. X moved on along the bar to the rear of the café, crossed between writhing dancers to some small booths on the other side of the room. He slipped into one of the booths, eyes and ears on an unpleasantly plump man of about thirty-five who was seated at the bar, emphasizing every point of a drunken lecture with vigorous wags of his dirty white cap.

The cap the man wore looked as though it had once been part of a naval uniform. The rest of his clothes might have belonged to

She drew a long breath...
raised the gun.

almost any occupation or to almost any other person than the man who wore them. His duck trousers refused to button at the top and stuck to his fat hips by virtue of a length of hemp rope which ran through belt loops. A shirt of blue denim hadn't a button on it and exposed a crop of coarse, black hair on the man's chest.

"H'it's only a matter of weeks," bellowed the fat man, accenting "weeks" with a nod of his cap, "before this whole bloomin' ocean'll be bubblin' with war. America'll be up to 'er ears in war, that's wot!" He plunged a bulbous nose into a glass of *okolehao*.

The Agent's eyes wandered along the bar. His eye picked out the particularly bizarre dress of a woman. It was fashioned from multicolored silk of Oriental design, cut low in the back. His eyes widened. Even though he couldn't see her face, he instantly recognized Myra Silinski. Next to her, a man was leaning sideways against the bar, drinking, admiring the woman's profile with jetty eyes. The man, too, X recognized as Rex Gorham, the retired submarine commander he had met at Marden's dinner party. Rex Gorham's carefully pressed white suit was the only completely clean thing in the Golden Lotus. In spite of his attitude as he stood at the bar, Gorham still looked the part of a naval officer—an officer at ease.

Gorham was talking to Myra Silinski. His waxed mustache twinkled now and then with a word, spoken so low that X could not catch it above the din.

Across the table from him, in the dim corner of the booth, X detected a slight movement. He glanced from the bar and across the table. There, huddled in the corner, was Janet Lane. Her large, dark eyes were fixed unblinkingly upon the back of Myra Silinski. Her small body was shivering, as though her shoulders felt a chill draft that couldn't have existed in the stifling atmosphere of the Golden Lotus. Her right hand, on the edge of the table, clutched an automatic. So intent was the girl on watching Myra Silinski, on *aiming* the tiny, dangerous weapon at Myra's back, that she had not noticed the Agent's entrance into the booth.

Janet drew a long, quivering breath, as though to steel herself. She raised the gun.

X's arm darted across the table. His hand fell upon her wrist. Her eyes jerked to his. The name of "Barry" was startled from her lips. She let the gun drop from nerveless fingers.

Behind the rimmed glasses X wore, his gray eyes became grim. "Janet," he said gravely.

The girl uttered a sob, put both hands out to clasp his arm, dropped her head on her arms.

GENTLY, the Agent released himself from her grasp, got up, rounded the table, and sat down beside her. He put his arm around her, lifted her head from the table.

"Janet," he whispered into her ear, "what are you doing here? What were you going to do?"

She wouldn't answer for a moment. Then words tumbled with tears. "I wanted to kill her. She was killing me by inches. Robbing me. Taking you away from me. You love her. You know you do. That's why you came here tonight. I knew you would. That's why

I slipped away from Marden's and came here to watch. And you came. You were going to meet her here. It's true. *It's true!*"

X winced. The girl was sick with jealousy, mad with jealousy. Her love for her husband was more than love; it was a mania. And her husband was dead. He, Secret Agent X, was deceiving her into thinking that Barry Lane was alive. And he was powerless to right the wrong this deception was doing—powerless, because duty demanded that he keep silent. If only there was some way that he could create an illusion that would prove to her Barry Lane had remained faithful to her. Then, later, if he could quietly slip from the picture, he might leave a more pleasant memory of her dead husband in the eyes of Janet Lane.

He picked up the gun Janet had dropped and pressed the butt of it into her hands. "Go ahead," he said coolly.

Tear-glistened eyes looked at him in bewilderment. "Wh-what do you mean?"

"Go ahead and kill her, Janet, if you're still under the impression that she means anything to me. Better kill me, too, because I'm not anxious to see you in court."

She dropped the gun a second time, stared at it with eyes that must have realized for the first time that here was a weapon of murder.

"Barry!" her whisper sobbed. "What have I done? I—you—can you ever forgive me? Can you forgive me for doubting you?"

He smiled slightly. "Sure. Why not? I guess it's only natural. I've tried to explain that any time I've seen that woman it's been because duty demanded it. You didn't seem to understand. Maybe now you can, because, dear, you're really all that matters, see? I'd be glad if Myra Silinski was dead. It might save a lot of trouble. Do you think if I'd cared anything for her, I'd stand here and watch Rex Gorham make love to her?"

"No-no," the girl hurried. "I didn't think. I wasn't thinking. Oh, I don't think I have anything to think with. I've been a fool—a silly little fool."

X pressed her head against his shoulder. "Hush," he whispered. "I'm trying to hear what that drunken lout in the dirty white cap is saying."

The fat man at the bar had continued his lecture. "I gives um two weeks," he bellowed. "Just two weeks from now the bloomin' Americans will be shippin' men to the East. H'it'll be some war, that's wot!" he nudged the man next to him. "And when the Yanks' guns are blazin' out there, yer'll awsk yerself wot started h'it all. And wot did, uh? Tell yer wot. H'it'll be Pudge Mason hisself, see? Me, I'm the bloke wot started h'it. I'm the bloke wot dropped the match in the bloomin' powder keg!"

"What does he mean, Barry?" Janet whispered.

"Possibly just drunk and shooting off his mouth," X said.

His eyes shifted to Rex Gorham. The dapper, mustached ex-naval officer had left his position beside Myra Silinski and was moving down the bar toward the fat cockney who called himself Pudge Mason. Gorham nudged his way in between Mason and Mason's drinking companion. He didn't say anything. He called for a drink, stood there drawing lines on the top of the bar with his forefinger.

The drunken Pudge Mason watched Gorham's finger with bulging eyes. He wiped his mouth with the back of his hand, licked his lips, gulped, as though to swallow words he had spoken. And he was staring at the spot on the bar where Rex Gorham's finger had been, even after Gorham pulled away from the bar and went to escort Myra Silinski out of the café. And then Pudge Mason faded back from the bar and staggered toward the door.

AGENT X stood up, filled in the place at the bar that Mason had vacated. He called for an "oke" while looking down at the spot where Gorham had drawn his finger. Nothing visible, except a faint smear against the polished surface. While the barkeeper was getting the liquor, X reached over, picked up a container of powdered sugar from the bar and spilled some of its contents on top of the bar where Gorham had written with his finger. He blew the excess sugar off, while white particles of it clung to the moist smear Gorham's finger had made. There, clearly visible against the dark background of the bar, was the scrawled word: "*Death.*"

The Agent's eyes narrowed. Gorham, the dapper ex-naval officer, and Pudge Mason, the cockney sot, were both involved in the scheme. And there was not the slightest doubt in the Agent's mind but what at least a portion of the cockney's drunken babbling had been fact. Someone was planning to involve the United States in the Eastern war. What that plan was and how it was to be checked, he had no idea. But it had to be checked.

A few moments later, the chef of the Golden Lotus came out of his filthy kitchen and left the door ajar. Through the open door, X saw that the kitchen was empty; saw, too, the door in the floor that obviously led to the basement.

He turned swiftly from the bar, crossed to where Janet was sitting, and took her hand. "Come on," he whispered. "Quickly. Don't want to take you with me. But you're not safe here." He took a quick glance over his shoulder, saw no watching eyes, and pulled the girl into the kitchen.

"Below the Golden Lotus—" That portion of the cipher message could mean only one thing: the basement of the café. X stooped, pulled open the basement door. A flight of worn, unclean steps led downwards.

"Barry, why—" began Janet.

"Hush," he whispered, as he helped her onto the stairs and then let the door drop over their heads.

"It's dark," the girl's voice quivered.

"Sh-h," he warned.

He stepped cautiously in front of her, ventured a flash from his torch down into the basement. The room was apparently empty. Its walls were of stone block for a stretch of about six feet above the floor. There, upright oak piles took up the burden of supporting the building above. A brass lamp hung from the beams above and contained an electric globe which X turned on as soon as they had gained the concrete floor.

"Find the map eight blocks from west corner three from the bottom," X's mind repeated the words of the cipher. The blocks probably referred to the stone blocks of the wall. He hurried to the west corner of the room, closely followed by Janet. He counted the blocks—six, seven eight, and the third row from the bottom. He knelt, tapped the block the message had indicated, with his fingertips. It wasn't stone. It was only a piece of fiber board carefully decorated to resemble stone.

He pulled out a jack-knife and inserted the blade in what appeared to be mortar, but was only sand glued to the edge of the fiber board. He pried the board away, revealing a small, dark cavity. He reached inside. His fingers clutched a roll of paper.

"Got it!" he whispered triumphantly. "Back now. Keep behind me." He turned, started swiftly toward the stairs, stopped.

Somewhere in the room was a faint noise that might have been made by a rat or mouse. X drew his gun, moved quietly along the wall.

"Mmmm—" A half-choked cry from behind him. He jerked his head, saw Janet in the grasp of black, naked arms. As he did so, something swished air above his head. He raised his eyes, saw too late the shadow of the Hindu squatting on the wall above his head, the club in the Hindu's hand descending in a swift arc.

Ducking was but a futile movement. Had he moved with ten times the speed, he could not have escaped the blow that crashed into his brain, bringing night and sky spangled with flashing bombshells. And then only night....

CHAPTER V

GUARDIAN OF CORPSE-HANDS

X WAS FIRST conscious of the shadow. Cast against the stone wall of the basement, the shadow was of toothpick proportions. It was the shadow of a man whose body was as gaunt as famine. The Agent raised aching eyes, saw the figure of a Hindu, fully six and a half feet tall, standing over him, arms folded. The man wore a turban of pale-blue cloth and a black suit of ancient cut. His arms were folded.

What was his name? The Agent's semi-dazed mind groped backwards to that seeming far-distant time when he had dined at Marden's. Dal Rama. The tall, grave-eyed Hindu who had been profusely polite had been called Dal Rama. X sat up, for he recovered consciousness far swifter than most men because of his superb physical condition.

Three other Hindus were in the room. All bore the strange trident case mark on their foreheads. All had cruel eyes and hungry mouths. One of them held Janet Lane's small body with one arm while a brown hand plastered over her mouth prevented her speaking.

Dal Rama reached inside his coat and extracted the long cylinder of paper which X immediately recognized as the map he had taken from the secret hiding place. As he did so, a door at the end of the basement room opened and another man stepped in. The man was no Hindu. Though a black curtain-domino mask covered his features, X could clearly see pink ears beneath a white panama hat.

Dal Rama bowed low to the newcomer. He held the map up. "These spies came here to steal this, *sahib.*"

"Burn it," said the white man in a muffled voice. "We are through with it. Our plans are thoroughly in mind." Eyes in the mask looked from X to the girl. The man asked: "What do you intend to do with them, Dal Rama?"

"*Sahib,*" said Dal Rama, "we have seen these unbelievers take into their unclean hands sacred corpse-hands from the girdle of Kali. It is fitting and proper punishment, then, that we cut off the right hand of both the man and the woman, and so let them die."

The white man nodded. "It is immaterial to me how the job is done, just so both are killed. Good night." The white man turned on his heel and left the room.

The Secret Agent patted his pockets. Dal Rama shook his turbaned head. "We are not such fools as to have failed to search you." The gaunt Hindu drew a long-barreled pistol from the pocket of his coat and leveled it at X. "You will have the pleasure of watching while my servants remove the lady's hand."

One of the Hindus drew a long, heavy-bladed knife. The man who held Janet forced the girl forward. His brute strength brought her to her knees in front of a wooden packing box. In spite of her struggles her arm was laid across the top of the box and held there. Above the gagging hand of the Hindu, Janet's eyes rolled appealingly toward the man she supposed to be her husband.

"Wait a moment," X drawled calmly. "No sense in that. Use your brain, Dal Rama. Goddess Kali will no doubt be delighted with the bloodshed, but without her girdle of corpse-hands she isn't apt to be happy very long. I've got one of your sacred withered hands, you know. It happens to be in a particularly good hiding place. You could tear down the walls of my house and still not obtain it. Shouldn't you consider that? Shed a drop of my wife's blood and your withered hand is gone for good."

Dal Rama held up his hand to stay the knife of the dacoit henchman. "Perhaps," he said to X, "you would reveal this hiding place if we promised a more speedy death for you and the lady."

X laughed. "Don't think so. My lady and I go scot-free or no withered hand. Take it or leave it."

He knew to just what absurd extremes the fanatical Dal Rama would go to obtain his relic. Dal Rama was not a criminal. He was a murderer chiefly because the doctrine of the worshipers of Kali prescribed assassination. He would, to fulfill his sacred duty, go to any end to obtain the withered hand. It was entirely through foresight that Agent X had been particularly careful to keep the withered hand to use as a whip, in the event such an emergency arose.

FOR SOME TIME Dal Rama stared at the floor. Then he raised his gaunt face to meet the eyes of X. "You drive hard bargains, Mr. Lane. Where is the Seventh Sacred Hand?"

"That what you call it?" X asked. "Well, I'd have to get it for you."

Dal Rama shook his head. "Do you think me quite a fool? Where is the Seventh Sacred Hand? Answer at once and truthfully, or we will proceed to sever your wife's hand."

"It's in a particularly impregnable strong-box, one which no one can open but myself," X said. "If you will bring the box here, I will open it and give you the hand. Otherwise, nothing short of dynamite would open the box, and that would also sort of spoil the Seventh Sacred Hand. Send one of your men to my house. The box is a cubical affair of steel, outside dimension about a foot."

"You could tell us the combination to the lock of the box," Dal Rama suggested.

X shook his head. "I couldn't. The box was made for me by a Chinese craftsman, and its secret is far too intricate to explain with mere words. Bring the box here. And when you have the Seventh Sacred Hand in your possession, you will permit us to leave unharmed. That a bargain?"

Dal Rama bowed his assent, but there was something in the man's eyes that told X that Dal Rama had not the slightest intention of living up to his part of the bargain. But X had foreseen even treachery.

One of Dal Rama's gaunt fanatics left the basement through the door which the masked white man had employed. X and Janet were permitted to relax somewhat, though Dal Rama's gun kept close watch upon them.

Above their heads sounded the din of shrill voices, the clink of glasses, dancing feet and discordant music. Twenty minutes later, his dark skin bathed in perspiration, his thin back bent under the weight of the cubical metal box, the Hindu returned.

Dal Rama took the box from the other, turned it over in his hands. There was no visible opening or lock. It was a solid block of metal to all appearances. Dal Rama handed the box to Agent X who was still sitting on the basement floor.

"No trickery," Dal Rama warned. "You will be watched closely."

X began fingering the metal sides of the box, pressing the plates from which it was fashioned. Small portions of the plates of each side were thin and flexible. When pressed simultaneously, the bottom plate of the box fell out, revealing a small knob like that of a combination lock, except that there were no numbers around it. Actually it was a combination lock, using in place of numbers a series of slick clicks which were inaudible but could be felt by sensitive fingers.

When X had run through the combination, he put down the box, took hold of the upper half and removed it. He made no attempt to reach into the box then, but extended it slightly toward Dal Rama. Inside was the withered hand—the Seventh Sacred Hand of the Girdle of Kali.

Dal Rama prostrated himself before the relic. His lean lips mumbled a prayer. Then, gloving his hands with silk, jewel-embellished cloth, he picked the mummified hand from the box, and wrapped it up tenderly.

X stood up, the lower portion of his strong-box under one arm. "Come, Janet," he said to the girl. "We'll be on our way."

Janet Lane ran across the room to his side. Dal Rama's lithe body whipped around. His long-barreled pistol snouted upward. An evil smile wreathed his thin lips.

"You do not suppose that you will be permitted to live after touching this sacred relic, do you?"

X frowned slightly. "I remembered that among men of your cult great honor rewards the most skillful liars. That is why I ought to rate a medal for tricking you, according to your code."

His right hand, as he spoke, stole into the metal strong-box there to press a scarcely discernible button which allowed a cleverly constructed false bottom to fly up against one side, revealing a padded recess beneath. The strong-box dropped from his hands, and in his right hand was a small, deadly automatic which he had snatched from beneath the false bottom. The crash of the box against the floor was accompanied by the angry bark of the little automatic. Dal Rama's eyes had followed the falling box, rather than the Agent's hands. And the next moment Dal Rama had dropped his gun and was clutching a bleeding wrist with his left hand.

CHAPTER VI

DRUGGED

"**D**ON'T MOVE ANY of you!" X warned, his voice becoming hard. "Dal Rama, you will tell me who the white man was who entered this room several minutes ago—the man you addressed as *sahib*. And you will tell me his name immediately. Otherwise, it shall be my duty to kill you."

"I have no fear of death," said Dal Rama mildly. "Had I such fear, I would not be able to tell you the name of the *sahib*, for I do not know. Kill me if you will, but do not imagine that you can escape death."

One of the dacoits moved, flicked a knife from his waist and threw it with lightning-like motion. The Agent's gun swerved, barked again, and at the same time his left arm shot out to brush Janet behind him. The knife-man slumped on the floor, for the Agent's slug had mashed his shin bone.

A warning cry from Janet, and X whirled around to bring his gun up in a blue blur that culminated in a blow to the side of a Hindu's face. But the instant he had taken his eyes from Dal Rama, the tall Hindu landed on X's back, his long legs wrapping about the Agent's legs to trip him and bring him to the floor. As X hit the floor, breath exploded from his lungs, his small gun slid from his fingers and along the floor.

As he fought to break the stranglehold the Hindu had upon his throat, X heard a cascading sound of running, tumbling footsteps on the stairs, glimpsed out of the corners of his eyes the drunken mob from the café above. Drunken women shrilled screams of delight. A shout went up from the sailors: "It's anybody's fight!" Another man cried, "Bust the heads of the damned foreigners!" and at the same time seized Dal Rama by the collar and yanked him from Agent X.

But this man was evidently no ally of the Agent's, for as X got to his knees, he tried a wild blow to X's jaw. But X jerked his head aside, felt the fist fan his cheek, came up under a shower of blows, and wormed in with a short, chopping blow to the unguarded side of the man's head.

X reeled out of the way as another man lurched in to take the place of the one he had just dropped. Across the room, he saw Janet in the arms of the drunken cockney who called himself Pudge Mason. X charged across the room, yanking a sailor from his path. His right hand dropped on Mason's shoulder and pulled the man away from the girl.

Mason wheeled, cried hoarsely: "Yah bloomin' swell—" Then, with fists swinging, he staggered straight into a left and right from the Agent that stretched him on the flooring.

X seized Janet's arm, pulled her through the excited crowd of dance-hall girls clustered about the stairs. He hurried her up the steps, through the café, and out the front door where Barry Lane's car awaited them.

"What does it mean?" the girl gasped. "Barry, I never was so frightened in my life. But you were perfect, knocking those men around the way you did. I never knew you could move so fast. You didn't seem to be the man I married at all."

X had nothing to reply to this last remark, and he remained silent the rest of the way to the Marden mansion, feeling more deeply than ever the injury his impersonation was doing Janet Lane. The girl *had* to know the truth. Twice he opened his mouth to tell her that he was not Barry Lane, but each time he did so, the hideous phantom of war passed before his eyes. For, as Barry Lane, he was making steady progress toward unraveling the plot that threatened the peace of his country.

He knew, for instance, that Rex Gorham was involved in the plot—perhaps the chief mover in the scheme. And when he thought of the dapper man who had once worn a navy uniform, plotting to throw his fellow Americans into the hell-brew in the Orient, he could have killed Gorham with his bare hands.

WHEN at last they reached the mansion, it was Marden himself who rolled his chair across the floor to open the door for them.

"Mrs. Lane!" he exclaimed on seeing Janet. "I supposed you were in bed long ago."

"I should have been," the girl said meekly. "But I couldn't sleep, I went out for a walk."

"And I haven't been able to sleep," Marden said, almost gleefully. "I haven't had so much going on around me since I was captured by bandits in the Chinese interior. Lane, your friend Holme has been a veritable dynamo of energy, buzzing around the house, sending cablegrams to Washington. Something about a submarine and South America. I happened to overhear. By George, I'm sorry I have to leave tomorrow."

"Leaving tomorrow?" X asked. He removed his glasses and began polishing them with his handkerchief, as he had often watched Lane do. "Why?"

"Business," Marden said. "Nothing very exciting, more's the pity. I had hoped to put off the trip until my leg had mended. But there's a N.Y.K. boat docking tomorrow, and I am leaving on her for Yokohama."

"Don't think I'd care to go to Japan at the present moment," X said with a yawn. "Where's Holme?"

"In the library, marching around the telephone, last time I saw him," Marden chuckled. "A man of action, Mr. Holme is."

X left Janet with Marden and entered the library to find Holme divested of coat and vest and pacing the floor in rather violent-hued suspenders. He whipped around as X entered.

"I'm waiting for you," he snapped. "What results? Get the map?"

X shook his head. "No, but I'm beginning to organize our potpourri of information. There seem to be three angles in the business—the Hindu thugs, directed by Dal Rama who is apparently joined with a white man he knows simply as 'sahib.' Then there's Myra Silinski, who changes her boy friends as she does her clothes. One of her boy friends happens to be Rex Gorham, an ex-navy man—a submarine commander, I believe, and he's associated with a cockney named Mason.

"All three angles seem to have a common point of focus—getting America in trouble in the Orient. What interests each represent, we don't know, except that Myra is evidently working for some power which has vast holding in the Orient. That power would rest considerably easier if it was certain that America would go to war with Japan, and save her the trouble, possibly, of protecting her own interests in China.

"By the way, there's a Japanese vessel docking tomorrow—"

"I know," Holme cut in. "One of the N.Y.K. motor boats. Marden said he was sailing on her. However, did I hear you say something about a submarine officer. Ex-officer, I think. Name of Gorham?"

X nodded. "Know him?"

Holme shook his head, shot a pencil of cigar smoke from puckered lips. "Point is, I've been looking at this drawing of Selwick's. Remember, we agreed it looked like a detail of a giant pump. It is. Checked with Washington on it. Selwick designed a new and better kind of submarine ballast pump. Submerges the vessel. Rather, pumps the water out of the ballast tanks. Details don't matter. Thing that matters is that there's only one sub ever carried that pump. A U-boat built on the coast by American workmen for use by the Chilean government.

"I thought, damned if we ought to mix Chile up in this. Much too involved internationally as it is. But when I learned Chile never got her sub, because the damned thing went to the bottom or was lost, or something, during delivery—well, then I got interested. What the devil was this Selwick doing here, anyway? He wasn't here for his health."

Somewhere outside the library sounded a crash and a sharp cry that could have come only from Janet. X and Holme broke from the library, heard Marden's voice in the curio room saying: "There, there, Mrs. Lane. It's nothing. Really nothing. Don't bother your pretty head over it at all."

"But you said it was priceless," Janet Lane said. Then, as X entered the room, she gestured in dismay at bits of broken pottery scattered over the floor. "The Burmese idol Mr. Harden prized so much—the one he showed us last night after dinner—I've broken it, Barry. The sleeve of my dress brushed it off the shelf. It can never be replaced."

"Now it's nothing at all," Marden said. "Please don't worry about it, Lane. The pieces can easily be joined with cement."

AGENT X dropped to his knees and started gathering the pieces of the hideous little idol together. As he did so, he noticed a label on the inside of a broken portion of the base. He frowned slightly.

"Somebody played a joke on you, I'm afraid. This image was made in Japan. Probably an imitation."

"What!" Marden cried. His fingers couldn't roll his chair fast enough to X's side. "Let me see." Excitedly he took the bit of pottery from X's fingers.

"By George. Japan! Of all the rotten swindles! I paid that guide a thousand dollars to take me to the place where it was kept, thought I'd risked my life getting it. And it's an imitation. Excuse me, Mrs. Lane, but I'll be damned!" He tossed the piece of the broken image into a corner of the room. "I'm glad you broke it, Mrs. Lane. You've done me a great favor. In my absence I'd be grateful if you'd break any more imitations you find in my collection."

The telephone rang. Inasmuch as all the servants had retired, Marden asked Agent X if he would answer it.

"I wonder who can be calling at this time of the morning," Marden said, as X left the curio room to go into the library.

X raised the phone, announced that this was the Marden residence.

"You, Barry?" It was Myra Silinski's throaty voice. "I've been trying to get hold of you for the past hour, Barry. I have some information that should be of inestimable value to you, if you care to come to the apartment and get it. Don't, please, bring the charming wife."

"Be right over," X said in Lane's voice. He hung up. He stopped at the door of the curio room and called Janet to him. Then he led the girl out far enough from Holme and Marden so that they could talk in private.

"That was Myra Silinski, Janet," he said. "I'm going over to her place. She says she has some information for me. You're not going to follow me or do anything foolish?"

Janet Lane smiled. "No, of course not. Barry, if you'd always thought to tell me when you went there, I wouldn't have acted like a little fool. I won't worry, because—because I'm really sure you love me, Barry." She stood on tiptoe to kiss him.

X turned away quickly as their lips parted, that she might not see the look in his eye. Never in his life had he felt so completely guilty. When he had assumed the disguise of Barry Lane it had been far more than deception. It was more like theft—the theft of affection that belonged to a dead man.

He pushed such thoughts from his mind, left the house, drove first to the Lane bungalow, where he went into the room that had been assigned to him when he had first arrived in Honolulu under the alias of Regan. "Because," he said aloud thinking of Myra Silinski, "there is something reminiscent of a Medici about the woman, I'd better go prepared." He searched in one of his bags and located something which he concealed in his handkerchief. This, and an automatic similar to the one Lane had carried, were the weapons of defense which he took to Myra Silinski's apartment above the Golden Lotus.

Even in King Street there was a before-dawn hush, and fresh perfume that heralded the morning had dispelled to some extent the unpleasant odors that had been so predominant the night before.

X alighted from the car and climbed the steps to Myra's apartment. There was no bearded watchdog in front of the door this time, and he entered without knocking. Myra, wearing full-cut pajamas of black silk, was lounging on the couch, waiting for him. She did not bother to get up, but waved him to a seat beside her. Her eyes were cold, her attitude almost indifferent.

"I do not know why I do this," she said, bending over a table beside the couch to pour liquor into two small glasses, "for I am usually the most selfish of mortals. I am probably prompted by a sense of duty toward my country, just as you must have been when you made love to me."

"The most pleasant duty I have ever been called upon to perform," X said.

Myra laughed. "I rather enjoyed it, too. But I was under the illusion that some of the words you spoke came from the heart instead of the brain. However, let's be friends about it." She raised her glass of liquor, pushed the other glass toward the Agent.

X raised his glass, drank quickly. At least he seemed to drink. Actually, he retained the liquor in his mouth. A second later, as he apparently wiped his lips on his handkerchief, he emptied his mouth into the collapsible rubber bag he had concealed in his handkerchief. He put down the glass and lolled back on the couch.

"Now," he said, "what did you have to tell me?" He retained the handkerchief containing the rubber sack in his right hand.

MYRA was watching him closely, with the cold-blooded interest of a scientist who chloroforms a rat. "Smoke?" she invited him, gesturing toward a taboret containing black Russian cigarettes and an onyx ash-tray.

X shook his head. "Don't feel like it."

Myra laughed. "Poor boy! You haven't had a minute's sleep all night, have you?"

"No, feeling a bit drowsy, too," X said. Through half-closed eyes he saw a look of triumph flash across Myra's face. Then it was instantly gone.

"Our countries have one great interest in common," Myra said.

"That so?" X said drowsily.

"Of course. We've discussed it often enough," she said. She got up, flicked ash into the onyx tray. "Barry, don't you want to lie down for a few minutes?"

"No. Go on. What were you saying? Better start over again. You said you had some important information." X passed a hand over his face. "Stuffy in here."

Myra laughed, sat down beside him, "No, it isn't. You're just sleepy."

"Keep on talking," X said. "Always liked to hear your voice." He yawned, closed his eyes, sighed. Myra's arm went about his shoulders. She pulled him toward her, pillowed his head on her breast.

"Poor, sleepy boy," she whispered. "Somehow I thought you too clever to fall for that old, old ruse. Just relax. It will all be over in a little while."

"What's that?" he struggled with seeming impotence. "What did you say?"

She laughed again, gently stroked his forehead. "I shall just keep you here a little while. And when you wake up, you may go back to your wife, if she will take you. When you wake up, Barry Lane, there will be nothing left for you in the world but me. Your superiors will have discharged you. Your wife will have nothing to do with you, because you have failed so miserably."

"Uh?" X grunted.

"When you wake up, it will all be over. Gorham has told me of the thing that is to happen near Egg Island. And when you wake up, Barry Lane, your country will be at war. It will be a great load off the shoulders of my country."

Sleeping, X might have appeared to be. But his brain was active. Egg Island. That was what Selwick had tried to say before his death. Something was hidden there—something that held the power of life and death over millions of Americans. And Myra Silinski thought that Barry Lane was the one man who could move to prevent the impending disaster. So she thought she was going to prevent the one man she supposed to be Lane from staving off some carefully planned international trouble.

And Myra Silinski's primary purpose seemed to allow that plot of someone else's weaving to go on unhindered. The plan was neither hers nor that of her countrymen, otherwise she would not have had to obtain this information from Rex Gorham. It was simply the policy of her country to permit the United States to become involved, thus allowing America to bear the burden of protecting foreign interests in the Orient.

The door to the apartment opened, and the bearded giant X had met on his first visit to Myra Silinski's apartment entered. Myra stood up, allowing X to fall back limply on the couch.

"Why are you here, Peter?" she demanded.

"*Bogu!* All women are fools. Even Silinski is a fool. Twice, now, I have watched through the keyhole to see this Barry Lane come in here and not do what Barry Lane always does. I have seen him do it much too often in past weeks, but last night and this morning he does not do it. Always he comes in, sits down, and starts turning that ash-tray over and over in his big fingers. And look at this man's fingers. They are not big. And he has not played with the ash-tray—he has not even touched it. I have watched. I tell you you are a fool!"

"What do you mean?" Myra demanded.

"I mean that this man is not Barry Lane. I have watched. I know. And I know who he is, if not Barry Lane. We heard of him in the Great War, though we never had the misfortune to meet him. He is more than a spy. He is the man called Secret Agent X. Who else could have impersonated Barry Lane so well that even you do not know the difference?"

"That—that is impossible." Myra turned her eyes on the motionless Agent. For the first time she seemed not quite sure of herself.

Peter drew a knife from a hidden sheath at his waist. "Lucky I am careful watchdog, Silinski!" He took a step toward the couch.

"What are you going to do?" Myra's tall, proud figure came between Peter and Agent X.

"Do? Like a dog I will kill him."

"But that isn't necessary. He's drugged. We will simply keep him here until it is impossible for him to stop this thing."

"Impossible? There is nothing impossible to that man until he is dead!"

Peter brushed the woman aside with one sweep of his powerful arm, sprang to the couch, his knife upraised.

CHAPTER VII

DEATH OF A CORPSE

NOT UNTIL DEATH was directly above him did Agent X move. Then it was only to squeeze the collapsible bag which was concealed in his handkerchief, thus shooting a stream of the drugged liquor from the opening in the bag into Peter's eyes.

Taken completely off guard, the bearded giant backed a step, blinked, digging at smarting eyes with a clenched fist. And then, before he completely comprehended what had happened, X was on his feet, fists swinging. He slugged through the giant's guard, landed a hard fist up in the man's beard, saw Peter's eyes rolling back. As Peter's knees buckled, X whipped out his automatic and clinched the victory by hammering the barrel of the gun to the top of Peter's head. The bearded giant stretched out on the floor, uttering a dull groan.

X waved his gun at Myra Silinski. "Sit down in that chair over there," he ordered quietly.

Myra Silinski raised shoulders and eyebrows in insolent submission to this sudden twist of fortune. She sauntered over to the chair, sat down, crossed her legs. She swung her foot impatiently.

"You," she said, "are Secret Agent X, I suppose."

"I am," he admitted.

"And what happened to Barry Lane?"

"Dead. He died the most horrible way a man could die. You might have saved him."

Myra Silinski paled slightly. "I?"

"Yes. Had you given him the information you are going to give me, it is entirely possible that this plot, which you and your countrymen seem to watch with such interest, would have been nipped in the bud. As it was, Lane was floundering around, getting too close to the truth without knowing it. So he had to die. I am much nearer the truth than Lane was, and I intend to live. Isn't it a rather nice thing to be alive, Myra?"

The woman shrugged again, looked away.

The Agent stepped nearer, centered his gun on Myra's forehead. "I have two questions. First, who is the man behind these murderous Hindus? Second, how do the plotters intend to precipitate a declaration of war between Japan and the United States?"

Her eyes met his steadily. "I have no idea of the answer to your first question, Agent X. I have no intention of answering your second question."

X sighed deeply. "I am sorry to have to do what I must do."

"Kill me? When one takes service with one's country, one ceases to possess a future. For the past eight years I have lived every moment of my life as though it were the last. Do your worst."

X stepped to the window and pulled down the silken cords that tied heavy drapes. "Unfortunately, you still have a future, Myra, and it's something to worry about."

She made no resistance as he tied her to the chair. She said: "You would hardly stoop to the barbarism of torture."

His eyes narrowed, became like twin steel points. "Do not deceive yourself," he said slowly. "You should know how thoroughly my country despises war. And if our foreign policy indicates this hatred of war, know that I, who lived through the last war and saw all its horrors, hate it even more so. I know exactly what advances have been made in militarism since the last war. I can foresee how much more terrible this next war will be when it comes. Do not suppose that I would permit one lone woman to stand in my way, knowing that she possesses information that may prevent that war? Do you suppose that my code is so rigid it cannot be stretched when there is much to be gained?"

She raised her blond head defiantly. "There is no pain you can inflict which I cannot endure, Agent X."

"We will see."

He moved across the room to a door, through it into a bedroom. In a bathroom that connected this bedroom to another, he found a pair of shears, a mirror and a razor which evidently belonged to the bearded giant, Peter. He returned to the living room.

HE PLACED the mirror in a chair, moved the chair up in front of the woman so that she could see her face and head. She watched all this in perfect composure. He went behind her and began removing the small pins that confined her hair.

"I give you one more opportunity, Myra. I know that you are not involved in this hideous plan to send thousands of Americans to their death. But I know that Rex Gorham is. And I know that it is to your country's advantage that this plot succeeds. But I must know just how it is to be accomplished. Tell me that, and I will immediately liberate you."

Myra forced a yawn. "Sunrise in Honolulu. I have seen it hundreds of times, yet it never fails to thrill me."

"There is one torment woman cannot endure," X said. "She may have courage to withstand physical pain, but the torment I have in mind for you is aimed directly at woman's vanity. Have you ever stopped to consider just how attractive you would be *with your head shaved?* You see, it's your hair that is responsible for the loveliness of your face. Without it, your face would appear much too long. And I think your ears will stick out rather grotesquely when your head is as bald as an egg."

"You forget," she said quietly, "that I am less a woman than a citizen of my country."

X raised a gleaming silver-gold strand of hair and snipped it off with the shears. He tossed it into her lap.

"And besides, I can always buy a wig," she said. "I could even have a wig to go with each costume."

X raised the razor and slashed through the silken cords that bound the woman. "Stand up," he ordered.

Myra Silinski obeyed, turned to examine him with eyes devoid of curiosity. The Secret Agent was smiling. "You may consider yourself under arrest, Myra Silinski."

She raised her eyebrows. "You've given up the idea of trying to make me talk?"

"No one," said X, "can ever say that Secret Agent X does not admire and appreciate the courage of his opponents. I have a car outside. The gun in my pocket will cover you until you are in the hands of the proper authorities. I will go to Egg Island at once."

"You will be killed, Agent X."

He bowed slightly, offered her his arm. "As you say, when one undertakes the services of his country, he ceases to possess a future."

In the library of the Marden mansion, Ronald Holme and Janet Lane listened intently while Agent X related to them what had occurred at Myra Silinski's apartment. The lovely spy was temporarily incarcerated in the city prison, and Holme had started making arrangements for her immediate deportation. Marden had gone to his warehouse to attend to important business before he embarked for Yokohama.

When X concluded his narrative, Holme, hollow-eyed from lack of sleep, looked up to meet the keen, never-tired eyes of Agent X.

"What's to be done? I'm at a dead end. I have Honolulu police rounding up every thing that looks like a Hindu. I've ordered the immediate arrest of this Rex Gorham and his cockney pal. All I can do is thunder over the phone. It's up to you. I haven't got a thought in my head. Go to this Egg Island? What with? The marines? Call out the Pacific Fleet? Hell can split before our ships can move. You can't fight before you know what you're fighting. Can't tell where these devils will strike."

"We charter a small cruiser," X said, "as private citizens bent on a fishing trip. We go to Egg Island. We may not know exactly in what direction the enemy will strike, but we know that this Egg Island is the source of the danger."

Holme bit off the end of a cigar, picked up the phone. "I thunder again. Damn it, why didn't that Silinski woman talk?"

"Because," X said, "she is as devoted to her cause as we are to ours."

While Holme phoned, X went to the bookcase and searched until he found a large folding map of Hawaii and vicinity. Never, except on this occasion, had he ever heard of Egg Island.

Holme slammed up the phone. "Done. We've got the cruiser and it's fully equipped; radio, crew, provisions. But the owner of the boat asked me where in hell Egg Island was."

X and Janet bent over the map. The girl pointed a slender finger to a little dot off the coast of Niihau. "There. That looks like an egg. It's called Lenua on the map. Do you suppose that's it?"

X nodded. "Someone down at the waterfront ought to know. Let's go, Holme."

"I'm going, too, Barry," Janet announced.

X hesitated. "Perhaps it would look more like a pleasure trip if you do. We'll stop at the bungalow on the way to the pier. I want to pick up some equipment." For, having only the faintest idea of what he was going into, Agent X was determined to be prepared for anything.

ON REACHING the pier, X found that the boat Holme had obtained was a trim seventy-foot cruiser which looked capable of speed. The crew consisted of two white men and a Polynesian cook. The eldest of the whites insisted upon being called captain. He was not entirely shipshape, judging from the odor of whiskey about him, but he declared that Egg Island was a little dot of rock north of Niihau and was generally known as Lenua.

"You see," Janet said triumphantly, "I am good for something."

"But," the captain said to Holme, "that ain't the best place for fishin'."

"Doesn't make a particle of difference," Holme snapped. "That's where we want you to go. How soon can you raise anchor or whatever you do to get this thing started?"

"Right away," the captain declared. "Soon as Jerry starts the engine."

Jerry, who knew engines and radios, wasn't long in getting started. The elderly captain took the wheel. The Polynesian cook went to snore in the galley. And the boat sliced the water, moved west past Slaughterhouse Point, hugged the shore so closely that the grim gray walls of Oahu Prison seemed like cliffs above their heads. The sea was smooth even when Kaena was the last visible landmark of Oahu Island.

Holme, X and Janet stood in the stern of the cruiser, watching the Pacific swallow the land. Janet, holding the Agent's hand, was engrossed in the graceful wanderings of white gulls against the sky. The Agent was almost grimly quiet, for within him was an unconquerable dread of what must follow if their almost-formless plans should fail. And Holme, probably because of that same feeling of impending disaster, was nervous, loud-spoken, restless.

"How in the name of heaven," demanded Holme, "can the slightest spark of war be created in these peaceful waters? If we only knew how, we'd know at least where to look. And how to duck when the blow comes. Figuratively, of course. Because we won't duck. We'll fight."

"The blow will come somewhere along this identical route we are taking," X said. "Egg Island wasn't chosen entirely because of its comparatively remote location. That Japanese motor ship passes the island going through Kamukahi channel."

Holme's mouth opened. His thin cigar went over the side unnoticed. "By George, Agent—Barry Lane. By George, Agent Barry Lane, that's it!"

"I'm afraid it is," X agreed. "I've been afraid so ever since I found out where Egg Island is."

"What, Barry?" Janet asked. "I don't understand."

"Well," X drawled, "if something should happen to that N.Y.K. ship in Hawaiian waters, Japan would hold the United States responsible. Inasmuch as the ship carries supplies for the war, and if whatever happened to it could be made to look like an act of war—"

"Why," Holme interrupted, "there would simply be war between the United States and Japan. No getting out of it, much as neither nation would want such a thing. The Jap ship is trailed by a destroyer. Destroyer would probably open up her guns on some of our ships in Pearl Harbor. Why, the lid of hell would pop right off!"

"But how can we do anything about it?" the girl asked. "Will they—these people who want to start the war—bomb the Japanese ship, or what?"

"If we were sure of that, we'd be that much farther ahead than we are now," X said.

It was shortly after noon when the cruiser rounded the north tip of Niihau, and the captain came to the rail to point out a jagged tooth of rock sticking out of the placid sea.

"Well, there's your Egg Island," he said. "Now that you've seen it, what d'yah want to do?"

"Want to go ashore," X said.

"But there ain't nothin' there," said the captain. "Not unless it's a couple of deserted fishin' shacks."

"Looks like a pier sticking out into the water a little way," X said, squinting toward the island, "Made of new boards, too. Don't put in too close. Better lie right here."

X tugged Holme to one side. "I'm going to swim for it, sir," he said. "If I'm not back in twenty minutes, better start looking for me—and for *anything*. Take care of the girl. Keep her attention away from me when I go over the side."

HOLME nodded, left the Agent, and went forward with Janet. X hurried into the tiny cabin, stripped to his trunks. Then he opened one of the satchels he had brought with him, took out an oilskin bag which was large enough to contain one of his kits of makeup materials. This bag, with makeup kit enclosed, he fastened to his back with cords. Then he padded to the stern of the boat and slipped over the rail into the water.

His lean, powerful arms worked like tireless oars as he swam for the island and the newly made pier. If he guessed correctly, the pier had been constructed to enable small boats to land supplies on the island. Egg Island was probably the base of operations of the plotters.

He climbed onto the black lava rock, which formed the island, a little to the south of the pier. His next move was to scale cautiously the highest point within easy access, with the idea of getting the lay of the land. The island, he judged, was not more than two miles long and half that wide. Down toward its seaward side he saw a couple of small huts and a newly constructed wooden shack. Except for a few lonely gulls, there was no apparent life on the island.

Nevertheless, he approached the shacks with caution, zig-zagging from one sheltering rock to another. Twenty feet from the nearest hut, he paused, listened. From the paneless window came the sound of lusty snoring. His bare feet made no sound on the hard surface as he crept to the window and looked in. Four men lay on the floor, dirty, unshaven, wearing a motley assortment of garments. Only one he recognized—the cockney of the Golden Lotus, Mr. Pudge Mason, who had boasted that when war started he was going to be the man who started it.

For a moment X stood there, his mind working with lightning rapidity, considering every possible course that he might take. Then, in the distance sounded the *putt-putt* of a gasoline motor. He went to the corner of the hut and looked out to sea. A motor launch, with a tiny cabin, was nosing in toward the island out of the great expanse of blue water. Where had it come from? So small a boat would scarcely travel over a wide body of water. He scanned the ocean anxiously, saw nothing that looked like a larger ship. Yet he knew instinctively that a larger ship was there.

X ran down to the shore, waded into the water. As soon as he had reached his depth, he began swimming straight for the launch. As his head broke water for a gasp of air, he saw that the launch had apparently a single man aboard—a Hindu....

Fifteen, twenty minutes passed at a snail-pace for Ronald Holme. And no sign of Agent X. No less anxious was Janet Lane as she scanned the island with the captain's glass.

"Why did you let him go?"

"Why?" snapped Holme. "I sometimes wonder if I could ever stop him doing anything he's set his head on. On his two shoulders rests the fate of a nation. If he fails—"

"He won't fail," Janet said. "Not Barry."

"Barry?" Holme caught his tongue in time. He groaned.

"Look!" The girl tugged at his sleeve. "There's a boat out there!"

"Where?" Holme snatched the glass and refocused it impatiently. "A launch. Two men aboard. Tiller's loose, the way she's going crazy. The men are fighting. By George, it's a Hindu and Agent—and Barry. Isn't that Barry, Mrs. Lane?"

He poked the glass into the girl's hand. She watched a moment, gripping the rail with one hand. Then a frightened cry escaped her. "Barry! Oh, he's fallen! They—they rolled down into the cabin, still fighting!"

"Here—" Holme grabbed the glass, focused it on the floundering launch. No sign of anyone on the tiny deck of the craft. He cursed aloud. He hadn't the slightest idea what to do, because he had no idea of the Agent's plans. Should he get the captain of their cruiser to try and overtake the launch? Should he try and help Agent X? He snorted aloud at the thought. Help Secret Agent X mop up the floor with a Hindu? Preposterous! But he had to do something. Why didn't X come back on the deck of the launch?

"Captain!" Holme bawled. "Damn it, where is the man. If he's sucking a bottle of Scotch, I'll break it over his head!" He shoved the glass into the girl's hand and went through the narrow hatch into the cabin. The captain was emulating the example of the Polynesian cook—taking a nap.

Holme shook the captain awake. "Where's your engineer?" he shouted. "Get him to move this thing."

The captain yawned. "Easy, now. You and me's too old to get excited like this. What's the hurry?"

"Hurry? A man's being killed out there. Fighting on a launch. Get this dishpan to moving, can't you?" And he shoved the captain from the cabin.

As he gained the deck, Holme saw Janet drop the glass, sway slightly forward. He sprang toward her and seized her just as she seemed on the point of toppling over the rail.

"Barry!" she sobbed. "Barry— Oh, Mr. Holme, he—he's dead. The—the Hindu came out alone—"

And Janet Lane collapsed in Holme's arms.

RONALD HOLME squinted across the water, saw the launch making steadily toward the little pier. At the wheel squatted the half-naked brown body of a Hindu, his head heightened by a white mound of turban. An oath dropped from Holme's lips. It was an oath of disappointment immediately followed by one of triumph; for, quavering eerily from the little launch came a high-pitched, birdlike whistle. It was the musical signature he had heard many times before—the whistle of Secret Agent X.

"Nothing impossible to that man!" he said delightedly to no one. "He's the Hindu. Agent X is the Hindu, by George! Impersonated the man. Knocked him out and then painted his body brown, altered his features, put on the turban. And, by George, he's on the inside of the gang, now!"

Then Holme's joy dwindled as he looked down into the sweet face of the unconscious girl in his arms. "But you," he whispered, "mustn't know the truth. Barry Lane is dead. He died twice. And the only death you need know about is the one you thought you just witnessed. Yes, sir. Barry Lane died heroically in the service of his country, that's all you need to know. Poor little girl!"

Something like a tear glittered in the hard eyes of K9 as he carried the unconscious Janet into the cabin of the cruiser. He placed her gently on one of the bunks and returned toward the hatchway, his footsteps less light.

"Hey, mister!" That was the voice of the captain.

Holme sprang forward. "Yes?" he snapped.

The captain was peering through the glass, out to sea. He beckoned with a horny thumb. "Want you to take a look at the damnedest thing I've ever seen. If my eyes are lying, I'd better change my brand, that's what!"

Holme looked in the direction of the captain's glass. His jaw dropped. Rising slowly out of the surface of the calm water was a wedge of dripping, gray metal, infinitely terrible in appearance to Ronald Holme. It was the conning tower of a submarine.

Holme cursed hoarsely, punched the captain on the back with his fist. "Move, man! Nose this boat back to Honolulu. Full speed. Where's your engineer? Get him to start that radio transmitter, do you hear? And if you ever moved, move now. That sub is surfacing. She'll have a four-seven rifle on her deck, capable of blowing a chip like this out of the water. We've got to outrun her!"

And as the captain ordered his combination engineer and radio operator to start the engine, Holme watched the little launch with the Hindu, who was Secret Agent X, making steadily toward the pier on Egg Island. Four men had moved out on the pier and were signaling the launch. Four men—a nice torpedo team for the monstrous gray shark that was pushing unalterably to the surface of the water.

Holme, who was not a religious man, found his lips mumbling prayers for that lone figure in the launch—prayers that he might be spared to save his country from the shell-ripped hell of war.

CHAPTER VIII

SATAN'S SUBMARINE

RONALD HOLME ELBOWED the young seaman named Jerry away from the little cruiser's short-wave transmitter. "Get to your engines," he snapped. "Get more speed out of them. I'll run the radio. Got to contact Pearl Harbor at once."

"But have you got a license?" demanded Jerry.

"License? Young man, I was eating Morse code for breakfast before you were born. Get to your engines. If that sub unlimbers her rifle before we're out of range, everything's over."

"Yes, sir!" And Jerry went back to his engines while Holme clamped his small head between ear phones and grabbed the transmitter key.

He didn't know the call letters of the cruiser's transmitter. But the spark signal of K9 was known by American army and navy officials the world over.

"K9 calling Pearl Harbor," the transmitter ripped out. "Calling Rear-Admiral Harkness, Pacific Fleet Pearl Harbor. K9 calling."

Then he ceased calling and listened, mumbling: "Pray heaven there's a subchaser in these waters somewhere!" Only a portion of the fleet had arrived at Honolulu for its customary spring practice, he knew.

After dragging minutes, during which Holme fidgeted and chewed halfway down a cigar, the answering call came through. And Holme clicked out:

"Advise position of any S.C. available for immediate action."

Immediately came the reply: "S.C. 86 in Pearl Harbor."

Holme rapped out: "Advise sailing time Jap mail ship Yokohama bound."

"Five P.M.," came back after a moment's pause.

Holme radioed: "S.C. 86 move full speed northwest on Yokohama shipping lane. Prepare for action. Watch for K9 to board S.C. from gasoline cruiser somewhere in Kaieie Channel."

A slight pause, and Pearl Harbor came back with: "Harkness asks explanation."

"Explanation be damned!" shouted Holme, as in the wake of the speeding cruiser, gun-thunder rolled, and a shot from the submarine's rifle shrilled overhead. "Can't you hear that, Harkness?" he yelled. "Explanation—" And then he seemed to recall that Harkness couldn't have heard and he clattered the key in the terse explanation: "Sighted renegade submersive off Niihau."

Pearl Harbor radioed: "Coming." And Holme sighed and switched off the radio.

Jerry stuck his head out of the engine pit. "Are we outstripping her, sir?" he asked.

Another shot from the sub's rifle cut through Holme's answer. Water spouted as the spent shell landed short astern. They were pulling out of range. But could the subchaser be put into action, steam into the danger zone before the sub got a chance to torpedo the Japanese vessel? Holme doubted it. His only hope lay in the fact that Agent X might have been able to board the sub. And if he did, could he stop the plans of the devil who piloted the sub?

Holme now understood much of the plan afoot. The renegade submarine, he was willing to wager, was the missing boat that had been built for the Chilean government. Don Selwick, the marine engineer, had been hired to put it into operating condition again. Then, getting some hint of the plan back of the sub's restoration, Selwick had sold out to Barry Lane, giving Lane all available information. Both Selwick and Lane had been killed by Hindus. Why these assassins from far-off Burma had been employed for the killings, Holme had no idea.

NOR, for that matter, had Agent X. No sooner had the Agent boarded the launch, which was steered by one of Dal Rama's dacoits, than he found himself in one of the wildest rough-and-tumble fights he had ever encountered. Only cool-headedness had enabled him to triumph over the dope-crazed fanatic. But when he had scored his knockout, his course lay clearly mapped out before him.

He had stretched the Hindu out on the floor of the tiny cabin, unstrapped the makeup kit he carried on his back, and set to work to remodel the full-cheeked face of Barry Lane, which he had assumed, until he was the gaunt, aquiline-nosed face of the dacoit.

Then deep-toned pigment had been employed to imitate the Hindu's coloring, and this he was compelled to smear over his entire body. He had then to put on the Hindu's loin cloth and turban. The latter gave him considerable trouble, but he at last succeeded in removing the turban from the dacoit's shaved head and putting it on his own head without greatly disturbing the intricate wrappings of cloth.

For a weapon, his disguise permitted him nothing but a knife. The Hindu, together with the Agent's makeup kit, had to be concealed in a small locker aboard the launch. He then left the cabin and got hold of the tiller of the launch. Hardly had he squatted at the wheel before he saw the conning tower of the submarine break water. And at the same time, Pudge Mason and his three companions moved down the pier of Egg Island and hailed the launch. The launch, evidently, bad been put out by the submarine to pick up the men on the island which seemed to have served as a base of supplies for the plotters.

X maneuvered the launch to the pier, where Pudge Mason, squatting on his heels, yelled: "Toss us a line, ye black devil."

The Agent obeyed in silence. Mason drew the launch in close to the pier, and he and his three companions boarded her.

"Let 'er go back to the sub," Mason ordered as he settled himself and began stuffing his pipe with a slice of tobacco.

"This man Gorham knows his U-boats, don't he, Mason?" asked one of the men worriedly.

Mason kindled his pipe. "Betcher socks 'e does. Far as runnin' 'em goes, 'e does. But h'it takes a man o' my wide experience to 'andle the white-'eads. H'l never fergits the time H'I blowed the 'ell outa that Dutch tanker in the Baltic. That were wot you called a neat shot!"

As they neared the sub, its superstructure now above the surface, the conning tower hatch was open, and Rex Gorham's handsome head appeared over its steel rim. Gorham and another man, who was clad only in a pair of khaki trousers, came out of the hatch to extend a narrow gangplank of steel equipped with grappling hooks which fastened to the rail of the launch.

Gorham, dark and dashing in his spotless white uniform, stood with legs widespread on the submersive's wet deck. A white-toothed smile flashed across his tanned face. "Come aboard, Mason. We've put her through her paces. She's a sound ship. Now that we've proved that, no need for you to be afraid any longer."

Mason reddened, shot a guilty look at his companions. His bloodshot eyes encountered the gaze of the Hindu who was Agent X, "Wot are you grinnin' about, ye bloomin' 'eathen?"

"Here," Gorbain said sternly. "That man wasn't grinning. One thing you can say about these Hindus, there's not a coward in the lot. Don't start throwing your weight around among the Hindus, Mason. We're apt to have trouble with them as it is. Come aboard."

They filed from the launch, Agent X last of all, through the hatch and down the steel ladder into the belly of the sub. Gorham and the man in the khaki pants remained in the conning tower, Gorham battening the hatch. Evidently the ship was ready for immediate submersion.

X took a quick look around the conning tower, saw that the controls and fathometers were of the most modern type. He felt certain that Don Selwick had done his best in repairing this ill-fated submarine that had been built for Chile and was now in the hands of Satan. Her most vulnerable spot would be the electric motors which would be cut in in place of the gasoline motors when the vessel was submerged. He intended to get aft to the engine room at once. There, a wrench thrust through a motor housing and into the whirling armature of a motor should cripple the further advance of the sub.

But on the way from the conning tower, Pudge Mason grabbed him by the arm. "For'ard torpedo room, 'eathen. Need a man of your muscle to 'elp rack a white-'ead."

X WAS led through a short companionway into the crew quarters. There, crouched over a small table, was Dal Rama, still wearing his turban and rusty black suit. On the other side of the table stood a man wearing white linen. His face was covered with a curtained domino mask. Though X could not see the man's face, he was certain that he was the same man whom he had seen in the basement of the Golden Lotus Café. The masked man was pointing out a spot on a chart spread out on the table, and saying to Dal Rama:

"Here is our present location. Here, we expect to cross the path of the Japanese vessel, put a torpedo into her. Gilbert Marden, your enemy, will be on board that ship. It is he who has the rest of the corpse-hands from the sacred girdle of Kali. He will be justly punished."

Dal Rama rubbed his hands. A hellish smile spread over his corpselike face. "Yes, *sahib*."

"Mason," the masked man snapped as the cockney and X were about to pass.

"Yes, boss?" Mason said.

"You and those three drunken louts you just shipped will be enough to handle the torpedoing. Let your three men do the muscle work. This Hindu understands engines. We're short handed. Gorham says we can use this man—" nodding at X— "as an oiler." To X he snapped. "Aft to the engine room. Take orders from Gorham or Maitland or myself. No one else."

"I beg your pardon, *sahib*," Dal Rama said, "but Langa Doonh is first of all my servant."

The masked man tapped the steel floor impatiently, with his foot. "Of course, but our wishes are in accord, are they not?"

Dal Rama nodded. "To a certain extent. My quarrel is with those who have laid unclean eyes upon the Sacred Girdle of Kali, and with them alone. Langa Doonh, my orders shall take precedence over all others. Go to the engine room."

X bowed. Nothing could be sweeter. He could do more damage there than anywhere on the sub. He turned, started back. Passing the entrance to the conning tower, he heard the voice of Rex Gorham ordering his assistant to admit ballast. The sub was going under to lie in wait for her prey.

Gorham came clattering down from the conning tower, followed X toward the engine room for a final check with the men in charge. X respectfully stepped aside to one of the steel bulkheads to allow Gorham to pass along the narrow way. Gorham nodded. "Go ahead," he said. "I have scruples about just whose eyes are watching my back."

As X, unmindful for a moment of the fact that he was wearing a turban, stepped away from the bulkhead to obey, the none too secure turban on his head caught on a steel hook suspended from above. His hand went up quickly, but not quick enough to prevent the unwinding of a portion of the turban—not quick enough to cover an unshaved portion of his head. Knowing immediately that the watchful Gorham must now realize that he was no more a Hindu than Gorham was, X started to turn around; started to reach for the knife at his waist. But Gorham had jumped forward instantly to bring the barrel of an automatic crashing down on the Agent's skull.

All the world became sky. And the sky was studded with spinning balls of fire. A roar that might have accompanied the destruction of the universe filled the Agent's brain as he sank to the floor.

HOW LONG he remained unconscious, X had ho idea. He knew only that coming to was like awakening to find that a nightmare had turned into a reality. Not once did his own dangerous position cross his mind. Not once did he think how thankful he should be that he wasn't dead. There was nothing in his mind but the sickening realization that he might be too late to save his country.

And then he began to take in his surroundings. He was in the submarine galley, lying on the floor, his legs roped from knees to ankles, his arms lashed from elbow to wrist. But his hands were bound in front of him. There was just a chance— His hopes vanished in a flash as the door of the galley opened slowly. He dropped his eyelids nearly closed and lay perfectly still.

At first he could see nothing against the dim outline of the door. And then he caught the white flash of eyes not more than two feet from the door. One of Dal Rama's dacoits was crawling toward him on hands and knees, a knife in his hand. A rescuer? X hardly dared hope the man was that.

He heard the rapid, steady breathing of the dacoit. The creeping man's shadow fell across the Agent's face. He opened one eye slightly. The dacoit's scrawny hand extended carefully, took hold of the fingers of the Agent's right hand. In the dim light, the Hindu's knife flashed upward, and X knew that in the fanatic's kill-crazed mind was the same design for murder that had doomed Selwick and Barry Lane. He intended to cut off the Agent's hand.

As the knife descended, the Agent's bound arms moved upward, both hands open to seize the wrist of the dacoit. The pressure of X's steel fingers brought a wince of pain from the Hindu. Then, as X's fingers dug deep into the hollow between the tendons at the dacoit's wrist, the Hindu let the knife drop from his fingers. The knife slid along the floor to within a few inches of X's head. The dacoit's inflamed eyes followed it. And X immediately relaxed his grip, for he knew the dacoit's next move even before the brown man realized it himself.

As the dacoit clawed out for the knife, his throat came within easy reach of the Agent's bound hands. Again X's fingers clamped, this time on the dacoit's windpipe. He pushed out and upward with his bound arms, partially lifting the squirming body of the Hindu, never relaxing his stranglehold for a second.

Gradually the man's struggles became more feeble. Finally they ceased altogether, and he hung, a dead weight, in the Agent's hands. X flung the fanatic aside, rolled over, got hold of the knife with his two hands. He sat up, slashed through the ropes that bound his legs. Then he reversed the position of the knife, worked its blade back and forth to saw through the cords at his wrists. Another moment to chafe his legs until he felt the tingle of blood in them again, and he got to his feet.

He moved cautiously to the door of the galley and out into a narrow companionway. In the crew quarters, he could hear the muffled voice of the masked man shouting orders up into the conning tower. "Bring her around, Gorham. Signal the forward torpedo room to make ready. As soon as you strike the Jap, dive and run for it! That'll do the trick." And this man who made wars single-handed uttered an evil laugh.

X stepped forward. On his lips was a fervent prayer for a little more time. He had to get to the torpedo room to check these orders—even if he had to kill Pudge Mason and his torpedo crew. It was now or never—the life of a few or the lives of thousands. The Agent's teeth clenched. He gripped the hasp of his knife....

CHAPTER IX

HELL BELOW

RONALD HOLME HAD never seen a more welcome sight than the low, gray deck of the submarine chaser when he hailed it from the deck of the cruiser. In mid-channel he boarded her, while members of the crew helped Janet Lane aboard. The girl had recovered consciousness, but she moved as though in a stupor as she was taken to the captain's quarters.

Holme stood on deck after boarding, his nervous tension relaxed somewhat by the assuring sight of twin depth-bomb catapults, looking like giant's slingshots against the late afternoon sky. Tersely he explained the situation to the commander.

"The renegade submarine will be in the shipping lane used by the N.Y.K. ship of Japan. Somewhere between here and Niihua, the sub plans to torpedo the Jap vessel."

"But who owns this submarine?" demanded the captain.

"That," snapped Holme, "is not the question. It is a question, of course, but a detail which is not of the greatest importance. What we must do is prevent the sinking of that Japanese vessel in American waters."

The commander's eyes shadowed beneath the bill of his cap, grew grave. "That would seem as though America were retaliating for various unfortunate accidents to American property in the zone of fighting in the East."

"It would mean war, commander. No apology or reparations would ever turn aside the juggernaut this damned renegade has started rolling. We've got to find that sub before the Jap boat does."

"Right. And sink her."

"And—sink her? Only as a last resort. There's still hope, commander, that the plan may fail because of the interference of our own Secret Agent X."

"What do you mean?"

"I mean that Secret Agent X is going to be on board that submarine. Probably outnumbered ten to one, but that man doesn't know the meaning of impossible."

"But, Mr. Holme, sinking the submarine means—"

Grim jaws clenched on his cigar, Holme said: "You don't think I haven't thought of that. It means that our country loses its greatest single crime-fighting tool. It means death for the man who has been more than my right arm. But if he fails, we must not fail. I know the man's mettle. He'd go down to the bottom with a grin on his face if he knew that he'd succeeded in staving off this impending war."

The commander looked at his watch. "The *Nagoya,* that's the Japanese ship, ought to be sailing now. She's trailed by a destroyer. If the *Nagoya* sinks, that destroyer will unlimber her guns. She could shell Honolulu before much of our fleet could get into action. Wouldn't it be wise to signal Pearl Harbor to have everything in readiness for an immediate battle?"

"Positively not!" Holme cracked. "Have the newspapers get hold of that? Not on your life! That would cinch the business. It's not going that far. That sub isn't going to sink the *Nagoya.* Get a man on your hydrophone. Pick up that sub's direction, and go after her!"

For an hour, the S.C. 86 was the scene of quiet, well-disciplined activity. On the afterdeck, men were busy with racks of spherical depth-bombs. And far below, the expert in charge of direction-finding was seated with his hands on what resembled bicycle handlebars, a pair of head phones clamped to his ears, and watchful eyes on compass and dynamo-frequency indicator.

Holme fidgeted at the direction-finder's elbow, poking him every now and then by way of question.

The man turned: "I can hear the *Nagoya* and the Japanese destroyer quite clearly. They're overhauling us at a smart clip, sir. No sounds of a submersive. The *Nagoya* has a heavy cargo."

"War chemicals, probably," Holme clipped. "Hence the guardian destroyer. You don't think—" He stopped, noticed a sudden tenseness of muscles about the direction-finder's jaw. The man turned to the commander of the subchaser. "There's a fathometer sounding to the northwest."

"What's that?" snapped Holme.

"He means that there's a submarine out there somewhere," the commander said grimly. "She's evidently motionless, sounding out her depth with an instrument for that purpose."

"Submarine's screw turning now, sir," said the direction-finder.

HOLME gripped his head with both hands. "Oh, hell!" he moaned. "I thought for a moment Agent X had— Well, do something about it, can't you? No, don't. Don't do anything till we're sure Agent X is helpless."

"Submarine moving along about fifteen knots," said the man at the hydrophone. "Heading for the *Nagoya*."

"She's sighted what she's going after, and she's going after it!" the commander cried as he sprang to the engine-room telegraph.

The point of his knife jabbed the small of Gorham's back.

Holme scrambled onto the open deck. A thin slice of sun was rapidly sinking. It was like a blot of blood on the western horizon. Smoke from the ships created an artificial range of dark and distant mountains.

To the right of the subchaser and a little behind, the *Nagoya's* clean, white shape cleaved the waves. Beyond her lay the low, gray lines of the Japanese destroyer.

Holme dashed back to the hydrophone. If he could only see what was going on beneath that placid sea. Placid sea? He laughed bitterly.

"Mr. Holme," said the commander gravely, "the sub is maneuvering to torpedo. She's surfacing slightly. We're in an excellent position to drop a depth-bomb. I'm going to signal the afterdeck."

"No!" Holme snapped, his face was chalk-white, his eyes haggard. "My man is on board that submarine. I—I can't give an order like that. I—" He stopped. His fists clenched. "You don't think there's a chance? Not a chance that Agent X could be bringing the craft up?"

"He's going to torpedo that Japanese boat if he is. It's now or never, if we're going to stop this."

Holme's arms dropped limply to his sides. "Go ahead."

For the first time in his sixty years of life, K9 walked like an old man as he stumbled to the deck. In the wake of the boat a geyser of water shot high into the air, spread out like a fan. The ocean twisted and writhed like a tortured, living thing as the first depth-bomb exploded. The subchaser wallowed like a drunken thing from the terrific detonation.

Holme seized the rail in both his hands and hung on to a spinning world. On the I afterdeck the grim order, "Give 'em another," sounded. Holme's lips moved almost imperceptibly.

"Good-bye, Agent X," he muttered....

As Secret Agent X stepped from the little galley into the crew quarters, the man in the khaki pants tumbled down out of the conning tower. "Boss," he shouted to the man in the domino mask, "Subchaser!"

The man in the mask whipped around. "What of it?" he snapped. "I said torpedo. I *meant* torpedo!"

"But the subchaser's in position to bomb—"

"And we are in position to torpedo!" roared the masked man. "Do as I say and be quick about it!"

"Yes, sir."

The man in the khaki pants saluted, turned, met Agent X at the foot of the conning tower. Probably, in the dim light, he thought X one of the Hindus. But not for long. The blow X handed the man, with the hasp of his knife, was a white man's blow to the temple. Gorham's assistant dropped without a groan into the Agent's arms.

X moved with swift, quiet precision to lay the unconscious man behind the conning tower steps. Then his bare feet carried him with silent speed up into the conning tower. Rex Gorham was at the controls, his eye glued to the periscope, his lips at the mouthpiece of the torpedo-room telephone.

"Get ready to torpedo," Gorham said. "When I say air, give it air! Ready—"

The point of X's knife jabbed into the small of Gorham's back. "Give the order to dive, you rotten, traitorous swine. Dive and run, you fool. The second that torpedo is loose, I run this knife through into your heart. Dive, do you understand?"

Gorham turned his head. If ever he had met murder in a man's eyes he saw it now in the gray eyes of Agent X. He turned to the phone. "Hold that torpedo," he said.

"Good!" X rapped. "Now the order is take ballast to thirty fathoms."

Gorham nodded a pale head. His hands went out to levers. The submarine responded immediately. The hand of the depth gauge swung downward, nose first.

From the quarters below sounded the masked man's roar: "What the hell!"

GORHAM swung around, made an effort to snatch up a gun from a small shelf beside him. But the Agent's left fist cannoned up to the point of Gorham's chin, knocking him out.

And then X turned to meet a new peril. The masked man had ducked into the conning tower and out again. He was shouting for men, shouting for Dal Rama's dacoits. Three dark, kill-crazed faces appeared at the door of the conning tower. And behind and above them was the face of Dal Rama.

"Kill that man!" ordered the man in the mask. "He is responsible for the loss of your sacred girdle of Kali!"

The three dacoits moved swiftly into the small room. Agent X held up his empty left hand. "Wait," he said in a low voice. "But a few minutes ago, you were to aid in sinking the Japanese boat because Gilbert Marden was aboard, and it was Marden who was responsible for the loss of the girdle. Now you say I am the man who stole your girdle.

"Does that make sense, Dal Rama? Don't you realize that the man who stole the girdle originally is your supposed friend, the man you call *sahib*? Don't you realize that he sent one of the withered hands to Barry Lane, then told you that Lane had one of the hands, simply so that you would be sure and kill Lane? And he urged you to kill Don Selwick by the same ruse. And all to gain his own ends. He doesn't give the smallest damn about your sacred hands. He wanted Selwick and Lane out of the way, that is all.

"I do not know where your sacred girdle and its remaining hands are at the present time, but I know the man who has them— *the man you call sahib;* the man who would have you aid him in sinking that Japanese vessel. How could you, Dal Rama, regain the sacred girdle if it was on the bottom of the ocean? Or did he tell you that a torpedo sinks a vessel it strikes?"

"I tell you to kill that man!" roared the masked master of the submarine.

And at that moment, the submarine quaked from stern to stem. Men fell over men. Hoarse cries of "Depth-bomb!" rang out from one steel wall to another.

And it was as though the bomb was a signal for warfare within the submarine itself. The dacoits, unable to determine whether it was Agent X or the masked man who was lying, divided themselves into two camps. Some threw themselves upon the masked man to be shot down by his roaring automatic. Others charged into the conning tower at Agent X. X met them with bare fists. Only when his life depended upon it did he use his knife.

As he was locked in a hand to hand struggle near the door of the tower, the second fearful detonation tortured the steel body of the sub, seemed actually to lift it and shake it. X and the dacoits were flung down the steep steel steps, clawing at each other as they tumbled downward. X felt the man beneath him go limp. He pulled his battle-scarred body out of a grip that death had frozen into the dacoit's fingers.

On his feet, X saw that the submarine listed sharply. Somewhere in the ship he could hear a horrible bubbly sound. His heart chilled. Any grave but this; any coffin but a thing of steel, wobbling helplessly to the bottom of the ocean.

He could hear the roar of the masked master, trying to marshal some of the whites to come to his assistance. X started through the companionway, bumped head on into Pudge Mason, white-faced and marble-eyed. Mason tried to draw a gun, but X's quick fingers drew it for him and jabbed it into Mason's fat belly.

"H'it's no time for quibblin', mister!" cried the terrified Mason. "We been 'it, that's wot. 'It astern, and the plates 'ave buckled. She's sinkin' fast!"

"Fast because we're still taking on ballast!" X snapped. "Get up there on the controls. Get those pumps working. Surface like all hell. And steer away from that subchaser, full speed."

MASON darted a frightened glance over his shoulder. "But the boss—"

"Up into the conning tower!" X rapped. "I'll hold them off. You've got about four chances—death at my hands, death from the boss, death from Davy Jones—or a possible chance to live if you can surface this sub. Which do you take?"

"With you to the last bloody trench, sir!" cried the cockney, and he sprang up the conning tower steps in time to escape a volley of shots from the masked man and a handful of loyal followers who were coming up the companionway.

X was hit. One of the slugs had ripped through the flesh of his left shoulder. Yet not so much as a grimace of pain changed the expression of his painted features. He retaliated with two quick shots that found marks, bounded up the steps, crouched at the door to fire two more shots with cold, deliberate aim.

"She's 'oldin' 'er own," breathed the cockney from his position at the controls. " 'Eaven 'elp the pumps. Selwick pumps, that's wot. Got the stuff in 'em!"

"Shut up!" snapped X. "Stick to those controls. The depth gauge is swinging up. We're winning."

"H'I'm stickin'," moaned Mason. "Keep 'em back, for the love of me Lord 'Arry!"

Two men were coming up the steps. X squeezed the trigger of the gun in his hand. An empty click resounded.

"Toss me Gorham's gun. Quick!" he gasped to Mason.

And then as one of the men came through the door, gun poised to kill, X flung the empty automatic from his hand full into the man's face. The man toppled backward. The muzzle of his gun bucked ceiling-ward as it went off. X sprang backward, scooped up Gorham's gun from the floor.

"Eight fathoms," breathed Mason. "And if the subchaser does drop another of them bombs, h'it's to 'ell with as. Seven fathoms! We're makin', sir. 'Old 'em off!"

X staggered to the door of the tower, sent shots crashing down at a handful of retreating men in the companionway below. "Keep her going up, Mason!" he shouted, and clattered down the steel steps to push his vantage to the fullest. The men scattered in front of his well-placed shots that weeded them out, knocking legs out from under them as they ran.

X turned, knocked aside a lunging Hindu who made a half-hearted effort to knife him. The dacoit was already bleeding from a half dozen wounds, still slashing because his drugged brain didn't know when it was dying. And X pattered swiftly forward, into the dim, narrow forward passage. Ahead of him, weaving in and out of the bulkheads, he could see the white coat of the masked master.

He knew what the man was up to. The masked master wanted to cripple the forward pumps. He preferred death in the submarine to disgrace and a far different sort of death that would be his if the craft was successfully surfaced.

X crept up silently, waited until he saw the masked master stoop over a hand-wheel which regulated one of the pump check valves. Then X raised his gun.

"I wouldn't do that," he said softly.

The masked man turned, fired hurriedly. X felt the teeth of the man's slug in his thigh even as he smoothly pulled the trigger of his own gun to shoot the automatic from the masked man's hand.

"You like action," he said in that same deadly, quiet voice. "You have one wound. I have several—"

The masked man lowered his head, charged forward, a bull's bellow on his lips, his arms swinging like windmills. He landed three times blindly on the Agent's muscular shoulders before a quick punch landed on his chin and straightened him up with a grunt. Then X proceeded to wear the man down with lightning-like, but not hard, punches that had the masked man reeling woozily from one side of the catwalk to the other.

X seized him by the collar and dragged him back toward the conning tower.

ON BOARD the subchaser, Ronald Holme's small fingers seemed welded to the rail. He looked out across the now nearly dark water, still heaving from the last of the depth-bombs. The Japanese destroyer had swung around and now lay between the N.Y.K. boat and the subchaser. Holme was suddenly conscious of feverish activity on the deck of the subchaser. He turned haggard eyes, dully watched seamen unlimbering the forward rifles.

"What," he asked sharply, "are you doing there?"

"Captain's orders. That sub is surfacing, out of range of the depth-bombs. We want to be ready in case those aboard show fight."

"Then—then the sub wasn't hit?" Holme gasped incredulously.

"Oh, she was hit, but not bad. Her pumps are pulling her up slowly. Maybe for a surrender, but we can't be sure."

A searchlight cut through the gray of impending night and swept its narrowed sword of light across the water. Holme waited breathlessly as the light weaved back and forth and then lingered on a spot of water that was broken by a gray wedge of steel. The submarine had broken the surface.

The sound came then of the clank of a steel hatch thrown back on the submarine's deck, and a rich, deep voice hallooing: "Subchaser ahoy! We surrender! We surrender. Come aboard!" And following the call was a strange eerie whistle that none about the chaser could possibly have explained except Holme.

Holme plunged his right fist into his left hand. "He's done it!" His lips quivered. "Done it. He's alive. No war. Tell the Japs it was target practice."

He had control of his emotions by the time he boarded the sub with the commander of the subchaser and a portion of the crew. Sailors, armed to the teeth, lined the prisoners up along the wet deck of the sub, dragged out the dead and wounded from below.

Agent X, when he could get his right hand out of the grip of Holme's fingers, gestured toward Pudge Mason. "I recommend a pardon for that man. In the last minute he strung along with me. It was he who surfaced the sub in spite of the leak your depth-bombs made."

"You could recommend him to a position in the executive cabinet and he could have it!" snapped Holme. "Who's the tall Hindu? Who's the man in the mask?"

"The tall Hindu is Dal Rama, guardian of the corpse of hands from the temple of Kali. Someone stole the girdle and brought it to

Honolulu. Dal Rama and his cutthroats followed. And the real thief passed the blame off on certain of his enemies by sending them withered corpse-hands. Then, posing as Dal Rama's friend, he told Dal Rama where those corpse-hands were, so that Dal Rama would kill the masked man's enemies for him. The enemies, of course, were Barry Lane and Selwick, who had made progress in unraveling the masked man's plot."

"But the masked man," Holme persisted.

"Is the man who is supposed to be on that Japanese ship sailing for Yokohama. That was merely to give himself an excuse for getting out of Honolulu. Actually, he went to Egg Island where he had been having the sub reconditioned for the sole purpose of sinking that Japanese vessel in American waters."

"You don't mean— Why, that's impossible. He was in a wheel chair—"

"His leg injury only faked, sir. Just another dodge to divert suspicion. Remember that little statue that Janet Lane broke in Marden's curio room—the one that bore the 'Made in Japan' label? Well, that made me suspicious. The night before, right after dinner, when I was in his mansion in the guise of Regan, your secretary, Marden had promised to show us a particularly gruesome relic from Burma. He wheeled his chair up to a steel cabinet, and naturally we supposed he kept the relic there. But at the unexpected entrance of Dal Rama, he quickly moved to one of the glass cabinets and removed that idol which Janet broke.

"YOU SEE, the gruesome relic was the girdle of corpse-hands that Dal Rama was after. He knew that to show it before Dal Rama meant that Dal Rama's cutthroats would kill him. So he picked up the first thing his hands touched and that happened to be that clay idol Janet broke. Marden told a convincing story, no doubt, concerning the idol. But when the idol was broken, and I saw it was of Japanese origin instead of Indian, I began to think that Marden had not showed us what he had at first intended to, and because he dared not show it in Dal Rama's presence. I could think of nothing except the sacred girdle that would have endangered Marden. Later, when I found out how the masked man was goading Dal Rama and his dacoits on to do his bidding all through faked information about the sacred girdle, I was sure of my man. But under the ocean isn't an opportune place to make an arrest."

Holme craned his neck. "Look! They're taking the mask off the man now. And, by George! It is Marden. And—"

With an unearthly cry, the tall form of Dal Rama lurched forward. A narrow-bladed knife, which he had somehow managed to conceal in spite of the sailor's searching, flicked from his fingers, buried hilt-deep in the back of Gilbert Marden. The millionaire's big body dropped to the wet deck as sailors crowded in around the struggling Dal Rama.

Holme shook his head. "Justice, though. His own double-crossing caught up with him. Marden. *Marden.* It seems incredible."

"Not at all," X contradicted gently. "All the vast fortune that Marden possessed lay in South China. If America had gone to war with Japan, Japan would have had to throw her weight around to meet the American attack. South China would have been saved—and with it Marden's interests. I needn't tell you that that is how wars are made. One man's selfish interests weighed against millions of lives of men who are never told why they are fighting."

From the deck of the submarine, X looked dreamily toward the subchaser. "Myra Silinski's motive was about the same, only she had the interests of her country at heart. If America had become Japan's new opponent, her country, with far greater interests in China than ours, would have looked quietly on. Now—well, who knows?"

"We'd better get back to the subchaser," Holme said. "The doctor will work on those wounds of yours."

"Mere scratches," X said quietly, "There's another aboard the S.C. 86 with a far greater wound. The doctor can't help her much."

"Janet Lane?" Holme darted a shrewd glance at the painted face of Agent X. "I don't know but what you helped her more than anybody else. You made her believe her husband was a far greater hero than he was. She'll never know the truth, I suppose?"

"Not from me. I'll never see her again."

"Sometimes," Holme said, "I wonder if you're quite sensible about some things. But your private life is your own—"

"And," X said flatly, "it is never permitted to interfere with what one might paradoxically refer to as the public life of a secret agent."

BOOK XXXVIII

THE CORPSE
THAT MURDERED

The long, grasping tentacles of the avaricious Golden
God were engulfing the poor-rich of Carrollton
City in a holocaust of death and disaster. And
Agent X, master of a thousand faces and a thousand
daring cases, found that the talons of the Golden
God belonged to a corpse—to an evil cadaver that
lethal weapons of mankind could not conquer.

CHAPTER I

THRUST OF THE SILENT DEATH

HE WAS A small man. His hair lay in waves of silver with the shine of pink scalp showing through. Years of poring over ledgers had rounded his back and bowed his shoulders. He screwed his mouth up when he made tiny blue-inked figures in the ledger. He clenched his knotty fingers about his steel penholder.

In the cone of light that cut down through the darkness from the green-shaded drop-light, he looked like an old gnome. He wasn't so old, though, as tired. His eyes were tired; they had been tired for thirty years.

He had worked hard in the newspaper office. He did nothing glamorous—not reporting, not even rewriting, not bawling out sarcasm like some movie version of a city editor. He did clerical work mostly, handling lots of figures and dollars on paper. And there wasn't any monotony in it for him, because when he was through at the office there were the wife and kids to go home to. The kids— well, he didn't go home to them very often because they were out a lot at night. Good kids, though, those two. Yes, they were really good.

He grinned at the columns of figures as if they, too, knew his kids. George, in college, and Dorothy working up front in the news office at the telephone switchboard.

Carter Leeds uncramped his fingers from the grip of his penholder and shoved the pen into the rusty wire spiral on his desk. He pulled out his watch to see if he could finish in time to go home with Dorothy. Soon she would be relieved by the other switchboard girl. He shook his head. Dorothy was off duty at ten o'clock; it was nearly that now. He wouldn't make it. Young Harkness would, though.

*His fist lashed out with
blurring speed.*

Carter Leeds' tired blue eyes winced as he thought of young Harkness. Tony Harkness had been keeping Dorothy out late pretty regularly these nights.

Carter Leeds drew a long breath and expelled it slowly through his pinched nostrils. That was one of the things you had to take. You had kids and built your life around them. If you were a good dad you kept reminding yourself that the kids wouldn't build their lives around you. This Tony Harkness was a nice boy. He'd probably make Dorothy a good husband. It was just that it seemed to Carter Leeds that he had had Dorothy, the little girl, for so short a time, and then she was Dorothy, the woman.

He couldn't blame Tony Harkness. He couldn't blame any man for falling for Dorothy.

Carter Leeds pushed his steel-rimmed spectacles up onto his forehead and rubbed aching eyelids with his fingers. He stopped rubbing and opened his eyes. The cone of white light, the desk with its neat little woodblock sign reading, *Mr. Leeds, Auditor,* matured out of red haze. He reached for his pen, but didn't pick it up. Instead, he turned his head slightly to the right, ducking it down between his shoulders.

His eyes squinted. Within the base of the cone of light he could see a man's polished oxfords, creased trousers and the edges of coat and vest. The man's head and shoulders were cut off by the sharply defined boundary between blazing white light and what, by contrast, was total darkness.

Carter Leeds pulled his glasses down onto his nose. His lips quirked into an uncertain smile. "You—you startled me," he said in an inoffensive treble voice. He swiveled his chair around, eyes puzzled by that line of demarcation between light and darkness. He liked to see the faces of people he was talking to.

The visitor did not move. He seemed perfectly satisfied with the comparative darkness that masked his features. He said: "Mr. Leeds?" His voice was something like the rattle of crushed stone in a rusty dishpan. "You the Mr. Leeds who's got a son George in college here in town?"

"Why, yes. George Leeds is my son." Leeds smiled. There was something wistful about Leeds' smile when anyone mentioned either of his children. Carter Leeds started to get up, but his visitor pushed out two thick fingers and planted them on Leeds' chest.

"Just keep where you are, Mr. Leeds," the man said;.

"You—you're a friend of George?" Carter Leeds asked doubtfully.

"Friend? Sure. And I don't want to see George get into any trouble, see?"

"Trouble?"

"Yeah. I guess you don't know George has been gambling lately, huh?"

CARTER LEEDS opened his mouth. He didn't say anything. A lot of things whirligigged through his mind. George needing more money for an honorary fraternity assessment; George saying he had lost his slide rule; then the theft of drawing instruments from George's locker. It had all run into quite a little sum he had had to give George lately.

Carter Leeds forced a laugh. "Why, yes. Yes, I knew he had put some money in a pool. They were betting on the outcome of a football game or something. George always tells me everything."

But that was something George hadn't told his dad. Carter Leeds hated to admit his son hadn't told him. But that was it, surely. Most of the boys bet on the outcome of a game. Still, maybe George had gone in for that sort of thing a bit heavily. He needed a lecture on the value of money. That would straighten George out.

The visitor, whose face was masked with darkness, laughed as though he meant it. "This wasn't no football game, Mr. Leeds. We didn't know he misunderstood. I guess maybe he thought it was just marbles for keeps he was playing. We don't want young fellows that can't afford to play coming in with pin money. The other night George lost quite a bit. He gave us a check."

"Check?" Carter Leeds mouthed.

"Yeah. Maybe you'd like to see." The man in the dark fingered out a slip of paper from his pocket and held it down within the cone of light from the drop lamp. Carter Leeds blinked.

"Recognize the signature, Mr. Leeds?" asked the man.

"Why, no. It's my name, but—" Carter Leeds jerked a shallow breath. His lips soundlessly formed one word too terrible to utter: "Forged!"

"Yeah," said the visitor. "You catch on quick. George forged his old man's name to the check, and we took it in good faith."

Carter Leeds extended a trembling hand for the check which was drawn away quickly just out of reach. "Two thousand dollars!" he gasped.

"Yeah. That's what he went down for the other night. Not much when you got it, but he didn't have it. And we always collect, even if it's cigarette money like that."

"Two thousand dollars," Leeds whispered. "Cigarette money?" His eyes squinted, tried to pierce the darkness to see the visitor's face. "There isn't that much in the bank account right now. If you will give me about a week, I can raise it. Then you could put the check through. I—I'll cover it some way."

"That ain't the point," the man said. His words were rattled by a deep-seated chuckle. "The point is that forgery is a crime. You can't just let such things go. If your son got by with it this time, maybe he'd try again. What we'd like to do is just destroy that check." The man put the check back in his pocket. "We don't want to make no trouble, understand?"

"No," said Carter Leeds dully. "Of course. Destroy that check by all means. I'll speak to the boy. I'll cut off his allowance. And I want you to know I am deeply grateful to you for coming to me. And for destroying the check."

"Good," cut in the visitor. "I'm glad to hear that—on account of there'll be a little charge for destroying the check. Say thirty grand."

Carter Leeds glared at that maddening darkness. "Thirty *what?*"

"Grand. Thirty thousand."

"Why—why—" Carter Leeds sprang out of his chair. Two thick fingers shot forward, rammed into his chest, punched him down into the chair.

"I SAID you was to stay in that chair, didn't I?" The visitor's voice had lost all trace of friendliness. "We don't mess around with loose change, see. You come across with the thirty grand or I'm afraid George is going to be a steady boarder in stir. It's going to cost you the thirty grand to beat this rap."

"But thirty thousand dollars! Why, if I sold everything I had and borrowed—why, I couldn't raise half that amount. I wouldn't. I wouldn't do it. Why, it's blackmail!"

"We don't have to call nothing names, Mr. Leeds. What you been doing with the money you've taken in all these years?"

"Why, I've raised a family. I've saved what I could. I've put money into life insurance—"

"Yeah. That's it. Thirty grand in life insurance."

"But I can't touch that," Leeds faltered.

"No. But your widow can. And we're going to collect from your widow, Mr. Leeds. And while you're waiting to take it in the belly, just think what it means to be sent up for forgery. Just think that over."

Carter Leeds stood up. His weak-blue eyes were wide, staring, incredulous. The other man was backing into the shadows. Leeds could not see his face; could not see anything but indistinct blackness of the man's form and the blur of a white face above.

"You—" Carter Leeds whispered. "I know you. You must be— But it's incredible. *Impossible.*"

The shadowy figure moved swiftly. Then something silvery darted like a bird across the darkness. It flashed across the cone of light and came to rest in the breast of Carter Leeds. It was a knife.

Agony twisted Carter Leeds' small body, screwed his face into knots of pain. His ropy, blue-veined fingers clawed ineffectually at his chest. He tottered backward, fell into his chair. He lurched sideways. Only his frantic clutch on the desk kept him in the chair.

His eyes, with the sense of sight dying within them, wandered across the desk to where the pen rested in its wire spiral. He thrust out his right arm, inch by inch across the desk top. The ledger dropped to the floor. He was trying to reach the pen. He had to tell, had to talk with the pen after—after he was dead. There must be some record for the police, something to tell them—

The earth up-ended, threatened to hurl him into a swirling vortex of cold, gray mist. His fingers clutched convulsively on something he could not see. Yet the sense of touch told him what it was, and he clung to it. Perhaps they would know. Perhaps—

Carter Leeds tumbled out of the chair, into the cold, gray mist, dead....

Beyond the quiet of the auditor's room where Carter Leeds lay dead, was the front office of the Carrollton City *Clarion*. The door of the office opened and a man came in off the street. He was actually a person of commanding physical proportions. Yet his strength was effectually concealed by his choice of subdued gray tones in suit and topcoat. There was nothing remarkable in the formation of his features. He was one of those persons neither handsome nor otherwise; the kind of a man readily lost in a room containing half a dozen other men.

He had, however, one dominating feature which all his crafty ability in the way of self-effacement could not conceal—his eyes. They were gray in color, sometimes clear, soft and kindly; and again they attained an unfathomable quality as though they were machined from hematite. But always they were shrewd, inquiring, thrusting, hypnotic in their power.

But a short while before, those eyes had looked down upon Carrollton City with its picturesque hills, its landscaped Carroll University Campus, almost as a scientist might view some biological specimen. Those eyes had probed beneath the peaceful exterior and seen an ugly cancer of organized crime. Here a master hand, clad with a glove of iron, had whipped lawlessness into a hideous Gargantuan form. A thing to be feared by a nation, but a thing unseen save by the ubiquitous gray eyes of Secret Agent X.

WHEN crime lords war among themselves, they are dangerous. But Agent X knew that where underworld warfare ceased, organized crime began; and there, danger increased at a remarkable ratio. Once the crime lords learned what united strength could do, who knew where they would stop?

Frequently X had met such master criminals bent on organizing their weaker colleagues into an underworld army. And almost single-handed he had conquered them. But here was something new. Here murder struck and struck again; not at the wealthy, but at the vast group of patient, middle-class families who collectively controlled the bulk of the nation's riches.

To Harvey Bates, the Secret Agent's key man, Carrollton City had been the location of a veritable epidemic of murders and suicides—all without singleness of motive.[1] Puzzled, he had radiographed his chief. His message had reached the Agent in Honolulu. As always, X had answered that call for aid, and this time he found something more grave than murder.

Carrollton City's underworld was alive with whisperings, and X had listened. There was talk of a nameless leader among criminals. A man who pointed the way of nefarious enterprise, a being who lived and killed to tap one of the richest sources of gold in the world—who called himself the Golden God. And to suppose that that man, whose ambition compelled him to deify himself, would be satisfied with the control of a single city, was preposterous. The thirst for power is a drunkard's thirst. Carrollton City was but a stone cast in a quiet pond; the ripples from that stone would be far-reaching—if the Golden God remained unchecked.

Agent X allowed his gray eyes to travel across the newspaper office where the night force was hard at work at typewriters. News? These men knew not what they wrote. They wrote of murder, something they could see. But they neglected the invisible, overwhelming presence of the being behind the murder—the Golden God.

"Something I can do for you, sir?"

The Agent turned sharply toward a telephone switchboard at the right of the door. A girl was at the board—a petite, dark-haired girl with eyes that matched the happy sparkle of her voice.

X lifted his hat, smiled slightly. "I wonder if it would be possible for me to have a look at the newspaper morgue? I—" He went to the switchboard, took credentials from his pocket which identified him as a member of the F.B.I. The girl's eyes widened.

"Of course!" she said. "I'll have someone show you— No, there's my relief just coming in. I'm off duty now. I'd consider it a privilege to show you there myself."

---

1   AUTHOR'S NOTE: Readers may remember Harvey Bates as the most trusted lieutenant in the Secret Agent's network of operatives. His capability had obtained for him the high commanding rank in the Agent's organization during its chief's absence in Hawaii as narrated in "Claws of the Corpse Cult."

"Please do," X said quietly. And as the girl stood up he touched her on the shoulder, "No mention of my official capacity," X whispered. "None at all, if you please." [2]

The girl smiled. "I've always wanted to see if I could keep an important secret." She pushed open the gate of the waist-high fence that enclosed the office. X followed her between rows of desks and through a door at the back of the room. "Any particular item or personage you were interested in?" she asked.

"Yes," X replied. "A man by the name of John Sine. He died in prison some time ago. Was a native of this city."

The girl bobbed her head. "We've loads about him. He was sort of a local boy who made good in a bad way, so naturally we've got reams of material. He committed suicide in prison, didn't he? Took cyanide or something like that. Always interested me—" She paused a moment, waved her hand toward a lighted office door on the other side of the hall. The door was marked *Auditor*.

"That's my daddy in there," she said proudly. "Working his eyes out."

"Really?" asked X pleasantly. "Quite a—" The gray eyes narrowed as they reached the door of the auditor's office, saw through the clean glass into the room beyond. He saw a cone of white light which enveloped a desk and an empty chair. Empty save for a single white hand and arm which lay limply across the seat of the chair. It was something that the girl, because of her short stature, could not see.

"What were you saying?" she prompted. She paused with her hand on the knob of the door at the end of the hall and was looking over her shoulder.

"Quite a family of newspaper people," X said quickly. "This the morgue?"

The girl nodded.

"Then," X said, "you just run on back. I'll find everything nicely. Thanks. You have been most kind."

"All right," said the girl. "I'm in a sort of a hurry. I am expecting someone to meet me."

---

2   AUTHOR'S NOTE: *Secret Agent X is not an official member of the F.B.I. or any recognized law enforcement body. He has no sponsor except that of a certain Washington official who prefers to be known as K9. Through this medium X has obtained a number of credentials which permit him to impersonate federal officers.*

X smiled, his eyes appraising the girl's pretty face and figure. "No doubt of that."

THE GIRL flushed, and left him. X waited only until the door had closed behind her. Then he walked swiftly to the lighted door marked *Auditor* and looked in. A man, a pool of blood, a knife, his brain swiftly catalogued; the tiny girl's dad, murdered.

X shouldered through the door and into the room. He dropped on one knee beside the huddled form of the gray-haired, tired-looking man. He pressed one finger lightly to the man's right wrist, found no pulse, noticed something strikingly peculiar. In the man's right hand was one of those woodblock signs such as are placed on desks for identification. This sign read: *Mr. Leeds, Auditor.* It was like an epitaph.

Agent X gloved his fingers with his handkerchief and pulled the knife from Carter Leeds' chest. He stood up, held the knife close to the light. It was narrow-bladed, razor-sharp, perfectly balanced. As he stared at the knife and then back at the man on the floor, a far-away look came into the Agent's eyes. He thought of this dead man's daughter, heard her gay voice say: "That's my daddy in there."

Her daddy—this mild, meek, hard-worked man. Her daddy—this corpse....

A whisper of sound behind him. X had no time to turn before a heavy body cannoned into him. Long arms whipped around his neck. The full weight of a man's body bowled him over. The knife dropped from his hand. Both his hands slapped sharply like a gun report as they struck the top of the desk flatly. For a moment he was pinioned to the desk top by sheer weight. Then every agile muscle of his body came into play as he twisted over, rolled both himself and his opponent from the desk to the floor. They hit the floor, X on top, lungs of the man beneath emptying explosively.

The clumsy grip around X's throat relaxed. X squirmed over, jerked his head out of the way of a desperate blow from his winded assailant's right fist. He crouched an instant beside the man, then hopped back upon him, jamming his knees against the man's shoulder. His left hand hooked to the man's tie-less collar, his right hand balled threateningly.

Red-faced, gasping, the man on the floor glared up at him. He wore overalls, a blue denim shirt. His hair was red and snarled. He looked Irish.

"What's the big idea?" X asked. His mild voice, by comparison, emphasized the threat in his eyes.

"That's what I'll be after findin' out myself," panted the red-faced man. "I'm a janitor here, and when I see one man bendin' over another with a bloody knife in his hand, I don't have to ask me mother is it murderin' that's been goin' on."

"Faith, and you don't," X mocked. "But you might ask your mother whether that determines the guilt of the man with the knife."

"It's good enough for me," said the janitor. "Who are you and what are you up to, I'd like to know."

Again X produced his wallet and the card which identified him as an F.B.I. man.

The janitor's heavy jaw sagged, "Why didn't you say so in the first place? Let loose of me, will you?"

X released his grip, rose. The janitor stood up, wiping his hands on the seat of his overalls. He looked down at the corpse on the floor. "Dead, is he?"

X nodded.

The janitor took out a handkerchief and dabbed at his eyes. "And not a better man in this world or the next. Mr. Carter Leeds hadn't an enemy in the world. Now it's dead he is. Murdered!"

"Your job is to get in touch with the local police," X said quietly. "And do so from a phone outside this building. I'm thinking of the girl. It will go hard with her. Someone who can break the news gently to her will have to tell her."

"I'm thinkin' of the little girl meself. She that was so devoted to her pa. I'll not breathe a word of this to her. I wouldn't be the one to break her heart if I was being paid for it."

"Then go get the police," X ordered. He followed the janitor from the room. Instead of going to the back door of the newspaper building as the janitor did, X went out the way he had come.

In the front office, he saw Carter Leeds' daughter standing talking and laughing with a tall, grave-looking young man who wore thick-leased glasses. His beak of a nose lent something comical to his otherwise serious demeanor. His mouth was rather small, puckered as though he were tasting tea. He struck X as being a peculiar sort of hybrid with the body of a Greek athlete and the face of a potential college professor.

As X approached, he heard Carter Leeds' daughter say: "Anyway, Tony, whether it's a show or a dance, I've got to have my coat. I'll be ready in a moment." She turned, ran into a small room off the office.

X went up to the young man with the grave face. "Tony," he said in that same quiet voice, "I don't happen to know your last name."

The young man gave him a shrewd glance. "Harkness," he supplied. "And you?"

"Brown will do," X replied. "You are a friend of Miss Leeds?"

Tony Harkness nodded. His eyes half closed when he nodded. "I've known Dorothy for a long time."

"Then I'd like to speak with you outside." X placed a hand on young Harkness' shoulder and walked him through the door and out into the street. "That kid is in for one hell of a shock, Harkness," he said confidently. "Her dad has just died."

"Died? Carter Leeds?" Harkness gasped. "You can't mean it!"

"In fact, he was murdered," X said. "I'm leaving you the unpleasant task of breaking the news to Dorothy. You look like the sort to make it as easy as possible. The police have been informed. Keep the girl away from the body."

"But, Mr. Brown—" Harkness began.

"That's all," X said. "I'm going to be rather busy. Good night. Take care of the girl."

X stepped from the curb into the street. He crossed the street, eyes on the single lighted window of the office building opposite the news office. Black letters across the window read:

FRED ARCHER DETECTIVE AGENCY

Agent X entered the stairs leading up to that office.

CHAPTER II

CHALLENGE TO
THE GOLDEN GOD

MR. FRED ARCHER was not embarrassed, though there was lipstick on his mouth and a gorgeous red-haired girl on his knee. At that moment Agent X entered the office. Archer lifted the girl to her feet and whispered: "Customer, Miss Cromer."

Miss Cromer was tall, almost slender enough to be lanky. She had eyes that were greenish-blue and lustrous, lips that had been slightly smudged. Her carefully arched eyebrows gave her a look of habitual wonder. She wasn't pretty. She was, rather, beautiful, amazingly so inasmuch as the exact reason for her attractiveness was difficult to define.

Archer was of about the Agent's own height and build. He was dressed to emphasize the breadth of his shoulders. He had a face that was like an inverted ace of spades. A wide forehead with a forelock of black hair cleaving it in the center, a sharp chin, slanting brows above dark, narrow eyes. His nose was large, straight, rather bulbous at its tip. He had a deep, very husky voice.

There was a half-filled bottle of rye on his desk and a couple of paper cups. Cigarette butts were methodically arranged about the circumference of a bronze ash-tray.

The redhead withdrew to a mirror in one corner of the room to do things to her hair and lips. Archer ground the heels of his palms together. X reflected that it was remarkable to find so charming a smile on a face that resembled Satan's.

He had learned a little about Archer. He was fairly honest but also greedy. He had the knack of making the local police look foolish and was, therefore, not popular with them. He was apparently on the best of terms with certain underworld leaders and for that reason he was a little feared by them; for he was obviously a man who knew too much, who hadn't talked yet, but might almost any time.

"What can I do for you this time of night?" asked Archer.

"I don't know," X said. "That's why I'm here to find out." He introduced himself as Arthur Brown, shook hands with Archer.

Archer said: "That'll be all tonight, Miss Cromer." He opened the door of his consultation room at the back and waved X to enter. Archer started to follow, retraced his steps, picked up a bottle of rye and a couple of fresh paper cups.

"Women are funny," Archer said. He gestured with the bottle toward the door that had just closed behind Mies Cromer. "You take Jane Cromer, my secretary—"

"I'd be delighted to," X said seriously, "but some other time. Carter Leeds has just been murdered."

"So?" Archer exhibited no surprise. He poured whiskey into the paper cape. "Someone I ought to know?"

"The auditor on the paper across the street," X said, dropping into the chair toward which Archer waved.

"Oh, another one of those," Archer said. He handed X one of the cups. "You know, Mr. Brown, no one interesting ever gets murdered these days. Used to be able to say—" Fred Archer sat down at his desk and drank—"you used to be able to say no nice person gets himself murdered. How, it's different. Take this Leeds. He's probably a man making twenty-five to thirty hundred dollars a year, got a family, no skeletons in the closet, sticks to his wife. And what happens? He's murdered. No reason."

"There is always a reason for murder," X contradicted quietly.

Archer shrugged. "Okay. Name one reason for these murders that have been going on around here recently. Comparatively poor people getting knocked off. You name a reason."

"Perhaps the Golden God has a reason."

THE AGENT'S gray eyes watched Archer closely. Except for a tightening of the lips, Archer's face remained unaltered. He studiously said nothing. His dark eyes expressed nothing. For fully thirty seconds, X remained silent. And so did Fred Archer.

"I was wondering, the other day," X began at length, "about the suicide of Joe Sine, the forger. He killed himself up at the state pen, you remember. He took cyanide poison, and no one ever got a clear idea of where he could have obtained the poison."

"What's that got to do with all this—this murder of Leads, for instance?" Archer asked. His eyes, X thought, were slightly hostile.

"I don't know. I was in hopes you could enlighten me. Previous to Sine's death, there wasn't a whole lot of crime in Carrollton City. But within one week following Sine's death, other sudden and violent deaths occurred here. There's been a steady string of them. I wonder if, previous to Sine's death, you ever heard anything about the Golden God? What do you know about that person, anyway? Have you ever seen him?"

Archer's face darkened. His jaws clenched. He stood up, towered over the seated Agent. His clenched fists rested on the desk top.

"Who the hell are you, mister? And what's the idea of putting me through this catechism?" Then the clenched fists, the jaw muscles relaxed. Archer's lips smiled.

"Look here, Brown," he addressed the Agent, "you put me in a spot. Here you are, a prospective client, I take it I'm supposed to impress you with my detective ability. If I say I don't know of this Golden God, you, as a prospective client, may lose faith in my ability. If I say. 'Sure, the Golden God and I are like that,' how the hell can I be certain I'm not speaking to the Golden God right now?"

The gray eyes of Agent X met Archer's shrewd eyes steadily. "All right. How do I know that I'm not addressing the Golden God?"

Archer laughed. When he was through laughing, he poured another drink. He lighted a cigarette. "Listen, Brown, you've been down to the police headquarters talking with the boys down there."

"I have not," X said. "What makes you say that?"

Archer shrugged. "Because down at headquarters I'm apt to be called anything, even the Golden God. Listen, those flatfeet have framed me so often I'm beginning to feel like Whistler's Mother. They don't like me. Now this Golden God—I hadn't even heard of such a thing until about a month ago.

"Then I got wind of a story that was going around. Somebody had got in with Al Curzon, Steve Lannigan and other toughs in this town. That somebody had formed a sort of criminal's union. The idea behind the scheme was to unionize all the crime in the country.

"How far that union has spread, I don't know. Personally, I don't think the Golden God's power goes beyond this town. Not yet. I hit the 'yet' hard, for I happen to know that this Golden God is somebody. Boys like Al Curzon aren't paying a big per cent of their total take to the Golden God for nothing. It means the Golden God offers them either protection or some big new racket. Maybe both. I don't know."

Archer took a long drag on his cigarette. He shook his head. "Damned if I know why I've been shooting off my face. Drinking too much. Anyway, you've got everything I know about the Golden God. When I first heard about him or it, I started to do a little investigating. I didn't get to first base before I was knocked out of bed one night by the damnedest racket. It was a bell ringing. For a long time, I couldn't locate the bell. Then I found it enclosed in a cake of ice in my refrigerator. Sounds screwy?"

He paused, studied X's face for some reaction. But none was forthcoming. "Well, the whole device was so hellishly clever, see? It was enclosed in a white glass container in the center of the cake of ice. When I took it apart after breaking the ice, I saw it was a complete bomb. Not a detail missing except the explosive. In place of the T.N.T. there was this bell and a message. The message read: 'See how easily I can kill you any time you get in my way.' "

Archer put down his cigarette carefully on the edge of an ash-tray. "So," he concluded. "I am the Three Wise Monkeys; I hear no evil, speak no evil, see no evil—about the Golden God."

Archer's phone rang. He regarded the instrument moodily for a moment. Then he jerked to his feet, excused himself. He went out into the outer office to take the call on the extension phone out there, obviously to avoid X overhearing.

BUT NO sooner had Archer closed the door than X had his hand on the phone in Archer's consultation room. And when he heard Archer remove the receiver in the outer office, X promptly removed the receiver of the phone in his hand. He listened closely.

"Listen. Archer," said a voice that was scarcely more than a whisper, "we don't know what you're up to, but we don't like it. You keep your nose out of things and keep those stool-pigeon cops of yours out also. The Golden God doesn't want to have any trouble with you."

"Now, listen—" Archer's voice had a noticeable quiver in it.

"You're doing the listening, Archer. My advice is to grab a rattler and get out of town. The Golden God—"

The whispering voice didn't finish, because Archer's voice cut in, husky but steady. Steady, because it came from the lips of Secret Agent X!" [3]

"To hell with the Golden God," X roared into the phone. "And you tell him I said so, too!"

In the outer office Archer broke the connection. As X hung up, the private detective burst through the door, his face black with rage, his slanting brows almost meeting in a scowl, his fists clenched.

X regarded him mildly. "Something wrong?" he inquired.

"Wrong?" Archer brought his fist down on the desk top, making the paper cups dance. "Why, damn you, what was the idea? Don't you know what you've done? Slapped the face of this guy who calls himself the Golden God. How was that bird on the phone to know X wasn't yelling that? I might as well order flowers. Why, you lousy meddler, I'm going to break your skull. I'm going—"

Archer stopped, he bent over his desk, his face close to the Agent's. "Fer hell's sake, say something before you start choking on your teeth."

"Before who starts choking on whose teeth?" X asked. His voice had lowered a pitch, had become husky; it was, in fact, like an echo of Archer's own voice. "You don't have to worry about the Golden God, Archer. You just won't be around when hell starts popping."

For no sooner had X heard the whispered warning over the phone than he was determined to impersonate Fred Archer. For some reason, the Golden God had the idea that Archer was dangerous to his welfare. He would, after the insult X had hurled at him over the phone, make some sort of a move to intimidate or perhaps kill Archer. And when that move was made, Agent X wanted to be ready to take anything the Golden God could hand out—and return it with interest.

---

3   AUTHOR'S NOTE: *One of Agent X's most remarkable gifts is his ability to impersonate any male voice after he has heard it even for a short time. Without this gift, his skill as a makeup artist would be of little use to him. Having a naturally flexible voice, rigorous training and long practice have enabled him to achieve these deceptive vocal effects.*

CHAPTER III

TWO TOUGH EGGS

AGENT X STOOD up slowly. The movement was deception itself, for it prepared Archer for the surprise to come. Archer dropped both hands on X's shoulders, probably with the idea of turning him around and kicking him out of the office. The effect of Archer's effort was something like tossing a lighted match into a tank of gasoline. For the tall, inoffensive man that X appeared to be, suddenly exploded.

His left fist pounded into Archer's hard-muscled middle. Archer's hand dropped, his body hinging forward from the waist. That brought his chin to the terminal of a fast-traveling right uppercut that knocked the private detective out on his feet.

Archer didn't hit the floor. X caught him, let him come down easily into the chair at the desk. Then X walked to the door of the consultation room, closed and locked it. From the inner pocket of his coat, he took out a flat leather case which contained his miracle-producing makeup material.

The cover of the case became a triple folding mirror which enabled X to view all angles of his own face clearly. Tubes, held into the lining of the case by loops, contained plastic volatile material. Then there were pigments for tinting the volatile material to resemble any sort of coloring. And finally, metal face plates to aid in the simulation of facial contours.

For moments after applying the plastic volatile material over the inconspicuous features he had already assumed, the Agent was virtually faceless. Then gradually the hopeless-looking mass of flesh-colored substance began to assume definite shape. Like a skilled sculptor X worked, glancing at his model, the unconscious Archer, and then into the mirror.

Then, when his face was like a pale death mask of Fred Archer, he added pigment to simulate Archer's deep coloring, subtle touches of wrinkles were added, and then shadows that gave his face perspective. As a final touch, he removed the gray toupée that had been a part of his disguise as Arthur Brown. In its place he put another toupée of black hair over his own brown hair. An application of pomade, a deft snip here and there with scissors, and he duplicated the forelock that cleft Archer's forehead.

His next move was to change clothes with Archer. The private detective's suit fitted him perfectly. Then, from a kit of special medicines he carried in his pocket, X took a loaded hypodermic needle. The injection of narcotic he gave Archer would keep him quiet for a long time.

X's makeup and medical kits he hid and locked in a drawer of Archer's desk. The gas gun X so often employed, he replaced with Archer's own automatic—a short-nosed .32 with a large magazine capacity. Archer's weapons, Archer's voice, Archer's appearance, and Archer's little habits—equipment that made Agent X virtually Archer himself. But an Archer of intrepid courage and far greater ability.

He had hardly time to thrust the unconscious private detective into a closet that opened off the consultation room before there was a knock at the door. X pushed over the latch, opened the door. In walked Jane Cromer, Archer's redheaded secretary.

Jane took a quick look around the consultation room, "That guy's gone?" she asked breathlessly.

She had evidently satisfied herself that the "guy" was gone, for she put both arms around the Agent's neck and drew his head down close.

"Listen, Freddy," she said, "you got to cut it out."

"What?" X asked huskily. Archer's smile played about his lips. "Cut out anything but you, baby. What's got into those eyes of yours? They look like you've been seeing ghouls."

Her bright-blue eyes searched his face. If his makeup could withstand such scrutiny it was good indeed.

"You know what I mean," she said earnestly. "You've been ribbing Al Curzon again. Haven't I told you to let dynamite alone? You get it into that head that you belong to me, see? If I ever get you in front of a church altar, I want you in a tux and me with flowers and a veil. But the chances are that you'll be wearing a wooden kimono. You should have seen what's just coming into the build-

*As the gun came up, the
Agent's fingers locked on
the man's wrist, forced the
barrel toward the floor.*

ing. A couple of toughs, and one of them looks like one of Curzon's torpedoes. Freddy—"

Somebody knocked at the door of the outer office. Jane Cromer bit her lower lip. "See?" she whispered.

"Sure," X said. "You're wonderful." He took hold of her arms and brought them straight down to her sides. "Quit worrying, baby. I'll handle this."

He stepped to Archer's desk, opened a drawer, took out a leather-covered sap. "You open the door, baby," he said quietly. "Two of them, you say? We'll talk with one—the second one through the door. Ready?"

The redhead nodded. "If you say so, but I think you're a dope."

"Dope? Think I'm going to take it sitting down—"

THE KNOCK came again. They went quickly into the outer office. X took his place, flat against the wall beside the door. Jane faced the door, took a long breath, reached out, grabbed the knob. The door opened a little way.

There was something about Jane Cromer that drew men's eyes in her direction—something that was indefinable but potent. This man who shouldered through the door was looking at Jane when he should have been taking care of his skull. Perhaps he relied upon his black derby to take care of his skull. Agent X noticed little about the man who entered, except the derby.

He brought the sap down squarely on the top of the hard hat. The derby went around in a wavering circle with its owner staggering beneath its broken crown. Then derby and wearer settled uncertainly to the floor. The second tough cursed, took a quick step backward, and reached toward his shoulder for his gat.

At that moment X stepped into the open door and in front of Jane. He said: "You walking in or going out—in the dead wagon?" He had Archer's gun in his right hand to make that something more than a suggestion.

The second tough, a tall, dried weed of a man, seemed to be worried about the destination of his hand. It fumbled around the lower button of his ill-fitting suit coat and then dropped to his side.

"Well," said X, "make up your mind, if any."

The tall man angled into the room. X planted the snout of the automatic against the man's vest and told him to put his hands up. Then he tossed aside the leather sap and employed his left hand in a quick frisk of the man's pockets. His search revealed a .45 gat and a pair of brass knucks.

X grinned, held up the brass knucks and tinkled them on his finger. "Look, sweetheart," he said to Jane, "we were in for a beating up. A sort of face lifting at the hands of this plastic surgeon. Some other day, maybe."

"Listen, mug—" the thin man had an exceptionally deep voice— "who do you think you are, socking my pal? Me and Bakers got plenty of weight behind us. A smart guy would cut his throat and forget this."

"Plenty of weight, eh?" X husked. "The Golden God sent you, I suppose."

"Yeah," growled the lean man, "and you'd better watch out who you're telling to go where. We was sent up here to give you a lesson—"

The Agent brought the automatic in his hand up in a swift arc to slap the thin man in the temple with the side of the barrel. The thin man broke like a toothpick and hit the floor with a bony sound. X immediately sprang sidewise, whirled, dived straight at the owner of the derby whom he had supposed to be unconscious.

Out of the corner of his eye, X had detected the man in the derby in motion—motion that demanded immediate action. For the man in the derby was making a try for his revolver. A short time later, X discovered why the man in the derby had not stayed out for the count—there was a skull-protecting steel plate inside the derby hat. But at the moment he was fully occupied in getting hold of and controlling the man's gun hand.

The man had attempted to sneak out his gun while lying at full length on the floor. As soon as he realized his deception was detected he had scrambled to his knees and yanked out his gun. As the gun came up, the Agent's fingers locked on his wrist, forced the barrel toward the floor. His little finger wedged in against the cylinder of the revolver and the gun frame, preventing the man from pulling the trigger. He tried to tear the man from the gun by sending a short left jab to the man's middle. But the owner of the derby retaliated by trying to kick off X's right kneecap.

A SWIFT change of tactics, and X forced the man's right arm back and up in a wrestler's hammerlock. The painful hold drew sweat out on the man's brow and from his lips a hoarse, "You're bustin' my arm." Then he dropped the revolver, and X hauled the man to his feet.

The man in the derby carried quite a bit of weight around the shoulders. He was short. His head was shaped like a tangerine, as though too many people had tried to flatten his skull. He had a wide mouth, the jerky eyes of a dope fiend.

X turned his head toward Jane. "Kick that chair over here, sweetheart, and we'll teach this ape how to sit down." To the man in the derby he said: "Your name's Bokers?"

"So what?"

Jane pushed the chair over and X shoved Bokers into it. X indicated the thin man on the floor. "Your pal's out for a long time. That makes you the spokesman for the team. Get busy and talk."

Bokers sniffed. "Well, what do you think of the political situation, dick?"

X smiled unpleasantly. "Not half as bad as your situation. I want to know who you are and who your boss is."

"He's one of Al Curzon's boys, like I said, Freddy," Jane Cromer put in.

Bokers sneered. "Sure, dick, listen to the dame. She'll talk and I won't. I've had better dicks than you work on me for hours and get the same results you've got up to now."

X shrugged. "Then I'll talk. You're Al Curzon's right hand, but Al takes his orders from a guy who calls himself the Golden God and chisels you punks out of half your profits. I'd like to get my hands on the Golden God, sure. But if you won't help, I've still got you, haven't I? I guess you know the local cops aren't wasting any love on me. But I can get in good with them by handing you over to them, see?

"You're a fall guy for a murder. Across the street, a man by the name of Carter Leeds was murdered. Tomorrow, citizens will start climbing the collars of the cops and the D.A. The public will want Leeds' killer. Well, they got him. They got you. I can hang the rap on you. And don't think I won't. Feed you to the cops in any kind of a flimsy frame, and I'm in right with the law. When you're railroaded to the chair, the law's in right with the public. Everybody's happy, including the daisies you'll be pushing up."

At the mention of the chair, Bokers' face paled slightly. His words, though, were brave enough.

"Keep it up," he said. "I'm laughin'. I'm laughin' 'cause I never heard of this guy Leeds."

"Maybe not," X said slowly. The full hypnotic power of his eyes made Bokers squirm. "Maybe not." He crooked his finger at Jane Cromer. "Get me something to tie this guy with. We'll fasten rope 'round his wrists and ankles. It'll be just like strapping him in the chair. I want him to get the picture of his own funeral. Ever been to an electrocution, Bokers? You know what gets the witnesses down, makes them want to vomit? It's the smell like roasting pork when they throw the switch. Only it isn't pork. It's you!"

And this time there was a definite gleam of terror in Bokers' eyes. X had found the one crack in this ten-minute egg's shell. Bokers was terrified of the electric chair.

That meant there was one way to make him talk—a way the cops wouldn't have thought of. Perhaps none but Agent X would have thought of such a plan and been thoroughly capable of carrying it out.

CHAPTER IV

THE LIVING DEAD

WITH WINDOW CORD supplied by Jane, X securely bound Bokers to the chair. Then he beckoned the girl to follow him into the consultation room. He closed the door, faced Jane.

"Honestly, Fred Archer, I think you're insane!" she snapped. "You think you're big. But if you weren't drunk you'd see you're not big enough to buck men like Curzon, let alone this guy who calls himself the Golden God. A while back you were saying, 'Hands off the Golden God. He's got ideas and power.' Now, with a slug of booze in you, you're—" She raised both hands in a hopeless gesture, turned on high heels, walked to the other side of the room.

"That's a nice back you're turning toward me," X said. Then he went over to the desk, pulled out a piece of paper from a rack, and picked up a pen. Swiftly, he filled the paper with curious cuneiform markings apparently as meaningless as Chinese to the Occidental. When he looked up from the paper, Jane had turned her gorgeous head and was regarding the paper with interest.

"Well," he said, "are you with me or without me?"

"Don't be a sap, Fred. I'm with you whether I like it or not." She came over to him, stood closely in front of him. "And I rather like it, don't you know."

He put an arm about her, clasped one of her shoulders in strong fingers. "Sure you do."

"Being with you," she said softly. "Not the other part of it. Not getting filled with machine-gun slugs."

X folded the paper and handed it to her. "There's an apartment house on Orange Street. Possibly you know of it."

Jane Cromer frowned. "You are drunk. I live there. Don't you remember?"

"I've been trying to forget," X said lightly, to cover the skip he had made. "Anyway, there's a man there in apartment B3. He speaks the same language I do, in case you're worrying about what I wrote on that paper." [4]

"I thought it was a symptom of your insanity," she said. "But who lives in that apartment?"

"A man," X said. "He'll be there alone and you'll know him from anybody else. His shoulders, body, jaw, head, everything about him is square. His hair is black and looks as though it had never seen a comb. He'll be dressed shabbily. He'll leave a lot of what he has to say to your imagination—something of a missing word contest. Give him the paper."

"Umm. He doesn't sound like anybody's big moment, that's sure," Jane said.

"Maybe next time I'll have you take a letter to Robert Taylor. The point is, you're to do whatever he tells you to."

"*Mister* Archer!"

"Scram!"

Jane Cromer went through the door of the consultation room. As soon as the girl was gone, X went to Archer's desk, unlocked it and took out his makeup kit. From this kit he removed a small paper envelope and a large rubber envelope. He went to the water cooler, opened the metal corner of the rubber envelope, put about two cups of water into the envelope. To this he added the powder contained in the paper envelope. Having closed the rubber envelope, he slipped it beneath his vest.

FOR TEN minutes he was occupied with the gun he had removed from the pocket of Bokers' pal. Gun in hand, he returned to the outer office where Bokers was tied. His weedy-looking colleague still lay unconscious on the floor.

"Just going to be sure you're tied for keeps, Bokers," he said. "Because if it takes a year, we're going to sit here until you decide to talk."

"Suits me," Bokers said. "I guess I can stand it as long as you can. Maybe a little longer,"

---

4   AUTHOR'S NOTE: *Agent X and his aides make frequent use of code and cypher in their communications, as well as a unique system of shorthand of the Agent's own invention. Probably this note entrusted to Jane Cromer was written in this shorthand.*

X busied himself with Bokers' bonds. Curiously enough, he changed the square knots he had put into the ropes into "granny" knots. These appeared to hold tightly, but with very little exertion on Bokers' part would loosen up. Then he pulled a chair up close to Bokers, put the automatic he had taken from the other tough on a small table near the door. Then he sat down in the chair.

For a time, he continued to eye Bokers. Once in a while his head would nod forward on his chest. His eyes appeared sleepy, but now and then they would steal a sharp glance at his wrist watch. Much depended on correct timing.

The nods became more frequent. At last, he seemed to have fallen asleep. Actually, his ears were keenly aware of Bokers' every breath. Through long lashes of his lowered lids, he could watch Bokers' feet. He knew by their cautious movements that Bokers had discovered that escape simply meant straining against the ropes. X saw the ropes loosen, drop from Bokers' ankles to the floor. He saw Bokers' big feet move out of the circle of rope, saw the toes of Bokers' shoes widen as the man stood up to tiptoe toward the door.

Instantly, X came out of his faked sleep. His hand started toward the pocket where he had Archer's automatic. At the same time, he called: "Hold it, Bokers, or take a slug in the spine."

But he was purposely slow on the draw, and Bokers had seized the automatic X had so conveniently placed on the table near the door. He attempted a gun threat to prevent X from drawing, but the movement of X's hand toward Archer's gun was unchecked. Bokers shot then, two thunderous reports. Secret Agent X dropped in his tracks, the fingers of both hands clawing at his chest. Deep crimson squeezed out from between those clutching fingers as X pitched to the floor at Bokers' feet.

"You asked for it, didn'tcha?" Bokers growled. He shoved the gun into his pocket and pulled open the office door. Then he froze in his tracks.

In the hall, a gun in his hand, was a man. His proportions would have awed a heavyweight boxer. His jaw followed the square, ponderous lines of a dredging engine. His shoulders were wide, thick, and square-cut. He wore no hat; his black, shaggy hair lent ferocity to his dark eyes. He didn't say anything, simply stepped forward and dropped a ham of a hand on Bokers' shoulder.

BOKERS was no pygmy, but his stocky body was shaken in the grasp of the shaggy-haired giant who wrested the gun from Bokers' hand. Then the square-jawed, square-headed man shoved Bokers into a chair, kept a dark eye on him, went over to where X lay. He stooped ever, made a brief examination.

He straightened. "Dead," he said. "Murder." He shoved a thumb into the arm hole of his vest and Bokers got a flash of a police badge.

"I—I—it was in self-defense," Bokers stuttered. "Sure it was. That guy, that Archer, he had me tied up."

"Kill him with a glance?" the square man chopped out.

"No, no. He tried to keep me from leaving the office. I—I didn't mean to kill him. I—"

"Wait." The big man took a deep breath as though talking was going to be an effort. "Can't talk yourself out of the chair. Caught red-handed. Good as convicted. One of Curzon's torpedoes. Maybe you could make things easier if you came out with the truth."

Bokers squatted on the edge of his chair. His thick legs were quivering. He didn't say anything.

"Listen," the square man clipped. He shoved a thumb toward Agent X. "No friend of mine. No friend of the cops. Seeing you get a murder rap no feather in my cap. But if I could nail the man higher up. If you'll tell the truth— Don't know. Maybe to get the man higher up, we'd have memory lapse or something. Huh?" His dark eyes shifted to the unconscious, weedy-looking man whom X had knocked out. He pointed: "Who's that?"

"Slim Kieffer," Bakers said. "You—you'll give a guy a break if I talk? Listen, copper, ten minutes. That's all I ask is ten minutes to blow. You can do it. Say I gave you a fight and slipped out on you. Say anything. Just ten minutes, and then you and the other bulls come after me. You got Slim there, if you need a fall guy."

"Yeah. Got Slim," the big man clipped. "Ten minutes? Give you twenty. Spill it."

Bokers twisted his hands together. "It's a deal. You're a white cop. It was an accident, me bumping Archer."

"Don't give a damn about Archer. What'd you come here for? Who sent you?"

"I'm gettin' to it," Bokers said. He wet his loose lips. "Al Curzon told me to pick up one of the boys and come up here. The Golden God had a job for us, Al said. We was to beat up this Archer, knock in his face. Not kill him, just hammer him down. Make an example of him, was what Al said. So I said, sure it'd be a pleasure. I got Slim and we come up here—"

The square-headed man checked him with a gesture. "Who's this Golden God?"

"That's what I don't know. Nobody knows, I guess, except maybe Al Curzon and some of the big shots. Anyway, the Golden God runs this town. From what Al says, he's going to run the country some day. He's got big ideas. He's got smart guys like Al under his thumb. He's a per-cent man, collecting from guys like Al. But that's okay with guys like Al, 'cause they're in on big money, see?"

"Know Joe Sine?" the square man cut in.

Bokers nodded vigorously. "Joey? Sure, we were cellmates up at Michigan City. I was with him when he bumped hisself. I was in the same cell, see? He took poison. The doc in stir said he was dead, only—" Bokers paused. There was a queer, terrified look in his eyes.

"Only?" the square man prompted.

Bokers rubbed the back of his neck as though there was a cold chill there. "Only I ain't sure about Joey Sine. Al Curzon—well, him and Joe is brothers—was brothers. Joe changed his name, see. Joe told me about it in stir. So after Joe killed hisself, I got out of stir. I'd finished the rap, see. And I went back to Al for a job.

"Well, I been with Al some time. Once—it was a hell of a dark night—Al says come on to me. Let's go for a ride. We got in Al's heap. In the back, the windows of this heap were closed up with black paint. I couldn't see where we were going. First I thought I was on the dot, only just Al and the driver of the heap was along, and Al don't touch killin' personal. When the car stopped, it was in a garage. We went upstairs in the garage and down a hall which was connected with a house, I guess, because we was in a house then. Al said we was goin' to get some new Tommy-guns for the boys and I was to help him load up the car."

HE STOPPED, looked at the square man questioningly, as if uncertain as to whether he should go on. He must have decided yes, because he cleared his throat.

"Al, he left me in a room upstairs and he went through a door. It was when he opened the door I got the shock of my life. I won't say it's true. I hadn't had a shot all day, so it wasn't dope. And I only had a little liquor, so it wasn't that. There was a guy sittin' in the room. Al went in. Al said hello to the guy and shut the door. But I got a good look at the guy's face. It was Joe Sine. Joe Sine sittin' there. And he was alive. I heard him speak, say, 'Hiyah, Al,' just like that."

"Screwy," commented the big man.

"Hell, it's the truth. I ain't Joe Sine's cellmate for all that time and not know him. That's the way it was."

"Go on," the big man said, sternly.

"That's all," Bokers said. "So help me, I ain't in the know on everything. I just do what I'm told and get paid."

The office door opened. The big man turned slightly. Jane Cromer stood in the doorway. Her large eyes darted around the room, came to rest on Agent X, became wide with horror. For a moment, any movement save the rapid rise and fall of her bosom seemed impossible for her. Then she darted forward, fell on her knees on the floor beside Agent X.

"Freddy!" She raised his head to her thigh, rocked it back and forth on both hands. *"Freddy!"*

The square-headed man said: "Told you to stay away."

Jane didn't seem to bear. She bent her head, covered her face with her hands.

"Don't act so tragic," a husky voice said. "I willed you a case of rye."

Jane dropped her hands. Her indrawn breath screamed. For the husky voice was unmistakably Archer's. The eyes of the man supposed to be a corpse were open. His lips were smiling at her.

"Fred Archer!" Jane slapped the Agent's cheek. "I could kill you for that trick!"

"He ain't dead?" gasped Bokers.

"He ain't," said X sitting up. "Fake bullets in the gun you used on me. Fake blood flowing out of a rubber bladder inside my vest. But, you talked.... Nice work." This last remark he addressed to the square-jawed man, Harvey Bates, the Agent's able assistant.

Bokers' face was the color of flour. "I—I talked. You ain't dead. I'm not pinched. It's a fake. It's a dirty fake."

"But," X said, "you talked. Who's this thin pal of yours?"

"Kieffer? A new guy with Al's bunch," Bokers said miserably.

"Then he wouldn't know any more than you do," X said. "Well, you can go now."

"Go?" gasped Bokers. He got up from his chair. Sweat stood out on his forehead. Both fists were clinched, he advanced toward X. "Damn you," he said through clenched teeth. "They'll kill me. Kill me for talking, see? It'll be murder. You killed me, get it? You killed me, makin' me talk."

X eyed him coolly. "That's tough. Well, get out. We'll dump Slim on the steps where he can pick himself up when he comes to. And that's a door behind you, Bokers. We don't want you or any like you around here until we get air-conditioning. Get out!"

He seized Bokers by the shoulder, whipped him around. Bokers rode a kick out of the office, and X slammed the door.

"Bates," he rapped at the big man, "follow Bokers. Keep him within sight day and night. He's a dopey. When he needs a shot he'll go back to the boss. Back to Al Curzon, or possibly the Golden God. Take this—" indicating the weedy man on the floor—"out with you and roll it somewhere. Keep Bokers in sight. Everything he said had the ring of truth in it. We've got to work on it."

"You'll do nothing of the sort!" Jane Cromer said. "You—" she turned furiously to Harvey Bates—"if you put him up to backing this mob, I hope you choke on that phony badge you're wearing. You're no cop. If you get Freddy into a mess I'll beat your ears in."

X laughed shortly. The redhead turned on him. "What's the laugh, Fred?" she snapped.

"You beating Bates' ears in." He nodded toward the door. "Get going, Bates." Then he turned on his heel and started toward the consultation room. Jane followed, seized him by the arm. He turned, looked down at her.

"Fred, we're taking the next train out of here," she said.

"Are we?" he said coolly. "Why?"

"Because—because, I love you, damn you!"

X TOOK her small chin in thumb and forefinger and tilted her head. "We don't start a war and then take a powder, do we, kid? We spend a lot of time thinking about ourselves and how to clip clients at both ends to make both of our ends meet. That's what we've been doing. We're through with that. Guys like Carter Leeds get murdered. No millionaire. Just a hard working guy like you and me, see? Only he works harder and lives better because he's got kids. So we stick a thorn in the side of the guy who killed Carter Leeds and a lot of others. Do we take a powder, kid, when we really got that killer yelling? Or do we stick and finish the job?"

Jane's lips quivered. "We aren't big enough, Fred."

"I am," X said. "How much salary do I owe you?" He released her chin and put his hand on the doorknob of the consultation room.

She said nothing, crossed the office to the window and stared at the reflection of herself in the dark glass. She twisted the curtain cord. He waited, looking at the clean, trim lines of her figure. She turned, made a helpless gesture with her hands.

"You—you can't fire me, you big sap," she choked out. "I'm sticking. I'm sticking and ordering funeral sprays for us both. What do you want? Chrysanthemums and baby-breath?"

"Garlic," he said, and went into the consultation room, closing and locking the door behind him.

Alone, Agent X opened the closet where the unconscious Archer was confined. He hauled the private detective out, went to Archer's desk, and took out his makeup kit. He quickly applied plastic volatile material to Archer's face, formed new features, added pigment to color the plastic. He worked swiftly, calling on his imagination in the formation of a mask for Archer.

When that was done, he went to his medical kit and filled a hypodermic needle with narcotic. As soon as he had cleaned up his makeup material and locked it in the drawer again, he opened the door and called Jane.

She came in smiling. The smile faded, when she saw Archer, now totally unrecognizable to her, stretched out on the floor.

"What is this, a morgue?" she asked.

X shook his head. "This one isn't dead. He's taking a rest cure. He's an important witness who might get the wanderlust if he came to. I'm going to show you how to give him dope. You've got to keep him snowed under until I get back."

"Where are you going?"

"Away," he said. "I'll be back in a few days. Maybe sooner. You're head man. Bates may drop in now and then. He may have a report on Bokers. Bates is okay, see?"

"Who is he, Fred?" she asked. "I thought I knew all your operatives."

"You've got quite a bit to learn about Bates and me before we are through," he said cryptically.

CHAPTER V

MADMAN AT LARGE

FOR TWO DAYS Jane Cromer did not see the man she was calling Fred Archer. Much of that time she devoted to keeping the real Fred Archer under the influence of the narcotic which Agent X had left her.

Then on the morning of the third day after X's departure, while she was in the act of administering another hypodermic shot to Archer, she heard footsteps behind her, she turned, saw Agent X, still wearing the Archer disguise, standing in the door. He was smiling and rubbing the heels of his palms together in an entirely self-satisfied manner.

She sprang to her feet, threw her arms around the Agent. He lifted her lightly, kissed her, put her down. He stared at the unconscious Archer, grinned. "Now I know how I look when I'm asleep," he chuckled.

"Freddy!" Jane Cromer sat down on his lap. "Next time you go off on a vacation, I'm going too. I've been through hell."

"Yeah?" his fingers played with the soft waves of her hair. "You don't look it. You look like you'd just passed through heaven. What was wrong?"

"Nothing. Only not hearing from you. I imagined everything had happened to you. I haven't slept a wink."

He looked down into her eyes. "And I thought those circles were eye shadow. Sorry, lady."

"And I imagined you were in prison—and then that you were dead."

"Woman's intuition," he said. "Do you think it will ever replace the old-time ouija board? Because I was in prison and I spent some time with an undertaker and some time in a graveyard. I've gone places and done things, sweetheart. I was on the trail of Joe Sine, the convict suicide up at the pen. It wasn't so much a trail as a shadow."

"Tell me about it," she urged.

"Well, Bokers was Joe Sine's cellmate in stir. And Bokers confessed that he thought Joe Sine was alive. Even though he had witnessed Sine's death, and the prison doctor had signed the death certificate. So I went to stir and checked up. The prison medico said there was no doubt but what Sine was dead. Sine had taken a lethal dose of cyanide poison, had been pronounced dead. His mother had claimed his body. I might have stopped there, only I looked up certain records and found that Sine didn't have a mother. Only living relative he had was this Al Curzon.

"The mother business, the fact that the local epidemic of killings and suicides didn't start until after Sine had died, a lot of little things like that, kept me interested. I went to the undertaker who had prepared the body for burial. He, too, told of Sine's old mother and how she had paid for the funeral and how he, the undertaker, had personally attended to everything. He said Sine was not only dead but carefully embalmed. And after an undertaker gets through with you, you stay planted until some future generation excavates you and calls you an ape man."

"And that ought to have satisfied you," Jane said.

"Nothing satisfies me but you, Red," he said. "So I keep on plugging. I went to the town where Sine was buried—little burg up north. But the town was up on city law, and so I couldn't dig in their cemetery even if Joe Sine was a criminal. So I had to wait for a dark night when I played ghoul."

Jane shuddered. "You're lying, but it's good."

"Well," he said, "if I am, the newspapers had quite a column about the grave robbing. And if what I dug up was Sine, then time was not kindly to him, for the corpse was that of an eighty-year-old man who had been rather badly cut in a railroad accident. I later found out from the undertaker that the man was a tramp who had fallen off a freight and forgot to duck when the train kept rolling."

"The same undertaker who swore he'd embalmed Sine?"

THE AGENT nodded. "He'd already collected for embalming Sine, so he panned this corpse of the tramp off as Sine. He didn't want to lose his fee and his reputation by coming out with the fact that Sine's body disappeared within ten minutes after it was delivered to his mortuary."

Jane sat up straight on X's knees. "That's funny!"

"Yeah. I laughed myself sick. If you want a real pleasant vacation, go see your undertaker and dig up some stiffs. Somebody swiped Sine's body."

"Sure. But that doesn't alter the fact that he was dead," she objected. "And it doesn't hook up with the Golden God or anything around here."

X didn't say anything for a moment. Then he suggested they have a drink. Jane got the rye and the paper cups. She poured the liquor, gave him one of the cups.

"So what?" she said.

X put the cup down, the liquor scarcely tasted. He leaned forward in his chair, regarded her earnestly. "When Carter Leeds was murdered, he was found clutching a woodblock sign in his hand, reading, *Mr. Leeds, Auditor.* Just one of those tombstones they stick on your desk when you get to be an official in an office. Was Carter Leeds trying to identify himself? That's nuts. Was Carter Leeds grasping for a weapon of defense? There was a paper-knife on the desk that would have made a better weapon. Did the killer put the sign there as though it was a headstone? Maybe. Or was Leeds trying to tell the cops who his killer was? S-I-N-E, Joe Sine's name. And it's pronounced the same way as S-I-G-N, isn't it?"

Head on one aide, Jane considered the matter. "It's far-fetched, but I suppose if Leeds was dying it was the best he could do. Still, he must have been wrong. Joe Sine is dead."

"Was dead," X said, "undoubtedly. But cyanide happens to be the one poison that works so fast that it stops the heart before it actually kills. By that I mean that theoretically if the heart could be started again, a man *might* live. It worked with a dog in laboratory tests. Why not with a human? And another factor—one of the beet authorities on the subject is in our local institute of higher learning. I mean Professor David Harkness of the Department of Biological Research."

"Harkness," Jane tasted the name. "Isn't there a lad by that name over in the newspaper office across the street?"

"Tony Harkness runs around with Carter Leeds' daughter," X said. "And Dorothy Leeds works for the paper. Tony is the professor's son, and he looks as though he'd be insulted if you said he was a newspaperman. I think he's doing graduation work at the university."

"Where are we now?" asked the girl. "I mean, in connection with the Golden God?"

X shook his head. "I don't know. Except that Sine had one of the most brilliant criminal minds of today, in addition to being a clever forger."

The door of the outer office opened and the sound of an earnest male voice came to the ears of Agent X. He could make out the words quite clearly.

"But, Dorothy, it's a waste of money, I tell you. The police are doing everything they can and this man is mercenary."

Dorothy Leeds said angrily: "It's my affair, Tony, positively!"

And then Agent X told Jane Cromer to go into the outer office while he restored the drugged Archer to the closet. A moment later, he went out to join Jane, Dorothy Leeds and Tony Harkness. Dorothy looked small and helpless. The death of her father seemed to have taken all the color from her cheeks. Tony Harkness, owlish and grave with his thick-lensed glasses, was standing a little behind Dorothy, pulling his long nose. His mouth looked sulky.

Dorothy took a hesitant step forward. "Mr. Archer," she began, "I came about my father. He was—was killed, you know."

X took both her hands in his. "May I offer my sincere sympathy, Miss Leeds. And, if it's worth anything, my assistance in any way possible."

"See, Tony?" Dorothy said triumphantly, turning to the young man. "He will help me."

X LOOKED Tony Harkness' tall, athletic body up and down. The young man met X's gaze with steady eyes. X said: "Were you under the impression I wouldn't help, Mr. Harkness?"

"No," Harkness replied bluntly. "I simply thought It was a waste of money employing you inasmuch as the police are working on the case. I have been to see the district attorney, and he promises results in twenty-four hours. So I advised Dorothy against employing you."

"District attorneys have been making those twenty-four hour promises for years," X said with a smile. "Sometimes they really have something. Sometimes they don't."

"But you will help me, won't you?" Dorothy persisted.

X nodded. "Of course. It's my business. Just step back here and we'll talk it over."

Dorothy entered the consultation room. Tony Darkness started to follow, but the girl checked him with a wave of her hand. "I'd rather talk with Mr. Archer alone," she said coolly. "I don't think you have been much help, Tony."

Young Harkness frowned. "Well, I'll be waiting right here in case you need me."

X followed the girl into the consultation room, offered her a seat, then dropped into the chair behind the desk. He held out some cigarettes. She shook her head.

"Daddy didn't like me to smoke," she said. A tear sparkled in her eye. She kept her lips firm with considerable effort.

A gentle, sad smile that was more the property of the Secret Agent than an imitation of Archer's smile, curved X's lips. Then he said: "Harkness doesn't trust me a whole lot, does he?"

"Oh, Tony's like that," the girl said. "He's really been an awfully good friend. Sometimes, though, he's a little too possessive."

X looked into the girl's small, pretty face and understood clearly why almost any man could be possessive where Dorothy Leeds was concerned.

"Well," he said finally, "What can I do for you?"

"Do—do you charge much?" she asked hesitantly.

"What can you afford to pay?" he returned.

Dorothy Leeds opened her pocket-book and took out a tight roll of bills. "Will two hundred dollars be enough?" she extended the roll to him.

X counted the money and thrust it into his pocket. "Yes," he said. "You want me to find your father's murderer."

"I do."

"Okay. Had your father any enemies, male or female?"

She shook her head. "Everybody loved him. He was the best man who ever lived. He always did what he thought was right. I can't think of anybody he ever harmed except that miserable forger."

A gleam of interest cams into X's eyes. "Who?" he questioned quietly.

"Joe Sine. Daddy testified at Sine's trial. Sine stood up in court and said he'd get Daddy for it. But you remember. You were in the courtroom."

"Of course," X lied. "But then, Sine is dead, so that doesn't help much."

"No," the girl sighed. "I guess it doesn't. There just doesn't seem to be any motive except maybe vengeance, and no one could be behind that except Sine."

X nodded. "That was what your father thought. Could there have been any way that killing your father would have brought anyone any money? Any other children besides yourself who might benefit by his death?"

"No," the girl said quickly. "There's my brother George in college here. But of course all the life insurance named mother as beneficiary, so no one could have got any money out of the—the murder."

"Dad leave mother pretty well fixed through the life insurance?" X asked.

The girl's soft lips trembled. "No. We haven't anything except my job. George will have to quit school. The house we live in isn't worth much, though it's nearly clear. The strange part is that mother always supposed she'd be pretty well off because dad had thirty thousand dollars in life insurance. But mother said today she'd found out the life insurance wasn't worth anything."

"Why?"

"I don't know. It was with the Central Reserve Company, and I always thought they were pretty strong. But mother just said it wasn't any good."

X remained silent for a moment, scowling thoughtfully. Then he stood up. "Can you give me anything more in the way of information?"

The girl shook her head. "Do you think you can do anything?"

X smiled. "Pretty sure of it. You've given me a start. I don't mind telling you I think we're bucking the most dangerous criminal group in the country. Vengeance may have been the motive behind your father's death. But there's something else, too."

THE GIRL stood up. X opened the door and led her into the outer office. Tony Harkness was standing in front of Jane Cromer's desk. Jane was sitting on top of the desk, fixing a red rose, from the bouquet on her desk, into Tony's buttonhole.

"There!" Jane exclaimed. "That gives you a finish, doesn't it?" She was in a flirtatious mood. Her five-hundred-power charm was turned on young Harkness. All that was earnest had gone out of his face. He was warming in the redhead's flaunted flame. He turned around quickly as X and Dorothy entered. His cheeks flushed.

"All through?" Tony asked because he felt he had to say something.

Dorothy nodded. If she was at all hurt at what she had seen, she concealed it. X judged that she cared less for Tony Harkness than he had first suspected. Jane Cromer was possibly disappointed.

As soon as Harkness and Dorothy Leeds had left, X turned to Jane. She was standing in front of a mirror, preening herself. He watched her, made some remark about Jane having been the red-headed woman who inspired the St. Louis Blues.

"Oh, I'm not that old, darling," she said.

"Well, you hop on the phone and find out if Central Reserve Life Insurance paid off anything on that insurance that Carter Leeds had. And find out to whom paid."

"Okay," she said. "Got a lead?"

"Got nothing," he said. "Plenty of it." He went back into the consultation room and called the Private Branch Exchange at Carroll University. He wanted to speak to Professor Harkness of the Biological Research Department. A minute later, a deep, sonorous voice came over the phone.

"Professor Harkness," X said, "this is Fred Archer, the private investigator, speaking. I'd like to have a little talk with you sometime today. Can you spare me a few moments?"

The professor cleared his throat. "I believe I can after classes this afternoon. Say about three-thirty. I shall be in my office next to the biological laboratory."

That suited X perfectly. He hung up. Then he sat down and waited until Jane Cromer came in to report that the life insurance company had settled the Leeds' claim immediately. Thirty thousand dollars, with a check payable to Mrs. Leeds. Mrs. Leeds had cashed the check.

"Now who's lying?" Jane asked. "Something definitely screwy somewhere, isn't there?"

X nodded. "Maybe we'll be able to put our noses on something definite this afternoon. I'm going around to see Professor Harkness. Want to discuss the possibility of bringing a victim of cyanide poisoning back to life." He settled himself comfortably and lighted a cigarette....

Agent X found Professor Harkness a smaller man than Tony. His hair was mixed sand and silver. White, transparent skin, a lipless mouth and pink-lidded eyes made him appear cold. Like his son, he wore thick-lensed glasses.

"Well, sir?" he said brusquely, looking the Agent up and down. He offered no chair, so X went over to the corner and got one which he brought to Harkness' side and sat down. The professor seemed to resent such close proximity; for he rolled his chair back a way, wheeled it around angrily. He looked at his watch and growled: "Be as brief as possible, Archer. I'm a busy man."

"Okay," X said. But he removed a cigarette with exaggerated deliberation, put it in his mouth, and scratched a match on the edge of Harkness' desk before beginning to speak. All of this was annoying to the professor. X intended it to be. He was certain that Professor Harkness' brusqueness was a mask to conceal extreme nervousness. Why the man was nervous, he had no idea. But he intended to find out.

"Ever hear of Joe Sine?" X asked. He flamed the cigarette and squinted at the professor through a cloud of smoke.

"Never," Harkness shot out.

"He was a criminal. A damned clever one. He was especially smart in the matter of forgery. A local boy, too. I thought maybe you knew him."

"Criminals," the professor said with a sneer, "are not frequently found on college campuses."

AGENT X flipped away the match. "I don't know about that," he said. He shot a sidelong glance at the professor to surprise a startled gleam in the weak eyes.

"Joe Sine killed himself in prison," X continued. "He took cyanide poison. He was pronounced dead. My question, professor, is this: Could Joe Sine have had some friend on the outside who restored him to life as soon as his body was removed from prison?"

"Preposterous!" Harkness exploded.

X frowned. "Cyanide is a peculiar poison. Most deadly of all, there is, nevertheless, a specific antidote, discovered only a few years ago. I thought perhaps you had heard."

"Heard?" snapped Harkness. "Mr. Archer, do you happen to know the man you are addressing? I assure you that there is nothing about cyanide poisoning and its antidote that I do not already know. Why, experiments—" Harkness paused.

"Go on," said X mildly.

"I— Mr. Archer, I have already told you that my time is limited. I am not here to listen to fairy stories and idiotic suppositions concerning the revival of the dead. Experiments have proved such to be impossible."

"Got to contradict you there, professor," X said. "There have been successful experiments along that line." [5]

Professor Harkness leaned forward in his chair. "This wondrous news," he said acidly, "has failed to reach my ears. I know not one single case in which a dead man has been brought back to life. I do not refer to those experiments of a fellow scientist of mine who has spent much of his lifetime killing dogs to make them live again. Such death is not truly death. The heart may have stopped, respiration may have ceased. But that is not death. Nor, to my knowledge, has the life he has restored to them been life. I may take the legs of a frog, entirely dismembered from its body, and I may stimulate the nerve in the frog legs with electric current and cause those dismembered legs to kick. That is not life."

Professor Harkness stood up. "These newspapers! How they jump to conclusions. A college sophomore keeps a chicken's heart alive for days, keeps it beating in physiological salt solution. Some newspaper hears of this and prints headlines to the effect that science has mastered death. And then some detective, Mr. Archer, comes to me and claims that a convict who has taken cyanide poison in prison is still alive!"

"I make no claims, Professor Harkness," X said. "But men have taken cyanide poison in lethal doses, have to all appearances died. Yet they have been brought back to live their normal span of life by means of an injection of methylene-blue dye." [6]

Harkness drew himself up haughtily, "Sir, I am well aware of such instances. But Sine was dead. Pronounced dead by the prison physician. Some time later, his body was called for. It was taken to an undertaker's establishment. Considerable time elapsed before it

---

5   AUTHOR'S NOTE: There are certain research foundations in the country today devoted entirely to the study of reviving life after death. Up to the present time, scientists have had to confine their efforts to experimental animals, chiefly dogs. Medical records show, however, that physicians are daily widening the borderland between life and death. Cases of heart failure, which a few years ago would have been considered hopeless, have been treated by injections of adrenaline direct to the heart, causing that organ to function again. In some cases, these heart patients have been literally brought back from death.

6   AUTHOR'S NOTE: This is a matter of record.

would have been possible for anyone to have made such an injection of methylene-blue—"

"How do you know, professor? Were you there?"

Professor Harkness became as pale as a corpse. Then color flooded his face. "You are intolerable! Didn't I say I didn't even know the man. Didn't I—"

"Yes, and then contradicted yourself a moment later by giving detailed facts on the time element elapsing between the moment of Sine's taking the poison and the time when—shall we say, when you stole the corpse and attempted to revive it?"

Harkness sprang at Agent X, seized him by the neck. He would have dragged him to the door had not X been rather difficult dragging for a man of Harkness' build. With a movement that seemed scarcely more than a gesture, X knocked the professor's hands down.

"I was merely jumping to conclusions, professor," he said quietly. "Someone did steal the body. It might have well been you. Now I know my conjecture was correct. You revived Joe Sine—"

"You lie!" roared Harkness. "Leave this office at once, or I will have you thrown out!"

"Just a minute, Dad."

X GLANCED toward the door. Tony Harkness stood there, one arm braced against the door. He had evidently just come from or was on his way to the school laboratory, for he had a white smock over his arm. He was wearing a dark suit, with a limp-looking yellow-white rose in his buttonhole.

"I don't think this lying gets us anywhere, especially when Archer seems to have ferreted out half the truth. Why not tell him all?"

"Anthony," the professor rumbled, "I demand your silence."

"Sorry, Dad," Tony Harkness said. "I think you've forgotten that Archer has no official capacity. Private detectives being what they are, I rather imagine we can persuade him to keep quiet. I intend to tell him the truth. Then, if it's money he wants—"

X smiled. "That's right, professor. The kid's got the right idea. Let's have the truth."

"Dad happened to have a friend working at the state penitentiary," Tony Harkness said. "That friend reported the suicide of Joe Sine a short time after it occurred. As soon as the body had been taken to an undertaker. Dad and I engineered the body snatch that seems to have aroused your interest. And we did attempt to revive Sine in a little laboratory we had prepared for just such a purpose in Michigan City. This was the opportunity Dad had been waiting for to try out his theory of reviving the dead. We didn't care if the man was Sine or who he was.

"I need not go into the process we employed. We did inject methylene-blue as you supposed. That was only part of the experiment. Dad withdrew from the laboratory for a few moments. And I must confess I dozed off for a little time. When Dad re-entered the lab and awakened me, I found that Sine was gone.

"That's all there is to it. That's the reason I was not anxious to have Dorothy employ you. I have always felt that the crime that has been going on unchecked in this city began that night in our laboratory. Because I believe Sine walked from that laboratory alive! Naturally, I wasn't anxious to have our little crime made public, though at the time of our experiment, we never considered the possible results."

"Tell him about the brain," Professor Harkness said hoarsely.

Tony Harkness nodded. "That's worth mentioning. It may also explain the fact that police seem to be able to find no motive for these murders. You see it's relatively simple for dad to restore a supposedly dead heart to beating again. Circulation may even be restored to such a point that the animal body may be able to move again. But to restore complete circulation to the brain is something that has stumped every scientist. So if Joe Sine is really alive and roaming the streets, it's highly probable that he is a maniac."

"Yes," concluded the professor. "A raving, maniacal killer!"

CHAPTER VI

THE GOLDEN GOD SPEAKS

JANE CROMER SAID: "You missed the law by a couple of watch ticks." She was seated at her desk in the front office of the Archer Detective Agency, eating peanut brittle.

Agent X went over and helped himself to some of the candy. "What did I miss?"

"The law," she repeated. "I know you're practically ignorant of its existence but the law in the form of a headquarters dick named Demotte was in here a while ago. He wanted to talk to you, said he'd wait. He got his eye on that half-filled bottle of rye you had in there. I guess he drank it all and ate the bottle. Anyway, if you want to drink a toast to my eyes you'll have to use water."

"That'd be good enough," he said. "Anything else happen?"

She shook her head. "The office was dead, but it is just as well to get used to a lot of silence. What did you find out talking with the local brain trust?"

"That Tony Harkness and his old man snatched Joe Sine's body," he said. "That they not only think that Sine came to life after they attempted to revive him, but that Sine is crazy."

A shudder writhed Jane's shoulders. "I don't like that. And say, how long are you going to keep that poor devil shut up in the closet back there? Realize he hasn't had any nourishment but dope for three days?"

"He's husky," X said. "Any word from Bates?"

"That big lug? Oh, sure—he called about ten minutes ago. Wanted you. He said he'd call back. I asked him if he'd managed to shadow Bokers—wasn't that the guy's name?—and he intimated by a lot of silence that he didn't trust me. What has he got against women?"

X smiled. "You don't flatter yourself much, do you? Because he didn't fall on his knees before you, you think he's off the species entirely."

Jane pouted, "Gosh, you're nasty. You haven't said I'm wonderful since you got back."

"You're wonderful," X said. Then he went over to pick up the ringing telephone. The man on the other end of the line was Bates.

"You, chief?" asked Bates.

"Yes," X said, and at the same time tapped out the letter "X" in Morse code on the mouthpiece of the telephone. Thus having identified himself to his lieutenant, he listened to what Bates had to report. Bokers had been in hiding ever since he had left Archer's office. And Bates had faithfully watched the lodging house where the man had been holed up. Evidently Bokers feared the Golden God would discover that Bokers had been tricked into talking.

Bokers, Bates said, was in need of a shot of dope. His nerves were fraying out, and Bates was of the opinion that Bokers would venture out of his hiding place very soon in quest of a dope ration. X learned that Bates was phoning from a drug store directly across the street from where Bokers was hiding. X promised to join Bates as soon as possible....

Night had scarcely fallen, but a chill rain out of the east had put people indoors at an early hour. The street, where X was to meet Harvey Bates, was not one to attract pedestrians even in the most pleasant weather. Tonight it was a narrow way of puddles, burbling gutters, with the smoke of a nearby factory smothered down by the damp. The brightest spot was the corner drug store, and even that was bright only by comparison.

Beyond the area of fuzzy light from the drug store, was a spot of red light like an eye that came and went with the regular rhythm of a danger signal. The spot of glowing light came from the square bowl of Harvey Bates' pipe. Bates was standing on the curb, the personification of patience, when Agent X touched his arm.

"Is he still there?" X asked. And his voice was not the husky voice of Fred Archer; it was lower, richer, vibrant—the true voice of Agent X.

BATES turned. His square jaw released his pipe, its bowl was lost in his big right hand. "Can't say how glad I am to see you, sir," he said, with simple sincerity. "Glad to be working with you again." [7]

"The pleasure is mutual," X said quietly. His next words concerned Bokers, whom Bates had been shadowing.

"Lighted window across the street in an old brick house," Bates pointed out. "Bokers put on a coat minute ago. Turned out light. Nervous. Ought to be out in a second."

Across the street, a door eased open. The stocky figure of Bokers emerged from the shadows, moved with cautious steps along the front of the building. He stopped every few steps and glanced back over his shoulder. Then, ducking his head as though he expected something to land on his skull any moment, he moved swiftly up the street.

"Let's go," X whispered. "Stay on this side of the street. His dope connection may be at the Golden God's own headquarters."

On the other side of the street, Bokers turned into a narrow alley so suddenly that it was almost as though the earth had swallowed him. X nabbed Bates' sleeve and jerked him toward the curb. "Hurry," he whispered. "He'll give us the slip if we don't step on it." And he sprinted across the street to the mouth of the alley.

As he entered the alley, X turned, looked past Bates, saw two men walking swiftly up the sidewalk. Was someone else interested in Bokers' movements?

Just inside the alley, X and Bates paused, listened to detect Bokers' footsteps ahead of them now breaking into a run.

"After him," X whispered, and his long legs cut the distance between himself and Bokers in half.

Suddenly twin headlight beams blazed out from the middle of the alley. Bokers was silhouetted midway between the walls of the building, his body crouched, half turned like a panic-stricken animal. But if the lights of the car that bottled up the alley disclosed Bokers, they also revealed Bates and Agent X.

"Trap," Bates clipped, as he caught up with X.

---

7   *AUTHOR'S NOTE: X's recent investigations had drawn him away from New York, his usual headquarters. In leaving Harvey Bates in charge, X felt his secret work in that city in good hands. Not knowing exactly when his chief was to return from Hawaii, Bates had left New York, acting on his own initiative, when he learned of the exceptional crimes in Carrollton City.*

X pulled out Archer's automatic. "A trap for Bokers, and we're in the middle of it. Men coming up behind. Get to the opposite wall. I'll be on the other side of the alley. If the pair coming up behind are Bokers' executioners, we'll catch them in a little cross-fire."

As X and Bates moved to take positions on opposite sides of the alley, Bokers tried to duck out of the relentless rays of light from the parked car. But a spotlight in the car was turned on, and every step Bokers took, the spotlight followed him. Bokers staggered, reeled as though the light was a web that tangled the feet of a fly. It was torture. It was a hell for Bokers, created by the man he had failed—the Golden God.

Bokers yanked out a gun. "Damn you!" he sobbed. "Damn you. Take it, then!" He raised a wavering gun and fired three times in an effort to knock out that spotlight. Three times he failed, and then a man leaned way out over the car door and X saw the thick, black body of a sub-machine gun in the man's hands.

It was murder. It was the rotten rat justice of the underworld. And X hated it as much as anything in the world. Oblivious to his own danger, X ran from the protective shadow of the building into the yellow rays from the car. He ducked through a tracing line of bullets from behind, gained a position behind a telephone pole. The machine gunner was in range of the small gun in X's hand. His keen eyes jerked the sights into line. The little automatic barked like a terrier.

The machine gunner was hit. He brought the muzzle of the gun around to the spot whence that wasp sting of a ballet had come. The gun bucked, emitted its death chatter. Slivers of wood and chips of brick rained around X's head. And then from directly across the alley a single shot roared. Bates' gun, X knew by its cannonlike blast. And the machine gunner spilled forward on his face from the car.

Bokers, saved for the moment when X had drawn the killer's fire, tried again to outrace the beam of that spotlight. He was running toward the point where Bates was concealed behind a barricade of ash cans. Within a scant two yards of safety, a bullet from someone in the car cut him down. He struck the pavement on his left shoulder, rolled, crashed into the ash cans and lay still.

X SAW Bates stand upright and unprotected, trying to see what had happened to Bokers. And then from a doorway, twenty feet behind Bates, an arm and a steady gun appeared.

"Drop, Bates!" the Agent's voice rang out. He sprang from shelter, rushed the doorway, firing from the hip. The man in the doorway whipped around, retaliated. X uttered a sharp, clear whistle that rang out above the crashing echo of gun thunder. It was a signal for retreat. The Golden God's brand of justice had reached out for Bokers. It was up to X and Bates to save their own skins. And X's attack on the man in the doorway was Bates' chance to slip out of that death trap alive.

But at the other end of the alley a motor roared. X glanced away from the doorway that had been his object of attention, saw the car bearing down upon him. In that searing light he could not hope to escape the guns of the men in the car. He sprang backward to a building wall. Eyes on the car, fingers groping for some niche of concealment, he moved as quickly as possible to retreat before that car.

There was no cranny, no doorway, only black wall that targeted him perfectly. And the car ate up the short distance that separated X and his mortal enemies. Another moment, and it would be his marksmanship against theirs.[8]

Suddenly, powerful arms reached out, seized X's left arm, pulled him off balance. Two men landed on him simultaneously to pinion his arms, to stamp upon his gun wrist until pain forced him to release his weapon. A kick to the temple half stunned him. Through swirling clouds of mist, a voice said: "Sack Archer. Boss's orders." Something soft, black and velvety, shutting out all light, dropped over X's head. A cord knotted at his throat, all but strangled him.

He was rushed to the car, thrown to the floor. The motor raced, the car accelerated. Far in the distance, a police siren wailed. Too late for the law of the law-abiding. The law of the greedy Golden God had taken its toll.

Blinded by the sack that covered his head, all sense of direction muddled by the twisting route, X had no idea where he was when the car stopped. He was lifted by two men, taken up a stairway, seated in a chair. Steel clamps fastened wrists and ankles to the chair. The cord of the sack was loosened and the sack taken off.

X found himself looking into the perfectly hairless face of a tall, stooped man whose rawboned hands were holding the sack that had blindfolded X. The man had a lantern jaw, high cheekbones; his convoluted forehead merged into a smooth, bald cranium. He

---

8   *AUTHOR'S NOTE: Though X prefers not to use lethal weapons in his investigations, certain impersonations, such as that of Fred Archer, demand that he use the weapon commonly employed by the man he is impersonating. For that reason, he keeps himself always in good shooting form; and with a revolver or automatic, he has few equals.*

looked more like a farmer than anything else, except that the black stare of his small eyes was accentuated by his paper-white skin.

"Hello, Archer," the bald man said. His soft, smooth voice was deceivingly close to kindly.

"Hi," said X. His eyes took in his surroundings. He was in a small hall paneled with light-finished oak. There were doors at both ends of the hall. The door at one end opened. A man with a bullet head and close-clipped albino's hair appeared.

"Okay, Mr. Curzon," the bullet-head addressed the bald man. "The Golden God wants to speak to Archer."

So the man with the bald head was Al Curzon, one of Carrollton City's big-shot racketeers. Curzon moved behind the chair that confined X, and for the first time X noticed that the chair was on wheels. He was pushed forward to the door from which the bullethead had appeared, shoved into total darkness. The door behind him closed and latched.

"Just a minute, Mr. Archer," said a voice within the room. "I am removing my mask. You will be one of the few who have seen the Golden God face to face. I think it will impress you. The very purpose of our meeting is to impress you.... Now!"

Lights were turned on. X was at one end of a long, barren room. At the opposite end, curtains of black velvet hung against the wall. In front of these curtains was a desk. Behind this desk sat a man. Perhaps the most powerful man in the underworld, he who had welded opposing forces of crime into a single unit—the Golden God, as he called himself. But X knew him by another name. He had seen too many pictures of this man in rogue galleries to ever forget that face, though it was thin and sickly-looking now.

IT WAS a face with high cheekbones, a long, pinched chin, a nose that was cleft at the bridge by a pale-blue scar. Shaggy black brows jutted over cavernous eye sockets. The head was bowed slightly and motionless, the black hair cut close to the head. The hands were hidden in the man's lap. On the desk beside him was a mask that appeared to be gold and which would have covered the face of this master of hell completely. Master of hell indeed, for he had journeyed there and returned.

The man behind the desk was Joe Sine, forger, murderer, convict, suicide, corpse—now crime's all-powerful master.

"You will excuse me if I don't rise to greet you," came from the motionless man behind the desk. "This returning from the dead is a slow process."

"You are partially paralyzed then?" X asked.

"Yes. But we have not met to discuss my health—but *yours*. You have repeatedly ignored my warnings, presumably because someone has paid you to ignore them. I know a good bit about you, Fred Archer. We've met before. We have one thing in common. Our ruling passion for money. I am not entirely sure that our means of obtaining it have been very different, either."

"That depends upon the point of view," X said with a laugh.

"And the amount of money involved. My total take in the past few months you would trade for all the money you've earned in a lifetime. And it is only the beginning. Here in this city is the nucleus of a business that will spread throughout the country. I have taught racketeers how to increase their earnings by working together. They pay me a liberal per cent for protection, settlement of their bickerings and new enterprises they would never have thought of. I have taught them to tap sources of wealth hitherto beyond their grasp. I am not being too optimistic when I say that my system may even become international."

"Yeah," X said, "but where do I come in?"

"You're a meddler, Archer. You annoy me. I am going to give you one more chance to keep out of my affairs. Then I intend to kill you. But I am liberal and will make your non-interference worth while."

"How much?" asked X eagerly, never forgetting the dominant urge of the man he was impersonating.

"Fifteen thousand dollars," said the Golden God.

X shook his head. "Make it thirty."

"Fifteen," said the Golden God. "And that means your hands off definitely. It might even be well for you to leave town at once."

"Okay," X agreed. "Where's the dough?"

"You will be given it on your way out. It is agreed, then. I will demand that you live up to your part of the bargain. You forfeit your life if you don't."

Black curtains swung silently downward to envelop the desk and the man behind it. "Al," the voice of the predatory Golden God called from behind the curtain, "Archer is leaving."

The door behind X opened. Al Curzon entered, took hold of the wheel chair to which X was secured, and rolled it from the room.

X turned his head, looked up into Curzon's long-jawed face, "Wait a minute. I get fifteen grand for this."

"You'll get it," Curzon said. He walked away from the chair to the door at the other end of the hall. X was left alone. Silently, he cursed the steel bands that kept him in the chair. Had he been able to break one of them, one hand would have enabled him to wheel himself into the Golden God's court. One hand would have enabled him to strangle the sickly, greedy, grasping monster who ruled the organization that victimized such men as Carter Leeds.

But he could not move. And furthermore, he noticed that a small knot in the oak paneling was centered by something that glittered and moved—a human eye.

It was less than a minute before Al Curzon returned. He had a packet of bills in his hand. He stood in front of X and counted them aloud. There were one hundred and fifty hundred-dollar bills in the lot.

"Satisfied?" Curzon said.

"Okay. I'd like to count them myself, but these bracelets would sort of prevent that," X said.

CURZON stooped over and thrust the money into the inside pocket of X's coat. He straightened, took from his pocket the velvet bag which had enveloped X's head during his journey to the house of the Golden God. The bag was replaced, the drawstring tightened. Darkness again and maddening helplessness as he was removed from the chair and rushed from the house.

This time he was placed in a coupé, between the driver and another man. Only the gun of the man at his right continued to menace him. Agent X could scarcely repress a laugh as he thought how different the outcome might have been had the avaricious Golden God only known he had been entertaining Agent X and not the mercenary Archer. How the Golden God would have been pleased to know that the fifteen thousand he had spent to buy Archer would go to the family of Carter Leeds.

These reflections were abruptly interrupted by a remark from the driver of the car. He said to his companion: "Say, I saw Al hand this bird fifteen grand just before we brought him out. How's about you and me lookin' out for ourselves for a change?"

"You mean liftin' the wad?" asked the man with the gun. "Nix. I don't double-cross the Golden God. Look what happened to Bokers tonight for messin' up a job. I was in on the kill. I don't want no slug in my back."

"How's anybody to know?" asked the driver. "And we can do a clean job."

"You mean bump him? Bump Archer?"

"Why not? Find a lonely spot just out of town, take the dough, put a slug in him, and roll him in a ditch. The G.G. ought to give us a medal for bumpin' the nosey dick."

"Nobody would know," reflected the man with the gun.

"Okay then. Soon as we're through town, you bump him, get your hooks on the dough, and we split fifty-fifty."

Then silence, save for the purr of the motor. Three men were alone with their thoughts. Two plotted murder. The third plotted for his life. And the third man could not even see to strike his first blow.

Noises about him informed X that they were going through the city and that it was not late enough for traffic to have thinned out much. He was passing through what was undeniably the safest part of his one-way trip. Now, with potential witnesses on the street, his two self-appointed executioners would be reluctant about using their guns. At the same time, his only chance of escape was a dangerous one, dangerous not only to him but to others.

Still, when he considered that his escape might be of vital importance to citizens in general, he dared not hesitate.

He kicked out blindly with both feet. One foot he tried to ram down on the driver's foot that stepped on the accelerator. The other he swung in the direction of the ankle of the man with the gun. He missed the accelerator entirely, but connected on the shin of the man with the gun.

Instantly, X felt the gun against his side jerk away as pain doubled the man over. At the same time, X grasped out for the steering wheel. He got hold of a spoke, pulled the wheel way over.

The car lurched, jumped a curb. Then there was the crash of glass and a scream of twisting metal. X was hurled forward in his seat. The instrument board struck him high on the chest. Pain racked his body. Shock tortured his brain and nerves. Still, he kept his mind clear. His hands came up, ripped at the drawstrings of the sack, pulled the sack from his head.

Like a speed lens of a camera, eyes and mind took in the situation. The roof of the coupé was partially caved in on the driver's side by a steel lamp post. The driver was either dead or unconscious, his body jammed up against the steering wheel. The man at X's left was partially stunned. Flying glass had raked his face. Still, his hands were fumbling in an aimless sort of way, perhaps in an effort to retrieve his gun or stop Agent X from getting out of the car.

THERE WAS a knot of excited people standing around the car. A cop pulled open the door at the right-hand side, made an effort to draw the partially conscious hood out. But X scrambled out over the man, gave the cop a stiff-arm blow that knocked him back into the arms of bystanders.

Then X was out, thrusting his way through the crowd, knocking down hands that would have attempted to stay him.

"The man's knocked silly!" cried one bystander.

"Ought to be in a hospital!" yelled another.

And then their cries became inarticulate mumbles as X's strides took him to the corner and around on a side street. Every muscle of his body rebelled against the punishment he gave it. As he burst open the door of a corner taproom and lurched to a phone booth, men at the bar might have mistaken him for a drunk.

He shoved a nickel into the slot of the phone and rang Archer's office. It was a man's voice that answered. Not Archer's voice, but a deep, gruff voice he failed to recognize.

"Who's talking?" demanded the man in Archer's office.

X quietly hung up. Something extreme—coplike about that voice. He scowled. Suppose police were there. Suppose they searched the office and found the real Fred Archer, If they examined the man's face closely and removed some of the makeup—

But he was more concerned over the safety of Bates. Had Bates succeeded in escaping the death trap that had been set for Bokers?

He left the taproom. At the curb stood a taxi, the driver lolling at the wheel taking a nap. X got into the cab and out of the rain, reached over, and shook the driver into waking up.

"Howdy, Mr. Archer," said the man sleepily, "Rotten night, ain't it?"

"Hell of a night," X said. Evidently the driver was acquainted with Archer. "Get me to my apartment as quickly as possible."

"I'll have to have the address on that, Mr. Archer," said the driver as he churned the cold motor into action. "I guess I've taken you everywhere except home."

X snapped out the address of a west side apartment building not far from the college campus. Though he had never been there, he had noted the address in the identification card in Archer's wallet. He had been carrying the wallet ever since he had stepped into Archer's shoes.

As the cab stopped in front of the building, X saw a tall, slim figure pacing up and clown in front of the doorway. As X ducked out of the cab, the tall man hurried toward him.

"Mr. Archer!"

X looked up, saw that the tall man was Tony Harkness. "Hello, Harkness," he said briefly and hurried toward the door of the apartment.

Young Harkness followed. "Mr. Archer, may I have a few words with you?"

"If they are few," X said. "Come on up." And he entered the hall and ran up the steps to the second floor. He took out Archer's keys from his own pocket and opened the door of an apartment which overlooked the street.

"I tried to get you at your office," Tony said as soon as the door had closed behind them. "But you weren't there. I came over here in hope of getting in touch with you."

X shook a cigarette from a pack and lighted it. He tossed the pack to Harkness. "You go in person to my office?"

"No, I called on the phone. A man answered. He said you weren't there."

X swung through the living room, bedroom, bath and kitchenette. He half hoped that Harvey Bates had come to the apartment on not finding X in Archer's office. But no sign of Bates, not even so much as a crumb of the big man's shaggy pipe tobacco lying around.

A ringing telephone brought him back to the living room. He picked up the phone.

"Freddy!" came from the receiver. It was Jane Cromer's voice.

"The hotel, right now. I gave the cops the slip. Your office is filled with them. But I've got the key to the consultation room. Unless they break into it, that doped witness of yours is still in safe keeping. You're in a jam again, Freddy. You know how the cops love to frame you. This is something new. You're wanted for the Leeds murder."

"Leeds' murder? How do they figure that?"

"Oh, your fingerprints were among a lot of others in Leeds' office. Yours were on top of the desk. I phoned the janitor, and he said he hadn't seen you in the newspaper building for a month of Sundays. That doesn't help much, though. The murderer naturally would take pains not to be seen."

AGENT X remembered then how the janitor had landed on his back, flattening him out on the desk top. Those were his prints on the desk, not Archer's. But the cop who had called at Archer's office earlier had not come simply to drink Archer's whiskey. He had taken the empty bottle along with him and got X's prints from the bottle. X's prints, but the cop had naturally supposed them to be Archer's. And they had corresponded with the prints on the desk in Leeds' office.

"That's not all, Freddy. Dorothy Leeds called to tell you that she needed help. She said that her brother George had been at the Smart Owl taproom, down by the river, George was drunk. His dad's death and his having to quit school must have laid him out. He's going in for drink, and Dorothy was scared that he was going to kill himself. He was shooting off his mouth about bridges and rivers and forgetting it all."

"And Bates," X snapped. "Have you seen Bates?"

"Oh, the big lug. Sure. He scared the wits out of me. Called up the office to see if you were there. He sounded as though he thought something had happened to you. He wouldn't enlighten me. Why don't you teach that guy how to speak?"

"Where is he now?" X asked.

"Hunting you, I suppose."

"Well," X said, "be a good girl. I have an idea we can remove the cops from the office if they haven't been in the consultation room. We'll give them something to keep them busy." He hung up.

Tony Harkness was at his elbow, pulling his long nose, staring with owlish, earnest eyes at X. "Mr. Archer," he began, "I believe all our fears have been fully realized."

X went to Archer's closet and grabbed a topcoat. "Yeah?" he said as he slid into the coat.

"That was early this evening. I've been trying to get hold of you ever since."

"What was early this evening?" X demanded huskily. "I'm in one hell of a rush."

"I saw Joe Sine. He was in a car going north. I wanted to follow, but was on foot and there was no cab in sight. It might be that if you went to some of his old haunts—"

X nodded. "I'll do that later." He hurried Harkness from the apartment, locked the door, and ran down to get into his waiting cab. Murder had marked the Leeds family. Now suicide threatened. Hand in hand, murder and suicide stalked in the wake of the greedy Golden God.

Why? *Why?* The question hammered continually in the mind of Agent X. But if he could save George Leeds, there might be a lead. Would this one take him only to a blank wall to have that eternal *why* echo back to him again?

CHAPTER VII

DOUBLE-TIME FALL GUY

AS THE TAXI in which the Agent rode neared the river front, X tapped the driver on the shoulder. "Pull up," he ordered. "Damned if I can see through that windshield from back here with all this rain. I'm moving up front."

When the driver had braked his cab, X got out and climbed in beside the man. "Now," he ordered, "take in all four of the bridges that keep this town in one piece. Take them at about twenty-five miles an hour. Be ready to brake if I say the word."

"What you looking for, Mr. Archer?" asked the driver.

"Ask me something easier," X said. "Look here. If you were going to commit suicide, which of these bridges would you dive off?"

"None of 'em," said the man. "Water always gets up my nose when I swim. If I wanted to commit suicide I'd drink myself to death or something pleasant. Who you expecting to do the high dive?"

X didn't answer this question. His eyes seemed to strain from their sockets as he scanned the rain-swept bow of the Black Street bridge. He wondered what possible chance he would have of stopping George Leeds from taking the jump even if he did see him.

By the time he had patrolled each of the four bridges, he was ready to admit that the search was well-nigh impossible. He didn't even know what George Leeds looked like.

It was when they reached the end of the Mark Street bridge that a man jumped from the sidewalk into the street and waved his arms wildly at the cab.

"Stop!" X ordered. The driver stamped down on his brake. X sprang from the car, ran back toward the man who had frantically signaled him.

"Get a policeman!" shouted the man. "There's a young fellow down there." He jerked his thumb toward the river.

"Jumped in?" demanded X.

"No. I don't think so. Not yet. He's nuts. I found him on the bridge, leaning over the rail, looking at the water and muttering to himself. He said something about everything soon going to be over. Then he went to the end of the bridge and down toward the concrete embankment. That was just before your cab came in sight. I know he's crazy, I know he's going to jump."

X ran to the end of the bridge and down the steps that led to the top of a concrete flood wall that hemmed in the river. Ahead of the Agent, a lank shadow crept along the top of the wall. It stopped now and then in its forward movement to inch to the precipitous edge of the wall. It was during these momentary halts that X held his breath and offered a mental prayer that this man might wait only a few seconds.

Then as the suicide turned his back on the Agent and continued his slow walk toward his intended grave, X sprinted silently along the wall on rubber-soled shoes. He dared not call out. One single word might be the spur that the suicide needed to plunge himself into the dizzily whirling waters below.

Again the man halted at the edge of the wall. And this time he dropped to hands and knees and thrust his head out over the edge. Whether this was the place he had intended for his finish or not made little difference. Another second of looking into that swift current would make the man so dizzy he would fall in.

X kept moving. All of his will power was expended in an effort to project a single controlling thought into the crazed mind of the man on the brink of destruction. *He must not jump.* Whether his mental effort really accomplished anything, he never knew; for the next moment he was expending every physical effort in a mighty leap that landed him flat on his face. His left hand was clutching the shoreward side of the wall, right hand clinging to something he hoped was a man's arm.

"Let me go, damn you!" a thin, hysterical voice pleaded. *"Let me die!"*

MUSCLES swollen until it seemed they must burst through his skin, X hauled the man back from the brink of eternity, inch by inch. Then, when he had dragged the struggling man far enough back so that he dared to alter his position, X got to his knees. He slapped the man's white blur of a face—two sharp, stinging blows with the flat of his hand.

"Fool!" X panted. "Blind, crazy fool. Can't you find anything better to throw your life away on?"

The man drew a long quivering breath. "It's my life," he murmured, "to do with as I please."

"You're wrong!" X snapped. "You're George Leeds, aren't you?"

"Yes, I'm—"

"And what in hell do you think your mother and sister will do without you?"

The young man laughed bitterly. "Do without me? If it hadn't been for me, they wouldn't have got into such a mess. I stole from them. I stole everything that was rightfully theirs. I didn't mean to. I didn't know what I was doing—"

"So you'll jump in the drink and they'll have to float another mortgage to give you the kind of a burial you don't deserve, eh?" X snapped. "Stand up on your feet!" X jerked the man's slight form upright and held him there a moment until his nerves had steadied.

"I—I never thought about that," George Leeds whimpered.

"What are you shivering for?" X demanded, shaking the youth angrily.

"It's chilly out here in the rain. I—" George Leeds laughed. "I guess it would be colder in the river, mister."

"Now you're beginning to have a little sense. Spit it out, now, the whole truth. I want to know what you've done. If it's such a crime as you think it is, stand up and take your medicine instead of passing the buck to your mother and sister."

"Who are you?" whispered George Leeds.

"Try and believe I'm your friend," X said earnestly. "Anything you tell me is strictly confidential. I won't criticize you for anything you've done. But I'd damn you the rest of my life if you went into that river. I'm not going to tell you you were acting cowardly in trying to kill yourself. It takes a certain kind of physical courage to plan your own death. No, you're not yellow. You just can't talk things over with yourself and get an answer that makes sense. This time, try talking to me."

"I—I forged my father's name to a check," George Leeds whispered. "I didn't know I did it. I was too drunk to know. I didn't know until this afternoon when mother took me into her room and told me I'd have to stop school. She said we didn't have any money.

She said the thirty thousand dollars she had got from the life insurance company on Dad's death—the money that should have taken care of her for the rest of her life—she'd had to spend it to keep me out of jail.

"That was because of the forged check. Somebody got hold of the check and showed it to mother. Whoever that was said she'd have to come across with the thirty thousand or I'd go to jail. You know how mothers are?"

"Yes," X said huskily. "I know. They'd spend their last cent on a son who would kill himself rather than live and try to make such a sacrifice pay dividends. How'd you happen to forge this check?"

"I—I don't know. I was drunk, I tell you. I had been gambling. A lot of fellows in college go out there. Some of them take in quite a little money. I did, too, once. And then I lost. I must have lost a lot more than I supposed. I don't remember making out the check and putting dad's name to it. I was drunk. It wasn't a crime, because I wasn't in my right mind."

"You don't have to excuse yourself to me," X said kindly. "I know how it is. The drinks and the girls. They give a lot of synthetic courage, make him want to spend and show what a good sport he is. Then comes the awakening and the headache. Sure, I know. But where did you do this gambling?"

"Out at Steve Lannigan's Plantation."

"Lannigan," X mused. "Another of the big-shot racketeers; another branch of the Golden God's empire.... Okay, George, I'm going to take you back up to the street. In your pocket you're going to find fifteen thousand dollars."

"Fifteen thous—" the youth gasped. "Say, who are you? Santa Claus? What is this? A loan?"

"No," X said. "It's part of the money that's due your mother. It came from the rotten devils who gypped her out of it. And there's going to he more." He took out the wad of bills the grasping Golden God had given him, thrust them into George Leeds' pocket. Then, hanging onto the youth's arm in a friendly manner, X led him back to the level of the street.

THE TAXI driver and the excited individual who had hailed X and Tony Darkness were standing there. Harkness, insistent that X act upon the fact that Harkness had seen Joe Sine in a car, had got into his own roadster and followed X to the spot.

But for the moment, the earnest young Harkness had forgotten Joe Sine. He seized the sopping shoulders of George Leeds' coat. "George!" he gasped, "you weren't going to—"

"Hell no, he wasn't," X cut in generously. He turned on the excitable man who had hailed him. "It's a good thing you didn't call the police," he snapped. "This man was down there looking for his watch. He lost it somewhere around here this afternoon. That right, George?"

In the light from the cab headlights, X got a look at George Leeds' face. It was a thin face, oddly reminiscent of the face of Carter Leeds, but lacking the fine lines of character that years had given the youth's father. A trifle weak, X thought, but then George Leeds was hardly more than a boy.

George Leeds glanced shyly up at the Agent. "Say, you're Fred Archer, the private dick, aren't you. Say, I've always been interested in your work. You couldn't give me a job, could you?"

X laughed. "Maybe. When you're out of school, we'll see about it. You've got to go through school, now, you know. Harkness, suppose you take Leeds in your car. The loss of his watch has sort of upset him. You see that he gets home. Have a smoke on the way and talk things over."

"Glad to," Harkness said earnestly. "Let's go, George. I'd like to drop in on your sister, anyway."

The youth and the young man walked off toward Harkness' small car.

X turned to the excitable man. "You like walking—in the rain?"

The man nodded. "Yes, but that boy did say something about jumping—"

"Get on, then," X cut in. "There's a lot of rain to be walked in." And he got into the cab and told the driver to take him back to Archer's office. He had yet to take care of the matter of a murder charge against him.

He got out of the cab about a block from the office, hurried to the alley back of the building. The fire escape led him to the second floor. With a bit of wire thrust between the sashes, Agent X clicked over the latch of the consultation room window. Then he had slipped across the sill into the dark.

"We'll get Archer if we have to wait here all night," X heard a voice in the outer office say. "I sent a couple of the boys around to his apartment. He's bound to show up at one place or the other. He can't get out of town, because we've got men at the depot and on the main roads watching for his car."

"Yeah," said another cop, "we got him sewed up, all right. But have we got enough to hold him? After all, there were about ten people who had fingerprints plastered all over Leeds' office."

"Sure," said the other, "but we got to nail somebody, even if we can't hold him. The newspapers are climbing the D.A. The D.A. is climbing me. What the hell can we do?"

"No use talking," X thought to himself, "you got to have a fall guy." And in the dark he crossed to the closet where the real Fred Archer was confined. He unlocked the door, hauled Archer across the floor by the shoulders of his coat Then in the darkness the Agent's skilled fingers worked, removing the plastic material that covered Archer's face.

When that was done, he went to Archer's desk, unlocked the drawer, and withdrew his medical kit. His keen sense of touch enabled him to find the correct antidote for the narcotic he had employed on Archer. Having loaded a hypodermic with the antidote, he made an injection in Archer's arm.

HE CROUCHED there in the darkness, waiting for the powerful stimulant to get in its work. He felt Archer's lax muscles gradually tighten, heard his lips mumbling. X stood up, hauled Archer to his feet. Cautiously, he moved the still groggy detective across to the door.

"What's going on, huh?" Archer sighed. "Go away and let me sleep. It's still night."

Half supporting Archer with one hand, X unlocked the door with the other and swung it back a little way. A gentle push served to send Archer staggering into the room—into the hands of the waiting police. X sprang back into the shadows, flattened himself against the wall. He waited until he heard the outer door close behind the cops and the protesting Archer. Then he breathed again, lighted the light and stepped out into the outer office.

Less than a minute later the door of the office opened and Jane Cromer and Harvey Bates entered. Jane was saying: "But they framed him, I tell you. The cops in this town hate Fred because he gets the jump on them so often. He's said himself—"

And then the redheaded woman's blue eyes darted across the room, saw Agent X. Her jaw dropped. She took a deep breath, started to scream. But Harvey Bates' big hand came up to clamp over her mouth. Bates kicked the door closed with his heel, still holding the girl.

"Let her go, Bates," X said in his own deep, soft voice. "The cat, we might say, is out of the bag now. She saw the cops taking Archer out of here?"

"Right," clipped Bates. "She wanted to war with them about it." He released Jane Cromer.

The tall girl stood there a moment, staring at X. And then she found her tongue. "Of all the lousy tricks. Who are you, anyway? Some impersonator? What's your racket? You framed Fred—"

"Didn't you help?" X asked coolly. He was smiling a calm, assured smile. "You've been poking drugs into him for me, haven't you?"

"Then—then all this time you—you've been Freddy instead of Freddy being Freddy," she gasped. "You've sat here in this office— Why, damn you, you even kissed me."

"You can hardly blame me for that, Jane," X said. "As for framing Archer, just wait until the police take his fingerprints. Those happen to be my prints they've got in Leeds' office, so neither you nor Archer have anything to worry about. I simply fed the cops your employer and boy friend to keep them interested while I go after the Golden God."

"Then you're not a crook?" Jane asked.

X smiled. "I've been called that lots of times."

"You—you're the man called Secret Agent X!" she cried triumphantly.

"I've been called that, too," X said. "But you'd better stick to calling me Freddy. Because I'm not through with this face yet. Tell you what you do, sweetheart," and to Jane's utter amazement, his voice gradually drifted into Fred Archer's tones and manner of speaking, "you get into your glad rags. You and I are going to take in Lannigan's Plantation Club. I want you along to make it look as though I'm Fred Archer out for a large evening. Then, I kind of like your company."

"You and I—me?" Jane Cromer rested both hands on the top of the desk and leaned over to peer into Agent X's face. A slow smile spread across her warm, inviting lips. "I kind of like your company, too, Mr. X. And I like the way you get things done. Only one thing, you got to assure me Freddy's safe."

X nodded. "No safer place than jail."

"Then I'm safe," she said. "I'd hate to have Freddy see me with another man—even if the other man was his own reflection."

CHAPTER VIII

THE WORLD'S
WORST CRIME

STEVE LANNIGAN'S PLANTATION was well warmed up by the time Agent X and Jane arrived. They didn't linger as long as Jane would have liked to in the legitimate dine and dance portion of the building that fronted for the gambling.

There wasn't much secrecy about the big game room in back. Just enough to make it interesting to those patrons who wouldn't have been there if it hadn't been against the law. You had to be okayed by a big bruiser who stood at the door.

"Archer," said a big doorman, sticking out his hand, "you haven't been here for a long time. What was it Steve said about you coming here?"

"Steve said he didn't like the idea of a private dick playing roulette," said a pleasant, soft voice to the left of Jane.

X turned to see a man standing in the door of what he took to be an office, for the half-open door was marked private. The man was short, slight, handsome. He had a small, square mustache, beady eyes hung in puffy hammocks, sleek hair parted in the middle. He didn't look particularly like a man who would be called Lannigan, but that was what the big bruiser called him.

Lannigan came forward, smiling. He shook hands with the man supposed to be Archer. "You're forgiven this time, Fred," Lannigan said. "Go in and have yourself a time. I can even stand having a private dick around when he brings something as ornamental as that." Lannigan pointed a look at Jane Cromer.

So X and Jane were told to go into the gambling room, which was situated beyond what appeared to be the doors of a bank vault. The doors were not locked but could be on a moment's notice. That made the entrance to Lannigan's gambling place simply appear to be a large wall safe. Beyond lay a miniature Monte Carlo, glittering beneath the rays of a crystal prism chandelier.

Jane had been there before, but she had never played roulette. X bought her chips, stood behind her, pretended to give her tips on placing her bets. He was occupied chiefly with close scrutiny of the patrons of the place. They were young men, mostly, students from the university. And the feminine charm that warmed them into throwing their money away had not come from the campus. The women, to X's experienced eyes, were considerably older than the men. They were Lannigan's professional hostesses.

As the fascination of the game took hold of Jane, X slipped away, left the gambling room proper and headed for Lannigan's office. There was no one in the hall outside. The big doorman and Lannigan were in the office. So were a couple of young fellows. Lannigan was shaking hands with one of them as X glanced around the door.

"Anybody who's a friend of Wilson is all right with me," Lannigan was saying in his too pleasant voice. "Play here all you want. You'll have to register, of course. It's a little formality we've always held to. It fixes you up so that the doors of the Plantation are open to the best people only, see."

Lannigan took from his desk two crisp, square papers. From where X stood, they looked like printed forms. Lannigan put the papers down on his desk.

"This one," Lannigan pointed out, "you put your name on and your address, occupation, and so on. The other one, you write your father's name, address and so on. You see why we do that, don't you? We might get hold of some poor sport who would lose and then want to squawk to the police. But if we've got your old man's name down, why, then, any chiselers who'd like to squawk to the cops are in a sort of a spot themselves. We just say, 'You squawk to the cops and we tell the old man you've been gambling.' See how it works?"

The young man nodded and eagerly filled out the slips of paper.

AS SOON as this was done, the big doorman took the two college boys by the arms and conducted them toward the hall. X slipped behind a small fountain that was set into the center of the hall, watched the two young men being led into the gambling room. X's teeth clenched. He was beginning to get an insight into the world's worst crime. Something that only the mind of a perverted genius like the avaricious Golden God could have thought up.

X then slipped back to the door of Lannigan's office. There was a woman in there with Lannigan this time—a curvaceous blonde wearing a cheap fur coat. She had evidently just come in, for the raindrops in her hair sparkled in the damp light.

Lannigan was placing the crisp registration papers, which the late suckers had just signed, into an envelope. He put a stamp on the envelope and handed it to the girl. "Mail this, Marsha. And here—" Lannigan unlocked a drawer of his desk and took out four or five long slips of paper. "You put these in the usual spot for safe-keeping. We wouldn't want them to turn up if there was a raid. When the Golden God is ready to apply the pressure, I'll get them from you."

"Okay, Steve," the blonde woman said, putting the slips into her purse.

"Why, hello, Mr. Archer!" said a quiet voice behind X.

X turned quickly, saw Tony Harkness a few feet behind him. The tall, grave man was looking at X somewhat in the manner of a Sunday-school teacher who finds his pupils playing marbles for keeps.

X strode up to young Harkness. "What are you doing here?"

"Following George Leeds," Harkness said. "He got away from me. Told me to let him out at a drug store up here, and then he slipped out of the drug store and came this way. I shadowed him, saw him come in here. I don't know what his idea is—"

"Damn!" X cracked out. He knew what the idea was. X had given George Leeds fifteen thousand dollars to take to his mother. George had the crackpot idea that he might come to the Plantation and win back enough to make the thirty thousand he felt obliged to pay to his mother.

X turned swiftly from Tony Harkness, strode back into the gambling room in time to see George Leeds approaching the cashier's desk. Just as the youth put his hand into his pocket for the money with which to buy chips, X seized his arm. He spun the boy around.

"I ought to land one on your jaw, you young sap!" he husked. "Where is that dough? Hand it over, or I'll take it out of your hide. You're not old enough to take care of street-car fare. I'll mail it to your mother."

"Look here, Mr. Archer—" began George Leeds lamely.

"Hand over the dough. You're playing no games tonight." And when George Leeds made no move to hand over the money, X reached in the youth's pocket and pulled out the wad himself. X jerked his thumb toward the door. "Now you make tracks out of here. I guess once a sap always a sap."

"Just a minute, Archer."

That was Steve Lannigan who spoke. He was crossing the floor in short, swift steps. There was a troubled, angry frown on his handsome face.

"What's the idea of putting your nose in my affairs?" Lannigan snapped. "If this man has money, he's free to play here. George Leeds is one of a select group—"

"Group of suckers!" cut in X. "Well, he's not playing here with money that doesn't belong to him. You keep out of this, Lannigan, or you're apt to be choking on your teeth."

Lannigan's right had made a swift gesture toward his pocket. X's left fist lashed out in a short, swift arc that caught Lannigan on the point of the chin. Lannigan was cold when he struck the floor.

X jerked a glance over his shoulder. Many of the patrons had left the game tables to watch the scene between Lannigan and X. Jane was among them. X said: "Come on, sweetheart." He grabbed her arm with one hand and George's arm with the other. He hurried them through the vaultlike doors into the hall outside. Tony Harkness was there, staring owl-eyed.

X shoved George Leeds into Harkness' arms. "Get that infant home and to bed," he snapped. "You're big enough to give him a licking, Harkness. Do it, if he doesn't behave."

"I will," Harkness said earnestly. "I'll do that very thing." He took off his glasses. His strong fingers clenched on George Leeds' sleeve. "You going to come or do I have to drag you?"

Young Leeds decided that it was far safer to come.

X and Jane hurried from the building and got into Archer's car.

"Just as I was winning, too," Jane sighed. "You didn't even give me a chance to cash those chips."

"I'll cash them personally," X promised as he started the car.

HE DROVE about three blocks and then stopped the car in front of a drug store. He had had every intention of following the blonde called Marsha Kent from the Plantation, but George Leeds had spoiled that. Somehow, he had to get hold of those slips of paper the woman had put in her purse. He had heard Lannigan say she was to keep them until the Golden God was ready to use them in his extortion scheme.

In the drug store, a glance through the phone directory gave X the address of Marsha Kent. She lived down in the business district, probably in an apartment over some shop.

He drove downtown and found the address without difficulty. It was an apartment over a small dress shop. Next door was a gaudy-fronted jewelry store. X parked the car out in front. He craned his neck out through the window and detected no light in the apartment above.

"Nobody home, evidently," he said to Jane. "I'm going to do a little fancy housebreaking. If you see a well-upholstered blonde covered with a lot of rabbit skin, approaching this place, a couple of blasts on the horn and I'll skip out a back window. After you've tooted, drive around to the west end of the alley and pick me up."

"Be careful," Jane warned, "this makes me nervous."

X got out, climbed the stair between the dress shop and the jewelry store. He worked for a minute with a master key on the lock of the door at the top. It opened and he found himself in a small, richly furnished apartment. There was living room, bedroom, bath and kitchen. He began a search that lasted approximately ten minutes and took in all the rooms with swift thoroughness, but revealed no sign of a clue. Then came Jane's warning signal on the horn of the car. X went into the bathroom, raised a window, stepped out on the fire escape and pulled the window down again.

He hurried down the steps, into the alley, and ran to join Jane in the car.

"What luck?" the girl asked.

"None. You saw the blonde?"

"Sure. She came on foot, started up the steps."

"Good," X said. "Wait here. I've got a screwy notion that I'm going to rob a jewelry store."

CHAPTER IX

CHECKS OF SEALED FATE

A **GENT X HAD** a triangle of handkerchief tied over the lower part of his face. The collar of his topcoat turned way up, and his pulled-down hat concealed the handkerchief. He had a half of a brick he had found in the alley in his left coat pocket. Fred Archer's gun was in his right coat pocket.

He wandered along the street, past the dress shop, past the stairway that led up to the blonde Marsha Kent's apartment. Then he went to the window of the jewelry store. The diamonds in the window were probably fake. No jeweler would have left genuine stones of such size in his window at this hour. Fake or not, it made little difference to Agent X.

He simply pulled the brick out of his pocket and hurled it through the jeweler's window. He stepped back quickly to avoid the flying glass, then darted forward to thrust an arm through the broken pane, scoop up a handful of glittering jewels, and stuffed them into his pocket.

Across the street a window flew open. Someone yelled for the police. But by that time there was no evidence of the burglary except the broken window and the looted case. Agent X was already on his way up the steps leading to Marsha Kent's apartment.

At her door, he could hear the shrill toot of the police whistle. He chuckled. That would lend considerable credence to the tale he intended to tell. He knocked on the door.

"Western Union," he said, in a voice that sounded as if it belonged to a boy. At the same time he turned down his collar and pulled his gun.

The door opened a crack, and he saw the round, pink cheeks of the blonde. He thrust his foot into the crack and shoved with his shoulder. His gun was the first thing into the room. He said: "Don't yell, lady, and you won't get hurt none." Then he forced his way into the room and slammed the door.

"Whew, dat was a tight spot, lady!" He reached in his pocket, pulled out a handkerchief with which to wipe his brow. As he did so, he spilled some of the jewelry intentionally on the floor. The woman's eyes widened, followed the tumbling glitter covetously.

"What is this?" she demanded in a strident voice. "A stick-up?"

"Dis ain't, lady," X said. "Dis is de lam after I cracked de joint. Cops are on me tail, see, and you're tellin' dem I went the other way, see. I'm stickin' here until things cool down. Pick up dat ice and give it to me." He waved his gun toward the woman. She watched him steadily for a moment, and then obeyed.

"Hundred grand in dis haul," X said. "Nice night's woik, ain't it?"

She dumped the gems into his outstretched hand. X backed to the door, put his ear against the panel. He could hear heavy footsteps on the stairway.

"Cop," he breathed. He sprang lightly across the room to the bedroom. "Listen, lady," he said. "I'm watchin' you over a gun from in here. Tell the cops you seen nothin'. Try any tricks and I let you have it."

The woman was breathing in shallow gasps. She nodded her pale head. "What's it going to be worth to me?"

"Your life, lady," X said, and sprang into the bedroom as big knuckles pounded on the door.

Marsha Kent opened the door. "Yes?" she said in a steady voice.

"Sorry to bother you at a time like this, miss," said a thick voice, "but somebody broke in Carson's Jewelry Store. Did you see anybody running away?"

"No," said the woman. "I didn't see anything. I heard a crash of glass, but didn't think to look out."

"Hear anybody on the stairs out here? Anybody come to the door?"

"No," said the woman.

"Okay. Sorry, miss."

Marsha Kent closed the door.

IN THE bedroom, X had spread a handkerchief out on the bed and was depositing the glittering array of stolen jewels in the center of it. His gun was lying on the bed, but a good long reach away.

Actually, he was perfectly aware of Marsha's entrance, but he apparently paid no attention to the woman. He kept his eyes on the

*She flew at him, suddenly
realizing she had a weapon
in her hand—the ice pick.*

heap of gems. Aloud, he calculated the imaginary sum some fence
would give him for the loot. All in all, he knew the imitations that
had been used for window decoration were probably worth little
more than twenty-five dollars.

The blonde woman made a swift, catlike movement forward. X
was slow turning his head. And when he did look around, Marsha
had his gun in her hand.

"It's a cinch," she said, "I plug you and yell for the cops. Maybe I
get a medal for knocking off their jewel thief, see."

"Easy, lady," X whined. "You wouldn't do that. Say, how about one of these rings wit' about two carat of shiner in it? I was goin' to make you the present anyway for standin' off the law."

Marsha's rouged lips curled into a smile. "I'm giving you a break. Scram, and don't touch those jewels."

"Don't touch— Why of all de noive! Listen, lady, you can't do dat to me." X sprang to his feet. The gun in the woman's hand steadied on his middle.

"I'm not kidding," she said. "Scram. I'll count ten. One... two... three.... You'd better start moving."

X cursed. "I'll get square wit' you for dis, lady."

"Four... five... six..."

X moved across the room, into the living room. He opened the door. The woman followed him. She had the handkerchief filled with jewels in her left hand. Her right hand held the gun as though it had been especially made for that purpose. X went out of the door and slammed it. He heard the key turn in the lock. The blonde woman withdrew the key. He could hear her laughing to herself. X ran noisily down the steps, turned around, tiptoed back. He dropped to his knees in front of the woman's door and looked through the keyhole.

She was in the center of the room. She had kicked back a scatter rug and was kneeling on the floor. She had an ice pick in her hand. As near as X could make out she was pushing out what appeared to be a nail head on one of the narrow strips of oak flooring. As X watched, the woman pushed down on the strip of flooring with her fingertips. It dropped back on hinges, revealed a narrow opening from which she took a thin box of black-painted steel. She opened the box. Inside were narrow strips of paper such as X had seen Lannigan give her.

Marsha reached into the bosom of her dress and pulled out the handkerchief which contained the jewels she had taken from X. She intended to place them in her secret hiding place, just as X had hoped she would do. His plan had worked to perfection. There was nothing to do except open the door, go in and take the slips of paper from the box. He thrust the same master key he had used before into the lock, turned it, opened the door and sprang into the room.

The woman was on her feet, lunging toward a small table where she had left the automatic X had carried. X's hand came down on her wrist at the same time her fingers clutched the gun butt. A quick twist, and she was disarmed.

He picked up the gun, turned it on her. "You can have the jewel for your trouble, Miss Kent," he said. "All I want are those papers you were keeping for the Golden God."

He crossed to the steel box and scooped out the papers. She flew at him, suddenly realizing that she had a formidable weapon in her hand. The ice pick she had used to open the secret compartment. The Agent's gun jerked up. Its silent threat stopped her in her tracks. Her face blanched.

"No," she said hoarsely. "They'll kill me. Take the jewels."

X shook his head. "They're only worth about twenty dollars. These pieces of paper are worth several human lives. Take my advice and get out of town tonight. The Golden God's throne is crumbling under him. Better take a powder if you don't want to be crushed when it falls."

And with that X left the apartment. He removed the handkerchief from his face and hurried to join Jane Cromer in the car.

"Got them," he said. "Take a look." He pulled the slips of paper from his pocket and held them under the dash lamp.

"Checks," she said. "All payable to the Plantation."

"Checks that would never be cashed," X said. "See how it works? Whenever one of those college boys comes to the Plantation to gamble, he is asked to fill out registration slips. On one of those slips, he has to fill in his father's name and address. The criminals take these registration slips, cover the name of the father, written by the boy, with some sort of removable film which is impervious to bleaching agents. Then they treat the slips with chlorine gas or something of the sort, and that removes all the ink except the father's name.

"The slips are trimmed to the size of check blanks, carefully printed so as to look like check blanks, with the father's name, as written by the son, appearing on the signature line at the bottom. The rest of the check is filled in, and the criminals have a check to which the boy has apparently forged his father's name. The check is made out to cover the boy's loss at the games.

"They get the boys drunk so that they don't remember what they have done. They use the check to extort money from the boy's father. They demand the amount of money the father has in life insurance, because most of the men they tackle aren't wealthy enough to make any other sum worth while. Then they kill the boy's father. The boy's mother collects the insurance, and then the extortionists tackle the mother, make her pay it all over to them under threat of exposing the boy as a forger. The mothers make easy victims. And it's a way to get at wealth that crime so far hasn't touched."

"It's rotten!" Jane said. "The filthiest racket I ever heard of. So that's what's back of these killings here in town."

"Yes. And back of that, the Golden God. I'm going to get that guy!"

Bates was waiting for them back in Archer's office. "Any luck," sir?" he asked.

"A lot," X said briefly. He hurried back to Archer's desk, took out the medical kit that he had left there. From it he removed a small paraffin vial of acid. "I may be able to test these checks and make sure of the bleaching chemical used on them," he said. "There's the chance that that might tell something about the man who did the dirty job."

Wax vial in one hand, checks in the other, he paced the office, scowling. Then he thrust the vial into his breast pocket and used both hands to fold the checks into his wallet.

"That won't be necessary," he muttered. "I think we've got something—something in the past that puts the finger on the killer." His face brightened. He took from his pocket the fifteen thousand dollars he had taken from George Leeds. He handed it to Bates. "Get this to Mrs. Leeds. When you're through with that, keep your eye on Marsha Kent. She lives over the Susie Lou Dress Shop. It she's smart, she'll get out of town. If she sticks around, she's apt to be murdered. And we don't want any more bloodshed."

"What are you going to do?" asked Jane.

"Going to visit Al Curzon. I think he'll take me to the Golden God—without knowing it."

CHAPTER X

THE GRASP OF
THE GOLDEN GOD

AL CURZON IN a dress suit was like a skeleton in armor. With every step you expected to hear the bony clatter of his ribs against his shirt front. He wasn't moving much at the present time except to reach to his ash-tray and pick up his cigar for a few puffs. He was sitting in his living room in the Colonial Hotel, which he owned and operated. The hotel had been a cheap little flop house which the enterprising Curzon had turned into a racy night club. It was on the main street of the city and boasted considerable patronage.

Across from Al Curzon's lounge chair sat the man Curzon supposed to be Fred Archer. Al Curzon was frankly puzzled.

"Every time you pay me a visit, Fred," he said, "I expect to get shaken loose from a lot of cash. What is it this time?"

"Not money," said Agent X. "So just relax. You've always played square with me. Now I'm playing square with you. Your brother is Joe Sine?"

Curzon nodded. "Joe Curzon. Sine was an alias he took some time ago."

"And you think the Golden God is Joe Sine?"

Al Curzon nodded. "I know it. You know it. You talked with him the other day. He's pretty much of a physical wreck, I guess, but his brain is still working."

"I wonder if it is," X said quietly. "You're paying the Golden God a big per cent of your total take, aren't you, because he's organized the underworld and made new sources of revenue accessible for you and Lannigan, and others of the same stamp? He's put down mob warfare. He's made it worth your while to pay him his per cent."

Curzon nodded. "I thought you agreed to keep your nose out of the Golden God's affairs?"

"You'll be glad I didn't before I'm through. Do you think that your brother committed suicide in prison?"

Al laughed. "Of course he didn't. The first time I saw him after he was out he told me that he had taken some sort of a drug that had stopped his heart beating. He was passed off for dead. Then he revived and went back to work, though his recovery was never complete."

X nodded. "He can't move a muscle. And still he took that risk when he had only one more year to complete his stretch in prison. Is that logic? Don't answer. It isn't. The drug he took was cyanide. That's what the newspapers said. That was the truth. It was undoubtedly cyanide. You think he took it of his own free will? If he did, it was because he thought it was a drug that would enable him to escape. Somebody deliberately poisoned your brother. Got any idea who might want to do that?"

Curzon leaned forward in his chair. "How do you know this?"

"I've got proof that Joe Sine took cyanide poison. The medical records of the prison show this, and the doctor there is on the square. I argue that he wouldn't have taken cyanide of his own free will. He couldn't have got it in prison. So somebody smuggled it to him from the outside, telling him it was a drug to assist him to escape. Now, who might have wanted to kill him? Who was it that had reason to fear Joe Sine so much that he didn't dare risk Sine's leaving the prison alive?"

CURZON pulled on his bony chin. "I don't know the man's name. But Joe said when he got out of prison he was going to blackmail somebody and be on easy street the rest of his life."

"That's it, then," X said. "Well, here's some more. If Joe Sine is alive today, it's only due to the fact that a certain scientist used him as a subject of an experiment in reviving the dead. That scientist may have been partially successful. Theoretically, his experiment should have worked. But if it did, Joe Sine hasn't a brain, because it's impossible to fully restore circulation to the brain once the heart has stopped for any length of time."

Curzon stood up, leaned over the Agent. "That's over my head. All I know is I've seen Joe and I've heard him talk."

"Ever see him move?" asked X.

Curzon shook his head. "He's paralyzed."

"If he's paralyzed, it's the fault of the man who tried to kill him by sending him the cyanide in prison."

"But," Curzon objected, "do you think Joe would have taken anything in the way of a drug that an enemy had sent him."

"Don't be a sap," X husked. "The man who killed Joe Sine wouldn't have smuggled the poison to prison, himself. He's have sent somebody to do it and told that somebody to say it was from you."

"Listen. Archer," Curzon whispered tensely, "if you know who it was killed or tried to kill my brother, spit it out. I'll pay you your own price—"

X held up his hand. "There isn't any price. I just want to get things straight. The man who killed your brother by smuggling the cyanide into prison is the Golden God. You *think* Joe Sine is the Golden God. Well, your brother is just the fall guy. If he's alive, he's being framed."

Curzon dropped a bony hand on the Agent's shoulder and shook him. "You're lying, Fred! How could that be?"

X shrugged off Curzon's hand. "I've got proof. The Golden God ordered you to deliver me into his hands. He wanted to talk to me, to buy me off, didn't he? He paid me fifteen grand to keep my nose out of his business. Figure a reason for that. A lift of his finger and he could have had me bumped. It would have been a lot easier than the other murders he's pulled. But no, he pays me fifteen grand to stay out. And why did he appear before me without a mask? Only one reason for that. So I would see that the Golden God was Joe Sine; so that when the blow-up eventually came, I would be the witness that would say the Golden God was Joe Sine, when you and I damn well know that he isn't!"

Al Curzon's pale cheeks reddened slightly. "That makes sense," he said.

"And," continued X, "the Golden God is framing your brother to take the rap that's due the Golden God because your brother is helpless. I think I'd look into the Golden God a little closer, Al."

X got up, put on his coat, and left the room. Bat he did not leave the hotel. He lingered around the corridor, listened at Al Curzon's door. Finally, he heard Curzon using the telephone. To somebody on the phone, Al said: "Have the mob at 1452 Paragon Street in three quarters of an hour."

X's mind instantly recorded the address. Was it the headquarters of the greedy Golden God, or simply a meeting place for Curzon's men before they would go to hammer on the Golden God's door? Either way, X intended to be at that address....

1452 Paragon Street was a huge-frame house, set far back from the street in a jungle of shrubbery and neglected trees. It had every evidence of being uninhabited. X noticed, however, that there were marks of tire treads in the mud of the drive that led to a garage attached to the house. Cars had obviously been there lately.

X hurried up the drive, splashing into puddles in the rainy darkness. He was certain that when Curzon had brought him here the first time, they had entered the house through the garage. So it was toward the garage that he went now. The lock on the garage door was a flimsy latch which yielded readily. Once inside, he unlocked the door connecting garage and house with one of his master keys. He stepped into the house where every creak of the floor told of emptiness.

FROM HIS pocket, he took a small pencil flashlight which he beamed around a large reception hall that was devoid of furnishings. He glanced into a living room that was equally empty. Then he stole up the stairs to find himself in a hall paneled with light-finished oak—the identical room to which Al Curzon had brought him. He was in the headquarters of the Golden God!

He stepped to the end of the hall and quietly opened the door. Beyond was the long, low room where he had spoken with the Golden God. At the end, velvet curtains were drawn. There was no sound within the room. Nothing but darkness, unbroken save by the darting beam of X's flashlight.

He tiptoed to the curtain at the opposite end of the room, parted them with cautious fingers. The silvery needle of his light stabbed into the thin, white face of Joe Sine.

Only the quiver of the light beam betrayed X's excitement. Joe Sine's glassy eyes remained fixed and staring. Not a muscle of the ghastly face moved. No muscle in that face would move again. For Joe Sine was dead, as he must have been from the moment he had taken the cyanide poison in prison. Not only was he dead, but the body had been artfully embalmed and posed. Joe Sine's deadliest enemy had been the Golden God himself.

X stepped in behind the curtains where the corpse sat at the desk. He got behind the corpse, drew back the chair a little, stooped. Beneath the chair was a conical radio reproducer. The means by which the real Golden God had spoken apparently through Joe Sine's dead lips. All to frame a dead man, so that if an emergency

*The Golden God leaned forward, plunged
the hypodermic needle into X's throat.*

arose, the real Golden God could let the blame fall upon the shoulders of a man he had killed.

And by thus posing as Joe Sine, Al Curzon's brother, the Golden God had enlisted the aid of Al Curzon and his mob. Without them he would have hardly been able to weld the underworld into a single, powerful fighting unit.

X opened the drawers of the desk one by one. Inside one drawer he found a complete book of records which told of the tremendous sums that had sifted into the grasp of the money and power greedy Golden God. Here was a list of every crime and its perpetrator. Here was doom for each and every member of the Golden God's criminal army. But to catch the Golden God himself—

X hastily put the book back into the desk drawer. There was one way to do that. He had sufficient makeup material in the hollow heel of his right shoe to enable him to make over his face to resemble that of the corpse in the chair. Then he could hide the corpse, take exactly the same position, wait motionless until the Golden God returned.

Back toward the opening in the curtain, X studied the thin, pallid face of the corpse. He stooped, opened the compartment of his hollow heel, and removed a tube of makeup material. He straightened. A familiar chill raced along his spine as he did so, for the chill originated at the muzzle of an automatic pressed into his back.

"Put up your hands," a whispered voice ordered.

X obeyed.

"Keep them up. Turn around."

X turned slowly. Between parted curtains stood three men. Two of them were hard-faced criminals with kill-for-a-nickel eyes. Between these men was a tall figure dressed in a well-fitting black suit. His entire face was covered by a mask made of some metal that resembled gold. The Golden God had returned.

"Secret Agent X, good evening," said the Golden God. "I just witnessed the release of Fred Archer from the local jail. So of course you are Agent X."

X eyed the three men, saying nothing. All three had guns in their hands. There wasn't half a chance of breaking through that death ring that hemmed him in.

The Golden God said: "You men remove the body of Sine from that chair. Under the circumstances, we need a new fall guy."

The Golden God's henchmen obeyed. Their chief said: "One of you throw the corpse down the steps."

SENSELESS though the order might have been, one of the men took the corpse in his arms and carried it across the room. The Agent could hear the body tumbling down the steps. The henchman returned. A nod from the Golden God, and one of his men removed the gun from X's pocket.

"Now, Agent X," said the Golden God, "you may sit down in that chair. Perhaps you came here to impersonate the Golden God. I am going to give you that opportunity."

The two henchmen forced X into the chair. A cord was tied to one leg of the chair, wrapped around X's ankles. It was brought up across chest and arms and tightly tied beyond all hope of reach at the back of the chair.

"Few things," said the Golden God, "go on of which I am unaware, in this city. Very soon now, as my organization grows, the underworld of the nation will be within my grasp. It is well to have you removed in the very beginning." The Golden God turned his head slightly. "The hypodermic," he said softly.

"I take it," X said evenly, "that you are under the impression I am about to stop bothering you and your kind?"

"You put it bluntly. Yes, I will be much relieved to know that with you removed nothing can hamper the growth of my empire. Even the federal government shall feel my strength."

"I see," said X. "And I've little to do but submit. Just when did your crime career begin?"

The Golden God laughed. "Years ago. It had a small beginning like all truly great things. And no one ever guessed."

"No one except Joe Sine. Sine had something on you that he intended to blackmail you with as soon as he was out of prison. So you managed Sine's death by sending him cyanide poison."

"Perfectly true. I sent it to him through a drug merchant who was working the penitentiary at that time. Sine wasn't a drug addict. He thought it was a drug that would produce artificial catalepsy and enable him to escape from prison. I had hired the drug merchant to tell him that and to give the impression that it was his brother who was trying to help him escape."

"And the Harkness attempt to revive Sine was an absolute failure," X said. "You stole the body, leaving the impression that Sine had revived and walked away."

"Exactly. Sine would make the perfect fall guy for the extortion scheme I was planning. Sine being a forger, suspicion would naturally have fallen on him if the forged check racket I had planned failed at any time."

The Golden God turned as one of his henchmen came back with a small silver case in his hand. The Golden God opened the case and took out a small hypodermic syringe filled with some dark fluid.

"We've talked enough, Agent X," he said quietly. "I am well aware that Al Curzon is on his way here with a group of armed men. I think when he finds the body of his brother at the foot of the steps, he will be sufficiently disturbed to come up here and kill you. Because you will be wearing the mask of the Golden God. You will not be able to move from the chair. And should Curzon hesitate, I have a few words that will urge him to shoot you.

"You see, you will not be able to talk or in any way defend yourself. And by means of the same loudspeaker system through which I made the corpse of Joe Sine speak, I shall also speak for you."

And with those words, the Golden God leaned forward, plunged the hypodermic needle into X's throat first on one side and then on the other. A strange, tingling sensation spread over X's throat. The sensation became one of cold. He tried to move his tongue, but was unable to tell whether he had moved it or not. There was a peculiar tightening of his vocal chords.

"The effect of the drug will soon pass," the Golden God said, "but you won't have to worry about that. You will simply be unable to cry out when Al Curzon kills you. Al should be here any moment. I am going to take that record book from the desk."

The Golden God opened the drawer and removed the ledger which recorded the crimes of his combine. "And now you'll have to excuse me. One of my men will be behind the curtains until Curzon arrives, in case you try one of your miracle escapes I have heard about. And now, lights out for a moment."

There was an interval of darkness. Something cold was pressed over X's face—the mask of the Golden God. And when the lights came on again, X saw an empty room through the slits of his mask. A dull weight of helplessness rested upon his shoulders. There was no escape from this web. No conceivable way out.

CHAPTER XI

STAKE OF AN EMPIRE

NEVER HAD X found himself in such a hopeless predicament. Unable to move, his power of speech temporarily paralyzed by the narcotic, he might better have been unconscious. That way he could not have heard the approach of his own doom. For now there were footstep, on the stairs, slow and quiet but regular as the ticking of a clock that measured X's allotted moments on earth.

Curzon would find his brother on the stairway. His appetite for vengeance would be whetted. He had come for the blood of the Golden God, and to all appearances X was the man Curzon sought. And X could not even voice a denial.

As X strained against the ropes, he was conscious of something hard pressing against the left side of his chest. He glanced down, remembered instantly the wax vial of acid he had thrust into his breast pocket when contemplating the possibilities of chemically testing the fake checks that he had received from Marsha.

His heart gave a bound. That acid was retained in a wax bottle because only wax was impervious to its corrosive action. Glass could not have kept it. Once out of the flask, it would eat through cloth, flesh and rope. And the rope that confined him passed directly across the vial.

He exerted all his efforts to strain the rope against the pocket where the wax flask was concealed. He heard a faint pop, like the cracking of an egg shell, and then a lance of pain shot across the flesh of his breast. He closed his eyes against the strong fumes that arose from the broken flask. He ground his teeth in an effort to withstand that branding anguish.

Then, as the knob of the door turned slowly, he glanced quickly down at the pocket, saw shreds of cloth dissolving in the fuming liquid. Would there be enough to reach the rope, or would it spread through his clothing, eating only into his skin?

He looked up. The long, skeletal frame of Al Curzon centered a group of five men who had entered the room. Al Curzon had a gun in his hand. The others had their right hands poised over pockets and shoulder holsters.

"Don't move G.G.," warned Curzon as he took cautious steps forward.

Not any danger of him moving!

"This is where you pay for the rotten double cross you handed me, G.G.," Curzon went on as he advanced. "I want you to go out slow. You'll get the slugs way down in your belly. I want you to have plenty time to think over what you did to Joe."

"I've thought about that a lot." It was the voice of the Golden God, apparently coming from Agent X. Actually its source was the radio loudspeaker under the chair in which he was sitting.

X was living through moments of hell. Seven feet away from him were the man and the gun that were to kill him. And within his breast was a gnawing pain of liquid fire. Acrid fumes coiled about his face, choking him. The rope. Was the acid attacking the rope? He couldn't see. He could only hope blindly while the Golden God goaded Curzon to a passion by means of the reproducer under the chair.

The Golden God gleefully boasted of how he had killed Joe Sine because Sine had threatened him with blackmail. How he had sent a message to Sine in prison, using Al Curzon's name, telling him of the escape he had planned for Sine by means of a drug Sine was to take. How that drug was poison.

Expert on signatures that Joe Sine was, he nevertheless had had no reason to question the message he supposed was from his brother. For, boasted the Golden God, the signature was Curzon's signature which had been appended to a note Curzon had written to the Golden God. By the same process by which he had bleached the registration slips the players at the Plantation were required to fill out, the Golden God had bleached out all the writing in that letter except the signature. It had then been a simple matter to type in the message that had led Joe Sine to take the poison.

"Okay," Curzon said. "I'm killing you personally, G.G. This is a personal matter. I want you to die slowly. I want you to—"

THE ROPE across X's chest snapped. The acid had eaten through all but the last strand and X's strength had taken care of that. Even as Curzon would have pulled the trigger of his revolver, X made the only move that could have possibly saved him for even a split-second. He needed surprise, and surprise was what that movement achieved. His left hand shot up to the golden mask and jerked it off his face.

Involuntarily, Curzon's trigger finger relaxed. *"Archer!"* he gasped. "Why, you dirty—"

He didn't get any further. There wasn't time. X burst from the ropes, sprang from the chair. His left arm shot out with speed that made his clenched fist a mere blur of white that became something more than that only when the biceps of Curzon's right arm stopped it. Fingers of Curzon's right hand stiffened. Numb as they were by the blow, he fumbled his gun. X scooped it out of mid-air, side-stepped to bring Curzon between him and one of Curzon's men.

The burning acid that was eating into X's skin was like a spur to a racehorse. He moved like a cyclone gone mad, but coupled with this appearance of madness was lucid thinking.

Holding to Curzon's throat, he dragged the man, backing all the time toward the Golden God's desk. Beneath Curzon's arm, he fired, but low; for no one hated to kill more than Agent X.

As his hips touched the desk, X flung Curzon away from him, kicked up with both feet to pivot around and slide to the other side of the desk. From this barricade, which Curzon's men were rapidly turning into a sieve, X shot deliberately to extinguish the lights in the room.

In darkness, gun flame splashed the walls with momentary light. There were at least ten men in the room. That meant that the Golden God's personal staff had joined the battle, determined that Agent X should not escape.

X's hand dropped to the floor. He felt the cold, metal face of the Golden God's mask. He picked it up, stuffed it inside his pocket, got to his feet. He ran toward the door. There, slivers of gun flame told him, a man waited. X took out the guard at the door with a well-placed shot, and instantly marked himself as a target. A slug grazed his left arm, but it was hardly noticeable because of the pain the burning acid was causing.

He reached the door, seized the knob, twisted. In his hands the door opened and closed like the shutter of a camera. Wood of the door was slivered by a hail of lead. But X was already clattering down the steps.

Outside the house, sirens wailed. As X ran out through the living room toward the hall which led into the garage, police were thundering on the front door, trying to break it down. It was the fall of the Golden God's empire. But where was the Golden God? If he escaped, all of the Agent's efforts had effected only a remedy rather than a cure.

Gun in hand, X burst into the garage. There was a car there now. A man had one foot on the running board, and the motor was idling. The man turned, drew a gun, fired without aim. More deliberate, more accurate, X fired, saw in the dim light the blood that striped the man's gun wrist. The man's gun clattered as it dropped to the garage floor.

The man, heedless of X's gun, threw himself forward, punching with both fists. He was powerful. His reach was long. He had had training, perhaps, but panic put fighting sense to rout. X's right arm shot out, wormed in behind a hastily raised guard. He shot a short punch to the chest that rocked the man into the side of the car. X followed the punch by ramming the muzzle of his gun into the man's middle.

"Don't move, Tony," he warned. "You're through. Finished, for all time."

TONY HARKNESS crumpled up against the side of the car. His fine body was wilting under him, weakened by stark terror. His face was the same, grave stoical mask it had always been. His owlish eyes stared steadily at Agent X. He said nothing.

"You, Tony Harkness, are the Golden God," X accused.

"How absurd," Harkness said. "How utterly fantastic, Archer."

"Call me Agent X, as you did before," X said. "The moment I discovered how the forged-check extortion scheme of yours worked, I knew you were the man. Chlorine gas is the most powerful of all bleaching agents. The flower of the rose is particularly sensitive to it. Remember when Jane Cromer put one of her roses in your buttonhole? It was a red rose. Yet when I visited your father at the university, that rose had changed strangely to a sickly white shade.

"It had been bleached by some of the chlorine you were using to prepare the Plantation registration slips by bleaching out everything except the 'forged' signatures of the gambling victims' fathers. Unfortunately, at the time I did not know how your extortion racket worked."

"And," Tony interrupted, "I have destroyed the incriminating rose, leaving you no proof."

"No proof but the record book on the seat of the car behind you," X said. "The record is in your writing. Police want no greater evidence than that to land you in the chair for the worst series of heartless crimes I have ever encountered. All of your efforts to frame others for your crimes have failed.

"Through the loudspeaker system, you confessed to the slaying of Joe Sine. That is enough to insure your death. All of that talk about seeing Sine in a car tonight was an effort on your part to prevent me from finding George Leeds and to divert suspicion from yourself. Yet you might have succeeded in all your plans, had it not been for the rose. Crime is like that. There's always some little thing to slip on—"

Tony Harkness flung himself straight against the Agent's gun. His breath was sobbing in his throat. It was as if he hoped to die now in an effort to evade the lingering, tortured progress of justice. But there was no compassion in the Agent's stern eyes. He did not kill. His left hand flicked out, pounded young Harkness back. His right clubbed his gun, brought it down on Harkness' head. And the Golden God plunged into oblivion.

X lifted the man into the car beside the incriminating record book. He placed the golden mask over Tony's face. Then he ran to the garage door, anxious to escape before police overran the place and started to ask embarrassing questions.

But in the gray light of early morning, the unkept lawn before the old house was swarming with police. Trying to avoid those in front, X found himself in the center of a detail approaching from the rear. And in the center of this group of police was the real Fred Archer.

For a moment, Archer just stood as though he was seeing a ghost. One of the police, quicker witted, pulled a gun.

"Damn it!" the cop exploded, "one of you Archers is that impersonator Mr. X, and I intend to find out which. You're both under arrest."

"No!" a feminine voice cried.

All eyes turned toward Jane Cromer. She was running across the lawn toward them holding up the long skirt of the green satin dress that sheathed her perfect form. "I can tell you," she panted. "I know. This man is Fred Archer. The other is Secret Agent X."

And as she said, "Secret Agent X," she pointed at Fred Archer. For Agent X, she had a quick wink of a blue eye which told him that she knew exactly what she was doing. Perhaps the suit X wore had told her that he was Agent X. Or perhaps it was some intuition that enabled her to recognize the greater of the two men and to unhesitatingly make her choice.

INSTANTLY, the police fell upon Archer, trying to scrape makeup off his face. It was the Agent's chance, and he took it, a smile of thanks on his lips as he looked one last time at Jane.

Then he was off, running like a hare through undergrowth to gain the street. A car glided up beside him. A deep voice clipped: "You, chief?" For the man at the wheel was Harvey Bates.

X sprang into the car, and Bates gave the motor all it would take. Soon Carrollton City would be behind them. New adventures and new crimes would spread the web of mystery and danger before them. Carrollton City would soon forget Agent X, for the credit for the capture of the Golden God would go to the police.

But somewhere in that city were four persons who would not forget: George, Dorothy and Mrs. Leeds were not to forget. For the following day they received a package of money which would enable George to continue his studies and which would insure Mrs. Leeds a home for the rest of her life. Affixed to the package of money was only the penciled letter "X."

Nor would Jane Cromer forget. Perhaps she would never look upon the face of Fred Archer without her heart swelling with the futile hope that it was but a mask covering the features of another.

BOOK XXXIX

CURSE OF THE CRIMSON HORDE

Across six thousand miles and spanning two continents
an unseen hand moved living pawns over a chessboard
of death. The stake was the life blood of a nation, the
symbol—the Red Maggot—a fire to unholy ambition, the
possession of which bound a man's soul to the Devil.

And Secret Agent X—man of a thousand faces and
conqueror of kings of crime—found himself parried by
the ageless weapons and black magic of the Far East.

CHAPTER I

DEATH ON FIFTH AVENUE

THE TALL, MAHOGANY-SKINNED man was breathing quickly, white teeth slightly apart. His obsidian eyes sparkled with a purpose undeniably sinister. A faint spot of crimson glowed darkly in each cheek. Then his teeth clicked together like an inexorable steel trap, and his lips curled like those of a starved wolf scenting its kill.

He pulled his expensive overcoat closer about his shoulders. The night was cold, far below freezing. Bitter weather for this man who bore the stamp of warm and tropical climes.

A block away an advertising clock gave the hour as three minutes of seven. New York's Fifth Avenue was singularly free of pedestrians and motors cars. The bitter cold had sent office workers scurrying homeward from the icy blasts yowling in from the river. Tonight even taxicabs and the lumbering double-decked buses seemed scarce.

The scattering of pedestrians staggered breathlessly against a battering wind. It was too cold for any thought save that of warmth and no one paid the slightest attention to the tall man at the curb.

Up the street a few yards, a smoldering tar vat of the portable type was being attended by an employee of the Department of Streets. The employee adjusted the oil flame under the bubbling mixture and inspected a heat gauge. Apparently the mixture within the vat was not yet ready to pour into the small spot in the street needing repair.

The dark man noticed the repair outfit, and a fleeting smile twisted his red lips into a snarling grin. With some difficulty he extracted a white Sumatra cheroot from a silver case and held a wind-proof lighter flame to its tip. He sucked in the smoke, turned his head slightly. His profile was vulturine, sharp as if hewn of brown flint. But what he saw made the brief grin return to his red lips.

A man, also in the garb of a city employee, was working over the brass spout of a fire plug between two stores. The quiet elegance of the store farther from the dark man told of its exclusiveness, that its patronage came only from the wealthy. The neat sign affixed to its marble front read simply:

VAN der VEER

Pearls

That was all, just those few letters. But behind that sign was an establishment famed wherever fine and costly things were appreciated. Henrik Van der Veer dealt only in pearls. His far-flung group of agents purchased pearls from every section of the world, dispatched them to Van der Veer shops in New York, Paris, London and a score of other cities.

And as the dark man shot another glance up and down the street, his dark eyes suddenly became pools of ominous flame, narrowed to glinting slits. He peered sharply at the entrance to the Van der Veer store. Inside, standing near the door, he saw the small, slim figure of a man. The dark man on the curb saw a white

handkerchief show as the one within the store wiped at the glass of the door.

From down the block came a faint *bong-bong-bong*....

It was exactly seven o'clock.

The tall man tossed his cheroot aside on the instant, strode toward the door of the Van der Veer establishment. As his slim fingers found the latch, the last stroke of the hour sounded, and there was a sinister finality to it that again made the dark man's red lips twitch into a fleeting wolfish grin.

HENRIK VAN DER VEER, fabulously wealthy owner of the pearl establishments, was short and rotund. He had the apple-rosy cheeks which are a part of the Dutch makeup, sea blue eyes of twinkling and ready friendliness, a trim goatee of white. His hands on the

The next instant X was looking into the muzzle of an automatic....

desk were a bit pudgy but they felt tenderly of a bulky something encased in a bag of softest Carpathian chamois.

"You are about to see the Red Maggot, *Herr* Pope," Henrik Van der Veer said with no trace of accent to the man seated across the desk. "It is wondrous, the Red Maggot. A wondrous but terrible thing. For it kings and princes and just plain people have died. It has devastated whole countries, *mein freund,* has the Red Maggot.

"The possessor of this pearl is accursed, for the lust for power seethes in the brain of its owner. It is true, what I tell you. Just as the destroying maggot enters the bodies of all living creatures after death and consumes them, so does the Red Maggot destroy the brain and *soul* of its possessor. That is why it bears its unholy name. I tell you this because you have asked, because tomorrow you are to leave for the Far East on a scientific expedition."

"But you, sir," Arnold Pope, famous explorer, said gently, "you are not accursed because of the Red Maggot."

Arnold Pope was a man of forty-one or -two, rather tall and slim, deeply tanned of face and with eyes that were half-narrowed as if perpetually squinting against a tropic sun. He was in dinner clothes, wore a small white carnation in his coat lapel. He ran slim fingers through black hair slightly tinged with gray at the temples, smiled at Henrik Van der Veer.

The owner of the pearl store shook his head, "For two reasons, *Mynheer.* One is that I do not trust myself to look upon it save on occasions such as this. The other is that I hold it in trust, as it were, for the safety of that territory we call the South Seas. Should the Red Maggot return to that hell of islands, there would be revolt from Manila to Batavia, from Bangkok to the far Fijis. Who knows but what America might also be embroiled before it was over? I speak truth, *Herr* Pope.

"I leave tonight by plane for San Francisco, the first stop on my regular trip to my pearling interests in the Far East. But I dare not carry the Red Maggot with me. The knowledge of its return would spread like an electric spark, cause the superstitious natives to believe the overthrow of the foreign races was at last possible. I would destroy it—utterly—before I would allow its return! But look yourself, *Herr* Pope, and feel its malignancy like a blow in the face. The Red Maggot, *Mynheer,* the only blood-red pearl I have ever seen!"

With the words Henrik Van der Veer loosened the drawstrings of the chamois bag and placed what it contained before Arnold Pope's eager eyes.

The explorer gasped. Before him on the desk glowed the immense pearl that was the Red Maggot. Strangely, it was in the shape of a heart, but a living, pulsing heart! It seemed to expand and contract under Pope's staring eyes, to exude red, incandescent life. Yet it was a malignant life, a red malevolency that had all the horror of aeons of unspeakable outrages concentrated in its baleful being. For the Red Maggot had a being, an entity.

Arnold Pope closed his eyes, drew a sharp breath. The huge blood-red heart beneath his eyes had all at once seemed to intensify its demoniacal influence in waves of ruby light that battered into the explorer's very soul. He could understand how this accursed thing would gnaw at the brain and reason of men.

Arnold Pope covered the pearl with a trembling hand. It was soft as velvet to his touch, yet an electrical emanation from it coursed through his veins like liquid fire.

"O-o-over five hundred and fifty grains of—of concentrated evil!" [9] Arnold Pope faltered. He averted his gaze, narrowed lids cloaking what was in his eyes.

Through the door of the private office he saw Jebel Zeck, Van der Veer's New York manager, wipe something from the glass of the street door. An elderly clerk was arranging display trays in a showcase. A small clock at Pope's elbow on the desk softly began chiming the hour, seven o'clock.

"*Ja,*" Van der Veer nodded somberly. "That is why I keep the Red Maggot in a new type safe that only I, and Rika, my daughter, can open. It is too evil a thing for any man to touch who knows the acid bite of greed, the ambition of unwarranted power. I have not seen it for three years until tonight."

He slipped the chamois covering over the pearl. "Should it return to the South Seas it would mean native uprisings, strife, murder—"

---

9   AUTHOR'S NOTE: *The Red Maggot weighed 551.375 grains, which made it possibly the largest pearl in history. Its red color, brilliant as gushing blood, has never been explained, although pink pearls are fairly common. Many jet black pearls also have been found. It must not be thought that a pearl of this size is fantastic. The pearl known as La Peregrina weighed 126 carats—504 grains—and was brought from India to Spain in 1620. It once was owned by Princess Youssopoff, of Old Russia, and at that time was valued at $135,000. The pearl that Cleopatra is said to have melted in vinegar and drunk as a toast to Anthony was valued at $400,000. A Shah of Persia once owned a pearl valued, in 1633, at over $300,000. But none of them would exceed the value of the Red Maggot with both size and exotic coloring considered.*

Henrik Van der Veer broke off short as a black shadow fell athwart the desk. Pope, whose gaze had been riveted to the chamois bag, looked up. A man stood in the doorway of the office. He was tall, coppery-skinned, had hair as black as India ink. His fulsome red lips were parted in a twisted smile over white teeth. It was the dark man of the sidewalk.

"*Herr* Van der Veer?" the man asked shortly but there was a hissing quality to the tone remindful of a cobra's warnings. "I am Milo Sabbat, of—of Singapore. I desire a perfectly matched string of pearls as a gift. I want them as quickly as possible...."

THE REVERBERATING sound of a dull explosion silenced the man's words. He looked in simulated amazement through the door and to the street. Arnold Pope was on his feet, brow wrinkled in puzzlement.

In front of the Van der Veer shop, Pope saw, a portable tar vat had exploded, was burning fiercely and spewing up vast clouds of inky smoke. The smoke veiled the large window of the store. Then Arnold Pope gasped. Jebel Zeck, Van der Veer's manager, had suddenly gone mad with fear. He dashed to the door, threw it wide.

"Fire!" he screamed. "We'll burn! Run—*hurry!*"

Then an incredible thing happened. The explorer saw it dimly through the murky fog of black that now filled the shop. He recalled seeing a city water department employee working on a frozen hydrant as he entered. Apparently it had burst. Water cascaded onto the window and sidewalk.

Pope's frown deepened. For the water froze on the window almost upon contact, completely covered it with an opaque curtain of white ice.

Under cover of the eddying wraiths of black that blanketed the small private office, Milo Sabbat's hand came from the pocket of his overcoat. In his slim fingers was a small glass ball. He surreptitiously dropped it to the rich Chinese rug underfoot and broke it with the heel of his shoe. Instantly an unseen gas permeated the pall of smoke. Sabbat held a small filter-type gas mask to his mouth and nose and his snapping eyes peered at the weaving forms of Van der Veer and Arnold Pope.

The explorer, through the smoke fog, saw a dark blob rush to the open safe, crash the doors closed, twist the combination knob. He was vaguely certain it was Van der Veer. He did not know what had become of the customer. Arnold Pope, keen brain racing, knew the burning tar vat and the broken water plug were not coincidences. They were planned by some master of strategy.

But now his senses reeled as the unseen gas found his nostrils, was gulped into straining lungs. But, he knew, the Red Maggot was safe, locked in the steel vault.... A terrible thought struck him. But was the pearl safe?

The gas was taking its toll of Pope's consciousness. Then, in the murk of the store, he saw Jebel Zeck lying across the threshold of the open street door. Ice was caked about him, covered his legs. Smoke funneled through the door. At Zeck's side lay the elderly clerk. The man's face was black. His mouth was open, the tongue protruding.

The fact that the clerk was dead wormed its way into Pope's numbing brain. The attempt at robbery perhaps was an abortive one, but a man was lying dead... it meant murder!

And just at that instant unconsciousness swooped down, and Pope's brain went blank....

THE MAN seated in the comfortable leather chair turned the pages of the rotogravure section with swift movements. His keen eyes swept over the pages almost casually, but each was photographed instantly and impressed upon his brain. As his gaze went over the last page it focused upon a picture there, held steady.

It was a picture of Arnold Pope, wealthy explorer and scientist, and told of his coming departure for the Far East to study coral growths by means of a newly perfected bathysphere. The man's gaze left the picture and went to a small bundle of letters on the desk by his side.

He picked them up, riffled through them. He chose one having the stamp of the Straits Settlements on the envelope. The postmark spelled out the place of mailing: Singapore.

A smile, brief and reflective, touched the man's lips momentarily. He nodded, got to his feet, the roto section under his arm. He stepped to the wall, and long fingers ran lightly up and down the expensive paneling. There was a soft click, and a portion of the wall slid to one side. The sliding panel automatically made an electrical connection, and brilliant lights flooded the small room behind the wall.

It was a strange cubbyhole. Directly before the man was a theatrical type dressing table with a full-length mirror. On this table, laid out in neat rows, were many jars and tubes of makeup materials. The man took off his dinner jacket, tie and shirt, sat facing the mirror.

He studied the picture of Arnold Pope, the explorer, with narrowed eyes. Then he did a curious thing. His fingers found a switch beneath the top of the table, and the lights were extinguished, leaving him in almost complete darkness.

Then, with incredible speed, the man's fingers darted from tube to jar, then to color pencil, liquid dyes and accessories. No sound was to be heard save the occasional click of the jars or tubes as they were replaced on the table. Then, not over sixty seconds later, the man's fingers flicked on the switch.

The man in the chair now had the face of Arnold Pope, explorer!

Again the brief smile played on the man's lips. He inspected himself closely, comparing the features in the mirror with those printed on the rotogravure page. He nodded in satisfaction.

A clock in the outer room boomed seven times. The man with the face of Arnold Pope walked from the cubbyhole and turned on a radio near the table for the "Vox Pop" broadcast scheduled for this hour each evening, returned to the mirror again.

As the commentator's voice came to him over the radio, the man sat in the chair and began removing the makeup from his face. The plastic material which had made his cheekbones more prominent, came away, was discarded. Thin strips of pinkish rubber came from behind each lip where they fitted against his teeth.

The man's face was remarkably youthful when free of the disguise. His eyes were alive with the clear brilliance of a penetrating and original mentality. The love of humor was in the curve of his mobile lips; but grim determination and unflinching courage were there, too. Strength of purpose was in the hawklike lines of his nose, the broad forehead, the firm chin.

The man was Secret Agent X.

The assembling of a difficult disguise but a few moments before was one of the innumerable tasks with which he tested his amazing abilities. That it was done in the dark with uncanny results put the hallmark of genius on his effort.

Many times had Secret Agent X been forced to adopt first one disguise and then another, with his life as forfeit should he fail. Always on his person was a small flat box of makeup materials. And often, with only seconds of grace, he had saved his life by the application of a new disguise.

Suddenly Secret Agent X tensed as excited words from the radio communicator came to him. He got to his feet with a lithe movement, strode into the library. His eyes now were narrowed, sharp, as he listened to the commentator's rapid flow of words.

"I'm giving you an eye witness account, folks, of an accident happening on icy, wind-swept Fifth Avenue. This is the 'Vox Pop' radio hour and it happens I'm stationed tonight in the Gigantic Building across from the Van der Veer pearl store. As you know, it is very exclusive and sells some of the finest pearls in the world. But something strange has occurred.

"A Department of Streets employee was attending an asphalt repair outfit in front of the store. It's afire, and great clouds of smoke are rushing into the store. A man is lying in the doorway. Another workman was thawing a water hydrant and it suddenly burst. The water has formed a coating of ice over the show window. I can't see inside...."

Agent X turned with lightning speed, strode back to the mirror. His hands chose certain tubes of plastics, volatile makeup materials, with unerring accuracy. This was worked over his face, tinted with consummate art with dyes and ingenious pigments. From the library the radio voice continued.

"The man at the threshold of the street door is overcome by the smoke fumes. Another man is beside him. This man, folks, appears to be—be dead! Wait! A tall man has rushed from the shop and he's half carrying, half leading another. I believe the dazed man is Van der Veer, but the smoke's so thick....

"A bystander has just told me he saw Arnold Pope, the famous explorer, go in the shop ten minutes ago. He must be in there now! There's an ambulance! The tall man helps Van der Veer into it. It drives off. A crowd is gathering, folks...."

X gazed at his features in the mirror for a moment, nodded in wordless satisfaction. From a shelf beside the table he picked up a phone hand-set, swiftly dialed a number.

"Gem Garage?" he asked. Then: "This is A.J. Martin, Associated Press. I'm on my way there now. Have my car ready for me. Leave the motor running. I'll be there in five minutes."

With quick movements Agent X turned off the lights, closed the secret door, hurried from his apartment and, on the sidewalk, stepped into a taxicab.

"The Gem Garage as quickly as possible," he rapped out to the cab driver.

CHAPTER II

THE GIRL IN THE ROAD

WHEN SECRET AGENT X arrived in front of the Van der Veer store, he saw the police had the situation well in hand. The tar vat had been extinguished and the fire plug was frozen solid. Within the still murky shop an oxygen squad worked over the form of Arnold Pope.

As the Agent entered, the explorer moaned, sat up. He was groggy but would fully recover after a few minutes in the fresh air. Sergeant Watts, whom X knew, was in charge. Seated in Van der Veer's private office, swathed in coats and blankets belonging to the oxygen rescue squad, was Jebel Zeck. He grinned weakly at the Agent's nod of greeting.

"A curious accident, Mr. Martin," Zeck said huskily. In brief sentences he told what had happened. "I suppose you'll be writing it up for the wire service?" Zeck asked.

"Perhaps," X said crisply. His face was bland, innocent, when he questioned Zeck. "There's nothing missing?"

"Missing?" Zeck said sharply. Then he laughed. He was a small man, had sandy-hair, greenish eyes, an oval face. He had a nervous habit of rubbing at his chin with a forefinger when he talked.

"I'm afraid, Mr. Martin," he said rather stiffly, "you are trying to be as melodramatic as the police."

He smiled at the scowling Sergeant Watts. "I've told this police officer time and again there was no attempt at robbery, that nothing is missing. I opened the safe in his presence. Nothing was disturbed. Mr. Pope was rather emphatic he saw Mr. Van der Veer lock up a—er—certain pearl during the thick of the smoke."

He shrugged. "It was just an accident, and there's no need of making mountains of molehills." Zeck snuggled into his blankets.

Agent X swerved on Sergeant Watts. "Sergeant, did you locate either of the two city men who caused all this smoke and ice?"

"No, Mr. Martin," Watts admitted. "It'll be tomorrow before I can check with the proper officials and find who were assigned the jobs. But there's nothing else we can do, sir. Mr. Zeck says there was no attempt at robbery, so that lets us out." He nodded to a uniformed officer, shook hands with X and walked out.

"The clerk is dead. Mr. Zeck?" Agent X asked of the manager.

Jebel Zeck nodded and pain flashed over his oval face. "Yes. He was in wretched health. Heart, you know. The excitement was too much for him, I suppose." He sighed, shook his head sadly.

"How about this man who was in Mr. Van der Veer's office at the moment of the explosion? I understand from Mr. Pope his name was Sabbat."

"I'd never seen him before. He walked into the store with such assurance I naturally thought he was either expected or was a friend. He left during the excitement. That's all I know."

Secret Agent X, narrowed his eyes thoughtfully, looked around the room with keen gaze. He turned back to Zeck. "Mr. Pope says he was viewing the Red Maggot at the time. It's in the safe now?"

"It must be." Zeck showed surprise. "Why, I never gave it a second thought. I dimly saw my employer rush to the safe with something in his hand, thrust it in and lock the doors. I assume Mr. Pope saw the same thing. He was closer, in fact, in the same office. That—that damnable pearl is kept in the smaller inner safe."

Zeck's shoulders moved in evident disgust. "I never touched the accursed thing. Only Mr. Van der Veer and Miss Rika have the combination. She's at Eastern College, you know, fifty miles from here, taking a post-graduate course in chemistry."

"Ah, Miss Rika, eh?" Agent X nodded again.

In various disguises X circulated in a number of social sets. In that manner he was able to study people, hear things, learn of sinister undercurrents that often crop up accidentally in the most respectable places. He remembered Rika Van der Veer; in fact, once had met her while he was in the disguise of A.J. Martin.

"You've heard from Mr. Van der Veer?" X asked Zeck. "I understand he was taken to some hospital in an ambulance."

"Probably had a touch of smoke. He's a strong man, and—" Zeck broke off as the telephone rang. He reached for it, listened for a moment and then hung up. He smiled at Agent X. "That was the ticket office at the Newark airport. Mr. Van der Veer has just left for the West; he asked the ticket man to phone me.

"He was planning the trip, you know, and had to make this plane in order to connect with his ship in San Francisco. He recovered fully in the ambulance, caught a cab to his downtown apartment and picked up another hat and coat. He'd already had his bags sent to the airport."

Zeck shrugged once more. "There's nothing we can make of it, Martin, other than a freakish accident." His thin face sobered, and the forefinger rubbed at his chin. "By the way, if you don't mind, how did you get here so quickly?"

THE AGENT looked at Zeck and Arnold Pope and laughed. "The merest of accidents and one as strange as—as what happened here. I was in a cab fitted with a radio and on the way to my office. It was tuned in on the 'Vox Pop' program across the street in the Gigantic Building."

X briefly told the rest of the story. "Knowing Mr. Van der Veer, I decided to see if there was anything I could do. Then too," the Agent, grinned, "being a newspaperman I thought I saw a story."

"Well," Zeck laughed shortly, "I'm sorry you're disappointed, Mr. Martin. Just a happening, any one of your legmen could write up."

Agent X agreed, turned to Arnold Pope. "I've my car outside, Mr. Pope. I'll be glad to run you to your apartment." He reached for his hat on the desk, but it escaped his fingers and fell to the floor. He recovered it and stood erect.

The explorer nodded his thanks, shook hands with Jebel Zeck. X did likewise, and together they walked over the slippery sidewalk to where the car was parked at the curb. A moment later X shifted gears, took the corner at Fifty-first Street at high speed.

Arnold Pope looked his surprise. "Rather in a hurry, eh, Martin? Getting me home is no case of life or death—"

"To you, no," the Agent snapped. "But I think Rika Van der Veer is in deadly danger!"

"Nonsense," the explorer laughed. "You're like the police, Martin. Trying to make something sensational out of an accident. You might tell me of your premise." He laughed again. "Clues you newspaper and police fellows call them."

Agent X smiled grimly to himself. "You forget you were overcome by a gas, don't you?"

Arnold Pope laughed. "Why, that was nothing but the effects of the tar smoke. I'll admit it overcame me pretty easily. But a lethal gas!" He shook his head, a rather patronizing smile curving his lips.

"Pope, since when have you gone in for *green* carnations?" Agent X asked quietly.

"Green carnations! Why—" The explorer threw back the collar of his overcoat, took the flower from his lapel and held it so the dashlight shone on it. The carnation was a deep emerald green!-

"The reason you went under so easily, Pope," X stated, "was because there was a discharge of etherolate gas in that office. I know, because that particular gas will turn the petals of a white flower a deep green. It has an anesthetizing effect on humans, acts exactly as does ether. And here's another premise, as you call it."

Secret Agent X held out his hand. In the palm was a small filter-type gas mask.

"Perhaps you'll recall I dropped my hat as we were leaving. I did it to cover this mask. You don't find etherolate gas and filter masks in a room unless something nefarious is under way. Agree?"

"Definitely!" Arnold Pope exclaimed. "But why this mad dash toward Eastern College? Miss Van der Veer is undoubtedly safe in her dormitory. I can't see how she would be affected by this."

"Let's hope she is safe. The Red Maggot apparently is within the special vault, or Van der Veer would not have left on his trip. But I feel there's something queer to the whole thing. Zeck firmly believes nothing is missing. He may be right.

"But if Van der Veer and Rika are the only ones knowing the combination of the inner safe, and the robbery was a failure, it remains that her safety is endangered, for the ones trying for the Red Maggot may force the girl to open the safe. I honestly believe Zeck is unaware it was a planned attempt. For the time being we won't let him know it was an attempt."

SECRET AGENT X threw his speedy car around a corner, straightened out on the main road which led to the little town in which Eastern College was located. A feeling of danger, of menace, impinged on his subconscious. There was something deadly, malignant in the perfectly planned affair on Fifth Avenue which, in its perfection, implied menace yet to come. And that led, without doubt, to Rika Van der Veer.

"Get a look at this customer who appeared in the office, Pope?" X suddenly asked.

"Not a good one," Arnold Pope admitted. "Things happened pretty fast. I naturally thought he was a special customer. I got to my feet, stood back. Mr. Van der Veer apparently had covered the Red Maggot." The explorer briefly described the man known as Milo Sabbat.

"A sinister name," X remarked. "In medieval times it meant an orgy celebrated by demons and sorcerers. But go on."

"Well, the smoke and water started. Zeck went mad with fright. Anyone who lost his head so completely couldn't have had anything to do with planning the robbery, so that lets him out. The smoke was so dense I couldn't see anything. That's about all I know, Martin."

X nodded. "Van der Veer is a very wealthy man. Crooks have tried to get to him in the past, particularly for that damnable Red Maggot. I've known the old Dutchman for years, and he's told me of the attempts. It once was owned by some Khmer king. He lost his country because of the madness it instilled in his brain, they say. Van der Veer has been safe from this madness because he is stolid, unimaginative. Too, he has persuaded himself he holds the pearl in trust.

"The pearl was lost for a thousand or more years. Then an adventurer stumbled across it in a jungle-choked temple guarded over by white cobras! This adventurer sold the pearl to Van der Veer, then died of injuries received in the jungle. He had a daughter. But he left no address of her whereabouts, and Van der Veer has been holding the purchase money in trust for her. He's spent thousands trying to find her.

"The Dykas and Malays of the South Seas attribute weird things to the Red Maggot. But they are always tied up with murder, greed, unwarranted conquest. That's why the pearl should never return to the Malay territories; it would mean revolt. Van der Veer owns a coral island somewhere in the Java Sea, I believe, has an immense pearl bed there he nurses. He also has invented a way to make perfect pearls by some electrolytic process—"

"I didn't know of that," Pope said, interested.

"Yes. With his process Van der Veer discharges high frequencies through treated sea water, thus killing all impurities. Pearls are made, you know, by some minute bit of grit or foreign matter adhering to the inner side of an oyster or similar shell. Nacreous matter covers this impurity with many layers of 'skin,' which forms the pearl.

"The pearl, created by impurity, often has its value impaired by other impurities. This is the phase of pearl culture Van der Veer has overcome. He can make real pearls with astonishing speed by stepping up his voltage. If he were dishonest, he could break the pearl markets of the world—"

"Say, isn't that a fire ahead?" Arnold Pope interrupted.

"I've been watching it for some time," X stated, voice grim. "I believe it's somewhere close to Eastern College. Wait, there's a motorcycle scout. Perhaps he can tell us." Agent X pulled up at the curb beside the motorcycle policeman.

The officer threw the beam of a flash on the Agent, then grinned. "Oh, hello, Mr. Martin. You remember me; I'm Slim Leonard. The fire's the chemical lab at Eastern. Two girls were making a dangerous experiment, I hear, and it exploded on them."

He drew a slip of paper from his pocket, directed the beam of the flash on it. "One of 'em named May Eaton. The other," he peered again at the paper, "was named—Rika Van der Veer."

"Too late—too late!" Agent X whispered, face taut and drawn. His deduction had proved correct. This chemical lab fire was no accident, but a planned move by some mastermind of crime.

Suddenly Secret Agent X tensed. From afar had come the thin shrill of a woman's scream. Neither the explorer nor the motorcycle scout had heard it. To the Agent's left was an old road which wound around the base of the hill on which Eastern College was situated. X knew this territory well. Without a word he quickly meshed the gears, twisted the steering wheel to the left.

"What the—" Pope asked shrilly.

"A scream. Down this old road," X snapped. "This back road circles the college grounds."

The road was rough, full of holes in the asphalt. The Agent's car lurched and bounced, but he kept it moving at a dangerous speed.

"There, ahead!" X suddenly cried, and there was a triumphant timbre to his voice. "On my side of the road, Pope! Look, she's waving us down. It's a girl, and she's frantic with fear!"

X PULLED the car over toward the girl, jerked on the emergency. He jumped from the car, strode to the girl's side. In the light of the spot he saw her distended, fear-crazed eyes, her blonde hair in wild disarray. She held trembling hands to her face, and X saw her slim body was twitching with fright. Over her dress she wore a long white laboratory coat. She took her hands from her face, held them imploringly toward the Agent.

It was Rika Van der Veer!

"They—they're after me!" she faltered. "They tried—to blow me up with—with a bomb in the lab. I escaped and—and they saw me run. They passed a moment ago—looking. I hid behind the bridge approach—

"Heavens, here they come!"

She pointed wildly ahead, turned to run but the Agent's strong arms jerked her to him.

"All lights out, Pope!" X snapped. "We won't have time to get the car off the road. Hide behind it."

With the words the Agent ran swiftly toward the bridge, directly into the jumping beam of the light thrown by the headlights of the approaching car. As he ran the Agent's supple fingers worked at the cover of a little steel box in his vest pocket.

In a moment six or eight little glass pellets were in his hand. They were innocent appearing, but within the glass was a terrible corrosive acid that acted instantly. It would eat through toughest steel, sear flesh, like living flame.

From ahead came the sudden *rat-tat-tat* of a machine gun. X was twenty yards on the far side of the old concrete bridge now, running low and with amazing speed. He heard the staccato blasts of a .38, saw the flashes of livid flame. But every flash missed in the darkness. Then, the car almost upon him, X tossed the handful of glass pellets in front of the speeding murder car, arrowed for the side of the road.

The machine gun continued its spiteful yammer, and the Agent felt the shock of hot lead close to his flying feet. Then the aim was again changed to his own car outlined in the headlights. The murder car—he saw two occupants as it flashed past—was speeding close to sixty miles an hour even though it bounced dangerously.

There was a dull explosion as a tire blew out. Another followed. The acid pellets had eaten through the tire rubber within the space of ten short yards.

The car of death swerved, lurched, slammed the bridge abutment, careened in a mad, grinding half-circle. All was silent for a long second following the crash. Then a dull red eruption of fire spewed into the night. X ran forward, but he could not get close due to the terrific heat of the gasoline-fed flames. He ran past, joined Rika and Pope on the far side of the bridge.

"They're both dead," he said grimly.

"Too bad, they could have told us who is behind all this. That customer, Milo Sabbat, has to be the one." He turned to the girl. "You remember me, Miss Van der Veer?"

She nodded. "Yes, you're Mr. Martin of the Associated Press. I've heard father speak of you often. He left for Singapore tonight."

In swift, clipped words, Agent X told the girl of what had happened at her father's Fifth Avenue store. "I think," he said slowly, narrowed eyes reflective, "I'll write up a story and say you are— *dead!*"

"I—dead?" she faltered, paling under his steady gaze.

X inclined his head. "Yes, dead. I've an idea you were to be killed so you couldn't check up on your father. It will serve him best if the one behind this murder game believes the attempt was successful." He turned to the explorer. "I can depend upon you to keep silent?" The explorer's face was puzzled as he nodded. "Yes, Martin, but I can't understand a newspaperman wanting to keep a hot feature story out of the papers."

"I can't explain that yet, Pope," X said shortly. "Please believe me it is the thing to do. Later, perhaps, you'll understand more." X faced the girl again. "I believe you are the only one besides your father who can open the inner safe in which the Red Maggot is kept. We'll go back and have a look-see."

He broke off as he heard the sound of the motorcycle speeding toward the red blaze of the burning car.

X explained to the scout what had happened. "Wish you'd have the coroner in this district send anything he finds on the dead men on in to New York. Have him get fingerprints if possible."

THE ARRANGEMENTS made, X again got behind the wheel of his car, and sixty minutes later stopped in front of the Van der Veer store. Jebel Zeck had locked up for the night, but Rika had keys to the door. Soon she had the larger safe open, was working the combination of the smaller one.

At the Agent's suggestion, Arnold Pope phoned the airport to learn complete details on Van der Veer's movements. He completed the call, returned to the safe where X was watching the girl.

"Nothing new, Martin," he said. "Mr. Van der Veer and secretary left on the plane as scheduled. Mr. Van der Veer seemed weak from exhaustion and all information was given by the secretary—"

Rika Van der Veer looked up, face white. "Secretary?" she exclaimed. "Why, he never traveled with a secretary in his life! I don't—"

"It's Sabbat!" Agent X said quietly. "No one would know your father didn't travel with a secretary if you were dead! That's one of the reasons you were to be murdered tonight, so that fact couldn't be looked into. I expect Zeck also was to be killed. He—"

The Agent turned as he heard a gasp of dismay from the girl. She pointed in wordless consternation.

Secret Agent X peered within the inner safe built to protect the Red Maggot. It was empty.

"I thought so," he said quietly. He turned to the explorer. "The form you saw making for the safe in the smoke was that of Sabbat. He was doing that deliberately, making you think it was Van der Veer locking up the Red Maggot. In that way there'd be no immediate suspicions the pearl was stolen."

The Agent's smile was grim now, made his lips taut. "Pope, how would you like to have a new member along with you on your expedition? Two new members, in fact?"

"I—I don't understand, Martin," the puzzled explorer said.

"Rika and I would like to accompany you on your yacht to the Far East. We'll give this Sabbat plenty of rope, and then—"

Secret Agent X's jaw was set, his eyes hard as if of frozen agate. Without a word he led the way from the Van der Veer shop into the cold street.

CHAPTER III

FORTY FATHOM FIGHT

RIKA VAN DER VEER slowly shook her head at the Agent's question. "I'm not certain at all," she said. "My father was always secretive regarding the location of Lost Island. It isn't on the Admiralty charts. All I know is that it lies about halfway between the tips of Borneo and the Celebes in the Java Sea."

X nodded. There were, he knew, scores of tiny coral islands not shown on the various charts of the South Seas. Every once in a while some new one was discovered, so it was not unusual that Van der Veer's island wasn't generally known. He looked out the window of the speeding railroad car.

The Universal Museum expedition, of which Arnold Pope was in charge, had taken this private car and several baggage cars to hold the personnel and the large amount of baggage, scientific instruments and supplies. The museum's combination yacht and schooner, the *Wanderer,* was already in San Francisco harbor. The new and improved bathysphere, which was to be used in studying coral growths, was being loaded on the ship at the moment.

X turned to the girl, "Who knows the island's location besides your father, Rika?"

"Just two men. Even Jebel Zeck doesn't know it, and father trusts him implicitly. Of course Peter DeVery—he's the technical man in charge of the island—knows its location. The other is father's Singapore manager, Jon Smit. Uncle Jon, although he's no relation, is my father's closest friend. Peter DeVery is a brilliant scientist and chemist. Those three are the only ones knowing the location of the island outside of two or three government men."

"It would be useless to contact this Jon Smit by radio phone for the location," the Agent mused. "I doubt if he'd tell us anything even if we were face to face. I remember I've heard your father speak of him and I can tell he's a cagy individual.

"We'll set out for Singapore via the Java Sea in the *Wanderer*. I've already made arrangements to that effect with Arnold Pope and the Universal Museum officials. Maybe we can find this island if you're certain it's approximately halfway between Borneo and the Celebes."

She nodded. "But why try to find the island first, Mr. Martin? Don't you believe Sabbat will take my father to Singapore first?"

"Perhaps so. They will go there first if it isn't found out that the death notice I had put in the paper telling of you being blown to bits in the lab explosion is a fake. If it is discovered you are alive, then Sabbat, who undoubtedly knows the location of Lost Island, will hide there. But," he smiled, "you are officially dead. I know of no one outside of this party who is aware that you came through safely, not even Zeck."

"Yes," Rika said ruefully, looking at her soiled dress and lab smock. "I've been with you and Mr. Pope ever since you rescued me last night." She trembled. "It doesn't seem possible that just twelve hours ago I was being shot at with machine-gun bullets! Now we are on a train bound for San Francisco. And I haven't even a toothbrush! I—"

"Martin, here's something interesting." The words came from Arnold Pope, who hurried into the car. In his hand was a newspaper.

Secret Agent X took the newspaper, held it so the girl could read. They saw:

ATTEMPT AT PEARL STORE MANAGER'S LIFE

JEBEL ZECK ESCAPES

Jebel Zeck, manager of the New York interests of the vast Van der Veer pearl organization, was attacked by masked thugs en route to his apartment last night. The attack followed the mysterious death of Rika Van der Veer, daughter of the pearl millionaire, who was blown to bits in a laboratory explosion at Eastern College earlier in the night. Henrik Van der Veer, now on his way to Singapore via *China Clipper*, could not be reached.

Mr. Zeck could attribute no reason for the attack. Two thugs with automatics opened fire on him but the bullets luckily missed. Inspector Harry Clifford, chief of the Jewel Squad, is handling the investigation.

X NODDED, blue-gray eyes bleak. "We could put our hands on Milo Sabbat within a few minutes of sending a radio message," he said slowly. "But that wouldn't turn up the gang with him. And," his eyes glazed a wintry gray, "I believe Sabbat is only a lieutenant in this plot. The real man hasn't yet come into the picture. We have to catch the entire gang of plotters. That the Red Maggot is missing is conclusive that revolt against white dominion in the South Seas is the core of the plot."

Rika Van der Veer leaned forward, her hand on the Agent's arm. "I—I can't quite understand one thing, Mr. Martin. That's your interest in this. Why are you taking all this time to go on this trip? It undoubtedly will be dangerous should we catch up with the men who have my father. I would think your newspaper duties would keep you so busy it would be impossible to leave them."

Secret Agent X smiled, and there was warmth and understanding in it. But when he spoke there was a deadly quality to the words that made the girl and Arnold Pope blink in amazement.

"Rika," he said, "my particular writing job is a roving one and I make my own assignments. I already knew an attempt was to be made for the Red Maggot. It just came days before I expected.

"My first instructions when I joined the AP were to follow to a conclusion anything that might, in time, endanger America. Only your father and I realize what revolt in the Far East might eventually mean. And should this Sabbat be in the employ of a foreign government— It's a very definite threat toward America—a threat we can't allow to go unchallenged!"

"Rather like that nebulous Secret Agent X whose name appears in the newspapers every once in a while, eh?" Pope laughed. "He seems to be in the thick of things when plots against the country are hatched. I have a friend, though, who thinks differently. I'm speaking of Inspector Burks, New York detective. He seems to think this mysterious Secret Agent X is a bigger crook than any of 'em."

"I wouldn't know," the Agent said dryly.

Henrik Van der Veer sat with unseeing eyes, his face turned toward the window of the *China Clipper*. Underneath was the smoothly rolling Pacific, glinting under the rays of a horizontal sun. He seemed in a trance. The pupils of his blue eyes were pinpoints. When his eyes moved they jerked. His face was expressionless, showed no interest in the huge flying boat or the fact it was flying over the ocean.

Seated next to the pearl millionaire was a tall man with eyes of coal black. Occasionally his red lips curled wolfishly away from his startlingly white teeth. It was Milo Sabbat. He narrowly inspected his companion's face with his cold eyes. Then he pressed a button at the side of his seat. A steward came up, listened attentively.

"My employer would like a glass of orange juice," Sabbat said.

Shortly the steward returned but as he turned away he did not see the bit of white powder Sabbat dropped into the liquid. Van der Veer drank the juice at Sabbat's command, doing it obediently as would a sick child. The radio officer hurried toward Sabbat and handed over a radiogram. There was pity on his young face. Sabbat looked at the words on the radiogram, frowned in the presence of the officer. He said softly so that only the radio operator could hear: "Mr. Van der Veer is too ill, as you can see, to learn of the terrible death of his daughter. Please advise all who know of this message that he must not learn of it." The radio operator nodded, his face again filled with pity. He returned to his post.

"YOU SAY this island alee isn't on the Admirality charts?" Agent X asked the question of Bob Crandall, aviator and navigator for the expedition. Crandall shook his head. X nodded, looked through prism binoculars at the towering coral cliffs of an island to starboard.

The trim schooner-yacht had made the trip under forced draft. It was a strange vessel. In it were embodied some of the latest inventions which made it a speedy craft. Forward, a trim three-place seaplane was ensconced on a navy type catapult. Below decks a fully equipped machine shop and laboratory were situated, making it possible for a crew of trained technicians to carry on experiments even while at sea.

For two days now the *Wanderer* had beat up and down the Java Sea on a line with the tips of Borneo and the Celebes. Now, after hours of search, an unknown island of pinkish coral lay to starboard. The Agent was certain it was Van der Veer's Lost Island, the location of his fabulous bed of virgin pearl shell and the plant for manufacturing cultured pearls.

Secret Agent X, face taut, walked forward and entered the cabin occupied by Arnold Pope.

Five minutes later the explorer came on deck, beckoned for Crandall and two of his technical men.

"We're alee of the island and there's no sea to speak of, so I believe I'll test out the bathysphere. It's been air tested, is ready for a dive. I don't believe bottom is deeper than forty or fifty fathoms. We'll drop our sea anchors as close as possible to the coral cliffs there." He pointed. "Meanwhile, get the bathysphere ready. You two mind the lines and you, Crandall, get on the telephone." [10]

Within thirty minutes the sea anchors were in place fore and aft, and the *Wanderer* was stationary alee of the coral island, its cliffs only fifty yards away. The electric fathometer recorded bottom at approximately forty-two fathoms. Arnold Pope walked to the companionway leading below to where the bathysphere chamber was located.

The bathysphere was, like its name, spherical. To its top was affixed a steel rope fastened to the lowering drum. The telephone and air lines were played out with the steel rope with which the bathysphere was raised or lowered. The interior of the large ball was fitted out with numerous scientific instruments, auxiliary oxygen tanks, and had accommodations for three divers. While under the water it was possible for a portion of the sphere to open and allow egress to the floor of the ocean.

Within this pressure chamber were three diving suits, which could be donned while in the bathysphere itself. Then, by means of the inner controls, water was allowed to enter the pressure chamber until conditions outside the bathysphere were reached. Followed the opening of the hermetically sealed door and the diver was ready to carry on explorations with the bathysphere as a base for replenishing the air.

The new diving suits were self-contained. It was not necessary for cumbersome life and air lines to be attached to them; the oxygen was fed to the helmets from small tanks fitted to the heavy shoulder plates. Enough oxygen was stored within this small tank to allow the diver to live for an hour away from the bathysphere. A reserve supply good for ten minutes was stored in a small cylinder attached to the larger one.

The bathysphere was contained in a special room built into the hull of the yacht. Machinery raised this section of the hull, and

---

10   AUTHOR'S NOTE: *A bathysphere is a hollow ball of steel used for underwater exploring and scientific research. The greatest danger of a bathysphere is that it might develop a leak and the weight of the water pressure cause an implosion—the opposite of explosion. It must be remembered that Dr. William Beebe descended to a depth of 3,028 feet on Aug. 15, 1934, in the ocean 6 miles south of Nonsuch Island, one of the Bermuda group.*

the bathysphere was lowered down steeply inclined tracks until it reached the water and hung free.

Earphones clamped to his head, Arnold Pope gave directions through the fixed mouthpiece at his lips. The steel door was securely clamped, the air working perfectly. The explorer looked around, saw the various instruments were functioning. He spoke into the mouthpiece.

"Lower away! Stop at three fathoms for inspection."

The lowering drum slowly unwound the steel rope. The bathysphere began to sink, shortly stopped.

Inside the huge drum Secret Agent X nodded with satisfaction as he inspected the various gauges and tested the air. It had been necessary to take Arnold Pope into his confidence in the cabin ten minutes before. The amazed explorer agreed to remain within his cabin while X, in disguise, made the descent into the ocean's depths.

Everything was in order. The Agent's voice, perfectly duplicating that of the explorer's, gave crisp orders into the telephone.

"Lower away slowly. At thirty-eight fathoms let rate of descent be extremely slow. I'll tell you when I touch bottom. Stand by!"

THE BATHYSPHERE resumed its descent to the floor of the ocean. From the fused quartz windows with which the steel ball was fitted, X saw a myriad of brightly-hued tropical fish flash past. Sunlight, he knew, would penetrate many fathoms through the turquoise waters, allow him to view the wonders of underwater life.

Ahead of him lay deep shadow, undoubtedly cast by the coral cliff. A pilot fish darted past, and the Agent grinned. Somewhere in his wake he knew a shark must be swimming, probably eyeing with displeasure this strange trespasser in its domain.

Suddenly the sinking motion of the bathysphere ceased. X peered at the depth gauge, saw it registered thirty-eight fathoms. Then the steel ball slowly settled. He felt it grate against coral, flashed the signal through the telephone. The bathysphere gently rested on the floor of the Java Sea.

The Agent put his eyes close to the windows of the bathysphere. Outside it was dusk, but the water was clear and he could see dimly for yards in any direction. The huge steel ball had settled in a bed of growing coral fashioned in fantastic shapes. On the bed of the ocean were huge oysters, mussels, giant clams. Like a forest of tiny trees, rose the brilliantly colored coral growths.

But it was the shell that interested him. He could see that this bed of virgin shell had not been molested. Here, he assumed, Henrik Van der Veer recovered some of his most valuable pearls. No wonder the cagy Dutchman didn't want the location of this island to become known! Here, within reach, was a tremendous fortune in pearls of the finest water, worth the riches of a rajah.

The Agent's main purpose in disguising himself as Arnold Pope and making the dive in the bathysphere was accomplished. None but those who were members of the expedition could make a descent in the huge ball and, as Martin, X knew it would be impossible to secure permission. But, in the cabin, X had shown the explorer a letter from K9, in Washington, which put a different light on many things which Pope had thought strange in the past.

Too, the dive showed X that this was Van der Veer's Lost Island, for the pearl bed was as the old Dutchman had described it.

Secret Agent X, if he had wished, could have stood high in the realm of science. The bathysphere, to his trained perceptions, was simple. He had amazed Arnold Pope on several occasions, with his deep comments on scientific matters. Although this was the Agent's first dive in a bathysphere he had many times been underwater in a regulation sea diving outfit.

Now he was determined to get into one of the suits with which the giant ball was fitted and step to the floor of the ocean. There was a reason for this, one that was yet vague in his subconscious.

An excited smile on his expressive lips, the Agent entered the pressure chamber, took one of the diving uniforms from its hook. He struggled into the heavy suit, saw that the oxygen tank was in order. Then he lifted the helmet in place, clamped it. The air flow was a bit slow so he opened the valve. Then he screwed shut the bathysphere door, opened the valves which allowed sea water to enter the diving chamber.

Every detail of the intricate mechanism worked perfectly. Within five minutes, the pressure approximating that of the outside, X threw open the steel door. Through it he saw the wide reaches of coral, the semi-opaque world of water. He stepped from the steel ball onto the ocean's bed.

AND THEN, inexplicably, the Agent's lithe body became as motionless as the shadowy coral cliffs. His amazingly receptive mind had received some premonitive flash of menace from this waste of water and coral growth. He turned his head within the helmet, peered in all directions.

The knife advanced to stab into the Agent's rubber diving suit.

He took a step forward with ponderous slowness. Again the feeling of imminent danger, of some unknown, deadly force close by, filled him. But no fear was in his brain. He again stepped forward, blue-gray eyes glazed with the wintry enamel of grim purpose.

To his left a fish suddenly darted like a streak into the shadows. X turned. An involuntary cry of stark surprise escaped his taut lips. He thought at first it must be some strange reflection in the water, some concoction of his mind. But his mind was too well disciplined for imaginary figures to be imprinted there. There could be no mistake, no error.

Advancing toward him, a long keen stabbing knife held menacingly in front of his body, was a diver!

Slowly, inexorably, the diver advanced. The knife was held, rigidly forward, the point advanced to stab into the Agent's rubber diving suit. He knew that should the knife penetrate the tough rubberized fabric, the sea water would rush within the air-inflated suit, cause his death.

And then he did the unexpected. X, unarmed, advanced to meet the murderous diver making for him!

The mysterious diver hesitated. And in that moment of indecision the Agent stepped within range of the stabbing knife. The diver lunged forward. X parried the thrust, stepped to one side and threw the weight of his body and heavy suit against the other.

The strange diver slowly went back. In another instant X twisted the knife from the man's hand, dropped it. The other struggled to get to his feet. X tried to step forward, but something was clamped around his foot. He looked down.

The shell of a giant clam had closed on his foot, held it as firmly as if it were within the cruel jaws of a bear trap.

Then, with amazing swiftness, millions of air bubbles swirled and eddied the water, caused a blanket of white to curtain the unknown diver's form from the Agent's eyes. Swiftly, the bubbles disappeared. X stared. The mysterious diver had vanished.

CHAPTER IV

DEATH STRIKES
IN MID-OCEAN

TAUT LIPS CLAMPED above a square jaw, Agent X gazed down through the murky water at his foot trapped by the giant clam. He was aware that often pearl divers were caught by these huge mussels—held so firmly it was impossible to break loose—there to drown.

X surveyed his predicament, nodded as he saw the long stabbing knife he had wrested from the mysterious diver. By stretching his length horizontally among the coral growths he was able to touch the knife with his fingertips. Finally he reached it, slowly toiled upright once more.

The knife was a heavy one, was firmly embedded in a haft of bone. X attacked the tough muscles of the bivalve which held its shell closed. He got the stout knife between the lips of the two shells, pried upward. The pressure on his foot lessened and he was able to withdraw it. His face, little planes and angles making it craggy, broke into a momentary smile. He retraced his steps to the dangling bathysphere, entered the pressure chamber.

It was not necessary to undergo a long period of decompression so, five minutes later, he switched on the valve which blew the sea water from the diving compartment. Then he clamped the door, opened the one to the interior of the bathysphere. The diving suit was replaced on its hooks. He signaled Crandall to draw up the bathysphere.

A few minutes later X saw the face of Crandall peering anxiously at him through the fused, quartz window. He nodded, smiled. In a moment the door of the huge ball was unclamped and X stepped to the deck of the yacht.

Crandall's eager questions met the Agent's ears. "Say, Mr. Pope, what caused all those air bubbles? We thought for a moment an air coupling had worked loose. It worried—"

Crandall saw the dripping diving suit within the pressure chamber for the first time. "You didn't say you were going out in a diving suit! We couldn't get you for about ten minutes on the telephone but thought it was out of order. How'd the apparatus function?"

"Splendidly, Crandall," Agent X said. He smiled at the tense face of Rika Van der Veer, walked toward the explorer's cabin.

Something was in the Agent's mind now that he hadn't time to think about yet. The fight with the unknown diver, the clam trapping his foot—all had happened so quickly as to cause him to momentarily put out of his mind a fact that now was apparent.

There was an underwater entrance to Lost Island!

There had to be. No other ship was in sight, so it stood to reason the unknown diver had walked from within the island upon seeing the bathysphere make its dive. What deadly menace was now afoot? The Agent suddenly nodded to himself. He got that part of it now. Lost Island was in the hands of Sabbat and his men!

"Mr. Pope—Mr. Pope!"

X, still in the disguise of Arnold Pope, turned in the doorway of the explorer's cabin and saw the radio operator running toward him. X took the yellow sheet of paper. His eyes narrowed as he read it at a glance. His lips came together, made a thin line across his face. He beckoned to the girl and she came to him, her face showing white.

"Rika, it's from S'pore. A news flash that was picked up by the operator. Your father is very ill from some strange malady. He's in a hospital. I think you should know of it. I also believe you should go to him without delay."

"Oh!" the distraught girl cried, her face ashen. "It—it'll take hours and hours in the *Wanderer*. He—he may die before—"

"I think I know a way to get there in a very few hours, Rika," X said gently. He called to Crandall. "Make ready the *Gull*, Crandall! You had better come along." He swerved on Rika. "I'm going to fly you to your father."

But there was more than compassion for Rika Van der Veer in the Agent's decision. Lost Island was indubitably in the hands of Milo Sabbat's men. Henrik Van der Veer, in all likelihood, had served his usefulness to the gang, now was to be done away with.

For the Agent had no doubt that Van der Veer's strange malady was nothing but the effect of some virulent poison.

And, taking the girl to Singapore would serve another purpose. If the Dutch pearl merchant was there in a hospital, then Milo Sabbat was not far away.

X STRODE into the cabin, quickly made his arrangements with Arnold Pope. "I'm still going to keep on your disguise, Pope," X said briskly. "Although I've my own agents in S'pore, I think it best to reach there as Arnold Pope. You planned to go there anyway, so I'll be waiting for you. As soon as I leave the ship you come on deck.

"There'll be lots of questions, naturally. I think you can depend upon your crew to keep matters quiet after you've told them the sinister motives behind all this. "Bye."

X shook hands with the explorer and made for the catapult on which sat the *Gull.* A detail of mechanics swarmed over it, stripped it of protective canvas, saw to the oil supply—its power plant was a Diesel engine of high horsepower—emergency rations, flares, a medical kit and the score or more things with which it was equipped. Agent X personally installed near his seat his personal luggage and a small box of light steel.

The *Gull* was a three-place amphibian, fitted with a huge radial motor, a new type reversible-pitch steel propeller, and was constructed wholly of metal.

There was a burst of quick power from the special Diesel motor, and Crandall, the aviator, nodded from the cabin that all was in readiness. A mechanic placed three small bags in the luggage compartment, reached down for Rika's hand. In another moment Crandall moved over, and Agent X took his place at the controls. The motor was revving up smoothly, showing the necessary r.p.m. X switched on the silencer a moment, said to the girl:

"Put your head back against the headrest. A catapult take-off is a rather strange experience, but it lasts only a few seconds. Just lay your head back and relax. Ready?"

Face strained and white, she nodded.

Secret Agent X was a master aviator. Many years before, during the World War, he was attached to the British Camel Squadron 151 in dangerous night operations. Since then and in civil life, X had kept pace with the tremendous development in aviation and flew all types of ships. In fact, he owned two planes, the *Oriole* and the *Blue Comet,* flew them a great deal in his cases throughout the country.

Agent X, eyes glued to the temperature gauge, knew the r.p.m. of his steel prop was at the 1,700 mark. He raised his hand and a mechanic at the catapult's controls pressed a button. There was a dull explosion followed by the hiss of compressed gases. The catapult boom slid forward and literally threw the *Gull* into its element.

It shot away from the *Wanderer,* dipped a moment, and then the Diesel motor took up its throaty cadence of power. The plane lifted, circled the yacht once, then pointed its whirling propeller due east. In seconds it was but a dot on the horizon, a dot above a waste of water that was the Java Sea.

Rika Van der Veer, after her initial fear, relaxed and seemed to enjoy the flight, although X saw little gray ghosts of worry deep in her blue eyes. He surprised her several times gazing at him, wondered why she averted her eyes so quickly when he turned, why faint flushes of crimson toothed her cheeks.

It was mid-afternoon now and the *Gull* drummed along at a steady 250 m.p.h. X long ago had set the Sperry gyroscopic robot pilot, lounged in his seat. He brought out a package of sweet biscuits and a thermos jug of pineapple juice.

Suddenly X, keen eyes shaded against the glare of the sun, caught Crandall's arm and pointed below. Far away on the horizon lay a streamer of serpentine smoke. He got out high-powered binoculars.

"It's a tramp steamer, Crandall. Seems to be en route to S'pore. But look almost under us. That's what attracted my attention. Wait, I'll swing the plane around so you can have a look-see."

He disengaged the robot controls, banked the plane in a turn to port. He straightened out at Crandall's yell of surprise.

"It's a life raft, Mr. Pope, and there's somebody on it! How in the world did that tramp steamer miss seeing it?"

"That could be easy enough," X said crisply. He pushed forward on the control wheel, gently closed the throttle. The whistle and shriek of wind came to their ears as the *Gull* spiraled downward toward the surface of the water.

Fifty feet above the gently breaking waves the Agent opened the throttle once more, cruised in a tight circle around the life raft. Suddenly his eyes narrowed and puzzled astonishment parted his lips.

The person on the life raft was alive and, incredibly, it was a girl!

X made a perfect landing in a long swell of water, brought the nose of the plane about and blasted the tail around. In another ten seconds he was as close to the raft as possible. He unlatched the cabin door on his side, turned to Crandall when half out of it.

"We'll have to put her behind us on top of the baggage. She's apparently fainted, but I don't think she's been exposed much to the sun. At least her skin doesn't show it. Looks like a Chinese girl from here. I'm going after her."

WITH THE words, X dropped into the water, Rika gave a little cry of fright as his head vanished from sight. With two powerful Australian crawl strokes his fingertips touched the raft. A quick upward lunge brought him aboard.

Ordinarily, the disguises used by Secret Agent X would run coming in contact with water. But many of his disguises were water-proof, needing special chemical cleansers to erase. Knowing he was going down in the bathysphere with its hot, humid air, he had applied a special disguise when making up as Arnold Pope, the explorer. It would not run or smear in water.

The girl who lay supine before him was not Chinese. Probably an Eurasian, he thought. Her slightly long, oval face was the color of very light amber, her lips red, her cheekbones high. Hair black as obsidian was parted in the center, lay close to her shapely head. She wore Chinese costume, the knee-high slit of the gown disclosing a shapely leg encased in gossamer hose. She was alive, for the steady rise and fall of her bosom could be seen under the thin Shantung silk of her gown.

And then she opened her eyes. They were a deep slate-gray tinged with little flecks of gold. Her eyes slanted ever so little, lent an exotic touch to her appearance that made the Agent blink. He smiled down at her.

"You're all right, now. I've a plane here. You are to come with me. You'll soon be safe in Singapore."

"Singapore?" she asked. There was a melodious tinkling sound to her voice, and X was reminded of the little silver bells hung in the Musical Pagoda in old Pekin.

"Yes, Singapore," he said. Then: "You can swim?"

She shook her head.

"We'll have to swim back to the plane. You can trust me to keep your head above water. Slip into the water when I tell you, put your hand on my shoulder. Now!"

With the words the Agent slid into the water, turned toward the girl. She crawled to the edge of the raft. Her gold-flecked eyes studied him momentarily. Then, as if trusting him implicitly, she let her lithe body be drawn into the water. He felt the warmth of her slim fingers on his shoulder, could detect no tremble. He headed toward the plane, using his left arm for the stroke. He looked at her, smiled.

A frenzied shout from the plane made the Agent look up. He saw Crandall leaning from the cabin window, pointing frantically.

"Behind you, sir! Sea snakes! They're poisonous!"

Upon the instant the Agent leaped into wild action. He knew of the poisonous sea snakes infesting the waters of tropical oceans. The yellow-bellied sea snake, particularly, was feared. It is a slim killer hardly two feet in length but it is akin to the cobra, having a bite that is deadly.

And, X saw, Crandall was right. He and the girl were ringed about by deadly sea snakes, and even as he watched the circle grew smaller, cutting off their avenue of safety to the amphibian.[11]

The Agent saw something else now that brought a momentary frown of disquiet to his face. The *Gull* had drifted during his rescue of the girl and was now a good fifteen yards away. He had to go on as the sea snakes were between him and the life raft.

The Eurasian girl gave a low cry of horror. Apparently she knew and feared the sea snakes. Her slim arm went about the Agent's neck, and he felt it tighten, almost cut off his wind.

"Don't!" he commanded in a low, tense voice that stung her like the lash of a bullwhip. "Get behind me, put a hand on each shoulder. Quickly, or we're too late!"

GASPING, the girl did as commanded, but X felt the hotness of her breath on his neck. With fingers moving so rapidly they seemed a blur of action, he delved into a pocket, found a small metal box. His

---

11   AUTHOR'S NOTE: *This was one of the sea snakes, family Hydrophiinae. Quoting from Dr. Raymond L. Ditmars, Curator of Mammals and Reptiles, New York Zoological Park: "They (sea snakes) are, for the most part, of striking coloration and provided with fangs and venom so virulent, their rank must be among the most deadly of the poisonous snakes." Again: "The Yellow-bellied Sea Snake is widely distributed. It is common in the Indian Ocean, the waters of Malaysia and the tropical and semi-tropical Pacific generally." And again: "In the Indian Ocean and waters of the Malay Archipelago, Sea Snakes may be seen swimming in schools of several dozen individuals. My friend, Mr. Rudolph Weber, informs me that when nearing the coast of Sumatra upon one of the regular steamers, he was treated to an interesting spectacle. The sea appeared to become suddenly alive with brightly-banded snakes, swimming in every direction in graceful lateral undulations." The poison of these snakes is almost identical with that of the cobra.*

hand reappeared, and in it was a number of small tissue-wrapped packages.

He tossed one of the packages behind him into the very fangs of the sea snakes. Another went to his right and left, two in front of him. Almost instantly a white steam rose above the surface of the water followed by a furious boiling. The effervescent acid halted the attack of the sea snakes, burned their bodies.

Now with powerful strokes X flung himself forward, threw the girl's body onto the pontoon and into the waiting arms of Crandall. In another instant X was safe beside Crandall and the girl. There was no sign of the sea snakes.

"Gosh!" was all Crandall could say. He wiped dripping perspiration from his face, heaved a great sigh of relief.

The Agent said: "Help me get the girl into the plane."

Crandall nodded, the command bringing him out of his terror of a moment before. Between them they helped the girl climb into the cabin to a spot behind them in the luggage compartment.

X bent over the controls, fed oil to the motor. After a hundred-yard run he had the *Gull* on the step, pulled her into the air. He adjusted the robot control, turned and looked at the Eurasian girl.

"Well, how did you get on that life raft, young lady? You might tell us your name, too." His smile was friendly.

The Eurasian girl, her slightly slanting eyes narrowed, looked at him for long seconds before she answered. Then her musical voice came to him.

"My name is Alea, Alea Andrew. That name should mean something to this girl, and you—Secret Agent X!"

X started. He knew his disguise was perfect, that it had not betrayed him. But now he knew this girl being on a life raft in the Java Sea was no accident. It meant that Sabbat's gang knew everything, was leaving no stone unturned to capture them.

X smiled and nodded as he saw the puzzled faces of Crandall and Rika Van der Veer. He turned, looked at the Eurasian girl.

"Well?" he asked softly.

A sneer was now in Alea's voice as she daggered a look at X and Rika, "My father, Secret Agent X, was Carl Andrew, the adventurer who found the Red Maggot and sold it for a handful of silver to this girl's father! You are helping her, trying to keep the Red Maggot from returning to the Malay territory where it rightfully belongs.

"Yes, this is all a plant. A radio message from Lost Island told us you were bound for S'pore by plane. That tramp steamer you must have seen put me on the life raft so as to lure you to stop. Agent X," her tone was edged with steel, "you are returning immediately to Lost Island! There you, these other two, will meet your—*deaths!*"

Agent X blinked. With a quick, lithe movement, Alea Andrew had drawn a small object from some concealment. X saw a square of oiled silk on the floor at Alea's feet. The next instant X was looking into the muzzle of a small automatic.

"Turn back, Secret Agent X," Alea rasped. "Quickly! The South Seas are for those who live here, not you white peoples! Turn back, or I'll kill you! Death means nothing to me. Turn back!"

Secret Agent X laughed softly in her face.

The Eurasian girl, a scream of fury on her red lips, jerked up the automatic and X saw her finger whiten on the trigger. A shot made a vicious *spat* of sound in the tiny cabin of the plane. Something like white hot steel creased the Agent's cheek. He heard Rika scream, saw Crandall's startled face.

Again her finger tightened on the trigger.

CHAPTER V

PALL OF GREEN DEATH

THE AGENT'S MOVEMENTS for self-protection were impossible in the cramped quarters of the speeding amphibian. Ordinarily, his small anesthetizing gun would have served his purpose. But it was in the pocket of his dripping coat and his right arm was thrown back over his seat, his fingers inches away from where it was stowed.

But the Agent's left hand was busy under cover of his body. With quick movements he disengaged the robot control, quickly brought his knee behind the control stick.

And a split-second before the Eurasian girl again fixed he lunged forward with his knee. The *Gull* dived with a maneuver that caused her to vibrate horribly, scream seaward with a speed that threatened to shear the stubby wings from the fuselage.

The maneuver slammed the Eurasian girl against the ceiling of the cabin. X caught her, saw in a quick glance that she had been knocked unconscious by the force of the plane's dive.

X turned, leveled the plane, reached for the throttle. Strangely, the motor was just ticking over, and X had to dive again to regain flying speed. Then he saw what had happened. The enraged girl's second bullet had smashed the throttle segment and X could not feed oil to the Diesel engine.

A landing now was necessary to repair the broken throttle.

Agent X flashed an anxious glance downward and a taut look overspread his face. They were no longer over the Java Sea. Below was a blanket of undulating green. It was jungle. Then X knew where he was. It was Borneo.

A forced landing here would mean their deaths, for as far as the eye could reach there was nothing but the pall of green. It meant death, a horrible death. But there was no choice now.

On board the *Wanderer,* Arnold Pope was explaining to the members of the expedition Secret Agent X's impersonation of himself.

"I have been shown letters addressed to me by an extremely high official in Washington. There is no question as to their genuineness. I also received a code message this morning from the museum officials telling me to take orders from Secret Agent X. I am glad to do that, for there is more than an undercurrent of menace to America in the work the Agent is doing here in the South Seas. We must ally ourselves with him—"

A wild yell of excitement came from a member of the expedition and he pointed to port.

"Look—the sea's on fire!"

Arnold Pope led the rush to the rail. Twenty yards away from the yacht a huge column of flame spewed up from the water, leaped fifty feet straight upward!

"Volcano!"

Arnold Pope shook his head. "Impossible here. That fire is made by some human agency. Look! There's a metal can of some kind near the column of flame. That fire is to draw attention to the can."

He whirled on the ship's captain. "Captain Ott, I believe I'd raise the sea anchors at once and get farther from the island. Send a boat crew for that can and bring it to me."

"Aye, aye, sir," Captain Ott said crisply. He yelled out orders, and the crew jumped to their stations.

The boat crew returned shortly with a metal container such as unrefined spices are packed in for shipment. It was tightly sealed, but the ship's carpenter pried off the lid.

Inside was a message typewritten on a square of rice paper. The explorer read it with wide eyes.

It is known to us that Secret Agent X has enlisted your aid to suit his personal designs. The column of fire you saw a moment ago could have been used to cut the bottom out of your ship. Let it be a warning to you. All of you will die if any mention is made of this island or what happened here.

By the time you read this message Secret Agent X will be dead. The Red Maggot is to remain in the South Seas and help deliver this territory to the natives. Beware! Should you return your ship will be destroyed.

There was no signature on the note.

SECRET AGENT X, eyes glazed, shot a glance behind him and saw that the Eurasian girl was still unconscious. He held the rapidly sinking plane as steady as he could.

The plane glided earthward in a long, slanting circle. Now the tops of dank green trees were swishing the pontoons. In another ten seconds the staggering plane would trip on some treetop. It would somersault over and over and crash, throw them through the metal plates of the fuselage, crush their bodies to a bloody pulp.

And then he saw it. A ribbon of dirty water, moving sluggishly between narrow banks of hanging vines and drooping jungle growths. If he could break through the overlapping branches of the trees he would be safe. But then a new peril threatened.

He saw brownish rapids dead ahead and beyond, leaping water which told of submerged logs or rocks. But ahead of that was a stretch of smooth water.

X took the chance. He suddenly dipped the *Gull* through an opening in the overhanging branches hardly large enough for the plane. But there was no crash, no jar. He had made it! Then the Agent pulled the wheel back into his lap. There was a mighty splash, and water leaped up about them. The plane slowed, came to a halt.

"Close going, Agent X," Crandall said, with a tight grin. There was admiration showing in his level blue eyes as he surveyed the man at the controls.

X nodded, smiled at Rika Van der Veer. Alea, he saw, was conscious now and was surveying him with sullen eyes. She offered no excuse, no apology, sat silent, but X saw that inwardly she was boiling with baffled rage.

"We can stretch our legs a bit on the pontoons," X said. He helped Rika down, but Alea refused help and climbed down with a lithe strength that brought a look of admiration to the Agent's face.

"I've a hunch we're on the Barito River, Crandall," X said as he watched the aviator work on the jammed controls.

They were in the middle of the sluggish stream, hardly moving with the current. A hundred feet away, on both sides, was the green of the impenetrable jungle. Out there, X felt, were strange enemies in the shapes of wild beasts, deadly poisonous snakes. Unfriendly natives, too, who perhaps had never before seen the face of a white man. Armed with long *sumpitans*—blowguns—they were eager to aim their poisoned arrows at any trespasser of their jungle fastness.

The green of the jungle, in all shades from a light green to the darker and deadlier hues—engulfed them. It was everywhere, sinister, deadly, a pall of living, clutching death. As the Agent's eyes flashed from side to side he saw a sudden movement in a tree whose branches dipped into the water.

At first he saw nothing. Then his keen eyes caught an incredibly long shape, a triangular head. It was a Regal Python, the largest constrictor snake known. It was the dreaded. *Ular-Sawa* of the Malays.

Without moving, X's penetrating gaze went along the curtained bank of the Barito. He *felt,* rather than saw, menacing and deadly life there. Then a movement of a hanging tree branch attracted his attention. Again at first he saw nothing save the brilliant green of the growth, the glistening moisture emanating from the haze of heat rising from the water.

But now something was taking dim shape and form on the retinas of his blue-gray eyes. And then, in startling reality, he saw clearly. It was a Dyak, one of the natives of Borneo, and in his hands was a long, slim *sumpitan!* [12]

A splash of water near the pontoon drew his gaze. The snoot of a river crocodile showed momentarily and then sank from sight. The Agent saw other ripples, made out the dark bodies of the beasts ringing the plane. He knew that should one of them fall into the river there would be a concerted rush, a terrific fight....

A tiny movement against the leather of his light boots caused him to look down. Now the Agent's eyes were narrowed to grim slits. For imbedded in his boot was a stem arrow of bamboo. At the point was a dark brownish substance, thick and viscid. *Curare,* the deadly poison with which the Dyaks tipped their *sumpitan* darts!

X clipped, but his voice even: "Crandall, get the two girls in the cabin. *Quick!* Dyaks with *sumpitans* are on both banks. I think they are about to send a volley of poisoned arrows...."

"Looks like we're a little bit late, X," Crandall said softly.

With the words a piercing war yell split the stillness. Wild birds screamed, monkeys chattered. X looked up. From up and down

---

12   AUTHOR'S NOTE: *The blow-gun, or sumpitan, of Borneo is between 6 and 7 feet in length and made of ironwood. The arrows used, all of them envenomed with poison, are about 10 inches long, pointed with fish-teeth, and feathered with pith. Fair accuracy is gained for distances up to 60 yards, and at 20 to 40 yards the aim is deadly.*

the muddy Barito he saw war canoes heavy with Dyaks push away from the banks, make for the plane. Other yells added to the din.

These came from the Dyaks hidden on the banks on both sides of the river. Again water splashed, and a huge crocodile raised his ugly snout, bellowed a challenge. There was sudden quiet. Then a deep voice yelled out some fierce command.

The Agent's eyes narrowed. He stepped forward to protect the two girls, but they were on the opposite pontoon. But there was nothing he could do. Scores of poison-tipped *sumpitan* darts were arrowing at them from all sides!

In a moment they would strike, and then the swift virulence of the curare would bite and gnaw at their hearts....

RIKA AND ALEA screamed as they saw the tiny shafts of death arcing toward them. The Agent and Crandall, stony eyes hard, watched the poison-tipped arrows in flight. The Dyaks, eager for the kill, had badly miscalculated the distance. The little winged deaths fell short, made tiny jets of water leap upward as they fell harmlessly into the Barito.

Crandall jerked his automatic from its holster, made ready to fire, but the Agent's sharp command held his finger from pressing the trigger.

"Wait," X said softly. "I can make them understand. Meanwhile you get into the cabin. We're headed up the river. Work on that throttle. When I give the word start the engine, it may frighten them. Pass down that little steel box in my map case. But first give me a chance to placate them. That's the chief in the leading canoe. The wizened little savage beside him is the witch doctor."

X held up his hand and gained the attention of the natives while Crandall climbed into the cabin and passed down the flat steel box. Something in his fearless presence stopped the second command to fire from the chief. The Agent knew that all savages, living as they do in daily physical danger, admire courage in their enemies. The canoes were only twenty-five yards away now, and even with yammering machine guns they would be mowed down by a cloud of poison arrows from the *sumpitans*.

"*Tabe,*" X said easily, addressing the chief.

The chief of the jungle Dyaks looked surprised at being addressed in faultless Malay. He studied a moment, and X saw the witch doctor whispering to him. The chief stood erect in the bow of the canoe.

He was short, slight, a deep cinnamon brown. Around his waist was a bark loin cloth, and to it hung two hideous dried heads. He held a *sumpitan* in his hand and attached to his loin cloth was a small cylindrical tube of bamboo.

In that tube, the Agent knew, was the arrow poison in which the tiny shafts were dipped before being blown through the *sumpitans.* Around his neck was a triple necklace of crocodile teeth, yellowed with age. In his jet black hair several plumes of brilliantly-hued birds were placed, denoting his high position as chief of his *kampong,* or village.

"It is not a good day, as you say, white man, when you trespass in the land of the jungle Dyaks. We allow no one to come here—*and return!* Shortly my warriors will reach you with their *sumpitan* darts and your heads will adorn the ridgepole of my house. You are devil-devils. So says my witch doctor, and Rapa is right. I am the great M'Lo, chieftain of all this region. Even the *Nederlanders* and the *Inggris* have fear of M'Lo."

Secret Agent X answered him in swift Malay. "We mean no harm. Our api *tambangan*—air boat—came down to rest for a few moments. Shortly we shall leave and our coming will bring good fortune to your *kampong.* But I warn you, M'Lo, do not act on the advice of Rapa, your witch doctor, or great harm will befall you and all your men!"

"Rapa's magic is great, *poeti orang*—white man—and he has but to raise his hand and a hundred *sumpitan* darts will quiver in your flesh."

"I too have magic, M'Lo," X said.

As he talked his busy fingers had delved within the little steel box. They reappeared. He held up a small cylinder of light metal. "Ask Rapa if he knows magic such as this!"

With the words the Agent flung the small cylinder into the air. As he did so, however, his fingers pressed down on a concealed button. A red balloon blossomed at one end of the cylinder. The tube was filled with a highly compressed gas. The pressing of the button released it into the large red rubber balloon. Having tremendous lifting power, the gas filled the balloon and it rose into the air, growing larger as it ascended. The Agent smiled at the awed faces of the Dyaks.

Suddenly the balloon burst with a tremendous noise, and a cascade of red, green and blue fire erupted, from the cylinder. It was a "star bomb" such as is fired on the Fourth of July. But to the simple

The Agent's knife hand darted almost into the crocodile's mouth.

Dyaks it was a major miracle. There were gasps of fear from the Dyak warriors, and they looked uneasily toward M'Lo and Rapa.

Laughing softly, X reached down and jerked the little bamboo *sumpitan* arrow from his boot. He held it aloft so all might see. Then, with a quick movement, he jabbed it into his forearm!

Rika cried aloud in horror. The Dyaks gasped, looked at each other with wondering faces. X again laughed. He was adept at sleight of hand. So quick had been his movements that no one saw the steel pin he had taken from his belt, and palmed. Then, holding it so as to make the wound, he had jabbed it into his arm. It appeared as if the poison-tipped arrow had drawn the blood.

He held up his arm so all could see the blood. Then, contemptuously, he tossed the *sumpitan* arrow into the Barito, again palming the steel pin.

A MADDENED voice came from behind Secret Agent X. He swerved, eyes glazed in wintry hues. It was Alea, and she was addressing the Dyaks in Malay, inciting them to attack!

"It is trickery, M'Lo," she screamed. "This man is trying to win more of our islands for the white peoples! Look at me! Hear me! I am native to the Malays although my father was white. This man is your enemy! Have you not heard of the *mera mata hari*—the Red King—the great pearl-heart known to the whites as the Red Maggot?

"Truly, I say to you, this man wishes to keep the Red Maggot from returning to the Malay States so they, not *you,* may conquer the white man's dominion! Attack, M'Lo—*attack!"* Alea, screaming defiance, leaped into the muddy Barito and swam with lithe strokes toward the chief's war canoe!

"So you can swim now!" X said raspingly. He looked at M'Lo and the wizened Rapa, saw they were ready to attack. His fingers came from his belt and, with a sweeping motion, he threw something into the bow of M'Lo's advancing canoe.

It was a pellet of thin glass, and within it was a spoonful of acid similar to that which he had used on the tires of the murder car near Eastern College. The glass shattered against the floor of the canoe, and a burst of sulphurous yellow smoke flew upward in the very faces of M'Lo and his witch doctor.

Almost instantly the acid ate through the bottom of the canoe. A wild yell of fright screamed from a score of Dyak throats. Other canoes darted in to save the chief and the Dyak warriors.

And then, in the utter confusion of the rescue, a piercing scream of utter terror knifed the thick jungle air. The Agent swung about and a cry of horror escaped his lips. The cry had come from the swimming Alea. She was only ten yards away from the *Gull,* on the Agent's side, but within several feet of her was an immense river crocodile, its reptilian eyes beady, its huge mouth opening to snap at the helpless girl![13]

Another splash sounded as X's muscular body impacted against the water in a clean knife dive. He swam under water with powerful strokes, came up beside the terrified Alea. His strong hand got the girl by the hair. He jerked her from the path of the savage creature, pushed her backward with a mighty lunge of his shoulders.

Then the Agent's knife hand came above the water, seemed to dart almost into the mouth of the crocodile. But none saw the tiny ball of glass shatter against the bony structure of the saurian's upper jaw. Before X dived from view, the inert body of the girl in his arms, he saw the deadly acid take effect.

The crocodile coughed, bellowed, spewed out a cloud of the sulphurous smoke. Its terrific death movements roiled the muddy water, caused brown spray to cover the awe-stricken Dyaks.

Brief seconds later the Agent threw the body of the unconscious Eurasian girl onto the pontoon of the plane, clambered up himself and lifted her to safety. He turned, gazed at the silent Dyaks.

M'Lo, Rapa and the Dyak warriors had been hauled aboard other war canoes, had watched the rescue through staring eyes. Suddenly X heard gasps of wonder, saw the Dyaks pointing down stream. He followed their pointing arms with his gaze and a quiet smile hovered momentarily about his taut lips. The dead crocodile, white belly upward, was floating down the sluggish Barito.

"Do you believe now, oh M'Lo," he asked quietly, "that I too have much magic? I mean no harm to you or your *kampong*. I wish to go eastward in peace. I want your friendship, want to tell the great chiefs of the far cities that in M'Lo they have a friend, one who courteously treats visitors with the welcome he too would expect. Tell me, M'Lo, shall it be friendship or—war!"

Voice faltering, cinnamon-brown face working in fear, M'Lo once more got to his feet. In the flowery language of the Malays he told of how he had desired peace but for the urgings of the wicked Rapa. He—M'Lo—would see that Rapa suffered for the indignities offered the man-who-was-not-afraid-of-river-crocodiles. And, too, M'Lo wished to give a present to the white chief.

---

13   AUTHOR'S NOTE: *River crocodiles have been noted 30 feet in length in Malaysia, and 16 to 18 feet is rather common. The crocodile takes a terrible toll of native life each year.*

Voice now incisive, M'Lo commanded his Dyaks to paddle close to Secret Agent X. His hand disappeared for a moment within his loin cloth. He held something out to X, who accepted it with a grave bow. In return he gave M'Lo a metal mirror, and the Dyak chief looked at it in mingled awe and gratitude.

X looked down at the hard object M'Lo had placed in his hand. His eyes narrowed and a low whistle escaped his lips. It was an uncut ruby the size of a small egg!

The Dyaks stayed close to the *Gull* as Crandall tinkered with the oil feed lines, discovered that all was in working order. The two girls were helped into the cabin and X wound up the inertia starter. The Diesel motor caught. Its roar of power startled the Dyaks, but the Agent explained they had nothing to fear. M'Lo cleared a pathway for the take-off, and X, after a last wave of his arm, gave the ship the gun.

It was a narrow take-off, the river confined as it was by overhanging branches and trailers of green vine. The *Gull's* wing-tips brushed against the green of jungle trees as it soared into the late afternoon, its silvery prop again boring into the east. The Agent put the ship on its course, adjusted the robot pilot.

A noise of strangled sobbing came to him. He turned around and a slight smile curved his lips. The Eurasian girl was sobbing, her delicately oval face buried in her hands. Her shapely shoulders under the silken dress were shaking and trembling.

CHAPTER VI

THE PEARL KINGS

JON SMIT, VAN DER VEER'S Far Eastern manager, sat at the head of a small table, his nut-brown face and brown eyes troubled, tense. He was a small man, thin, had the bad color of one who had lived many years in the tropics. Sparse hair was plastered to his head with perspiration. Even through his look of worry, however, there was courage in his indomitable face, a shrewdness to his canny straightforward eyes.

Jon Smit toyed with the pineapple drink before him, swished it about in the glass so the ice made musical tinklings. He looked at the other four men in the room. One of them was an elderly Chinese. His name was Kwang. Dressed in pongee silk, like the others, he was fat, wore tortoise-shelled glasses, boasted a mandarin mustache with flowing ends.

Next to him sat a dapper Japanese, Jiro Yoshida. Across the table was a Greek, Anaximander Papapoulos. The last man was Abdallah, an Arab.

The five were seated in a private room of the Raffles Hotel, in Singapore. It was an ill-assorted group. Yet, at the least, these men represented millions of Straits dollars.

They were the pearl kings of the world.

Regardless of where a pearl was found, in the Indian Ocean, the Gulf of California, the Arabian Sea, a hundred and one little South Sea islands, it eventually passed through the hands of one of these five men before it reached a world market. Jon Smit, representing the fabulous Van der Veer interests, was at the head of the table.

"*Ja, Mynheers,*" Jon Smit said slowly, "it is a bad business. The S'pore market is flooded with magnificent pearls. I have checked with Batavia, with Padang, even with Amsterdam. None of my agents is able to explain it. Yet," Smit shrugged nervously, "the

220

pearls descend upon the markets. Already the price is down many Straits dollars here in S'pore. It is inexplicable."

"By Allah, we find the reason!" thundered the Arab, pounding the table with his brown fist. "These pearls do not come from the Arabian Sea or the Gulf of Oman, my territories. But in Cairo, my brothers say by radio, the price of pearls is down twenty *piasters* per grain. It is ruinous!"

"Yess," the Japanese said hissingly. "It is the same in Tokio. My firm will pay many *yen* to stop this illicit trafficking in these pearls. They are genuine pearls, as we all know. Perhaps some pearler has found some hidden cache, some—"

Jon Smit shook his head. "It cannot be that, *Mynheer.* We all know that. No one bed of pearls, even if left unmolested since the Mogul emperors, could yield so huge a number of first water pearls. I am mystified."

Anaximander Papapoulos, the swarthy Greek, leaned across the rattan table. His black eyes bored into those of Jon Smit. "Listen to me, Jon Smit. Rumors tell us that Henrik Van der Veer makes seed pearls by a secret new process. So far, we learn, these are very small and cheap pearls such as the Japs have in their culture beds. Could it be possible that your firm"—a sneer creased his oily face—"has discovered a way to make *big* pearls?"

He sat back, pulled an Egyptian cigarette from a diamond-studded case, held the flame of an ornate lighter to its tip. The heavy smoke was like incense in the room.

Kwang, the obese Chinese, leaned close to the Greek and tapped him on the arm, "Do not throw veiled hints as to the dishonesty of your co-workers or they may do likewise," he said in a softly nasal voice.

He looked at the others. "My friend Van der Veer, peace to his ancestors, is beyond reproach, higher than suspicion. We gain nothing by hurling words at each other. We must unite or lose the markets it has taken our firms a generation to build up, to weld together."

Jon Smit nodded, the worry lines imprinted in heavy crow's feet at the corners of his harried eyes. He had reason to be worried.

The pearl markets of the world were glutted with first water specimens. The five of them seated at this table, he knew, controlled the pearls of the world. They were doled out so as not to fluctuate the market, were handled so that the demand always seemed to exceed the supply. Long years ago they had copied the DeBeers system.

IN AFRICA, the DeBeers diamond mines doled out just enough gems to cause no flurry in the market, to keep the stones steadily increasing in price each year. They were doing the same with pearls here in Singapore.

Only now, from some source unknown, hundreds of pearls were reaching the world markets at prices considerably under those offered by the syndicate. It was a damnable thing. Should it continue, it meant tremendous losses.

Jon Smit said: "I cabled our New York office the other day and our good friend, Jebel Zeck, answered me this morning. He is distraught over the news. He says none of the pearls have apparently reached America yet, but he is worried. Mr. Zeck is checking in San Francisco personally to see if he can find out anything. There's a bare chance he may take the Pan American *Clipper* and visit us for a short while here in S'pore."

Jon Smit had other worries, too. His employer, Henrik Van der Veer had landed in S'pore as if in a trance. He was ill of some strange malady, unable to talk coherently, to think. In his company was a man by the name of Milo Sabbat. Smit did not know him. But he recognized the power of attorney Sabbat held and signed by Van der Veer.

Sabbat was listed on that paper as having full and complete charge of the vast Van der Veer organization. Already Jon Smit had been told in no uncertain terms that his employ with the organization was to cease in sixty days.

Then, too, the radio messages told Jon Smit that Rika, Van der Veer's only child, had been blown to bits in a laboratory explosion at a New York college. It all was so sudden, so discouraging after forty years spent with his employer. Jon Smit sighed.

He said, a shadow on his face: "I have bad news, gentlemen. You have wondered why I am taking the place of *Herr* Van der Veer in this conference. The truth is"—pain made his eyes close for a moment—"Henrik Van der Veer is—*dying!*"

Incredulous surprise made the others silent. Jon Smit continued. "His daughter and only heir was accidentally killed some weeks ago in New York. I do not yet know what will become of the firm—afterward."

He had received implicit instructions from Sabbat not to divulge the new ownership of the Van der Veer interests. Smit wondered where Milo Sabbat could be. He had sent Van der Veer to the hospital, then disappeared. Smit had tried to trace him but to no avail.

"But, gentlemen," Jon Smit's face now was gray with a worry that gnawed inside him, "that is not all. I have learned what I tell you now, from my own sources." He lowered his voice, whispered: "I learn the Red Maggot has returned to the South Seas!"

Exclamations in four different tongues met Jon Smit's ears. He looked around the circle of paled faces, saw the same fear there he knew lay mirrored in his own eyes.

"By Allah!" hissed the Arab, "that means all nations save the Malays will have to go elsewhere for trade! It means—"

"Sabotage—perhaps war!" agreed the little Japanese.

"But there is one gleam of sunshine," Jon Smit said slowly. "For some reason I have not heard from Peter DeVery, our technical expert on Lost Island where we have our culture station. In the past he communicated with me by radio once weekly. Perhaps something is wrong with the sending apparatus, I do not know.

"But a Dutch vessel picked up a radio message from there a few hours ago, the first in several weeks. It was relayed to me by the wireless operator, a nephew of mine. It said—" Jon Smit took a bit of paper from his point, read:

"Arnold Pope's yacht now at island. He leaving by plane after apparent receipt your news item. Have reason to believe Pope is Secret Agent X in disguise. Proceed with plan as discussed with Alea. X will see her adrift. She can force return to island after his yacht en route to Singapore. Watch X carefully."

"Gentlemen," Jon Smit looked at the others, "something very menacing has happened. I know Peter DeVery did not send that message. Lost Island is in the hands of pirates! I believe the man who is returning the Red Maggot to the Malay territory also holds Lost Island as his headquarters!"

"But who is this Secret Agent X?" queried the Greek abruptly. "Why should he concern himself with the Red Maggot, assume this deadly risk? I do not understand."

Jon Smit shrugged. "No one knows. We of the Far East have not heard of him, although I have known of him through *Mynheer* Van der Veer. In America he is known as the 'Man of a Thousand Faces.' He is one of the most remarkable men of the whole world, a scientist, a man who knows no fear. And," Jon Smit leaned across the table, "he is a man without fear!

"He fights crime, *Mynheers*. When the safety or peace of his country is at stake, you will find Secret Agent X in the thick of things. He always wins. I wonder," he mused, "if you realize what the return of the Red Maggot means to America? That country has no vast stake here as have my country, the British, the Japanese. But, gentlemen, they have Manila and the Philippines!"

Jon Smit nodded, touched a *vesta* to a slim Sumatra cheroot. "With unrest here, eventually the United States would lose Manila—the entire Philippine group—to our common enemy. We know that before long these natives would be banded together by unprincipled leaders, cause a war that might be the end of civilization. *Mynheers,* if Secret Agent X is on our side we have a chance—a bare chance."

Jon Smit looked at his watch. It was seven-thirty. He tapped a bell on the table and a Malay waiter opened the door. Behind him, in the hallway, were two others.

"You may serve the meal now," Jon Smit told him. "We are in somewhat—" Jon Smit frowned.

FOR THE Malay waiter had nodded, flashed a brief grin, and then closed the door behind him! With swift steps the Malay waiter crossed the room and flashed a glance from the low-silled window. He recrossed toward the door, opened it, turned to Jon Smit.

"*Saja, tuan,*" he said softly.

Again Jon Smit stared. He had caught a flash of the Malay's eyes, and they were not inky black. They were a deep wintry gray! Jon Smit turned to the others at the table, but they were talking busily, paid no attention to what had happened.

The waiter at the door was handed a huge platter covered over with a silver bell such as is used to keep foods hot while being served. He walked to a serving table, placed the huge platter in its center. The other two waiters followed, each with plates of salad.

The last one entering the private room carefully closed the door, and only Jon Smit saw him deftly lock it. The slight Smit started to his feet, gasped in sudden surprise.

For, with the speed of striking cobras, the three waiters turned. Jon Smit got a flash of the platter under the raised silver cover. He gasped, for there was no food there. *Only three revolvers fitted with silencers!*

One of the waiters spat out, his black eyes venomous points of flame: "It is the end, you fools! The perils of the world are represented by you five in this room. We have silenced guns. With your deaths we will control the pearl markets of the earth! Accursed foreigners, prepare to die!"

He, and one companion, raised their silenced guns, their fingers straining on the triggers.

And then an incredible thing occurred. The waiter who had first entered the room turned toward those with the guns. In his hand now instead of the silenced gun was a small weapon no larger than the breadth of two fingers. Suddenly from this weapon a thin gray spray issued into the faces of the two wild-eyed Malays!

They coughed, started to turn toward the man with the small gun. But unconsciousness struck them before their rubbery knees slumped and their bodies crashed to the floor.

Jon Smit was on his feet, face ashen. His right hand came into view, and in his fingers was a small Webley automatic. But there was something in the eye of the eagle-visaged Malay before him that caused him to hold his fire. And then Jon Smit understood. He said, and there was awe in his voice:

"You—you are Se—"

The Malay turned, the movement like a flash of light. "I am," he said softly, "a private operative working for Mr. Van der Veer. That is all that is necessary for you to know, gentlemen."

Jon Smit nodded, a quiet smile on his thin lips. *He* knew this man in the disguise of a Malay was Secret Agent X!

X knelt over the two men on the floor, beckoned for Jon Smit to join him. "These two men, and a third one unconscious in the hallway, will remain helpless for an hour. They should be locked in jail immediately. I don't expect we will ever make them talk, but we can keep them in safety. They are so filled with the superstitious fervor of the return of the Red Maggot to the South Seas that they will die before they tell anything."

He looked toward the door as he heard noise from the hallway followed by a pounding on the door. "They've discovered the waiter I anesthetized with my gas gun."

Outside in the hallway there was the hum of excited voices, then a sharp knock on the door. It opened, and an assistant manager entered followed by a British police officer. In crisp sentences Jon Smit told of the attack, the part X—whom he introduced as an employee of the Van der Veer firm—had played in the rescue.

In five minutes the police had cleared the room of the unconscious Malays, advised the pearl dealers that a guard would be posted outside in the corridor. At the Agent's whispered suggestion to Jon Smit, nothing was said of the suspected reason behind the murderous attack.

X crossed to the open window, peered out. Suddenly he fell back, motioned the others away and held up his hand for silence.

The startled Japanese and the Greek stepped away from the screened window. As they did so there was the quick *swish* of something flying through the air, the metallic tearing of the upper half of the screen. A streak of silvery light darted across the room, narrowly missing Jon Smit's neck. There was a sharp thud, then silence.

"Mein Gott, look!"

Jon Smit pointed with trembling forefinger at the wall behind them. The others turned, watched with incredulous eyes as the Agent strode to the wall, jerked a silver *kris* free from where it was imbedded in the paneling!

"I thought so," he said quietly. "An old trick to strike fear into a group of people. There's a note tied to the haft."

His flying fingers unwound a length of jute which held a folded sheet of rice paper to the haft of the Malay *kris*. He read it, looked at the pearl merchants, a quiet smile on his face.

"I think," he said slowly, "we will have to be very careful tonight. Our unknown enemy is determined to frighten us off. Too bad we can't let the British authorities know of the possibility of the Red Maggot returning to S'pore." He tapped the note in his hand, read aloud:

" *'Do not think that you have won even a small victory tonight. As the clock strikes midnight one of your number will die! Which one small it be? Only death will show you!'* "

The note was unsigned.

Jon Smit's somber voice said slowly, but vibrant with triumph: "I am not afraid—now!"

CHAPTER VII

STING OF DOOM

THE AGENT TOOK immediate command of the situation. The hotel manager was called and arrangements made for a large room on the top floor of the hotel. As they walked toward the elevator, Abdallah, the Arab, turned to the manager.

"Down below you will see a very devil of a man waiting for me. His name is Mohamid. Tell him to come up to this same room to be with me. If I am to die I want him to be at my side, and we'll see how many of these accursed natives go along with us to Paradise." His laugh was deep in his throat.

"This Mohamid," X asked, "you can trust him?"

"Aie," the Arab growled. "Even though he is a convert to my faith I trust the rascal." His laugh boomed. "Many a man have we sent on the long journey together, master!"

The Agent nodded, walked with the others to the safety of the room, closed and locked the door. Shortly afterward Mohamid joined them. He was a big man, wore the clothes of civilization awkwardly. His left eye had been lost in some misadventure of the past, and a livid *kris* mark slanted across one cheek and dented the beak of his long nose.

The Agent drew Jon Smit aside, whispered the news that Van der Veer was recovering. A subtle poison had been found in the old Dutchman's system, introduced in some diabolically mysterious manner. It was the Agent's knowledge of toxicology that first put hospital physicians on the right track.

Jon Smit also was told that Rika was alive. He was given a brief account of the happenings in New York, the fake article in the newspaper and the dash eastward in the *Wanderer*. X told of stopping at Lost Island, but did not tell of his underwater encounter with the diver. He was not surprised when Jon Smit did not mention the secret entrance to the island, and X surmised it must have been discovered by the plotters.

"The yacht will dock tomorrow night?" Jon Smit asked.

"Yes," X nodded. "The *Wanderer* is headed for S'pore under forced draft, should reach here about dusk tomorrow or a little later."

"So, you believe," Jon Smit pondered, "this Sabbat is the one behind these strange happenings? From what you say it seems certain he is the one who stole the Red Maggot."

His face became grave. "That accursed pearl has caused men to go mad for the lust of power these thousands of years! It makes of the brain a cancerous growth. Should it reappear in the Malay States, it means perpetual unrest until destroyed. But it must be utterly done away with!"

He thought a moment and looked deeply into the Agent's eyes. "I trust you," he said simply and stretched out his hand.

A knock sounded at the door. The Agent opened it, stood aside to allow Crandall to enter.

Crandall looked around in evident surprise, spoke to Jon Smit. "Sorry, sir. I expected to find a friend of mine with you. He goes by the name of—of Mr.—"

The Agent's dusky face, in the disguise of the Malay waiter, brightened in a quick smile. "You compliment my abilities, Crandall," X said to the aviator.

Crandall started, finally nodded. "It's perfect," he exclaimed, looking at the Agent's face. Then his expression became serious. "Bad news, sir. I allowed Alea, the Eurasian girl, to escape as you ordered. I thought I wouldn't have any trouble following her, but she slipped me. Sorry."

A momentary frown flashed on the Agent's face, then cleared. "I don't think any harm's been done, Crandall. The girl is only a tool of the man responsible for all this: Sabbat. Perhaps it will cause him to become careless, step out into the open."

CRANDALL nodded. He smiled again. "But why this get-up, sir?" He made a motion to the Agent's Malay disguise.

The Agent's smile was grim. "I was told Jon Smit was here in a certain room with the other pearl merchants. I went there to inform him that Mr. Van der Veer would recover. Out in the hallway I saw three Malay waiters.

"I managed to get there just in time to see them hide three silenced revolvers under a large silver bell on a platter. I called one of them around the corner, sent him on an imaginary errand. I followed, anesthetized him and—well—" X shrugged. Then: "Rika is at the hospital with her father?"

"Yes. Mr. Van der Veer is coming along nicely although still unconscious. It'll be several days before he comes around."

X nodded, was thoughtful for a moment. "I am worried about Peter DeVery, Crandall. He's at the island, and it's in the hands of Sabbat and his men. I understand from Rika this DeVery is a brilliant technician. Should he meet his death it'd be a terrible thing. And—I mean to prevent it! We must return to the island as quickly as possible and attempt a rescue—if it isn't too late."

In terse sentences X told why they were together in the room, of the warning on the silver *kris*.

Jon Smit, who had been listening, agreed. He told of the radio message from the island picked up by his nephew on the Dutch tramp.

"It ties up with what you've told me. Lost Island is in the hands of this Sabbat and his men. DeVery is absolutely trustworthy. Alea tried to trap you. Peter DeVery must be dead. We must watch very carefully. Sabbat drugged my employer, forced him to sign the power of attorney. He has vanished."

"Yes," the Agent nodded. "The motive becomes very clear now. The maggots of lust have entered the soul of Milo Sabbat. With it, the Red Maggot, and the Van der Veer process for making perfect pearls, he will be able to raise millions of dollars, control the superstitious natives, endeavor to make the South Seas a place only for the Dyaks, the Malays and the wild bush-men of the interior."

With the words the Secret Agent excused himself and entered the washroom. With sure, deft touches he removed the Malay disguise, took out his small box of makeup materials. With plastics, dyes and chemicals he donned the face of A.J. Martin, Associated Press reporter, returned to the room.

Crandall grinned at him, for it was the face with which he was familiar, the face he thought was the Agent's real one. The pearl kings looked their astonishment at this amazing man, but refrained from saying anything. Crandall, pleased, introduced X as A.J. Martin. There was a sudden sharp knock at the door. The Agent opened it, stepped back in astonishment as a slight, smiling figure stepped into the room. It was Jebel Zeck.

Zeck's jaw went slack with surprise as he recognized X as the newspaper reporter. "Why, what are you doing here, Martin?" he cried. He shook hands, turned to Jon Smit and the others whom he evidently had met before.

Zeck turned to X, a grin of excitement on his face, his green eyes flashing. He rubbed at his chin with his slim forefinger. "Don't tell me you're still trying to say that accursed Red Maggot is stolen, is back here in the South Seas?" he said.

"It is here in the South Seas, Zeck," X said softly. "I know because I was with Miss Rika when she opened the safe later that same night of the strange accidents. I—"

"Miss Rika—the Red Maggot!" Zeck cried. Then: "The girl—she is alive? The Maggot stolen! I—I thought it was all imaginative, a—a sort of melodramatic story you, as a newspaperman, was concocting for a feature story."

The Secret Agent explained what had happened after he and Arnold Pope had left the Van der Veer store that cold night in New York.

"That explains something else, then," Jebel Zeck said reflectively, forefinger rubbing his sharp chin. "Two days later I changed the recording paper in the door lock of the store and noted it had been opened much later that night of the accidents. I thought the lock was recording incorrectly, had it changed. So Miss Rika is alive, eh? But how is Mr. Van der Veer? I've just landed from a plane an hour ago."

He sighed, shook his head. "If I only knew what this is about! I received a cable from a man who signed it as Milo Sabbat saying he had taken over the Van der Veer interests. It was the customer who was in the store when the tar vat exploded. He—he says I will not be needed after the first of the month, and—" Zeck's face was taut.

"I understand," X said quietly, "you were attacked by gunmen that same night. I read of it in the newspapers as I came East after being assigned a series of articles here by my association. It happens my friend, Arnold Pope the explorer, was just leaving Frisco so I came along with him."

Zeck became excited. "Yes, and narrowly escaped death! That is one reason I am here, Martin. I believe there's something to this affair that's far deadlier than the mere taking of the Red Maggot. Look," he held up his hand, counted off the fingers as he spoke.

"The attempt at Miss Rika, then my own escape. That makes two. I just landed, but already have heard Mr. Van der Veer was poisoned, that you saved his life. Probably, Martin, attempts have also been made against you." His greenish eyes were wide.

The Agent's laugh was low. In clipped sentences he went over the events of his brief stop at the island—without mentioning the meeting of the diver—the flight in the *Gull* and the finding of Alea. Then he told of the attack by the waiters, the threat.

JEBEL ZECK suddenly was nervous. He looked at his watch. "Why, it—it's ten minutes of midnight now! All of us may be killed! They—this murderous killer—may start with—with me!"

Oval face pale, Zeck looked at the others. Jon Smit walked over to the little man, encouraged him. But Zeck was distraught. His face was streaming perspiration.

"I—I had to come all the way to Singapore to—to be killed!" he moaned. "I thought I might help my employer, and—and—" He was unable to finish the sentence.

Suddenly the Arab spoke, "By Allah, if I die it will be fighting!" he growled. From the waistband of his trousers he withdrew a long knife. Jebel Zeck stared at it in morbid fascination.

There was silence in the room. On the desk a small electric clock made no noise, but its second hand seemed to race around the dial. The minute pointer was but one space from midnight.

The Agent, grim in the background, heard Zeck's strained breathing. The little Japanese sat looking at his fingernails in utter disregard of all danger. The Greek, Papapoulos, was sweating profusely. Kwang sat blandly staring off into space. Jon Smit and Crandall were immobile in their chairs.

And then, at sixty seconds of midnight, something strange came to the Secret Agent's sensitive nostrils. He could not place the strange odor. It was musky, faintly sickening, smelled unclean. The Agent's every nerve was tense now, his entire being watchful, vigilant.

And then the telephone rang.

Jebel Zeck sucked in his breath in a strangled sob. The Greek was on his feet in a sudden start of terror. The others merely looked at the telephone. From blocks away came a metallic bong, then another.

It was midnight.

Slowly, showing no emotion, X raised the receiver from its cradle. He put the instrument to his ear, said: "Yes?"

"Ah, it's Secret Agent X!" The voice over the telephone was oddly flat, devoid of inflection. "Mr. X, the clock now is striking the hour. As its last stroke sounds one of you will die—horribly. Perhaps it won't be you—this time! But later, Mr. X, all of you will feel the bite of death!" There was a soft click as the line went dead.

Again, strongly now, came the odor of musk to the Secret Agent's nostrils. He looked at the men assembled before him. They knew the phone call was from the one heading the gang of killers. But they didn't know which one of them was to die....

"Ten—eleven—"

It was Kwang who was counting the strokes of the clock. They were a death knell in the hot night air, a—

"Twelve!"

And then, in a flash of understanding, the faint warnings in the Agent's subconscious became acute. Across the room he saw Abdallah's man, Mohamid, take a white handkerchief from his coat pocket, start to raise it to his streaming face.

And then the musky odor became as a blow in the face. It suggested unspeakable horror, a deadly and menacing *something* of mystery. X stepped forward, his face set, eyes blazing like twin beacons.

Then the incredible occurred. X, his senses warning him, leaped forward. Too late! Something horribly black and writhing was in that white handkerchief of Mohamid. The man, his face suddenly ablaze with a frenzy that made of it a mask of diabolic fury, drew back his arm. He threw the black thing straight at the face of Jon Smit!

Jebel Zeck screamed, was echoed by the Greek's hoarse cry. But the Secret Agent made no sound. His face was grim, but no fear showed there. Like a flash of lightning, far quicker than the stabbing strike of a king cobra, the Agent's hand, opened flat, darted out at that arcing, horribly squirming thing in mid-air. His hard palm slapped the thing aside where it fell to the floor.

Almost in the same motion the Agent's left came around, the granite knuckles made a sound like the blast of a revolver on Mohamid's brown chin. The man's eyes glazed. He sucked in a breath, fell headlong across the room. His lax, nerveless hand fell close to the half-crushed ball of black on the floor.

With a dying movement the black thing moved close on long, hideously hairy legs. Then, a few inches away, it hurled its loathsome shape forward. A black tail curled over its glistening back and stabbed once, then again. As if the effort was too much, the black scorpion's hairy legs wilted beneath the weight of the body. Its work of death was done.[14]

"The deadly black scorpion!" X said tautly. "It shows the lengths this Sabbat will go to in order to win his objective. He must have bribed Abdallah's man with a very large sum of money to do this, after his own attempt with the waiters failed. As you know, the black scorpion is utterly fearless, will attack the first thing it sees. I thought I smelled its musky odor but wasn't certain. The black scorpion was partially anesthetized, I presume, given just enough to last until the strokes of midnight.

"Mohamid had instructions to throw the deadly thing into Jon Smit's face. You see, Sabbat wants first to kill off all those in the Van der Veer concern. No one could prove anything on him, he would be safe. I think there'll be no more attacks tonight, gentlemen. I, for one, am ready for sleep. But," and the Agent's face became set again, thoughtful, "tomorrow night Sabbat will strike again!"

---

14   AUTHOR'S NOTE: Ordinarily speaking, a scorpion's sting is not necessarily fatal to man. Yet many cases have come to the writer's attention of fatal results after being stung by the large black scorpion. Black scorpions 8 inches in width are not uncommon. A number of deaths have been noted in the public press due to the bite of the Black Widow spider, many times smaller than an 8-inch black scorpion; therefore death is not improbable should one be stung by a scorpion of this size.

CHAPTER VIII

THE MAN WITHOUT A FACE

ON THE OUTSKIRTS of Singapore, on the hills overlooking the Kalang Reservoir, was a magnificent estate. It long had been known as a place of mystery, was unvisited by any person save in the dead of the tropic night. Stationed at the gateway of the outer grounds were two dacoits. These men originally came from India, but there are many Hindus in and around the Malay States.

These two dacoits—and others hidden from view by the screening shrubbery of flaming hibiscus, coconut palms and banana trees—were devotees of Thuggee, the terrible practice of killing indiscriminately to placate some pagan god. Within the grounds fierce dholes roamed. The dholes, huge wild dogs known to pack together like wolves and hunt down tigers, also were imported from India.

Should any man chance to escape the vigilance of the guardians of the gate the wild dogs would stalk him down, tear him to bits. It was an impregnable stronghold, one calculated to keep the mind of the dweller within the boundaries completely at ease.

Milo Sabbat, his white teeth hidden behind rather taut lips, sat alone in an immense room of this house. He was ill at ease for he knew the man from whom he took his orders had cause to be angry with him. Milo Sabbat had never seen his employer in this nefarious work.

Several months before he had been approached by a Malay he had known for years. In fact, they had been in prison together in Batavia. This Malay was the contact man for someone higher up, perhaps the head of the criminal organization.

Milo Sabbat's reputation always seemed to speed ahead of him. He was a murderer with a price on his head in Sumatra; an embezzler sought by the French in Cochin-China; and another murder charge was on him in Manila. Half the nations having mandated islands of the South Seas would give considerable amounts of money to lay their clutches upon the person of Milo Sabbat.

Strangely enough, he was practically unknown in Singapore. The knowledge of how thoroughly the British punish offenders had kept him away from the island. But this Malay friend had assured him he would be safe in Singapore, hence his secret entry into the city weeks before.

The game, Sabbat recognized at once, was a big one. It meant a great deal of money, a trip to New York where he was quite safe, for he had never been to America. He had made that trip. But, and Sabbat's dark face showed lines of worry about the black eyes, it had been unsuccessful in the main.

He had managed to steal a huge pearl called the Red Maggot, of which he had heard vague whisperings in the past but other things had gone wrong. As they said in that strange city of New York, everything had gone "haywire."

A slight noise from across the room made Sabbat start. He peered in that direction, but saw nothing save an ornate Chinese screen embroidered in reds, greens and gold with the figures of two flying dragons. Red fire shot from their open mouths and underneath was a paddy field devastated by the searing flame.

Somehow, it struck a responsive chord in Sabbat's brain. For some reason that tugged at his subconscious, he was certain he didn't like that picture at all. It was so suggestive of the threats his mysterious employer made when he—Sabbat—agreed to murder.

Again the slight noise came from behind the screen. It was very like the sound of the legs of a chair scraping gently against polished wood. Then, and Sabbat felt squeamish, a grotesque shadow showed on the screen. Sabbat's white teeth showed like bleached bones for a moment as his tongue moistened dry lips. There was a man seated behind the dragon screen!

And then Sabbat almost cried aloud. For a voice, a thin, reedy and menacing voice, issued from behind the screen.

"It is well, Sabbat," the voice said without inflection, "that you should contemplate your many errors of the past. People who make errors do not work for me—long! You have made many mistakes, Milo Sabbat, and now it is time to take stock of yourself so that more do not occur.

"Last night, in the Raffles Hotel, three of your men failed miserably when they had the pearl tycoons of the world closeted in a small dining room from which there was no escape. Later, the man you bribed, Mohamid, bungled when he threw the black scorpion at the face of Jon Smit. You have—"

"It was that damn Agent X who caused it all," Sabbat said quickly, and there was strain in his husky voice. "Everywhere I turn, his clever counter-attacks oppose me, defeat my most careful plans."

"Perhaps my judgment was wrong in thinking you were able to meet fire with fire, fight steel with steel." A regretful sigh came from the man behind the screen. "It would be too bad—for you— should I believe my judgment so greatly in error! But again, Sabbat.

"Twice in America your bungling men allowed Rika Van der Veer to escape; once at the chemical laboratory and again after she escaped. Then I was fooled for a number of days, as were you, by the fake news item of her death which appeared in the papers. It—"

"X again!" Sabbat interrupted fiercely. "He was responsible for everything, I tell you. I—"

"You will allow me to finish," the voice resumed, a menacing note in it now. "At Lost Island it must have been you who authorized the diver to attack this X underwater when he went down in the diving ball as Arnold Pope, the explorer. That was a particularly stupid mistake, Sabbat, for it told this adventurer Lost Island was in the hands of Van der Veer's enemies.

"And then, adding stupidity upon stupidity, you sent a radio message to the tramp steamer telling them to try and trap X as he flew toward S'pore. Any number of ships might have accidentally picked up that message.

"But before that you got panicky, radioed me in code here in S'pore to get the Agent away from the island as quickly as possible. It necessitated my having a man poison Van der Veer so his approaching death would be sent out on the radio newscast. I fear now that was an unnecessary thing to do. He was so completely in our power with the unknown drug that we had no cause for alarm at alL By the way, does that fool, DeVery, still refuse to serve as our technician in making the pearls on the island?"

"Y-yes, sir," Sabbat nodded, "Our man, LaPorte, says he doesn't need DeVery's assistance. I think though—" and Sabbat's red lips curled wolfishly away from his white teeth— "DeVery will change his mind before another week is past. He is in the vat of sea water, and the Coral Death is creeping up on him!"

"Splendid!" There was a note of sadistic triumph from the man behind the screen.

MILO SABBAT wished it were possible to see this man with whom he talked. But the screen hid everything save the grotesque shadow. He was talking with a man without a face.

Suddenly the man without a face clapped his hands together and Sabbat saw a second shadow appear on the Chinese screen. Then he heard the voice utter a sharp command.

"Bring Alea to me."

There was quiet for nearly a minute. Then Sabbat heard a slight shuffle behind him. He jerked his head around, gave a sharp sigh of relief when he saw it was the Eurasian girl, Alea. In her arms she held a small langur—East Indian monkey—and the intelligent creature had one arm about the girl's ivory neck. Sabbat's eyes brightened a bit, roved boldly over her shapely figure. He liked this girl, and later, perhaps—

"Be seated, Alea," the man behind the screen ordered curtly. He waited until Alea took the chair next to that of Sabbat's. Then he rapped out: "Twice you have failed, Alea, You allowed this X to throw you off balance by the sudden diving of his plane after missing him with your automatic at point-blank aim.

"Then, during the time of the forced landing on the Barito, in Borneo, you were silly enough to almost jump into the mouth of a crocodile. During the confusion this man not only saved your life but also awed the river Dyaks into thinking him a god.

"Then," the voice of the man without a face became scathing in its acidity, "you do not stay with his party when you had the chance. You steal away and return here. It would have been very easy for a woman of your—shall I say accomplishments?—to fool him, stimulate contriteness and thus better serve me—and yourself."

"But," she faltered, "you do not know this Secret Agent X. He—he can do anything—*anything!* He—he paid no attention to me. He had that other girl, Rika Van der Veer—"

"One of your beauty, and wiles, need fear no woman, Alea," the voice from behind the screen said softly. He sighed. "I fear this man loves the Van der Veer girl—"

"No!" Alea was on her feet, face strained and little fists in clenched knots. "No, I tell you!" She was panting now with terrible anger. "I—I will kill her, will— "

"But," the voice taunted softly, "I have reason to know he *does* love her, that he hates you! It isn't the girl's fault, Alea. It's the fault of Secret Agent X! Do you think if I were in your place I would allow him to flaunt my love? No! I believe I would teach him what love meant by giving him my hatred—and six inches of steel in his heart!"

"Yes!" Alea panted furiously. "I hate him! I *will* kill him! Oh, give me the chance, this last chance! I swear to you he will die before the night is over. I swear it!"

"I have a plan that may help you, Alea," the voice from behind the screen said softly. "But first, Sabbat, I'll have to admit you did two good jobs in capturing Jon Smit and Van der Veer for me. Smit is below now. I shall talk to him after a while. It was clever the way you got Henrik Van der Veer away from the hospital. You sent him to Lost Island by plane immediately?"

"Yes," Sabbat nodded, taking heart from the words. "I slipped him out about an hour ago. The girl had just left him for the night, won't check up until morning. My men told the hospital authorities the girl had changed her mind and now that her father was recovering, although still unable to talk, she wanted him with her. They fell for it."

His laugh curled the red lips away from his white teeth. Alea glanced at him, tried to restrain the shudder of dread that trembled through her body.

"That is fine. Now we have a hold on the girl, can talk terms with her, force her to turn over her interests. But back to my plan. Within the next two hours Pope's yacht will dock at the Old Wharf. As you know, the British fleet is just finished with maneuvers and occupy all but the old native docks.

"Where the *Wanderer* will berth is nearly deserted. The few craft there are native boats, a few Chinese junks and Indian dhows. X undoubtedly will meet his boat. He'll go down there in a ricksha, probably take his companion and Rika with him. Perhaps he may even take—ah—Zeck I believe his name is, the New York manager, along with him. He will be surrounded by my lascars and dacoits, will be allowed to make a run for it, and his party will be hemmed in so that the only safety that offers will be aboard this old dhow!

"No one knows I have installed silenced motors in it and you can put to sea in order to get rid of the bodies." The man without a face laughed and it had a reedy, eerie pitch that sent little prickles up and down Sabbat's back.

"There, Sabbat, on the dhow, you and Alea will form a reception committee of two and—" the voice became thick with menace and the promise of a terrible retaliation—"*you know what to do!* Secret Agent X, all who are with him, *must die tonight!*"

ALEA was on her feet, her almond eyes half-closed with evil purpose. Her breasts rose and fell under the stress of her emotion as she said, voice as brittle as ice dropping on glass: "I promise that Secret Agent X will die tonight!"

And as she hurried from the room she held the monkey so tightly in her arms that it whimpered in pain.

And Milo Sabbat, although experienced at murder, was visibly shaken as he mopped perspiration from his brown face, followed the girl from the room. He knew what he would do. This night he would make Secret Agent X pay for his victories. Pay not only with X's death but with agony that was worse than death....

The man behind the Chinese screen smiled softly to himself as he heard the others quit the room. His fingers went to a sling arrangement under his arm, and when it came into view a magnificent red pearl was in the hollow of his hand.

It was the Red Maggot. The man caught his breath with the sheer beauty of it. But it was a malignant beauty. It emanated evil in its blood-red rays, took the very soul of the man staring at it and twisted, turned it into that of a skulking beast.

Wild thoughts of conquest permeated the man's brain, warped and deadened it to all human sensibilities. The Red Maggot was truly a gnawing and consuming living entity within the brain of the man who held it.

He got to his feet, his face a mask of sadistic cunning. Beneath the floor on which he stood were the cellars, and there, confined in a small cubicle of concrete, was Jon Smit. The man slipped the Red Maggot into the pouch, walked eagerly toward the entrance of the stairs which led below....

The short dusk of the tropic nightfall was setting in. The Agent, Rika Van der Veer and Crandall stood at the curb in front of the Raffles Hotel. X held up his hand, and three rickshas stepped from line and advanced, putting their shafts to the street so the three could climb within.

"The Old Wharf," X directed in Chinese, for the three ricksha men were of that country. In a moment, the three rickshas abreast, they were proceeding at a leisurely pace toward the Old Wharf. The Agent had no way of knowing the three Chinese ricksha "boys" were Sabbat's men. But, within his mind, accustomed to danger, a premonitive stab of warning caused him to become restless, preoccupied.

The Secret Agent did not speak to the others regarding his feelings. He had no personal fear, but he feared for the safety of those accompanying him. Now he wished the girl had stayed at the hotel. She had had a harrowing experience the past forty-eight hours.

But her father, now safe in the hospital, was in a deep normal sleep, probably would awaken in the morning with no memory of his capture by Sabbat and the long journey from New York.

X looked about him. They were approaching the Old Wharf now, had left Occidental invention and improvement behind them. Here only native craft tied up. There were Chinese junks, *sampans* with lateen sails furled, huge dhows from India, a rusty tramp or two. Here were the smells of the Far East; the sourness of bilge, the stench of fish and all intermingled with the heady aroma of spices, the penetrating odor of green coffee.

Occasionally a furtive figure of a Dyak showed momentarily in the gathering dusk. The native would watch them with no sign of friendliness. And, several times, the Dyak would slip after the three rickshas with stealthy feet, keeping out of sight in the shadows cast by the godowns, or warehouses.

Rika Van der Veer and Crandall were carrying on an animated conversation. The girl wondered why X was silent, almost morose. And then Crandall, also wondering about the other's silence, looked at him.

Suddenly the Agent held up his hand. With a low command he ordered the three ricksha boys to halt. They did so, and to Crandall's astonishment vanished within the shadows. X stepped to the rotted boards of the wharf, motioned the others to follow.

From around them came a soft, *pat-pat-pat* of sound. The Agent frowned, wondered what it could be. And then, in a sudden flash of understanding, he recognized that macabre sound.

The patter of bare feet on the wharf! They were being surrounded by Sabbat's dacoits, his thugs and lascars!

"Good thing we brought our guns, Martin," Crandall said quietly.

"Don't use them," X said quickly. "We could get a number of them but they're too many. Wait." He was thoughtful for a moment, "I remember seeing an old Indian dhow up the wharf a hundred yards. The gangplank was down. We'll make for there, perhaps hold them at bay. Follow me. Walk slowly, don't talk. Our only chance is to make that dhow! Perhaps there's a boat we can launch, row back toward town. We can hold them off if we get on the water!"

THE COBRA DEATH

WALKING SLOWLY THROUGH the pungent darkness, occasionally stumbling on the rotted wharf, the Secret Agent led the girl and Crandall toward the old dhow which loomed ahead of them.

A sudden gust of air hot as from a furnace swirled around them. Followed an eerie clanking and creaking of lateen sails, the soft *slap-slap* of wavelets against the piling. It whimpered around masts that stuck up like dead fingers. A rat scampered almost from under their feet, squealed once and was gone.

The *pat-pat-pat* of feet seemed to be all around them. Dimly ahead a lone light glowed dismally, was so weak as to make no shadow. From afar came the slow ringing of a ship's bell. From miles away in the harbor a whistle sounded like a voice from some grisly sepulcher. No moon was overhead. It was as if the night were holding its breath, sitting back and ogling the play of death before it.

The three reached the stern of the old dhow. It was motionless, but a faint creaking reached their ears. It was as if the ghosts of a hundred years leered down at them, the ghosts of men murdered on a dozen seas and oceans, in strange ports.

Now, stronger than ever, the warning of impending danger surged through the Agent's mind. But there could be no turning back now. The gangplank of the dhow was a few feet away. It swayed under their feet, threatened to capsize and plunge them into the stinking water. X reached the top of the gangplank, stepped upon the seamed deck.

Then from the shadowy figures below on the dock arose a hissing sigh. X tensed for it seemed more like a murmur of relief than one of disappointment. And then the terrible truth impacted on his brain, momentarily stunned him. They were supposed to have taken refuge on the dhow!

X had led them into a cleverly set trap of death!

The old ship was as silent as the grave. No sound could be heard except an occasional, age-old creak of the teak with which it was made. From his pocket X took a small, heavy oblong of metal.

On the side of it was a crank that folded down into the oblong itself. He turned this crank perhaps twenty times. From within came the slight whir of cogs, a thin, almost soundless noise as if some small flywheel was spinning at a tremendous rate.

It was a pocket flashlight and the turning of the crank caused a tiny dynamo to generate electricity. A portion of the case folded back and uncovered a powerful light bulb. The Agent pressed a button and a brilliant beam of light knifed the deck of the old ship.

Rika Van der Veer almost cried aloud in startled surprise. Crandall caught her arm, drew her close to him, X threw a quick glance toward the dock. He felt, rather than saw, the massed brown bodies there, the fierce faces upturned. Escape from them was impossible by way of the wharf.

He turned back again. And then the ghostly ship became alive. Not with figures, with anything that could be seen, but with menacing and grim rustlings and eerie creakings. It was as if a company of phantoms had climbed the hull, took position on the high poop deck, descended rigging, emerged from the hold to ring them in a circle of death. Then the musky odor of sour, unclean bodies came to the Agent's nostrils.

The imminence now of death was felt by Rika Van der Veer. She stepped close to the Agent and he felt the warmth of her trembling body close to his, could hear her efforts to breathe, almost could catch the poundings of her heart.

He put out his steady hand, gave her shoulder an encouraging touch. The light had been out for long seconds now, for it would only disclose their position to the eyes hidden in the darkness.

There was the sudden opening of a door in the cabin of the dhow. X arrowed a beam from the flashlight toward the sound. He gasped. Rika caught her breath and it sobbed in her throat, Crandall cursed under his breath. For a girl stood in the doorway. In her arms was a small monkey that clung to her ivory throat with both small arms. It was Alea.

A TERRIBLE smile curved her red lips, heightened the slant of her eyes, accentuated the full cheekbones. X saw her bosom rise and fall as with some great emotion, noticed her hands were tight fists. She stood tall and quiet there in the doorway and the purpose of death was in every hard line of her face.

Heads outthrust, fangs dripping amber poison, the cobras inched forward for the death thrust....

"Secret Agent X—*at last!*" she spat out. Her lithe hands pulled the arms of the monkey from around her neck and the creature whimpered in fright, put small black hands over its face. Alea rasped out:

"No need to look for escape now. You are surrounded on all sides. Even heaven and hell is against you! Turn the beam of your light upward for a moment and see."

With a quick movement X pointed the flash beam overhead. Rika gasped. Directly overhead and some ten feet above the teak deck of the dhow three men hung at the ends of ropes. Their fiendish eyes sparkled in the beam of the light and the Agent saw gleaming *krises* thrust into their loin cloths.

There was the grating noise of sliding wood. The Agent brought down the beam of the flash. Almost at their feet a sliding hatch had been pulled aside disclosing a well of darkness. Even as he looked, the wide stairs coming to the deck itself were filled with dacoits, fiat-faced lascars. Each held a short stabbing *kris* ready for attack.

A hard laugh made X look up. It was from Alea. Her face was strangely taut, and there was a near hysterical note in her brittle laughter, in the way her eyes gleamed.

"The great Secret Agent X!" she taunted. "Made a fool of in front of the girl he loves! Well, Mr. X, why don't you work some of your miracles now!" She made a motion to the Dyaks. *"Now!"*

On the instant a score of brown bodies flashed at X, Rika and Crandall. The Agent's hard right found a dusky chin, and he heard the jaw crack under the blow. They had no time to use their guns nor any of X's private, secret devices. Nor would they have been of use in the swirling maelstrom of dark bodies. X and Crandall, the girl between them, fought like devils from hell, but as fast as they knocked aside a Dyak, his place was filled by others.

Something light brushed against the Agent's throat. He paid no attention, aimed a blow at a pair of glaring eyes in front of him. Then something cut off his wind with the suddenness of a lightning bolt. He gasped, tore and clawed at the string of silk that cut deep into his bronzed throat. He knew then it was the end, the finish.

Thug garroters had strings of silk about their throats!

As consciousness left X, he had one thought: Rika. He was responsible for her, and now— A well of blackness engulfed him....

Secret Agent X fought back to consciousness. He thought he was in a morass of black quicksand, and it was choking him as he sank deeper into the quagmire with every forward step. He made the bank, fell on it, exhausted.

He opened his eyes, looked about him. An oil lamp glowed in his eyes, was gently swaying from a chain fastened to the ceiling. They were in a room located in the hold of the dhow. X tried to move, found he was fastened with iron wrist gyves. His arms were chained above his head.

He saw they had their backs—for Rika and Crandall were likewise manacled against the ribs of the dhow, the same long wrist bar holding all of them. Undoubtedly the dhow had been in the African slave trade, and this room they were in had been a prison for unruly blacks who protested leaving their native land.

Across the room was a stout door of black wood which X took to be teak. Above the door was a transom probably eight inches in height, the only opening. He heard a strangling noise from his left and knew it came from Crandall. He strained his head outward, managed to see that the aviator was regaining consciousness. Then, in a moment, Rika Van der Veer shuddered, opened her eyes.

The Agent calmed her with low words. The girl smiled at him and nodded. "I—I am not afraid," she said.

A sound of a chain clanking came from the direction of the door. It was pushed open, and a breath of cooler air eddied into the room. A man stood in the doorway. Behind him was Alea. The man's swarthy face broke into a cruel smile as he surveyed Secret Agent X. His red lips writhed into a wolfish smile and disclosed teeth white as bones. It was Milo Sabbat.

"It's the first time we have met," Sabbat sneered.

He stepped into the room, strode to X. A sadistic smile on his evil face, Sabbat struck the Agent across the mouth. Blood spurted and coursed down X's chin.

X, blue-gray eyes glazed, softly laughed deep in his throat!

The low, amused laughter suddenly infuriated the maddened Sabbat. Again and again his brown fist flashed out, struck the Agent's battered face, knocked his head from side to side.

CRANDALL strained at his wrist bonds, tried to kick out with his manacled feet. Sabbat laughed now himself and there was more than an edge of madness to it.

"Another few minutes, X, and you will be through. Your dead body will be thrown overboard. The girl and your friend will join you."

His obsidian eyes gleamed fiendishly. "Nor will an easy death be yours. You shall pay hard for those first victories of yours. No more will Milo Sabbat be laughed at. When you writhe in your bonds, and scream, then *Milo Sabbat* will laugh."

Sabbat thrust his maddened face close to the Secret Agent. "You—all three of you—are to die the Cobra Death!"

A sob of terror came from Kika's throat. X smiled at her and she subsided, became calm. She said, her voice strangled:

"I am not afraid, Milo Sabbat. I wish father—send word to him—that I was not afraid. And then," her emotion almost overcame her, "I ask you get word to Peter DeVery for me. Tell him I loved him, knew at the end he loved me. That is all, do as you wish." Her head drooped as merciful unconsciousness descended upon her.

"Peter DeVery!" Sabbat laughed. "He is having a different death. The Coral Death!" He turned toward the door. "Ahmed—Talo! Come with my glass cage! Wheel in the Cobra Death! Let's see if the man who is supposed to have no fear can look my little pets in the eye!"

His screaming laughter filled the room. The little monkey in Alea's arms chattered and scolded in alarm, clung to the girl's neck.

The Agent glanced at her, and what he saw made a frown come to his face. He saw a great struggle seething within her, saw that her terrible hatred of a moment before had been replaced by utter horror. She was trembling, was biting her crimson lips to keep them from forming a scream of terror.

And then a noise came from the room or passageway outside. It was as if a piece of heavy furniture on casters was being pushed across an uneven floor. Alea stepped hastily aside, her face white, eyes narrowed in loathing. And then X gasped.

Through the doorway, pushed by two half-caste natives, a table on casters rolled into the room. But it was a strange table, a table of horrible, unspeakable death.

On all four sides of the table were panes of heavy glass extending upward fully four feet. One of the panes of glass was arranged so it could be pulled up by means of a lever extending from the back of the table. This would leave a space of several feet between its lower edge and the top of the table. And now the reason for pulling up that pane of glass was too apparent to Secret Agent X.

For on the table, imprisoned by the walls of glass, were six king cobras!

The diabolical scheme was simple. The table was wheeled in front of X, the girl and Crandall. It was only six inches away, the top level with the Agent's waist. When Sabbat raised the pane of glass the cobras would be unhampered, could strike at their unprotected faces!

"Sabbat, no—*no!*"

The frenzied scream suddenly came from the writhing lips of Alea. She threw herself upon him, tried to hold his arm as it reached for the death lever of the glass cage.

"You fool!" he cried, and pushed her back.

"Take me, Sabbat, not—*him!* I didn't know, I didn't know! I—I thought he loved the—the girl!" She fell sobbing to the floor.

Sabbat nodded to Ahmed, the half-caste, and he dragged Alea into the passageway outside.

Sabbat swerved on X, strode forward, his black eyes alight with utter madness. "Does your flesh crawl now, Mr. Secret Agent? Do the hairs on the back of your neck crinkle and quiver? Ah, fear is in your soul, withers your brain, your heart. You are mortally afraid now, you fool, for the Cobra Death soon will stab at your heart!"

But X said nothing; his lips remained sealed.

Milo Sabbat screamed, struck once more. He ran to the back of the table, jerked downward on the lever. The pane of glass swung up a full two feet. The writhing cobras within came erect, their extended hoods showing spectacled death's-heads. And then, heads outthrust, fangs dripping amber poison, their sinuous bodies inched warily forward for the death thrust.

A scream of laughter welling from his throat, Milo Sabbat turned and ran, slammed the door. X heard the chain clank into place, sealing the room of the Cobra Death!

CHAPTER X

MESSAGE FROM THE DEAD

BLUE-GRAY EYES GLAZED as if with enamel, the Agent gazed at the advancing cobras. His being was filled with a nauseous loathing, but there was no halting the clear thinking processes of his intellect. And, as calmly as if he were planning a movement on a chess board, he already had his strategy worked out.

A cobra is the most vicious creature known to man. It is utterly fearless, will attack in the twinkling of an eye. Any movement, when the snake is erect and prepared for the strike, will cause it to arrow forward, its death lunge often carrying the sinuous body forward several feet.

Secret Agent X knew that should he make any sudden movement one or more of the cobras would strike at his face, sink long fangs into flesh. Then would follow the chewing motion which most venomous reptiles have to make in order to sink their poison deep into the victim's veins. Then, in a few moments, death would follow.

Slowly, the Agent pulled his body upward by resting his weight on his manacled wrists. The cobras, seemingly bewildered, hesitated in their cage of glass. X's fingers found something concealed in his bushy dark hair. It was wrapped in a bit of cloth the color of his hair and attached to it by a strand of dark silk thread. It came free.

With sure movements he pulled away the tiny square of cloth, and a small glass vial was in his fingers. Then his forefinger flicked the little vial onto the table top. There was a tiny tinkle of crushed glass. The cobras turned, hissing horribly.

A glowing spot of red flame was created out of nothing. It grew, blossomed into a hellish red rose of fire, sputtered and spewed, and from it arose a single pencil of grayish smoke. It was a chemical flare of red which the Agent used for signaling purposes, much as a heliograph message is sent. The contents of the vial burst into red flame as quickly as air reached it.

The cobras writhed. One of them struck at the ball of red, fell back as the terribly hot chemical burned through its venom-dripping mouth. Another struck, pushed the ball into the coils of its mate. The cobras threshed about in the glass enclosure, made the table tremble with their death agonies.

But one of the snakes glided forward, stuck an inquiring head of triangular horror toward the Agent's taut face. Its head and neck arced backward like a mighty spring. It was ready for the strike.

Then another little ball of thin glass made an almost invisible parabola, shattered on the table. From it a low-hanging gray gas sprang into life, rolled in little clouds across the table top. This was a blistering gas similar to mustard, entered the system through the skin pores or wherever moisture gathered.

It touched the sinuous bodies of the cobras, caused the skin to raise into little mounds of blisters. The cobras writhed into balls of horror, struck at each other with vicious fangs.

And then, jarred loose by the cobras' wild movements, the lever slipped from its notch and the pane of glass crashed into place!

Crandall sighed, flashed a tremulous smile at X. "Oh, boy!" was all he could say.

The Secret Agent, face still taut, looked up as a noise from the door reached his ears. He stared, a puzzled look on his face. In the transom above the door was the gray form of the monkey, Alea's pet!

As he looked, it clambered through the opening, dropped to the floor. It chattered softly a moment as it passed the table on which the dead cobras lay. Then, with a quick spring, it jumped to the Agent's shoulder. A gasp of surprise escaped his lips. The monkey had something in its black hand which it pressed into that of X's. It was a key!

LONG FINGERS working speedily but with sure movements, X at last managed to fit the key into the lock which was at his end of the wrist shackles. He jerked, pushed outward. The wrist manacles came free.

The Agent stooped and placed the monkey on the floor, turned to Crandall, who was holding Rika in his arms.

"Chafe her arms and wrists, Crandall. I see Alea has had a change of heart. She's on our side now! If we can get out the door—"

A slight sound of metal outside the door was the answer. It swung slowly inward, and Alea stood in the opening. The little monkey hurried to her, swung to her shoulder. She was breathing hard and spots of color showed in her olive cheeks. Her dark eyes were alight from some inner glow, some compelling force. Crandall stared at her, then at Secret Agent X. He understood, pitied this half-caste girl who, for love of the Agent, risked her life.

"I managed to bring your guns," she whispered. "They're outside in the passageway. You must hurry. Sabbat and his men are in the cabin, drinking to your—deaths. The girl is coming to, can walk. Follow me. There's a secret stair leading to a hatch overlooking the dock. I think you can make it."

"And you, Alea?" X asked softly. 'You will go with us?"

A wild light of hope flared in the girl's face and then died. She sighed, and when she spoke again her voice was flat, dead. "No. I will disappear if I win free with you. Heaven help me, I am a half-caste!" A sob tore from her clenched lips and tears glistened in her dark eyes.

The Agent, face flaming, gathered the girl's hands within his own, pressed them silently.

Alea looked up into his blue-gray eyes, and a brave and beautiful smile caused her face to become calm. "Your friendship gives me everything—*everything!*" Then her mood changed. "Quick!" she breathed. "We must hurry—"

Muffled shouts came from the passageway. Alea screamed. X thrust her lithe body behind him, leaped into the passageway. His fingers delved beneath his shirt, came into view with some dark object showing. He had been unable to use this when they first entered the dhow because the Dyaks and lascars were too spread out. They had been all around the dhow, above as well as on all sides.

The dark object rolled toward the horde of dacoits and lascars boiling down the narrow passageway. Drops of diphenoloxide inclosed in glass of paper-thinness broke at the feet of the oncoming natives, filled the air with drifting, smarting fumes.

Thrown *krises* barely grazed the Agent's form as he stood in that passage of death and flung lead into the seething mass of flesh. Crandall, at his side, was pulling trigger methodically, but every leaden slug caused a death yell to twist from a dying man's throat.

X flung a fire ball of searing acid into the midst of the frenzied natives, and they broke and ran. Rika Van der Veer between them, X and Crandall rushed forward. They made the end of the passage.

Beyond lay the open deck. In a moment they were at the head of the gangplank. The Agent turned.

"Alea!" he called. "Hurry! Hurry!"

A strange vibration shook the deck beneath their feet. Agent X frowned. It was the sound of motors! The huge dhow started to move away from the dock. The gangplank was about to fall into the water. The Agent pushed Crandall and the girl down the trembling gangplank, followed more slowly. As he stepped to the dock the plank fell with a mighty splash. The dhow headed toward the open sea....

JON SMIT knew he had one chance in a million of leaving his steaming cell alive. Yet he showed no fear.

His hellhole of concrete was as hot as a bake oven, and the narrow slit of an opening near the ceiling allowed no breeze from outside to enter. The door of the cell was of teakwood, almost as hard as cast iron. A rude bench, bolted to the floor, was the only furniture.

Several hours before, just as dusk set in, Jon Smit was phoned by a man claiming to be Crandall, the Agent's friend. He was told that X had discovered amazing developments to the plot, that he then had the Red Maggot in his possession and Smit was to come to a certain estate near the Kalang Reservoir.

Jon Smit had hurried there without delay, noted fierce wild dogs roaming the grounds as he entered. He went into the house and was met by Milo Sabbat and a threatening grin.

Now he was in some cell beneath the house, a prisoner. From the slit in the concrete, which apparently led outside, he heard the snarls and whining cries of the fierce dholes as they roamed the grounds. Escape from that direction was impossible.

Men do not live long in the Far East before they acquire a feeling of fatalism. It is the creed of the East, one trait of the natives which the whites have no hesitancy in accepting.

Jon Smit was sixty-five years of age. From Amsterdam he had come to Singapore and given the Van der Veer organization practically all of his business life. Now, in some rather indefinite way, he knew his long and honorable career was finished. Just as the Far East breeds fatalism, so does it engender courage. Jon Smit was not afraid.

And then, with startling suddenness, faint whisperings came to Jon Smit's ears. They were mysterious, ethereal, seemingly came from nowhere. His brown eyes narrowed and he looked about the small room. In a corner of the cubicle of concrete he saw something he had not noticed before.

It was a small round hole in the wall. He inspected it and decided that once a water pipe entered the cell. Long ago it had been torn out, the iron pipe cut flush with the concrete wall and then plastered over. But the covering of plaster had not completely hidden the end of the pipe. A small hole allowed sounds from some room above to be heard in the cell working on the same principal as a speaking tube.

By straining his ears Jon Smit heard the voice of Milo Sabbat in conversation with some other man. He did not recognize this other voice when the man said to Sabbat: "It is well, Sabbat, that you should contemplate your many errors of the past. People who make errors do not work for me—long!"

There followed a long conversation, mention of Alea. In a moment she entered the room and Jon Smit heard this unknown voice taunt her with the fact that the Agent was in love with Rika Van der Veer. Jon Smit knew that was not true, that the girl was deeply in love with Peter DeVery, the technician on Lost Island.

And then he heard of the murder plot on the old dhow, the fact that Van der Veer himself had again been captured, was being flown to the coral island. Jon Smit knew the end was near—for him.

Strangely—this was a day of startling happenings—Jon Smit heard a hissing sound coming from the slit in the concrete which led to the outside grounds. He thought at first one of the wild dogs had winded him. But the hissing sound continued. Then Jon Smit's heart leaped with sudden hope. For a soft voice in Malay said:

"*Tuan* Smit! It is Mat Noh. You will remember I once was your houseboy. I work here now, *Tuan* Smit, and I am afraid. These people are fierce, do murder. I saw them capture you, take you to the cell. The dogs know me so I was able to come to this little window. Tell me what to do, *Tuan,* and I will do it."

"Listen carefully, Mat Noh. I have a pencil here and will write a note which I want you to deliver to—Mr. A.J. Martin. You probably will find him at the Old Wharf. His ship, the *Wanderer,* will dock there very soon now. Take this note to him, tell him to come without delay to help me. Wait."

Jon Smit took a slip of paper from his pocket. He started to write when again whispers from the pipe attracted his attention. He listened and a look of incredible amazement overspread his brown face. He knew the man behind this plot of murder!

Writing furiously, Jon Smit did not at first hear the footsteps in the concrete passage outside his cell. There was the sound of a key turning in a lock. Jon Smit jumped to his feet, but the message was unfinished. He got upon the bench of teak, put the message through the little window, whispered fiercely:

"Run, Mat Noh—*hurry!*"

As Jon Smit's feet touched the floor the door opened. In the opening stood a man. His face was covered with a mask of coral pink silk. In his hand was an automatic. Without word, without hesitation, the man raised the automatic and pulled the trigger three times.

The sounds were as blasting thunder in the narrow confines of the cell. Jon Smit, his proud face showing disdain, his chin thrust upward, fell on his face. He twitched once and was dead.

THE AGENT, Rika and Crandall stood on the dark wharf and watched the dhow pull out into the harbor. X said in hard, grating tones:

"I think we'll see Sabbat again, Crandall. He'll make for the safety of Lost Island now. We must return there. The final showdown is ahead of us now. The *Wanderer* will be here within the hour. We'll refuel with all speed, turn back again—"

He stopped, swerved, and his hand went to his automatic. X turned the beam of the flashlight up the wharf and it shone upon the staggering, nigh spent figure of a Malay. In his hand was a bit of rice paper which he held in front of him.

"*Tuan* Martin—*Tuan* Martin!" he gasped. "It is a message from *Tuan* Smit. He—has—just—been killed. I, Mat Noh, heard the shots—*Tuan* Smit's death sigh!" The native fell exhausted at the Agent's feet.

X hastily unfolded the grimy bit of paper, turned the beam of his flash upon it. He read aloud:

Trust Mat Noh. Have been captured by enemy. Mat Noh will lead you. Soon enemy leave for Lost Island by planes. Overheard their talk. Watch out for dhow of death. Protect island for Van der Veers. Van der Veer kidnaped from hospital, taken to island by plane. Hurry. Enter island under sea. One behind this is—

The note ended. Secret Agent X gently shook the Malay, questioned him in his own tongue. The Malay talked gaspingly. Then X stood erect.

Stray rays from the flashlight brought out his face in terrible relief. It was hard like steel, and Crandall could see the blue-gray eyes flashing in the darkness. He said, and the simple words were a prayer: "Heaven rest his soul! Jon Smit is dead!"

CHAPTER XI

SECRET OF LOST ISLAND

THE *WANDERER* DOCKED within the hour. The Agent and Crandall had an oil lighter already tied up at Old Wharf ready to discharge its cargo of fuel without delay. Aboard the yacht, X sketched briefly what had happened to Arnold Pope. Rika, shaken and weeping, was in a cabin.

The first horizontal rays of sunlight were slanting across Singapore harbor when the *Wanderer* put to sea, mighty Diesel engines at full throttle. Shortly afterward, but a speck on the horizon, the city disappeared from view.

Face tense, the Agent's blue-gray eyes were hard, wintry. He stood alone in the bow of the plunging yacht watching the unbroken swell of water pass beneath the prow. He felt as if something was lost to him. The death of Jon Smit had been a personal one. He deeply admired this little man who, under the spell of death, had died as only men die.

He wished he could have stayed in Singapore with Jebel Zeck and help pay his last respects. But Zeck would see that Jon Smit received every attention in those last earthly rites. Later, Zeck had promised, he would take a special plane and meet the *Wanderer* at Lost Island, to fight shoulder to shoulder with the others to protect Henrik Van der Veer, now Sabbat's prisoner there.

The Secret Agent wondered about Alea. His craggy face softened at the memory of her sacrifice. He wondered if Sabbat had killed her. Again his face hardened. It was another score to settle with Sabbat and his men. There was Peter DeVery, too. Rika loved him. He, too, was a prisoner of the island, perhaps dead by now. X slammed a hard fist into the palm of his left hand. There were many scores to settle!

Then he remembered that message from the dead Jon Smit. "Enter island under sea," he had written. He had overheard of the secret entrance before he died. He knew that X had a bathysphere aboard the yacht, had been told of the self-contained diving suits.

The secret entrance was the island's weak spot. Jon Smit knew it probably could be captured with a surprise attack *if entered from underwater!*

And, alone, not asking his men to share this terrible danger, X was determined to capture Lost Island!

All day and the following night the mighty propeller and twin screws of the *Wanderer* forced her westward toward the Java Sea. They passed the tip of Borneo, the mouth of the sluggish Barito, reached the Java Sea. And then, as dawn marched across the turquoise waters, a dim dot showed on the horizon, grew larger as they watched. It was Lost Island.

An hour later the *Wanderer* was hove to in the island's lee, the side on which the bathysphere lay concealed completely hidden from view.

While they ate a hasty breakfast the bathysphere was made ready for a dive. And then a new problem confronted Agent X. He did not want the others to know of the terrible risk he was taking. So, to allay their suspicions, he asked Arnold Pope and Rika to accompany him. He knew the dive would cause the girl to momentarily forget her father, that the novelty of it would bring her some ease of mind.

The bathysphere's door was clamped shut, and Agent X tested the air supply. Then he signaled to Crandall to lower away. At forty-one fathoms the steel ball rested on the bed of the ocean.

A misty haze hung over the island and below it was shadowy, silent death. Strange fish flashed past the fused quartz windows and brought exclamations of delight from Rika Van der Veer. But X noted something strange about their swift passage.

They did not float past in lazy contemplation, stop and stare through bulging eyes at this unusual round ball from another world. They swam fast, as if they were startled, as if some other enemy lurked in the shadows cast by the precipitous coral cliffs.

EYES STONY, like glazed steel, the Agent passed into the pressure chamber in which hung the three diving suits. He struggled into one of them, all save the helmet, opened the sliding door which led into the other segment of the bathysphere. Rika stared at him with startled eyes. He grinned bleakly at her, turned to the explorer.

"I've decided to go out for a few minutes, Pope. Want to look at something I think is near where the bathysphere rests."

"But," the explorer cried, "there's no need of you risking your life out there!" He jerked his thumb at the watery depths. "We'd better get aboard the *Wanderer*. It's broad daylight now, and we've got to get on the island!"

Then, in terse words, the Agent explained what he had in mind. He meant to enter the island by the secret entrance, try to capture it alone. He handed over a tightly folded sheet of paper.

"Read this when you get aboard the boat, Pope. Signal Crandall to draw you up as soon as I leave the pressure chamber. This note contains full instructions— *Look!*"

He pointed out the quartz window. Arnold Pope and Rika turned, and a cry of horror sprang from her throat. Advancing on the bathysphere, a curious rodlike thing in his hands, was the mystery diver!

X donned the helmet of his diving suit, stepped into the pressure chamber. He clamped on the heavy lead shoes of his outfit, twisted the clamps that sealed the door. Quick fingers twisted valves, and sea water entered the chamber. Other valves built up the air pressure so it approximated that of the depths. He opened the outer door, stepped from the bathysphere onto the bed of the Java Sea.

X had immediately recognized that rocklike instrument carried by the diver. It was an underwater cutting torch such as salvage crews use in cutting up a sunken ship so it may be drawn up piecemeal. The diver planned to cut the hoisting lines of the bathysphere, maroon them on the bottom of the sea!

The Agent saw a brilliant white light above the bathysphere. The diver had raised his cutting torch and even as X watched, the hoisting lines of the steel ball parted! The Agent moved forward as fast as the weight of his suit and the terrific pressure would allow. Again came the burst of bubbles, the roiling of the water. Helpless, X stood motionless. The bubbles ceased and the diver had vanished!

X turned toward the bathysphere, and a cry of fear for his friends within it sounded hollow in the confines of the helmet. The bathysphere, released of its hoisting wire, was slowly turning over!

X lunged backward, got mighty shoulders against the slippery steel, pushed with all his strength. He stayed the turning motion but even his strength could not hold out long.

The Agent twisted about and discovered one of the quartz windows of the ball was almost directly in front of his helmet. Within the bathysphere he saw Pope and Rika, the latter terror-stricken. But the explorer's face lit up when he saw the Agent peering through the quartz.

Using one free hand as much as possible, Secret Agent X motioned to his own diving helmet, then pointed to Rika Van der Veer and Pope. But his efforts to obtain purchase for his feet stirred up muddy silt, obstructed his view of the interior of the bathysphere.

After what seemed long minutes of effort X made the explorer get his meaning. Pope nodded, and X saw him turn and speak swift words to the girl. The Agent grinned in taut satisfaction. Pope understood.

X, great muscular shoulders strained almost to the point of breaking, held the bathysphere level. Through the quartz window he saw Pope help Rika don the diving suit, then climb into his own. X knew the air within the giant ball was becoming thin, soon would be nonexistent, heavily charged with carbon monoxide. Their only safety was in the diving suits!

The bathysphere rolled a bit. X thrust again with his shoulders and kept it from turning. Should it roll a few more inches it would be impossible for the explorer and the girl to open the outside pressure door; they would be doomed within the steel prison!

Flashing out desperate messages of *"Hurry—hurry!"* the Agent strained for purchase so his shoulders would not slip.

And then, when even his physical endurance could no longer hold out, the outer door opened and Arnold Pope and Rika Van der Veer stepped from the bathysphere. X motioned them aside, leaped away from the turning sphere of steel. It settled slowly, lay so the door of the pressure chamber, although now open, was almost flat against the bed of the ocean.

SECRET AGENT X rested momentarily against the steel shell of the bathysphere. He looked around, and a taut smile parted his lips. He bent, picked up a half of a shell which had somehow been left there.

Coral growths were all around him. With his heavy diving shoes of lead the Agent broke off a sharp pencil of coral. With its flintlike point he scratched words on the inner surface of the shell. Rika and Arnold Pope watched him intently, but the shadow would not let their faces be seen.

The Agent looked up. Dangling just above the bathysphere were the severed hoisting rope of steel strands and the telephone and electric light cable of rubber. X climbed up on the bathysphere, his shoes gaining a foothold on the bolts which held it together. He reached for the dangling hoisting cable.

It took him long minutes to unwind a strand of the wire but he finally made it. Then, working as swiftly as possible, he bound the shell to the cable's end, slid back to the floor of the ocean once more.

Weaving with fatigue, every pore exuding profuse perspiration, X motioned for the girl to get between them. He took her hand, led them toward the black shadows of the coral cliffs.

The Agent knew that nearby lay some means of entrance into the center of the coral island. Where it was he had no idea. But there could be little delay now. He had used up half his air supply in the terrible exertion of keeping the bathysphere from rolling. Escape had to be near....

For long minutes Secret Agent X searched the blackness, hands groping for some hole, some entrance way. He felt the air becoming thin in his diving suit. He was becoming groggy, thick-headed for lack of oxygen for his straining lungs. His hand went to the emergency supply and twisted the tiny valve. New vigor flowed into his veins as the pure air was drawn into his lungs.

He stumbled onward. The steel of purpose filled him, strengthened his lagging muscles. And then, when again the air was becoming thin and his strength ebbed from his muscles, he fell over a low shelf of coral. His fumbling hands found another shelf, still another. It was a stairway hewn into the coral of Lost Island!

Gasping, every taut muscle straining, his heart hammering and blood pounding in his temples, Agent X toiled upward step by step. It was agonizing, a labor threatening to end as each higher step was reached.

It took long and precious seconds for him to understand why his feet were so heavy, why the diving suit became a near unsupportable burden. He was leading them nearer the surface where the water pressure was not so great but the weight of the diving suits was greater in proportion to their closeness to the surface!

Escape, now, was but a few steps above them.

But could he make it? The Agent had no fear of his own death, but the responsibility of the girl and the explorer weighed heavily upon him. He must win free for them. And to eradicate forever the menace of the Red Maggot.

With clumsy fingers he unbuckled the heavy leaden shoes and stepped out of them, motioning for the others to do likewise. Strangely, the effort helped him, for now he took four or five more of the slippery coral steps with new-found strength. But the terrific exertion, he knew, was almost beyond his endurance.

He was crawling now, on weaving hands and knees. He reached upward, jerked back his hand. A warm something had touched his hand And then he knew. He was at the surface! They had escaped!

With his final strength X helped draw Rika up the last shelf of coral. With desperate hands he unclamped her heavy helmet, tore it from off her head. He saw she was white, almost trancelike with fear. He unclamped the helmet from Pope's suit, heard it strike the coral with a metallic clang. Then he worked upon his own helmet, managed to unfasten the clamps as if in a dream.

Sweet, fresh air rushed into his face like a blow. He sucked it into his mouth, felt his flattened lungs fill out, the blood rush through his veins. He smiled, lay supine for a moment. Then, revitalized, he sat up, looked at Rika Van der Veer. He touched her cheek, felt the warmth of her blood as it rushed to her face. She was safe. Arnold Pope, he knew—

A faint sound came to his ears. X started, twisted about, and a gasp of surprise welled from his throat.

Behind them, an automatic clasped in his long fingers, stood Milo Sabbat! Behind him were two Dyaks, their *krises* out, ready for attack.

"Welcome to Lost Island, Secret Agent X!" Sabbat sneered. "It was a good thing I came by air so as to be here to greet you! I think it is the end—this time!"

He stepped forward, his wolfish grin of triumph showing his white teeth, the madness in his black eyes.

CHAPTER XII

PRISONERS OF
LOST ISLAND

TRAPPED, UNARMED, WEAK from exhaustion, the Agent and Pope submitted to a search for weapons. The search was a thorough one, but Sabbat's fingers failed to locate certain little pockets in the waistband of the Agent's trousers or discover the fact the heels of his shoes could be taken off with a quick twist.

Herded before Sabbat and his two natives, X, Rika and the explorer were marched upward through a winding passageway hewn from the coral. The underground room they had just vacated was slightly higher.than the water level. The coral was a deep pink, glistened like the first red flush of the sun over the Java Sea.

Above them, fully fifty yards along an upward slanting gallery, they came to a large room. It was furnished with a large table, many chairs and a bed in one corner of the room. A telephone reposed on the desk, or table.

"This is the central room occupied by—" Sabbat laughed. He nodded to the Malays and they bowed and left. Sabbat, automatic ready, guarded the three. "But wait, here is your host now."

Footsteps sounded from across the room. The Agent drew a deep breath. He knew that now he was to see the man who was behind the death plots, who had stolen the Red Maggot in order that he might rule the superstitious natives, eventually win untold treasure through the manufacture of the pearls. To foment, perhaps, unrest, rebellion—to drive the whites from the South Seas so he could rule over them dictatorially.

A man entered the room. X stared. The newcomer wore a mask of coral pink which completely hid his face! He stood for a moment, this masked man, surveying his three captives.

Then a laugh of sneering triumph issued from behind the mask. He suddenly struck his hands together, and two fierce Dyaks came from the passageway behind, took up their guard in absolute silence.

"Welcome, visitors to Lost Island," the man of the mask said in a thin, reedy voice.

X started. That voice was vaguely familiar, yet he was unable to place it. He knew the masked man was talking in a higher voice than normally used, was disguising it.

"There are many strange and beautiful things here, Secret Agent X, or should I call you Mr. A.J. Martin?" His laugh was sneering. "Death is here, too, and even death can be beautiful as all of you will discover!

"You have thwarted me many times, but this is the end. Jon Smit died, Van der Veer and Peter DeVery are soon to die. Sabbat tells me you had no fear when king cobras were loosed almost at your throat. He tells me you have no fear. We shall see, we shall see!"

His laugh was keen, knifed the room like the snap of a whiplash. He resumed: "Yes, this is a strange island. At the foot of these cliffs untold hundreds of first water pearls lie in virgin shell. It was while diving for them that we found the underwater entrance.

"But now we go nature one better. We make pearls, priceless ones that cannot be told from the genuine! Already I have made millions by flooding the pearl markets of the world with these. I shall make many more millions.

"I have the Red Maggot now, Agent X. I soon will be ready to incite the natives to action, cause them to rise in their superstitious zeal and drive the whites from the South Seas. I shall rule over them myself.

"But something else about the island. That fool, Van der Veer, didn't know that when he discovered a way to make pearls he also, by the same process, could make coral! As you know, coral is made of the skeletons of little animals called polyps. By forcing carbonate of lime into electrically charged sea water we cause the microscopic creature to die faster, thus build up coral.

"And," his laugh was shrill with mad hatred—"you should see the Coral Death! Three people are undergoing it now, Mr. X. Van der Veer, Peter DeVery and—Alea! Yes, I brought her back so she could pay her debt to me! I'll let you speak to all of them after a while. But step over here."

Eyes narrowed, the Agent's gaze followed the masked man's pointing hand. He saw then how light came into this inner chamber. Small square holes were cut into the coral, and daylight streamed through! He walked over to one of the holes, looked out. Then he understood.

The room had been hollowed away so that a wall of coral was left standing. Then the holes had been cut. X looked down, saw beneath him the deck of the *Wanderer!*

THE CLIFF of coral was similar to the Rock of Gibraltar which has passages and rooms hollowed out within it, peepholes so that those in the passages may watch the ships steaming past. The coral cliffs of Lost Island had served the same purpose. The Agent did not wonder now why those of the island knew his every movement aboard the yacht. He felt almost as if he could reach down and touch it.

He saw Crandall, the aviator, and members of the crew pacing distractedly up and down the deck near the empty space where the bathysphere had rested. To them, he knew, they still were within the steel ball, marooned on the bed of the ocean.

"Look closely, Agent X," said the masked man's reedy voice. X saw him wink at Milo Sabbat. "Even now my diver is rising under the yacht, his electric cutting torch ready. Before those on the ship know what is happening it will sink beneath them!"

X started. It was all too true. The keel plates of the *Wanderer* could be cut. The yacht would sink instantly....

But there was a smile of triumph on the face of Secret Agent X as he peered through the hole in the coral at the deck of the *Wanderer.* For he saw that the winch was drawing up the severed cable. Suddenly he saw Crandall leap to the edge of the bathysphere room, lean far out and down.

The Agent turned back to Sabbat and the masked man, smiled in quiet derision. Sabbat's face paled and he muttered angrily to himself. He leaped to a coral window, peered below. A grin of wolfish triumph overspread his face. He motioned for the masked man to join him, look below.

The masked man was excited at what he saw. "They've discovered the ship is sinking!" he cried in a frenzy of enthusiasm, "LaPorte, our technical man and diver, has sliced through the—"

A sob of surprise came to the masked man's lips. The Agent peered below, saw a white cloud of air bubbles rising to the surface. He knew what had happened. The yacht was under way now, was headed toward the open sea. And, in some manner, LaPorte's lines had fouled the screws of the yacht. He had died a terrible death before he had a chance to cut the *Wanderer's* plates!

A terrible torrent of curses came from Sabbat and the masked man. They could not understand the strange phenomena of the yacht leaving its moorings at the last moment before it was to be sunk.

X peered through the coral window and saw the yacht disappear in the mist of the morning. Again his quiet smile played about his lips. Crandall had received his message of warning, had moved the ship immediately. And the Agent wondered if he had understood *all* that message.

"You won't escape so easily, Agent X," the masked man spat out with vicious anger. "You and the other two may wish you were still within that steel ball at the bottom of the sea! Come, let me show you a new death that will make fear surge through your body. Sabbat says you do not know the meaning of fear. But I know differently! You have not yet seen the Coral Death!"

The Agent, Rika and Arnold Pope were led down another passageway off which small, roomlike cells opened. A door was reached, and the man in the mask opened it, motioned the three prisoners within. X gasped in utter horror at what he saw. Rika screamed, fell against Pope who held her in his arms.

IT WAS a red room of horror, this cubicle of the Coral Death. On one side of the wall were three shallow tanks hollowed from blocks of red coral. The tanks were filled to the rim with water. Strange electrical devices hung over the water and the buzzing spit of high voltage could be heard.

And, moaning in delirium, three people were in the tanks of the Coral Death!

Van der Veer, Peter DeVery and Alea Andrew!

The horror of it tugged at the Agent's throat. For coral growths of red encrusted the three prisoners to the waist! The horrible red excrescence adhered tightly to the skin of the three in the tanks, was slowly but surely covering their bodies in a shell of crimson death!

In a few more days the red beastliness of the coral would sap their last living breaths, suffocate their bodies, then continue until they were encased in living rock.

"Poor LaPorte," the masked man sighed. "This was his crowning achievement! But how does it affect you, Secret Agent X? Does fear course your veins, make shudders of dread race your spine?"

X laughed.

The man in the mask raised his gun, then lowered it. "No," he panted, "a bullet is too quick, too painless. But we must work fast, Sabbat! These three now in the throes of the Coral Death will be covered in another twelve hours. We will finish them first.

"Then we will have to work fast, double the charge of electrical energy, for in a few days that accursed yacht will return, perhaps with reinforcements. We want the island to be free of all our enemies when it is inspected!"

The Agent, the still unconscious girl, and Pope were led to a cell next to the room of the Coral Death, locked in. The explorer placed the girl on a long bench cut from solid coral, joined X at one of the windows overlooking the sea.

"I see Crandall finally got your message," Arnold Pope observed. "Think he'll return in time to be of any help?"

"I think so," X nodded. He hoped Crandall could read the further message he had written at the last moment on the shell. The mist now was thick, rolled in on the island in banks of gray.

An hour passed and suddenly X caught Pope's arm, held it tightly for long seconds. Then a smile lit up his hard face, made it gleam with excitement.

"Are you ready?" he asked softly.

The puzzled explorer nodded. Agent X bent and wrenched the heel from his right shoe, then the left. Inside the hollow spaces disclosed were two "palm" pistols, a dozen small bullets. X divided the bullets, handed Pope one of the tiny 1-shot pistols. From the waistband of his trousers he took a tiny steel box which, when opened, yielded a handful of tiny glass balls.

Then he walked to the door, inspected the iron hinges. Careful not to break the glass balls before he was ready, he placed one on top of each hinge, resting it against the door itself. Then he tapped them with the small palm gun. The glass shattered and smoking acid ran down the iron hinge. It corroded the iron immediately, began to eat into the metal structure, dissolve it as hot water melts ice.

Then, with Pope's aid, he lunged against the door. It almost fell to the floor with the power of their shoulders, but the Agent caught it, laid it carefully against the wall.

"The central room!" X breathed softly into Pope's ear.

The little pistols concealed within the palms of their hands, the two stole silently toward the central room fifty yards away. They saw it ahead of them, saw too a portion of a man's back seated at the desk.

They reached the room. It was Sabbat seated at the desk. X, his jaw grim, his eyes hard, stepped into view, strode silently across until he stood at Sabbat's back.

"I've come for you, Sabbat!" the Agent rapped out.

Milo Sabbat leaped to his feet, face pale and lips curled away from his white teeth. He was panting with sudden fear, and his eyes stared wide. But rats fight when they are cornered. His arrowing form flashed at the Agent. They sprawled to the floor together.

The murderer fought like a tiger with kicking feet, nails, his teeth. X pounded in a flashing fist which caught Sabbat on the cheek. He went back and down. X was on him like a pouncing puma. Once more his fist flashed, and this time it found home on Sabbat's jaw. His body went lax. The Agent toiled to his feet.

"Stand where you are, Secret Agent X!"

ACROSS THE ROOM, gun in hand, stood the man in the mask! X, eyes wintry, shot the palm gun as he came erect. He had no time to get set, to aim. The bullet struck the masked man in the arm. He jerked back, faced the Agent.

But X had reloaded the palm gun. He took more careful aim this time, touched the release.

A terrible scream split the confines of the room, echoed and re-echoed through the grisly red passages. The man in the mask clawed at his hidden throat, fell forward on his face....

"Where's Sabbat?" Pope yelled.

X turned. Sabbat's body had disappeared! During the fight with the masked man Sabbat had regained consciousness, crawled away. Suddenly screams of fury rilled the room and a score of dacoits and Malays boiled at X and the explorer. The palm guns were good but for single shots and there wasn't time to reload.

X tried to get to the gas and acid bombs in his belt but he was rushed by a dozen Malays, borne to the floor. Stabbing *krises* barely missed his throat. Brown fingers scratched, tried to gouge out his eyes.

A fierce yell that sounded like a banshee of death split the ears of the yowling natives. The next moment Crandall, and an officer from the ship, guns pounding, were in the thick of the fray! Their guns bucked under their steady fists, threw death at the surprised natives.

The Agent and Pope had time to reload now, accounted for three of the dacoits. And then it was over. The island was conquered! And in the thick of the brown bodies lay the dead Milo Sabbat!

"I want to see this man's face!" Arnold Pope growled as he bent over the form of the masked man.

Secret Agent X laughed. "I can tell you who it is, Pope. It's— Jebel Zeck! I caught him several times rubbing his chin with a fore-finger, and I remembered Zeck's habit. He probably has the Red Maggot on his person. He was behind the whole thing. That phony attack on him in New York was to divert suspicion. On one of his trips to the Far East he must have made the contacts and plans for capture of Red Maggot."

Ten minutes later the three prisoners of Lost Island were free of the terrible coral growths, were weak but would recover. Rika Van der Veer was in the arms of her father and Peter DeVery. Alea, abashed, confused, stood in the background. Rika turned to the Agent.

"Alea says she'd like to stay on the island with Peter and me. I—I think she has suffered enough."

X nodded, smiled at Alea. He turned to Crandall. "I see you got my message from the shell to take off in the *Gull* and bail out in the mist with your 'chutes. You saved us, Crandall, you and that officer." He shook hands gravely. "I was sending you a message in the bathysphere to do what I finally had to tell you on the shell. It's still in the bathysphere, I suppose."

"The *Gull* is lost," Crandall said sadly.

"Yes, I know," Agent X answered. A shadow crossed his face at the loss of the valiant little plane. But he would replace it. No one had ever lost when aiding Secret Agent X.

Henrik Van der Veer raised his hand for silence. "There is noth-ing I can say, Mr. X, to thank you. I think you know how I feel. But there is one thing I want to do while we all are here. I want the memory of a gallant gentleman to remain with you—with us—al-ways. And," his smile was tremulous, "you are always welcome to return to—*Jon Smit Island!*

"I hereby dedicate it, erase for all time the fear of a superstitious force causing the natives to wish to drive us away."

With the words the old Dutchman dropped the gleaming blood-red pearl, the Red Maggot, onto the coral floor, ground it to dust under his heel!

Secret Agent X, the picture of Jon Smit large in his memory, brought his hand up in a stiff salute.

BOOK XL

CORPSE CONTRABAND

Ten thousand years ago it had been written in brass that the Yezidee would overrun the world with blood. And now Erlika, the daughter of Satan, had smuggled in the Yezidee to form an unholy alliance with the American underworld. And Secret Agent X—man of a thousand faces—found himself stalemated by ageless magic and barbaric cruelty.

CHAPTER I

CARGO OF CORPSES

AT DUSK, MORTON Edgewood peered out of the leaded glass window in the office of his Old Colonial Pottery Shop. It was an evening of deadly calm. A drowsy heat had settled upon the city. These were dog days. Some called it suicide weather, others the moon of madness.

The moon looked anything but mad. Above the stagnant, dust-gray leaves of the maples on the other side of the street, the moon showed its face, pallid and consumptive. Morton Edgewood sighed as he closed his account book. He anticipated without pleasure his bed in the rooms above the shop. The shop, which was in a residential district in the city of Maywood, was air-conditioned for the comfort of his fastidious patrons.

But Edgewood's narrow margin of profit had not permitted him to extend the air-conditioning to his bachelor quarters above. His rooms would be oven-hot tonight. He had half a notion to drag down a mattress and sleep in his office. Except for his old man's sense of modesty, he would have done that. But the large, leaded glass window of his office had no blind.

A droning sound, as hot and irritating as the buzz of locusts, came up the street. A dusty van stopped in front of the shop, its back facing the entrance to the shop. Morton Edgewood pulled his brassy-looking spectacles down half the length of his thin beak. The driver of the van was getting out, a notebook in his hand. Morton Edgewood was puzzled. The van bore a Texas license beneath one of its tail-lights.

The brass knocker on the door of the shop clacked imperatively. Edgewood straightened up from his book, opened the office door, stepped into the shop. The knocker clacked again. He took hold of the doorknob, pulled the door open, at the same time turning on the entrance light.

The driver of the van stood there with the stub of a pencil in one hand and his receipt book in the other. He shoved pencil and book at Edgewood. He was very tired. His gray shirt was nearly black across his chest because of sweat. Black hairs, visible at the open neck of his shirt, glistened against tanned flesh. He had a dull, heavy-featured face.

"What is it?" Edgewood demanded. "Haven't you the wrong address?"

The driver backed up, looked at the numbers of the shop. "Your name's Edgewood, isn't it? This is the Colonial Pottery Shop, isn't it? No, I don't have the wrong address. Sign on the bottom."

"I'm not expecting anything," Edgewood said. "There's some mistake."

The driver scowled. "Listen, if your name is Edgewood I got a load of Mexican pottery. It was shipped F.O.B. and I'm collecting the freight on this. One hunnert and forty-eight bucks freight charges."

"I am not expecting anything," said Edgewood. "You've made a mistake."

THE DRIVER shoved his hat back on his head. "You kiddin' me? If you are kiddin' me, get it that I ain't in the mood. I been on the road three days with this stuff and if you think it's hot here, you ought to sit over a damned truck motor and drive up from Texas some time."

"If you'll step inside," Edgewood suggested kindly, "you can cool off and have a glass of lemonade."

The driver laughed. "Listen, old man, you pay the freight and I'll buy my own drinks."

Edgewood stiffened. "I am sorry. I ordered nothing. I am overstocked now." And the driver took a belligerent step forward. Edgewood slammed the door and pushed over the bolt. The driver grabbed the knocker and clacked it angrily. He yelled: "If I camp here all night, you're goin' to pay me—through the pocket-book or through the nose."

"Young man," called Edgewood, "I don't like your attitude." He turned, walked stiffly back to his office. The presuming upstart! It was one of those rackets you hear about. It was—

The trapdoor opened. Scarred, cruel faces appeared—and flashing knives.

Having just opened the door of the office, Edgewood paused, took half a step backward, his lips puckering to form a silent "Oh." There was a woman in his office. She was dressed in a long, summery dress of frothy black stuff ornamented with a sprinkle of sequins that sent forth darts of light like stars in a dark sky. Her face he could not see because of her hat, which, to Edgewood's eye, untrained in such matters, resembled a Salvation Army lassie's bonnet.

Her costume was sheerest witchery, sleeveless, low cut, and in a measure old-fashioned. Tight little curls clustered at the nape of her neck. Fragile-looking, silvery sandals were on her small, narrow feet.

She had not looked at him, yet it seemed she knew he was there and was giving him time to digest the charm of her figure and costume. Then she turned her head slowly toward him. An unaccountably cold sensation passed along Edgewood's spine. Then it was gone and he felt, alarmingly, that he had lost twenty years of his life in as many seconds.

She smiled, and there was something in her smile, in the glint of her teeth, that burned a single descriptive word on Edgewood's mind—*rapacious*. And in her nearly black narrow eyes with their obliquely slanting brows, he saw cruelty.

She was at one and the same time the most charmingly beautiful and entirely wicked-looking young woman he had ever seen.

"Sit down," she said, patting the bottom of his desk chair with her dark, slender-fingered hand.

EDGEWOOD crossed the office with a sprightly step he had not known for years. He sat down. "To what—er—do I owe this—er—pleasure?" he groped back through the dictionary of forgotten gallantry.

Her smile was amused. "Men usually want to ask how I get in."

"Well," he said, feeling the perfect idiot and enjoying it, "how did you get in? Were you wafted through the keyhole on the breath of a tropic breeze?"

She laughed deep in her throat. Her laugh was like a bar of music from Satan's Mass. "Breeze from the tropics or an updraft from hell?" she whispered, leaning rather closer to him than he thought was necessary. Edgewood squirmed, delightfully uncomfortable.

She said: "You're rather a nice old thing."

"Old?" he muttered, and frowned at her laughter.

Her laughter stopped so suddenly that the silence startled him. For a moment of stark insanity, her eyes possessed him and he had an impulse to take her in his arms and crush her full red lips against his own. And then the deep tones of her voice came softly to his ears:

"There is a man outside with a load of pottery. I intend you to pay him what he asks and have the six large packages brought in here. The other pottery you may have, to do with as you will. But—the six great urns are mine."

"But—but," he stammered, "I ordered no pottery from Mexico."

"How do you know?" she said.

And without taking her eyes from his, she reached into a large, black bag made of the same frothy stuff as her dress, and produced a slip of paper. She held it out for him to see. It was an order blank filled out in his own handwriting and directed to a potters' firm in Mexico.

Edgewood looked up blankly. "I do not understand. I do not remember—"

"Of course not. But you will remember an odd feeling of sickness that came over you some weeks ago? You remember how unconsciousness stole upon you like night creeps across the horizon? How do you know *what* you did then, my friend? It was then that you wrote this order, for then you were mine. Then you belonged to Erlika, daughter of Erlik."

She leaned forward in her chair until her lips were within inches of his. "And do you know, when you were mine you didn't behave entirely as a gentleman should? Twice I had to remind you of your years." She shrugged. *"Hashish*—it is like that with some men."

Her hand touched his, and his first impulse was to jerk his hand away. But he let it linger and reveled in the thrill her touch gave him.

"You will pay the drayman like a good boy," she said, "and earn, perhaps, Erlika's lips for a little while."

Edgewood stumbled to his feet, left the office, went to the door of his shop. The truckster was sitting on the front steps. He turned, looked up at Edgewood.

"It's about time," he said. He stood up and handed Edgewood the book and pencil. Edgewood signed, reached into his pocket and took out a roll of bills. He counted out the money which the truckster carefully tucked away.

"I picked up a couple of loafers uptown," the driver announced. "They'll help me with the big packages. Where do you want the stuff?"

"Anywhere," said Edgewood dully. "In the shop, I suppose."

He stood back from the door to watch the unloading. There were a number of small cartons and six huge bundles packed in straw-lined crates which required two men to handle. Then the drayman and his assistants left the shop.

For a moment, Edgewood stood there in the absolute silence of his shop, staring at the large straw packages. A soft laugh from the door of the office caused him to turn around. The woman was standing there, lips and eyes taunting.

"Get a hammer, sweet old man," she ordered. "I want you to open these things for me."

WORDLESSLY, Edgewood obeyed. With hammer and wrecking bar he removed the thin slats that crated the big straw packages. The woman ripped aside the straw from one after another to reveal, in each package, a graceful urn of rust and blue striped pottery, fully five feet in height and two feet wide at the top. Six urns in all stood in the midst of six heaps of straw in the center of the floor.

Edgewood stared in open-mouthed wonder. "What on earth are you going to do with these things, Miss?" he asked.

She smiled at him. "Just call me Erlika. I do not care for formalities. And hand me the hammer. I will show you what is to be done."

Edgewood obeyed, as he felt compelled to do. Again he thrilled at the touch of her hand as she took the hammer from him. Then she approached one of the urns, struck its bulging sides a sharp blow with the hammer. The thin, brittle clay smashed, fell into bits. And tumbling out among the fragments was the body of a man.

Erlika whirled on the pottery dealer. "You will not cry out," she warned sternly.

But Edgewood had never been farther from crying out. He could only stare glassily at the body on the floor. It was a man, swathed in white silk, legs doubled under him, arms crossed and bound flatly to his chest. Fingers of the hands, visible above the wrappings, were long, talonous things with cruel, curling nails.

The man's head was hairless, deeply yellow. His face, perfectly composed with closed eyes, nonetheless seemed but a mask for something more hideous than appeared on the surface. The lips were full, sensuous, the nose broad and flat. Cheekbones were high like an Indian's, but the skin that covered them was yellow. A squarish block of black beard centered the chin. A mustache drooped from the upper lip, lending the face an aspect of cruelty and ill nature.

The man on the floor was like a Chinese. Yet Edgewood knew perfectly that the man was not Chinese—not the native of south China with which he was familiar, but a man from Black China, impenetrable Inner Mongolia!

The woman went from one urn to another, smashing them with the hammer. From each rolled the silk-wrapped body of a hideous, yellow-faced man. And on every face a common trait was deeply etched—cruelty. As each Mongol appeared, Erlika's laugh rang out. She named them one by one: Djedstung, Damba, Gheghen, Hutuku, Bogdo, and Hun Taigi.

It was immediately after the appearance of the sixth yellow man on the floor that the door of the shop was flung open and a man stepped into the room. It was the truckster.

Erlika whirled from the wreckage of the last urn, her soft velvety fingers moving with incredible speed to her black bag. When her hand darted from the bag, it held a small, black automatic. There was no smile on her red lips as she faced the truckster.

"Close the door," she commanded. "Why have you returned?"

The truckster gulped in air through his mouth. "The receipt. The old man didn't give me the receipt. What the hell's goin' on in here? These—" he looked at the six yellow sleepers on the floor, and his gesture tried vainly to express what his words could not.

One hand on her hip, the other nursing the automatic carelessly, Erlika took swaying steps to the truckster, avoiding the sharp bits of broken pottery. "You only want your receipt," she said softly when she was so close to him that the sparkling skirt of her gown touched the harsh, gray cloth of his trousers. "You would not go to the police and say what you have seen? Oh, no! You will not go!"

Her laugh taunted. Her black eyes cracked like twin whips at Edgewood. "Old man, you will pick up some of those cords and bind this man's hands and feet."

Edgewood hesitated. "I—I don't want to get mixed up in this."

Erlika's beautiful teeth gleamed. "You are already mixed up, as you say, in this. You were mixed up in it ten thousand years ago. When Erlik wrote upon tablets of brass in the Seventh Tower by the Lake of Spirits, you were mixed up in this. It was written there that an old fool would be mixed up in this. You will tie his hands, you old fool!"

EDGEWOOD stooped, fumbled with hemp cord that had come from the straw packages. He found pieces of the proper length and approached the truckster. Erlika watched, her head coquettishly cocked on one side. "He is so handsome a man," she said aloud, "that it is very unfortunate he is to die."

"Listen, sister," the truckster said, "I don't know what this is—"

"Stop, you pig!" Erlika's eyes flamed. "Erlika 'listens, sister' to no one. She is not your sister!"

The truckster gulped his words, mumbled beneath his breath: "Of all the screwy setups. Smuggling aliens in pottery!"

Erlika stepped back. From her black bag she took what appeared at first to be a lizard eight inches from snout to tail. The thing had an odd, metallic luster, yet so perfectly was it modeled that it seemed alive. She turned toward the astonished Edgewood, the lizard thing outstretched toward him. From the open mouth of the thing in her hand a blue-gray cloud hissed straight into the pottery dealer's face.

Edgewood choked, strangled. And when the paroxysm had passed, his eyes were strangely glazed. He felt at first a feeling of

Tumbling out among the fragments was the body of a man.

impotence. Erlika advanced, took his hand, pressed something into his palm. He looked down dully. In his hand was a slender-bladed knife. He stared at it in horror, yet something compelled him to cling to it. He raised his eyes to Erlika's black, penetrating eyes. The woman was standing beside the bound truckster.

"In one moment you will try to escape me, Edgewood," she said. "You will try to fight your way out of here. But standing in the door is a man—a big, powerful man. You will feel a desire to kill. You will have to stab him to clear the way to the door."

The room seemed filled with fog. Only Erlika's hellishly beautiful eyes pierced the fog and possessed his soul. Something like liquid fire was poured into his veins. Suddenly, he could see with startling clarity the door of the shop and the truckster standing in it. Everything else belonged to another world.

Morton Edgewood gripped the knife....

Morton Edgewood, age fifty-eight, bachelor, owner of the Old Colonial Pottery Shop, came shuddering from the realm of nightmare. There was in his mouth a bitter taste and in his mind a lingering reflection of his dream. He had stood on a ragged cliff surrounded by clouds. Above him he had seen a sky made of ink, yet twinkling with countless stars. Beside him on the cliff had been a man and a woman—a woman so beautifully made that he had thought her the most wonderful thing in the world.

He was young again, in his dream. The woman had given him a knife, and a promise. He had plunged the knife into the other man and derived a hellish pleasure from twisting it in the wound.

A prayer quivered on Edgewood's lips. He was on the floor of his own shop. All about him were bits of red and blue pottery and little heaps of straw. Near the door was the body of a man—a man in gray with a truckster's cap on his head. In the center of the truckster's broad chest was a small wound from which blood seeped slowly.

Morton Edgewood got to his knees. He seized the edge of a counter and dragged himself to his feet. Only then did he notice that his right hand was tightly closed on the hasp of a knife. Blood formed ruby drops at the tip of the knife.

Edgewood's eyes jerked from one corner of the shop to the other. He staggered to his office, looked through the door. The place was empty. There were no signs of hideous, sleeping Mongols, save the bits of broken pottery on the floor of the shop. And no sign of a woman, Erlika.

With a hoarse cry that stark madness drove from his throat, Morton Edgewood ran from the shop, plunged into the hot, fragrant summer night.

BACK in the shop, the truckster stirred. The ropes had been removed from hands and feet. His eyes opened. Dully, at first, his eyeballs took in their surroundings. And then the dullness passed and there was terror there. Terror spurred him to his feet. Terror compelled his leaden feet to carry him staggering from the shop into the street. He tried to run, fell blindly into the arms of a policeman.

The cop's strong hands gripped the truckster. "Great hell, man!" he gasped. "You've been knifed."

Words rattled in the truckster's throat. Forked fingers clawed at his chest. "Edgewood," he husked, "knifed me." He seized the cop's arm in a grip that told of approaching death.

"Listen, for the love of heaven. I'm dying…. There's a woman with all hell in her eyes—so beautiful you wouldn't mind dying, just looking at her. She came—gave the old man something from a lizard—You John Laws—they're smuggling yellow devils in—bring 'em up through Mexico. Like Chinks, only different…. They put them in big—urns…."

Blood that had welled into the man's throat choked him off. There was a final, strangled sigh, and he became limp in the policeman's arms.

There was no sense to it, the cop told himself, as he later surveyed the wreckage of pottery in the shop. Still, a report had to be made. He went to Edgewood's phone and called headquarters. There was no sense to it—yellow men in pottery urns, a woman with hell in her eyes, mild old Morton Edgewood stabbing a man.

But there was something in the report that made it imperative that the chief of police notify the Immigration Bureau at Washington—Asiatics sneaking across the border, coming up through Mexico in pottery urns. And eventually that report reached the ears of a gray-eyed, young-looking man seated in a visitor's chair beside an imposing desk. Behind the desk perched a small gray-haired man whose every birdlike movement indicated his highly nervous temperament.

"And that's the story," said the gray-haired official, his hands making a twitching gesture. "No man has seen hide nor hair—if they had hair—of the Asiatics. The man, Edgewood, is gone, too. Truckster's dead, so there you are. If you would like to run out to Maywood—nice town of about three hundred thousand."

"Why Maywood, K9?" asked the gray-eyed man in a deep, calm voice.[15]

"I haven't the slightest notion."

"Maywood," said the gray-eyed man, his lips curving into a slightly ironic smile, "is a nice town. Its people work hard and are so completely occupied with their own affairs that they seldom even see their own neighbors. Some of their neighbors would bear watching.

"There's Art Murdo, for instance. Mr. and Mrs. Citizen of Maywood don't know, but Art Murdo filches a goodly per cent of their

---

15   AUTHOR'S NOTE: Agent X's immediate superior, a powerful Washington official, prefers to be known only as K9, his number during the period of his life in which he served as an intelligence officer. K9 is the only official sponsor of Secret Agent X.

earnings from their pockets. He's the most high-handed racketeer in the country. And—" the gray-eyed man shrugged—"getting away with it."

He helped himself to one of K9's cigarettes. Behind a curtain of blue smoke, the gray eyes, infinitely brilliant and far-seeing, mused dreamily. "I wonder—"

"You wonder what?" K9 rapped. "My only objection to you—you're obscure. What are you wondering about, eh?"

The lips of the gray-eyed man twitched humorously. "I'd better go to Maywood where there are other obscure people like Art Murdo. But if it's any satisfaction to know, I was wondering if the very fact that Art Murdo makes his headquarters in Maywood isn't the reason why the Asiatics were shipped to Maywood. He could be in the alien smuggling business."

The gray-eyed man stood up, took the hand of K9. "By George," said the latter, "I'd like to go with you, but, damn it, my doctor never got through lecturing about my going to Hawaii with you that time."

The gray-eyed man laughed pleasantly. "The Yellow Peril scare never amounted to a great deal. This business at Maywood may not even prove interesting."

But deep within him that strange intuition that had more than once saved his life, warned gray-eyed Secret Agent X that deadly danger awaited him at the end of the journey to come.

CHAPTER II

THE MAN FROM MONGOLIA

THE NIGHT CLERK at the desk of Hotel Mayfair leaned forward as the man in gray tweeds approached. The new arrival was not a man of apparent distinction. His features were as commonplace as his subdued clothing. His hair was of an uncertain sandy color. Yet this man who accomplished virtual self-effacement was A.J. Martin, renowned feature writer of a famous newspaper syndicate. He was, also—though the clerk had no way of knowing it—Secret Agent X.

"We received your wire, Mr. Martin," said the clerk needlessly, "and have taken care of your requirements. I believe you will be entirely comfortable."

"Thanks." X wrote the signature of Martin on the register card. He turned from the desk and let his steely eyes wander thoughtfully across the elaborate lobby of the city's finest hotel. Little knots of young men with old faces who bore no baggage save tripods, flashlight equipment and cameras, were scattered across the room.

"Why the press convention?" X asked the clerk.

The clerk's eyebrows lifted. "Hadn't you heard? Really, I supposed that was what had brought you here, Mr. Martin. Prince Djamok, the Mongolian educator who has been touring this country for some time, was kidnaped. That is," the clerk corrected hastily, "almost. He claims to have routed his attackers—something which I was inclined to doubt, he is such a slight man.

"But not long ago one of the reporters who had tried to get into his rooms came out again very rapidly and was taken to the hospital. Prince Djamok refuses to see reporters and is quite ferocious with intruders, it seems."

"Huh," X grunted. "Where's his room, by the way?"

"By the way, Mr. Martin!" The clerk chuckled. "The instinct of a newspaperman is showing itself! Prince Djamok's suite is directly below yours. Unfortunately, there is no connecting fire escape. And I would not attempt to see this Mongol. After all, if he can manage kidnapers and reporters—" The clerk concluded his caution with a shake of the head.

X laughed. "Oh, I'll keep out of his way—at least for the next two or three minutes." And he followed the bellhop, who was laden with his bags, to the elevator.

Prince Djamok. X had heard of the enlightened Mongol chief who had come to the Western hemisphere to take Occidental culture back with him to his native land. The Mongol was a great admirer of the English speaking people, having had an English tutor. And Djamok was a man of fabulous wealth—a perfect target for American crime, were it not for the fact that he had methods, apparently, of protecting himself.

In spite of the clerk's warning, or rather because of it, X decided to pay the Mongol prince a visit. His trip to Maywood had been entirely without event, and a man of X's temperament could not long remain content with inactivity. No sooner was he installed in his new quarters than he carefully locked the door and proceeded to open one of his bags.

From this satchel he removed a circular metal disk about nine inches in diameter and not unlike a case for moving picture film in appearance. A metal hook protruded from the slot in one side of the case. On the opposite side was a leather-padded loop of metal that served as a hand hold. A triggerlike piece of metal extended from the case into the metal loop.

This device was the Agent's own version of the rope ladder, compact enough to be carried in one of the large pockets of his coat. Within the case was a fifty-foot coiled ribbon of highest tensile strength steel on a spring reel delicately balanced against the Agent's own weight. He had only to attach the metal hook to the inner side of the sill, roll up the screen that covered his window, seize the hand hold, and he was ready to descend the outer wall of the building.

HE HUNG to the loop, broke the rapidity of his descent with the trigger device in the center of the hand hold, and quickly and silently lowered himself to the window directly beneath his own. The roll type screen and the window shade of the Mongol's window were both pulled down tightly. He was prepared for this.

Hanging by one hand, he inserted a small wire hook into the mesh of the screen, pulled down, permitted the screen to roll to the top of the window. Then he reached in, cautiously took hold of the shade and raised it. Ahead was black uncertainty. Within that darkness was the man who had frightened away kidnapers and sent a newspaperman to the hospital. Agent X swung over the sill.

There was a box on the sill—something like a long, wood cheese box. In the darkness it might have easily been mistaken for the top of the sill itself. X did not know it was there. Not until it was too late to avoid its subtle trap.

As his hand touched the top of the box, the thing sprang apart. Its sides buckled beneath his weight, and the heel of his hand crushed down on something cool-skinned, slippery, alive. Cold coils whipped about his wrist.

X sprang into the room. His left hand darted to the breast pocket of his coat, came out with his pencil flashlight. He thrust the beam downward toward his wrist, and it centered upon the deadly beauty of a coral snake, its slender, striped body wrapped about his wrist, its head back and jaws open ready to strike.

With a swiftness that rivaled that of the striking snake itself, the Agent's left hand, bearing the flashlight, darted downward. There was no time to think. The angry little reptile had brought certain death within inches of the Secret Agent. Into the gaping, poisonous jaws, X jammed the end of the pencil light. He sprang to the right, encountered the elongated pulls of a floor lamp with his fingers, pulled, illuminated the room.

The dark venom of the snake spewed harmlessly over the metal body of the pen-light, drained each poison sac dry. Then X dropped the pen-light, his fingers darting to pinch directly behind the head of the infuriated serpent.

He pulled the writhing, sinuous body from his wrist, held it at arm's length, crossed the room to where a cigarette humidor rested upon a walnut table. He raised the lid of the box, popped the serpent inside, dropped the lid in place.

He stepped over to pick up his flashlight. As he stooped, he saw reflected in a decorative mirror on the wall, the door of the room opening. A yellow hand flashed through the door, shot across the top of a taboret beside the door, seized a knife. The hand was silently withdrawn and the door closed.

X calmly wiped the deadly serpent venom from his flashlight with his handkerchief, returned flashlight and handkerchief to his pocket. Then he crossed to the door through which had passed the yellow hand. It was not the only door which opened upon the living room of the prince's hotel suite, he learned a moment later. For as he opened the door, looked into an empty bedroom, a stealthy whisper of slippered feet behind him warned him that there was another entrance.

X pivoted, and the point of a knife met his throat. The man he faced was tall, slight. His features were delicately formed, his face oval, his mouth as sensitive as a woman's. His black hair was sleeked back from his forehead. On his chin was a small, neatly trimmed goatee. His almond-shaped eyes were soft, brown, deceptively gentle.

He was wearing green pajamas of American design, topped with a bathrobe of glaring, yellow Chinese silk. A Scotch pug pipe clasped in his white teeth was the final touch of grotesqueness. The yellow hand with which he held the hasp of the knife was marked with a bloody abrasion. Evidently, Prince Djamok had met with a slight accident. All of which did not alter X's predicament in the slightest. The prince was perfectly capable of pinning him to the door panel with that knife.

"Having passed the snakes which guarded your window, your highness," X said coolly, "I meet the snake's master. I should have much less difficulty draining your fangs of poison than I had with the snake."

Djamok's smile was not pleasant. "I have given fair warning to Yankee—" he pronounced it Yon-kee—"newspapermen that the next intruders coming in are going out dead."

X LAUGHED. Though the ripple of the laugh in his throat brought his flesh against the tip of the knife, still he laughed. "*Tokhta!*" [16] he said quietly. "Have you forgot that I drained your serpent's fangs of poison?"

Djamok's smile was unaltered. "Boasting of past achievements no defense against present predicament."

"Past achievement," X mocked, "excellent foundation for future ones. I thrust my handkerchief into the jaws of your coral snake, drained its venom, wiped the handle of your knife with the venom. With that abrasion on your hand, there is some doubt in my mind about your lasting long enough to thrust that knife home, Djamok."

---

16   AUTHOR'S NOTE: "Look out!" Mongol dialect.

Not thinking that it would have been impossible for X to have known that the skin of his right hand was broken, Djamok, his face suddenly turning pale, dropped the knife. X immediately planted his foot on the knife, shoved Djamok back with his hands.

X laughed. "We've had our fun. Suppose we sit down. And do not offer me any of your cigarettes. The snake is in the humidor."

Djamok looked bewilderedly about the room. Then his smile gained breadth, became more pleasant. He indicated a chair with a low bow. "Yankee cleverness," he admitted.

X grinned. Yankee nerve, perhaps. "You really are quite capable of taking care of yourself. It's no wonder that you foiled your kidnapers. Tell me about it."

Djamok sat down only after X was in a chair. He lighted his pipe. "I being most diligently reticent about unfortunate happening. I being not so sure of myself after you fooling me. I unacquainted with how Yankee newspaperman know Nomad-Mongol speech."

"I crossed Asia after the Red revolt in Russia," X said. "It was Mongolia or the firing squad. I chose Mongolia."

"My country was flattered," Djamok said.

X smiled grimly. "On the contrary, or else your country has very peculiar ideas about accepting compliments."

Djamok sighed. His brown eyes became sad. "I being very sorry for my country's ill manners toward strangers. Sometimes I being afraid my efforts wasted to tame my country."

"Were the kidnapers countrymen of yours, by any chance?" X asked, his eyes fixed shrewdly on the Mongol's face.

The brown eyes became inscrutable. "I being most reticent," Djamok insisted.

A short while later, X said good night to the Mongol. He returned to his room only long enough to reel up the steel ribbon with which he had accomplished his entrance into Djamok's rooms. Then he descended in the elevator to the lobby. His next move, he decided, was to visit Art Murdo, king-pin of Maywood crime. Murdo had done much to deserve such a meeting, and X was determined to put it off no longer....

Above an east side tavern was a room which contrasted sharply with the dingy exterior of the building in which it was situated. The criminals who thrived under the protection of Art Murdo had a high standard of living developed by a continuance of prosperity. So this particular rendezvous for criminals was luxuriantly furnished.

There were five granite-faced men in the room, lounging in the soft cushioned chairs, smoking, their eyes, habitually void of expression, fixed on the sixth man, their leader. The sixth man was Monte Crespis, wasp-waisted, square-shouldered, red-haired, ape-faced.

Monte Crespis had a reputation envied by every heist man in the business. Monte had brains. When he cracked a bank or lifted a payroll, it was a clean job, because he planned his jobs as carefully as an architect might lay out a building. After that, he would lay his ideas before Art Murdo.

Only after he had gained Murdo's approval did Monte Crespis take up the matter with his five henchmen. So a meeting of Monte and his henchmen was an indication that things were about to happen in Maywood.

ONE THING that made Monte's reputation for brains what it was, was the fact that he had never stooped to murder. When you were really smart, he argued, you didn't have to hurt a guy to get him to part with his money. And you didn't have to kill half a dozen coppers to cover your trail, if you were smart; if you were smart and on the good side of Art Murdo.

Monte spread a large, square piece of paper out on the table in front of him. He jerked his ape's head to indicate that his henchmen should move within the circle of light cast by the ornate bridge lamp behind Monte's chair.

"I want you guys to get this and get it straight." That was always Monte's preamble to his lecture on the subject of how a particular job was to be carried out. Then his voice lowered as his men huddled about him. His stubby forefinger traced lines on the paper. His blue eyes picked up the glow of enthusiasm.

In the middle of a sentence Monte stopped. He looked around at the five faces about him. A man muttered: "What's the matter, Monte?"

"Nothing," Monte replied. "Notice something? That piano downstairs stopped. All of a sudden. Everything is too damned quiet around here."

There was a tap at the door. Within the room breathing became shallow, jerky. Monte's eyes narrowed, slid toward the door. "See what it is, Cock," he said to one of his men.

A paunchy man with broken nose and flop ears pulled reluctantly away from the group. He slid back a small panel in the door, looked out into an unlighted hall. Enough light stole through the peephole for him to see the figure of the little shrimp Monte had placed on guard. Cock turned to Crespis. "Shrimp," he said.

"Open the door," Monte ordered. "What the hell's he bothering us about?"

Cock opened the door and Shrimp came in—not like he had ever come in before. He fell forward on his face, lay there in a motionless heap, a yellowish sliver of wood stained with blood sticking through his throat.

From the shadows of the hall, another man sprang into the room. In his hand was a gun. Beneath the low bill of his cap was a face such as none within the room had ever seen before. It was a face with cheekbones that belonged on a death's-head. It was a face with flat nose, almond eyes, sunken yellow cheeks. It was a face that might have been some mad sculptor's conception of the personification of cruelty.

One of Monte's men pulled a gun. He had no chance to level it before a knife flashed like a lightning bolt and buried itself to the hilt in the man's gun arm. He dropped his gun, stared goggle-eyed at five more yellow-faced men who moved with silent swiftness into the room.

Monte Crespis stood up as one by one his followers melted away from him, pressed back against the wall by the threatening guns and knives of the yellow men. Monte's lower jaw jutted defiantly.

"I told you guys," he said, addressing the yellow men collectively. "Told you and that guy who wears the fancy mask. Told you that I was damned if I was going to kick in with you. You may take my tip and get out of town before Murdo opens up on you. You can't—"

Monte stopped. He swallowed, and it was as though he had swallowed his glib tongue. The leader of the yellow men, a massive man with dangling, clawlike hands, advanced toward Monte. The yellow man's face was slit by a diabolical grin. In his eyes burned a strange, fanatical gleam.

Monte backed a step, bumped into his chair, sat down involuntarily. He slid out of his chair, his eyes never leaving the yellow man's cruel face. He kept going backwards. The yellow giant advanced, his arms drawing up, his claws clenching.

Monte bumped the wall. He stood still. Then he seemed to re-call for the first time that he carried a gun under his coat. His right hand flashed upward toward his shoulder and was snared by a yellow claw that had the strength of steel in its grasp. A second yellow hand disarmed him, flung the gun aside, then leaped to Monte's red hair.

At the same moment the yellow devil's hand darted beneath his coat, produced a compact roll of white cloth which rippled down to Monte's feet. Monte, his head jerked forward, his eyes on the floor, watched the mound of white cloth with glassy eyes that were perhaps keen enough to inform his terrified mind that here was his shroud.

THEN with incredible swiftness it happened—that which froze the blood of every white man in the room, made cowards of these hardened crimesters. The yellow man who held Monte without apparent effort, whipped out a fragile-looking sliver of bamboo from beneath his coat. The yellow man's knee came up, caught Monte in the middle, brought him groaning to his knees on the mound of white cloth.

The sliver of bamboo caressed Monte's neck, drew a thin, bloody line across the white flesh before its razor edge cut deep, severed blood vessels and cartilage, sawed with a circular motion that compassed the throat.

There was no cry from Monte—only a bubbling, liquid sound which escaped from the lip of the wound itself. Blood fountained. And then with one quick snap of the hand which held Monte's hair, the yellow man broke Monte's neck bones. The bamboo sliver cut cleanly through.

Hysterical cries of horror broke from the lips of Monte's companions. Heedless of the threatening guns about them, the men rushed from the room, falling over each other. In their minds was a single thought—to put as much distance between themselves and these silent, yellow killers as possible.

Within the room, the yellow murderer stepped over the body of Monte Crespis where it lay upon the white shroud. Blood blobbed from the severed neck. The yellow man held aloft the head with its hideously contorted face.

For a moment the yellow man's eyes flicked about the room, stopping finally on the ornate bridge lamp which stood behind Monte's chair. Then he strode majestically to the lamp, jerked off the shade. He jammed the severed head down on the sharp spear point of the lamp standard. He stepped back, turned to his companions for their approval....

Agent X had visited the city frequently before, and had obtained files of information on the activities of the underworld. He knew there was a certain tavern and rooming house in the east end where Murdo usually transacted business.

As X left the hotel door, a woman coming from the other end of the lobby fell into step beside him with apparent unintention. He gave her one of his sidelong glances, quick as the click of a camera shutter and as discerning as camera film itself.

The woman was startlingly beautiful. The dusky beauty of her face was accented by a gown of vivid scarlet. Curls of blue-black hair were carefully coiffured. She had a figure alluringly slender and she walked as though she expected to be looked at.

There was a single cab in front of the hotel. X made directly for it. As he put his hand on the handle of the door, a soft voice behind him said: "Taxi."

The driver of the cab sprang to the sidewalk, faced X squarely. "Sorry, sir, but the lady spoke first."

X turned, viewed the woman full in the face for the first time. The front view bore out all that he had anticipated from his glimpse of her profile. The nose, the mouth, the teeth were perfect. The eyes—there was something about the eyes. They were beautiful beneath their obliquely slanting brows. Beautiful eyes, yes—but there was something else.

"This," his mind muttered, "is the most dangerous woman I have ever met." Aloud, he said: "I beg your pardon. I did not know the cab was engaged."

She smiled. Her eyes passed appreciatively over his lean, square-shouldered figure. "Nor I," she said softly. "I did not engage the cab. Taxi service is intolerable in this city, don't you think? What direction were you going?"

"East," X answered.

"How fortunate. Why should we not share the cab?"

X held the door open for her. "Mine is the fortune," he said as he helped her in.

She paused while his hand was on her arm, looked back over her shoulder. "We will not argue, of course, but what with a kidnap attempted in the hotel this evening, I feel rather more secure having such capable company for at least part of the way, Mr. Martin."

Company for part of the way, she had said. Then she was determined that he should get out before she did. In other words, she was brazenly following him.

X GOT into the cab and found the woman occupying the center of the cushion. Her long-fingered hand pulled her scarlet dress back to make room for him beside her. X gave the driver an address that was a block away from his actual destination. Then he asked the woman how she had known his name.

"Was it black magic?" he asked.

She laughed. The gleam of her teeth sent an odd, cold sensation throughout his body. "I was in the hall when the Mongol prince said good-bye to you. I really was hiding behind the floor desk waiting to see the Mongol prince. Like all Americans, my curiosity where royalty is concerned is insatiable."

"And in exchange, oughtn't I have your name?" X asked.

She was searching for her bag on the seat beside her. As if by accident, her hand touched his. "I think," she said softly, "you may call me Erlika. Yes, I think I would like you to call me that."

"Miss Erlika?"

She laughed. "Only if you insist upon the 'Miss.' I am not married, if that's what you mean."

The taxi came to a stop in a dingy street bordered by old frame houses that had no common quality save the need of repairs.

"My corner, I believe," X said.

The woman extended her hand, and as he took it she grasped his fingers firmly and drew herself closer to him.

"The most dangerous woman in the world!" X's mind warned suddenly. Aloud, he said shortly: "Good-bye."

Erlika dropped back into the shadows of the cab. "But it is not good-bye," her soft lips murmured.

X closed the door of the cab, went behind it, and crossed the street at a brisk pace without looking back. He did not look back until he was well concealed in the shadows of the porch of a house he had no intention of entering. Then he saw the cab stop at the next corner east, and the woman who called herself Erlika got out.

X chuckled. She would need bloodhounds to follow him! He vaulted the rail of the porch, cut north between houses, crossed an alley, another lot, and came to his destination.

It was a two-story building, squared off at the top with a false front. The glass of door and window were painted red with the words: "BEER—WHISKEY." There was no illumination in front except that which managed to pass through these painted signs.

Silence greeted the Agent as he pushed open the door of the tavern. The front door opened directly upon the barroom. There was the bar without a keeper. There were half a dozen round-topped tables and they were without customers. At the back of the room, cones of light burned down on a pair of pool tables, but there were no players.

The Agent's footsteps pounded hollowly on the bare floorboards as he marched toward the back of the room. He moved with more caution than his steps indicated. A noisy brawl-house like this doesn't empty itself without reason. Something had happened.

He stopped a few feet from the nearest pool table. Something had happened, all right. A man's trouser-clad legs were visible beneath the pool table.

X walked to the table, stooped, reached beneath to seize one of the ankles, dragged the man out. He was a man in his twenties, long-legged, thin, round-shouldered. He had pink, waxy-looking skin that showed blue veins at his temples. His face was a triangle widened by a mop of tow-colored hair at the top and narrowing to a sharply pointed chin. Above the sensuous lips, he had a mustache that looked like corn silk and added years to his boyish face.

The blond man opened one bloodshot eye. "Go 'way," he said. "I'm dead."

"Dead drunk, you're right," X said. He slapped the man's thin cheek and got him to open both eyes. "Where's Murdo?" he asked.

The drunk rolled his eyes back and pointed with them toward the back of the room. "Mur's upshtairs." He turned over and pillowed his head on his left arm.

X stood up. "Skin-full, did you say Murdo or murder?"

There was no answer from the blond man on the floor. X started for the door at the back of the room. He opened the door carefully. Beyond was a stairway swallowed by blackness five steps up. X went up the five steps, then six. Blackness matted against his eyeballs like tar. Yet something warned him not to show a light. Then that happened which proved that had he not heeded that warning, he would not have lived.

HIS GROPING hand encountered a blade of steel in the darkness—steel that was slippery with *something*. X sprang backwards.

At the same time a flying body struck him full in the chest. His spine bowed backward from the impact. Long, lean arms gripped him around the waist. Weight threw him off balance, but as he fell, he pivoted halfway around on the ball of one foot so that he took the shock of the fall on his right side. The edge of the stair-tread gouged into his ribs, knocked breath out of him.

He heard the clatter of knife steel on the steps. Fingers he could not see hooked into his throat. X punched savagely into a face. A head snapped back with an audible crack beneath his blow. The stranglehold on his throat was broken. He tried to screw his legs around to get his body on the level of one of the steps so that he could sit up.

In his twisted position the vital function of breathing seemed impossible. But as he turned, his opponent caught him by the ankles, jammed on his legs, doubled his knees to his chest, shoved, sent him rolling down the steps.

The back of X's head thumped against the lowest step. The force of the blow dashed the blood-red rain of pending oblivion across his eyes. He ground his teeth as though his jaws had the power to cling to his senses. He blinked, rolled over, got dizzily to his feet. Somewhere within the building a high-pitched voice shouted: *"Toug ia glachako!"*

A coldness born within him by that wild, barbaric cry shocked him to his senses. He saw clearly now the empty taproom, the open door through which his assailant had passed into the night. He turned to the dark stairway and bounded up its length. His flashlight beam pointed out a door, open, and about four feet from the top of the stair.

He walked to the door, but no farther. For immeasurable long moments, he stood there, unable to move, held by the hand of horror. For within the room, only a short time before, had occurred the most damnable, barbaric ritual the world has ever known.

CHAPTER III

SHROUDS OF THE YEZIDEE

SEVEN BLOCKS AWAY from the tavern where Agent X had expected to meet Art Murdo, was a basement room beneath a barber shop. The door of this basement room burst open and five men tumbled over each other in getting in. Their fingers fumbled frantically clamping the three iron bolts into place, securing the door of their hideout.

Worn out, breathless, they melted down upon old chairs and boxes. They looked silently at each other and saw the paleness of their faces.

One of them, a paunchy man with a broken nose and flop ears, dug his fingers into his belly and groaned. "Wot they did to poor Monte is 'ard to stomick. The bloody 'eathen!"

"What they did to Monte is all right for you to worry about, Cock," said another man who was nursing a knife wound in his shoulder. "It's what might have happened to *me* that's worrying me."

Another little man who sat on an empty beer case and shivered, said: "Chinks. Where'd the chinks in this town get nerve enough to blow in on a high-class outfit like Monte's? And what's the idea behind it?"

The paunchy man nodded. "Wot's behind it? You've it there. If this was Lon'on, and some of the bloody brawls on Ropemaker Street, there'd be a point—just 'eathen against the whites."

"They ain't Chinks," said another. "I've seen a lot of Chinks, and these yellow devils ain't Chinks. Cock about had it right when he said they were heathens. Like Tartars, they are, sort of."

"What they are," said the fifth man, "don't make a whole lot of difference. The main thing is they're here and they finished Monte. They'd have nailed us to the wall with their knives if we hadn't lammed when we did. The question is, what are we going to do without Monte? Monte planned that payroll heist. We got our instructions. Can we go through with it without Monte? Or do we go to Art Murdo and tell him his pal Monte has been put on the spot? Monte paid a per cent of his heist jobs to Art Murdo and Murdo thought up ways to keep Monte and us out of trouble."

"We been payin' Art for protection, ain't we?" asked the wounded man. "Then shouldn't we go to Art and get that protection?"

No one answered the wounded man's question, for at that moment there was a knock at the door—a gentle, ghostly sort of tapping.

The five men looked at each other, mouths open and silent. The tapping came again.

"It ain't cops," one whispered.

"No, it ain't," said another.

" 'Oo's to know 'ow the 'eathen knocks?" asked the paunchy man.

"You take a peek, Cock," one suggested. "That little panel at the top of the door."

Cock moistened his lips, fidgeted.

"And get a slug in me peeper?"

The wounded man cursed. "I'll take a look." He stuffed a bloody handkerchief in under his shirt, got up, went to the door and slid back the panel.

He turned from the peephole to his anxious companions. "It's a dame," he said. "And a looker, too. What you suppose she wants?"

"I could do nicely with a dame right now," one said. "Why don't you ask her what she wants?"

The wounded man turned to the peephole. "What you want?" he asked.

"Oh, I would like so much to come in and talk a little," a soft voice said. "You are not afraid of me, are you?"

"Let her in," somebody whispered.

The wounded man started manipulating the bolts. "She'll knock your eyes out, boys. Evening dress and the whole works."

HE OPENED the door. There was a flash of scarlet from the darkness, and the woman called Erlika tripped into the room. She gave them a mocking curtsy, smiled her bewitching smile. Then she took a cigarette from the fingers of the little brown man on the beer case and put it to her lips. Her brown eyes covered each man's face, oblique eyebrows elevated.

"You like me, eh?" Erlika said. "I do not blame you. It is a very good thing you do because I have some things to tell you that you will not like. First of all, with Monte Crespis gone, you will need a new leader. I have a new leader for you. You will go right ahead with the payroll robbery Monte planned, but it will be executed a little differently."

" 'Oo's this new leader?" Cock asked.

Erlika smiled mysteriously. "He is a very powerful man."

"Has he been okayed by Art Murdo?"

Erlika sneered. "Art Murdo is on his way—out!"

"You mean we're to kick in with a guy we've never seen?" asked the wounded man. "Baby, you're beautiful but dumb."

"You are half right," said Erlika. "And you are going to kick in, because if you don't—" She shrugged. "How would you like to be thrust through in a hundred places with bamboo slivers? Or perhaps you would prefer the water torture where we insert a bamboo tube into your throat and pour water down in your belly until you burst like a poisoned toad? Or perhaps you would like to be fed to the rats? You could watch them eat off your flesh. Would that be nice?"

Five frightened faces loomed palely in the gloom of the cellar. The wounded man pulled a gun. "How would you like to be ventilated, lady?" he asked.

Erlika laughed. "I would not like it at all. I would bleed and that would be unpleasant. If you will look around, I think that you will agree that to shoot me would not be the thing to do at all."

The five men turned like five puppets operated by a single wire. The trapdoor in the ceiling of the basement room was open. Light passing down from above fell upon six scarred, yellow, hideous faces with flat noses, high cheekbones, and cruel slots of eyes.

"The 'eathens!" breathed Cock.

Knives flashed into the hands of the six Mongols.

The wounded man tossed down his gun. "Okay," he said. "We kick in, miss."

ONCE before Agent X had heard the Mongol battle cry, *"Toug ia glachako."* He had learned then what it meant, but never before had he witnessed the hideous result of the *iagla michi,* as the ceremony was called by the nomad Mongols.

He knew as he stood in the doorway of that room above the tavern, that he had to deal with the most barbaric religious organization in the world—the Mongolian Yezidee. Devil worshipers they were, serving the Asiatic equivalent of Satan, Erlik. Their creed was the annihilation of civilization, for it was written in their religion that they should some day overrun the earth, conquering with cruelty, creating rivers of blood from white men's bodies.

X knew that the Yezidee, like the similar cult, the Hassanis, which flourished to the south of Black China, used the drug *hashish* in all its forms. He knew that this drug created not only a fiendish desire to kill, but an oblivion of pain and fatigue. A Yezidee might be dying, yet still he would fight while a drop of blood remained in his body.

How such a cult had become rooted in the United States, he could only guess, but he knew that if the human beasts were permitted to multiply, to teach their creed to the American underworld, his nation faced its greatest danger since the World War. It was incredible, but the Yezidee had come to America. Directly before his eyes was mute testimony of the horrible fact:—the ceremony of *iagla michi*.[17]

The body of Mr. Monte Crespis, dude gunman who had planned a dozen successful bank and payroll robberies, was in that room. It lay across a pure white cloth, and its headless neck pooled blood onto the worn floorboards. The head of Monte Crespis was planted firmly on the spiked top of a metal floor lamp from which the shade had been removed. Ritual of the Yezidee prescribed that the head of the enemy should be mounted on a lance, and the lamp standard had offered an excellent substitute.

Wisps of red hair had been torn from Crespis' head and were tied in little knots at intervals along the lamp upright. Between these knots of hair were smears of blood. Only then had the Yezidee uttered the cry that had chilled X to the marrow: *"Toug ia glachako—the battle standard is anointed."*

For a time X stood there puzzled over the presence of the white cloth beneath Monte Crespis' body. And then it occurred to him that the cloth might well be intended for a shroud. The Yezidee thoughtfully provided shrouds for their intended victims. As the knights of old threw down their gauntlets to challenge an enemy,

---

17 AUTHOR'S NOTE: *Iagla michi, the ceremony of anointing the Mongolian tong, or battle standard.*

so the Yezidee threw down their shrouds as an unpleasant announcement that they were about to kill.[18]

The Agent's course was clearly set before him. Monte Crespis was in all probability one of the human tentacles of the criminal octopus, Art Murdo. If these Yezidee assassins had murdered Crespis, it was logical to assume that they would next turn on Art Murdo. With that in mind, X went down the stairs, into the tavern.

THE BLOND-MUSTACHED young man appeared suddenly crawling on hands and knees from beneath one of the round tables in the taproom. He had a heavy automatic in his right hand, and as X approached he sat back on his heels, raised the gun to eye level, and pointed it uncertainly at X.

X took a quick step forward like a football player attempting a drop kick. His right foot shot out, the toe of his shoe kicking the automatic out of the drunk's hand. The drunk looked dully with squinting blue eyes at his empty hand. "Pop," he said. Then he shrugged and lay down flat on the floor.

X seized the young man by the shoulders, hauled him to unsteady feet. He slapped the lean cheek of the pale, triangular face.

The tow-head shook his head and blinked. "Don't," he said. "I'm dead."

X forced the man into a chair, propped him up with one hand while with his other he removed his pocket medical kit. From this he removed a loaded hypodermic needle containing a powerful, but harmless, stimulant containing caffeine. He bared the man's arm, made the injection.

"You'll feel better," X said gently.

The man felt better almost at once, for he stooped, scooped his gun from the floor. He would have brought it into an excellent position to drill X through the middle had not X seized his wrist and given it such a twist that the man dropped the gun.

"Pain, too, clears the head," X said. "Now, what's your name?"

The man ran fingers through his mop of pale hair. "I'm Whitey, because my hair is like that."

---

18   AUTHOR'S NOTE: It is part of the Yezidee religion that none of their cult can expect to journey into the world of hereafter without having a suitable shroud. For that reason, since every Yezidee fully expects to die at any time, these Mongols carry their shrouds with them at all times.

"You're Whitey," X said, "and you're the sort who can lie his way out of almost anything. Make another try for that gun and your name will appear on a nice piece of granite."

He took from his medical kit a piece of rubber that looked like part of an auto inner tube. To this rubber was attached a pump and a small meter. This was actually a physician's device for checking on a patient's blood pressure, but Agent X used it for quite another purpose.

He wrapped the tube around Whitey's arm, made it tight by pumping air into it. Then he kept his eye on the indicator of the instrument. The device became a lie detector of the most elementary sort, for untruths would be immediately indicated by a jump in blood pressure.

"Now, Whitey, who do you work for?"

Whitey gave X a deadpan look. "Metro-Goldwyn—and the other guy. I'm stand-in for Mickey Mouse."

"You're a damned liar," X said mildly.

"Well, you don't need a lie detector for that," Whitey said sarcastically. "But that's the story I stick to."

X balled his fist and jabbed it at Whitey's mouth. Whitey's head snapped back. His blue eyes blinked. X said: "You work for Art Murdo."

"That's it—Metro-Goldwyn-Murdo," Whitey said. "What's the dingus say now?"

"It says your blood pressure will decline to zero if you don't come across. What happened here tonight? Were you in the room upstairs?"

Whitey made a face as though there was a bitter taste in his mouth. He shook his head. "I came here for a drink—"

"Which you had several times. Go on."

"Monte and the boys were upstairs, but I wasn't because I'm not in the mob. Crespis runs one end of Murdo's organization, but I hang around Murdo. I keep in the clear. After I'd had a few drinks, the yellow devils came in—six guys with faces that had been through a meat chopper, it looked like.

"They lit into the few of us guys that had been drinking and scared the pants off everybody but me. Me, I'm a hero. I crawled under a table and said I was dead. The yellow devils went upstairs and pretty soon hell broke loose up there and Monte's mob came tearing down the stairway. There was some yelling, so I went to sleep."

"All right," X said. "Now take me to Art Murdo."

Whitey blinked. "You wanta die?"

"Do you?" asked X coldly. "If not, take me to Murdo."

CHAPTER IV

SHROUD FOR AGENT X

THE CAB CAME to a stop in front of a swanky ten-story apartment building. Agent X had a gun in his pocket and this he kept pressed against Whitey. He nudged the young criminal to precede him from the cab, then followed closely.

"You can turn that heater another way, pal," Whitey said. "I'm enjoyin' this a lot, because I can see you stretched out in the gutter with a lot of cops standing around talking about the angle at which the bullet entered your peritoneum."

X, however, remained close to Whitey, the bulge of his right coat pocket pressing against the crook's side. They entered the building, crossed a lobby that was cool, dimly lighted, and softly carpeted. An elevator that moved without sound took them to the second floor.

Whitey indicated a door marked B2. X told Whitey to knock. So perfectly was the place sound-proofed that what sounded from the hall like a mumble of voices became the noise of an uproarious party when the door was opened by a tall servant.

"This guy wants to see the chief, Fish-face," Whitey said.

"In private," X said.

They were admitted into a small hall from which they could see half a dozen couples in the living room, drinking, dancing, necking. Only one man in the group looked like criminal stock. The others were of the sort pigeon-holed as "influentials"—men it was well for Art Murdo to be friends with. The girls looked like the usual run of bar-fly femininity.

The servant appeared a moment later, went to a door in the south wall of the hall and unlocked it. He held the door open for Whitey and X to enter. He closed, but did not lock it behind them.

They were in a small library with a single window which looked out on the parking ground back of the building.

Art Murdo had one hip on his walnut desk. He was a long-legged man, heavy across the chest and shoulders. His dark brown hair was brushed close to his well-shaped head. A few gray hairs salted his temples. A small lump above each eyebrow looked like devil's horns on the point of sprouting.

There was about him a certain attitude that placed him apart from the general run of men. It was something that was difficult to define, something that indicated that dinner clothes were the natural habitat of such a body. This attitude was perhaps the reason he was frequently referred to as the Magnificent Murdo.

"Guy wants to see you," Whitey said. He walked straight to the desk with X close beside him, reached coolly into the desk drawer, then swung around fast.

His left hand grabbed at X's pocket, twisting the barrel of the gun it contained to one side and at the same time drawing a gun out of Murdo's drawer. Whitey did all this with such smoothness and without any apparent thought for himself, that X was almost taken by surprise. X jabbed a short, straight left to the point of Whitey's chin.

Whitey reeled into the desk, bowed backwards across it under the force of the blow. He fired one wild shot and probably never knew that it drilled harmlessly into the wall of the building, for he rolled off the desk to heap at the Agent's feet, unconscious.

X pulled the gun from his pocket, pointed it at Murdo and pulled the trigger. The top of the gun flew up, revealing a package of cigarettes. He extended the smokes toward Murdo.

"Have one. But when Whitey comes around don't tell him about this. I've been bluffing him for half an hour with that trick cigarette case."

Murdo grinned. He had a pleasant smile in spite of his undershot lower lip. He accepted one of the Agent's cigarettes, put it in his lips and lighted it. "Your name's Martin, isn't it?" he asked. "A newspaperman?"

X nodded. "I've been here before. Having a shindig?"

Murdo shook his head. "Just a few of the boys who would like to be in the city hall next November. They won't get in, but I thought I might just as well get right with them—just in case. Sit down, Martin."

X chuckled. "You'd better sit down," he said cryptically. "I'd rather fall out of a chair than off a desk."

Murdo looked puzzled. He sat down in his chair, took another drag on the cigarette. "I don't get it," he said. "What's the joke?"

"You'll get it eventually," X said. "And please don't blow that smoke in my direction. It's drugged."

"Drugged?" Murdo looked at the cigarette and hurriedly stamped it out in an ash-tray.

"Yes. That's why I carry them in a gun. They're almost as capable of putting a man temporarily out of the way as a gun."

MURDO tried to get to his feet. He seized the edge of the desk, dragged himself half out of the chair. He was breathing in shallow gasps. His eyelids seemed to have weights attached to them.

"Damn you, Martin," he choked out. "Damn you!" Then he keeled over to the floor.

X stepped to the door of the room, opened it, saw no one in the hall. He removed the key from the lock, closed the door, locked it from the inside. He went over to Whitey, made sure that the tow-headed crimester was out for several minutes to come. Then he propped Murdo back into the chair, stood studying the man's face for a few minutes.

"Your name is Martin, isn't it. A newspaperman?" The exact words Murdo had spoken a minute or two ago now came from the lips of Agent X, but in a perfect imitation of Murdo's voice. The intonation, inflection, even that certain slovenliness with which Murdo pronounced his words were exactly counterfeited.

X quickly removed his coat, withdrew a flat, leather-bound case. When opened, this revealed a triple folding mirror, tubes of make-up material, pigments, pomades, flexible metal plates which could be used as the foundation for such characteristic irregularities of physiognomy as the hornlike bumps above Murdo's eyebrows.

Seated at the desk, the mirror in front of him, the living model of the man he was going to impersonate on the opposite side of the desk, the fingers of Agent X worked like those of a skilled sculptor. The commonplace features that identified him as A.J. Martin vanished. His nose became larger. The little bumps above his eyebrows formed. Plates and plastic plumped his cheeks.

Lastly, he removed the sandy colored toupee he wore, revealing his own naturally brown hair. He slicked down the waves of his hair with brown pomade. White pomade added the touch of silver to his temples.

As a final touch, he changed clothes with Murdo. The racket king's evening clothes were a little too loose, for Murdo had some superfluous flesh on his otherwise fine figure. This difference was easily remedied by pneumatic pads placed beneath the clothes.

When he was satisfied with his own makeup, he stooped over Murdo, altered the racketeer's face until it closely resembled the face X had recently worn as Martin.

That attended to, he gave Murdo a hypodermic injection that would be effective long after the drug in the cigarette had worn off. And then he was ready to revive Whitey.

The lean, tough, blond gunman came out of it blinking blue eyes, rubbing his chin. Then he sat up, brushed his tow-colored mustache, looked from X to Murdo. To his eyes the positions of the two men must have been exactly reversed—Martin unconscious in the chair and Murdo standing beside him.

"He packs a wallop, chief," Whitey said. "What'd you hit him with?"

X rubbed his knuckles. "My fist," he said, in imitation of Murdo's voice. "We got to get him out of here. He's a big-shot newspaper guy. Nosey, but not a bad guy to keep on the good side of."

"So," Whitey said, getting to his feet, "you knocked him out. That should help get on the good side of him, that should. What do we do with him?"

"Go out and tell Fish-face to run the guests out. Then we'll take Martin back to his hotel just as though he had had too many drinks."

As soon as Whitey was gone, X made a quick search of Murdo's desk. The racket king was too cautious to have anything incriminating in his apartment. X looked in the waste basket where he found what had started out to be a letter to somebody addressed as "Dearest Edna." That information might be helpful.

Then he picked up Murdo's gun which Whitey had borrowed for the purpose of polishing off Agent X. It was a serviceable .38 loaded, and X put it into his pocket. There was no room in Murdo's evening suit for X's elaborate makeup kit, so he took several items from it and dropped them into his pocket.

Other devices which he frequently employed, he removed from the coat which the unconscious Murdo was now wearing. These, with the makeup kit, he wrapped in a sheet of paper, intending to replace them in the room he had engaged at the hotel in the name of Martin. Murdo's keys and wallet passed into X's pocket.

WHITEY returned to announce that the guests had been tactfully got rid of. Together they raised the limp form of Murdo, whom Whitey supposed to be Martin, and dragged him from the apartment to the elevator, then out through the lobby of the building and into the waiting cab.

As they rode toward the hotel, Whitey said: "I don't think you can count on a per cent from that payroll job you laid out for Monte Crespis. I think something happened to Crespis. This guy Martin could tell you." And Whitey related what he had already told X about what had gone on at the tavern.

"Yellow men, eh?" X said, as though all this was news to him.

Whitey shuddered. "Yellow and hopped to the eyes. Like chinks, only not chinks. I don't know what happened to Monte's mob. They're probably still on the run."

X remained silent until they reached the hotel, where he and Whitey got out with the unconscious man between them. They entered the hotel, all eyes turned upon them, and approached the desk. The clerk bowed to the Magnificent Murdo.

X said, in Murdo's voice: "My friend Martin has had a drop too much. We'll take him on up to his room if you'll give us the key."

The clerk passed the key to a bellhop who accompanied them up to the rooms X had engaged. There X installed Murdo, locked his bundle of makeup material and other devices in his bag, and once again joined Whitey.

"I think, if you can spare a bed, I'll bunk with you tonight, chief. My old lady's plenty sore. She found out today that I been working with you instead of that job I was supposed to have for the past two years."

X looked at the blond-mustached man. The kid had a mother. Well, he supposed even gunmen had mothers. That didn't make it any easier for him to see that these criminals were brought to justice. He said: "And the old lady don't like the idea?"

Whitey laughed. "Not much. I was supposed to go to college and be a doc. Can you feature it?"

X forced a laugh. "Stick with me, kid, and some day you'll be able to buy your mom anything she wants."

"Tell *her* that!" Whitey scoffed.

They reached the apartment, and X showed Whitey to one of Murdo's three bedrooms. Then he went into Murdo's library and sat down at the desk.

He had not been seated more than a minute before there was a tap at his door. X's hand drifted down toward his pocket. He said: "Come in."

It was the butler whom Whitey had christened Fish-face. "There's a lady outside to see you, sir," he announced.

"Is there?" X asked disinterestedly. "What's she look like?"

"It's an old lady, sir. Mrs. Fauvre, she says her name is."

X nodded, though he hadn't the slightest idea who Mrs. Fauvre was. "Show her in."

The woman who entered must have been over sixty years of age. Her gray hair hung in strings from beneath her black straw bonnet. Her face was deeply lined, her eyes a moist blue, her hands crooked and hard-worked.

X stood up. "Won't you sit down?"

"No," said the woman in a scratchy voice, "Not in the same room with you. It should be poison to breathe the same air as you, you filthy beast."

X raised an eyebrow, took all this in Murdo's characteristic superior manner. "You're not very complimentary, mother."

"Mother! I'm not your mother, thank heaven! But I am a mother—somebody's mother. I can't forget that." Her voice broke, but she had it under control again. She kept shuffling toward Agent X, and her weak blue eyes gained new potency.

"I've come for my son. You're the man who's responsible for all his bad ways. I'm taking him away from here, you understand? I'll not let him associate with the likes of you. It's you that taught him to drink, and—"

X held up one hand. "Please. Who is your son?"

THE WOMAN eyed him sharply. "I'm Mrs. Fauvre. I want my Delmar back. You took him away and you can give him back. He's got the makings of a fine, upstanding man in him if you haven't taken all that away."

"Your son has very light hair, a small mustache?" X asked.

"Of course. Where is he? I'm taking him home."

X pressed a button on Murdo's desk. The servant appeared in the door. X said: "Tell Whitey to come here a moment."

At the sound of Whitey's foot-steps in the hall, the old woman's lips quivered. "My boy," she whispered beneath her breath. "My poor lost lamb."

Whitey stepped over the threshold, stopped, looked at his mother. The pink went out of his face. "Why, mom," he said gently.

The old lady went to him, arms outstretched. Whitey looked embarrassedly at X, lowered his eyes.

"Son, I've come for you. You've got to go home."

"No, mom," Whitey said. He yielded slightly to his mother's embrace. "Mr. Murdo's my boss. I'm working for him. It's honest work."

"Honest work!" The woman turned on X. "Art Murdo never did an honest day's work in his life. Men who associate with him don't do honest work. He'll use you, son, until he's through with you. Then he'll find a way of getting rid of you."

"You don't get it, mom," Whitey said.

"Oh, I get it. Murdo has told you you'll make a million dollars some day. Money got that way isn't any good, son. You're going home with me."

Knife upraised, a man sprang into the room.

X shrugged, looked at Whitey. "It's up to you, Whitey. You can quit now if you'd like."

Whitey's sharp chin jutted. "I'm sticking with you, chief."

The old lady's shoulders wilted. She turned without a word toward the door and tottered out. Her shoulders shook with sobs no one heard. On the face of Agent X was an expression of profound sympathy, utterly out of keeping with the hard features of Murdo. This expression changed quickly as Whitey looked toward him.

"Mind if I see the old lady home?" Whitey said.

X shrugged. "Go right ahead. Be back though. I may need you."

Whitey left in an embarrassed hurry. X looked at his watch. It was after midnight. The servant came to the door. "The guards have come, Mr. Murdo. May I leave now?"

X nodded. Guards? What kind of guards? He waited until the servant was gone, then he went to the hall door and looked out. A thug-faced man in a checkered cap was lounging in front of the door. He touched his cap. "Hi, Mr. Murdo."

"Hi," said X. He closed the door. He went to the rear of the apartment which opened on a porch. There were two men out there, their coat fronts bulging. Art Murdo took no chances.

But Agent X did not know that there was one more watchman, a hard-jawed ex-burglar who had given up his profession to become the keeper of keys in Art Murdo's modern castle. His position was at a door at the end of the hall—a door which was cleverly lined with steel and fitted with a lock of his own design.

The key was a small, flat piece of metal with wards of unusual design. He kept it in his pocket, and his big, puffy right hand on top of it. So even if he dozed in his chair, as he frequently did, no one could have possibly obtained that key by stealth.

And that night he dozed. It was something more than a doze, for he had taken on more than his usual ration of beer. He was aware that someone was approaching him, but it was impossible for him to shake off his drowsiness before that someone got close enough to drive the muzzle of an automatic into his chest.

The watchman opened his eyes, stared up into a face that was masked with a triangle of handkerchief.

"Give, quick," said a husky voice. "Give us the key to Murdo's flat and make it snappy."

The watchman's eyes strayed into the shadows beyond the masked man. There was another somber figure waiting in the background. The watchman said: "I ain't got the key, I ain't." Then lent some truth to his statement by shoving the narrow key through the worn lining of his pocket and letting it go sliding down his pants leg.

The masked man ordered him to stand up. The watchman did as he was told, planting his right foot on top of the key which had fallen to the thick carpet from his trouser leg. The masked man gave him a quick frisk.

"Where's the key, damn it?" the masked man demanded.

The watchman raised plump shoulders. "I can't think where it is, I can't."

PUSHING the automatic against the watchman's spine, the masked man forced him out into a waiting car. There, a black sack was tossed over the watchman's head. A swift ride in the dark, direction and destination unknown. Then he was hustled from the car, stretched flat on his back on a wood floor, tied helplessly with ropes. And then the sack was removed.

He had swift visions of the most beautiful woman he had ever seen; a brazen statue of monstrous form, leering down at him; tall, lean men with yellow faces more inhuman than that of the brass image; and then a man who had no face at all except a grotesquely hideous mask of gold.

"The key. Tell me where the key is," came a muffled voice from behind the metal mask. "You know where the key is. Tell me."

The watchman tried to speak, gagged on the words. He shook his head. Terror of these exotic surroundings and strange people possessed him, but loyalty to Murdo was not easily shaken.

The masked man bent low. "The key, you fool. Have you any idea how long a time we can take to kill you? Have you any conception of the torment of which we are capable?" Again the watchman shook his head.

The masked man turned. "Bring," he said, "the hungry one."

The watchman closed his eyes. His mind prayed and blasphemed. And when he opened his eyes again, it was to see yellow fingers cutting away the front of his shirt with a knife that tasted blood twice in the process.

"Good!" the watchman heard a woman's voice say. "The smell will tempt the appetite of the hungry one."

The watchman saw one of the yellow men approach him bearing a large coconut husk. Another carried a strange ventilated box from which came sharp, animal squeaks. He would have cried out then against the torture that threatened him had not his tongue actually stiffened with fear. He could utter only inarticulate sounds.

Bending over him, the yellow man dumped the squeaking contents of the box into the coconut husk and then clapped the husk to the watchman's naked chest.

"A Burmese rat," the masked man whispered. "A rat that has been on a fast. He is hungry, my friend. Now where is the key?"

Little feet scampered over the watchman's chest, driving him mad with their tiny, scratching claws. A cold snout sniffed at his blood. Then needlelike teeth sank deep.

The watchman uttered a wail of agony and lapsed into unconsciousness. Icy water drenched his face. He came to, sobbing: "The rat! Take it away. Take it away."

"The key, you fool. Where is Murdo's key?" The masked man was bending over him, his golden face like that of some god who watched a human sacrifice with avid glances.

"The key," the watchman shrilled. "In the hall. On the rug. Dropped it—when— The rat! Take it away. It's eating...."

Then blissfully another interval of unconsciousness.

The masked man turned to the woman. He said: "He must have pushed the key through his pocket. If it's in the hall, everything should be easy." He gestured to one of the Mongols. "Take the rat away."

The Mongol grinned, uttered something in a guttural tongue. The masked man looked at the woman. She translated swiftly: "He says let the poor beast feed. There is no better food for it...."

X returned to the library, started a pedestal fan, took off his coat. He was restless. In the stifling heat, the unaccustomed quiet, lurked an unknown quantity that prodded that intuition of his. The air breathed danger.

There was a scratching on the window screen. X sprang toward the window, remembered that his gun was on the other side of the room in his coat. He backed toward the coat, his eyes on the window. Something tapped on the door. X turned to the door, and at that instant the window screen rattled, fell away, and a lithe, powerful man sprang into the room.

The man wore ragged Occidental garments, but they seemed strange to him. And no wonder! The yellow, scarred face, the flat nose, the high cheekbones proclaimed him a native of Mongolia. In his talonlike hand was a long-bladed knife.

X sprang toward his coat, but something tugged at his trouser leg, *thucked* into the wall. The right leg of his trousers was pinned to the wall with a Mongol's knife. And the cloth of Murdo's suit was strong stuff. The door of the library opened and another hideously yellow-faced man entered.

The new arrival held a gun in one hand and in the other a long white roll of cloth. X stooped, seized the hasp of the knife, pulled it from the wall. At that moment, the yellow Yezidee tossed one end of the roll of cloth at the Agent's feet.

Before X spread his shroud.

CHAPTER V

FOOD FOR RATS

BEFORE THE MONGOL had a chance to release the other end of the shroud, X seized the end of the cloth near his feet. He gave it a jerk that brought the yellow man within reach of a nasty haymaker that the Mongol took on the shoulder. The yellow man rocked back, caught himself by seizing the back of a chair.

At the same time, his companion, who had entered through the window, thrust a three-joint length of hollow bamboo almost into the Agent's mouth and blew upon the other end of it. A vaporous something clouded from the end of the tube and was dragged into the Agent's lungs by his inhalation.

The vaporous stuff had the unmistakable odor of *hashish*. Its effect was almost immediate in spite of all the will that X exerted against it. The Agent felt as though red-hot spurs were biting into his flesh. He went mad, completely berserk. Under the insidious influence of the drug all the inhibitions of civilization dropped from him like discarded garments. He had one desire and that was to kill.

A knife thrust along his side passed unfelt. He was in a world of fog, peopled only by hideous, scowling Mongol heads. He lashed out with fists and feet. He tore up chairs from the floor and hurled them at the yellow heads.

But for all the stimulation his normally Herculean strength had received, his fighting lacked direction and he had no defense. He never knew exactly when the blow that brought him down, was struck. There was simply an explosion in his brain and total darkness.

When they saw Agent X upon the floor the two Mongols went to the window of the library. There hung the rope by which one of them had gained entrance to the apartment. As soon as they had worked it loose from a hook above the window, they carried X and the rope into the living room, one end of which opened on the sun porch at the rear of the building.

On the porch lay the two bodyguards Murdo had employed. Both stretched out on the floor, narrow slivers of razor-edged bamboo thrust into their throats. They had bled to death soundlessly. The two Mongols exchanged a few guttural words, then, walking softly on green-soled shoes, they rounded the pools of blood on the porch floor, carrying X with them.[19]

One end of the rope they looped around the Agent's body, lowered him over the edge of the porch and into a waiting car in the parking lot below. They then slid down the rope, detached its grappling hook from the rail above when they had descended.

There was a man waiting beneath the steering wheel of the car. No sooner had the Mongols joined the unconscious Agent X than they sped across the lot into the alley.

But a pair of horrified eyes had watched all this from the shadows. And as the Mongol's car moved off, the slim figure of a girl darted across the lot, climbed into Art Murdo's flashy roadster.

THE AGENT'S first sensation was that of being hurled through empty space. Cold empty darkness was all about him, and there was a sickness in his stomach such as an aviator, power diving from the sky, might feel.

Then there was the dawn of light, a graying of the blackness, and the nausea passed. He sat up, looked dazedly about him. He might have been transported by magic to secret Asia. A smoky, yellow light coming from a brass-screened storm lantern of ancient design illuminated the room. Directly in front of him and back against the wall was a hideous, crouching demon, fashioned in brass and gaudily painted. Cruelty was cast into its metal face.

On each side of the brass god stood three tall, sinewy Mongols clad in white, tuniclike garments of silk. Their shaved heads were covered by peaked white caps around which scarlet silk was wound, turban fashion. The Mongols were as motionless as the hideous image they guarded.

X turned his head. On the other side of the room a white man was stretched on the floor, his torso stripped of all clothing. To all appearances the man was dead, or blissfully unconscious. His

---

19   AUTHOR'S NOTE: The Mongolian Yezidee, to show his contempt for the religion of the Moslems, wears green, the color sacred to the Moslems, beneath his feet.

hands and feet were roped to rings in the floor. A half of a huge coconut husk rested on his chest, and from beneath the husk came greedy, squeaking sounds. Cold chills wound around the Agent's spine like serpents. He had heard of such things, but he had never expected to see them.

X got to his feet. His powers of recuperation were truly remarkable. There was a slight pain in his head and a sensation of dizziness. Aside from that, he felt fit for anything—anything except *that,* as his eyes returned to the man on the floor, to the coconut husk that retained the hungry, squealing thing.

A door opened. Through it came first a small, gray-haired man with brassy-looking spectacles. X recognized the man immediately as Morton Edgewood, the pottery dealer who had so strangely disappeared; for X had seen Edgewood's picture in the newspaper before he had left for Washington. There was an expression of utter despair in the pottery dealer's eyes.

Behind Edgewood came a man and a woman, arm in arm. The man was tall and lean. Very little else could be told about him, for his face was masked by a golden Yezidee devil mask, fully as leering and hideous as the face of the brass god guarded by the Mongols.

The woman—it was she who called herself Erlika. Erlika dressed in flaming yellow, her long, dark hair coiled upwards in two horns about a conical, pagodalike cap of gold. Her lovely face was flushed. Her mouth smiled. In her eyes was an unholy animation, a gleam that softened immediately and became strangely alluring as her eyes fell upon Agent X. Resting in the girl's hand was a sort of scepter to which was attached a lifelike image of a lizard, its tiny jaws open.

"Welcome to the temple of Erlik, Art Murdo," she said to the Agent, and then she stood aside for the man in the devil mask to approach X.

Said the man in a muffled voice: "Erlik has spared your life, Murdo, that you may serve him better alive than dead."

"Nice of Erlik," replied X lightly in the voice of Murdo.

"I think that we have sufficiently demonstrated our power tonight," went on the masked man. "Your bodyguards had their throats slit, since their blood was deemed unworthy to grease our *toug.* One of your guards, the man who is now dead or dying on the floor, yielded keys to your apartment after he had been subjected to the torture with which you are doubtless acquainted. A hungry Burmese rat is imprisoned beneath the coconut shell, you see."

"That's a new one to me," X said calmly. "I must try it on someone some time. It would be more persuasive than burning the soles of the feet with cigarettes, I suppose."

"You were brought here for the purpose of urging you to join our cult," said the masked man. "We have a high regard for your abilities."

"Thank you," said X. "The only trouble is that when I join a lodge, I want to be head man right off. You'd have to let me have your devil mask and run the show. By the way, what does your organization do besides commit murder for the fun of it?"

"Blood is the food and drink of Erlik," said the masked man sternly.

"Erlik should be well fed," X commented. "But aside from feeding Erlik—"

"YEZIDEE are the rightful masters of the earth. It is written on top of the world that we shall annihilate civilization. This is but the beginning of things. We sow the seed which our followers shall reap. America is the logical place for our beginning.

"First of all, those who live outside the law, like you do, Murdo, shall be drawn into our folds. From them we shall gain new riches and capable followers. For months, perhaps years, citizens will go on living their lives, while within those dark corners where America's criminal element gathers, the cult of the Yezidee shall hold forth, controlling with its power the lives of government officials until the day when all America shall be ours.

"From the Eight Towers of Black China, the power of the Yezidee shall stretch like tight strong arms to embrace the world. From Baga Nor—"

"Excuse me for interrupting the travelogue," X said, "but what was that about getting wealth from America's criminal element? Do you have the idea that I'm going to toss my take into your bank account to stretch a telegraph system like eight strong arms from the leaning tower of Pisa to the Lakehurst mooring mast or something? Brother, you and I aren't going to get along!"

"Do you mean that you refuse to join with us?"

"I think that you've got the idea," X said, lips smiling disdainfully. "Besides, you're nuts."

Erlika took swaying steps to the side of the masked one. "We have ways of persuading the unwilling. Look at Morton Edgewood. He would lay down his life for me, would you not, nice old man?"

Edgewood looked frightened. Erlika tapped his head gently with the lizard wand she carried. She laughed. "You are not going to be stubborn, Art Murdo?"

X smiled. "Lady, a beauty like you could probably get anything out of a man. But when you touch Art Murdo's bank account you're fooling with dynamite. I'm getting out of your temple and I'm coming back. And when I come back, I'll have the best choppers and rodmen in the country with me. You think you can take over this town after I've run it for years? Well, the whole world can join your crazy lodge if it wants to, but this town is mine!"

The masked man glanced at Erlika. She stepped swiftly toward X and extended the lizard wand toward the Agent's face.

But at that moment, the door of the room swung open. The silhouette of an automatic snouted into the room, spat orange-yellow flame. The screaming slug of lead smashed the lizard wand from Erlika's hand.

CHAPTER VI

MURDO'S GIRL

SELDOM, OUTSIDE OF the vortex of a cyclone, do things happen as quickly as they did in the Yezidee temple immediately following that mysterious shot that had saved X from he knew not what. But what he could imagine.

First of all, there was the sudden and unaccountable presence of the person who had fired the shot. That red-haired, angel-faced person sprang lightly into the room, grinned at X, flung the gun she had used in X's general direction. X had to leap high and to one side to yank the gun out of the air. When he came down, it seemed one of the Mongols was almost under him, knife in hand.

X let the yellow man have the barrel of the gun across the side of the head with such force that the Mongol pivoted dizzily and struck the floor. X took a split-second to look around. Erlika was standing at the base of the brass devil god, eyes flashing, shouting out orders in Mongol dialect.

Two of the Mongols had closed in in front of their masked leader. Another Mongol was taking catlike bounds toward the red-haired girl. Two more were coming at X from different directions. Gray-haired Morton Edgewood, pale-faced with fear, was creeping behind the brass image of the devil god.

X had to make a quick choice. One of the Mongols was in an excellent position to knife him from the rear. But across the room, another had come to grips with the redheaded girl. X thought of himself last and delayed his move for self preservation long enough to shoot a leg out from under the yellow man who was trying to knife the redhead.

Instantly X dropped almost to all fours in time to catch the Mongol who sprang from behind him, by means of a body-block which pitched the yellow man heels over head. Straightening, X met the flash of a knife in his face, seized a yellow wrist of his second attacker. He held off the knife, spilled the man over his extended leg.

The Agent sprang toward the two Mongols who seemed to be guarding the masked man. If he could but lay the leader by the heels the whole elaborate and deadly scheme of the cult might be defeated. The two Mongols parted suddenly before X's onrush.

His hand, cupping the gun, brushed the ear of one before he could check the blow and save his strength. Directly behind that point where X expected to find the masked leader, there was a closed door. Then he heard the redhead's frantic cry: *"Art!"*

He turned, dashed across the room to where one of the yellow men had the redheaded girl by the throat. X socked the Mongol at the base of the brain with his clenched fist. The man went down, still clinging to the girl's throat with the relentless grip of the jaws of a bulldog. The redhead fell on top of him, and X had to hack the wrist of the Yezidee with his gun barrel until bones splintered, before he broke the hold.

Then he dragged the girl to her feet, shoved her toward the door. He darted a glance over his shoulder, saw two of the yellow men coming through another door. They were burdened with an antiquated machine gun which could nevertheless make a man's body look like a sieve. There was a time to run and a time to fight.

This, X decided, was the time to run, inasmuch as he was fully responsible for this heroic and fascinating redheaded girl who had risked much to save him. He tried one more shot over his shoulder before pushing the girl through the door.

X slammed the door on the way out. The girl, who evidently remembered perfectly the way she had come in, led right and left through a short hall, came to a door and flung it open. Ahead was the darkness of the night.

"The roadster," the girl cried. "Over there!" She pointed at a flashy car parked in the center of a rough and rolling lawn and about a hundred feet from the house.

The machine gun came to life, spat lead promiscuously. Mongols had gained the door and were firing with automatics. And then a head, an arm, and a gun thrust up over the edge of the rumble compartment of the roadster toward which they were running. The gun in the car streamed slivers of flame.

FOR AN instant X thought they were caught between two fires. But glancing back, he saw the Mongols had ducked back within the door and were firing with more caution, though very little better aim. The person in the roadster rumble was covering their escape with a wild fusillade of bullets.

They gained the car. X shoved the redhead in and followed. The man in the rumble stood upright, yelled in a mushy voice: "How'zat, chief?" And then as X started the car forward, he nearly tumbled out.

"Whitey!" gasped the girl. "How did you get here?"

Whitey took the wind in his teeth, leaned forward so that his tow-colored head came between the Agent's and the girl's. "You brought me, toots, though damned if I knew anything about it until the fireworks began. Where in hell are we?"

Lights of the roadster had picked out a drive. X nosed the car into the drive, wheeled it around a curve that edged the corner of a dilapidated cemetery. To the south of the road, X saw the lights at the outskirts of the city.

"It was this way," Whitey was yelling in X's ear. "I had a drink or two on my way back to your place. I got to thinking it was too damned hot to sleep indoors, so when I got to your place I just thought the rumble seat of this fire engine would make a better bed than a bed would. Next time I deep outdoors, don't anybody wake me up like that again. Gives me the jitters."

X stole a glance at the girl beside him. With the wind streamlining her hair, his eyes caught a perfect profile against the moonlit horizon. A forehead with a babyish bulge, a saucy nose, rather large lips, a determined chin, the smooth curve of her bare throat. Was this, he wondered, "Dearest Edna?" Now was as good a time as any to find out.

"Edna—" he began.

"Yeah, what?" the girl answered.

"How come you happened along when you did?"

"Well, I tried to get over for the party, as I said I would, but dad had an emergency case out in the country and I had to go with him and help. So I was late getting to your apartment. Whom should I see but Art Murdo, the Magnificent, being lowered from his apartment on the end of a rope. I simply followed in your car. You told me I could use the roadster any time. And what was that crack you made once about a respectable doctor's daughter not making the kind of a gal for you?"

X smiled. "I'll have to take it back. You were wonderful."

She looked at him sharply, then bounced across the seat until she was as close to him as possible. "Where do you get that past tense, Art? I still am wonderful."

X put his arm across the girl's shoulders. Her head nestled against his chest. In the rumble seat, Whitey yawned. "Don't mind me, folks," the tow-head said.

It was queer—two kids drawn into crime by the magnetic personality of Art Murdo. One of them, the man, not amply supplied with wit, and what brain he had sodden with alcohol, would naturally have followed a stronger character than his own. It was unfortunate he had chosen Murdo. And the girl, evidently a physician's daughter, enlightened, brilliant, brazen, deliberately seeking the searing flame that was Murdo, like the moth that dances into the candle flame.

Lips against the girl's hair, an expression of pity escaped X. "Poor kid!"

"Lucky girl," she sighed, and was very still for the rest of the short trip across town.

THERE WERE cops in Murdo's apartment when X arrived—a couple of plain-clothes men who addressed X as "Art" and wanted to talk with him in private. Whitey and Edna disappeared into another part of the apartment while X took the two dicks into the library.

"Now, what went on here tonight, Art?" asked one of the dicks, settling himself in a chair. "Folks heard the sounds of a row and investigated, found three of your men lying in their own blood, slivers of bamboo in their throats."

"I was kidnaped," X said.

"And you won't talk about it, like that Mongolian prince in the hotel, huh?"

"On the contrary, I don't mind telling you that I was kidnaped by Mongols. The same six Mongols, I believe, mentioned by the truck driver who was assassinated in the Edgewood pottery shop. Furthermore, I saw Edgewood himself. He seems to be the tool of this gang of cutthroats. I was taken to a house on the edge of town near an old cemetery. You can go there and raid the place, and about all you'll find is another of my men, dead, his body partially eaten by a Burmese rat and possibly a big, brass idol too big to move."

"Are you kiddin' us?" asked the other detective.

"I was never more serious in my life," X said. "If you want me, you'll know where to find me." He stood up. "So long."

After the police had left, X sat in the library for some time, his mind occupied with what had taken place in the Yezidee temple that night. The six Mongols and the leader, plus Erlika's witchery, plus the knowledge of the use of the drug *hashish* in forms with which the Occidental scientists were unfamiliar, made a combination hard to beat. The savagery of the Yezidee and his philosophy of destruction presented for the first time a genuine danger to the western world.

The Agent's thoughts were interrupted by the sudden appearance of Edna, attired in a pair of Murdo's pajamas rolled up at the trouser cuffs and the sleeves. She sat down on the arm of the Agent's chair and fingered his hair.

"You don't mind if I stay here tonight? You see, dad will be out with his patient—"

"It looks very much as though I'll have to invite you to stay," X said, looking up into innocent blue eyes.

"Dad won't mind," she said. "He knows I can take care of myself."

"Your dad is a fool," X said coldly. And then, because she looked hurt, he took her hand, fingered an enormous diamond solitaire upon her third finger.

"I'd like a plain gold band to go with that," the girl said.

X laughed. "Drop into the jewelry store tomorrow and get one," he said, putting into the sentence a harshness that cut the girl deeply.

He knew precisely what he was doing and what Art Murdo had done. Murdo had begun his conquest in the guise of a gentleman, but X knew the man too well to suppose that he had any intention of carrying out any promises he had made the girl. So through his impersonation of Murdo, he wanted to make the girl see the ruthless racket king in his true colors.

The girl went to the door, a pitiful yet comical figure in the baggy pajamas. At the door, she turned half around. X saw the glint of tears in her eyes. "You—you'd better get some rest," she said. "Good night."

"Good night," X mumbled. He leaned back in his chair and closed his eyes. He heard the soft footsteps of the girl, felt her lips brush his timidly and tenderly. He did not open his eyes. But he did not sleep.

IT WAS at dawn that Agent X left Murdo's apartment, but not as Murdo. Though he wore Murdo's clothes, his face had once again become that of A.J. Martin. In this disguise he returned to the hotel and to his room where the real Murdo, disguised as Martin, still slept beneath the dose of drug that X had given him.

As soon after breakfast time as he thought fitting, X phoned the room of Djamok, the enlightened Mongol prince.

"Martin speaking," he announced. "I intend to have a talk with you. Shall I come in through the window or shall it be the door?"

Djamok laughed. "I being most happy to welcome you at the door," he said.

Two minutes later X was installed in a chair facing Djamok who cuddled his Scotch pipe. The prince listened politely as X related the happenings of the night before, keeping himself out of the picture entirely, and acting as though the adventure had happened to Art Murdo. When he had finished, Djamok asked:

"How do you know all this, eh?"

"Murdo told the police, and I have ways of getting information from the police," X said.

"I being familiar with Mongol Yezidee, I will tell you what I know," Djamok began. "First, understand all Mongol not being Yezidee. This Erlika, she being but a symbol of Erlik's daughter. She being one of many white women chosen by the Yezidee, one white woman each generation, to serve as Erlika, goddess. She probably brought up from babyhood in Yezidee temple and being taught unspeakable things and magic the Yezidee practice."

"I think I understand," X said. "Where do these white goddesses come from?"

"This one probably American baby traveling with parents in Asia," Djamok explained. "Otherwise, how she come back to America. You hearing of kidnapings of white travelers by Mongol bandits? When a new Erlika is needed, bandits search for new white baby girl to take old Erlika's place. She being brought up like goddess, eh? Erlika is Erlik's daughter—the devil's daughter, eh? She being brought up bad and learning things not knowing about devil-magic."

"But the other Mongols—how could their entrance into this country be managed?"

There was a far-away look in Djamok's soft, intelligent eyes. "Many things I not knowing about Yezidee. Many things no man knowing—strange things. The Yezidee may sleep like death—what you call it?"

"Catalepsy?" X suggested.

"So. Artificial catalepsy, sleeping like dead. The Yezidee makes the effort. He willing himself to sleep like dead thing. In that state, he not being in need of food. He being like dead, he could be shipped on boat concealed in some box marked something else, eh."

"Could be shipped in a big urn, for instance," X said.

X thanked the Mongul prince for his information. It had been more than information he had been seeking. Djamok was an enigma, and X had sought to see behind the kindly, mild face of the yellow man. He had not succeeded.

Returning to his room, X once more assumed the disguise of Art Murdo. Choosing an opportune time, he went down the fire escape at the end of the corridor and walked briskly to a cab stand where he engaged a taxi to take him back to Murdo's apartment.

The phone was ringing as he entered the apartment. X hurried into the library where he found Edna had picked up the phone. He took it from her hand, said hello in Murdo's voice.

A frightened, miserable old man's voice came over the phone: "This is Morton Edgewood speaking. Last night I heard you defy Erlika and her yellow devils, so I am calling you instead of the police. I escaped during the fighting. I am only hoping that my information may help you in ridding the country of these terrible people. I know you are a criminal, Mr. Murdo, but I know you have a selfish purpose in trying to get rid of Erlika and her devils."

"Yes. Go on," X urged impatiently.

"I dare not call the police. I am wanted for murder which I did not knowingly do. Erlika uses some drug which puffs from the mouth of that lizardlike thing to enslave men's minds. I was not conscious of what I was doing when I killed the truck driver in my shop. I want to clear my name before I die."

"Chin up," X snapped. "You're not going to die."

"There is no escape. Listen, while there is time. The Mongols have added to their gang a group of criminals once directed by a man by the name of Crespis. Tonight at nine o'clock, an armored car bearing the payroll for the Wayde Machine Company will be at the corner of Hurst and Salter Streets. As the car passes that corner there will be a holdup.

"It will be the most horrible thing of its kind in the history of crime, for if there is any resistance, not a man in the car nor any policemen or any bystanders will be permitted to live. The Mongols have hideous ways of killing, and they delight in bloodshed. And Mongols will direct whites in this crime. That is all."

"Wait. Where are you now?"

"I am hiding in the basement of a deserted garage on Orange—" From the receiver of the phone at the Agent's ear came a cry of mortal terror.

X CLACKED the receiver back on its hook. He turned to Edna. "Where's Whitey?" he asked.

"He said he was going out and get tight because I didn't love him."

"He would, when I need him!" X snapped.

"Can't I help?" the girl asked eagerly.

"Yes. You can drive me to Orange Avenue in my car. I may need both hands to shoot with. Mongols again."

X searched the drawers of Murdo's desk, found an automatic, pocketed it. The girl had grabbed up her purse and was already running toward the door. X followed. Out in the parking space behind the building they got into Murdo's car, Edna at the wheel.

The girl knew how to drive fast and get away with it. Eight minutes later, X sighted the deserted garage on Orange Avenue. He said to the girl: "I'll get out here. You drive around the block and pick me up, say about five minutes later."

The girl looked at him, her lips set. "I will not!"

She braked the car to the curb and was out of it as soon as X was. The Agent led the way to the sliding doors of the garage, found them locked from the inside. The door of the garage office yielded after some coaxing, and X entered, flashlight in hand, Edna behind him.

The girl got hold of the tail of his coat, hampered his movement as he crossed the greasy concrete floor of the big building, now and then venturing a beam of light, searching for the entrance to the basement. When he found the basement entrance, it was somebody's old door set in the floor, the doorknob replaced with a ring. A tiny string of light passed up through the keyhole of the door.

X dropped to his knees, took from his pocket a little rod that resembled a very lean lead pencil. It was actually a miniature periscope and very well adapted for the purpose to which he put it. He thrust the instrument through the keyhole and squinted in the end of it, turning the instrument slowly from right to left. What he saw caused a hoarse exclamation to explode from his lips.

He stood up. "Stay back, Edna. They've gone. They've left a souvenir you wouldn't want to see."

He opened the door and descended rickety steps. The basement was floored only with packed earth. A broom handle had been stuck in the floor to act as the wooden neck for the head of old Morton Edgewood. Wisps of gray hair had been tied to the wooden upright. Blood still dripped from torn blood vessels. The decapitated body had been thoughtfully provided with the white Yezidee shroud.

X turned from the revolting scene and hurried up the steps to rejoin Edna. The girl sought his arm in the darkness and squeezed it hysterically.

"No nerves, now," X said. "You get in the car and run back to the apartment."

"What for?" she demanded.

"Because somebody has to be there to answer the phone in case Whitey calls," X told her. He was expecting no call, but he had to have an excuse to get rid of the girl.

As soon as she was gone, X crouched in the darkness. He needed no light and no mirror other than his supersensitive fingers for re-shaping his features and becoming once more Mr. A.J. Martin. He left the garage, walked up Orange Avenue until a street car bound for the center of the city came within sight. He boarded this and rode down within a couple of blocks of police headquarters.

As he left the car, he failed to notice a plump-faced man with flop ears get off behind him, follow him to the police station, even enter the corridor of the building.

At the desk, X demanded to see the chief of police and was told that the chief was busy.

"He will see me, nevertheless," X said, "in regard to the where-abouts of Mr. Morton Edgewood, wanted for murder. I know the truth about Mr. Edgewood."

The desk sergeant got up and personally escorted X to the chief's office. The plump man with the lop ears walked calmly from the police station, saying to a cop at the door: " 'Ow's the weather? 'Ot enough for you, I 'opes."

SEATED across from the chief of police, X quietly and calmly related all that Edgewood had told him over the phone concerning the payroll robbery that was to take place that night. He also revealed the place where Edgewood's body might be found.

The chief listened gravely. "The payroll robbery," he said finally, "won't be a success, thanks to you, Mr. Martin. We'll have men there to take the wind out of those yellow devils' sails."

X smiled slightly. "I do not think you will be troubled with the yellow devils. Your chief job is to take care of the remnant of Monte Crespis' gang." For X believed that before the time for the payroll heist, he would be able to take care of the Mongols personally....

The fat man with the lop ears entered a corner saloon some distance from police headquarters. The nickel in his fingers found the slot of a booth phone. He dialed a number, whispered his message and went out.

On the other side of the city, the shell-pink ears of Erlika received that message and she in turn employed a telephone.

"Beloved," she said in the transmitter, "Cock ran into the newspaperman, Martin, entirely by accident, though he claims to have been shadowing him. He followed Martin to the police station. Edgewood must have been talking to Martin when our men found him, for Martin gave information concerning Edgewood to the police. Martin will have to die, you understand. And you will have to take care of the job yourself, because by the time Martin has returned to his hotel, we will need the Mongols for the proposed robbery.

"It will be absolutely safe for you to kill him. I have planned the murder so cleverly he cannot escape and you will be absolutely safe. Listen closely...."

CHAPTER VII

SLEEPERS IN THE TOMB

ONE HOUR LATER, Agent X, again in the disguise of Art Murdo, crouched behind a tombstone in the old cemetery near the house at the edge of town in which he had been held a prisoner the night before.

He had already explored the house and had found it deserted, as he had expected. But the cemetery—six ferocious Mongols had to be kept somewhere. And if the Yezidee practiced artificial catalepsy, the deathlike sleep, what better place to keep them than one of the three old stone vaults in the cemetery?

X had dressed in the darkest business suit he had been able to find in Murdo's extensive wardrobe. Beneath his suit coat, and attached to his belt, was a mysterious black box of metal. In spite of the heat of the night, X wore black leather gloves, the palms of which were covered with a strong metal mesh.

He had not long to wait until the pale moonlight showed the figure of a woman dressed in black, picking her way delicately among the old graves and approaching one of the vaults. The woman's face was nearly concealed by a hood of black pulled over her head. But there was no mistaking that alluring figure. The woman was Erlika, child of Satan.

She stopped at the door of the vault and X heard her key grate in the ancient lock. There was a snarl of rusty hinges as she pushed back the heavy door and entered the world of the dead.

X sprang from his hiding place, hurried to the door of the tomb. He pressed gently upon the bronze panel with his gloved hands. Erlika had locked the door from the inside, and it would have taken the strength of six men to have battered in that door. Time and patience alone would accomplish an entrance.

X dropped to his knees, searching his pocket as he did so to procure one of the simplest and yet one of the most important tools which he carried—a needle-nosed *oustiti*.[20]

With breathless care, X inserted the tool in the lock, felt around until he could grasp the tip of Erlika's key. Holding the handles of the tool tightly, he turned it small fractions of an inch at a time. When he had turned the key completely around, he withdrew the tool with the same caution.

There was no possibility of opening the door quietly so he simply gave it a kick with his right shoe and stepped into the vault.

With a swift glance, X recorded the scene within the vault. Six of the crypts had been entered. Six old coffins had been removed. In the dark crypts moldering bones of the rightful owners of the coffins were nakedly exposed. The six coffins occupied the center of the floor. But in only one, enfolded on the soft dust of decayed cushions, lay a Mongol. The others were evidently away on some errand.

As X entered, Erlika straightened up from the coffin where the lone Mongol lay in his cataleptic sleep. In her hand was a small glass vial. Her red lips peeled back from set white teeth in a snarl. Her eyes flashed. Yet even in her fury she was the most beautiful woman X had ever seen. It seemed incredible to find her here breaking the evil spell which she herself had probably induced upon her sleeping servant.

Erlika uttered a single guttural syllable, and the Mongol over whose coffin she had been stooping sprang to his feet, snatched a knife from his garments.

Agent X, legs wide-spread, empty-handed, waited for the yellow man's lunge.

THE MONGOL hurdled his coffin, knife upraised. The Agent's gloved fingers flexed and were patient. The yellow man, slightly surprised that X made no move to protect himself, paused a moment, then seized X's throat in one hand, drove down at X's upturned face with the knife.

Swiftly, surely, X's right hand shot upwards, closed upon the knife wrist of the Mongol. His left hand came up as far as his belly,

---

20   *AUTHOR'S NOTE: This device belongs primarily to the burglar who makes a practice of entering hotel rooms locked from the inside. It is a slender-nosed pair of pliers, the inside of the jaws of which are concave and knurled so that the tip of the skeleton key inserted in the lock from the other side may be grasped and turned.*

touched a switch on the front of the black box strapped there. The Mongol took a writhing half turn to the right and collapsed on the floor, unconscious.

For a moment, the look of triumph on Erlika's face became one of bewilderment and then immediately one of fear. For X stepped over the fallen man and approached the woman. On his face was a smile of deadly determination. He said in Murdo's voice:

"Come here, sweetheart. Let's see if the electric glove matches your devil magic."

Erlika backed to the farthest wall of the tomb. Her hands crept along the cold stone, groping for something—some weapon, anything with which to stop this man.

"Come, Erlika," X urged. "If you're a good girl, I won't turn on the juice into these gloves. Besides, I gave your Yezidee such a dose he'll probably never come out of it. I doubt if the battery could stand much more."

The girl sprang to the right and at the same time drew a gun from the folds of her dark gown. But X leaped at the same time, seizing her in his arms, crushing her gun hand against her own chest. He held her a moment.

"Pull the trigger, Ekrlia, and save the hangman a very unpleasant task."

She spat at his face. "Son of a pig!" she snarled. "Release me. I am the daughter of Erlik."

"You are a very beautiful, completely spoiled, thoroughly wicked woman," he said with a laugh. "And nothing more."

She raised her head suddenly, and her teeth snapped at his throat. At the same time the hard, pointed toes of her pumps kicked his ankles. And then, as his hold upon her became even more firm, she dropped her gun, melted toward him. Her lips, less than an inch from his, whispered while her eyes brimmed with tears.

"Please. You do not understand Erlika. I have only been in this country a year. Think! I was taken from my mother as a baby and brought up in the Yezidee temple. I know nothing else. I came here because I wanted to be with my people. I was tired being worshiped as a goddess by yellow-faced men. I wanted to live like Americans do—to have a home of my own with some nice husband. I wanted to have children and worry about them catching measles. I wanted to have to worry about the grocery bills—"

X laughed. "Lady, as long as you can act like that, your ambition to worry about the grocery bills can't be realized. Hollywood will find you."

The red lips quivered. "You do not believe me. You think I know nothing of love?"

"I think you know quite a bit more than you ought to," X said.

"Please let me go, Art Murdo. Or better, take me with you. We could do much together, you and I. Is it a bargain?"

X nodded. "I have every intention of taking you with me."

"Then kiss me."

X kissed the inviting lips, then released the girl, and seized her right wrist in his firm grasp. "Oh, I forgot to add when I promised to take you with me that you will be held a prisoner. You can, in fact, consider yourself kidnaped."

"Pig!" she cried. "Deceiver!" And she struggled to free herself from that grip which was like a bracelet of steel about her wrist.

"Ah-ah," X cautioned. "I will let you feel the sting of the electric glove."

OBEDIENTLY she subsided and together they left the vault, X taking the precaution to lock the Mongol inside the vault. But he was only one out of six. Where were the other Yezidee? Perhaps they would soon be looking for Erlika. Yes, Erlika would be the bait that would bring them and the man in the metal mask, the big boss of the mob, within X's reach.

The drive back to Murdo's apartment was one which X was never to forget. Three times Erlika tried to throw herself from the speeding car. Twice she tried to wreck them by jerking the wheel from X's hands. She tried to scratch out his eyes once, and finally embraced him passionately in an effort to make him crash into a street car.

X drove the car directly into the basement garage of the apartment. No sooner had Erlika spied the garage attendant than she yelled: "Help! He's kidnaping me!"

X looked at the attendant and winked. The man remained grave until X passed him a twenty dollar bill which brought an answering wink and a whispered: "The last one didn't have so much spirit, Mr. Murdo."

X got the girl into the elevator and from there to Murdo's apartment. As he was about to unlock the door, it was opened by Whitey, who evidently possessed a key to the place. Beyond Whitey, X saw Edna just removing her hat in front of the mirror.

Whitey took a look at Erlika. His mouth fell open, and for a moment he seemed powerless to move or speak. Finally, he backed away from the door, asked: "Where did you get that angel, chief?"

X raised his eyebrows. "She came from the farthest extremity from the natural habitat of the angels, Whitey."

"Why, it's—" Edna began, immediately recognizing Erlika.

Erlika gave the redheaded girl a haughty stare. "You will all pay dearly for this!" she threatened.

"I know," X said dryly, "you're dynamite. But we've a place for dangerous things."

Between the two spare bedrooms was what had been intended for a dressing room. It had only one window and it was secured by means of a metal grill closely resembling a Venetian blind from the outside. The single door was backed by a steel plate and fitted with special locks.

Murdo had evidently found it convenient to use this room as a prison for some of his enemies. It was to this room that they took Erlika. After he had locked the heavy, sound-proof door, her angry cries could not be heard more than three feet away.

He started back to the others, but Edna came running to him. Her blue eyes were frightened, her cheeks slightly pale. "There are policemen outside, Whitey says. You'd better get that woman out of here."

X shook his head. "Unless they have a search warrant, we don't have to worry on that score. Open the door, Edna. Where's Whitey?"

Whitey was in the living room thoughtfully smoking a cigarette. X joined him and waited for Edna to usher the police into the room. Two plain-clothes men entered followed by old Mrs. Fauvre, Whitey's mother.

Whitey dropped his cigarette, stood up. "Mom," he said hoarsely.

The old woman ran around the cops, tried to take her tall, lanky son in her arms. "My boy! My poor, misguided boy! You didn't do it. Tell them you didn't do it!"

Whitey looked blankly from his mother to the cops and then to X. The old woman suddenly released her son and directed her entreaties to Agent X.

"Tell them he didn't do it, Mr. Murdo! You've got to help him. He's always been a good boy at heart. He wouldn't kill anybody. Anything that's bad about him you taught him, Mr. Murdo. Now you owe him something—help, at least."

X looked over the old woman's head. "Will you two coppers kindly come to life and let us in on something?"

One of the dicks stepped forward and put a hand on Whitey's shoulder. "I've got a warrant for the arrest of Delmar Fauvre for the murder of A.J. Martin."

FOR A FRACTION of a second, X nearly lost his composure so necessary to his impersonation of Murdo. There was only one man who could possibly have been mistaken for A.J. Martin. That man was Art Murdo himself, disguised as A.J. Martin, and now in a drugged condition in the hotel rooms X had engaged in that name.

It was the most natural mistake in the world for the murderer to make, and at the same time it created a number of confusing possibilities. As soon as the body was subjected to close scrutiny, it would be discovered the supposed Martin was Murdo. Then if Murdo was dead, the Agent's scheme of impersonation would be discovered.

"Where did this happen? When did it happen?" X demanded.

"In the Maywood Hotel," the dick said. "We don't know exactly when, because the coroner's physician had not yet arrived when we left. But it's open and shut. One of the room service girls at the hotel saw this Delmar Fauvre—she called him Whitey—going into the room with a knife in his hand. And the clerk remembered signing this Whitey Fauvre for the room directly across the hall from Martin. So—"

X started for the door. "Let's get over there immediately. I want the lowdown on this. Edna, stay here. I want to—" He left the sentence in the air and made eyes in the direction of the room in which Erlika was imprisoned. Then he led the way from the room with the two dicks, Whitey, and Mrs. Fauvre trailing behind.

In the police car driving to the hotel, X turned to the silent Whitey. "Well, what about it?"

"I didn't do it," the towhead said, moodily pulling at his mustache. "But what in hell's the use if some jealous dame wants to tell the cops that I did?"

"If the chambermaid is lying, we'll break her story," X said, more to cheer Whitey's mother than to hearten Whitey.

The kid was hard. He had been with Murdo long enough to have learned to look callously upon murder. And if he had been drunk, as he usually was, there was no telling what he might have done.

The first move on arriving at the hotel was to take a sample of Whitey's writing and compare it with the hotel register card the clerk claimed he had filled out. The writing on the card was extremely shaky. It would be difficult to obtain an accurate comparison of the two samples.

X was eager to get to the scene of the crime, but he first made Mrs. Fauvre comfortable in the lobby and assured her that he would do as much as possible for her boy if he was innocent.

"Oh, he is innocent!" the old woman sobbed, wringing the Agent's hand. "You've got to make them believe he is, Mr. Murdo."

X smiled and hurried after the police and Whitey to the elevator.

Fortunately, the coroner's physician had not yet arrived, X reflected as he entered the suite of rooms he himself had engaged. The man who looked like A.J. Martin was lying on the bed in the same position in which X had left him. He had been stabbed in the heart. There was nothing to indicate a struggle, naturally, and no evidence of attempted robbery, the police pointed out.

"All right," X rapped. "Let's see the room across the hall that Whitey is supposed to have engaged for this murder business."

A detective produced a pass key, unlocked the door of the room opposite the murder scene. He let X walk in ahead. Everything was in perfect order. There was no evidence of recent occupancy, nothing except the smell of something burning—not tobacco. The bathroom was the source of the burned odor. X led the way into the bathroom and there saw the brown metal waste basket, which would have ordinarily rested beside the writing desk, standing in the bathtub. Inside was a wad of newspapers partially burned.

X seized the paper before the detective could lay hands on it. The burned portion crumbled beneath his fingers. The remaining portion was tinged a slight yellow. He unwrapped the wad, held the open paper in his hands. In the very center of the paper was a tow-colored false mustache, a little spirit gum clinging to the center of it.

"I'll be damned!" The dick pounced upon the mustache and bounced triumphantly from the room.

X went into the hall. Whitey and the detectives were crowding around, staring at that little piece of crepe hair.

"I guess," one of the dicks was saying, "this just about clears Whitey of the charge. Somebody was trying to frame him and didn't get away with it. The disguise the killer wore in order to make himself resemble Whitey didn't burn as it was intended to. I guess you can go tell your mother the good news."

Whitey grinned, mumbled his thanks, and hurried off.

AGENT X looked up and down the hall. A red light at the rear of the hall indicated the fire escape. It was barely possible that the scheme would work. It *had* to work. He felt that he was too near the climax of his fight with the Mongols to risk having his scheme upset by police interference. And he would be assured of such interference as soon as some of the officials discovered that the supposed A.J. Martin was Murdo.

Without any further thought on the subject, X reached into his pocket and took out a sphere about the size of a large marble. This he threw with all his strength toward the end of the hall nearest the elevators and farthest from the fire escape.

The little ball struck the wall and bounded around the corner. There was a faint pop as the percussion cap it contained ignited the fuse. The ball was a simple firework device with which X hoped to produce a mild panic.

The end of the hall where the little ball landed was suddenly filled with dense black smoke tinged with red flame. X shouted, "Fire!" pointed at the smoke, and immediately the police dashed toward the source of the smoke.

X sprang into the room where the corpse lay, lifted the body, slung it over his shoulder and got out into the hall. The corridor was already crowded with excited people, rushing through the smoke. Several were making toward the fire escape. Others were rushing in a panic in the opposite direction. In the general confusion it must have appeared that X was making a heroic effort to save a man from the fire.

He got to the fire escape, clattered down flight after flight of iron steps, passing one person after another in spite of his burden. Not until he reached the alley below did a hitch occur in his plan. Out of the shadows stepped a man. A flashlight beamed into X's face. Reflecting rays of light caught on the badge of a uniformed cop.

"Let me give you a hand, brother," said the cop. "Put the man down on the ground. He's probably suffocated from the smoke."

"Got to get him to the hospital," X panted and made an effort to get around the cop. But he was all but exhausted from having lugged the body down the fire escape, and he could have scarcely hoped to have escaped the cop.

The officer got squarely in X's path. His pop-eyes saw the blood that stained the shirt of the murdered man. At the same time, someone above, who had undoubtedly discovered X's hoax, shouted: "Stop that man!"

There was only one thing that X could do and he managed it quite effectively. He stumbled forward, bent low to allow the corpse to slide down to its feet. Then, with all his strength, he shoved the body into the cop. Corpse and cop went down together. X darted from the alley, his energy rapidly returning to him after he dropped his burden.

The cop had regained his feet and drawn his gun. His were not the bullets that followed X as he sprinted up the alley. Some of the police who were in the hotel tried hard to check his bumblebee flight, but he was beyond the accurate range of hand weapons.

At the end of the alley, he ducked into the back door of a tavern on the corner. The place was darkened for the dancers who struggled around a small dance floor to the swing of an electric organ and a pair of saxophones. X passed the dancers, came to the front of the tavern. On his way, he picked up a check intended for four patrons who were on the point of leaving.

The foursome seemed drunk enough to take a joke, and X promptly stepped into their midst, laughing, slapping the men on the back, calling them by names he made up. When they reached the cashier, X paid the check, and there were no objections made.

"Get us a taxi, toots," X said to the cashier.

One of the men in X's adopted party tapped him on the shoulder and said: "My car's out in front, pal. Where you live?"

X gave the man an address within a block of Murdo's apartment. The man thought it was fine because he was going in the same direction. They walked out the door and across the sidewalk just as a pair of policemen came running along, looking, no doubt, for the Agent. X stepped into the car with the others, suggested that the driver step on it.

He was working now desperately against time. If the police got to Murdo's apartment in time to prevent him from reaching Erlika, his plans would be hopelessly defeated. In kidnaping Erlika, he had intended to sit back and wait for the leader of the Mongol pack to attempt a rescue. Thus he would have the leader and the five remaining Mongols.

But now he would have to find some other place to hide the girl, inasmuch as the police would naturally cover Murdo's apartment closely. Where that other place could be, he had no idea.

HE HURRIED up to Murdo's apartment, unlocked the door and was immediately greeted by Edna's cheerful cry: "That you, Art?"

She came out of a bedroom, holding a gun in her hand. X took the gun from her and put it in his own pocket. He seized her shoulders in both of his hands. His eyes were so earnest they broke the girl's usually level stare.

"I'm in a spot," X said tensely in Murdo's voice. "Getting Whitey out of the jam, I'm in one myself. The police are after me, and we've got to get Erlika out of here. We can't let her go. Where will we take her?"

"How about your country place?" Edna suggested promptly.

"Right! I hadn't thought of that." The simple reason that he had overlooked this hiding place was that he did not know of its existence. "You'll drive. You know the way?"

"Of course. We've been there half a dozen times at least."

"Then I'll get Erlika. We're in for a showdown soon, I hope. Otherwise, you can visit me in jail."

"Art," she caught his arm as he turned to leave the room.

"What?" he demanded impatiently.

"You didn't kill that Martin fellow?"

X laughed. "How could I have—when I was kidnaping Erlika at the time?"

"I don't know," she said softly. She raised her arms, placed them about his neck, wove her cool fingers together, drew herself up to him.

"I just want you to know that it wouldn't have mattered if you had killed. Or done anything else. I know what people say about you. I know where you get your money. It isn't right, the way you get your money."

"Go lecture to the Y.M.C.A.," he said harshly.

She clung to him. "What I mean, no matter what you've done, it doesn't make any difference. I used to think that I liked being with you because you were—well, because you were Murdo the Magnificent, king of the rackets. I thought I was just having a little adventure. Tonight, though, and last night, it's been different, and it's made a difference with me. I love you, Art." She rested her head against his chest and burst into tears.

"No, you don't love me," he said more gently than Murdo could have said it. "You can't, because you don't know me. No one knows me. No one must ever know me. You don't understand. You'll never understand, but I'll try to explain as we drive. We've got to get Erlika out of here before the police arrive."

He broke away from her. As he went toward the door behind which Erlika was a prisoner, he took from his pocket his cigarette lighter. It was something more than it appeared to be. Within the lighter case was a small cartridge containing a powerful anesthetic gas. A touch of a button and the gas could be directed into the face of the Agent's victim.

X unlocked the door with one hand while the other held the lighter. As the door swung open, Erlika sprang at him like a tigress, fingers clenched, long nails threatening him like ten tiny knives. X flicked the lighter. A puff of vapor clouded the girl's face.

"Better than *hashish,* Erlika," he said as she fell limp and unconscious into his arms.

He carried Erlika back to the door of the apartment where Edna awaited him. They crossed the hall, brought up the automatic elevator, got in, sent the elevator creeping toward the basement garage. The garage attendant's curiosity had evidently been satisfied by the tip X had given him earlier, for the man asked no questions as X lifted the unconscious woman into Murdo's roadster. With Edna at the wheel, the car was soon cruising down the dark street.

X glanced at Edna's young, pathetically eager face as she handled the car skillfully across town.

"Keep your eyes on the road, Edna," he said softly. "You've told me tonight you love me. Whether it's love or just a young girl's infatuation for an older man who accomplishes a little bit of the task before him, I do not know. We won't argue about it. But in fairness to you, I've got to tell you something."

"Is—is there anybody else? A wife somewhere," she faltered.

"No, Edna. No. You know, I think I ought to call you Eddy. We've been pals like a couple of boys. And pals are about all we will ever be. You see, Eddy, I'd make a poor excuse for a husband. And besides, I'm not Art Murdo."

She was silent for a moment. Then: "Well, why not go on?"

"That's about all there is to it. I'm not Murdo."

"I know," she said. She breathed a slight sigh. "You're Secret Agent X."

"YOU SEE," Edna explained, "when you told me to drive the car back to the apartment after you had discovered the body of Morton Edgewood in that garage basement, I didn't go quite as soon as you supposed. I hung around across the street until you came out. But it wasn't Art Murdo who came out. It was that newspaperman, Martin. At first, I thought something had happened to you. I went back into the garage, couldn't find any Art Murdo. That and what you said about no one knowing you—well, two and two, you know."

"I see," X replied.

"And then it makes it easier for me," the girl continued, "I took a job with the D.A. trying to get some convicting evidence out of Murdo. I was supposed to make him fall in love with me—a nice job for a nice girl!"

"Your job has just about played out, then," X told her. "Murdo was murdered." And he explained briefly how Murdo had been mistaken for Martin.

While they had been talking, Edna's foot had not relaxed on the accelerator. About ten miles outside the city limits she turned the car up a steeply inclined cinder drive. The drive ran into a garage at one side of a three-story frame house that looked as though it had undergone recent remodeling. X handed Edna Murdo's keys.

"You probably can find the right one quicker than I," he said. "Beside, I've got to handle Erlika." Erlika was showing signs of reviving, X had noticed, and he was anxious to get her into the house before the trouble began.

With Erlika in his arms and Edna leading the way, X entered the house. He made a brief survey of its layout and decided the most strategic position for them to await the coming of Erlika's rescuers was a large game room on the third floor. Windows of this room commanded an excellent view of the winding, moonlit drive below.

"Now nothing to do but wait and make ourselves comfortable," X said to Edna, after he had placed Erlika in a chair. "We've all the comforts of home—radio, billiard table, comfortable chairs, though a trifle too modern to suit my fancy. Ah, there's a bar apparently well stocked. A drink wouldn't hurt us." X headed for a small, ornate bar at one end of the room.

"Erlika's coming to," Edna warned.

"Oh, we'll mix a drink for her, too," X said. "How about it, Erlika?" He looked over his shoulder to see the lovely, dangerous woman open her eyes and stare about her bewilderedly. She made no effort to get from the chair. She tried to burn Edna to ashes with a scornful look.

X went on mixing the drinks, came back to the two women a little later with three tall glasses and a plate of spiced wafers on a tray. He put the tray down on a small table which he placed between Edna and Erlika. Then he pulled up a chair for himself and sat down.

"Do not be so complacent, Art Murdo," Erlika said scornfully. "You will not escape. For this thing you have done to me, you will die a hundred deaths. Do you suppose I will not be found?"

"I'm not," X said in the voice of Murdo, "supposing you won't be found. I'm looking forward to it, in fact. Otherwise I should have simply given the name of the leader of your mob to the police and allowed them to clean up the mess. I'd rather handle the matter personally, thus saving the police some bloodshed, and saving me 'loss of face,' as the Chinese say." He lifted his glass. "Here's to a short future and a merry one."

EDNA raised her glass. Erlika stared moodily at hers. She reached across the table with her bracelet-ornamented arm and took one of the spiced crackers. She nibbled it. She said: "That is too old a trick to fool me. You have poisoned my drink. I know that you have."

X shrugged. "Then we'll trade. I'm immune to poison."

He exchanged glasses with Erlika. Erlika drank slowly, suspiciously. Edna seemed tuned to Erlika's uneasiness and got little enjoyment out of her drink. X tossed his off quickly, wiping his mouth with his handkerchief afterwards.

Erlika put down her glass, leaned both elbows on the table, fastened her eyes on X's face. X leaned back in his chair. He pulled Murdo's automatic from his pocket, stroked its sleek, polished barrel affectionately.

"Yes," he said, "we will be more than a match for your Mongols when they come. I presume that the leader of your mob will come tearing down here with them. That is as I would prefer it. Then we can do a thorough job." X rested his gun in his lap. His eyelids looked heavy, drooped.

"You see, Erlika," he mumbled, then paused. "What was I going to say?"

"That you feel sleepy?" Erlika prompted, her smile widening.

"Now that you mention it, I—I—" X struggled to sit up, but seemed to lack the strength. He passed a trembling hand over his forehead. "Stuffy in here—"

Edna sprang to her feet with a cry of alarm. Her horrified eyes were fastened on X's face which had become strangely lax. X muttered: "Not so much noise. Want to sleep—"

And then he tumbled sidewise from his chair to the floor. The gun dropped from his lap beside him. Both Edna and Erlika sprang for the gun at the same time. Edna was inches nearer to it, but as she stooped, Erlika kicked her mercilessly on the wrist, shoved her out of the way, swept up the gun, turned it on Edna. Erlika's eyes flashed. Her laugh rippled musically.

"Now, we shall see who is the cleverer," she cried. "I drugged my own drink with a tiny tablet which I dropped from the hollow bangle on my bracelet when I was reaching for the crackers. He is so gullible, this Murdo. I had no trouble getting him to trade glasses with me, you see?"

She turned the gun threateningly upon Edna. "You will make no move to interfere with my plans, redheaded ugly one, or I will shoot you."

On the other side of the room, the ringing phone interrupted Erlika's threat. She took catlike steps toward the instrument, beckoning Edna to follow her. Edna obeyed.

"Pick up the phone," Erlika ordered. "Hold the receiver several inches from your ear so that I may hear also."

Edna obeyed woodenly. She gave the immobile Agent X a frightened glance. "Hello," she said tremulously.

"This is Whitey," came loudly from the phone. "Edna? The chief there with you?"

"Yes," she replied.

"And the kidnaped female, huh? Well, listen, what the hell am I supposed to do? Sit here and chew my nails?"

Erlika said loudly: "Tell him to come at once and bring the boys. You understand. Bring the boys. The trap can work both ways."

Edna repeated the message word for word at Erlika's dictation.

"I get it." Whitey said. He broke the connection.

The phone slipped from Edna's fingers to the floor. Erlika ordered her to pick it up.

"I know that trick, too," Erlika said. "You would shout for help and hope the exchange operator heard you. Sit down in that chair." Erlika indicated a chair which faced the spot where X lay on the floor. Edna obeyed.

Erlika raised her skirt and pulled a lean-bladed knife from her garter. She said: "Now you will see how long it takes a man to die." She dropped to her knees beside Agent X.

CHAPTER VIII

DESIGN FOR DYING

EVERY MUSCLE IN Edna's body quivered. She was caught in the riptide of two powerful forces. Self preservation demanded that she remain quietly seated under the watchful eye of Erlika's gun. Yet it seemed she could not sit there and watch the deadly work of Erlika's knife on the Agent's body. If there was only something she could do.

But Erlika had designed her vengeance with a mind trained in the cruelty of the Yezidee sect. Death for this man who had defied her; slow, agonizing, mental torment for the girl who loved that man.

"You will watch him bleed to death from a thousand cuts," Erlika's smiling lips said.

Three times she thrust downward with the point of her knife, to check it a hair's breadth from the Agent's face each time. Three times Edna screamed shrilly, hysterically. And Erlika, laughed.

"He has a nice face," Erlika said. "His lower lip is too long and we will have to cut it off. And I would have him have a deep scar on his face. Several such scars would prevent his friends from saying how natural he looks when they look into the coffin. American racketeers have such nice funerals, don't you think?"

With the point of her knife, Erlika drew a delicate cut across X's cheek. But no blood flowed. Erlika scowled and Edna held her breath. The knife had only pierced the layer of makeup material on X's face.

"What is this thing he wears for a face?" Erlika puzzled. "It is like flesh, yet it does not bleed. How very odd. I should like to peek beneath and see what kind of a man this is, I should—"

The door of the room opened. In spite of Erlika's threatening gun, Edna sprang to her feet. Whitey? Was it Whitey and Murdo's men?

Yes! The men who crowded through the door looked like gunmen, caps and hats pulled low over their faces and collars turned up. Erlika laughed, and her laughter struck cold despair to Edna's heart. Erlika made no move to protect herself from the men who had entered the room.

And then as light crept under the bill of one of the men's caps, Edna saw a hard, cruel, yellow face. Mongols! X's scheme had worked as he had planned. But X lay helpless on the floor.

Edna's hand flattened over her mouth to check a scream. In the center of the group was one man whose face was masked with a demon mask of golden metal—the leader X had tried to trap!

Then someone in the hall cried out in English: "Cops!" There was a moment of silence in the room during which all listened to the wail of sirens on approaching squad cars. The police, Edna knew, had discovered that the man they supposed to be Murdo was someone else—was Agent X. To all appearances, it must seem to the police that Agent X was the murderer of the real Murdo who had died wearing the disguise of Martin.

Erlika spoke rapidly to the men in a language that Edna did not know. The men turned, ran from the room, drawing automatics as they hurried to the stairway. Erlika's laugh rang out madly. She whirled toward Agent X, spoke to his immobile figure:

"You are the one who is responsible for all this. You should die a thousand deaths, if there were only time." Then she dropped to her knees, lips drawn back from clenched teeth, the knife raised above her head.

"Stop!" cried Edna. She sprang toward Erlika. Erlika's left hand carried a gun she had taken from X. She jerked the trigger as soon as her sights had covered Edna.

But no sound came from the gun save an empty click. She flung the gun at Edna, drove down with all her strength with her knife—straight toward X's chest.

THE AGENT'S two hands flashed upward, seized Erlika's knife wrist, twisted. The knife dropped to the floor. Erlika sprang to her feet. She had been tricked—tricked by the man who had so frequently cheated death, who seemed immune to drugs, who had palmed off an empty gun on Erlika and laughed. Erlika whirled, ran through the door.

X was on his feet in a moment. He had every intention of following Erlika, though he knew there was little chance of her escaping. He had heard all that passed in the room. Clever as Erlika had been, she had not been able to conceal from X's keen sight that momentary movement when she had dropped the drugged pill into the glass of liquor that X had apparently taken into his mouth.

Actually, X had allowed the drink to pass his lips. But immediately afterwards, pretending to dry his mouth with his handkerchief, he had spit out the drugged liquor into a rubber inter-lining of his handkerchief. It was a trick he had frequently used, but never with better success than tonight.

No sooner was he on his feet than Edna threw herself into his arms, clung to him passionately. The girl seemed to have forgotten entirely that such action on her part prevented X from following Erlika.

Quickly, but not unkindly, he broke Edna's embrace. Downstairs, the Mongols had opened up with their guns. Outside, the police had laid siege to the house. Gunsmoke rolled in clouds through the door. Or was it gunsmoke? There was more the smell of burning tar about it.

X plunged into the smoke-filled hall. At the rail of the circular stairway that wound its corkscrew way from the third to the first floor, a man shoved a blazing can of tarlike stuff over the banister. Like a comet with a tail twenty feet in length, the can rocketed downward as X lunged at the man at the rail, his only weapon the knife he had taken from Erlika.

The man turned. Beneath his hat, there was no face—nothing but a demon mask of golden metal. The man raised both hands above his head. X thrust the knife against the man's chest, reached up and jerked off the metal mask. Beneath the mask was the smiling yellow face of Prince Djamok.

Djamok bowed as much as the threatening knife would permit. "I not knowing you, but enemy of Erlika same as friend of me. I being annoyed by too many kidnaping by Erlika and misguided fellow countrymen."

"You mean they kidnaped and forced you to come here?"

Djamok bowed, shouted above the noise of the gun fire: "I being forced to wear devil mask without knowing why."

X knew why well enough. The leader of the Mongol mob had needed a fall guy badly. And what better fall guy for the leader of the Mongols than another Mongol? If anything went wrong with the leader's plans, he had only to toss Djamok to the police.

Black smoke rolled like a monstrous dragon up the circular stairway. In the light of scarlet flames below, X could see black shadows that were men running to escape the flames. The gun fire had abated but little in spite of the fire that Djamok had caused.

Djamok looked proud of his work. He had escaped from his captors at the time of the police attack and had started the fire with this roof patching compound that he had found in a storeroom. X did not think that firing the house was the wisest move Djamok could have made, for the flames would only drive the Mongols into the upper portion of the house. But the damage had been done and had to be made the most of.

The leader of the mob must not escape. X's mind was firmly made up on that point. Ordinarily, he preferred to hand criminals he captured over to the police so that justice might take its course.

Gunfire rang out over the crackle of flames.

But in this case, justice to the leader would only mean injustice to one who had already suffered too much. But how to trap the man? How to make certain of his death?

X turned to the storeroom Djamok had indicated and returned at once with a length of rope he had found there. Djamok at his heels, X ran back into the game room. He glanced around. Edna— where was Edna? He sprang to the window, dropped the rope to the ground, looped the end around the radiator and tied what appeared to be a secure knot.

The knot, however, was one of those "melting" slip knots which magicians often use in rope tricks. Any weight on the dangling end of the rope would result in the knot coming untied. X had only to steer the mob leader toward this means of apparent escape and his task would be over.

HE TURNED from the radiator. Now to find Edna. Then to drive the mob leader toward the one avenue of escape—the window that meant death.

Djamok was eyeing X with a puzzled expression upon his face. X said: "The red-haired girl—did you see which way she went?"

"She not going very far, certainly," Djamok said. "I being most happy to help find." And he followed X from the room.

The upper reaches of the house were filled with smoke. X held a handkerchief over his face, stumbled from room to room. Now and then he would remove the handkerchief long enough to call out the girl's name, but it was doubtful if she could have heard above the roar of the flame and the intermittent sputter of gun fire.

And then he saw the figure of a woman, flying wraithlike through the murk ahead of him. He shouted, broke into a run, falling over furniture in his effort to catch her.

The woman ran into the game room. "Edna!" X shouted. "Stop!"

The woman laughed, turned her head. X saw for an instant Erlika's gleaming smile. It was Erlika whom he pursued, not Edna. And Erlika was at the window—the window that was death's door.

X lunged forward, hands outstretched. But before he could reach her. Erlika was over the sill, had the rope in her hands. And the knot slipped. The end of the rope whipped from around the radiator.

X heard Erlika's piercing scream out of the blackness of the night. And before he could touch it, the rope was snapped over the sill. There was no screaming then, no laughter, no sound but the mocking crackle of the fire.

X pivoted. Above the roar of the fire, he heard Djamok's voice calling: "I have found her. She is safe!"

X rushed to the door, brought himself to a stop. The hasp of Erlika's knife was clasped in his right hand. Directly in front of him, his triangular face pale, his tow-colored hair scorched, his blond mustache awry, was Whitey Fauvre. He had a heavy automatic in his hand and it centered unwaveringly on the Agent.

"I'm getting out of here," Whitey said. "You're not stopping me."

The eyes of Agent X became as stern as granite. The muscles of his jaws were set. "You're not going anywhere, Whitey, if I have to kill you to make you stay. You are the leader of the Mongol gang, even though Erlika might have been the brains.

"When you phoned here a while ago and Edna answered the phone, Erlika told Edna what to say loud enough for you to hear Erlika's voice and know that she had the situation in hand. You were to "bring the boys"—bring your Mongols and finish the job.

"But even before that I knew you were the man who killed Murdo, who you thought to be A.J. Martin at the time. It was cleverly done, all right.

"It was smart of you to frame yourself for the murder which you actually committed. And smarter to leave evidence to prove to the police that you *were* framed. But didn't it occur to you that if someone had wanted to kill the man you thought was Murdo and at the same time throw the blame on you by disguising himself as you, that the killer would have taken every precaution to *prevent* the false mustache from falling into the hands of the police?

"Of course it occurred to you. That's why you tried to make it appear as though the murderer had wanted to destroy the false mustache. You wrapped the mustache in a piece of newspaper and set the paper on fire, first making sure that the portion of the paper containing the evidence you wanted the police to find could not burn. You had fire-proofed that portion of the paper by dipping it in ordinary water glass, I imagine.

"Police overlooked the fact that *had* someone been trying to frame you by impersonating you, the logical thing for that someone to do was to simply put the false mustache in his pocket and walk away. Not try to destroy it until he had it far away from the scene of the crime."

THE AGENT paused, eyed Whitey's automatic. The gun was held straight and level. X decided to keep talking.

"You are the man who should have rightfully worn the Mongol devil mask tonight. You were the man who wore it last night when you tried to get me to join the Yezidee cult. That story about you having been asleep in the rumble seat of the roadster when Edna followed my captors was just a story.

"When Edna and I succeeded in breaking up your Yezidee meeting, you simply ran out. You beat us to the car and alibied yourself by pretending to cover our escape from the house.

"You did that because you were yellow, Whitey. You're too yellow to drop that gun and fight it out man to man. You're so yellow that I can't permit your blubbering in the prisoners box in a court of justice when your sentence is pronounced. You're not leaving this building alive, because that poor old mother of yours would never live through her boy's murder trial. I'm thinking of her when I'm killing you!"

The Agent's hand shot out, palm up and open, Erlika's knife lying in his hand. With incredible swiftness he moved, and the knife traveled the short distance to Whitey like a ray of silvery light. Whitey's gun bucked, roared. X swerved to one side, felt the tug of the bullet through his coat.

Whitey would not shoot again with his right hand, for Erlika's knife showed its glittering handle against Whitey's right forearm. The blade had thrust cleanly through flesh and muscle.

As soon as he had delivered the knife, X launched himself in a low leap. His arms caught Whitey around lean thighs. Whitey had got his gun into his left hand and hacked down with it to X's head as they fell to the floor together. For a moment, X was blinded by the blow. His brain was a whirlpool.

Several moments he fought instinctively, pounding telling blows into Whitey's chest. And then he felt the shock of cold gun steel touching the side of his head. He brought his head down hard, his face flat against Whitey's chest as the gun roared. At the same time, he reached up and back, seized Whitey's left hand, twisted the gun from Whitey's grasp.

He flung the weapon aside, kept up that relentless pounding of the killer until Whitey's resistance became feeble and finally failed altogether.

X got to his knees. He was pulling in great lungfuls of smoke-laden air. In front of him, the rail of the circular stairway had teeth of red flame. It occurred to him that quite possibly this was the end.

There might be no escape. He and the killer might well go down into the burning wreckage together. Had he been sure that Edna and Djamok had escaped, he would have accepted his exit cue as something which Fate had written into her strange drama. But he had to know what had become of the girl.

Smoke curled up from between the floorboards in the hall. Flames were hungry tongues that whipped from the walls to taste his flesh, as he staggered on, searching the ruddy darkness with seared eyeballs for a glimpse of Edna.

Ahead of him, a door burst open. A woman's voice, hoarse with smoke, screamed: "Agent X!"

Edna! She was standing in the doorway of the storeroom calling to him. And then between him and the girl a curtain of flame roared to the ceiling, died down almost immediately as a section of the flooring sagged downward like a piece of limp paper.

X ran toward the flaming gap in the floor and leaped. He landed on all fours, the burning floor scorching his hands. Then he was on his feet, running toward the girl.

"Quick!" she gasped. "Djamok has found a way out. A ladder in the storeroom—"

X seized the girl around the waist, all but carried her through the door. At one end of the low-roofed attic storeroom, a gable window was open. Through it, X could see the end of a ladder disappearing. He ran to the window and looked out. Ten feet below, on a metal roof that jutted out over a large bay window, stood Djamok trying to pull the twenty-foot ladder through the window.

X steadied the wavering end of the ladder and as soon as it was clear and mounted on the tin roof below, he helped Edna get out the window and swing onto the ladder.

While she climbed down, X's fingers moved swiftly, skillfully over his face, altering the features that identified him as Murdo. Murdo's wallet and keys, which might have identified him, he tossed over his shoulder into the flames. Then he, too, swung out of the window, got to the ladder and climbed down to the roof.

THE WHOLE building seemed to tremble beneath them, and X and Djamok lowered the ladder from the tin roof to the ground. Flames writhed to the black roof of the sky, shrieking like tormented beasts. One whole side of the building had given way.

The ladder was in place, held at its foot by police. Djamok went first to aid Edna while X lingered on the roof, making sure that the change in the contours of the plastic which covered his face had made him unrecognizable. Then he, too, descended to the waiting police.

The police had readily identified Edna and Djamok. They were uncertain about X.

"What's your name, buddy?" one of them asked, preparing to write it in his notebook.

"He's my brother from Chicago," Edna spoke up.

"Okay, lady," said a cop. "We'll have to have his full name for the report."

"Edward Carse," Edna said.

The cop looked queerly at X. "Can't you talk for yourself?"

X shook his head. "Painful. Face burned."

The cop turned to Edna. "Guess you'll have to speak for the trio then. The prince's English isn't so hot. Your brother is tongue-tied—"

But X heard no more. With a flashing smile at Edna Carse, he turned, and slipped into the shadows.

Oddly enough, Edna could not satisfy the police officer at that moment. She burst into tears....

The following morning, another woman was to burst into tears because of a man—a different sort of a man. This woman was old and gray-haired. She sat at the window of her meagerly furnished second-floor room and opened a paper packet that had come by post.

To her amazement, ten green pieces of paper, each one a thousand-dollar bill, fluttered to the floor at her feet. On top of the packet was a typewritten note which read:

Dear Mrs. Fauvre:

I am indeed sorry to report that your son Delmar "Whitey" Fauvre lost his life last night. It may console you a little to know that your son died for the cause of law and order. He was engaged in a secret mission to wipe out crime and corruption in this city when he fell.

In appreciation for what Delmar Fauvre did, I beg you to accept and enjoy to the rest of your days, the enclosed.

Sympathetically,

A CITIZEN.

And "a citizen" who was gray-eyed Secret Agent X, sat in the office of K9 in Washington and told his story.

"You see, K9," X concluded, "this woman known as Erlika, who had been born of American parents—who were later murdered by Mongolian bandits—evidently came across her birth certificate which proved she was an American citizen. From Mongolia she journeyed to America, probably gaining the Mongol's permission by promising to establish a Yezidee sect in this country.

"Probably Erlika traveled over the country, enjoying herself with riches the Mongols had provided for her. She arrived at Maywood, where she met Whitey Fauvre. Probably, Whitey made love to her, something no one could have blamed Whitey for.

"Erlika returned that love, but she had been brought up to believe herself a superior being, a Mongol goddess, the reincarnation of the daughter of Erlik. She naturally felt that it would be beneath her position to mate with a common gunman like Whitey."

K9 nodded. "So she decided to elevate Whitey to a position of importance in the underworld. By George, that's it! Make Whitey king of crime and she could then be queen. She imported her devil-worshiping servants, knowing what an impression Mongol cruelty could make upon the American gunmen. But what became of this Erlika? By George, she was a type!"

"She fell from the window, caught in the trap I had intended for Whitey," X said. "The spot where she fell was shortly covered by the collapsed wall of the burning building."

"Then there's not a chance of her being alive," K9 said. "Not a chance, unless there's something in this devil's daughter business."

"I don't know about this devil's daughter business," X said, "but she couldn't have escaped. I think we can dispense with any and all romanticism about Erlika. She was beautiful, but her kiss was a death kiss—and very often a horrible death. We may feel sorry that one so beautiful made mockery of justice, but we cannot feel sorry that justice finally prevailed.

"She claimed to be the devil's daughter and—I don't mean to pun—she went to the devil."

BOOK XLI

YOKE OF THE CRIMSON COTERIE

Out of a grim medieval castle they brought her—
Madam Death, the beautiful one, whose touch
meant destruction. And when the Crimson Coterie
sought to erect the yoke of world empire upon
her hell-brought bondage, Secret Agent X found
himself manacled to the pyre of her lethal flesh.

CHAPTER I

DEATH'S BURNING TOUCH

THUNDER AWOKE STRANGE echoes in the black halls of Strada Castle. It was as though long dead feudal Magyars, who had built its towers in the fastness of the Little Carpathians, trod its floors again with ponderous, iron-clad feet.

The six-foot-thick stone walls reduced the storm to impotence, and the wind howled with disappointment within the hundred niches and crannies of the ancient structure. Lightning; which had effortlessly split a sky of seeming impenetrable blackness, blunted its silvered sword on Strada's hoary battlements. Strada Castle rivaled the endurance of the mountains that were its foundation.

Within the tall, topmost room of the round west tower, a woman worked busily. She was surrounded by an array of strange scientific instruments that glittered in the rays of a powerful compound electrical lamp which was attached by jointed shafts of stainless steel to blackened beams that were a part of the ancient roof structure.

No hideous crone, this woman, with claws that clutched on mystic vials. Simple though her plain white uniform was, it could not conceal the perfect symmetry of the form beneath, Nor could the heavy, insulating gloves she wore conceal the graceful movements of her fingers as she worked. Hair the sun had gilded piled high upon her lovely head. It seemed a shame that such perfect features were more than half masked by square-lensed, metal-framed goggles of black glass.

On a porcelain-topped table before her stood a metal ring closed at both ends. Within the tube, supported by delicate wires, was a single, jewel-like flame, so brilliant that it eclipsed the lightning which now and again thrust its rays through the narrow windows of the tower wall.

A curved piece of metal shielded the tube and its brilliant treasure from the girl and the spectroscope with which she worked, in an attempt to classify the mysterious fire within the tube. There was nothing like it in the world—that flaming element which pierced the metal shield with its searing rays. And yet the woman who worked within the laboratory showed no indication of excitement. She was as emotionless as a machine, oblivious to the power within her grasp—a power such as mankind had never known before.

A DOOR in the floor of the tower room opened slowly upon complaining hinges. An old man, whose knees seemed made of the same rusty material as the hinges of the door, climbed through the opening. He wore a clean suit of denim. His long, white hair framed a kindly face that saddened as his glinting blue eyes fell upon the woman at the spectroscope.

The woman looked up slowly. One gloved hand passed across her brow and when it had fallen wearily to her side, a slightly annoyed frown formed above her black goggles. The old man shuffled nearer and the woman reached quickly across the table to rotate the metal shield so that the rays from the glass tube did not shine on the old man's face.

"My child," spoke the old man's rusty voice, "you are working too hard. The Doctor has no right to keep you working so late with such a terrible storm outside. Come, it is time you were in bed. You must have sleep."

The woman's frown deepened. She rested elbows on the table and cradled her sweetly rounded chin against the clasped knuckles of her gloved hands.

"Who are you?" she asked slowly, bewilderedly. "You are vaguely familiar. I cannot seem to associate the face and the name." She pressed gloved palms to her forehead.

"Who—who am I?" repeated the man. "Who am I? I?" His thin hands danced up and down on his chest. "Good Lord! What has happened to your eyes, child? Has it hurt your eyes? Tell me, for the love of heaven!"

A look of intense anxiety on his face, he hurried across the room toward the woman. She warned him back.

"The ray! Keep back from the ray, whoever you are. It is astralite. It destroys, burns, blinds!"

The old man stopped. For a moment, he stared open-mouthed at the beautiful woman. "Look at me," he said hoarsely. "You do not know me—me, your own father?"

The woman shook her lovely head slowly. "I cannot remember you."

"But you saw me only this noon, child! You are ill. Where is the Doctor? He must not let you work this way."

"I—my memory is fogged," said the woman in her soft, unemotional voice. "I do not remember you."

"It is your eyes, child!" gasped the old man. "The Doctor said the new element was more dangerous to eyesight than radium. You must stop this work. You will be blinded."

"I see you perfectly," the woman said. "Odd, though, I have a strange ache in my head. I feel within my blood a feverish glow, as though my heart was made of solar fire. And in my mind there is nothing but a voice—a voice that cries out to me to work, work, work. Please go, old man. Interruptions are annoying."

The old man threw his hands to his head. "My child! She is mad!" He turned, fled toward the stairway, shouting: "Doctor! Doctor! My child, she is mad!"

The woman shook her head, turned back to her work, only to be disturbed a moment later by the return of her father with a much younger man who wore full evening dress, but whose face was half-masked like the girl's by black-lensed goggles.

The man in evening dress looked at the girl a moment. "Come here," he ordered crisply.

The girl got up from the table, came toward him with slow effortless steps. He kicked a metal stool toward her, told her to sit down. He went to the table in the center of the room, picked up a pair of gloves, put them on. Then he returned to the girl, taking a physician's stethoscope from his pocket as he did so. "Unbutton the bosom of your smock," he ordered. When the girl had obeyed, he pressed the disk of the stethoscope to her flesh.

"You feel ill?" the man called the "Doctor" asked.

She shook her head. "I seem to have lost feeling. I do not know. My head aches. Inside, something burns. And I do not seem to be able to determine the course of my own thoughts. It is as though someone else were thinking for me. That someone else has been telling me to work."

"I have been telling you to work," said the Doctor. He put away his instrument.

The old man leaned over his shoulder, asked: "How is she, Doctor?"

The Doctor shook his head. "It is alarming, frankly. You understand, we have been experimenting with an element which up to a few months ago, we did not suppose existed at all. Until the present time, I do not think it ever did exist on earth. It came from a meteor which struck the earth near Bratislava. I suspected the existence of this element, and by spectrum analysis discovered that the meteor was giving forth an unclassified ray.

"Far more potent, this new ray, than radium itself, I set about extracting the element from the meteor. Astralite, I called it. I informed your daughter fully upon the danger she might encounter working in this laboratory. Even so, she insisted upon the position as my assistant. I greatly fear that the ray has poisoned her."

"But—but," mumbled the old man, "she is my child. My only daughter. You do not know what that means, Doctor."

"I do not," said the Doctor. "I am sorry. And I am greatly surprised. I cannot understand this mental weakness. How docile her mind is to my will!"

The Doctor stood up, pointed a gloved finger at the woman. "Go to the cage and bring me one of the experimental rats. Take off your gloves first."

WITHOUT hesitation, the girl obeyed. Her aged father gasped an oath. "But she is afraid of rats! Doctor, do not make her do this thing. She may be bitten!"

The Doctor checked the old man with a gesture. "Watch!" he whispered tensely. "It is barely possible—barely possible, understand, that—"

On the other side of the room, the girl turned from the cage of experimental rats. One lovely hand extended in front of her, she approached the Doctor. Her white, slender fingers were closed upon a white rat. And from the furry body of the creature, pale gray wisps of smoke arose toward the ancient black beams above. The little animal was dead.

"Drop the rat," the Doctor commanded.

The woman obeyed, watched dully while the Doctor bent over the rat.

"Good Lord!" muttered the Doctor. "Dead!" He straightened. A white-toothed, exultant smile flashed momentarily across his flushed face.

"Another rat!" he ordered. "Bring me another rat!"

"She—she killed it," husked the old man. "It was as though a bolt of lightning—"

"More potent than lightning!" the Doctor cut in. "Look, she touches another rat. It dies in its steps, smouldering. Good Lord, what a find! What power! And it is mine. *She* is mine—body and brain!"

"No," said the old man quietly. "No. She is my child. My only daughter. Either you will give her back to me and give her back her health, or I will kill you, Doctor."

"Stand aside!" the Doctor cried. "There are other experiments."

Determinedly, the old man blocked his path. "You will give her back her health," he croaked. "Or, so help me, I will kill you with this knife!" And from the belt of his trousers, the old man jerked a horn-handled hunting knife.

The Doctor uttered a short, derisive laugh. His right hand shot out, rammed into the old man's face, knocked him to the floor. Erect, threatening, the Doctor stood over the old man. His goggled eyes sought out the girl at the other side of the room. Speaking in a harsh, commanding voice he said to the girl:

"Touch this old man with your bare hands. My will commands it."

The girl turned from the rat cage and with slow, unfaltering steps approached the old man on the floor.

The old man got to his feet. He blinked incredulously at his daughter. "No," he murmured. "My own daughter. My own child. She would not hurt me. She would not do to me what she did to those rats. She wouldn't— Don't touch me!"

He shouted then, sprang back out of the way of the woman whose outstretched hands were the touch of death. His terrified eyes jabbed at the trapdoor in the floor. The Doctor blocked off the exit. And the woman, whose mad brain was in the clutch of the Doctor, lunged again.

With a wild cry, the old man ducked, scampered toward the other side of the room. Looking back over his shoulder as he ran, he crashed into the table laden with apparatus, then sought shelter behind a steel cabinet of chemicals. His gnarled fingers gripped his knife, raised it above his head as the woman approached. Then his shoulders drooped dejectedly. The knife fell from limp fingers. His face turned toward the thundering heavens.

"Forgive me," he mumbled in prayer. "I have raised a knife against the life of my own daughter. Forgive me—"

Pale slender fingers reached out but barely touched the old man's throat. He toppled forward into his daughter's embrace, into the embrace of death.

FOR AN instant the smell of burning flesh filled the air as tendrils of gray smoke whisked upwards from the old man's body. The girl's arms unclasped. Her father's lifeless form crumpled to the floor.

She looked down at her father, and above the heavy goggles she wore her perfect brow was again marred by a frown of bewilderment. She turned to the Doctor, gestured with her deadly hands toward the body.

"He does not move. What have I done to this man I do not know?"

The Doctor neither moved nor spoke. So wild his hopes and speculations at the moment, that he did not notice the fire that burned within the room; did not see that the old man had knocked over the tube containing the priceless and only existent quantity of the newly discovered radioactive element that was a hundred times more potent than radium.

The tube had broken and the substance the Doctor had named astralite had immediately burned through the planks of the floor. Not until the flames from the floor shot to the beams above, born of a draft that passed up through the tower as though through a factory chimney, did the Doctor jerk himself from his dream of power.

Then suddenly he ran across the room, skirted the rapidly spreading flame. He seized the girl by the arm, his own life protected by the heavy insulating gloves he wore. His triumphant laughter rang high above the roar of the storm and the crackle of the mounting flames.

"Madam Death!" he cried. "What a weapon for the Brotherhood!"

That night the round tower of Strada candled the black hills for miles around with lurid flames that lashed through narrow windows. It was as though the watch fires of the ancient Magyars burned again....

ONE NIGHT, eighteen months later, eight men whose features were covered by black domino masks, gathered about a table in the basement of a café in Bratislava. At the head of the table, the chairman rose to speak. He was an imposing figure with his black cloak draping from square shoulders. His mouth and chin, visible beneath the mask, had the decisive lines of a Napoleon.

"My friends," he began, "leaders of the Brotherhood, we have accomplished much. Within a short space of time, all of Europe will be in the hands of dictators, either actual or *sub rosa*. And these men who hold the power of Europe in their hands are answerable to me and to me alone. The cyclonic progress we have made in the past few months is due in great part to one man. Doctor, will you please rise."

The man from Strada Castle stood up. "Yes, Master?"

"Doctor," the Master said, "I wish to thank you in behalf of the Brotherhood. Had you not been instrumental in removing certain stubborn, but ignorant believers in the principles of democracy, our progress would have been impossible. But your work is not yet complete.

"Our eyes turn to the West, cross the seas where lies America, wealthiest, most powerful nation of them all. There we succeeded in establishing our organization, but it does not flourish. There are certain influential men who have stamped it un-American, and therefore, in their ignorance, refuse to see that our plan for complete concentration of world power in one man is the only solution to the dilemma of modern civilization.

"Of these Americans who stand in our path, I have picked five men as most dangerous to our progress. Listen carefully, Doctor, as I name them. America is finding a new leader in Rex Durmont who is rapidly climbing the political ladder toward what he hopes will be the presidency. Such a leader must be removed.

"In order that our cause can succeed, our American Brotherhood must be armed. One of our own men is in a position to become the head of one of the greatest munitions plants in the world. He will gladly arm our followers, secretly, once his immediate superior is removed. The superior I mention is George Sarles, president of the Sarles Munitions Company.

"Third on our list of men who must go, is the conservative labor leader, Boise Marquod. Once his fiery tongue is silenced, the laboring class will quickly fall in with our new ideals.

"Fourth is Gordon Service, a radio commentator with millions of followers. His keen ears are aware of our activities in America, and he has warned the public against us. He must die.

"The fifth of these doomed men will be the most difficult of all to check. While facts concerning the other four may readily be learned, I can tell you in a few words all that is known about the fifth. He is, apparently, a sort of secret policeman. The exact extent of his authority is not known, but he is sponsored by some official in the United States Government. He is a great character actor, a marvelous impersonator. No one has seen his real face. He has no name of his own, but travels under thousands of names. He has served his country in the intelligence department during the World War, so naturally he is a master of intrigue.

"This fifth man is the most dangerous foe we have to face, for he fights with weapons unknown to others, and he is unhampered by the law. The orthodox police fear him as a criminal. And the criminals fear him as the longest arm of the law. But for all that, I believe we can match his cunning with Madam Death."

"His name?" interrupted one of the masked men.

"He has no name," said the Master. "Must I repeat? He is called Secret Agent X. Doctor, you will leave on the next boat for America."

The Doctor bowed. "I shall be perfectly at home, Master. The five men you have mentioned will trouble our organization no longer, for Madam Death shall accompany me."

"You will need, perhaps, several Madam Deaths," said the Master. "This is not an easy task."

The Doctor shook his head. "There can be but one like Madam Death. All of the astralite, the rays of which poisoned Madam Death, was lost when Strada burned. Madam Death, herself, is slowly consumed by that invisible fire within her. We must work fast while she lives. But fortunately, though her death is so near that it can be foreseen, her power to kill increases as the poison spreads throughout her body. It seems that—"

ONE OF the men sprang from the table, strode across the room and jerked open the door. Against the gloomy gray of basement steps moved the shadow of a man.

The Master flung an imperative arm toward the fleeing figure. "After him! We have been spied upon. The spy must not live!"

Through the dark streets of Bratislava the spy moved like a frightened fox, now running with swift silence, now creeping along in the shadows a few feet away from the men who hunted him. At last he gained a tiny cottage behind which a mast of a short-wave radio transmitter reared its skeleton frame.

The spy crept into the building, moved familiarly through dark rooms to the panel of his powerful transmitter. He touched a switch. A pilot light on the panel glowed, revealed the taut muscles of his angular face, his haunted eyes.

Tubes warmed, current buzzed. The spy's nervous fingers touched the rubber grip of a telegraph key. Morse code beamed westward, its long finger of dots and dashes searching for a listening ear in the United States.

"Calling W2XJK," snapped the transmitter. "Bratislava calling W2XJK."

The transmitter paused. The spy switched in his receiver, his eyes searching the shadows in the room behind him. The receiver was silent. Again the spy called in frantic desperation as though from a sinking ship.

This time came a far-away, shrill answering message. The spy cut off the receiver, seized the key. Outside the cottage, he fancied he heard footsteps.

"This is Special Agent, League of Nations, identity number G58. Listen," sang the spy's transmitter. ""Five men doomed by secret organization known to be operating in America and seeking to overthrow democracy. These five men, Rex Durmont, George Sarles, Boise Marquod, Gordon Service and Secret Agent X."

The spy paused, glanced over his shoulder. Behind him, a window opened. His head snapped back to the transmitter and the telegraph key sang again:

"Brotherhood agent known as the Doctor to operate in America for removal of five doomed men. Arriving by next boat with Madam Death—"

Crack! Gun flame lanced through the open window. The spy jerked. His left hand fumbled up toward his back, came away, fingers moist. But, like a machine, his right hand kept tapping on the key:

"Madam Death most dangerous killer. Can be identified by—"

Crack! Again the long sliver of flame through the window. The spy spilled forward, head dropping across the brass key of his transmitter.

Out across the night, beaming westward, stretched the finger of radio in one prolonged dash that spelled death for the League of Nations spy.

CHAPTER II

THE VEILED DOOM STALKS

THE HEAD WAITER of the Brock-Broadmoor Hotel stood at the door of the elaborate dining room and surveyed the assemblage of American labor leaders with discerning gray eyes. At the speakers' table sat Mr. Boise Marquod, his rough, gray face and grizzled jowls readily distinguishing him from all others present.

Beside him sat his brother, Arnold Marquod, a far less serious man. His bright-eyed, happy face and flushed cheeks denied his otherwise middle age. The name of Marquod had for generations meant money, but the two brothers had sought happiness in early life by the application of two entirely different philosophies.

Boise Marquod had believed that money unearned rooted evil, and in his youth he had entered the ranks of labor to work his way from apprentice to the high position he now held. Throughout his life he had never touched the fortune that was his rightful inheritance.

Arnold Marquod, on the other hand, had lived the life of an epicure, buying his happiness at the expense of thousands of dollars, searching for happiness in the four corners of the earth. Yet in spite of life that had centered about self, it would have appeared that Boise was the happier of the two.

Tonight Boise Marquod was to make a speech, not for the ears of such men as Arnold Marquod, but a warning to labor organizations, against the insidious inroads of the un-American organizations. Boise Marquod was a man of intrepid courage. But to the mind of the steely-eyed man who was head waiter tonight, Boise Marquod's courage was hardly less than foolhardiness.

Three times had Boise Marquod been warned that his life was in danger. Yet Marquod would not forego his pleasure of lonely ramblings through the city streets unattended by any bodyguard save his perfectly good-natured and comparatively harmless old German shepherd dog, who was somewhat unappropriately named "Grouch."

The head waiter at the Brock-Broadmoor knew of these warnings, because he had been their source. His letters had told Boise Marquod that he was one of five men, doomed by the very organization which Boise Marquod cried out against. The head waiter had pleaded with Boise Marquod to meet with the other four doomed men that they might plan a defense against the danger that might strike at any time. The head waiter knew of the five doomed men because he was one of the five. The pleasant, obsequious face that he revealed that night was but a mask for the real features of Secret Agent X.[21]

Yet in spite of these repeated warnings, Boise Marquod walked alone. That he would not return home alone tonight was simply a matter of chance, for his brother Arnold had unexpectedly arrived in the city only a few hours before. And Arnold Marquod looked like anything but a capable bodyguard for his elder brother.

The danger which threatened Boise Marquod, Agent X and the three other doomed men, X believed to be imminent. Several weeks ago, a mysterious plane had crashed in a deserted portion of the eastern shores of Canada. Investigators had failed to find any sign of the occupants. The plane was of European manufacture and the unusually large size of the nearly empty gas tank gave reason to believe that the plane had flown from Europe.

IT SEEMED logical to X, who had been one of the few to see the League spy's incompleted message of warning to America, that the dangerous man called the Doctor as well as Mysterious Madam Death would have chosen some other way of crossing the ocean than by means of a ship. For the Doctor must have known that every ship from Europe would be carefully watched.

So X believed that the passengers of the mystery plane were that same Doctor, that same Madam Death who intended to accomplish murderous work in the name of the powerful organization they represented.

---

21 AUTHOR'S NOTE: Agent X owes his ability to impersonate any man to a particular plastic volatile material which closely resembles human flesh and which he uses to mold his own face into an artful imitation of the man whom he impersonates. This material, plus unequaled ability to imitate voice and mannerisms of other people, has placed X far above even the most capable police investigators in the country.

But until Boise Marquod complied with the plans of the other doomed men—to unite themselves against the common danger—very little could be accomplished against this pair of murderers. As his searching gray eyes photographed every characteristic movement of the gruff grizzled man who was Boise Marquod, a plan formed in X's mind by which he thought he saw a way to force Marquod to consider more seriously the warnings he had received.

X quietly left the hotel dining room and descended into the basement where were the locker rooms for the hotel employees. From a locker room which had been assigned to the head waiter whom X was impersonating, X removed a suitcase which he carried to a small washroom.

He locked the washroom door behind him, opened the suitcase, removed a dress suit, dark topcoat and a black hat similar to the one worn by Marquod. Within the suitcase was a compact makeup kit containing his plastic volatile material and a number of realistic toupees as well as pigments for achieving any particular skin tone he desired.

Opening his kit in front of the washbasin, X went to work on another lightning change of disguise. The thin lines of the waiter's face were plumped. The appearance of aged lines and sagging muscles gradually formed beneath X's skillful fingers. He then covered his own natural brown hair with a shaggy gray toupee.

Next he changed to the dress suit, all the while talking softly to himself as he worked—testing on his own ears his ability to impersonate Marquod's gruff voice.

A few minutes later, just as the real Marquod was beginning his speech, X, a somewhat too slender but otherwise perfect replica of the great labor leader, left the hotel through a basement exit. Grouch, Boise Marquod's old dog, was leashed in a little court at the side of the building, and to lend a final convincing note to his disguise, X untied the dog and walked off with him.[22]

A distance of about ten blocks separated the fine old Marquod residence from the edge of the business section of the city, and X set off at a brisk walk just as Boise Marquod might have done. Grouch fell in with X's stride, keeping his leather leash taut. Several persons who were evidently acquainted with Boise Marquod

---

22   AUTHOR'S NOTE: *The Agent's magnetic personality is nowhere better evidenced than in the influence he has over dogs. Even the most vicious watchdog seems to recognize in X a friend.*

addressed X by that name, and he had every reason to believe that his disguise was perfect. Whether or not it would fool the attractive widow whom Boise Marquod had taken a few months before for his bride, remained to be seen.

As X turned into Hart Street, where the Marquod home was located, he was conscious that someone behind him had been walking with almost the same speed ever since he had left the business section of the city. Light heel taps indicated that his follower was a woman.

When he judged that the woman was directly beneath the corner street lamp he had just passed, X turned his head quickly. He beheld a woman of exquisite proportions, smartly dressed in a black suit with sable fur. A black veil, rather heavier than the tantalizing cobweb most women affected, reached to the tip of her nose and concealed the upper portion of her face.

X increased his pace and realized that the woman's heel taps came more frequently. Undoubtedly she was following him, or rather following the man she supposed him to be. Oddly enough, Boise Marquod's dog had noticed the follower. Now and then he would stop to sniff the air and would immediately move forward at a more rapid pace, as though to hurry X.

MADAM DEATH—the name had conjured up a far different image in X's mind than that of the woman who followed him. That this woman purported to be so dangerous to the lives of men, should be young and beautiful seemed somewhat incongruous. Not but what X had met women who were both beautiful and dangerous.

But Madam Death was a murderess. Exactly how she accomplished destruction of life, X did not know, but he found it difficult to picture his follower with a gun or knife in her hand.

But after all, he decided as he came within sight of the Marquod house, he had no reason to believe that this was Madam Death except that she was following him with the dogged determination of a hound. Furthermore, he felt perfectly well equipped to take care of himself against any woman, Madam Death included.

The Marquod house stood upon a high bank into which a drive had been cut to the garage attached to the back of the house. This driveway, walled on either side by concrete, was particularly dark that night, for the night was cloudy. X tugged Grouch into the drive, went halfway up to the servant's entrance, stopped. Grouch hunched against his ankles, lifted his muzzle, whimpered strangely.

"Hush, boy," X whispered. He transferred the dog's leash to his left hand. His right went to the pocket of his coat and gripped the butt of a serviceable automatic.

Above him, a light in some room of the house was turned on and its rays illuminated a portion of the drive. X stepped back into the shadows and Grouch followed him, crowding his feet. The dog whimpered again, its muzzle pointing toward the opening of the drive, its ears pressed back against its head.

The woman had reached the mouth of the drive. She paused a moment, and it appeared as though she was either nervously picking her fingers or removing gloves. Then she turned into the drive and her steps clicked like clockwork as she approached the Agent.

Grouch growled; bristles rose on his back. And the growl became less terrible than terrified. The beast's flanks, pressed against X's legs, quivered, and for a moment its fear transmitted a cold chill throughout X's body. The dog got to its feet, pressed back against X until X was forced to take a step backward to retain his balance. Light from the window above glinted on the blue metal of X's gun.

When the woman was within twelve feet of X, the Agent said, in perfect imitation of Marquod's voice: "Stand still. Raise your hands."

Either the woman was deaf or blind to the gun which was in plain view, or entirely void of the emotion of fear. Her pace did not alter from the crisp, determined steps with which she had entered the drive.

Grouch snarled, and with no further warning, leaped at the woman's throat before X could pull back on the leash.

But no sooner had the dog touched the woman's flesh than it fell dead at her feet, legs rigidly outstretched, eyes staring glassily from their sockets. The odor of singed hair hung in the air.

And the woman, an entrancing smile on her rouged lips, calmly stepped over the dog, came on toward Agent X, her hands extended.

CHAPTER III

PLAN OF DEFENSE

I**F HE WAS** unnerved by what he had just seen, Agent X gave no indication of it. In fact, he took a step toward her, thrusting out his gun. "I warn you," he said grimly, "to put up your hands." His mouth tightened.

Hardly had he spoken the words than he heard the scuff of footsteps behind him. A hand fell heavily upon his shoulder. X turned, accompanying that movement with a hard, driving right to the midsection of a man. The man grunted, reeled back to the concrete embankment of the drive, only to launch himself in a furious attack that found X off balance and hurled him to the ground.

"Moll buzzer, eh?" the man grunted, and drove a fist at X's face.

X turned the blow aside, saw in the dim light that he was fighting a policeman. "What is the meaning of this?" he sputtered, in imitation of Boise Marquod. "I'll have you discharged for this deliberate assault, officer."

The cop checked his nightstick in mid-air. "By all things holy," he gasped, "and I believe it's Mr. Marquod I've collared! Let's have a look at you."

Still sitting astride X, the cop turned a flashlight into his face and immediately scrambled to his feet. He seized X by the arm, helped him to his feet. Eagerly he sought to repair the damage the struggle had done to the dress suit X wore.

"Sure, sir, I didn't know it was you, what with the dark and the light of it and your telling the lady to put up her hands. I thought it was some johnny troublin' an innocent woman. A woman—I thought it would be your stepdaughter back from Paris, sir, and it never entered me head it would be you in person, sir."

372

"Yes, yes," X said gruffly. "Your apology is quite satisfactory. Quite, indeed." X was starting toward the street. There was no sign of the veiled woman anywhere.

"And what's this, sir?" asked the cop, pointing to the dead dog. "Someone hurt your dog? Now ain't that a pity."

"Pity, indeed. Pity you couldn't have helped me to stop that woman. She was a criminal, I tell you."

The cop grew round-eyed. "Then I'll be after her. I'll whistle up Clancy from the next block and we'll comb this end of town for her. Was it stealin' she was up to?"

X shook his head. "And don't bother to look for her. I would not press charges against her if you did find her."

"Sure, now, she shouldn't be at large," the cop argued.

"I said you need not pursue her," X said stiffly, for he had no desire that the conscientious law officer and "Clancy from the next block," be subjected to the same treatment poor Grouch had received. "Merely go on about your business, my man, and don't worry about me."

The cop chuckled. "I'll not be worryin' too much about you, sir. Not with a wallop like that. You fair made me ribs ache with that punch. You're stout for sure, for a man of your years."

X smiled one-sidedly, said good night to the cop. He walked up the drive and approached the front door of the house. That he had no keys worried him not at all. As soon as the butler had come in answer to his knock, he said gruffly, "Forgot my keys," and strode into the hall.

He turned to the butler. "Where is Mrs. Marquod?"

"In the library, sir," said the man, indicating a door with a nod. "I trust tonight's meeting was a success?"

"Yes, yes. I trust so, too, of course," X growled, and turned into the Marquod library, shutting the door behind him.

A PLUMP, pretty little brunette woman got out of her chair and came toward him, smiling. "You're early, dear, and I know why. You're just as anxious to meet your new daughter as I am to have her again in my arms. Just think, it's four years since I've seen her. And you've never seen her at all."

"Yes, of course," X said hurriedly.

Mrs. Marquod frowned. "Yes? you mean no, dear. You've never met Doris."

"Of course not," X said. His mind was busy, searching the file of memory, trying to think up Boise Marquod's stepdaughter's last name. Hadn't Mrs. Marquod been a Mrs. Stevens before her recent marriage to Boise Marquod?

"And she won't be here for a whole hour or more," the lady sighed. "Well, we can just sit down and have a quiet talk until it's time to get excited about her coming. I wonder if I should have let her go to a wicked city like Paris for four whole years? Do you think it was right, dear?"

"Of course." X dropped his hands on the woman's shoulders. "Dear, we've got to move," he said. "Right away."

"Wh-what? Leave this dear old house?"

"No—no. You don't understand. We have to go away right now to a hotel. At least for the night. It's dangerous to stay here. So just run upstairs and throw some things in a bag—"

"Boise, are you out of your mind!" the woman flared. "We can't go away now when we're expecting Doris."

"We can and must," X insisted. "We can leave a note for Doris with the butler, telling her where to find us. Our lives may depend on this. Remember those warnings I showed you?"

The woman stared at him bewilderedly. "You've showed me no warnings. Someone threatening your life?"

"Yes, yes. If I didn't show them to you, I meant to." It would be like Boise Marquod to keep such things to himself rather than worry his wife with them. "And it is imperative that we go away from here at once. An attempt has been made on my life just outside the house, not five minutes ago."

Mrs. Marquod turned white. For a minute, X feared that she was the fainting type. But her chin stiffened and she nodded. "Of course, dear. Whatever you say. I'll go upstairs, throw our night things in a bag. And I'll have to write a note to Doris."

She took quick steps across the room to the door, saying over her shoulder: "You just sit down and rest, dear. Just relax completely. Everything will be all right—you just wait and see if it won't."

X smiled after her. He rather hated to trick a woman like that. As soon as he was certain that Mrs. Marquod was upstairs, he went to the hall and looked out. No servants in sight. He returned to the library, went to the phone, dialed a number.

"That you, Mike?" he asked softly, in a voice that seemed of a far younger man than Boise Marquod.

"Me? Sure it's me," a snaggy voice replied.

"This is A.J. Martin speaking," X said.[23] "Tell Mr. Sarles that the doomed men will meet at the Seville Hotel tonight. In about an hour. Come to the suite of rooms reserved for Mr. and Mrs. Marquod. Have Mr. Sarles contact Rex Durmont and Gordon Service, deliver the message to them. I'll be responsible for seeing that Marquod is there this time."

X hung up and immediately dialed the number of the Brock-Broadmoor HoteL Still speaking in Martin's voice, he said: "Put Mr. Boise Marquod on the phone."

"That is impossible, I am afraid," said the girl at the hotel switchboard. "Mr. Marquod is delivering a speech at the labor banquet at the present time."

"It is immaterial to me if he is addressing St. Peter," X said. "Get him on the phone at once. This is a matter of life and death. I'll hold the phone until you manage to get him."

X WAITED for nearly three minutes before Boise Marquod roared furiously into the phone. "Listen, Mr. Marquod, we've got your wife," X began.

"What?" yelled Marquod.

"We've got your wife. If you expect to see her alive again, listen closely. And stop yelling like that. I'm not at all deaf."

"Yes, yes," Marquod said, more quietly though his voice was trembling. "What is it you want me to do?"

"One hour from now you are to come to the Seville Hotel. There will be a suite of rooms reserved in your name. We will meet there to discuss the terms of ransom. Return to the banquet now and do not indicate in any manner that everything is not to your satisfaction. Do not inform the police. Do exactly as I have told you and your wife will not be harmed. Otherwise—well, you get the idea, Marquod."

X hung up, smiling slightly. If Marquod only knew the truth—that his wife simply believed that she was walking out with her husband!

The door of the library opened. There stood a putteed chauffeur with a bag in hand to announce that Mrs. Marquod was ready. X calmly walked out of the house to join Mrs. Marquod in the drive.

---

23   AUTHOR'S NOTE: A.J. Martin, A.P. news correspondent, is perhaps the most famous alias of Secret Agent X.

The chauffeur backed the car from the drive, got out, helped Mrs. Marquod into the car, then whispered to X:

"I took the liberty of removing poor old Grouch, Mr. Marquod. I thought the sight of him might be upsetting to Mrs. Marquod."

"Quite right, indeed," X said. "Upsetting to all of us. Quickly now, to the Seville Hotel."

Mrs. Marquod maintained silence until they were nearly at the end of their short trip uptown. Then she said: "You don't think Doris will be in any danger, do you? I feel terribly guilty, as though I were deserting her."

X stroked the woman's hand. "Now, now. Doris will simply read your note and come to the hotel at once. Nothing to worry about. Nothing at all."

At the hotel, X engaged a suite of rooms on the twelfth floor, signed Marquod's name to the register without hesitation, reflecting as he did so that he could have made a fortune at forgery had he been so inclined. Then he accompanied Mrs. Marquod to their rooms, tipped the bellhop and immediately excused himself.

Down in the hotel washroom, X removed the shaggy gray toupee which had been part of his disguise as Marquod, and substituted a sandy-colored one for it. His fingers worked swiftly over the plastic material that covered his face, ironing out wrinkles, adopting a disguise he had used countless times before—that of A.J. Martin, a commonplace appearing individual with a reputation for being on the spot when the great news stories broke.

Returning to the Marquod rooms, he found that Mrs. Marquod had retired to the bedroom. X quietly locked the door of the bedroom and sat down to await the arrival of the doomed men. He had not long to wait before George Sarles, wealthy munitions manufacturer, put in his appearance. But Sarles was not alone.

X might have expected that big, redheaded Mike Kafore, who strained his words through a fist-flattened nose, and hovered around Sarles like a hen mothering her only chick, would be there. Mike was Sarles' bodyguard.

But there was also Sarles' physician, a black, spidery man with snapping blue eyes and a lipless steel clamp of a mouth. And there was tall, gangling John Leonard with his hollow eyes and thin, sad cheeks. Leonard was vice president of the Sarles concern, having worked his way to that office from a position as Sarles' personal secretary.

"You see, Mr. Martin," Sarles explained, "these men were present when your call came." He stroked white hair that was so perfectly groomed it seemed molded from porcelain. "They were my guests and I couldn't very well order them from the house. Certainly anything that affects me affects my business and consequently Mr. Leonard here."

"I can withdraw if I am not wanted," said Leonard sourly.

"No need of that, Mr. Leonard," X said. "You're here and you might as well stay. I had hoped to keep the meeting entirely secret."

"I can assure you I have no intention of withdrawing," Dr. Dynes said sharply. "Mr. Sarles' heart is in no condition to withstand undue excitement. If this danger of yours, Mr. Martin, turns out to be a fizzle, I'll not forgive you in a hurry."

"I can assure you," X said quietly, "that the danger will not turn out a fizzle."

Mike Kafore thumbed his barrel of a chest. "And it's a cinch Pop ain't goin' nowheres wit'out me, ain't it, Pop?"

SARLES' SMILE formed stiffly on handsome lips. "I long ago tired of trying to escape from you, Mike." He looked around the room. "Where are the others? I understand that Gordon Service is giving his repeat broadcast for west coast listeners and will be considerably late. Where is Rex Durmont?"

As though in answer to his question, a knock sounded at the door. Mike Kafore took it upon himself to answer the knock, his right hand thrust into his pocket which ill disguised the size of the automatic he carried. He opened the door only a little way, like the doorman of an old-time speakeasy. He turned his battered face toward X, said:

"It's Durmont now. Biers is with him."

Biers' presence was logical, X had to admit, for he was the millionaire backer of Durmont's coming political struggle for governorship. Biers was a heavily made, dark complexioned man. He preceded Durmont into the room, completely eclipsing Durmont by his jovial greeting of all those present.

Durmont, a young man at forty, with black, gimlet eyes that looked as though they never slept, came over to X and pressed his hand.

"What we thought would be a quiet meeting of five men seems to have turned out to be a convention," he said. "I can't say that I like it. I met Marquod and that brother of his down in the lobby.

Pleasant chap, his brother. I asked Boise Marquod if he would go up with us, and he said he'd be damned if he would. Acted rather agitated, almost frightened, but he refused to pitch in his lot with us."

X laughed lightly. "That's because Boise Marquod is here to deal with kidnapers, or so he expects. That was the only way I could get him here at all—by kidnaping his wife. He'll be up in a moment and find that he has joined the doomed men in spite of himself."

"What's that?" Maurice Biers cut in. "Kidnaped Marquod's wife?" He slapped X on the back. "Martin, that's ingenious! How did you manage it?"

"I'd rather not go into that," X said. "That's probably Marquod at the door now. Let him in, Mike. You look like you might be up to kidnaping a lady."

"Okay, Mr. Martin," Mike Kafore said, "only you ain't exactly much when it comes to passing out compliments. Pop thinks I'm an angel, don't you, Pop?"

George Sarles nodded, stiffly smiling. "But you talk too much."

Mike opened the door with the same caution, closed it again immediately. He turned. "It ain't me pal Marquod. It's a guy with a nose like a pickle. Maybe it's that deathly dame."

"Madam Death does not have a nose like a pickle, Mike," X said, going to the door. He opened the door, looked out at a man who wore a derby hat and tilted a cigar at an approved house detective angle. He was no house detective. He was Steve Wienhardt, Gordon Service's agent. He said:

"Wienhardt's the name, brother. I'm representing Gordon Service, the radio commentator. Mr. Service is busy right now with a broadcast, so I hiked over to see what all this is about. Five doomed men, huh? Ought to be a smart publicity angle in this for my client."

"Come in," X said. "You don't look like a man who can be kept out of anything."

"That's right," declared Wienhardt, not in the least offended. He walked in, looked about the room, now somewhat crowded. "Quite a little gathering of the cream, I'd say. Durmont, Sarles, Biers. And hi there, Doc! How are the patients dying? Who's that—" pointing at John Leonard. "The undertaker?"

"Get this," X said, taking Wienhardt by the sleeve. "There's no publicity angle in this for anybody. If there had been, I'd have scooped it for the papers. If you ever met anything serious, this is it."

Wienhardt shrugged. "I could get Service a cross-country lecture tour with this publicity."

"You won't," Durmont said in a quiet, penetrating voice. "You are working Service to death as it is."

Wienhardt sighed. "You should kick. He's on your side of the political fence."

"It's the Marquod brothers outside now, Mr. Martin," Mike Kafore announced. "Tell pickle-nose to button his lip."

MIKE OPENED the door and Boise Marquod strode into the room, looked bewilderedly about, shook his mane of white hair, asked: "What's the meaning of this, Sarles? What's the meaning of this, Durmont? I've told you I am not the least interested in your united defense against some crank who sends threatening letters."

"Now ease up a bit, Mr. Boise," Arnold Marquod said. He entered from behind his brother, looking buoyantly happy, greeting those he knew and those he did not know with a pleasant smile and a nod. "You'll have to excuse my brother's brusqueness. He was told to come to this room to negotiate with some criminals regarding the kidnaping of his wife. It is little wonder if he seems upset."

"Little wonder indeed!" Boise Marquod growled. "What kind of a farce is this?"

"You'll die of cerebral hemorrhage if you don't stop throwing these tantrums, Boise Marquod," Dr. Dynes snapped.

Boise Marquod flushed, stamped his foot. "Damn it, I'm not throwing a tantrum!"

"You see," Sarles said, "It is the only way we could get you to listen to reason, Boise. You'll admit you are hot tempered. And we thought that if we kidnaped your wife—"

"*You* kidnaped my wife?" Marquod pounced at Sarles.

Sarles smiled stiffly. "*I* didn't, now Boise—"

Mike Kafore grabbed Boise Marquod by the shoulder. "Shall I lay him out, Pop?"

"Of course not," Sarles said, somewhat annoyed by Kafore's zeal. "I think that if Mr. Martin will explain why we are here, you'll see things straight, Marquod."

"I'm damned if I will!" Marquod exploded. "Doomed men! Damned jackasses!"

Arnold Marquod took hold of his brother's shoulders, and with unexpected strength forced him into a chair. "Listen to reason,

Boise. These men aren't the sort to be taking some hoax this seriously."

"Mr. Marquod," X got in hurriedly before Boise could break out in another tirade, "you are one of the five doomed men—key men who uphold democracy in this country. The very organization which you cried out against tonight is threatening your life. We know, because of a radio message which leaked out in spite of efforts of the European branch of this organization, that a man known as the Doctor and a woman known as Madam Death, are in America for the sole purpose of murdering you and four other men.

"We believe that if the five doomed men unite, go to some solitary stronghold, Madam Death and her Doctor will follow us. When they do we hope to be ready for them."

"Sounds like a very interesting adventure to me," Arnold Marquod said, beaming upon Agent X. "A murderous woman, a mysterious doctor."

"Sounds like damned melodramatic clap-trap!" Boise Marquod said, somewhat less vehemently. "Madam Death! I remained a bachelor for fifty-eight years. I guess I'm a match for any murdering woman."

"But a woman got you finally, didn't she?" Steve Wienhardt put in. "That's what I tell Gordon Service. Keep away from women and you'll get to the top."

"Where is my wife?" Boise Marquod bounced to his feet. His brother quite promptly shoved him back into the chair.

"Your wife is perfectly safe," X said. "To return to the subject, I can tell you all that Madam Death is a reality. An almost unbelievable reality. I have seen her work tonight. *She kills at a touch of her beautiful hands.*"

THERE was an interval of silence occasioned by the grave tone in which X spoke. The men looked uneasily at one another. Finally, Arnold Marquod said, his eyes fixed on X.

"Beggin' your pardon, but how does it happen you are so well informed, sir? I don't believe I quite got your name."

"An excellent point," John Leonard put in, "Though it's no business of mine, except my interest in the welfare of Mr. Sarles."

"There's something in that, Martin," Maurice Biers spoke up. "How did you happen to get wind of this?"

"It concerned me personally," X admitted. "The doomed men are Sarles, Durmont, Service, Boise Marquod. And there is a fifth on the list of prospective cadavers. I am the fifth doomed man."

Boise Marquod cleared his throat. "That throws a new light on it."

"Doesn't it?" his brother said, "because if this is clap-trap as you've claimed, Boise, and a lot of old-woman fears, it's rather odd finding a newspaperman mixed up in it. What I mean, Mr. Martin, newspapermen are not usually cowards."

"Never knew one that was," Marquod said, shaking his head, "Gentlemen, you can deal me in. Martin's plan sounds like horse sense—baiting these murderers by going to some lonely spot. Then we'll crack down on them, by hell!"

"And there's no better spot for the place," Durmont said quietly, "than your seaside mansion, Marquod. I suggest that we leave immediately. We can pick up Service at the Broadcast Building. I advise you to leave your wife here, Marquod. I have no intention of taking Mrs. Durmont."

"Sure, make it a stag party," Wienhardt said.

"It won't be a party," X said, "and there's no reason to include you among those present, Wienhardt."

Wienhardt tilted his cigar belligerently. "Listen, wise guy, as long as he is earning ten thousand bucks a week, my client don't get out from under my nose."

"He couldn't," Mike Kafore said. "Not that nose. Do I hammer it in for him, Mr. Martin?"

X paid no attention to the Kafore-Wienhardt squabble. He went over to Boise Marquod's chair. "Your wife," he said, "is in the next room, if you'd care to say good-bye to her." He gave the bewildered Marquod the key to the door....

While the doomed men and their friends hurried about their own individual business which preceded their departure from the city, a lone and very lovely woman whose hair was like threads of gold, whose face was concealed by a black veil, picked up a telephone in a small, two-room flat in an unpretentious quarter of the city. Her movements were mechanical, weary.

"Yes," she said flatly into the transmitter.

"Listen," came a clear, commanding voice from the phone. "This is the Doctor."

"I failed miserably, Doctor, because a policeman intervened. You have ordered me to keep away from policemen, since our presence must not be publicized. I was somewhat delayed in disposing of the man's dog which attacked me. By that time, the policeman had put in his appearance."

"I know. Listen closely. You have seen the face of Gordon Service. He must die tonight before he is joined by the others. You will proceed in this fashion. You will immediately dye your hair dark brown. Proceed to the Broadcast Building where you will await the arrival of a certain young man who will be bearing a satchel.

"You will lead him to some secluded alley nearby and there dispose of him. You know who this man is, as I have pointed him out to you several times. Take the satchel which the young man carries. It contains clothes. You will proceed exactly as planned. I will give you a mental command when to move against Mr. Service."

The voice stopped. Madam Death slowly replaced the phone on its cradle. Her fingers went to her golden hair, touched it lovingly. She sighed. In her poisoned brain sang the order of her master. "You will dye your hair dark brown...."

ONE HOUR later Rex Durmont, Maurice Biers, Steve Wienhardt and Agent X left for the Broadcast Building in Durmont's car. The Marquod brothers, Sarles, Mike Kafore, John Leonard and Dr. Dynes followed in the doctor's car. It was not as X had wished it.

He would have preferred that the five doomed men segregate themselves completely from their friends and associates. But he had to remember that each of those doomed to die was a leader in his respective field—a born leader is not easily led.

The two cars unloaded outside the bronze doors of the Broadcast Building. Even the granite-faced doorman was slightly flustered by the appearance of such a distinguished assembly; he even forgot to give his usual snub to Steve Wienhardt, who hailed him with: "Hi, your majesty."

X led the way to one of the high-speed elevators. Service's office and studio were on the tenth floor. X gave the floor number to the elevator operator.

"Don't ever have to bother with them when I'm along, Mr. Martin," Steve Wienhardt declared. "Everybody knows where I'm headed for. Everybody knows me."

"Ain't that everybody's misfortune," groaned Mike Kafore.

And then the elevator opened and they walked out upon the tenth floor.

An exceedingly handsome page boy dressed in the blue and orange uniform of the Broadcast Building stiffly awaited them in the hall. With white gloved hands he motioned them into a beautifully furnished waiting room.

"What program were you expecting to hear, gentlemen?" Inquired the page, his fair, young face as emotionless as a doll's.

"We will wait for Mr. Service to conclude his program," said Sarles. "He is expecting us."

"Tell him Steve is here," Wienhardt announced. "He's never too busy to see me, Wienhardt means money."

They filed into the waiting room, and the page, instead of obeying Wienhardt's order, stood stiffly just outside the door. The men found seats, with the exception of Kafore, who hovered around Sarles' chair; and Agent X, who stood in such a position that he could watch the page.

The boy interested him strangely. The clear, rather high voice in which he had addressed them was rather feminine. The modeling of his features was nothing short of exquisite, which, on the face of a man, was not entirely attractive.

The men fell to talking of politics and Rex Durmont's chances of election, until Durmont declared he felt quite like a cadaver at some medical school demonstration and asked if it wasn't time that Gordon Service showed up.

"Why not have the page boy go to Service's office and tell him we are waiting?" Boise Marquod suggested.

Sarles, who sat near the door, turned his well-groomed white head toward the immobile page. "Boy," he said, extending a crisp greenback toward the page, "please go to Mr. Service's office and tell him Mr. Sarles and party are waiting for him."

The page did not so much as look at the money which Sarles extended, but walked stiffly from the door into the hall. Sarles looked at the money in his hand, smiled stiffly, stuffed it into his pocket.

"That young man doesn't grab at opportunity, does he?" said Dr. Dynes.

But the doctor was not the only one who had witnessed the page's odd departure from the usual rule of accepting tips. Secret Agent X was immediately on the alert. The appearance of the page, his wooden attitude, the blank expression on his face—all contributed to an unpleasant chill which moved along X's spine.

He stepped into the hall, watched the page approach the door marked with Service's name. And the page did an extremely odd thing. He paused a moment before the door to remove his gloves.

As X moved quickly to follow the page, the door of one of the large studios opened. A flood of people who had been watching the broadcast moved into the hall, blocking X off from the brilliantly-colored figure of the page.

X elbowed into the crowd, fighting its tide which would have carried him in the opposite direction. He jammed his right hand inside his coat, gripping the butt of an automatic. If he had to shoot to kill, that page must not reach Gordon Service!

CHAPTER IV

FATE'S FRAME-UP

"WHO YOU THINK you're pushing?" a red-faced giant of a man demanded, blocking X's path. The man planted both hands in the middle of X's chest and shoved him backward. Had X not been so intent on trying to see if the page had entered Service's door, the red-faced person would have found him a difficult thing to shove. But as it was, he lost ground and precious seconds.

X got his elbows going, shoved himself forward, cleared the crowd at last. Service's door was closed and there was no sign of the uniformed page.

X put his left hand on the doorknob, drew his gun, but kept it out of sight and close to his body. He turned the knob, thrust open the door, walked into Service's office.

It was a small room. The sound-proofing which covered the walls was decorated to closely resemble fine walnut paneling. Against one wall were two high-backed chairs, uncomfortable enough to have been placed there for visitors. The center of the room was occupied by a desk, lighted by a small lamp.

A door in the wall opposite the visitors' chairs was partly open. In a padded swivel chair in front of the desk sat a man, a pile of thin copy paper in his hands which was resting on his lap. He had a shrewd face, pale in the lamplight. Black brows beetled beneath curly black hair. There was a thick oblong of mustache above his mouth. He sat strangely still.

Gun in hand, X crossed on tiptoe to Gordon Service, bent over the man, stared down into the face. Service's whimsical little smile was frozen on his lips. No more would his shrewd criticism and cutting sarcasm wake up a mentally lazy public to evils within their country which they, by united antagonistic opinion, could eradicate. Gordon Service had died while looking over the script for tomorrow's broadcast.

The half-open door creaked. X looked up. In the opening stood a girl, slender, attractive, dark-haired. She was wearing gloves, a hat with a black veil attached, a dark suit. He saw little else about her, for suddenly she was screaming.

X sprang toward her, would have shoved her out of the way, in order to see if the page had escaped through that door, if she had not thrust out her hands in an attempt to catch and hold him. X stopped.

How could he know this woman was not Madam Death?

The girl opened her mouth and screamed, "Murder!"

Almost at once the little room was jammed with men—elevator boys, pages, building officials, radio artists. X was literally smothered with humanity. His gun was wrested from his hand, lost in the mad scramble to prevent him, a supposed murderer, from escaping.

They pinned him to the floor, two men holding each arm, for there was not one among them who had not felt the power behind his fists. X looked up through a forest of tousled heads, saw the stern faces of two uniformed police.

The girl who had screamed was crying out: "Arrest him, officer. He's a murderer. He killed Gordon Service. I saw him. There's his gun over there on the floor. Don't let him escape."

"Don't worry, lady," said the cop. "Houdini couldn't get out of this room." And X was perfectly willing to admit that neither could Agent X.

"Just a minute, officer," X protested as one of the cops planted a knee on his chest and forced his wrists together, while the other clamped handcuffs in place. "The young lady is badly mistaken."

"You can't very well argue with an eye witness, buddy," said the cop. "And there's the body over there, ain't there?"

"Clear the room. Get out of here, you men," the other cop bellowed. "We got him red-handed. Everything under control. Don't get excited."

THEY FILED out, muttering disappointedly, until there was no one in the room except the cops, a plain-clothes man, who had put in his appearance, X, and the girl. They dragged X to his feet, set him down in one of the high-backed chairs.

"A quick confession on the spot will help to make things a lot easier for you," said the plain-clothes man.

X sprang up....

"You won't get it," X said, "though it would speed your promotion, I've no doubt. At the Olympic games, you should win a prize for conclusion jumping, if the girl doesn't nose you out. Ask her how she happened to turn up at the precise moment."

"I'm Mary Ferris," the girl explained quickly. X judged she was on the point of tears. "I'm Gordon Service's secretary. I mean, I— was Gordon Service's sec—secretary."

Her gloved fingers fumbled with the clasp of her bag. She brought out a handkerchief and raised her veil slightly. X studied her and found her an agreeable subject. She had clear, blue-green eyes, babyish lips which were trembling slightly at the moment, a warm, healthy-looking complexion. And this might be Madam Death!

"Mr. Service had just announced that I might go home. I went to the closet, which is just down that little hall—" pointing to the door through which she had come. "He—he was alive and smiling when

I left him. And after I got my things on, I came back to say good night to him. And I saw him in his chair, that man bending over him with a gun. I knew Mr. Service's life was in danger. I screamed."

"It looks to me," X said, "as though this final good night to Mr. Service was rather superfluous. Isn't that your particular shade of lipstick on his cheek?"

The detective wheeled on X and let him have a blow on the mouth. "You'll speak when you're asked, buddy."

X shrugged. "That's what you think."

Mary Ferris' bosom swelled proudly. "It *is* my lipstick. Gordon and I were to be married next spring. And now—now—"

She burst into tears, turned, ran into the hall from which she had come. X started after her. Perhaps Madam Death was escaping. How easily the kiss she had planted on Service's cheek might have been the last thing the man was conscious of.

The dick planted himself in front of X. "Are you going to come across?"

X nodded. "There's a card in my wallet explaining that I am A.J. Martin, newspaperman. I can assure you that I had nothing to do with Mr. Service's death. I was, in fact, trying to prevent it."

"Yeah, with a gun," the dick sneered. "Well, you want us to get your story the tough way. I guess we can do it, all right. Punch it out of you, if that's what you want."

X shrugged. "You don't know what a good punch is, fella. Take off these bracelets and I'll improve your education."

The dick thumbed at the door. "Take him away. I gotta get going on this."

IT WAS an odd situation X found himself in. As far as his own personal danger was concerned, no sooner had he been popped into the basement prison cell at police headquarters to await further questioning, than he became entirely beyond the reach of Madam Death.

At the same time his entire purpose was defeated, for he was effectively cut off from the four men he had sworn to protect. He could not tell the police the truth because—even if they should believe him, which was doubtful—it meant that the names of the doomed men and their hiding place would become public property. That way it would be comparatively simple for the murderer to hunt them out, kill them while they were deprived of X's protection.

His mental summing up of his predicament was cut off by the appearance of the same detective who had brought him to police headquarters. The dick opened the grating, motioned X to come out. There were two armed harness bulls behind the dick, and not the ghost of a chance, at the moment of X's making a getaway.

"Detective Lieutenant Dhiel wants to see you, Martin," the dick said. "You'd better make up your mind to come out with the truth. Because if you think I'm tough, wait until you meet Dhiel."

X gave the dick an insolent glance. "But then I don't think you are particularly tough. Your muscular development seems to have been confined entirely to the enlargement of your bellows."

The dick bared his teeth, yanked at X's arm. X brushed the man's hand down with a sharp blow. He said: "You show me the way. I'll get to your hard-boiled lieutenant under my own power."

Lieutenant Dhiel turned out to be a short, wide-shouldered person with a low forehead, an aggressive chin. There were two other detectives in the small, hot, windowless sweat room to which X was taken. X was told to sit down in a chair. Lamps, with the brilliance of photo-flash bulbs, were turned on him.

Dhiel passed backward and forward in front of X like a bear in a cage. Conversationally, he began: "This isn't a pinch, Martin. We don't want you to look at it that way at all. This man Gordon Service threw plenty of weight when he was around. Everybody thought a lot of him. Murder just doesn't go in this town, much less the murder of some influential person. What we want from you is help, that's all."

"Well?" X challenged.

Dhiel stopped pacing, moving in closer to X. "Just tell us the facts."

X nodded. "I entered Service's office and I found him dead. His secretary, Miss Ferris, entered the room a moment later, saw me bending over Service, supposed I was the murderer—a very mistaken but understandable conclusion."

"Listen, Martin," Dhiel spoke a little more harshly, "I've heard of guys gargling just before they go into somebody's office, but they don't usually pull a gun."

"I had reason to believe that an attempt might be made on Service's life," X said. "I was trying to prevent the threatened attempt."

"Yeah?" Dhiel acted interested. "Who was going to make that attempt?"

X shook his head. "If I knew their names and where to find them, I would have handed them over to the police before now."

"But you don't deny you had a gun in your hand?" Dhiel insisted. "Did you hear the shot that killed Service?"

"No. Because there was no shot."

DHIEL pounced on that. His right hand closed on X's shoulder, fingertips biting into muscle. "So he wasn't shot, eh? You *know* he wasn't shot. How in hell do you know that?"

"There was nothing that looked like a bullet wound on him," X explained calmly.

"No, you bet there wasn't! He was poisoned, wasn't he? Ever see this before?" Dhiel held out what appeared to be a gleaming cigarette case beneath X's face. The case caught the brilliant lamp light and turned its searing rays into X's eyes.

X blinked. "What is it?"

Dhiel flipped open the case. It contained three small cylindrical bottles of opaque glass and a hypodermic syringe.

"Where did you find that?" X demanded.

"In the waiting room near Service's office in the Broadcast Building. Now, what we want to know—"

"What's in those bottles?" X persisted. "What kind of poison?"

"We haven't got an analysis yet," Dhiel explained. Then his face flushed. He put one foot on the edge of X's chair, rested an elbow on his knee, put his heavy chin in his hand. "Say, listen, who's asking questions, you or me?"

"Listen to logic, Lieutenant," X rapped. "If Service was poisoned and I did it, and that case contained the poison, what was the poisonous murder weapon doing in the Broadcast waiting room while I was murdering Service in Service's office? Where in the waiting room was that case found?"

"On the seat of one of the chairs. You planted it there—"

"The truth of the matter is, Lieutenant," X's voice rang out accusatively, "you're on a spot. You know the public is going to clamor for the scalp of the killer of Gordon Service. So you hop on me, when you've only the flimsiest circumstantial evidence against me—evidence you won't even examine closely because you're afraid it won't hold water.

"You haven't the slightest idea what killed Service. Nobody has. So you're trying to rig up a lot of hooey that will make you look good in the eyes of the public. Not that I blame you a whole lot. You've got a job to keep. It's not that you're doing anything crooked. You're just trying to look plenty efficient, when the truth of the matter is, some reporter ought to print, 'The Police Are Baffled.' "

"What's the matter with Dhiel?" one of the subordinate dicks whispered to his companion. "This guy's got him stumped."

"This guy's too smart for his pants," the other growled.

Dhiel, his hands clasped behind him, paced over to the other detectives. He said: "You got to dig up something else. Try to get an angle that will connect Martin with the other killing. He's mixed up in this some way, only he's right when he says we haven't got anything on him. Slap him back in the cell."

So they took him back to the cell, and the dick who had been responsible for the pinch kicked X into the tiny coop and slammed the door. X went to the grill and called after the dick:

"What's your name?"

"Rossi," replied the dick.

"Thanks," X said. "One of these days I'm going to alter your face so much you'll have a little trouble remembering who you are."

X went back to the narrow bunk and sat down. Perhaps at this very instant, somewhere else in the city, Madam Death crept upon one of the doomed men. And X was powerless to prevent it.

X checked over the limited equipment he himself carried in secret compartments which even the police searching had failed to reveal. There was a quantity of makeup material concealed in the hollow heel of his shoe. Inside the case of his watch was a coiled saw of watch-spring steel, which, in time, would have enabled him to saw his way out of the prison cell. But in addition to time, he had to have solitude, and there were a number of cops in the basement hall outside who had settled themselves for a game of cards.

Hours of the night dragged on. The police outside continued the game with renewed interest. X had stretched himself on the bunk and was forcing himself to relax, when Detective Rossi came to the grill and said: "On your feet, Martin."

X rolled from the bunk. Rossi was extending a French type telephone through the bars. He said: "Just say a few words into this phone. There's a gal who thinks she can recognize your voice. If she can, then we'll see whether you've got an alibi for the Service job or not."

A puzzled frown darkened X's face. He took the phone, said hello. A woman's voice said: "I want to say a few words to you. Mr. Boise Marquod is here."

"Let me speak to Mr. Marquod," X insisted.

"Fine," Rossi cut in. "Let's have that phone, Mr. Martin."

ROSSI took back the phone and retired with it. A moment later Dhiel and Rossi came to the door of X's cell. Dhiel said: "That about clinches things, Mr. Martin."

"Clinches what things?" X demanded.

"That you're the guy that kidnaped Mrs. Marquod. That girl you talked to was the switchboard operator at the Brock-Broadmoor. She says that yours is the same voice that called Marquod and informed him that his wife had been kidnaped."

X laughed. "That kidnaping was a joke on Marquod. All you have to do is get hold of Boise Marquod and ask him. Or ask Durmont or George Sarles."

"Murder isn't a joke, Martin," Dhiel said, "And Mrs. Boise Marquod died exactly as Gordon Service died. It was pretty smart to kidnap a woman, say it was a joke, and then kill her."

X seized the iron bars that separated him from Dhiel. "You're talking nonsense. How could I have killed Mrs. Marquod when I was in police custody?"

"You weren't," Dhiel contradicted. "Mrs. Marquod died some time before Service did. We'll take down your confession whenever you're ready to give it. You're too smart a guy to make it hard for yourself."

X laughed harshly. "I'm smart enough to know that you don't dare get tough with me. Because you know well I'm going out of here and it wouldn't do to have any rough stuff get into the papers."

Dhiel shrugged—it was rather a helpless gesture—and he and Rossi went away.

Dawn came, and other cops replaced those in the card game. X lay sleeplessly on his cot, mentally chalking up the passing hours, wondering what dire things might be taking place while he was incarcerated here. Eight o'clock came, then nine. Detective Rossi put in his appearance, glumly unlocked the door of the cell.

"You got a lawyer, Martin," Rossi said. "We're letting you see him."

"Letting?" X repeated. "You couldn't very well keep me from it, could you?"

Inwardly, he was puzzled. Was it perhaps a trick of Madam Death and the' Doctor to get X out in the open where he would be their prey? Had the remaining doomed men already been disposed of?

He left the cell, walked with Rossi down the labyrinthine corridor toward steps leading from the basement of the headquarters building. They veered to the right at the foot of the steps, turned into a small office—a room with a desk, a couple of chairs, a clothes closet.

Rossi locked the door from the inside, remaining in the room. A blond young man with sharp eyes stood up, said to Rossi: "This is highly irregular. I have a right to see my client alone." He took off a green felt hat which was slightly too large for him, put it down on top of his brief-case.

Rossi growled. "You're alone."

X laughed. "We are indeed."

The lawyer shook X's hand. "My name is Bilsman. I'm interested in your case."

"Is that so?" asked X gravely. "Who interested you, Mr. Bilsman?"

Bilsman coughed. "I was specifically asked not to reveal the name of your benefactor. Let's consider exactly where you stand."

X and the lawyer sat down in the chairs. Rossi stood over against the wall and considered them contemptuously.

"Now, Mr. Martin, the information which I have indicates that you were seen by Miss Ferris bending over Gordon Service with a gun in your hand. Mr. Service was dead. He was not shot. Now, it occurred to me that we could make it look rather absurd to the jury, your bending over a dead man with a gun in your hand. Surely, had you been Mr. Service's murderer, you would know that he was dead and therefore the precaution of holding a gun on him would be quite ridiculous, unless you had just shot him, which the police must admit you did not."

X stood up directly in front of the lawyer. His right hand in his coat pocket balled into a fist. "Then you think I have a pretty good chance to beat a murder rap?"

"I think," the lawyer said, "that if the police went into court with the evidence they now have, we could make them look pretty absurd. It is obvious—"

X crouched slightly. His fist came out of his pocket fast, arched up to the point of the lawyer's chin with all the power which X had impatiently leashed during the past hours. The lawyer did not have a chance to leave his chair until it had gone over backwards with him and then he rolled from it, eyes closed, body limp, quite as though he didn't care about anything any more.

CHAPTER V

THE TRAIL TO NOWHERE

THE BLOW X handed Attorney Bilsman was actually a brief incident in the move he had been planning in his mind for the past five minutes. He moved with such swiftness and such precision that it seemed the plan was the result of hours of thinking.

The next incident, and one which was of lasting importance to Detective Rossi, consisted of three successive leaps which brought X to meet Rossi just as the latter showed his gun. X seized Rossi's gun hand in such a manner that his forefinger wedged in between the trigger and the trigger guard, making it impossible for the detective to fire.

Then X handed Rossi a punch along the side of his nose. If Rossi had a cry of pain in his system, he was given no opportunity to vent it before that driving left fist was back again, this time to land back of Rossi's ear. And by that time Rossi was in no condition at all to remonstrate against such treatment. He folded across X's shoulder, and as soon as the Agent had deprived the lax fingers of the detective's gun, he lugged Rossi to the clothes closet, opened the door, thrust him inside.

X paused a moment, drew a breath, held it, listening for any possible commotion in the hall. Police headquarters was remarkably silent. The Agent's little war had been conducted with a swift silence that had disturbed no one except the lawyer and the detective. X knelt beside the lawyer.

"Now, Mr. Bilsman," he said to the unconscious man, "you and I can carry on our conversation without any eavesdropping from our friend Rossi."

As he spoke, X's voice drifted away from the deep, resonant tones of Martin, became the higher-pitched, sharper voice of Attorney Bilsman, himself. And while he crouched, his fingers were busy with the heel of his shoe, removing a portion of the heel to reveal a cavity which contained a lead tube of plastic, volatile material.

With so limited a supply of equipment, it would not be the most perfect disguise he had ever achieved, but he was counting on perfect acting and sheer bluff to carry it across. The sandy toupee he wore, as part of his disguise, wasn't very much like the golden locks of Bilsman, but beneath the attorney's hat, the toupee scarcely showed.

Since he was still wearing the full dress suit he had worn the night before, X had to change clothes with Bilsman. The attorney's green-gray trousers were slightly large around the waist and a couple of inches too short, but an adjustment of suspenders took care of the difference sufficiently so that the trousers would look all right when he had put on Bilsman's topcoat.

His disguise as complete as he could make it, X lifted Bilsman and carried him to the closet where the attorney joined the detective. Rossi was showing signs of regaining consciousness so X knew he must put his plan into effect at once.

He grasped Bilsman's brief-case, pulled Bilsman's hat down as far as possible, went to the door, unlocked it. He stepped out into the hall, almost into the arms of a policeman who eyed him strangely.

X calmly turned his back on the cop, spoke, in Bilsman's voice: "I'll see you this afternoon, Mr. Martin." Then he shut the door, nodded at the cop, walked to the stairs.

The cop opened the door of the little room where X, Rossi, and the lawyer had been. X didn't turn round to see what the cop was doing. He heard the sound of the door opening, knew exactly what would follow, and went up the stairs three at a time.

DOWN in the basement, somebody uttered a hoarse alarm. But X was on the move, and moving faster all the time. He brushed through the side door of the building quite as though there had been no door there at all.

After that, it was what he didn't do rather than what he did, that was important to his safety. He didn't dash into the street, race down the sidewalk and hail a passing taxi. Nor did he make any effort to lose himself in the swiftly moving morning traffic in the street outside.

He simply walked down the side of the building, to the back entrance, walked coolly into police headquarters again, up half a flight of steps to the main floor, into the room with *Laboratory* lettered on its opaque door.

A white-coated technician looked up from a comparative microscope, blinked to relieve obvious eye strain. X, his hand in the pocket of Bilsman's coat, produced one of the lawyer's cards. He said:

"I'm interested in the case of Mr. A.J. Martin, who is being held under suspicion of murdering Mr. Gordon Service. The police attach considerable importance to a little cigarette case which contained three small vials and a hypodermic needle. This case was found in the waiting room where Mr. Martin and a number of other men awaited Mr. Service. Would you mind telling me what your analysis revealed?"

And if the technician did mind, X was fully prepared to extract that information from him by force. Before Service's death, Durmont, Sarles, Dr. Dynes, Mike Kafore, Steve Wienhardt, Arnold Marquod, Maurice Biers, John Leonard, Boise Marquod, had been in the waiting room where the case had been found. X was certain that it had not been there when they had entered, which would indicate that one of the above men had dropped it. He was anxious to see what position, if any, the police had assigned it in the puzzling murder problem which faced them.

"I'm ballistics," said the technician. "Dr. Hughes made the analysis and he isn't here at the moment. However, I see no objection to letting you see the somewhat surprising information Hughes obtained. A remarkable man, Hughes. His chemistry has cracked more cases in this town than all of Dhiel's third degrees."

"You'd think, then," X could not refrain from commenting as he followed the technician into a tiny office, "that Dhiel would forsake the worship of brawn for that of brain."

The technician laughed. "Not Dhiel. I expect he's been nearly frantic in the past twenty-four hours trying to keep up with murder. First the discovery of Service's murder. Then Mrs. Marquod— and Dhiel hasn't got to first base on that unidentified corpse they scooped out of the river three days ago. Not that you can blame him, for the body had been pretty well mutilated. These moron killers are the hardest of all to get. Let me see, Hughes showed me that report. Here somewhere."

The technician fumbled with paper in a wire basket on Dr. Hughes' desk. He nodded his head. "Here we are. I don't suppose you'd be interested in the technical end of it. Contents of the first flask were insulin."

"Insulin? Isn't that the stuff people who have diabetes have to take?" [24]

The technician nodded. "Perfectly harmless stuff and an absolute necessity to those suffering from the disease you mention." His eyes returned to the doctor's report sheet. "Contents of the second vial—insulin."

"And the third?" X urged.

"The third? Well, that was filled with insulin, too. Which merely means that the owner of the case suffered from diabetes, which isn't a sin, according to any laws I know. Dhiel will be quite thoroughly disappointed."

"I shouldn't wonder," X said. "And has no one claimed the case?"

The technician shook his head. "It does seem that a person suffering from diabetes would notice his loss immediately. Not but what he could obtain his ration of insulin easily enough. But that case is a mighty handy way to carry it."

"Maybe," X suggested, "he doesn't want to admit that he has diabetes. Some people are sensitive about their health. By the way, just what did kill Service and Mrs. Marquod?"

"If I had an answer for that one," the technician replied, "I'd rate a medal. Both died apparently from the same cause. Condition of the heart, Dr. Hughes said, indicates radium poisoning, which, of course, is about as likely as that they were run over by steam shovels. Neither of them ever had any occasion to receive radium treatments. And, besides radium poisoning is a slow process.

"I looked in on the autopsy last night, and it looked like an electrical shock had done the damage to me. And that's just as far off as the radium theory. Frankly, we're stumped. If this Martin did the killing, he's a wizard and nobody will ever be able to catch him with anything that will hold."

"I sincerely hope that is a fact," X said, and having thanked the technician, he left headquarters by the back door, unnoticed by police who were probably hunting him blocks away....

---

24   AUTHOR'S NOTE: It is evident that X was anxious not to appear too well informed in scientific matters lest he betray himself. Actually he is well versed in medical, chemical and biological knowledge.

THE YOUNG woman in Attorney Bilsman's office was not attractive. She had coarse, pinkish hair, small eyes magnified by thick-lensed glasses. She was industriously filing her nails when she was surprised by the entrance of a man she had every reason to believe was her employer.

Agent X had journeyed from the rear of police headquarters to the building where Bilsman had his office, without exciting any suspicion. Because the disguise he wore was perfect for obtaining the material he now needed, he had made no attempt to alter it. He was playing his bluff to the limit, knowing that at any moment the game might end with his capture by the police.

The young woman dropped her nail file and it made an astonishing noise as it hit the floor. She said rather dully: "Why, Mr. Bilsman!"

"How often have I told you that when I am out of the office I expect you to conduct yourself exactly as though I were here?" X asked in Bilsman's voice.

"Why, I never heard you say anything like that," the girl said. "Really, I didn't."

Which X reflected, might be entirely true. He said: "Well, remind me to tell you that some time. I've just been out talking to this fellow Martin the police have slated for the Service murder. Remember who engaged me to take the case for Martin?"

The girl blinked. "Why certainly. She was here early this morning—"

"All right," X cut in, "who was she?"

"Why—why—" The girl gasped and goggled. "Are you serious, Mr. Bilsman?"

"Answer my question, please."

"But I don't know who she was. You acted as though you knew her well enough. You took her into your private office and I'm sure I don't know what you said to her there."

"What did she look like?"

The secretary looked worried. "Are you sure you feel perfectly well, Mr. Bilsman? Because you didn't seem at all blind when you met her. In fact, well—" she flushed— "you noticed her pretty well, if you don't mind my saying so."

"I don't mind in the least. I just want you to describe her to me. Would you call her pretty?"

"Yes—that is. Well, of course she was pretty. Who wouldn't be in a dress like that? I've never seen a prettier shade of blue. I couldn't help noticing how much better it would have looked on another woman—say a blonde—than on a person with her brown hair."

X shook his head. "Never wear blue—not with your color of hair. Stick to greens. Tell me some more about this woman. Was she tall?"

"Why, I think she was tall, though she had on high heels. Yes, you'd call her tall."

"Did she wear a veil?"

"Why, I think she had one on her hat, but it was pushed back from her face."

"Good! We've got to her face. What was it like?"

"Oh, pretty," said the girl vaguely. "Blue eyes, or maybe they were green. Not brown anyway. She had on the dearest gloves—blue, just a shade darker than her dress. And her coat had cute, boxy shoulders. You must have noticed all that didn't you, Mr. Bilsman?"

X sighed. Bilsman's secretary had accurately described at least five hundred women in the city, one of them Mary Ferris, or possibly Madam Death.

The phone on the girl's desk tinkled. She asked if she should take it, and X nodded. She picked up the phone, listened for a moment.

"Why, Mr. Bilsman just walked in. I—"

And she had time to listen to perhaps a score more of spoken words before she dropped the phone, turned horrified eyes on X, uttered that peculiar noise cartoonists designate by "eek!" and fainted.

X picked up the phone and replaced it on its stand. If he was anything of a judge, the irate voice which was calling upon a "Miss Irwin" from the receiver of the phone, was that of Attorney Bilsman. X sprang into Bilsman's private office, removing the attorney's hat as he did so.

His eyes cast about the room, saw an old raincoat of the usual trench type hanging on a clothes rack. He took off Bilsman's topcoat, put on the raincoat. He removed the sandy colored toupee, revealing his own brown hair, quickly altered the shape of his chin and nose by deftly pinching the plastic material that covered his face.

HE WALKED out of the office, past the unconscious Miss Irwin, went out into the hall whistling. Attorney Bilsman had evidently called his office from the cigar stand on the main floor of the building, for he came bounding out of the same elevator which X nonchalantly entered and immediately employed to descend to the street level.

X engaged a taxi to take him to the Brock-Broadmoor Hotel. There he had engaged a room as soon as he had arrived in the city. He remained there only long enough to obtain clothes which fit him better than the garments he had taken from Bilsman, and to make certain alterations in his makeup.

Then he removed a leather letter case from his suit case and found within its folds an official-looking police detective badge and certain credentials which only the most careful examination would reveal as forgeries.

Thus identified as a police detective, he took a taxi to the office of Dr. Franklin Dynes whom he had met in the company of Sarles on the previous evening.

The doctor had not yet returned from his morning calls and X was forced to wait until nearly noon before Dynes made his appearance.

"Well, well, unless you're dying, young man, I must insist upon you calling at the regular hour this afternoon. I am not a man to forget my noon meal."

Dr. Dynes' steel clamp of a mouth chewed off the words as he whirled into the office, swinging his satchel. Then his penetrating blue eyes fixed upon X and he added: "I must say you don't appear to be dying."

X quietly removed his police badge from his wallet and showed it to the doctor. "We'd certainly appreciate your help, Doctor, in a little matter of solving a murder."

Dynes looked so hard at the badge that for a moment X wondered if he had detected the fact that it was fraudulent. Then he scurried into his consulting room and nodded to X to follow. Behind closed doors, Dynes extracted his pipe from a desk drawer, stuffed and lighted it, put it in a mouth that seemed made for the purpose.

"Open the window," he directed. "I don't care to have my consultation room stinking of tobacco smoke, and if I'm to play the role of detective I really ought to have a pipe, eh?" He laughed. "Hope

She held the gun on X as he slashed at the guard.

I can be of some use to you. Nasty business, that Service murder. Got to hand it to you for pouncing on the murderer, though."

"If you mean Martin," X said dryly, "it would have been a good pounce if we had caught the right man." He lighted a cigarette to keep company with the doctor's pipe. He said: "I believe you were in the waiting room just before the murder occurred. Mind telling me who else was there?"

Dynes pulled reflectively a moment. "The room was quite crowded. All the chairs were taken and two of us were forced to stand. Let's see. There was Rex Durmont, the political candidate for governor. And Maurice Biers, his wealthy backer was there. Oh, quite a distinguished gathering. Sarles was there—George Sarles and his Mike. Sort of a bodyguard, this Mike Kafore. And, let's see, Boise Marquod was there. Boise Marquod's brother, too—Arnold Marquod, I think his name is, though I never saw him until last night. And there was another fellow I'd never seen."

The doctor snapped his fingers. "The name slips my mind, but he was an agent of some sort. Something to do with Gordon Service. I remember Mike Kafore called him pickle-nose or something like that"

"Steve Wienhardt?" X suggested.

"That's it. That's the man. Wienhardt. There was this fellow Martin, too. You see this Martin had it in his head that Boise Marquod, Service, Durmont, Sarles and himself were in line to be murdered. And maybe he was right. Talked about five doomed men. Sarles has told me something about it, and it's evident that Sarles swallowed it, too."

"Don't you swallow it?" X asked.

"Well, until you said something just now about Martin's innocence, I believed it was just some sort of a scare this Martin fellow was throwing into the four wealthy men. Guess I'm not much of a detective, because there isn't much logic behind that. Oh, yes, there was John Leonard in the party. Nasty case of dyspepsia, John Leonard."

"And I presume you're intimate with all of these men?" X asked.

"You presume incorrectly. I treated Sarles, of course. Bad heart case. He has to avoid undue excitement. And I've treated Leonard, too. I looked Mike Kafore over a couple of times, just to please Sarles. And I am Durmont's regular physician. Biers I know only by sight. Dr. Jim Tracy is his physician. I believe Tracy looks after Boise Marquod, too."

X nodded. "What we're trying to find out is if any of these men have diabetes."

DR. DYNES frowned. "I can speak only for my own patients, of course. None of those men in question whom I have treated are troubled with that disease, I am glad to say. I could call Tracy and check up on Biers and Boise Marquod. Like me to?"

"Please. It may not be important. If we can find out that one of the men in the waiting room had diabetes, it isn't important at all."

Dynes was already on the phone. He tried Tracy's office, finally locating him at his residence. He hung up a moment later, shook his head. "Neither Biers nor Boise Marquod are troubled with diabetes. That leaves this man Wienhardt. I'll call his office and see if his secretary knows the name of his physician."

"Why not ask Wienhardt himself?" X inquired.

"Oh, he isn't in town. Went to Marquod's seaside home with the rest. It's this doomed men business. They all trouped out there as soon as they heard of Service's death. I'm going this evening to check on Sarles' heart. Bad case, but I guess I told you, Sarles can't stand too much excitement."

"You mean," X put in, "that John Leonard, Mike Kafore, Maurice Biers—they all went to Marquod's place with the doomed men? Of course Arnold Marquod would go with his brother. But Wienhardt—he was only Service's agent and his interest in the business should have ended with Service's death."

"Well, he went, anyway. Boise Marquod's stepdaughter is with them. Poor girl! To come home after years of study in Europe, to find her mother dead, and her stepfather a perfect stranger to her. But I'll check up on Wienhardt for you."

But when he had located and called Wienhardt's physician, he turned from the phone to shake his head. "No diabetes. Your man must be Arnold Marquod. We can check to be sure, of course. Arnold Marquod wasn't at home very much, I gather, but I do remember seeing his name in the hospital notes about three months ago. I said to myself then, 'Do you suppose that's Boise Marquod's brother?' "

Dr. Dynes turned to the phone, called the City Hospital and there discovered the name of the physician who had operated on Arnold Marquod some time ago. Another call and he had discovered that Arnold Marquod, too, was blissfully without the ailment of diabetes.

"Looks like we're getting nowhere," Dr. Dynes said.

X nodded. "That eliminates all but two of the men who were in that room; Martin I've checked up on before."

"Who's the other?" Dynes demanded.

"You, Dr. Dynes. Do you have diabetes?"

Dynes laughed. "I can assure you that I'd be the last person to be troubled. I watch myself too closely. I'd be a poor physician if I let myself in for anything like that, wouldn't I?"

"Still," X persisted, "physicians have the habit of dying, don't they, in spite of the fact that they are daily employed to outwit death? You weren't carrying a small case containing insulin and a hypodermic syringe last night, were you?"

Dynes shook his head. "Sorry to disappoint you. I was not."

X got up. "It must have been two other guys," he laughed. "Well, thanks a lot."

X left the office building and once again returned to his hotel. This time he occupied himself with selecting certain special equipment which included an elaborate makeup kit which he put into a voluminous secret pocket of his coat.

"So Dr. Dynes is going to the Marquod seaside place tonight," X mused. "To see Mr. Sarles—which may only be his excuse for getting at the doomed men. Well, he'll have us all together, if that's his motive, for I'll be there, too."

Completely equipped to face every known danger, but somewhat at a loss as to what to depend upon in case he met Madam Death, he left the hotel to go to a rental garage where he intended to obtain a car. On his way to the garage, he stopped at a bakery, entered the front door of the shop, asked if he might see the baking room.

The clerk said he would be only too glad to show X around, and led him into the baking room at the rear of the shop. The clerk began to point out the three ovens, the baking tables, the power-driven mixing equipment. But X's interest was centered on something which stood on a small table near the window. It was a large, cylindrical fly trap.

"I'll give you five dollars for that fly trap," X said to the baker.

The man goggled at him. "You'll what?"

"I want to buy your fly trap for five dollars," X repeated.

"Well, mister, you can buy one at the hardware store for a buck."

"Will you or won't you accept five dollars for your fly trap?" X persisted.

The baker looked from the money X extended to X's face, "Sure, if you're bound to have it. Will you," he added sarcastically, "take it with or without the flies?"

"Oh, with the flies," X replied airily. "You see, I'm going to a scavenger hunt tonight, and I have a tip that one of the things I must obtain is a fly trap filled with live flies. So if you don't mind—"

The baker accepted the money, handed over the wire cage of buzzing flies, vowed that all the fools were not dead yet. And Agent X went out to hunt the Doctor and Madam Death with live flies.

CHAPTER VI

THE FORTRESS OF DOOM

BY SEVEN O'CLOCK that evening, a blackness that was midnight's own descended upon the earth. The temperature had risen to an unseasonable high. Far out to sea, the pallid ghost of lightning fluttered restlessly, and now and then came the mutter of thunder.

As Agent X pulled his rented car to the side of the narrow road that skirted the high, ragged shore line, the abysmal sky relinquished its uncertain hold upon the rain. No passing shower was promised. It had begun to rain relentlessly—steady unchanging volumes of water, falling as though lead-weighted, straight down through stagnant air.

X, wearing a black slicker, carrying a flexible, water-proof bag, which covered the baker's fly trap, got into the car. The disguise he wore was that of the plain-featured, sandy-haired man known as A.J. Martin.

He had given some thought to the choice of this identity. Martin was wanted for murder by the police, it was true, but it was as Martin he had first approached the doomed men, and as Martin he had gained the trust of George Sarles and Rex Durmont. He hoped it was the disguise that would admit him to the Marquod house, where the doomed men had sought sanctuary from those who had marked them for lasting oblivion.

The Marquod house, perched giddily upon a precipice of rock, was a many-gabled affair of gray stone and green tile, approached by a tortuous drive. As X drew nearer, he could see that the lighted windows were striped by bars of iron. The place looked capable of withstanding a long siege.

When he reached the house, X's first move was to quietly explore its exterior to ascertain if there was any means of entrance which the entrenched doomed men had overlooked. A barred window near the massive front door revealed the battered profile of Mike Kafore. Kafore undoubtedly served as guardian of the portal.

X tiptoed around the foundation, testing the iron bars and latches of the windows. He was in the act of crouching by a rusty iron coal window which he had uncovered from behind overgrown shrubbery when he felt the cold snout of a gun muzzle at the back of his neck.

"You will stand up and raise your hands."

The voice was that of a woman, clear, level, so filled with desperate determination that X knew that to disobey that order meant death. He straightened slowly, raised his hands.

"You will turn around."

X turned slowly, looked down at the woman. Gloom cloaked her figure. He could only distinguish the black of her veil against the white of her face, the black of her gloves against the gleaming metal of the gun she held. The voice, he was certain, was that of Mary Ferris, the late Gordon Service's secretary.

"Miss Ferris, I believe," X said quietly.

"Never mind. I am going into that house. You are going to help me, whoever you are, do you understand?"

"Of course. My intentions are exactly the same as yours—up to the point of getting into the house, Miss Ferris. Remember A.J. Martin?"

"You?" she gasped. "You're Martin?"

"The same. You ought not to have forgotten me, since your testimony managed to put me in jail for a number of uncomfortable hours."

She said coldly: "And after I had had time to think, I engaged a lawyer to get you out again."

"Why?" asked X, though if Mary Ferris was indeed Madam Death the answer was obvious, regardless of what she might reply. For certainly Madam Death could not have reached out her deadly hands for him in jail.

"Because," came the reply, "I took time to think, to check up on Gordon Service's dealings with his agent, Wienhardt. Wienhardt had a very good motive for killing Gordon, Wienhardt wasn't on the level, took considerably more from Gordon than his commission. He might easily have killed Gordon to cover up his treachery."

"And you," X said, "want to get inside this house because Wienhardt is there. Suppose, since I cannot believe that you have any good intentions toward Wienhardt, that I refuse to help you to enter this house?"

"Then, I shall kill you without the slightest hesitation," the girl replied in a level voice.

"With a gun?" X inquired mildly.

"What else?"

HAD HE known for a fact that Mary Ferris was not Madam Death, he would not have hesitated to force her to give up the gun. But if she was Madam Death, then the mere touch of her flesh might mean not only his own end but that of the men he was trying to protect.

"Very well," he agreed. "How do you propose to enter this citadel?"

"Through the front door."

"As simple as that?"

"As simple as that. You will stand at one side of the door, out of sight. I will knock. They will not hesitate to open the door to a woman, and whoever comes to the door you will knock out."

"Oh, so they won't hesitate to open the door to a woman," X said with a slightly ironic laugh. "Well, if you'd like to try it, let's go."

Mary Ferris did not put away her gun, however. X felt its muzzle nudging him at intervals as they moved to the front of the house, mounted a small porch, and approached the door. It was not until she saw that X was flat against the wall beside the door that she hid her gun in the pocket of her rain-soaked woolen coat.

Without hesitation, she raised the ponderous knocker and clacked it twice. Immediately the hall light, which glowed through the window, went out. X could imagine that Mike Kafore was taking a look at his visitor.

The doorknob turned. X reached into his pocket, grasped his own automatic. The door opened and Mike Kafore stepped through the opening, his left hand holding a revolver of cannon proportions.

"So you came, did you?" Mike said through his teeth. "Well, Madam Death, I'm ready for you!"

Mary Ferris stepped slightly back, indicating X's presence with an involuntary look. Kafore turned his head, moved far less fast than Agent X, who rushed him. X got one hand on Kafore's throat, brought his gun barrel slashing down to the center of Kafore's forehead.

Kafore dropped heavily. X rolled him to the edge of the porch, gently lowered him to the ground. He turned around, saw that Mary Ferris was watching him closely, her gun showing now.

X stepped ahead of the girl into the black entrance hall, having first recovered the zipper bag he had brought with him from the city. The girl followed him, and X closed the door. A glimmer of light through a crack between sliding doors to the left marked the girl's location as its rays fell upon her gun.

X moved swiftly, first opening his bag, then driving into the mesh screen of the fly trap with the blade of his clasp knife. He ripped the wire wide, was gratified to hear the buzz of flies that swarmed about in the cage. He dropped bag and trap, closed his knife, and with hands bare, sprang straight at Mary Ferris.

Never had X been less sure of the outcome of a struggle. With only that narrow blade of light from the crack in the door to guide him, he had to seize the woman by her hands—and her hands alone. For her hands were gloved, and it was the touch of Madam Death's flesh that was deadly.

Crushing, steel-hard fingers of Agent X closed upon her hands. The girl lunged forward, but he kept her at arm's length. "Don't make a sound," he whispered. "Not a sound."

A fraction of an Inch at a time, his fingers crept up the girl's right hand to her wrist. Still his fingers contacted the protecting leather. "Now," he whispered, "drop your gun. Drop it, before I break your wrist."

The gun dropped. In the silent darkness of the hall it made a thunderous noise. Sarles' voice called tautly from the next room, "What was that, Mike?"

Instantly, the Agent's marvelous ability to impersonate voices came to his aid. "I just took off one of me shoes, Pop. Me dogs are killin' me."

He raised his hands to his face. Given time, in spite of the fact that he would have to work entirely from memory, he thought that he could rework the plastic that covered his face so that it would closely resemble Mike Kafore's homely visage.

BUT THERE was no time. Hardly had he spoken in the voice of Mike Kafore before Mary Ferris screamed. Whether X's vocal impersonation had been the final surprise that had snapped her strained nerves, or whether she had some definite purpose in call-ing the men, X did not know.

All he knew was that the sliding door sprang open and Arnold Marquod hurried into the hall. The smile on his smooth, flushed face was incongruous to the gleam of gun steel thrust threaten-ingly from his right fist. Behind him, loomed Maurice Biers' clumsy largeness, George Sarles' dignified form, and Dr. Franklin Dynes' spidery body. All three were armed.

"Surprisin'," Arnold Marquod said pleasantly. "We were expec-tin' a gentleman and a lady. Expectations apparently fulfilled. Mr. Martin, isn't it? And the lady—" Arnold Marquod's face paled a trifle as he realized how close Mary Ferris stood to him.

"Martin? Martin out there?" That was Rex Durmont's voice. He crowded past Arnold Marquod, thrust forth a hand to X, but Ar-nold Marquod jerked him back.

"Forgettin' that the police arrested Martin for the murder of Gordon Service, Mr. Durmont?" Arnold Marquod said. "He looks all right to us, but he's not denyin' he entered stealthily and brought a lady with him. And where's Mike Kafore?"

"All right," X said. "I entered stealthily because I had no idea what my reception would be. It would seem that I did not enter stealthily enough. I brought no one with me. Miss Ferris can speak for herself. I suggest we go into the next room. You men can sur-round us with your guns, shoot at the slightest provocation. Some-one will have to bring me up to date on what has happened."

"Logical reasonin' there," Arnold Marquod said. "Dr. Dynes, suppose you stand on one side of the door. I'll be on the other side. We'll be holdin' our guns on our visitors while they enter the room."

Dynes nodded. "Just as you say."

Durmont and Sarles backed into the room while X stood aside to permit Mary Ferris to enter, then followed the girl.

X looked around the room. In addition to Dynes, Arnold Mar-quod, Durmont, Sarles and Maurice Biers there were Steve Wien-hardt, the dyspeptic John Leonard, and a beautiful, pale-faced, neurotic-looking girl with dark hair and blue eyes, who sat apart from the men, quietly sipping a small glass of claret. This was Boi-se Marquod's stepdaughter, X supposed.

The men, all armed, formed a ring around Mary Ferris and X. X, however, was careful to stand some distance from Gordon Ser-vice's former secretary.

"Where's Boise Marquod?" X demanded, for he had noticed the labor leader's conspicuous absence, as soon as he had entered the room.

"My brother is upstairs restin'," Arnold Marquod said.

X nodded. "And I presume the lady is—"

"My brother's stepdaughter, Doris," Arnold Marquod explained. "Now, suppose you tell us *your* story, Mr. Martin."

A fly buzzed past X's ear. He smiled slightly. "There's very little to my story. Miss Ferris managed to land me in the jail when she testified that I was bending over Service's body with a gun in my hand. The police, completely baffled, had to name someone as the possible murderer, and I was that someone. Have there been any attempts on the lives of the remaining doomed men?"

"Not one damned thing has happened until you showed up." Wienhardt said, as though somewhat disappointed. "I think this is all a lot of eyewash to conceal the real motive behind Service's death."

"Exactly!" Mary Ferris spoke for the first time since their entrance into the room. Her blue-green eyes drilled Wienhardt's face. Wienhardt only blinked at her.

"The fact that nothing has happened may prove one point," X said. "It may prove that the murderer known as the Doctor and his assistant, Madam Death, have waited until my arrival to begin their murderous work. The Doctor now has all his prospective victims grouped beneath one roof."

GEORGE SARLES got half out of his chair, fell back again. His hands quivered on the arms of his chair. Dr. Dynes said: "Steady, Mr. Sarles. Mustn't get excited, you know."

John Leonard pointed an accusing finger at X. "Or," he said, "the fact that nothing has happened up to now may prove conclusively that Mr. Martin is the murderer. Naturally, he couldn't hurt anyone if he happened to be in jail."

X nodded. "Logical, except for the fact that I am one of the doomed men."

"Now, lookin' at it another way," Arnold Marquod put in, "how do you know you're one of the doomed men? My brother, for instance, might stand in the way of this mysterious organization which is tryin' to overthrow our democratic form of government. Gordon Service was another champion of the American system.

"Mr. Sarles seems to be something of a large toad, though I don't claim to be an authority on how much influence a wealthy munitions manufacturer might have over his government's policy. And certainly Mr. Durmont, here, as a potential political leader, may lay claim to greatness in the eyes of this organization. But you, Mr. Martin, an ordinary newspaperman—"

"I," X interrupted, "do not happen to be an ordinary newspaperman. Actually, I am a secret agent of the United States Government. Call me a G-man if you will. But I assure you that I am in such a position that no secret and criminally directed organization could get much of a foothold in this country without my knowing it."

Rex Durmont's penetrating black eyes were fixed on X's face. "Are you, by any chance—" He paused, turned to Maurice Biers. "Maurice," he said, "perhaps you have a better right to ask the question than I. You have contributed more money to the employment of a certain secret service agent than I."

Biers nodded his ponderous head. He stood up slowly. "I have never revealed this to a soul outside a certain circle of wealthy men who have contributed to a common cause. But because we believed him to be the.most pointed tool our country has for digging out and disposing of the criminal element, myself, Mr. Durmont, and a number of other public-spirited men, yearly contribute to a fund to be used by the man known as Secret Agent X!"

Dr. Dynes' spidery body jerked around. "You, Mr. Biers! Why, everyone knows that Secret Agent X is a criminal of the most dangerous type."

Rex Durmont leaned forward in his chair. "I must contradict you, Dr. Dynes. No one knows what Agent X is. No one has ever seen his face. This I know of him—that, regardless of what his methods may be, no man, no group of men can point more pridefully to a larger number of criminals who have received their just deserts at their hands than Secret Agent X. No one man has contributed more to the safety of our nation than Agent X. Are you, Mr. Martin, Secret Agent X?"

For an answer, X raised both hands to his face. Deft fingers moved with lightning speed over his features, and when his hands dropped to his sides, his entire appearance was altered. His nose was flat, broken-looking. There was what appeared to be a deep scar in his chin. There were apparently little knobs of fat at his cheekbones.

In a voice that was entirely unlike that of A.J. Martin, he said: "I would be rather un-human not to thus accept the extravagant flattery Mr. Durmont has just voiced."

There was an interval of stunned silence. Even the pallid girl who was Boise Marquod's stepdaughter seemed somewhat impressed, for she got to her feet and announced her intention of going to call her stepfather to witness this miracle of face switching.

As she left the room, Dr. Dynes said: "We may as well lower our guns."

"Wait," John Leonard said sourly. "Suppose all this is true. What about the girl—this Miss Ferris. Will Agent X vouch for her?"

"I will vouch for no one but myself," X said, his eyes following the crazy flight of another fly which had drifted in from the hall.

"Say, I'll vouch for Mary," Wienhardt spoke up. "She's Gordon Service's gal friend. I found that out when I tried to date her once. A bit snooty, but otherwise a right gal."

Mary Ferris turned cold eyes on Wienhardt. "I want no recommendation from you!"

"Can you assure us that Miss Ferris is—what she appears to be?" Sarles asked nervously of X.

THE AGENT shook his head. "I repeat, I can vouch for no one but myself. Someone in this group, and I include Mike Kafore and Boise Marquod in this statement, is certainly *not* what he seems to be."

"What do you mean?" Arnold Marquod frowned, batted at a fly that settled persistently on his cheek.

"When this group went to the radio studio yesterday," X said, "one man dropped a case containing insulin, the specific remedy for the ailment diabetes. I have made a most careful check. With the exception of Dr. Dynes, I know that no one here is *supposed* to be suffering from that disease."

"I can assure you that I haven't got it," Dr. Dynes snapped. "I told a police detective that today."

"I know," X said softly. "I was that police detective. When I asked you if you had diabetes today, you denied it, and I was inclined to believe you, because I saw no point in your denying it if you did have diabetes. Right now, there is a definite point in the guilty party denying he has diabetes."

"Why?" demanded Maurice Biers.

"Because, Mr. Biers, as I have just stated, no one here is *supposed* to have diabetes. Yet someone habitually carries insulin with

Each man knew her touch might mean death.

him—someone in this group. He carries it because he cannot live without it, because he is a victim of diabetes. If I prove that one of you has diabetes, that will indicate clearly that one man in this group is not who he is supposed to be."

"A masquerader, eh?" said Arnold Marquod.

"Exactly."

John Leonard smiled sourly. "Then, Mr. X, doesn't it strike you that you have just trapped yourself? You are the only masquerader in the group."

"But I admit that I am not what I seem," X insisted. He rested his hands on the back of a chair, leaned forward, his keen eyes traveling from one face to another. "Will the other masquerader admit that? Will he step forward?"

No one moved. There was no sound in the room save the faint footsteps of Boise Marquod's stepdaughter in the hall, and the steady drizzle of rain on the window panes.

"One man in this group is not what he claims to be," X said in that same quiet voice. "I do not mean that he wears makeup on his face as I do. It seems impossible in a group where every one claims to know every one else.

"Yet one man in this group is that high official of the nefarious and sinister organization which seeks to overthrow our government—that man known as the Doctor, the murderer who threatens the five doomed men."

"And Madam Death?" Sarles whispered hoarsely.

"And Madam Death is here, too," X said. "A woman—"

Mary Ferris' eyes snapped. "I haven't the slightest idea what you are insinuating, but it's obvious that I am the object of those insinuations." She jerked the sodden collar of her coat up tightly about her neck, and walked from the room. No man moved to stop her; no man knew but what to touch her meant his death.

Rex Durmont appealed to Agent X, "Have you no idea who this murderous Doctor is?"

And it was then that X decided to throw his bluff—the only weapon of protection he could possibly devise against the strange power that had killed Gordon Service and that doomed them all. He nodded.

"Yes, I know. And that is why there will be no more murder. I have deduced the identity of the Doctor. I have written his name and given a full description of him on a piece of paper which I have sealed in an envelope. I can assure the Doctor and his Madam Death that should one more of the original five doomed men die, that envelope will be immediately placed in the hands of the police. The Doctor and his murderous lady could not leave this country alive."

WELL KNOWING that there was no such paper, that as yet he had not determined the identity of the killers, X spoke on, his voice intensely dramatic:

"So I am in a position to extend an ultimatum to the Doctor. He must first of all destroy the power of Madam Death—he must deprive her of this power to kill at a touch, even if he has to sacrifice her life. He must leave this country immediately, never again to return. Then and only then will I withhold the evidence I now have—evidence which will land him in the electric chair."

"No," said Sarles sharply. He was staring at the walls of the room like a man gone mad. "It won't work. If *she* kills at a touch, then nothing could stop her. It won't work. The Doctor couldn't kill her, because she would kill him first. She'll go on and on like a typhoon, sweeping over the country—"

"Mr. Sarles! Mr. Sarles! Get a grip on yourself, man!" Dr. Dynes stepped between X and Sarles. The munitions king's shoulders were shaking with sobs.

"I—I've got to get out of here! I'm not going to sit here and be killed by *her*. I'm getting out, I tell you!"

And as Dr. Dynes would have prevented him from leaving the room, Sarles landed a surprisingly powerful blow in the doctor's middle. Dynes slammed backward against X, and X was thrown against the wall. Sarles shot through the door into the hall before anyone could prevent him. They heard the front door open and then the sound of a body falling.

Dr. Dynes, jittering around in front of X, delayed the Agent for only a second; then X sprang to the door, thrust Arnold Marquod aside. George Sarles was stretched across the front door sill, every muscle of his body rigid. Mary Ferris standing on the porch, was screaming. Boise Marquod's grizzled face looked like some hideous gargoyle as he bent over the stair rail on the second floor.

The men crowded out of the living room—Wienhardt, Arnold Marquod, Dr. Dynes, John Leonard, Rex Durmont and Maurice Biers. Crawling over the edge of the porch to frighten new screams from Mary Ferris, was Mike Kafore.

A sob choked in Kafore's throat as he saw Sarles. He came across the porch on flabby legs, staring at Sarles. "Pop!" he sobbed. "Pop!" And then he yanked his gun from his pocket and turned it on those in the house.

"What damned louse did this to him? Step out and die, damn you to hell!" Kafore snarled in open defiance of Madam Death and her Doctor.

X alone was calm, to all outward appearances. Inwardly, he knew that he was on the verge of making his most triumphant discovery. Flies swarmed in the hall, scores of them. They circled around the heads of the men. They crawled over the hands and face of Arnold Marquod, returned persistently when he absently brushed them aside.

"Look at Sarles' hair!" shouted Arnold Marquod. "The back of his neck looks as though it had been singed!"

"His hair's smoldering!" cried Maurice Biers.

"As though he had been burned!" said Wienhardt.

"Yes," said X, "the touch of Madam Death. I made no error when I said that the Doctor was among us. He is. And the name we know him by is—"

But while the Agent's discerning eyes moved toward the face of the man he was about to accuse, John Leonard, from behind, seized a heavy pottery vase from a stand in the hall, shattered it on top of X's head. Oblivion was instantaneous.

CHAPTER VII

THE SIXTH DOOMED MAN

COOL RAIN SPLASHING in his face was the Agent's first sensation. He peeled back feverishly hot eyelids from aching eyeballs and looked up at the starless night. He raised his head with difficulty, saw that he was on a narrow, rocky ledge illuminated with sickly yellow light from an oil lantern. His ankles were tightly bound with rope, and his wrists, he judged, had been treated in a like manner, having been tied behind his back.

Near the lantern was the angular figure of a man squatting on his heels. His right hand, which lay across his knees, held an automatic. The yellow light made a death's-head of his hollow-cheeked face.

"Mr. Leonard, I believe," X said lightly. "Where are we? I believe that is the usual question to ask upon coming out of a coma."

"I think," said Leonard, "that if you listen you can hear the sound of the surf drumming on the rocks some hundred feet below. Above us, and a little back from the precipice, is the Marquod house. More exactly, your position is one directly between life and death."

"I couldn't have gained better information as to my location from a gasoline station, could I?" X said pleasantly. "So you, Mr. John Leonard, are a member of the Brotherhood. And now that Sarles is dead, you will be in an excellent position to secretly arm your colleagues from the Sarles Munitions Plant.

"I see now why Sarles' death was of such vital importance. And I presume you understand thoroughly that as soon as the news of Sarles' death reaches the city, the identity of the Doctor will be revealed to the proper authorities?"

"I understand thoroughly," Leonard said. "That is the only reason why you are alive at the moment, because you will tell me where that information is and I will destroy it before the police can see it."

"Possibly," X said, knowing that there was nothing possible about it, since the evidence that would nail the Doctor was written nowhere in the world except in his own mind. "And since I am to give you this information, would you mind telling me about Madam Death? Who is she? What is she?"

"You will make her acquaintance shortly," John Leonard said, smiling sourly. "I do not know her name, so I cannot satisfy your curiosity on that score. She is at the present time out searching for Rex Durmont who bolted from the house. All the others are locked in the Marquod house and I have the key. So once we have disposed of Rex Durmont, you and the one remaining doomed man will give us little trouble.

"Madam Death is a product of the Doctor's laboratory—I might say an accidental product. She was his assistant in the attempted classification of a substance which the Doctor called astralite. Astralite is one of the missing elements in the series of radioactive elements. It is many times more potent than radium, and while it may exist on other planets, does not exist on our earth except in compound with the body of Madam Death."

"That is enlightening," X commented. "And how was it obtained?"

"I cannot but believe that it was given to the Brotherhood by some higher power," said Leonard devoutly. "It was found by the Doctor on a meteor which fell in that mountainous region between Hungary and Czechoslovakia. In working with the element, Madam Death became poisoned with it. Her flesh radiates rays of astralite to such an extent that her touch is death. Its poisonous rays also affected her mind so that she is completely under the mental control of the Doctor."

"And I suppose," X said, "that the Doctor fixes it firmly in Madam Death's mind just who she is to dispose of. At the present time, the unfortunate young woman has been sent to search out and kill Rex Durmont."

"That is entirely right," John Leonard said coolly. He stood up and considered X for a moment. "I am sorry I cannot make you more comfortable."

"Considerate of you," X said with a laugh. "Rather odd to find a considerate murderer."

"I am not a murderer," said Leonard in a shocked voice. "I simply have aided in the removal of certain men who stand in the path of the Brotherhood. I am doing America a service."

"Of course," X said, "in your opinion. I imagine that the high officers of the Brotherhood have convinced thousands of men like you that they are devoted to a noble cause—the cause based upon a somewhat contradictory principle that men are free only when they are completely shackled. You are no doubt prepared to die in the service of your ideals. I *hope* you are so prepared."

JOHN LEONARD, head on one side, had been listening intently to something which X, from his position, had not heard. He turned suddenly, moved along the rock ledge to natural steps that led upward to the flat land above.

No sooner was Leonard out of sight than X sat up. He was well prepared for such an emergency. The ropes which bound him meant little to him, given a moment for manipulation.

His first move was to strain his head downward to bite at the edge of his coat lapel with his teeth. Three times his teeth snapped before finally they clasped the back of a single-edged razor blade which was cleverly concealed within his coat lapel. Now, to get his hands to his mouth where the keen edge would quickly sever the cords about his wrists!

But before he could accomplish this, a baby avalanche of loose stones down the natural stairway announced the return of John Leonard. X dropped flat on his back, not daring to relinquish the hold he had upon the razor blade, yet not daring to expose its keen edge to the rays of the lantern.

John Leonard was not alone. Driven ahead of him by the goading of Leonard's gun was Rex Durmont. Durmont's forehead was gashed as though he had fallen among the rocks. He was limping painfully, favoring a sprained ankle. He looked half dead, but his eyes were the same black gimlets that darted this way and that, seeking a possible means of escape. And there was none—no way to escape the cold-blooded killer except over the edge of the cliff to the water one hundred feet below.

"Back against the wall, Durmont," John Leonard said. "It is just as well that Madam Death has not found you. You may be the means of extracting vital information from Agent X."

His back to Agent X so that he could face Durmont, John Leonard looked over his shoulder at X. He said: "I am going to shoot Durmont in a number of places. I do not want to kill him. I only want him to suffer, you understand? If you would save him all this needless pain, you will tell me where that envelope which contains evidence which you have collected may be obtained."

"Don't do that, Agent X," Durmont said grimly. "He'll kill us both anyway. We'll live only as long as you keep that secret."

X, unable to make any reply without running the risk of swallowing the razor blade, simply nodded his head. The secret would be safe, because there was no secret.

Leonard placed the lantern so that its rays fell upon Durmont. The latter, his hands flattened against the wall of rock, his legs wide-spread, looked as though he were posing himself to attempt the impossible—duck the bullets from Leonard's gun.

Leonard stepped back a pace, raised his gun. He said: "I'm waiting for your reply, Agent X. I shall count four. At the count of four I shall place my first shot along Durmont's thigh. One... two...."

X inched his way a little closer to Leonard. His legs doubled.

"Three," said Leonard. "Fo—" He got no farther.

X's legs shot out like pistons. His shoes rammed in at the back of Leonard's knees. At the same time, Leonard fired, his gun high in the air as he vainly attempted to keep his balance. His bony frame struck the ledge of rock. He rolled sideways, screamed as he felt himself going over the ledge.

There was a sound of ripping cloth as the ragged edge tore at his clothes. X jerked to a sitting position, saw that Leonard's fingers gripped the ledge of rock while his long body dangled helplessly in the air.

"Help!" Leonard shrilled, his voice sounding as though he were down in a cistern.

Durmont groaned. X glanced toward the rocky wall. Durmont was heaped on the ledge. There was a second wound in his head—a scalp wound. Evidently Leonard's one wild shot had creased Durmont's head, stunning him.

X DROPPED flat, threw his bound legs up and back, as though to turn a back somersault. His bound arms made a wide loop beneath him. Feverishly he worked, bringing the loop of his arms up around hips, the back of his knees. He drew his legs in close to his body, inched his wrists in under his heels, then his toes.

Regardless of what John Leonard might have done, X intended to save him if at all possible. He got his hands in front of him, brought his wrists up to his mouth, sawed on the rope with the razor blade clamped in his teeth. One strand... two strands... three.... The rope popped. X spat out the razor blade, at the same time working his wrists free.

"Hold on, Leonard. I'm coming. Hang—"

Rock crumbled. X turned over, reached out free hands toward the ledge in a mad effort to keep what he knew was inevitable from happening. For a split-second, he saw John Leonard's white fingers clutched on a bit of broken rock and then they disappeared over the edge.

The terrified scream of a man plunging to certain destruction was carried shrilly to X's ears on an updraft of air that brushed his face as he looked out over the ledge into seemingly bottomless black.

X wriggled back from the edge. His searching fingers found the razor blade flat against the stone. Again he plied it, ripping through the ropes that bound his ankles. In another instant he was free. He sprang toward Durmont, immediately altering his course as he heard the sound of rapid steps on the rocky stair leading from the level land above.

X leaped to the inclined cut in the rock wall, stood at its mouth, waiting. Possibly, he waited for Madam Death. His heart pounded madly, but his nerves were relaxed, his mind calm and clear-thinking. If it was a man, he would—

"Leonard," said a muffled voice, coming from the rock stairway, "who was that screaming?"

A man appeared in the opening only to drop flat as Agent X sprung full weight upon him. Once, twice, the Agent's left fist slashed out. And the second blow caught the bobbing, ducking head of the man just behind the ear. The man expelled breath in a low groan, lay still beneath X.

X got to his feet, stepped back, warily watching the fallen man. The man was lying face down, but X had no need to see his face. He knew it well enough.

X stepped back to Durmont, bent over him, shook him gently by the shoulder. Durmont opened his eyes, blinked back blood that seeped into them. He said: "X?"

"Yes. The job is two-thirds done. But Madam Death is still at large, hunting you. Can you get to your feet? We've got to work fast."

"The Doctor?" groaned Durmont, trying, with X's help, to stand upright.

"Over there. That's where you've got to go—beside the Doctor."

"Who—who is he?"

"I don't know his real name. I may never know it. But he is the man who posed as Boise Marquod's brother. He can't really be Marquod's brother because Arnold Marquod did not have diabetes, and this man has. Didn't you notice how the flies lighted upon him? Flies are always more attracted by persons suffering from diabetes than others, because of the increased sugar content of the blood of a diabetic."

"But—but wouldn't Boise Marquod know his own brother?"

"Of course. He knew this man wasn't his brother. He must have. It isn't probable that Marquod's brother and the Doctor are doubles. There's something about this we won't know until we've talked to Marquod. Sit down. Sit down beside the Doctor, Durmont."

Durmont, bewildered, did as he was told; he watched dully

Madame Death came relentlessly on.

as X extracted his makeup kit from the inner pocket of his coat. X opened the kit, glancing at Durmont's face in the lantern light, selecting such pigments as he thought would match Durmont's skin.

"What are you going to do?" demanded Durmont.

"I am going to engineer the death of a fiend," X whispered grimly, "if there is only time enough."

He reached over, turned the unconscious Doctor, the man they had known as Arnold Marquod, face up. Then swiftly he set to work, adding plastic material to the Doctor's face, fingers pinching it in place, his practiced eye recreating the contours of Durmont's face on the face of the Doctor.

"Madam Death," X whispered, "hunts for you, Durmont. Now, do you see? There is no better way. Those who live by the sword, you know."

"It's uncanny!" whispered Durmont, as he watched the facial change that came over the man they had known as Arnold Marquod.

"Not the best job I've done, but perhaps it will do. Remove your coat, Durmont. And help me get off the Doctor's coat."

DURMONT had evidently forgotten the pain of his wounds, for he fell to with good will to help X manage the change of clothes. And when that was done, the Doctor showed signs of returning consciousness.

X pocketed his makeup kit and brought out a small case of special narcotic agents which he put to many uses. From this kit he took a hypodermic syringe and a small dropper. He loaded the dropper from one tiny vial and the syringe from another. He handed the syringe to Durmont.

"Hold this. Now a few drops of this substance beneath the Doctor's eyelids—"

"What for?" whispered Durmont.

"To paralyze the muscles of his eyes," X whispered. "He may be able to control Madam Death with his eyes. The drug will also prevent him from seeing clearly. Understand?"

As soon as he had doped the Doctor's eyes, X bared the Doctor's arm, took the syringe from Durmont's hands, drove the needle point into the Doctor's flesh.

"A simple stimulant to hasten his recovery. And now to place his gun where he can reach it on coming to—"

"Listen!" Durmont husked. "Someone coming?"

X slid the gun from the coat he had removed from the Doctor, placed it near the Doctor's hand. Yes, he heard soft footsteps coming down the natural rock stairway.

"If—if that's Madam Death," Durmont stammered, "we're blocked. We won't be able to get off this ledge except—" He sent a shuddering glance toward the edge of the cliff. "We can't get past her that way. She'd only kill us."

"On your feet," X whispered. "The Doctor's coming to. Back. Get as far back from the rays of the lantern as you can. I'll stand in front of you." He shoved Durmont backward along the ledge to a point where the ledge was barely a foot in width. "Don't look down," X whispered. "Don't even think. Keep your eyes on the Doctor."

The Doctor was sitting up. Instinctively, his fingers closed upon the automatic beneath his hand. His left hand rose to his eyes. He got cautiously to his feet, stumbled toward the edge of the cliff. The booming surf below warned him back. He groped to the wall.

"My eyes," he muttered, "foggy. I don't understand."

The figure of a girl appeared from the mouth of the natural rock stairway. A beautiful girl, pale-cheeked, brown-haired, blue-eyes. The blue eyes turned on the Doctor and some of their world-weariness dissolved. She came forward, step by step, bare hands outstretched.

"It—it's Boise Marquod's stepdaughter!" Durmont breathed.

"Hush," X cautioned.

"Voices," mumbled the Doctor. "I hear voices somewhere." He half-turned, his fuddled vision coming to focus on the approaching woman.

"Naida," the Doctor said hoarsely. "Is that you, Naida?"

The woman came relentlessly on. On her lips was a triumphant, unbeautiful smile.

"Naida!" the Doctor cried. "Great heavens, what are you doing! Don't you know me? Where are your gloves? Don't touch me, you fool. You'll kill me!"

"Your voice does not fool me, Rex Durmont," said Madam Death, coolly. "The Doctor said I must find you. I have walked a long way, searching in every dark corner. Now, Rex Durmont, I find you."

Sweat beaded the Doctor's brow. He sprang back against the wall of rock. "No, Naida. No. Are you mad? I am not Rex Durmont. Look into my eyes. My eyes—damn my eyes!"

And then the Doctor raised his gun. "Naida, I will kill you!"

Madam Death laughed. "I, who am already doomed to die? I who burn cell by cell, ounce by ounce with the poisonous fire within me?"

And then she sprang upon the Doctor. And at the same time that she would have clasped him in her deadly embrace, the Doctor fired.

ONE HAND leaped to the bosom of her dress, then Madam Death lurched forward. And as she fell, her right hand closed on the Doctor's gun wrist.

The Doctor's body writhed like an eel caught upon a fisherman's hook, then suddenly grew rigid. Pale wisps of smoke arose from the wrist that Madam Death clasped. He pitched backward to the rocky ledge. Madam Death, one hand pressed to her bosom now tinged with the red of blood, dropped to her knees beside him. A look of utter bewilderment came into her face as she looked down upon the Doctor.

"Who are you?" she choked out. "So odd, that since I have been working in the laboratory with astralite, my memory at times is bad. I do not recall your face. Why do you lie so still?"

"Naida," X whispered.

"Don't attract her attention!" Durmont cautioned from behind X. "She is still alive."

X knew that the girl was dying. He took a short step forward, repeated her name.

She looked at him, a sweet, sad smile on her paling lips. "Someone else I do not remember calls me by name. Can you help me? There is something within me that burns like unholy fire. It has burned for so long. It began in the laboratory. Won't you do something for me to stop the pain?"

Durmont seized X's arm. "Don't go near her."

The girl's head sagged. Her body wavered forward, flattened on the rocks. Her deadly hands pressed to the surface of the stone. She said: "Cool."

In spite of Durmont's protestations, X stepped nearer. "Naida," he whispered, "you are going away. It will be cool where you are going. Is there anything I can do? Have you a father or mother somewhere who would like to know where you are going?"

"No," the girl whispered hoarsely. "A father—yes, once I had a father. In the laboratory, the Doctor showed me my father. He said

I was to catch my father with my two hands. Like I caught a rat. Ugh!" a slight shudder convulsed her. "I hate rats."

X leaned closer, whispered softly: "Naida. Naida." Her eyelids flickered faintly, and he continued: "Do you remember—a girl—Boise's stepdaughter? The girl you impersonate? You remember?"

She shuddered slightly. "A girl? Boise?" She paused. "The Doctor told me— Yes... on board ship, with one of the Brotherhood—in the furnace room—"

Her words came very softly now. X could hardly hear them. He leaned closer. "Go on," he urged gently.

Her eyes closed, a frown appeared between her brows. She seemed struggling to remember. "Before she.... They tortured her—to get information before—she died." A faint smile came over her lips, as though she could relax now—now that she had succeeded in remembering.

She jerked up her head, looked squarely at X. "Don't—don't touch me. Once, I touched my father. He—he died. I am not like other girls. I am poison. My touch—" She turned her head, seemed listening intently. "What is that rushing sound?"

"Only the surf on the rocks below," X said kindly.

"Water. Water down there? Cool water?" Breathing in shallow gasps, the girl dragged herself to the edge of the cliff. "Cool water," she repeated, "to quench the fire within me." And with her last ounce of strength, Madam Death rolled herself over the edge of the cliff. There was no scream, no sound below save the deep, eternal voice of the sea.

THEY returned in silence to the Marquod house—Agent X and Rex Durmont. X had brought the Doctor's heavy automatic with him, and with it had no trouble shooting the lock from the door.

Inside they found Boise Marquod, Steve Wienhardt, Mary Ferris, Maurice Biers and Dr. Dynes, a frightened group huddled together in the living room. Mike Kafore had died, trying to prevent John Leonard from locking the others up. The rigid body of George Sarles was stretched out in the hall.

"I think," X said, after all these seemingly mad things that people say when finding friends unexpectedly alive, had been said, "that the doomed men, the three remaining, may consider themselves comparatively safe."

"Madam Death—what happened to her?" asked Dynes.

X shook his head. "After inadvertently disposing of her creator, like the Frankenstein monster she was, she died. She was, of course, not Boise Marquod's stepdaughter, as she claimed to be. And that accounts for the motive behind Mrs. Marquod's murder. Mrs. Marquod would have known, of course, that Madam Death was not her daughter. Boise Marquod, who had never seen his stepdaughter, wouldn't be any the wiser."

Boise Marquod ran his gnarled hands across his haggard face. "No," he muttered. "No, of course not. And to think my poor wife—" He stopped, shook his head hopelessly.

"Would you mind telling us," X said kindly to Boise Marquod, "whatever prompted you to pass off that murdering villain as your brother?"

"Stubbornness," Marquod choked. "Nothing else but stubbornness. I haven't the slightest idea where my brother is at the moment. Traveling in Asia somewhere. He hasn't been home for more than a few weeks at a time during the past score of years. This man you call the Doctor—why, I've known him for years. He's visited me many times. Not more than a week ago, I ran across him on the street."

"I think rather he ran across you," X said dryly. "But go on."

"I hadn't seen him for ten years," Boise Marquod explained. "I asked him to the house to dinner, of course. He had been traveling in Europe. The name I have always known him by is Carver—Walter Carver. He was a scientist, a soldier of fortune, adventurer—almost everything you wouldn't expect him to be from appearances.

"It was about that time that I got your first warning. I showed it to Carver, and he suggested that until the danger blew over he should act as my bodyguard. He said that he had nothing particular to do for a couple of weeks."

"Nothing but commit murder," Durmont cut in.

"Well, I didn't like the idea of having a bodyguard," Marquod said. "Still, I didn't feel any too secure. So I simply hit up the plan of introducing him as my long absent brother. He promised he wouldn't reveal my secret—"

"You can bet on that!" Steve Wienhardt said. "Of all the damn fool tricks! Talk about mothering a viper, or whatever the saying is, you sure done it, Mr. Marquod."

Marquod bowed his head. "That's right," he said meekly. "Just a stubborn old fool. I wouldn't co-operate, yet I was secretly afraid of my life. So I—well, it's over. And I guess I am, too."

"Not at all," X insisted. "America needs you. You've got to carry on the fight, just like the rest of us. Rex Durmont goes back to beat all rivals in his campaign for governorship. We'll want him for president later on. And you, Boise Marquod, you've got to hang on to your job, too."

"And you?" Durmont asked.

X laughed shortly. He turned to Mary Ferris. "First of all I owe this young lady a sincere apology. And some thanks, too, for what she did for me. She hired a lawyer to get me out of jail, after she thought what trouble her accusations had made for me."

Mary Ferris lowered lovely eyes. "I got to thinking how foolish I'd been. And I really did think Steve Wienhardt had a good motive for killing poor Gordon. I didn't want to do you an injustice, Mr.—well, I guess it's Mr. X, isn't it?"

X smiled, put his hand on the knob of the door. "Take a good look at me so you will know me again, all of you. Good night."

He opened the door and walked out into the darkness.

BOOK I

PYTHON MEN OF LOST CITY

A fiery curtain of doom dropped on the first act of the
Phoenix's sinister murder spectacle. And that curtain
eclipsed the drama of the reptile-skinned stowaway
from nowhere. But it was just the first act, for the
Phoenix and his barbaric battalions of Python Men
were staging a weird welcome for the one man who
defied them. That man was Capt. Hazzard—peer of
perilous adventure and master of modern science.

INTRODUCING—
CAPT. HAZZARD

WHEN I FINISHED writing the chronicle of the "Python Men of Lost City," the editor asked me for a brief word of introduction for this column. To tell the truth, I didn't know just where to begin. For, in the story, I told that Captain Hazzard had been blind for fifteen years of his boyhood; and how he had studied and developed his mental powers far beyond those of an average person; how he had regained his eyesight, and then marshaled a group of assistants—scientists, chemists, mathematicians, adventurers—and flung a challenge to the criminals of the world. So I was at a loss as to how to give you a real insight into the character of this remarkable man—until I remembered what had happened on that glorious day when Hazzard's eyesight was restored to him.

As the doctor unwound the bandages over Hazzard's eyes he warned that the eyes could only be used for three minutes the first day. Young Hazzard reached out and took my arm, saying:

"There are three things I want to see. Will you get them, Hawks?"

I squeezed his arm. In a quiet voice, he made his first request:

"Let me see a picture of my mother and father."

That sorta choked me up. For both of his parents had died while he was blind. He had known and loved them—but had never seen their faces. "You shall see that picture, lad," I said.

His next request was a simple one. Most of you see it every day of your lives. Hazzard's voice had a strange thrill in it when he asked:

"I want to see—the American flag. Those stars, and the red, white and blue must be a beautiful thing to see."

I told him that a person has to look a long way to see a more beautiful thing than Old Glory. And then came his last request:

"The picture of Blind Justice—the lady holding the scales, and with the blindfold over her eyes.... I want to be her eyes."

Well, friends, this is the best way I know of introducing a brave, dashing—and sincere man.

Chester Hawks.

CHAPTER I

THE MURDER CURTAIN

THREE MEN STOOD beside a dusty gray auto at one side of Pier 52, North River, and watched the American liner, *Liberty,* slide into her berth. Their faces mirrored a tenseness mixed with a haunting, brooding dread. Some hidden conflict seemed to be twisting their nerves to springlike tautness. Stark terror of a force outside themselves was lashing them pitilessly to do a thing they feared.

Floodlights bathed the pier as the great ship touched the dock with a rumble of winches, a clatter of gangplanks, a shuffling of feet. White-coated stewards, carrying luggage, were the first to reach the pier. Then came the passengers, smiling, waving, calling excited greetings to friends and loved ones on hand to welcome them home.

But there was no love, no friendship in the eyes of the three men who stood beside that dusty, queer-looking auto.

One was tall, thin-lipped, with a sickly pallor accentuated by blue-black hair. Another had a powerful body, a heavy bloated face. The third was small, swarthy, vicious, his sharp teeth showing in a servile, hyena grin. He wore goggles and a chauffeur's cap.

They made no move to meet anybody. They stared fixedly through the door of the pier shed at the lights of the great liner. Not till all the passengers were off and had passed through customs did the tall, pallid man stoop and whisper something to the one with the bloated face. The heavy man nodded, set off at a fast walk diagonally across the street.

The swarthy chauffeur slipped behind the wheel of the gray car and started the motor. He sat on the front seat with the alertness of a cat waiting to spring. The pallid man climbed into the back and drew the side shades carefully. The car waited, its engine purring.

Fearful, smothered cries
ripped from their throats.

But something moved on top of it as the man inside slowly cranked a handle. It might have been a collapsible radio aerial. It rose up thinly, forming a low tripod. The handle inside continued to move. From the top of the tripod thin black rods pushed out of tubular metal framework. They were slender, almost invisible to anyone standing more than a few feet away. But they crisscrossed into a design that was horribly like the antennae of some great insect.

There were still finer, hairlike rods branching out from them and these trembled with the vibration of the car's engine, reminiscent of the feelers of a giant deadly centipede getting ready to strike.

The man inside ceased to turn the handle. He crouched forward, staring through a peephole in the side curtains at the big pier entrance. Once he moved to another peephole on the opposite side of the car and glanced intently in the direction that the bloated-faced man had gone.

There was an empty store diagonally across the street here, its windows broken and dusty. Dimly seen on the roof of this building was the rod framework of another small tripod. The hairlike antennae were invisible, but the metal tubes in which they were mounted reflected a faint gleam of light.

The dark-haired man's pallor increased, and his hands trembled. He again took up his station at the peephole nearest the dock. His black eyes held a savage gleam of impending murder.

There was excitement at the top of the *Liberty's* forward gangplank now. Several dapper ship's officers led a strange-looking figure forward, a stowaway who had been discovered in one of the holds after the vessel had come through quarantine.

The stowaway's clothing was tattered, stained, his body emaciated. But the most startling thing about him was his face. It had the dry, scaly look of a reptile. All life seemed to have gone from the skin. Brown, dead-looking, it was cracked into unsymmetrical sections like the hide of an alligator.

SEVERAL officers kept at a distance from him, as though they feared they might become contaminated. But two immigration men, accustomed to handling all sorts of queer characters, came up and grabbed him by the arms. One said:

"Come along, buddy, we're gonna take you places."

The reptile-faced man made no answer. His dull, glazed eyes were focused on some horror only he could see. He moved sluggishly, letting himself be pulled forward. The few people left on the dock recoiled as he passed, staring with open-eyed amazement.

The immigration officers led him through the pier shed toward the exit. Here another man, short, stocky, keen-faced, pleasant-looking, was lingering purposely. He stepped forward as the trio reached him. "My name's Crawley," he said. "Any idea where that chap came from? I picked up a message on the ship-to-shore telephone and heard about the stowaway."

One of the immigration officers waved him back. "You press people give me a pain," he muttered. "Our department will make a report when it's ready."

"The *Liberty* put in at several South American ports," persisted Crawley. "Maybe this man's an escaped prisoner from Devil's Island."

"Yes, and maybe he isn't!" snapped the officer.

Crawley shrugged, stepped aside. But he followed at a distance. His own car was parked outside along the block. He had instructions to learn the identity of this strange man who had somehow stowed away on a crack passenger liner.

He was fifty feet behind when the stowaway and the two immigration men passed through the exit. For a moment they were on a line with the gray car parked outside the pier and the metal tripod mounted up there in the darkness on top of the empty store building. Crawley was the first immediate witness of the shocking, extraordinary thing that occurred.

The night gloom outside the pier entrance changed suddenly. It grew lighter, with a wavering, eerie incandescence as though the sky had been fired with the glow of an aurora borealis. Tongues of shimmering, uncanny light slid through the air, wavered, intermingled, touched and retreated, only to reappear again. But they were not in the sky. They were in the air close to the earth—forming a weird, pulsating, radiant curtain between the tripod on top of the gray car and that other tripod on the roof of the building. A curtain of horrible death! For the stowaway with the reptilelike face and the two immigration officers stood paralyzed in this ghastly web of writhing fire.

Muscles strained under their clothing. Veins stood out on their faces, swelled, seemed about to burst like over-ripe grapes. Their eyes started from their heads. Their mouths opened, tongues protruding. Fearful, smothered cries ripped from their quivering throats.

The two immigration officers sagged on legs gone limp as jelly. The stowaway took two jerky steps forward. He seemed to possess inhuman stamina—for he almost stumbled out of the curtain of light. Then he, too, paused, staggered and dropped.

Crawley did a strange thing for a reporter—a strange thing in the face of that maelstrom of murder. He calmly closed his eyes, seemed to go to sleep. His features looked peaceful, trancelike for a moment. He seemed almost bored by the terror of the night. What went on in his mind made no show in the visible world. But odd systaltic vibrations stirred in the inner, unknown realms of etheric space. Crawley's horror and the image that fell on the retina of his eyes, was transferred in the flash of a split-second by telepathic influence to the brain of another man ten miles away.

THIS MAN was sitting quietly in an inner chamber of a great building on Long Island. It was a laboratory, a workshop and an airplane hangar. There were high walls of reinforced concrete around him, electrically charged barbed wire on top of that, and then other walls of steel and hardwood. But Crawley's mental image, his feelings, came through them by telepathic impulse with speed of light.

The man in the quiet laboratory received the same image, the same impressions of horror. His mind, connected by the mysterious bond of extra-sensory impressions, which make up the new science of telepathy and clairvoyance, known collectively as "parapsychology," actually seemed to see through the eyes of Crawley. The impressions came dimly at first, wavering, disturbing, out of a fog apparently, like an image from a projector being focused. Then they were clear, true, awful as the thing itself. And the man in the laboratory chair sat breathing deeply, gripping the edge of his desk with tense fingers, staring fixedly at the blank wall before him.

His name was Captain Hazzard. He was young, ruggedly built, broad-shouldered, dark-haired, with a face that was a mixture of dynamic youth and mature power. It was hard to place his age. He seemed to be in his middle twenties. He might have been younger or older. There was a changeable quality in his blue-gray eyes as there was about his face. The irises had the clearness of a blue flame, but, when his moods varied, a wind seemed to blow across the flame, and darker glints glowed beneath.

He was a man about whom many legends had sprung up. Many strange stories had been told of his actions, his powers, his career. But hardly any of them as startling as the truth itself.[25]

---

25   AUTHOR'S NOTE: Captain Hazzard, America's Ace Adventurer, was blinded in infancy and spent the first fifteen years of his life in total darkness. Denied normal pleasures and activities, he had been thrown back on himself, on his own cleverness and imagination. He had learned the Braille system of reading by sense of touch. More than this, in those long dark years when the outer world was beyond his sight, he had developed his latent mental powers to the point where they extended much farther than the average person's. He had studied all the phenomena of the mind: hypnotism, the various schools of psychology, Yoga and other forms of Oriental mysticism including the shamanistic beliefs and practices of the Lamas of Tibet, and telepathy.
When a delicate surgical operation had finally restored his physical sight he had dedicated his life to adventure, action, and the extension of man's knowledge of the world about him. He had gathered together certain chosen assistants, brilliant young scientists, chemists, mathematicians, adventurers. A few hand-picked men he tested for telepathic

In his mind's eye now he saw the stowaway pitch forward. He saw the two immigration men lying in huddled heaps. He saw for an instant, as did Crawley, that one end of that weird curtain of death was somehow connected with the parked gray car.

He sat stiffly in his chair while the action unfolded, while Crawley, his agent, continued to send out the telepathic impulses that were registering in his own excited brain.

The strange curtain of livid light disappeared as suddenly as it had come. It flashed off, leaving the darkness darker. And in that darkness the grinning chauffeur behind the wheel of the gray car touched levers and the car sped away.

Crawley pointed, cried through trembling lips: "Those men did it!" A policeman heard him, ran for a patrol car. Crawley himself turned and raced for the spot down the street where his own coupé was parked. He swung it around, tore after the gray car that was now only a ghostly blur up the long waterfront street.

Captain Hazzard, in his laboratory, grabbed the desk edge still more tightly, as though he himself were driving Crawley's coupé. It gained on the gray car. A police radio cruiser with a powerful motor, nosed up and went by Crawley. It continued to outpace him, creeping up on the gray car ahead. Crawley stepped on the gas, hugged the wheel more tightly.

Then Captain Hazzard rose from his chair as an idea struck him. He broke into the telepathic reception he was getting from Crawley, sent out a mental message of his own: "Look back, Crawley! There may be another car behind you. Tripod! Curtain of death!"

The message flashed through etheric space to Crawley's mind. Crawley got it, faintly at first, then more clearly as he felt the pow-

---

powers by means of card symbols, using the method of Doctor Rhine of Duke University. In this way, he had formed a small group of close associates who could send mental messages and images to him, and receive his in turn under certain conditions. The telepathic powers of the mind are not perfect. But some day, when the world is older, Captain Hazzard believes they will be. At present he has learned to make use of many. The common experiences which people everywhere have of telepathy, mind-reading, foresight, and psychic contact, prove that mankind is on the threshold of new and vaster discoveries in the realm of the mind. Captain Hazzard is a pioneer in this great new branch of science. And his brilliant researches and inventions in his Long Island laboratory, as well as his startling world adventures, have brought him not only wealth and fame, but recognition from his government. For certain secret advice of a military nature, which has helped to make America safe against foreign attack, he has been given the honorary rank of captain in both the army and navy air corps.

erful brain impulse of Captain Hazzard. He stared back, and his mouth opened.

Captain Hazzard breathed an oath as all went blank in his mind—blank, because Crawley had stopped sending, stopped receiving. Something had gone wrong! It was as though a switch on a radio had been turned off.

THE HAND of Captain Hazzard dropped to an inter-office telephone. He snatched the instrument up, barked a swift order: "Tell Crandall to warm Z2."

He slammed the instrument down. In ten quick strides he crossed and yanked a door open, walked down a short passage and through another door made of case-hardened molybdenum steel. He passed by a glass-partitioned office where absorbed young men were bent over long desks, passed a machine shop where other men were working, and a laboratory where white-coated chemists stood quietly in front of instrument-strewn tables. He crossed a foundry room where the latest scientific electric crucibles were mounted and where molten metal hissed.

Heads lifted as Captain Hazzard's tall, erect figure moved by. Men saluted or nodded in respectful greeting. He was the brains, the heart, the soul of one of the greatest private laboratories in the world. Loved as a close friend by the men around him, his word in this whole, vast, busy building was law.

He walked down another passage, stepped into a small automatic elevator that shot him up to the roof of the plant. The hum of a powerful airplane motor warming up filled the whole night air. The water of Long Island Sound gleamed close at hand. The plane itself was standing on a catapult, such as are mounted on the decks of battle cruisers.

It was a single-seater amphibian with twin pontoons, retractable landing wheels and a giant radial motor of six-hundred horsepower. A grave young man in the cockpit was watching the temperature gauge intently. He stepped out, saluted as Captain Hazzard came up.

"She's almost ready, sir," he said.

"Stand by to release me, Crandall," Captain Hazzard replied.

He got into the narrow cockpit, adjusted flying helmet and safety belt, watched the temperature gauge creep up. In thirty seconds, he raised a gloved hand and Crandall pressed a button. There was a dull explosion, a hiss of compressed gases. The catapult boom swung forward and literally hurled the amphibian out into space away from the roof.

It shot across the water, sailed in a long trajectory, dipping down till the motor burst into a full song of throaty power. Then it lifted, banked, climbed into the night sky on its silver wings and whining steel propeller.

Hazzard made the ten miles to New York's waterfront in exactly three minutes. His plane banked high over the city, shot down like a bolt from the heavens, came to rest on the river close to the stern of the *Liberty*. He taxied into the slip, threw a dockhand a rope, made his plane fast and climbed up a ladder.

Radio police cars were gathered around the three dead men. Cops formed a stalwart human barricade. They bristled when Captain Hazzard pushed through the crowd of curious people that had gathered. Then an inspector of detectives recognized him and nodded. The police opened a path to let him through.

The inspector said: "This is a hellish business, Captain Hazzard. Five men have been murdered, and the criminals have got away."

"Five?"

"Yes. These three poor chaps here and two officers in a pursuing radio car. They were knocked out the same way as these fellows. An electric ray or something. A car sneaked up behind them with a tripod gadget on it and lined them in a death zone with the car ahead."

"What about a reporter named Crawley?" asked Hazzard tensely.

"He was trying to follow the killers, too, Captain. He must have got nervous and lost control of his car. He swerved and hit a lamp post. They've taken him to the hospital with a case of concussion. I think he'll pull through all right."

Captain Hazzard breathed more easily. But his face was mask-like in its harshness as he looked down at the three dead men. The blueness of his eyes had given way to a wintry gray.

Morgue attendants were preparing to take the bodies off on stretchers. Hazzard looked down at the still figure of the strange stowaway. The police inspector said:

"It'll be hard now to find out who he was, Captain. We've been through his clothing. Nothing there to identify him. And look at his face! I doubt that he will ever be identified. His own mother wouldn't know him."

Hazzard nodded, bent down and examined the dead man. He took it for granted that the police had searched the clothing thoroughly. But something might have been overlooked. And suddenly Hazzard's hand darted to the corpse's thick hair. His fingers slipped through, snatched at a tiny object. It was a rolled-up cylinder fastened by fiber to several strands of hair close to the scalp. The light end of it had attracted his attention.

He swiftly palmed the cylinder. Then he rose, asking the inspector the name of the hospital where Crawley had been taken.

The inspector offered to lend Hazzard a police car, but Captain Hazzard declined. He passed outside the circle of cops, slipped through the crowd, to pause at the edge of it under a street light. With taut fingers he unrolled the tiny cylinder. It was a strange message to find on such a man in such a place. Printed in inked letters on tissue-thin parchment, it said:

> The poison of red-ant bites is filling my brain. The Jewel Men are close behind me. Spies of the Phoenix are waiting along the coast. Even if I can stow away aboard some ship and reach New York I won't be safe from them. That's why I've written this to put in my hair. Maybe they won't find it when they kill me—and maybe somebody else will. If so, tell Mary Parker that her father and some of his party are still alive at N. Lat. 15.10., W. Long. 89.27, prisoners of the Phoenix. The others who tried to escape with me were killed. It would have been better if they'd got me, too.
>
> John Roan.

Hazzard read it through twice, then a sudden sense of uneasiness made him close his fingers over the parchment, and whirl around. But he wasn't quite quick enough to see the furtive men on the roof of the empty store building who, through the achromatic lenses of a powerful prism monocular, had got the message by reading it over Hazzard's shoulder.

Hazzard made an impatient gesture, feeling that something was wrong. Then he strode to a telephone booth, grabbed a big directory and began thumbing through its pages looking for the address of Mary Parker.

CHAPTER II

THE WHISTLING DEVIL

HE FOUND IT, and a swift taxi sped him on his way. At the edge of town, in one of a row of big brick houses, an aged maidservant answered his quick tug on an old-fashioned bell.

Stepping past her into the hallway. Captain Hazzard saw a beautiful golden-haired girl standing as straight and tall as some exotic statue. She had curved red lips, humid eyes, heart-shaped features. Her face held a curious expression. Her expression showed that she recognized him and was puzzled at this visit from a man whom she regarded as a great celebrity.

When he reached her side he said in a quiet voice: "You know me, don't you, Miss Parker?"

"Yes." Her dark blue eyes roved over his face with a mixture of awe and curiosity. "I've heard of you, seen your picture often. You travel over the earth. You're a great aviator, an explorer, a scientist, who sometimes helps people in trouble. But—" her voice shook uneasily—"something extraordinary must have happened to bring you to my house. Tell me, has it anything to do with my father?"

He nodded gravely, looking into her eyes. "Yes."

"Oh!" The clear, rich coloring of her cheeks began to fade. She came closer, laid her hand on his arm. "Don't be afraid to speak the truth, Captain Hazzard. What have you heard from him? Is—he—"

For answer, Hazzard took the thin bit of parchment from his pocket and held it out. He watched her closely as she read the brief message. He saw her face grow strained. Her eyes lifted to his and there was stark fear in them.

"Where did you get this?" she asked.

He told her then about the stowaway with the hideous face who had been slain by the weird death curtain. Her cheeks turned paler. "John Roan was one of my father's men," she said breathlessly.

"What could have happened to him? And who—who is this man whom he calls the Phoenix?"

Captain Hazzard shook his head. "You may be able to help me piece the puzzle together. What was your father doing in Central America?"

"You knew he was down there then?" asked Mary Parker in surprise.

Hazzard indicated the figures of latitude and longitude in the note. "Those tell the story, Miss Parker. That compass point is somewhere on the frontier between Guatemala and Honduras, close to the Espiritu Santo range."

She dropped her eyes for a moment, then raised them, and looked deeply into his piercing blue-gray ones. "I promised father I wouldn't tell anyone where he'd gone or what he was doing, Captain Hazzard," she said. "But I can talk to you, trust you, and I've got to have help now that my father is in terrible danger.

"He's an engineer who has been interested for many years in mining properties down in Central America. He has a partner living down there, a clever metallurgist named Kurt Gordon. Gordon and father work together extracting ores.

"Two months ago father went down to Guatemala with a small group of experts to see Gordon about the development of some big deposits of platinum. They didn't have much capital. Rival mining companies would have tried to beat dad to it if they'd got wind of it. That's why the thing had to be kept secret. But now—" she broke off, and tears glistened in her eyes.

"How long has it been since you've heard from him?" asked Hazzard quickly.

"Four weeks. I've radioed both my father and Mr. Gordon, and they couldn't be located. I didn't know what else to do. But now that I know father's whereabouts hadn't I better ask the governments of Guatemala and Honduras to help me? Couldn't I cable our American consuls?"

Captain Hazzard didn't answer for a moment. He was trying to guess what was back of this weirdly murderous organization that reached from the tropical jungles of Central America to the crowded streets of New York. Presently he said:

"It's big, Miss Parker. Something that must be handled with gloves. I've told you what happened to Roan. We don't want to do anything that will put your father in greater danger. If you asked the help of those Central American governments and then they should blunder—"

"You're right!" Fear darkened the girl's eyes again. "Whatever happens—whoever the Phoenix is—I must save my father. And you, Captain Hazzard—couldn't you—would you consider the possibility of organizing an expedition to help me rescue him? I'll do anything I can. I have some money—"

He made an impatient gesture. "I intended to help you when I came."

"Then—"

"Wait!" Captain Hazzard tensed suddenly and lifted his head. He looked around the room in which they were talking, and his nostrils flared. The blueness of his eyes gave way to a slaty gray. A deep instinctive sense of danger had come like a sinister psychic whisper, tingling his nerves.

He began to move about the room uneasily, peering, prying, like a savage trying to find spoor. He came to a stop abruptly in front of a big bay window, from which he could command a view of the front stoop of the house. He stared, and the muscles under the tanned skin of his face went rigid.

Mary Parker came and stood beside him, staring, too, then lifted a trembling hand to her mouth in horror. "It's crepe!" she gasped. "Black crepe! It's hanging on the door of this house as if someone were dead."

"It wasn't there," said Hazzard, "when I came in."

She gave a stifled gasp. "Can it— Do you suppose it means that father's dead?"

Hazzard shook his head. "It means something else," he said, "something quite different. It means that the men who killed John Roan knew about that message and know that I came here. It means they intend now to kill us both."

THE TRAGIC look on the girl's face vanished. Personal danger didn't shock her so much as fear of her father's death. Hazzard felt a quick glow of admiration for her nerve.

He pulled her away from the window, drew the shade, and stood for a moment thinking. His psychic feeling of menace was like a chill fog now. They were in deadly danger, and he knew it, but he didn't know from what direction the thing would strike.

A noise interrupted him, the sound of a car drawing up outside. Hazzard thrust his fingers under his coat and grasped the butt of the heavy army Colt automatic he wore in a shoulder holster. He listened and heard feet scraping up the stoop.

The bell rang loudly in the still house, stirring echoes, but Molly, Mary Parker's maid, didn't show any sign of coming to answer it.

Keeping his hand on the Colt, Captain Hazzard motioned the girl back and strode to the door himself. He stood wide-legged, his

Capt. Hazzard

young face grim, drew the lock back and opened it.

A man in a gray uniform, wearing a visored cap, and holding a white slip of paper stood there. A big black truck was drawn up at the curb. The man said: "Is this the home of Miss Mary Parker?"

When Hazzard nodded, the man held out the paper slip. "Ask her to sign this please, and let me know where she wants 'em."

"Wants what?" asked Hazzard.

"The two caskets. We're making a rush delivery after receiving cash payment as per instructions. Will I have 'em put downstairs or up?"

Icy prickles ran along Captain Hazzard's back. But his face was masklike, inscrutable. It was plain to him that this man in uniform was genuine; merely carrying out orders for the quick delivery of two coffins which someone else had bought. Hazzard said quietly: "Bring them in. Take them right to the drawing room." He went back to Mary Parker and spoke soothingly. "Don't be frightened. Our friends are enlarging on their little joke. Now they've presented us with our caskets."

She stood wide-eyed, silent, stricken as the boxes were brought in. Hazzard had them placed in the drawing room. There was a bleak, hard smile on his face, like sunlight flashing over steel. He looked to see that both coffins were empty, signed the receipt, then dismissed the men.

The macabre black boxes so close at hand were mute reminders that they were both marked for the same dread fate. Hazzard asked:

"Where is your maid's room?"

Mary Parker's hand clutched his wrist, clawlike in its tenseness. "We must find Molly! She should have answered the doorbell."

They went down the old-fashioned, narrow stairway that led to the kitchen and the servant's quarters. Hazzard moved ahead, his big army Colt in his hand.

And it was he who first caught sight of the crumpled, pitiful body of the gray-haired maid. She lay on her back on the kitchen floor staring with wide, glazed eyes at the ceiling. There was a wire around her neck, tied tight in back.

Mary Parker gave a sobbing sigh when she glimpsed the body and crouched on her knees beside it.

Captain Hazzard crouched, too, but with every nerve alert. He understood something that the girl had failed to grasp in her sorrow. Molly's wanton murder meant that some of the agents of the Phoenix were already in the house.

Even as this thought came there was a faint sound of movement in the dark doorway beside the stairs that led to the servant's bedroom, Hazzard's hand flicked out, flung Mary Parker forward, sent her sprawling flat on the floor, and then dropped himself. He rolled over and over with the snapping suddenness of a tempered spring released.

Bullets followed him. Bullets beat a tattoo along the floor at his heels, like the fangs of Death snapping for his life. The snout of a sub-machine gun with a cylindrical silencer on it gleamed in that black doorway beside the stairs. And a man's eyes gleamed behind it.

It seemed impossible that he could miss. He was turning the snarling gun on its axis, hosing bullets at Captain Hazzard. And the wall of the kitchen was directly in front of Hazzard now, barring further movement.

But before he reached it, even as he was rolling over and over, Captain Hazzard's fingers flashed down to his belt, flashed up again with something in them. His wrist snapped out. The air was filled suddenly with sparkling pellets.

Drops of diphenoloxide enclosed in eggshell-thin glass rained at the feet of the gunman, broke open, filled the air with drifting, smarting fumes. The machine gunner choked and cried out, his eyes streaming. His weapon ripped plaster from the ceiling as he tried vainly to center its sights on Captain Hazzard.

Hazzard was up in an instant. He turned, bounded across the kitchen floor, ducked sidewise to avoid the wildly swinging stream of slugs. His gun muzzle lashed out and cracked down on the skull of the gunman, stunning him. The sub-caliber weapon fell. Hazzard snatched it up. Then he helped the girl to her feet and ran for the back door that led to a garden.

It was unlocked, half open. But caution stayed Hazzard before he bolted through. Caution made him fling the door wide, let his shadow precede him, and freeze in his tracks.

It was well he did so. There was a sudden snapping hiss in the darkness as lead from other silenced sub-calibers converged on the spot where his body would have been.

The slugs came close. They bit at the door frame and forced Hazzard back. There was a grim smile on his lips. He hadn't really expected that there would be an easy way out. Left to himself, he might have played a game of death with those men outside. But there was the girl to consider.

He closed the door quickly, snapped a bolt into place, put the lights out and caught Mary Parker's hand. He led her through the gloom of the kitchen, around the body of Molly, toward the stairs. She was sobbing softly.

He had marked the location of the stairway, and he went to it as easily as though it had been light. Darkness held no terrors for him. He had lived in the dark too long himself to fear it. When he reached the upstairs hallway he switched out the bulb there, left Mary Parker for a moment, and strode to the front door. He opened it, looked up and down the street cautiously.

A gray car was parked a few yards along the block. Metal rods gleamed on top of it like the antennae of a huge, malignant scorpion poised to strike. On the other side of the house, a hundred yards away, another car was parked. Between them, already visible, was a faint aura of eerie luminescence.

Hazzard gritted his teeth. He and Mary Parker were trapped. Guns waited in the yard behind them. In front, ready to sweep them into oblivion, was that weird, pulsating curtain of unholy death.

CHAPTER III

STAIRWAY TO HELL

HE COULD FEEL the strange influence of it even as he looked. Dizziness filled him. He raised the gun, but his fingers shook so that he couldn't aim it. He wasn't afraid. It was the unseen, unknown force of that weird, deathly light striking the cells of his body that made him shake. Two steps closer, he knew, would spell certain doom.

He backed up, shut the door quickly, and saw Mary Parker coming toward him along the hall. Her face was white. She said through tight lips:

"There's someone moving upstairs. I just heard footsteps."

Hazzard heard them, too, knew that the agents of the Phoenix were closing in.

Mary Parker's voice was a dry, taut whisper: "The telephone? Can't we call the police?"

He went to it with her, but found as he had expected that the line was dead—cut.

He could send a mental message through space that would summon his own assistants. But he dismissed all thought of that. To call them without giving full information of what they would find would only be leading them to slaughter. And even Captain Hazzard couldn't pretend to transmit telepathically details of the complex situation he faced. His only course was to fight it out alone.

"There must be a skylight," he muttered. "They've come across the tops of the roofs and broken through it. Now they're coming down."

"Yes. All the houses on this block are the same height."

Hazzard asked quickly: "The one next door, on the right—who lives in it?"

"It's vacant."

"Then we've got to go up." His voice was vibrant. His eyes held a light of battle.

"But they're waiting there now!" she whispered. "They'll surely kill us."

He didn't answer. Experience on the wild frontiers of the world had taught him that all life is a gamble when death is close. And Hazzard had some dice of his own to toss on Fate's table.

His belt was strong and wide and made of pliant leather. It had many small pouches, apparently for cartridges. But the compact spaces held a score of objects other than shells. In them he carried some of the gadgets that were the product of his inventive skill, articles he had turned out during his spare time in the laboratory on Long Island.

Hazzard chose a small, greenish, oval-shaped object with blunt excrescences on it. It looked like an enlarged bronze model of some sort of scarab. But the blunt points had tiny holes in them. Hazzard called it his "Whistling Devil."

He touched a button on one end of it and a faint sputter sounded in the strange thing's interior. Acid began to eat through a tinfoil wall. In a moment, when it touched another acid, a gas would be generated and pressure would build up.

He tossed it into the room with the two coffins, then pulled the girl cautiously toward the stairs.

A minute passed and hell seemed to break loose in that darkened chamber. A fiend appeared to be whipping itself into a stark raving fury. A shrill screech came as gas shot through a whistling vent. The screech mounted. Other screeches joined it. Gas under terrific pressure in the bronze jacket spurted through a dozen whistling holes. The force of it pushed the thing around the room like a whirlwind. It banged into chairs, hit the wall, leaped toward the ceiling, screeching, jumping, clattering.

In the midst of the din, Hazzard took Mary Parker's trembling hand and drew her up the stairs. He knew that the "Devil's" noise would drown out the creak of their steps. It was dark on the stairway. The men above would hear nothing except that startling, nerve-racking sound below.

HAZZARD'S eyes stabbed the gloom. At the first landing, he suddenly thrust the girl behind him and leaped, hurling himself like a projectile on a dim human form he had glimpsed straight ahead. A

man was standing on the stairway, gun in hand, eyes alarmed, trying to make out what that fearful racket was.

He saw Hazzard, and tried to raise the weapon. Hazzard knocked
it from his hands, then caught him around the waist in a football
tackle and lifted him bodily. The man struggled, yelled. Hazzard
threw him over the banisters in a savage, lightning heave that sent
him hurtling to the floor below. The gunman landed on his head.
His striking body made a thud, but no sound of it came above the
wail of the Whistling Devil.

He drew Mary Parker on to the second-story hall. There he
paused, peered up, and caught dim movement somewhere between
him and the glass skylight of the stairwell. Downstairs, the sound
of the Devil was growing fainter now. The gas was almost exhausted. Soon the creak of the stairs under them would be heard. It was
time to toss another of his dice.

He whipped a handkerchief from his pocket, turned to Mary
Parker and whispered close to her ear: "I'm going to tie this over
your eyes and nose."

"What for?" Her voice was a thin gasp of fear.

"Smoke bomb," he said quietly. He placed the handkerchief over
her face, knotted it in back. Then he drew a cylinder from his belt
containing carbon tetrachloride, sand, zinc dust and magnesium. It
was a miniature smoke pot having the same chemical basis as the
type used in wartime to hide military ground maneuvers.

He pressed a spark igniter, hurled the cylinder up the stairwell
to the floor above. In a moment even the dim glow of the skylight
was shut off. Smoke so thick it seemed to have solid substance
mushroomed out, filling the whole house. It rolled down the stairs
in a stygian cloud, floated up in a sable curtain. Through it, Hazzard faintly heard the oaths of startled men.

He took a deep breath, closed his eyes. Death might still strike
through the smoke, for those above had guns. They couldn't see,
but they might shoot at random, lay a barrage of lead that would
spell destruction.

That was a chance he had to take. He made Mary Parker walk
behind him, held her fingers in his left hand, and climbed quickly,
keeping the banister on his right. Close to the second floor Mary
Parker stumbled as her high heels caught in the stair carpet. She
gave a choking gasp. Instantly movement sounded.

Hazzard pulled her down beside him a moment before bullets
snarled above their heads. He couldn't see the flash of the guns.

The silencers on the sub-caliber weapons almost deadened the sound of the shots. It was erie having silent lead come at him out of that black cloud. But he heard the deathly whine of the slugs close above him, felt the wind they made.

His own finger pressed the curved trigger of the gun he had taken from the man in the kitchen. He heard a vicious slap as his slugs struck, heard the cry of a man mortally wounded. A human form came bounding down the stairs, struck his shoulder a glancing blow, and caromed on behind him.

Mary Parker, flattened against the steps, barely missed being hit by the hurtling body. Another gun hissed into life. Cold fear clutched Hazzard's heart. Fear for Mary Parker's life. He snapped more shots at the gun above until it grew silent. But the weapon in his own hands went silent, too, the drum exhausted.

He had his automatic, but he wanted to save its shells. They might be needed later. Even if they reached the roof there would be killers waiting.

HOLDING the sub-caliber gun as a club, Hazzard sprang on up, pulling the girl with him. A man stumbled into him, and Hazzard struck. There was a groan, a thud. Hazzard plunged on through the smoke cloud, reached the top hallway, and a cool draft told him that the open skylight was just ahead.

The black fumes of his smoke bomb were even thicker here. They poured out through the skylight cover in a volcanic cloud. Hazzard half lifted the girl up with him, and reached the roof.

He could see no stars. The black smoke funneled upward hiding the sky. But it would thin presently. Then eyes in the surrounding darkness would see. Crouching men on other roofs would fling lead at them. There might be a dozen, a score of the Phoenix's killers around them for all Hazzard knew. They would guess soon enough that he and the girl had reached the roof. They would figure on a running flight along the housetops as the obvious way of escape.

But Hazzard never did the obvious. He moved to the right, to the roof of the empty house next door. Here he stopped again. The billowing smoke still hid them. He had a few seconds in which to work. His hands felt for the skylight.

"You're not going down there?" muttered Mary Parker, her voice muffled by the handkerchief.

"Yes."

"But you said their car was parked outside. You said the death curtain—"

"That's why I'm doing it. They won't expect us. They'll think we're running."

He didn't say that he had another plan in his mind. He drew a thin hacksaw blade from his belt, slipped it under the skylight cover, and cut the hooks. In a moment he raised it softly, stepped in and drew the girl along. He whipped the handkerchief from her face.

"Hurry!" he said.

They moved down the stairs of the dark empty house like a pair of ghosts. Hazzard peered under a drawn shade at street level and saw the killers' gray car standing directly outside. The faint aura of the death curtain was still visible, but only in front of that hair-like antenna. If he could take those men in the parked vehicle by surprise....

That was the plan that he had formed on the roof—to capture that gray car, to escape in it, learn the nature of the fire curtain's devilish mechanism.

But he could see a head on the front seat now. And there must be one or more men in back. Hazzard turned to the girl. "I'm going to open the door and rush them. You stay here and watch. If I beckon, you come running."

Before she could protest, he flung the door wide and went down the steps, shooting. His first bullet glanced off the car's engine hood. The man behind the wheel, the vicious-faced killer with hyena teeth, turned and a gun came magically to his fingers. Flame lanced and lead brushed close to Captain Hazzard. But Hazzard's next two shots were deadly. They seemed to lift Hyena-face in the car seat and batter him to the floorboards.

Other bullets streaked from the rear of the car from a curtained side window. Hazzard smashed lead savagely till spidery cracks appeared in the non-shatterable glass. The gun-flame behind the glass suddenly ceased. Taking a desperate chance, Hazzard turned and motioned to Mary Parker.

She didn't hesitate an instant. Her nerve raised his respect for her. She came down the stoop with her eyes wide and her golden hair flying.

Hazzard held his breath for fear she mightn't make it. He saw chips dance close beside her on the walk as cupro-nickel slugs whipped at her feet from guns on the roof above. Then she was close to the open door of the car. Hazzard heaved out the dead driver, pulled the girl in and took the wheel.

The motor was running. In a moment the gray car moved. But that other car, with the antennae on it, was parked ahead. Men leaned out now, firing. Hazzard backed, twisted the wheel savagely, bounced fat tires up on the sidewalk, and made a desperate turn with lead crashing into the gray car.

He got the headlights pointed in the opposite direction and pressed his foot on the gas. There was plenty of power under that long gray hood. The car leaped ahead like a racehorse given the whip. But the car behind was moving, too, following them swiftly.

Mary Parker crouched beside him, her cheeks flaming with excitement. He was glad they were close to the suburbs where traffic was slight. He could hold the motor wide open, gamble on his driving skill to get them away.

He sped through quiet streets, whirled onto an open highway, braked daringly and flung the big car on a hairpin turn into another road that ran off at right angles from it.

But bullets still glanced off the gray car's roof, bit into its body, threatened to tear its tires to shreds. And suddenly a dull explosion sounded a few feet from their backs.

Hazzard whirled. Lead had found a mark somewhere in the strange mechanism that made the veil of deathly light. Following that dull report smoke commenced pouring out of both side doors, and he could see flickering light around the edges of the shade that covered the glass behind the driver's compartment.

The gray car was on fire. But to stop now, even to slow up beside the road, meant being mowed down by lead.

CHAPTER IV

EXPEDITION TO NOWHERE

MARY PARKER WAS gamely silent even when the shade began burning and the window behind them gave out a sinister snap. Hazzard could feel the heat of it on his neck and he glanced back.

The shade had fallen. For the first time, he looked into the car's interior and got a glimpse of the man his bullets had felled back at the house. The murderer of John Roan and four others was now a corpse himself. A horrible human torch with head lolling and hair and clothes on fire. His thin-lipped features made a ghastly grinning mask in the light of the flames.

A black box holding part of the mechanism of the weird death curtain was burning, too. It was out of this that the hottest flames were leaping. Its deadly power was destroyed. But by an ironic twist of fate it still menaced their lives.

Hazzard's face was strained. His knuckles curved whitely over the black rim of the wheel. The car had become a seething comet. If they stayed in it another few moments, they would be swept on to a flaming death.

He looked for some way out. All hope of saving the death curtain mechanism for investigation had vanished. His only thought now was to save their lives. The ignition would burn through presently, the engine would go dead, the car would stop, and they would be easy prey for the guns of the armed men behind.

Hazzard raced on a few seconds longer, until he saw a field of high dry weed stems. He felt a sudden surge of hope. The wind was bending the dry vegetation toward them. A stiff gale was sweeping the stalks almost flat. There was a flimsy fence in front of the field.

Hazzard called to the girl to hold on tight. He twisted the wheel with sudden violence. The gray car almost turned over. It left the road, bounced over a ditch, struck the wooden fence at a sharp angle.

Rails splintered, and the windshield cracked. Hazzard brought the car around in a wide curve straight into the wind, and plunged through the dry weed stalks. The engine died suddenly, the headlights winked out. But the fire behind them made a glow like a giant torch.

"Jump!" Hazzard literally threw the girl from the seat. She fell on her silken knees in the grass. Now that the car had stopped moving, the flames licked forward into the driver's seat. The glass behind it burst, and the fire reached for Hazzard even as he jumped.

He heard the squealing brakes of the killers' car in the road. Over his shoulder, he saw its headlights goggling as it turned and came through the fence. He kept Mary Parker from rising as lead cut the stalks over their heads.

The killers' car raced toward them. Hazzard had his automatic out, was shooting; but he was facing men armed with sub-machine guns. His few bullets couldn't stop their attack. His hope centered on something else.

Then it happened! The pluming flames that the wind beat back from the burning car caught the dry grass. The grass went up like tinder. It fanned out before the gale on both sides, making a barrier of flame and smoke that bore down on the attackers. This was what Hazzard had planned when he had swung the burning car into the field.

"Now!" He pulled the girl to her feet and drew her after him in front of the shielding wall of flame. They reached the other side of the field, and Hazzard heard the shrill whine of a laboring motor as the killers' car backed up.

There was a grim, tight smile on his face. He had used the fire which their bullets had set to start another fire which had stopped them. He hurried with the girl across lots and found a road that led to the city. Twenty minutes fast walking brought them to a suburban street where he hailed a cab.

"Whitestone Avenue, College Point. The Hazzard Laboratories," he said.

The cabman started when he recognized his distinguished passenger's face. Those piercing eyes, that hawklike nose and rugged chin had been pictured often in the papers. He touched his cap respectfully, said: "Yes, sir, Captain."

HAZZARD leaned back with eyes closed as the cab slid through the night. Mary Parker looked at him enquiringly as though she thought he were ill. His face was rapt, trancelike. But something about his appearance awed her, made her keep still.

She didn't know that his mind was concentrating, sending out telepathic impulses of directing energy that sped through space ahead of the cab.

When they reached the laboratory on College Point, lights sparkled and the whole great building seemed to hum. Off to the right was a big flying field and a group of hangars. The door of one was open. Men in denim were swinging the tail of a huge two-motored monoplane around on a dolly. Skilled mechanics were walking along the torpedo-shaped fuselage toward the giant motors. The ship crouched on its fat airwheels, facing the field lights like a colossal moth ready to take wing.

A young, keen-faced man stood by the watchman at the laboratory gate. He came forward eagerly when the cab with Captain Hazzard and the girl rolled up.

"I got your orders, Captain. You wanted the *Silver Bullet* tuned and made ready. You're going south tonight."

The girl stiffened in surprise. Captain Hazzard hadn't stopped along the way to use a phone. She didn't see how he could have transmitted any orders.

But Hazzard made no explanation. He said, simply: "This is one of my assistants, Miss Parker. Mr. Martin Tracey. He's going with us. You can tell him everything. I'm going to leave you with him for a while."

Tracey saluted and his tanned face cracked into a grin. "Thank you, Captain." He took Mary Parker's arm and followed Captain Hazzard into the big lab.

Hazzard was already twenty feet ahead. He went to his private sanctum and found another of his assistants waiting, a tall, bald-headed man of forty whose shrewd eyes were owlish behind steel-rimmed spectacles. This was Washington MacGowen, called "Wash" for short, a mathematical physicist and one of the most skillful laboratory technicians in the country.

Wash's face was long and solemn now. "I've been worried about you, Captain," he muttered. "You've been in danger, fighting a group of men who tried their best to kill you in some peculiar way. Why didn't you call some of us to help?"

Hazzard smiled. Wash, too, was able to receive and transmit telepathic messages. He was among the few hand-picked men who knew Hazzard's secrets. Along with Martin Tracey and Crawley, Hazzard had given him the card test for telepathy and clairvoyance when he'd first come to the laboratory to work.[26]

Hazzard said quietly: "I didn't call you, Wash, because you're too valuable to lose. And you'd have been killed if you'd come to my assistance." He described the strange action of that curtain of death.

Wash shook his head and looked still more solemn when Hazzard had finished. "If I could only get a look at that thing, Captain, I might be able—"

"The apparatus caught fire when bullets struck it," said Hazzard. He quickly swept up the phone on his desk and he put through a call to the police commissioner of New York. When the commissioner answered, Hazzard spoke tersely.

"Your men have found a burning car in a lot at the edge of town by this time. There's a dead man in it. I killed him. I'm not interested in the body. But I am interested in the car. If you'll have it rushed to my place as soon as it is cool enough to handle, I might be able to give you some information on those death-curtain murders. I'll hand the car back as soon as my men have finished with it."

He listened a moment, snapped the instrument up and turned to Wash. "The commissioner is agreeable. If they get it out here soon enough, you may be able to go over it before we fly."

"Then you plan to take me with you?" There was sudden eagerness in Wash's voice.

Hazzard nodded. "I couldn't risk leaving you behind, Wash. Before we crack this riddle, we'll all need all the brains we've got. And now—" Hazzard pressed a button—"I'll need Crandall to take care of the *Silver Bullet*. And where's Cole tonight?"

Without waiting for Wash to answer, Hazzard spoke into an inter-office amplifier that sounded in every room of the lab and even out in the hangars. "Hazzard calling. Will Jake Cole please come?"

---

26   *AUTHOR'S NOTE: This is the test worked out by Doctor Rhine of Duke University. Twenty-five cards are used with five different symbols; a circle, a square, a cross, a star and a wave design consisting of three lines. The subject reads the symbols without seeing them, or attempts to do so, and, by a count based on the law of mathematical probability, they unerringly tell whether or not he is gifted with psychic perception.*

A TALL, lanky man entered Hazzard's office in a couple of minutes. He had a stiff crest of straw-blond hair, a deadpan face, ungainly hands and feet and a nose which sometime or other had been broken. He was chewing gum. He slouched in with seeming negligence and looked at Hazzard blankly without a salute or even so much as a nod.

He was Jake Cole, ex-cowhand from Montana. He knew nothing about science, could hardly add a column of small figures. An auto engine was a deep enigma to him. His tests with the telepathic cards had proved his extra-sensory powers non-existent. But he had certain talents of his own. He was a wizard with a lasso. He could shoot like an Apache with rifle or six-gun, and he was one of the best trackers in the West. No man or horse could leave a trail too faint for Cole to follow.

Hazzard said: "Get your guns oiled, Jake. We're starting for the banana republics in about an hour. I think we may see something of the jungle."

"Suits me, Captain." Cole's jaws worked rhythmically. His deadpan face didn't show any emotion. But Hazzard, who could read his mind like a book, knew that Cole was seething with excitement. He smiled as Cole turned and shuffled off to pack up his equipment he always carried in the hot countries.

Then Captain Hazzard began the serious business of organizing the expedition to go in search of Mary Parker's father.

A half hour before the time set for the take-off, the car in which Hazzard and Mary Parker had taken their wild ride was brought by police escort out to the gates of the lab. Wash MacGowen and three young technicians began a searching examination of the car's interior.

They tore out what was left of the fire-curtain mechanism, made measurements with micrometers, poked and pried with delicate instruments. Wash covered scratch pads with hastily sketched designs and long mathematical equations; then made his report to Captain Hazzard.

Wash was a cautious man, not given to sensational statements, or emotional moods; but Hazzard could see now that he was excited to an abnormal degree. His voice shook as he stood tensely by Hazzard's desk, peering down through his steel-rimmed spectacles.

"I hesitate to make positive statements, Captain. But the thing doesn't appear to be electrical in any ordinary sense. Some electrical amplification may have been used. We found a socket that might have held some sort of tube for a carrier wave. There was also something that looked like a saline condenser. But the rest of the thing is mystifying.

"The rods on top aren't radio antennae. They're made of barium wrapped around a core of tungsten. The other metal we found is an alloy containing gold, molybdenum and rhodonite. I wouldn't want to be quoted, but my guess is that this thing generated, or used, a force outside the field of every-day physics."

Hazzard nodded. "Maybe some form of molecular or atomic energy."

"Yes, Captain, but good heavens—"

Hazzard interrupted him. "If you'd seen the light rays as I did, felt the effect of them, and seen those poor chaps who were killed by them, you wouldn't be afraid to follow almost any line of reasoning. We're up against an enigma, Wash. And the man who invented this murder weapon is either a homicidal paranoiac or a scheming criminal. We don't know who he is or anything about him. All we know is—he's going to make our trip south mighty dangerous. Now—" Hazzard glanced at his wrist watch—"let's get going!"

They took their places in the spacious cabin, Wash owlish and silent, peering through his steel-rimmed spectacles. Jake Cole chewing gum and with a high-powered rifle slung over his back. Tracey chatting and explaining things to Mary Parker. Crandall in the control room with Captain Hazzard.

The mechanics stood away. The rumble of the motors rose to a vibrant roar. The great plane quivered, then rolled forward into the wind with Hazzard at the controls.

The ship gathered speed, leaped into the night with a majestic thrust of unleashed power. Her silver wings canted. She left the ground so easily that Mary Parker didn't guess they were up till she saw the lights of the field and hangars falling away.

Hazzard banked, swept out over the Sound for a few minutes, then rose higher, pointing the *Silver Bullet's* nose straight south. He climbed till the tall skyscrapers of Manhattan thrust up into the sky behind them, till Brooklyn and Queens and the Bronx spread out as on a table. He climbed still higher on the wings of the wind till New York fell away, became lost in the haze, and the coast of New Jersey unrolled below them like a glowing bas-relief map.

Then Crandall, looking around with an airman's alertness, suddenly spoke. "There's something in the sky behind us, sir. It seems to be getting nearer. You don't suppose—"

"Yes," said Hazzard. "I've been watching it for the last two minutes. It's another ship following us, hanging right on our tail."

CHAPTER V

THE SKY SHARK

THE STRANGE SHIP was a light blur in the dark sky back of them. The dogged way it followed them made it seem sinister. It disappeared for seconds when mist intervened, appeared again as starlight glinted on its wings.

Hazzard climbed still higher and advanced the throttle. The *Silver Bullet* roared up through the night sky, seven thousand, eight thousand. The air began to get thin and cold. Hazzard flattened, advanced the throttle still more, watched eagerly to see whether the plane behind could still keep up. It did. More than that, it was climbing for still greater altitude, getting a thousand feet above their tail.

A sense of danger filled him. He saw the blur of the other plane change its outline. He got the impression that the tail was up now, the nose down. The ship grew bigger, its superior altitude giving it increased speed. It was in a fast power dive.

Then a searchlight winked from the nose of that other ship. It stabbed across empty space like a spectral finger, and rested on the fuselage of the *Silver Bullet*. Hazzard's plane hung in dazzling light like a moth caught in a flame.

Sparks suddenly shot off from the beam of the searchlight. They were tracer bullets from a machine gun and they snarled close to Hazzard's ship. Slugs were mixed with the tracers. One snapped through the *Silver Bullet's* wing.

But only one. Hazzard side-slipped away quickly. The beam of the searchlight left them. The other plane went roaring by. Hazzard got a glimpse of it. It was a small, fast, low-wing monoplane with a single motor. It was coming back now. It had the flashing speed of the fastest army pursuit job, and it seemed invincible.

But Hazzard gave an order to Crandall. "Raise the L.O. motor—then stand by."

Crandall reached forward and pulled a small lever. There was a faint grinding vibration in the ship. For a moment it lost speed as something obstructed the smooth flow of the slipstream above the fuselage. Thin metal panels in the top of the *Silver Bullet* slid back. From between them a thing like a huge torpedo reared up. It rose on powerful steel supports till it was six feet above the fuselage, pointing back and well above the tail assembly. There was a round vent in the after end.

"All ready, sir," said Crandall.

HAZZARD threw a switch on the instrument board and the strange torpedo-shaped thing began to hum a deeper note than the forward motors. It was another motor, an auxiliary rocket motor, using a mixture of liquid oxygen and high-test gas, and based on the same general principles as Fritz von Opel's rocket engines, used successfully on cars in Germany. It was one of many reasons why the *Silver Bullet* was no ordinary ship.[27]

A faint glow appeared at the end of the vent. The glow became a blush of light, then a shooting flame, reaching back suddenly across the sky. It seemed to burn a vacuum in the air. The pilot in the other ship must have thought he had set Hazzard's ship on fire. The shooting, powerful stream of gas from the torpedo-shaped motor was like the fiery tail of a comet. It aided the two forward motors of regular design.

The *Silver Bullet* surged forward. A hundred miles an hour was added to its speed. The long stream of fiery gas stretched back across the sky as straight as a string. The *Silver Bullet* was set on a plumblike course for the south. No turns or quick maneuvers were possible while the rocket motor hummed.

For a moment the hostile plane was visible in its light, a dancing hornet in a giant sunbeam. But its sting was ineffectual now. It fell away behind, disappeared in the mist as Hazzard's ship outdistanced it with a speed no ordinary plane could match.

---

27   AUTHOR'S NOTE: *In creating the first efficient rocket motor for use in airplanes, Captain Hazzard first studied the ground already covered by such experts as Valier, von Opel, Doctor Goddard, Hermann Oberth and others. His success lies in the great improvement of his carburetor-type injection nozzles, through which the freezingly cold liquid oxygen is fed into the combustion chamber. The main drawback of Hazzard's, and all other rocket motors, is their tendency to overheat.*

Mary Parker saw the glow in the sky behind them and stared with frightened eyes. Martin Tracey put her fears to rest by explaining how the rocket motor functioned.

With the aid of that auxiliary power unit the *Silver Bullet* was traveling at terrific velocity now. But, while the rocket motor was running, Hazzard watched the temperature dial with a wary eye. The liquid oxygen, close to one hundred and ninety degrees centigrade cold when it was injected into the combustion chamber, soon became fearfully hot. Overheating was a constant menace.

The *Silver Bullet* roared through the night, crossing cities, counties and states as it sped ever southward on its strange rescue quest....

IT was somewhere over Mexico, just before dawn, that the temperature reached the danger line, and Hazzard stopped the rocket motor. The sudden decrease in the speed was apparent instantly, though the *Silver Bullet* was still doing two hundred and eighty miles an hour. The rocket motor would have to cool for at least an hour before it could be restarted.

And, as though the malign intelligence of the Phoenix had arranged it, his agents chose that time to strike again. Terror reached out of the skies at Hazzard's party, terror that made even Hazzard feel fear.

For as dawn came over the mountains of Mexico like a silver, ghostly thing, two planes rose swiftly in the sky to meet the *Silver Bullet*. Two planes flying three hundred yards apart, holding their course steadily like ships in army formation.

At first, Hazzard thought they were government ships, planes patrolling in connection with the Mexican *Rurales*.

But when he changed his course a little and climbed higher, the planes ahead changed, too. Not only that, they seemed to be hedging to get the *Silver Bullet* between them.

Then Hazzard's sharp eye saw something that brought him up taut with dread. On top of one ship, dimly outlined against the first dawn light, was a spidery web of rods and wires—one of the strange tungsten-barium aerials of the Curtain of Death.

Hazzard pressed a button that sounded a gong in the ship. Crandall came running. The others sat up quickly, their faces strained and ghostly in the faint dawn light. Hazzard's four assistants knew that the sound of that gong meant deadly danger.

Hazzard snapped orders. "Man the machine gun, Crandall. Martin, look out for Miss Parker. See that she fastens her belt. Jake, get in the turret with your rifle."

Hazzard side-slipped and veered. Wind shrieked in the wings of the *Silver Bullet*. One of the strange, death-curtain planes dropped formation suddenly and dived to the right. The maneuver almost got Hazzard between them. Across the sky, like a faint and horrible aura, stretched a spotty curtain of fire. The shimmering, uncanny beams spread out, touched, retreated, touched again.

There was sweat on Hazzard's forehead. The nose of the *Silver Bullet* was aimed straight at that death light. It seemed that nothing could stop it from diving through. Hazzard knew the horrible end that faced them if it did. The image of John Roan's corpse was before his eyes.

He shoved the throttle to the quadrant stop. He pulled the stick back into his lap and brought the plane's nose up in a hurtling, roaring zoom. The *Bullet* climbed like a demon as though terror had even struck at its own steel heart. Up till it was hanging on its propellers, up still farther till it was over on its back. And, as it made the mighty zoom, its tail surfaces brushed that cloud of light.

Hazzard felt again that fearful dizziness that had come when he was standing at the top of Mary Parker's steps. He flipped the *Silver Bullet* over in an Immelmann turn, knowing that he had saved himself and his party from death only by a few spare feet. He was roaring in the opposite direction now; had lost speed in the zoom. The other ships using their quicker maneuverability, headed him off. The light curtain swept toward him.

This time Hazzard waited, while the nearest of the hostile planes bored in. He seemed to be inviting the death they held on to him. He let his ship stall, drop off into a falling leaf—as though it were out of control.

Then suddenly, with the weird light almost upon them, Hazzard brought the *Silver Bullet* back under control. He flattened her out, side-slipped directly *toward* the nearest of the two approaching ships.

HE HEARD the *crack* of Jake Cole's rifle. Looking back he caught a glimpse of Jake standing in the turret. The lanky cowboy was shooting with the nonchalance of a rodeo performer. He was actually chewing gum. His jaws worked rhythmically. *Crack, crack!* His rifle spoke twice more. Hot shell casings leaped out of the ejector as though in savage glee.

PYTHON MEN OF LOST CITY

The nearest plane with the tripod on it suddenly canted its wings and fell away. The light curtain sank down after it; a weird mesh drawn by those spider-web rods. The sky ahead of the *Silver Bullet* was clear. Then the curtain vanished entirely as the mechanism in the strange plane ceased to function. The plane swooped earthward in a long erratic dive.

They watched it go down; saw the dawn light strike the wings, saw it fall straight toward the rocky side of a mountain. Then suddenly a red rose seemed to blossom on the cliffs. The rose was followed by black smoke and the plane disappeared. The second plane had fled....

They reached Guatemala three hours later, and the great volcanic peaks of San Pedro, Santa Maria and Tolimán lifted up on the horizon. The *Silver Bullet* sped over green jungles, high mountain ridges dotted with Indian villages and shimmering clear blue lakes. Hazzard decided to fly to the compass point John Roan had mentioned in his note before trying to land.

Tracey explained to Mary Parker that they were close to their goal now. She came forward to where Captain Hazzard studied his compass. He had a map of Guatemala in front of him painted on transparent membrane, set in a boxlike frame. Thin lines of light from mirrors underneath showed on the map. They moved slowly. Where they crossed was the position of the plane.

It was another of Hazzard's inventions, his telautographic compass. He had many such transparent maps of all sections of the globe. By fitting them into the frame he could see his exact location in relation to topographical points.

The lines were converging now at north latitude 15, west longitude 89. Mary Parker's cheeks flushed as the plane sped forward, and the lines crawled ever closer to the Espiritu Santo range.

The mountains were under their nose now, high, volcanic, rugged. They crossed the main ridge, swept over a deep basin of dense jungle stretching for several miles. Another peak rose in its center, conical and grim. The plane bored on. The cone-shaped mountain had a feather of smoke stuck in a crater at its top. It came steadily nearer. They were close to it now—over it. The lines of the map showed 15.10—89-27.

"Now!" Captain Hazzard pointed. Mary Parker gasped in sudden dismay. "That? It can't be! It's a volcano. There's nothing on it. No one could live there!"

CHAPTER VI

GREEN FURY

CAPTAIN HAZZARD, TOO, stared tensely at that forbidding peak. Tumbled cliffs. Barren slopes. Deserted ravines. Not a vestige of grass. The green wall of the jungle halted at the edge of the volcanic rock as if eruptions in the past had put a dreadful curse on all growing things.

"How—how shall we find him?" Mary Parker's face showed that she had already lost faith in the search for her father.

But Captain Hazzard said nothing. He kicked the rudder, thrust the stick sidewise, brought the *Silver Bullet* around in a steep-banked turn. In descending spirals, he lost altitude. The black, sinister crater of the mountain rose to meet them.

He passed directly over it. Heat from those subterranean depths made bumpy air. The *Silver Bullet* rocked and bucked. He circled then, skirted the outer edges of the crater.

"Dead as the moon, Captain," said Jake Cole grimly. "I'll be a horned toad if even a gopher could pitch tent down there!"

Martin Tracey nodded. "Those figures Roan wrote in that message must be off. Maybe the ant bites made him nutty."

"And yet," Wash MacGowen stroked his long chin judicially, "doesn't it seem a little strange that those numbers should exactly correspond to this peak? It is the only mountain in this immediate jungle area. More than coincidence, I should say."

Hazzard was thinking the same thing. Though nothing showed on that grim mountain, he wasn't satisfied that John Roan's figures were wrong. From the first the Phoenix had been clothed in mystery.

Mary Parker repeated her question. "How can we find my father?"

Hazzard turned to her. "There's only one way—investigate that volcano."

"But there's no place to land, even if—"

"No." Hazzard looked at his map. "Lake Izabal is forty miles away. The nearest landing field is fifty. But there's an Indian village ten miles back. I saw it when we came over. Some of us will land there in 'chutes. Then we can reach the mountain through the jungle."

"Some of us!" The girl repeated the words and a look of consternation crossed her face. "You mean you won't take me?"

"Have you ever made a 'chute jump?" asked Hazzard.

"No. But I'll do anything—anything to be with you when you find my father." Her face was eager. There was no fear in her eyes. Hazzard nodded approvingly. She had the right stuff in her.

"All right," he said. "I'll give you a special 'chute we have, one with a self-operating ripcord. You jump—it does the rest."

He headed the plane's nose north, swept over ten miles of jade green jungle and saw the Indian village again. The architecture told him it belonged to a tribe of Chicastenangos.

They came running out to the streets as the plane swept low. They had queer costumes of bright red and blue. The men wore big-brimmed hats. The women had on *halos,* twenty-foot strips of red-and-blue hand-woven cloth wrapped around their copper-colored bodies. Their hair was black as night. The village was a tiny cluster of adobe houses perched on a terraced hillock that rose out of the jungle. There was a small square in it.

Hazzard noted the wind direction. If they bailed out at just the right altitude from just the right position it would carry them into the village. He turned the controls over to Crandall who could be depended upon to jockey the ship properly.

Wash went first. All of Hazzard's men had made 'chute jumps before. Wash made the drop as unemotionally as he'd add a column of figures. There was a special trapdoor in the *Silver Bullet's* floor. Wash simply climbed into his 'chute harness and slid through. Jake followed, chewing gum rhythmically as he went. He claimed that the movement of his jaws helped him to count off the seconds before he pulled the ripcord.

Hazzard dropped the parachutes of equipment next. Wash and Jake would be on the ground before they landed, so the Indians wouldn't appropriate them.

The air was filled with steel-shafted spears.

Then Tracey jumped, looking anxiously at Mary Parker. He'd already come to feel a proprietary interest in the girl. But Captain Hazzard put her into the auto-ripcord 'chute. There was a small, clocklike device on the back which could be set to jerk the ripcord at any given moment. Hazzard set it carefully and led the girl to the trap. Her face was pale, but she was smiling. She looked trim and athletic in her tropical shorts.

Hazzard strapped an automatic and a hunting knife around her waist, tied a first-aid kit containing anti-venom for snake bites and a water canteen on it. "After the 'chute opens," he said, "just pull the shroud lines in the direction you want to go. Spill a little air out and you can steer the thing like a glider."

She nodded, stepped to the trap and said: "Okay."

HAZZARD pressed a button and Mary Parker dropped into space. He watched to see her 'chute open, then got ready to jump himself. "We'll keep in touch with you by radio," he said to Crandall. "You can let us know where you land."

Crandall nodded, grinning. Taking care of the *Silver Bullet* was his especial pride.

Hazzard stepped easily through the trap and plunged into space. He didn't pull the cord till the ground was a few hundred feet below. The delayed jump let him catch up with the others. He touched at the same time Wash and Jake did, and he was able to help Mary Parker gather up the folds of her 'chute when she landed close to the little square.

Indians swarmed around them, staring curiously. Some made signs to ward off evil spirits. Others grinned, showing ivory teeth. Most of the Indians in Guatemala were friendly. Naked, copper-colored kids ran up and poked at their 'chutes and equipment till Hazzard shooed them away.

He was an expert linguist and he addressed the Chicastenangos in their native dialect. "Quichi lana," he said, pointing to the cone of the volcano ten miles away. "Fire mountain." "*Un nihongi atlan*— I go through jungle. *Tulul cuintla pan zumala*—we need a guide."

A change came over the Indians. Their faces sobered. Many backed away. Others shook their heads. "*Chal! Chal!*—No! No!" they cried. "*Huetenzo!*—Accursed!"

There was fear in their eyes and they began to talk vehemently. They told Hazzard that people from their village never went to the mountain now. A few had in the past and never came back. No trace of them had ever been found. The mountain was *Huetenzo,* cursed in some strange way. It's name was Omoxotl, which meant Terror's Shadow.

Besides that there were murderous Indians in the jungle, fierce Tzutuhiles left over from the tribes that even Cortés' lieutenant,

Don Alvarado, had been unable to subdue. There were poisonous snakes and dangerous animals.

Hazzard glimpsed one Indian at the edge of the crowd who didn't seem as excited as the others at the talk of going into the jungle. He wore a spray of the rare *figa-figa* berries in his hat, which meant that he understood jungle magic. And in his belt was the fang of a python which meant he was a great hunter.

"Your name?" asked Hazzard, pointing suddenly.

"Ulzi," said the Indian promptly.

"You are a mighty hunter," said Hazzard. "You know the jungle trails. You are a great witch-doctor. The evil spirits cannot scare you. You will lead the people-who-dropped-from-the-sky to Omoxotl."

Still the Indian looked doubtful, and there was a glint of fear in his eyes. Hazzard continued: "I, too, am a great witch-doctor.... Watch!"

He always carried a kit of chemicals in his knapsack. These, along with the gadgets in his belt, made a wide range of chemical "magic" possible. He brought two small empty test tubes out now and a piece of white cloth that had been dipped in cobalt-chloride. Ulzi nodded, grunting skeptically.

Hazzard slipped a lump of calcium in one tube and held his finger over it. This absorbed moisture, making the air inside the test tube dry. He drew his thumb away quickly, put the white cloth in, then again covered the top of the test tube.

"Look!"

Before Ulzi's startled eyes the white cloth turned a vivid blue. The Indians watching exclaimed in admiration. Ulzi looked awestruck; then quickly drew his face into a mask to show that he was not impressed.

Hazzard took another strip of the white, cobalt-chloride-treated cloth and placed it in the second test tube, along with a drop of water to make the air damp. This strip turned a vivid pink. Ulzi couldn't prevent his eyes from growing wide with wonder.

Then Hazzard took a small nickel-plated flashlight from his pocket and gave it to the Indian. "For the great hunter and magician," he said, "who will lead the white witch-doctor through the jungle to Omoxotl."

Ulzi nodded and struck his chest, his pride aroused by Hazzard's flattery and his competitive spirit stirred by Hazzard's trick. "Ulzi's own magic is so great he does not fear Omoxotl," he said.

Hazzard picked up his knapsack and pointed toward the forest. The other members of his party gathered their things. Following Ulzi, they started down the terraced hill toward the green wall of the jungle. The Indians watched them go, shaking their heads and muttering. Just as they reached the jungle, the Chicastenangos began a chant; low, wailing, monotonous, rising and falling in a minor cadence. The chant for great hunters doomed not to return from the never-never land....

THE JUNGLE grew ominously still after they had been walking for two hours. The monkeys ceased chattering. The bright-colored birds kept out of sight. Ulzi rolled his eyes nervously. Hazzard felt the first vibrations of a psychic warning that danger was creeping close.

The stillness of the jungle wrapped itself around them like a brooding, malevolent thing. It seemed suddenly to Hazzard that eyes were watching them—hostile eyes, baleful and murderous.

Hazzard's gaze darted upward suddenly. He saw movement in the great Ceiba tree ahead of them under which the trail wound. He called a warning, but not quite soon enough. Something streaked down like a flash of light from its green branches.

It struck Ulzi in the chest, and the copper-skinned hunter fell with a piercing cry. He lay still with a green-plumed spear sticking out of his body.

Hazzard fired at almost the same moment. There was another cry in the Ceiba's dense branches. The foliage moved, rustled. A body hurtled from it and fell beside Ulzi at the edge of the trail. The black vultures flapped their wings greedily.

Captain Hazzard ran forward. The man who had speared Ulzi lay on his back with his eyes open, glaring. There was a hole drilled through his head. It was no wonder Hazzard hadn't seen him till too late. He wore a green cloak of quetzal feathers, brilliant as the foliage. His face was the color of the reddish tree branches. The only conspicuous thing about him was the metal headband that held a bright, gleaming green jewel in the center of his forehead.

Ulzi gave a moan. *"Chlan cuinali,"* he said.

"What does he mean?" asked Wash somberly.

"The Jewel Men," said Hazzard. "They are Tzutuhiles—the worst Indians going. But—" His hand reached forward and touched the spear in Ulzi's body. Ulzi lay still now. He was dead. And Hazzard's eyes were bright with consternation. "This spear has a metal shaft—made of hollow tubing like a golf club."

"What!" Wash felt the spear, too. So did Jake and Tracey.

"It means," said Hazzard, "that some white man has armed them recently—some white man who is using them as guards to keep everyone else away. The Phoenix!"

Even as he spoke, something whispered through the branches. If he hadn't ducked instantly a green-plumed spear would have stretched him beside Ulzi.

"Run!" Hazzard pointed toward some black rock formations where huge vultures perched. Sinister as the rocks and their sentinels looked, they offered the only place of refuge.

CHAPTER VII

SLAVES OF FIRE

THE AIR WAS filled suddenly with steel-shafted spears, whistling, hissing, thudding. One came so close to Hazzard's face he could feel the breeze of it. Another zipped past his back. Hazzard opened fire with his automatic.

Martin, Jake and Wash began shooting. Cordite fumes drifted through the leaves. The crack of their weapons made a steady tattoo as they ran for the rocks.

Another Indian hurtled out of a high Ceiba tree where he'd been hiding. He did a somersault in the air, landed on a lower limb and hung there gruesomely for a moment, blood dripping from his neck.

A savage fifty feet to one side came running out of a bush, took three steps forward with a bullet in his heart, then dropped. Jake was taking steady toll with his high-powered rifle. He shot as fast as he could slide the bolt action and pump the trigger. But the whole jungle seemed filled with savages. Bullets alone would never let Hazzard's party reach the rocks.

Hazzard tugged desperately at his belt and drew out another smoke bomb. This one gave off white vapor and Hazzard used it in conjunction with a pair of infra-red ray goggles. He slipped the goggles on now, wishing he'd brought others, enough for the whole party. But he hadn't. The lives of all of them depended on this single pair.

He pulled the striker of the bomb, tossed it tensely and heard it explode with a violent *pouff*. White smoke spurted. It was denser than fog. It slipped through the leaves in ghostly streamers, crept along the ground.

Hazzard heard the Tzutuhiles yelling. The infra-red ray goggles, picked up light waves on one end of the spectrum only, the end which the white smoke did not touch, enabling him to see dimly through the vapor which blinded all the others.[28]

Martin, Wash, Jake and Mary Parker were already turned around, groping helplessly. Hazzard ran up to them, made them hold hands, and put Jake at the head. He told Jake, whose ears were sharp, to follow the sound of his footsteps.

Strung out so, Hazzard led his party toward the rocks. But the Tzutuhiles hadn't been scared off. They were fierce, murderous warriors eager for the kill. Hazzard saw one of them directly in his path. The Tzutuhile couldn't see him, but the Indian's ears, sharp as Jake's, had detected the sound of feet.

The Jewel Man had a piercing cry which told his fellow tribesmen that he had located the prey. It was like the cry of a killer wolf calling the slavering pack. He raised his spear to fling it in the direction of Hazzard's footsteps.

Hazzard dodged when the spear came whistling past his head. Then he ran forward toward the Tzutuhile. The man shrieked again, and stood his ground, eyes glaring, lips curling away from hideous teeth that had been filed to points. He tried to see through the smoke. He whipped out a long knife and ran at Hazzard.

Still Hazzard didn't shoot. He crouched on one knee quickly, seized the knife wrist of the leaping savage, and used the Indian's own momentum to lift him and hurl him through the air.

The green-robed Indian whirled over Hazzard's head and struck the ground with a thud. The knife flew from his hand. He bounced up and came back at Captain Hazzard. Hazzard felled him this time with a blow from his gun butt.

The rocks were directly ahead now. The vultures were lighting up on broad wings as the smoke rolled toward them. Their furious croaks mingled with the war screams of the Tzutuhiles.

Three of the Jewel Men came together and seemed to agree on some stratagem. Holding their steel-shafted spears in line they ran straight at Hazzard's party.

Hazzard knew then that the smoke was thinning, that the Indians could see. He pulled his goggles aside and made sure of it. The

---

28   AUTHOR'S NOTE: *Captain Hazzard got his idea for these when army aerial photographers recently took pictures of New York City through a bank of dense clouds. They used an infra-red ray filler on their lens. They couldn't see the ground, but the camera films were affected by the infra-red rays coming up through the clouds.*

Tzutuhiles' arms were drawing back. Another instant and at least one of Hazzard's party would be pierced by knife-sharp steel.

"Drop!"

Jake Cole and the others obeyed Hazzard's order as two of the spears came whistling over their heads. The crack of Hazzard's automatic broke the arm of the third Indian. The two others came on with their knives. Hazzard fired twice more and the Tzutuhiles fell back yelling and nursing broken fingers.

But there was no time to lose. The smoke was vanishing rapidly. From all sides the Jewel Men were closing in.

CAPTAIN HAZZARD mounted the rocks and helped Jake Cole after him. Jake pulled the rest of the party. The first fringe of volcanic boulders ended sharply. Behind them was another higher group, pitted with potholes and caves. Some gigantic upheaval of nature thousands of years before had left these weird monuments. There were natural bridges, caverns, huge upthrust spires.

Hazzard found a great, high-roofed cavern that had only two places to enter and here they stopped. They could stand off the Tzutuhiles. If their bullets failed, Hazzard had some tear-gas pellets.

The green-robed Indians appeared on the outer wall. But slugs from Jake's rifle made them hesitate. Every time a jeweled forehead showed itself Jake made powdered rock spurt in the Indian's face.

When the Indians showed no sign of making a rush, Hazzard stationed Jake at one entrance, Martin at the other. Then he announced:

"When it gets dark, I'm going to visit Omoxotl. The four of you can stay here till I get back. That should be in five or six hours. You've got the portable radio. If I don't show up by daybreak call Randall. Get him to use the high-power radio in the plane to get in touch with the government of Guatemala. They'll send soldiers to rescue you."

Mary Parker's dark eyes were filled with apprehension. "But the Indians will kill you! They're waiting in the jungle. How will you get through?"

"Don't worry about that, ma'm," said Jake Cole grimly. "The Captain could slip in an Indian's ear and the varmint would never know it. But—" he looked at Hazzard pleadingly, "you'll be needing company. You'd better take me with you."

"Sorry, Jake, I can't. The girl has to be guarded. The Tzutuhiles might take it into their heads to attack in the dark. As it is we've got to roll rocks up to both entrances."

They spent the afternoon making the cave safe against a rushing attack. Hazzard was sure that Jake and the others would be able to hold it unless something utterly unforeseen happened. But he wasn't so sure that he could get back. Visiting Omoxotl at night was like a challenge hurled in the teeth of Fate.

YET, WHEN night came, he slipped out quietly. The tropic blackness swallowed him. The trees seemed to enfold him in their branches. Those long years when he had been blind himself, living in darkness, had borne strange fruit. His muscles were trained like an animal's to act on instant reflexes. He had learned to walk swiftly, warily on springy toes. His mind, with its uncanny powers of clairvoyance, made him aware of things that the physical eye couldn't see.

He passed across the outer wall of rocks until a musky smell in the air told him that a lurking Tzutuhile was close at hand. The feeling of danger, the mysterious telepathic vibration that a hostile mind gave out, made it possible for him to avoid the savage. He moved on quickly, stealthily into the solemn terror that was the jungle night.

Hazzard heard the death scream of some small animal being struck down. He heard the horrid bubbling smacks of a jaguar feasting on fresh-killed meat. Once his senses screamed a different warning. The inner realms of his mind whispered: "Snake!"

A muskiness quite different from that of the Indian odor reached his nostrils. It was pungent, sickening. A reptilian odor this time. He crouched back behind a tree and waited while a great, forty-foot anaconda writhed its terrible crushing coils across the jungle floor.

Then Hazzard caught the smell of a man again. He crouched and waited. The shuffle of bare feet sounded soon. That meant he was near a trail. And as he crouched, one of the Jewel Men went by, walking in the direction of Omoxotl.

Moving silently, running from tree to tree like a specter, Hazzard followed him mile after mile. All the while his sense of direction told him that they were getting nearer Omoxotl.

He was sure of it when the ground began to rise. The sponginess left the earth. The trees began to thin. Suddenly they ceased altogether and Hazzard was out in a world of barren rock.

The footsteps of the Indian were fainter now, more muffled. Hazzard hurried ahead till he felt a sudden warm eddy of air on his face. The air, besides being warmer, had a different smell to it, a faint odor of sulphur. Hazzard guessed that he was standing close to a passage through the rocks.

He moved in and heard the feet of the Indian just ahead of him. The man muttered something, and another guttural voice replied. A guard! Hazzard crept forward as stealthily as a jaguar. When the Indian he'd been following went on, Hazzard sprang at the guard, ducking the spear that was thrust toward him. Hazzard stilled the cry on the guard's lips by a smashing blow of his gun. He lowered the limp body and sped after the Indian who was his unknowing guide.

The passage went up now. It seemed to go interminably through the very heart of the rock. An endless corridor of stifling, sulphurous darkness.

Then Hazzard glimpsed a faint glow ahead of him, reflected on the smooth sides of the passage, making it possible for him to get a dim silhouette of the man in front. He stopped a moment later, peering along another passage that ran off sharply to the right. There was a great room at the end of it, a room with a domed ceiling; a natural cavern in the mountain with great, high stone-buttressed walls.

But it wasn't the chamber that caught his quick interest. It was the men in it. Chained men, toiling at some unknown task before gleaming holes in the rock.

THE SULPHUR smell was stronger now. A faint acrid haze hung in the air. Out of those furnacelike holes came glowing light. The men's bodies were bathed in sweat. He could see the glisten of it. He wasn't close enough to see their faces, to know whether Mary's father and his partner, Kurt Gordon, were among them.

He couldn't even tell whether these were white men. Their skins were blackened, burned. But they were slaves obviously, chained to some grueling work, held against their will before those weird holes of fire. And Hazzard realized in a flash that the Phoenix was using the power of the great volcano, Omoxotl, for some strange purpose of his own.

He crept closer, trying to get a better look at the men. He noted then that there were other weird figures in the room not chained—Indians dressed in hideous costumes made from the skins of anacondas, with the gaping heads of the great serpents serving as parkalike hoods. The fangs had been left in. The eyes had been ornamented with green jewels. Python Men!

And they had whips, long scourges of plaited leather. As he watched, a whip flashed out with a crack like a pistol. It flayed the naked shoulders of a chained slave who had dared to pause in whatever he was doing. The slave gave a choking scream of pain and stumbled back to his work.

Hazzard's nerves went taut. This was like some nightmare; like a world of fantastic horror such as a madman might conceive. He tried to glimpse more. His curiosity spurred him on. His boldness brought him close to disaster. For a sudden whisper of sound in the darkness back of him made him turn. He was almost too late.

Three silent Python Men, dressed in snakeskins, had crept upon him. He could see the gleam of their coal-black eyes, the shine of their faces. They had whips, too. They were evidently guards who had come to relieve the others in the big chamber watching over the slaves.

He leaped straight at them—a thing they didn't expect. They lifted the heavy butts of their whips, tried to rain stunning blows on his head. He snatched one whip away, cracked a man with its butt, then grabbed him as he fell and swung him violently, knocking the others down. He leaped between them before they could rise and grab his legs. It would be fatal to everything if he were caught by them now.

He ran into a side corridor that slanted off darkly to the right. The Python Men were following, and he knew by their cries and the sounds of other footsteps that the guards in the slave room had joined them in pursuit.

They followed him for perhaps five minutes, then stopped abruptly. Hazzard stopped, too, listening, wondering why they'd seemingly given up the chase. There was no sound now. The silence was weird, forbidding, and Hazzard's scalp prickled with an intimation that something was wrong. He clicked on his flashlight.

For a moment he saw nothing strange. He was standing in a rock-walled passage. It had an uneven ceiling pitted with holes. It sloped ahead of him on a gentle grade. Then Hazzard noticed that there was a black vent close to the floor of the corridor about ten feet away, two more farther on.

And as he looked something came through them—wisps of yellow, writhing, sulphurous smoke. The smoke became red suddenly, red with glowing flame.

Hazzard moved toward it, eyes wide with wonder. The flame broadened. The glowing smoke had substance to it now. It was thick, bubbling, oozing forward steadily out of the holes. It hissed on the floor, spread out like pancake batter. It was molten lava, he realized, poured purposely into the passage through those vents to head him off.

He took two steps forward, stopped as the hideous, bubbling pool crept toward him. A fiery arm of the stuff reached out like a tentacle to clutch nim. Hazzard could go no farther. He was trapped.

CHAPTER VIII

THE WHISPERING SCOURGE

BACK IN THE cave, Jake, Martin, Wash and Mary Parker were filled with unreasoning dread. Hours had passed. No sight or sound of Captain Hazzard had come.

Mary Parker got a cigarette from Martin and smoked it in short nervous puffs. She paced back and forth. Her boots stirred whispering echoes that mingled with the strange sounds of the night. Those night noises scared her. The weird cries of the howling monkeys sounded like lost souls calling out there in the dark. And the bats! They kept slipping into the cave entrances, swooping low and staring at her out of small malevolent eyes.

But most of all she was frightened about her father. Now that darkness had fallen, now that Captain Hazzard didn't come back, all her fears returned. She stopped before Martin Tracey finally.

"Why—why do you suppose Captain Hazzard doesn't come back?" Her hands were clenched fiercely. Her eyes were big and dark.

And Martin wasn't his usual smiling self. His face looked pale, strained.

Mary noticed it. "You're frightened, too, aren't you?" she said.

He nodded. "Not for us—I'm thinking of the Captain. He's in a tough spot. I can feel—something has happened."

"Oh!" Mary Parker let her cigarette drop.

Martin turned to Wash, and in the bald-headed man's eyes he read somber agreement. Something had happened to Captain Hazzard. All was not well with him. Discordant vibrations which meant trouble were coming through the unseen ether. Even Jake Cole seemed to sense them faintly. His jaws moved with melancholy slowness as he stood, rifle ready, at one door of the cave.

Then in the troubled silence that followed, Mary Parker suddenly said: "Listen! What's that?"

They all heard it—a new sound out there in the darkness, a strange, uncanny whispering that seemed to fill the whole air.

"The wind maybe," said Martin. "It's been still tonight, but now I guess it's rising. Those must be leaves."

Jake Cole shook his head. He was all attention suddenly. His jaws had stopped. "Can't be the wind. That noise ain't in the trees—it's on the ground. Put out the candle, Wash. Let's see if there's anything comin'."

Wash snuffed the candle and the cave suddenly was pitchy dark. They could hear Jake close to the entrance, leaning against the piled-up rocks. "Nothing to see," he muttered. "No Injuns. But that noise—"

It was louder now—a steady, persistent whisper that got on Mary Parker's nerves. "The light, please!" she gasped. "I don't like it. I—I'm frightened."

Wash lighted the candle again; but the noise did not cease. It was louder still.

Jake Cole was tense before the entrance, prowling, peering, sniffing. "It beats me," he said. "It sounds like something crawling. I never heard nothin' like it before—except—"

"What? What is it? If you know please tell us," said Mary Parker. "It's coming here."

Jake didn't answer; but the sound was almost upon them now. It was in the grass outside the cave entrance. It was the restless, persistent movement of millions of insect feet.

"Ants! I thought so!" Jake was pointing now. Then he sprang forward and slapped at the stones that filled the entrance, beating furiously with his hands and hat.

Red ants were swarming over the rocks in an endless, scurrying stream. The cave door was blocked up so the Tzutuhiles couldn't enter, but space had been left for air. Through this the ants were coming. Jake's efforts were making no more impression than a straw stemming a raging tide.

The ants came on. For every dozen he crushed a hundred entered. They were the red ants of the jungle, the dread carnivorous insects that strip human flesh from bones. They had glistening eyes, waving antennae, eager jaws. They poured through the hole in the rocks, slipped through chinks, wriggled from underneath.

Martin and Wash began beating at them, too. But the ants came on. A thin line of them, the boldest vanguards, started up Jake's trousers. He slapped and a half dozen of the vicious insects clamped their mandibles in his skin. He brushed them away and they left red marks behind them.

Then Wash ran to his knapsack and drew a bottle out. He uncorked it, poured liquid in a thin stream around the entrance through which the ants were coming. It was strong carbolic acid for cauterizing wounds. Its pungent smell filled the air of the cave. It lay in an oily line on the floor.

The ants drove Jake and Martin back now. Their fight centered on brushing away those which had got on their clothes. They slapped them, dashed them to the earth before stepping over Wash's carbolic acid moat.

THE ANTS came on. The foremost of them reached the acid and paused. Others pushed from behind and crawled over them. These fell into the acid, fumed, shriveled and died. Still others fell on top of them. They died, too, their red bodies smoking; but their corpses made a bridge presently over which the rest could cross. The space behind the acid line in front of the cave doorway was filled with millions of swarming, crawling insects now. They were still pouring over the stones. They swept across the line in regiments of thousands.

"It's no use!" gasped Mary Parker. "They're coming. We can't stop them. They'll drive us out."

Mary screamed as the ants swarmed up her slim legs and bit her. They made red spots on her hands. She brushed them down, stamped on them, backed away. Jake ran across the cave and clawed at the other rock wall they had so carefully built. Wash and Martin helped him, knowing what he planned to do. The ants were driving them out into the darkness, out where the Indians waited with their deadly spears. And there was no help for it. "If only the Captain was here!" groaned Jake as he worked.

They got the stones out and quickly grabbed their knapsacks. Running, brushing the ants from their clothes as they went, they scrambled through the cave exit. Behind them, steady, persistent as doom itself, came the sound of a myriad feet.

But they knew they could outrun the insects. They didn't fear being caught when it came to mere speed. It was the black night itself that scared them. And they didn't know where to go.

There was no sound of the Indians, no faintest sign. They ran blindly for a hundred yards across an open space, until another rocky hillock loomed ahead.

"It's better than nothing," said Jake. "We've shaken those crawling varmints. We'll build up rocks and keep the Injuns—"

He stopped. A gasp of sheer amazement came from his lips. The others gasped, too. For there was a whisper in the air above them. A streak of brown stuff fell in the beam of Jake's flashlight. They tried to leap away. But they couldn't escape the meshes of the woven vine net that fell upon them.

It came down swiftly, layer on layer of it, criss-crossing around their heads and shoulders, dragging them down to the ground with its weight.

Above the swish of the net they heard the shrill, triumphant cries of the Tzutuhiles ranged in the bushes on top of the wall....

IN THE heart of Omoxotl, Captain Hazzard climbed desperately through a narrow, stifling flume. It was in the roof of the passage through which he'd been running when the red-hot lava had come.

He had seen the fumes of sulphurous smoke drawn up to this vent. He didn't know where it led. He wasn't sure he'd get through it. He'd climbed into it as the only alternative to being burned to death or captured by the Phoenix.

His skin was sore, burning. He knew now what had made John Roan's face have that reptilian look. The man had been chained, of course, in front of one of those furnace holes in the rocks. He had been exposed to these caustic, sulphurous gases for many days. It had taken all the oil from his skin, made it dead-looking.

The stuff was tearing at Captain Hazzard's throat. He stopped long enough to open his kit and slip on the small gas mask he always carried. He never went without it. It had helped him often. Its scientific respirator strained whatever good air there was. As the fumes got thicker his life depended on it.

The climb seemed endless. It was an hour before he finally felt the air getting cooler, the fumes thinning. Then at last the flume opened into a horizontal passage. Captain Hazzard flung himself exhausted on the rocks.

Suddenly he sat up. Tautness filled his whole being. His senses tingled. Those strange psychic whispers of danger to which he was given raced through his mind. Not danger to himself this time.

But danger to those for whom he was responsible; danger to Mary Parker and the others left in the cave.

Hazzard stood in a frozen trance as the psychic whispers became stronger. He could see now dimly—see the pictures in his mind's eye of what was happening; see Mary Parker, Martin, Jake and Wash being carried on poles through the jungle night by jubilant savages. He saw the strange barbaric procession entering the passage to the volcanic stronghold of the Phoenix.

Hazzard broke from his trance and ran along the passage with fear clutching his throat like an icy thing. He had got them into this. He had brought them to the jungle. He must get them out, save them somehow.

But a great earthquake tremor shook the rocks as though to mock his efforts, as though to show the helplessness of one human being in this place of titanic forces.

High above his head in the vaulted roof of the passage stones loosened and came down. They crashed at his feet. They made him trip and stumble. Then one struck his head and Hazzard pitched forward, still with the vision of calamity before his eyes.

CHAPTER IX

THE PHOENIX

MARY PARKER HAD never known such terror. She hung head downward on a long pole slung over the shoulders of two giant Tzutuhiles. Her wrists and ankles were lashed together above the top of the pole with palm fibers that cut cruelly.

All around her were Indians carrying torches. Their hideous faces shone. Their sharp spears gleamed. Their slitted black eyes were filled with venomous hatred as they looked her way. Each had a green jewel in the center of his forehead which seemed like a third baleful eye.

Behind her Jake, Martin and Wash were being carried on poles, too. All their equipment dangled from another pole carried by two savages who brought up the rear.

The procession was entering the rocky opening in the mountain. The Indians plunged in, walking in single file, and Mary Parker began to choke. There were fumes in the air that stung her throat and face. The place was warm and stifling.

The trek continued up now into the heart of the mountain.

The Indians stopped at last and dropped her and the others joltingly on the floor of a big rock vault that was empty and had no door. The equipment was dropped, too, all but the rifles and automatics. Then the Indians shuffled out, leaving their prisoners tied.

But Martin spoke tensely the instant they had gone. "There's no door," he said. "No way to lock us up—and no guard posted. We can get these cords off and make a break. Roll over, Jake, and I'll untie you."

Jake twisted till his hands were close to Martin's fingers. Martin quickly got the cords loosened. Then, as soon as Jake's hands were free, he untied the others.

Martin moved cautiously toward the open entrance of the room, then stopped with a savage exclamation before he reached it.

Something more implacable than any door appeared suddenly between him and freedom. A wavering, eerie curtain of pulsating light glowed and shimmered from floor to ceiling between two black screens set close against the walls. The death curtain itself was being used to hold them in.

MARTIN backed away, his face twisted. Then he pointed toward the knapsacks. "We've still got the radio! We can get in touch with Crandall. We can ask him to send out a message that will reach the government of Guatemala. Maybe they'll send help—before it's too late."

The savages hadn't had the wits to remove that small box. The guns they had recognized and taken, but the radio looked harmless.

Martin crossed the floor and bent over the radio mechanism with feverish haste. It was built for telephonic communication, and was one of the smallest, most compact two-way sets that the Hazzard Laboratories had created. Powerful chemical batteries made it run. Its range was seventy-five miles. Yet it took up a space no larger than a cigar box.

Martin unsnapped the earphones, clipped them on his head. He adjusted the small mouthpiece, clicked the switch and twirled the dials. "ML calling GC," he said. "Calling GC. Calling GC...."

A thunderous volley of shots drowned out his speech. They came in quick succession. The radio set on the floor began to dance fantastically. Its tubes popped into splinters. Its cabinet split. Its parts flew in all directions as slugs hammered into it.

Martin whirled dumbfounded. Behind the curtain of light a dim figure stood—a man with a gun.

His face was indistinct until the light thinned a little in its weird ebb and flow. Then Martin glimpsed it.

The features were wizened. The head was shrunken, matted with long stringy hair like a mummy. The nose was hawklike. The skin was cracked by the fumes of the mountain into hideous reptilian scales. The eyes shone with evil intelligence from deep-sunken sockets.

The man didn't look quite human. The way his head rested on his shoulders, the way his shoulders humped, gave him the appearance of a hideous vulture. But his thin lips opened. He spoke in perfect English.

"Four shots, and I didn't miss once."

There was silence in the room, tense, expectant, till Mary Parker gasped:

"Who are you?"

The vulture man's evil gaze turned slowly, explored her from head to toe. He spoke finally with a mocking smile twisting his shriveled features. "Who I am is one of life's riddles," he said. "But—" he peered at each of them in turn, shaking now with silent, evil laughter—"you can call me the Phoenix."

The room was hushed again for seconds as all eyes focused on that sinister, skull-like face. The Phoenix! The man who had been responsible for those murders back in New York. The man who had tried to kill them. The man who had taken Mary's father prisoner and been the cause of their coming south.

The Phoenix touched his chest, lifted his wizened head. Emotion glared in his sunken eyes, when he thundered:

"I am the Phoenix, who, like the ancient bird of imperial Egypt, have got my strength from the living heart of fire. I am the master of Omoxotl, ruler of the great volcano—and I shall become the ruler of the world!"

Words burst suddenly from Mary Parker's lips. She couldn't be silenced longer. "What have you done with my father and Kurt Gordon?"

"What!" The thoughts of the Phoenix seemed to come back reluctantly from intoxicating vistas of egotistic grandeur. His eyes fixed themselves on the girl again and his harsh laughter filled the room. "I'll take you to him," he said, "if you want to see him?"

THERE was something in his tone; something about his words that made the girl whiten. But she moved forward to the curtain of death, going as close as she dared.

The Phoenix stepped to the side of the room and touched something. "I'll let the girl through," he said, "but if any man tries to follow her, I'll shoot him dead. You've seen how good my aim is!"

The curtain faded. Mary Parker walked through as in a trance. None of the others followed. They read death in the Phoenix's eyes. Then the curtain came on again, shimmering as before. The man and the girl moved off together.

Seen close, the Phoenix's features were so horrible that Mary Parker thought she might faint. They were like a shrunken mask of intolerable evil; like all the sins and cruelties of man merged into one hideous face.

The girl kept her eyes away. She shrank from any contact with that shriveled body. She followed his shuffling footsteps until they came to a small opening in a wall of rock.

"Through there," the Phoenix said. "You can see him. The third from the end."

Mary Parker looked and her heart seemed to twist inside her as if it were skewered on a knife. Her eyes widened. Her hands felt cold. She was looking into a room where the chained slaves toiled. And the man who labored third from the end nearest her in the row before the fire holes in the rock was her father.

Her father—emaciated, sweating, corpselike! She knew! She could tell in spite of the way he'd changed. There were steel rings around his ankles, chains attached to them.

Mary Parker called out in a choking voice. "Father, it's Mary! Father—look—it's Mary!"

Only for one brief moment did the man turn his head. Then it was more like a reflex movement than a conscious action. There was no awareness in his sunken eyes. They were stupid, vacant, glazed.

And Mary Parker broke into a sudden spasm of hysteria. She screamed. She turned and struck the Phoenix. She clawed at his horrible face with her nails. She lashed at him with her tightly clenched fists.

The Phoenix didn't give ground. He merely snarled in his throat and struck back. He slapped her face with blow after blow that sounded like whips cracking. He drove her from him with a cold fury that made his eyes look like a devil's. He continued to slap her till she fell on her knees before him, her golden hair streaming, her face white.

She lifted her hands to her smarting cheeks, moaned on the stone floor of the passage outside the room where her father toiled.

THE PHOENIX bent over her trembling body like a vulture ready to feast. His eyes were blazing, malevolent, "This is a man's world. This mountain is a place where important work is being done. Work, do you hear! Great work—work that the ages won't forget. And you are useless. You are a girl, weak, foolish. There is no food for useless mouths in this mountain. But—" he paused and looked down as her as though giving consideration to a problem—"there is a useful way to get rid of you."

She paid no attention to what he was saying. Sobs wrenched her slim shoulders. The Phoenix went on with grating emphasis.

"My Indians have customs carried down from long-dead ancestors. They are nature worshipers, animists. The beasts, the birds, the reptiles, even the rocks to them are sacred. They have their especial fetishes and idols. It will please them to give you to the sacred serpents of Omoxotl; the great white pythons that have lived near the heart of the mountain since long before the coming of Alvarado. For centuries the Indians have fed them, made living sacrifices to them, thrown their enemies to them so that the wrath of Terror's Shadow might be appeased. But you will be the first white girl given to the White Lords of Omoxotl. To the Indians it should be a time of especial rejoicing."

Some of his words reached the girl's consciousness. She raised startled, terrified eyes. What was he saying? White pythons! Lords of Omoxotl! She cried out suddenly, gasping in horror, lifting herself to her feet.

The Phoenix looked pleased that his words had filled her with fresh terror. There was an inhuman, a sadistic light in his eyes now. She had struck him, scratched him, given insult to his megalomaniacal ego. Her abject fear was like a balm to his pride.

"They like only living things," he said gloatingly, "warm flesh still quivering."

Mary Parker fainted mercifully, unable to stand any more bombardments of horror after the strain she had endured. Two Indians took her back to the prison room. Then the Phoenix summoned other Indians with chains. These he exhibited to Jake, Wash and Martin.

"We have them always available," he said cruelly. "The work is such that the workers fall by the way, making room for others. There is no unemployment problem in Omoxotl."

Hazzard's three aides considered making a break for it as the Phoenix switched off the light curtain to bring Mary Parker in. But a dozen Indians with knives and spears stood grimly in the doorway. To fight now would be suicidal. Nothing would be gained by throwing their lives away. And they sensed that Captain Hazzard wouldn't want it. Mysterious psychic forces told them that he was still alive somewhere. The only way they could help him, co-operate with him, and help themselves, was to wait till some opportunity presented itself.

But there was a fearful finality about the feel of those steel rings on their ankles. With the Indians walking beside them, holding spears against their bodies, they were taken to the room with the furnacelike holes.

Two places were empty and at the third a slave had collapsed. His head lolled horribly. His mouth was open. His tongue, black and swollen, was thrust through cracking lips. He was dead, killed by the fearful labor, and his body was removed to make room for Jake to take his place.

The Phoenix had come in, too. He looked on coldly while the Indians chained the new slaves in the toiling row. The others hadn't stopped their work for a moment. They held long ladlelike implements. They thrust these into the fire holes with some sort of brownish rock in them. Every few minutes they drew the ladles out, plunged them into a vat of liquid for a moment, then thrust them back into the holes again. They kept this up till the rocks turned black. Then they dumped the rocks to one side and began all over with fresh ones.

Jake was given one of the long-handled ladles, together with a chunk of rock. He was told by the Phoenix to follow the movements of the others. Indians dressed in hideous python skins, clutching long whips, stood around with masklike faces.

Jake knew they were there to keep the slaves busy. But he was curious about the rocks and ladles. He stared at the Phoenix, pointed to his chunk of rock. "What's that for?" he asked grimly.

"Questions are forbidden!" the Phoenix snapped. He made a quick gesture. The nearest Indian brought his whip down on Jake's back in a blow that cut the skin cruelly. Jake didn't wince. But he thrust his ladle sullenly into the fire and whispered to Wash, who was chained close to him: "I'd rather be a horned toad in hell than fork my fuzztail permanent with this herd of sour-bellies."

CHAPTER X

ALTAR OF THE PYTHON MEN

CAPTAIN HAZZARD, TWENTY-FOUR hours later, was still lost in the mazelike passages of Omoxotl. There had been hours of desperate searching, of exploring air flumes and narrow crevices. Hours of sounding the lava walls for possible spots where an opening might be made.

His psychic senses told him that Jake and Wash and Mary Parker were still alive. He had established telepathic contact with Martin. He knew now something of what had happened. The three men were chained in the room with the slaves. Through Martin's eyes he had even got an impression of the Phoenix; of a personality more fiend than man. Of Mary Parker he knew only that she had gone out from the prison room to see her father and had been brought back in a faint. He had no inkling of the fearful fate that lay ahead of her.

And neither Martin nor anyone else could help him with his immediate problem. That was to find a way out of the tomblike rock cavern in which he was trapped.

He had tried almost everything. He had burned smoke powders and watched the way the vapor drifted in an effort to discover drafts that might lead to hidden openings. He had found several, but they had been only minute cracks. In sheer desperation he began to climb as high as he could get on one side of the wall. As he climbed he swept his flashlight over the ceiling.

It was thus that he discovered a small black hole in the roof of the vault. Did it lead to another, higher chamber, or was it merely a pocket left by a falling rock? Hazzard didn't know. But at the risk of a bone-shattering plunge he climbed up to it. Reaching out from a narrow ledge he thrust his arm in the black air pocket. Excitement gripped him instantly. There was a faint draft there.

Tensely, he took one of the small bombs from his belt. He set its chemical fuse to the maximum explosion point of five minutes, then wedged it in the hole. He wasn't sure it would give him time to get down. But he must risk it. He descended hastily, taking long chances. At the last, as seconds flew by, he jumped to the stone floor from a height of thirty feet, bending his knees as he landed to break the shock. The instant he hit he turned and fled down the passage and swung himself flat.

The explosion overhead filled the corridor with shattering, ear-splitting echoes. Showers of rock came down. Great boulders fell a few feet behind him. And after the explosion Hazzard's pulses raced.

For there was a gaping hole in the roof now; a black opening large enough to admit his body. He climbed up once more, squeezed through the space he'd blasted, and found himself in another chamber. There was a tight feeling around his heart as he ran along it. Since the mountain was honeycombed with passages this might be a blind one, too.

But a faint glow appeared ahead at the end of five minutes. Daylight this time! Daylight after hours of wandering in darkness. The sight of that opening in the rocks gave Captain Hazzard new vigor.

He crept forward cautiously. He wasn't sure where he was, or when he might run into prowling savages. But as soon as he reached the opening he saw that caution was for the moment needless. He was far up on the side of the great peak. Below him was the gorge through which he'd followed the Indian. Spreading out was a vast panorama of the jungle, with the Espiritu Santo range on the far horizon. Hazzard began moving along a narrow ledge on the face of the mountain. Cautiously but swiftly he descended, climbing down toward a spot where he had glimpsed what appeared to be another passage mouth.

But it took time to reach it. The going was harder than he had thought. He had to slip down the bare face of the rock in spots, hanging on precariously. When he did get near the opening he paused abruptly and listened.

From out of that cavelike hole in the rock came weird, barbaric music, the sound of many voices, wailing, chanting. It seemed far off, ghostly. It rose and fell. It had a persistent rhythm. And to Hazzard, who was sensitive to the tones and moods of even the most savage races, there was in it a note of unearthly horror.

MARY PARKER, too, heard that chanting. But it wasn't far away from her. It didn't reach her ears through hundreds of feet of rocky passage. It was all around her. In front—in back—beside her, beating against her eardrums in wave on wave of shuddering dread.

It seemed to be bearing her along on an evil tide of sound. But it was the Indians themselves who carried her. She wasn't slung beneath a pole now. She sat on a royal couchlike litter of ocelot skin trimmed with the waving plumes of the sacred quetzal.

She, too, was dressed in the bright-green feathers. She wore a cloak of them. The Tzutuhiles had made her disrobe and put this feathery garment on her slender body. It hung from her white shoulders all the way to her ankles. Over her lustrous blond hair they had slipped a band of gleaming gold ornamented with a bright-green jewel. It was the sacred emerald of the Tzutuhiles. The flawless gem that came from the rocks of this wild country. She was being borne along like a queen in state. Four chanting Python Men held the corners of the litter.

But her hands and feet were bound. She was not a queen in reality, but a slave. A slave of horrible death on her way to serve her awful masters.

She knew who those masters were. The Phoenix had told her. She knew, and yet her mind could not meet a thing of such unspeakable horror. It shied away from it, drew back dazed, dared not even contemplate it. Twice in the past few minutes she had nearly fainted away.

But close at hand, bringing that horror home to her, was an Indian with hands bound and head bent walking just ahead of her litter. He must have sinned against the Phoenix. The quivering features of his face, the look in his eyes, stabbed like sharp blades across her nerve fibers. The masters whom she went to serve were to have him, too.

THE PROCESSION moved on singing, carrying torches in the dim catacombs of the mountain. Mary Parker lay on the litter with a white face and eyes dark with steadily mounting dread.

They came at last to a chamber that was roofed high like a vault. There was a rocky floor in front. Toward the back the floor ended sharply, giving way to a steep-sided pit. In the air of this big room was a faint, musky scent that made the girl's body tremble.

The singing ceased in a moment. The Python Men ranged themselves around the edge of the pit. In the silence that followed, Mary

They lifted Mary Parker and carried her to the python pit.

Parker heard a slithering, scraping whisper of sound that was hateful, spine-chilling.

Drawn by a dread fascination that was stronger than will, she turned her head and stared down when the Python Men brought her close to the edge of the pit.

There under the light of the torches she glimpsed the scaly white bodies of the snakes. They were moving slowly, curling, unwinding, writhing over each other—a squirming, horrible mass of giant pythons, bleached almost to milky whiteness because the sun had not reached them or their ancestors for untold ages.

They thrust their great heads up. They glared with their cold green eyes. Their forked tongues flickered. Their scaly necks swayed, dropped back, rose again.

The Indians took their bound comrade and suddenly hurled him down into the pit among those writhing, twisting reptilian bodies.

Mary Parker dropped forward on the litter, hiding her eyes, stifling the scream in her throat among the green feathers of her robe.

But she couldn't shut out the awful sounds that came up from the pit. She couldn't close her ears to those hideous cries, those snappings and crunchings. It was only when the sounds reached their climax, when two of the great pythons had thrown their coils tightly around the Indian's body and were crushing the life out of him that Mary Parker again mercifully fainted away.

When preparations for the horrible feast in the pit began, when one of the pythons drew into a corner with his human prey to crush it and knead it, Mary lay unconscious on the litter. She didn't feel the rough savage hands that clutched her limp body and raised her slowly aloft.

Then the chanting started again. A high priest of the animist cult lifted the green jewel from Mary's forehead. They held it up on a feathered arrow, walked with it to the serpent pit and made other mystic passes.

The pythons thrust their ghostly heads up again as if their cold brains told them that another victim was to be thrown to them. These walls had echoed to that strange chanting often before. Never had it failed to mean food for the snakes.

The chanting was louder, deeper, more fervent. The priests were trembling with an emotion close to madness as they lifted Mary Parker and carried her slowly to the edge of the pit.

CHAPTER XI

HELL'S CONTROL ROOM

THEN IT HAPPENED—A thing that made the Python Men freeze into rigid statues of abject fear. A light glowed suddenly in the pit of the serpents. A light as bright as a ruby and as red as blood. It flared out of the semi-darkness, making the pythons hiss and crawl away.

The Indians hadn't heard the faint stir of the tiny cone that sailed over their heads. They hadn't seen it in their preoccupation with the awful ceremony being enacted.

It had landed on a python's writhing body which deadened the sound when it fell. An instant after it hit it burst into flame, spurting red fire at its narrow tip. And now it was burning weirdly, fearfully to the Indians' eyes. In its glow the white pythons seemed to be bathed in blood.

The Indians drew back staring. The red light seemed to indicate that Omoxotl was angry. Its sudden appearance was a sign that they had done something wrong.

And as they stood, filled with superstitious dread, staring at that strange blood-red fire, something moved across the stone floor behind them, rolling almost to their feet.

It came to rest finally close to the edge of the serpent's pit. It was a silvery ball about the size of an egg. There were holes in it. As it rolled a slender black cord hardly larger than a thread unwound from it, and trailed behind it.

The Python Men didn't see the cord. They didn't know where the silver ball had come from or what it was. They stared stupidly from it to the flare in the pit.

Then a sound rose from their very feet—a thin, ghostly voice, as though some spectral being dwelt in the floor of the room.

"Nihongi! Nihongi!" It was one of several words common to most of the Indian dialects of Guatemala. *"Nihongi!"* the voice said again. "Go!" Then the voice rose till it seemed to fill the whole chamber. "Leave the maiden! Go! Go!"

The Indians broke suddenly into a wild stampede of terror. With contorted faces, waving arms, rolling eyes they turned from the pythons' pit and fled toward the door. The evil, blood-red glow of the strange fire seemed to follow them. Their panic increased with every step they took. Omoxotl was angry. Omoxotl had spoken. They had seen his fiery eye. They had heard his awful voice. He had spurned their sacrificial offering.

They bolted through the door of the room, yelling, clawing, knocking each other down, trailing their green feathers. They let their torches fall and sputter. In a surging, frenzied human wave, they turned left and rushed down the long rock passage up which they had come.

As the sound of their thudding feet diminished, a shadow detached itself from a dark recess at the right of the door. A tall figure strode quickly into the sacred pythons' room.

It was Captain Hazzard, and he went at once to the prostrate girl. He bent over her, saw that she was still alive. Before picking her up he paused long enough to rewind the black cord on the tiny spheroid loudspeaker that had saved her life. It was made of aluminum, light as a feather, but could amplify the human voice many times.

Hazzard had developed it, together with a buttonhole microphone, as a means of communicating with friends or assistants in out-of-the-way places. The spheroid speaker slipped easily into his pocket.

He lifted the girl in his arms then, turned and moved quickly out of the room and strode after the fleeing Python Men. There was no time to lose. When they told the Phoenix what had happened the Phoenix would grow suspicious and would start an investigation. But if Hazzard could reach the part of the mountain where the Phoenix lived there might be a chance to make some investigations of his own while the panic-stricken savages held their master's attention. It would take some minutes to convince them that Omoxotl wasn't angry.

He broke into a run, swinging the girl in his powerful arms. The sound of the Indians was far away now. Burdened as he was, he couldn't expect to catch up. But he kept them within earshot, ran down dark, twisting passages, crossed natural vaults in the mountain. Some few of the savages had clung to their torches. When the passage was straight he could see their glow and this helped him to follow.

Mary stirred in his arms presently. The draft on her face was reviving her. And, even though she was unconscious, the magnetic power of Captain Hazzard's brain and body seemed to be driving the clouds of horror from her mind.

By the time they reached the level of the chamber where the chained slaves toiled, Mary's eyes were open. Hazzard had come closer to the torches of the Python Men. In their light, Mary Parker got a glimpse of his face. Her hands clutched him. Her voice came in a thin whisper like someone talking from the grave.

"Captain Hazzard!" There was hope, disbelief, amazement in her tone.

He nodded; then said: "Let me know when you feel strong enough to walk."

She said nothing for a few minutes. Her body relaxed and she seemed to sink into a trance. He could guess how weak she must feel after those moments of unforgettable horror.

Suddenly she roused herself. "I can walk now."

He wasn't sure of it, but he let her feet slip to the floor, and in an instant she was running along beside him.

"Hurry!" she whispered. "I've seen my father. He's here—alive. But they're torturing him. He's dying. If there's any way we can save him, we must!"

The Python Men had paused now. He could see their torches flaring down at the end of a long rock corridor. He could hear their voices jabbering. They must be clamoring outside the private chambers of the Phoenix—to tell him of the dread thing that had happened. Here was the opportunity for which he had hoped.

He moved stealthily toward the frenzied group of green-robed Tzutuhiles. Other Indians were coming from all directions; slipping out of doors and passages, running to see what the excitement was about.

As one door opened, Hazzard caught a glimpse of a big, lighted room filled with strange machinery. When the Indian who had come out of it disappeared in the direction of the yelling group, Hazzard whispered:

"This way. Come!"

HIS ARMY automatic was in his right hand now. In his left was another of those walnut-size bombs. As a last resort, he stood ready to fling it to save their lives. But the big room was empty except for one man, a slave chained before a great work table strewn with delicate instruments.

The man raised startled eyes. He was Teutonic in appearance, small, intelligent, with a blond-bearded face. There was suffering written on it, deep-seated fear in his small blue eyes. He looked at Hazzard and the girl as though he saw two ghosts.

Hazzard put his finger to his lips. He understood the situation at a glance. Here was one of the Phoenix's trained technicians. A great brain probably, a scientist or scholar who had somehow fallen in his hands. The Phoenix made slaves of civilized men, chained them, worked them to death under the cruel whips of his barbarous Python Men.

Hazzard spoke to the bearded worker in English and the man answered with a Germanic accent: "Vat iss it you are doing here? Und der girl! Don't you know der Venix vill kill you! Get oudt. Run!"

In clipped sentences, Hazzard told who he was and what had happened, and he saw hope flare in the chained man's eyes. The man said his name was Beckhardt. He was a chemist working for a mining company and had been captured by the Tzutuhiles, then brought here.

Captain Hazzard placed a chair for Mary Parker.

Beckhardt waved his short arms and whispered hoarsely. "Der Venix iss mad—mad vid a crazy ego dat makes him vant to rule der vorld. But he iss a great genius. Look!"

Hazzard stared around the room with its strange assortment of levers, dials, huge metal coils and giant valves. It looked more like a power substation in a great city than a chamber deep in the heart of a volcano. It was incredible, the work of a great brain, a mighty energy. There were whirring dynamos, electric lights, huge switchboards. But what of the power to run all this?

Hazzard guessed the startling secret even before Beckhardt stabbed one stubby finger dramatically at the floor. "Down dere. All of it. Dere in der volcano's crater!"

That was the answer. The Phoenix had harnessed the subterranean fires of Omoxotl. Hazzard knew that daring engineers had proposed such a thing. They had theorized, pointed out in scientific papers that there was enough power in the average volcano, enough heat units to run a mighty modern city. But no one had dared act upon the idea—except the Phoenix. It had taken a half-crazed brain, a man obsessed with limitless ambition, a man who held human life cheaply. It had taken a personality half genius and half fiend.

Captain Hazzard stepped to the wall of the room where there was a huge diagram in a frame. A diagram of Omoxotl, showing the course of the crater, its depth and structure. And here before Hazzard's startled eyes were the details of the vast engineering task. The Phoenix had thrown a giant valve across the crater, five hundred feet below its summit. He had capped the volcano, controlling the mighty gas pressure, as lesser engineers cap oilwells.

Steel girders such as are used to build bridges had been set in the rock, reënforced, roofed over with other girders and plates of steel riveted together. The valve in the center was worked by a system of giant worm gears operated by an electric motor.

Hazzard shuddered when he considered the toll of human life that this vast project must have taken. How many workers had fallen screaming into the fiery depths of the crater? How many others had perished in the stifling gases? And how many thousands, how many millions of dollars had this thing cost?

Mary Parker sat motionless in her chair, watching the two men.

HAZZARD'S excited gaze continued to run over the design, comparing it with the machinery in the room. He saw the delicate instrument under a glass case that made second-by-second recordings of the pressure of the subterranean gases. He saw that it operated a safety control attached to the great central worm gear.

This gear was in ceaseless motion, opening and closing the huge valve, letting gas escape or shutting it in, to keep the pressure constant. It could be varied by a rheostat. Except for this the mountain might blow up, or the pressure that the Phoenix needed in his work might vanish if the subterranean fires sank below a certain point.

Then Hazzard saw another control, another series of lines on the diagram. These showed how the pressure could be built up by letting water from an underground river fall into the crater. The water turned to live steam before it struck bottom. The steam turned to superheated gases.

Hazzard tensed suddenly as his mind grasped what would happen if the one control was closed and the other opened. He remembered the great volcano, Krakatoa, in the strait of Sunda, near Java. Sea water had fallen into Krakatoa's crater and it had erupted with an appalling loss of life, blowing a whole island to bits and filling the atmosphere of the entire earth with dust motes. Yes, the Phoenix was playing with forces so great that they staggered the imagination.

And what of his light-wave curtain? Hazzard spoke to Beckhardt about it. The German chemist shrugged. "I do not know. Only der Venix knows. But dere are pabers—dere in dat safe iff a man could open it. Dere are plans showing it. Maybe iff—"

But Hazzard had already darted away. He was kneeling before the safe, moving the dials, listening to the tumblers. He must have more knowledge. Their lives might depend on what he learned in the few moments left to him. He took a silencer from his pocket and slipped it over the barrel of his automatic. He laid the gun on the floor beside him. He would shoot—shoot to kill if he was interrupted.

Mary Parker's dark-blue eyes followed Captain Hazzard's every move.

And in a moment he had the safe open. In a moment his tense hands were shuffling through the papers. Then he found it, found what he wanted. He ran across the room to Beckhardt. They studied them together. But Beckhardt could make nothing of them. He didn't have the vast training, the super-technical skill of Wash MacGowen.

It was Hazzard himself who understood those diagrams and complex figures. Wash had been right in assuming that the thing might be atomic. The Phoenix had used the power of Omoxotl to break down individual atoms into their component electrons. Sending the electrons into space on alpha rays from a Roentgen tube he had built up an atomic barrage of deadly power, a protoplasmic oxidizer that congealed the blood and brought death quickly. It was a thing of horror, of far-reaching potentialities.

And there was literature in the safe to show that the Phoenix intended to develop this into a weapon that would make the nations of the earth bow to his will. Through agents, he was corresponding even now with certain European governments. He hadn't let the secret out of his hands as yet; but he had drawn up plans of the whole world as one vast corporate state with headquarters in Omoxotl and himself as supreme dictator.

Here was the dream of a megalomaniac; but a dream that could spread untold misery and horror if it wasn't nipped in the bud.

Hazzard knew that the small light machines tried out in New York and in the air were only the beginning.

Mary Parker called a swift warning as one of the Python Men suddenly came through the door. The savage stopped in amazement and opened his mouth to shout.

Without an instant's hesitation, knowing that he was acting in the interests of humanity, Captain Hazzard sent a bullet from his silenced gun into the Indian's brain. He rose swiftly and pulled the body out of sight. Then he drew a ring from the savage's belt and found a key that unlocked the shackles on Beckhardt's ankles.

Beckhardt came forward, a slave no longer, with deep-heartfelt gratitude shining in his small blue eyes. Hazzard thrust one of his tiny, deadly bombs into the chemist's hand. He showed him how to use it, then said:

"Stay here—you and Mary Parker. Don't use that bomb unless you have to—but use it if you must to save her life. I'm going to leave my automatic with her."

"Und vare are you going?"

"To try and free some other slaves."

Hazzard handed his army Colt to Mary Parker. "In case anything should happen to me," he said, "it will be better if you have this?"

She understood. "Yes. I'll use it—on myself—if they try to take me back to the pythons."

He knew she would. Nothing could make her face again that nightmarish horror. Hazzard went to the door then, looked out, and stepped swiftly into the passage. Moving as stealthily as a shadow, he hurried along the dark corridor toward the room where the slaves toiled.

CHAPTER XII

THE RUBY OF OMOXOTL

JUST INSIDE THE doorway stood a huge Indian, dressed in a hideous python-skin hood, and holding a steel-shafted spear.

There was no time for finesse. Other savages were already drifting back to their posts, and the group of Tzutuhiles who had fled from the python pit in terror were coming out of the Phoenix's private chamber with their frenzy calmed. In another few minutes Hazzard knew that the Phoenix would begin an investigation of that weird happening at the pit. In another few minutes every savage in those vast catacombs would be warned and alert.

Hazzard flung himself recklessly on the tall, armed guard. He hoped to knock him out, quiet him, and grab the spear before two other guards with whips, standing in the far side of the big room, came running.

But for once Hazzard had underestimated the lightning rapidity of savage reflexes. As well try to take a dozing jaguar by surprise as one of these grim Tzutuhiles.

The man turned in the flash of a split-second; turned before Hazzard's hands had touched his body. Like the claw of a striking cat, the spear flashed out. The Indian snarled deep in his throat. Hazzard leaped aside as the spear point brushed him. Its steel blade sliced his clothes. He felt the Indian's hot breath on his face.

Then Hazzard struck straight at that evil face. His blow would have felled a white man; but it failed even to stun the savage. The Tzutuhile let out an angry roar. Head down he came at Hazzard with the spear again. And behind him now Hazzard heard a determined patter of feet as the two other guards came running.

Desperate, Hazzard took a chance at strategy. He gave ground for a moment before the spearman. He turned and fled as though in terror. He heard the man's steps close behind him. He gambled his life on seconds. Just as the Indian drove the point forward to spear his back, Hazzard leaped aside. His hand flashed out. He caught the spear as it shot by him. He gave a savage tug, then tripped him and sent him sprawling on the floor.

The two guards with the whips were close now. Hazzard wrenched the spear from the fallen man's hands. As the Indian leaped up and came at him like a raging beast, Hazzard brought the weapon down on his skull.

He did not even wait to see the man fall. He whirled with the spear in his hand. The two guards had discarded their whips and had drawn long knives from their belts. They came at him from different directions.

The spear flashed out twice, its steel point gleaming like lightning. Twice, and the Python Men fell with limp-hanging arms and broken shoulders. Hazzard stunned them both with blows on the head.

Then he snatched a key ring from the man he had first felled. Quickly, deftly, knowing that he had only a few minutes to work; he went down the line of slaves before the fire holes and unlocked them. Jake Cole first, then Wash, then Martin. Then other men whose names he did not know. Finally he reached Mary's father.

Some of the slaves took a few stumbling steps and collapsed at this sudden freedom. It was too much for them after the routine they had known.

"Help them!" said Hazzard. "Quick. Follow me. We've got to get back to the control room."

A mad, a desperate plan was shaping itself in Hazzard's brain. He must reach the control room of the lost city again. He must have Wash there to help him.

Already the noise that the guards had made had attracted attention. As he stepped into the corridor three more Indians came running toward him. They paused only an instant, then, with shrill cries, leaped forward holding their spears. Jake, Wash, and Martin, helping the slaves who could not walk, were close behind.

HAZZARD flung pellets of tear gas which hindered, but did not stop the Indians' attack. With streaming eyes and distorted faces they came on through it. They hurled themselves on Hazzard and the others. For a moment there was a mad, hand-to-hand conflict.

Jake got one of the spears away and bashed a Python Man over the head with it. He swore like a mule driver. Hazzard knocked a second savage out with a blow to the body. But the third Indian let his spear fly and it caught one of the men who had been chained, in the neck. It pierced him, almost sliced his head from his body. The man, who a moment before had had the hope of freedom, went down with his troubles ended forever.

Hazzard plunged on along the passage, the others after him. They reached the door of the control room as a howling mob of Indians, aware now that a break had been made by the slaves, came charging from the direction of the Phoenix's chambers.

Their spears whistled through the air even before Hazzard had marshaled his men through the control room door. When the last man was in, he slammed it, shoved a bolt home. He had noticed this before he left it. It was part of his plan.

He turned to Wash, and explained briefly what he had discovered about the death curtain. While the Indians beat on the door, he showed Wash the plans he had taken from the safe.

Wash knitted his brows as calmly as though death were not howling outside. "Amazing," he said. "Extraordinary. You were right, Captain, I shouldn't have been afraid to follow any line of reasoning, however wild it might seem. This thing utilizes the force released from the breakdown of atoms. The force is discharged between two terminals and carried on alpha rays. We shall have to call in the quantum theory to explain it."

Wash was like a school-master giving a lecture, so absorbed in his subject now that he had forgotten all about their danger. Hazzard brought him back to reality.

"I know, Wash," he said tensely. "It's atomic all right. Alpha rays are the carrying agent. The point is, can we build up a defense against it?"

"I don't know," said Wash. "It would take some research."

"Research!" Hazzard laughed grimly. "There are a bunch of Indians out there waiting to do some research with spears and find out what our insides are made of. No, Wash. We've got to act quickly. We've got to take a chance."

"But how—"

"Look. We've got to break down the polarization of the carrying agent. We can't hope to touch the atomic factor itself. We don't know enough about it. But mightn't we blast through it, upset the polarization with a dose of the same poison? I mean, use more alpha rays to cut through and bisect the carriers?"

Dawning comprehension made Wash's eyes glow brightly. He rubbed his long chin excitedly. "It's possible, Captain—barely possible. But even that would take time. We'd have to have an X-ray outfit."

"Over there," said Hazzard. "But it's too big to carry. We need something portable. Can you strip it down, Wash, make it lighter and still have it work?"

"Time," said Wash. "I can do anything—given time."

"There is no time," snapped Captain Hazzard. "Get busy on that X-ray, Wash. Leave the rest to me." With a light in his eyes that even Wash couldn't interpret, Hazzard strode toward those two controls that held in leash the mighty power of the great volcano. The one operating the worm gear in the giant valve; the other which could send a river pouring into the crater. He swung the rheostat needle all the way over.

Delicate mechanism inside the glass case was transmitted to the huge electric motor, multiplied a thousand times, till tons of metal revolved as the great valve in the crater cap moved shut.

Then Hazzard opened that other control till a quivering needle on a clock-faced dial registered a flow of water. Tons of it began pouring down into the crater. Hazzard was beginning the greatest gamble of his life.

He turned and left the controls for a moment. Something was thudding on the outside of the control-room door. The Python Men had a log battering-ram and were going at it systematically.

There was a small sliding panel in the door, a peephole covered with a meshed grating. There were indications that the Phoenix had planned to use this room to withstand an assault in case his Indians ever became rebellious.

Hazzard opened the peephole and stared out. He saw a sea of fierce copper faces. Even if Wash succeeded in condensing the X-ray outfit so they could carry it, it seemed impossible that they would ever get through this cordon of howling savages.

BUT THE Indians were stepping aside now to make way for someone. They were opening a long path. Through it came a hideous, vulturelike figure. A man with a wizened face and evilly burning eyes. The Phoenix!

Hazzard waited breathlessly. The Phoenix came straight up to the control-room door. He spoke in a quiet voice as though addressing a business confrère. "I see, my friend, that you have succeeded in stirring up quite a bit of trouble. I believe I have the pleasure of speaking to the famous Captain Hazzard!"

"And you're the Phoenix," said Hazzard grimly. "The man who thinks he can conquer the whole world."

The Phoenix's eyes darted venomous fire. His thin lips curled back from his yellow teeth. "Fool! Because you have succeeded in barricading yourself in that room with a handful of slaves, you think you are in a position now to mock the Phoenix." The Phoenix drew himself up in fierce, bombastic pride. "You cannot even make terms with me. My Indians will batter the door down presently. Every one of your party will be tortured to death.... But, because I value the safety of certain instruments I have there, I'm going to offer you an alternative. Open the door, come out quietly, all of you and you will be allowed to live in slavery."

Captain Hazzard laughed. "What you say about the safety of your instruments is well put. And your Indians won't batter this door down. I'm going to stop them. Once in the past hour they tasted the wrath of Omoxotl. My red flare and my projected voice drove them out of the pythons' pit. Now, by the wrath of Omoxotl, I'm going to drive them away from this door."

"They're superstitious morons," said the Phoenix. "But I am with them now. Nothing you can say to them will have the slightest effect."

"No!" Captain Hazzard's voice was mocking. He spoke suddenly, a few clipped sentences in the Indian dialect. "Go. Leave this door. Let me come out in peace—or the wrath of Omoxotl will descend upon you. I am a white god, a greater god than the Phoenix."

The jeering voices of the Indians rose. They drove their battering-ram against the door more fiercely as the Phoenix spurred them on.

Hazzard then spoke in English, addressing the Phoenix. "I've closed the valve in the crater. I've let loose the underground river."

"What!" A note of shocked amazement was in the Phoenix's tone. He came nearer the door with his lips sliding away from his teeth again.

Hazzard said: "Listen."

There was a rumbling at his feet. A rumbling that came from vast depths in the earth, a rumbling that seemed to make the whole great mountain quiver.

"The voice of Omoxotl!" said Captain Hazzard.

A SICKLY, terrible pallor spread over the wizened face of the Phoenix. He commenced to tremble violently. "Shut it off, you fool!" he screamed. "Shut it off—or you will blow us all to destruction."

Without waiting for Hazzard to answer, he spoke to the Indians. They renewed their attack on the metal door.

Hazzard shouted: "Stop! Stop! The wrath of Omoxotl will be on your heads. The voice of Omoxotl speaks already."

Some of the Python Men left their places at the log battering-ram and stepped away. The Phoenix drew a revolver from his pocket and waved it.

"Back! Back," he shouted in their dialect. When the Indians didn't move, he deliberately opened fire on them. Hatefully, ruthlessly he sent bullets into their eyes, into their chests. The Phoenix was like a madman now. His eyes rolled. There was a froth on his thin lips. His yellow teeth were like the fangs of a jackal. Fear of him bit into the Indians' hearts, fear greater even than their fear of the mountain. Sullenly they clung to the battering-ram and shoved it at the door.

The room was shaking now. But not because of their blows. It was shaking because the whole mountain was shaking, because all hell was bubbling, seething down there thousands of feet below the rock. It was shaking because river water continued to flow into the crater and there was no way for the pent-up gases to get out.

Hazzard leaped back to the control board. Dial needles were quivering, trembling like mad things. A red liquid was pulsing furiously in an upright tube with coils below it. He turned the rheostat controlling the giant worm gear a little, opened the great valve a few feet.

A roaring shriek of gas escaping under terrific pressure came from somewhere in the mountain. It was a sound that none of them would forget as long as they lived. All the furies in hell seemed to be screaming at once. The floor shook. The walls rattled.

Outside the door Hazzard heard the frenzied, terrified shouts of the Indians. Their shouts were punctuated by the staccato reports of the Phoenix's automatic as he murdered them brutally, drove the rest back to the battering-ram.

Hazzard looked across the room and saw Wash working over the X-ray outfit. Bent, absorbed, Wash's face was as owlish and placid as though he were working over some interesting problem in the Long Island laboratory. He looked at Jake. The big cowboy was chewing gum lazily. His deadpan face was the same as usual. And Martin was doing his best to comfort Mary Parker.

But she didn't need much comforting now. She had her father with her. There were tears in her eyes, tears of joy. The thought of death didn't seem to trouble her as long as her dad could go out with her. Hazzard felt a lump rise in his throat. The lives of these people depended on him. He was taking long chances. He was gambling unmercifully. He was playing with death to keep death at bay.

He looked out the peephole. Most of the Python Men had fled except for the group that terror of the Phoenix had held together. The corpses of the men he had shot lay slumped on the floor. Hazzard wondered at the awful fear he must have inspired.

Then Wash spoke above the banshee shriek of the great mountain.

"It's ready, Captain. This is about as light as I can make it."

He hefted the X-ray cabinet, which he had stripped of all non-essentials. In twenty minutes of patient work he had put the experience of a lifetime into these changes. He had shifted delicate tubes, changed wiring, disconnected and reconnected batteries.

Hazzard picked the instrument up. It weighed about sixty pounds but he could carry it easily.

He did a strange, desperate thing then—the climax of his hairbreadth plan of escape. He walked to the control board, shut the great valve again, and deliberately smashed the mechanism with a wrench, wedging it so that the valve couldn't be opened. Then he did the same to the control which governed the flow of water.

He whirled, picked up the radio cabinet and said: "Let's go!"

CHAPTER XIII

DEATH'S GAMBIT

CAPTAIN HAZZARD SNATCHED the tiny bomb from Beckhardt. He took another one from his belt. He made the whole party retire to the far side of the chamber.

He ran forward, placed a bomb close to the door, touched the striker. Then he joined the others against the far wall. A ripping, roaring explosion came which momentarily rose above the rumbling of the mountain. The door was torn from its hinges and crashed outward, killing two Python Men, wounding others.

It almost struck the Phoenix. The vulture man fled away. The Indians followed him. At a nod from Captain Hazzard, the people for whose lives he was responsible followed him out.

Gun flame lanced down the corridor. Bullets screamed by their heads. The Phoenix was shooting, wildly, furiously. Hazzard grabbed his Colt from Mary Parker and fired till the Phoenix took cover.

Then they ran along the passage toward a far-off glow that was the light of day. Hazzard was alert for trouble. He knew the Indians would gather somewhere, make a stand.

He saw them grouped together at the mouth of the exit. Spears came his way. Shrieking, furious savages ran to head off the escape of these men who had a short time ago been abject slaves.

Hazzard touched the striker of another of his small grenades and hurled it. It was life against life now. The mountain was trembling, roaring. They must leave it soon or be swept into oblivion.

The bomb struck the foremost Indians, and they seemed to disintegrate. They died instantly and the others fell back shrieking. This seemed to be more evidence of the might and wrath of Omoxotl.

They retreated, leaving the passage clear, and they didn't try to molest Hazzard and his party further. But there was another barrier that Hazzard feared far more. Indians he could fight, with guns, with bombs, with his bare hands even. But that other barrier, dim, intangible, awful would be flung across the trail, barring their way.

Earthquakes were shaking the sides of the mountain. As they passed down the trail great rocks fell near them. They had to keep a constant look-out to be ready to dodge. Staring up, Hazzard saw a cliff break away and tumble with a roar like a hundred Niagaras. The earth under them trembled. There was terror in the air—terror, horror, madness. The awful shadow of the Phoenix seemed to hover over them still.

And then they came to a bend in the trail, and Hazzard saw the thing he dreaded. The curtain of weird luminescence hung between the two walls of the gorge. It danced, quivered, touched, retreated. Even the earthquake tremors which shook the mountain didn't affect it. It seemed worse now, more sinister, more symbolic of the evil of the Phoenix.

MARY PARKER clutched her father. Some of the slaves, miners and halfbreed Indians, whose nerves had been shattered by their awful experience, gasped in fear and crowded together. But they saw Captain Hazzard walk steadily on and they followed.

He was close to the death curtain now. Then, looking through it, he saw a line of green-plumed Python Men drawn up. The Indians set up savage exultant cries as they saw Hazzard's party.

Captain Hazzard set the X-ray cabinet down, switched it on. He made the others stand back while he advanced, holding the Roentgen-ray tube before him, letting its rays strike out toward the light curtain.

He walked closer and closer and nothing happened. The waving, shimmering mantle of dread light still hung there. The Indians' cries increased. Hazzard went closer, closer, till his head began to ring, till that strange dizziness came which was the first warning of a bloodstream being affected. He went closer still, till he could hardly stand. He pushed the power switch of the X-ray machine farther over.

Wash called a warning to him. Hazzard was reeling now, swaying on his feet. Anger, disappointment, despair beat in his brain. They were hemmed in by death. Death behind them in the form of the mighty mountain. Death in front in that ghastly curtain that seemed to have baffled him.

"Look out, Captain. Don't go any closer! Here, let me hold it."

Wash came forward. Jake and Martin followed. If Captain Hazzard was going to walk into that curtain of death these loyal friends and assistants wanted to follow him. A lump rose in Hazzard's throat. A haze swam before his eyes. Yes, if he gave the order, they would follow him. They would stay at his side, marching like soldiers in the face of withering fire, marching straight into that shimmering light curtain.

Wash was stumbling. Jake's jaws had stopped working. He was pushing forward slowly like a man walking against a hurricane sweeping over a desert. The light was making him dizzy. But they had faith—faith in Captain Hazzard. He had contrived this thing to battle the light waves. He had said it would work. If he said it, it must be so.

Then suddenly the miracle happened. Hazzard trembled, stared. The X-ray cabinet almost slipped from his hands. Then he held it tighter. Ahead of him, straight ahead, where the alpha rays from the mechanism he was holding bisected those other rays, the curtain of death was thinning. The hideous aura didn't quite touch now. When the shimmering points of light approached there was a weakness, an indecision about them.

Hazzard moved further into them, fiercely, exultantly. Jake and Wash and Martin followed. Into the curtain of death, into it like four comrades of a lost legion storming their way through terror.

And now the light was melting rapidly, cleaving away, leaving a tunnel for them to pass through. Hazzard called to the others. "Get the girl, Jake. Get her father. Have them all come. Hurry!"

Jake ran back, rounded up Mary Parker and her father; got the dazed men who had been his fellow slaves into motion. Gasping, trembling, they stumbled into the curtain, in through the tunnel that Captain Hazzard had made. On they stumbled, on to where the Tzutuhiles stood facing them.

Then another miracle happened—a miracle that followed logically on the heels of this first. Hazzard was ahead, walking resolutely toward them. And suddenly one of the Python Men went down on his knees. He bent his green-plumed head to the dust. He said: "Zuma! Zuma! Master! Master!"

The other Indians followed suit. They had seen with their own eyes what the Phoenix had told them could never happen. They had seen men, living men, walk through that curtain of spectral light and still stay alive. They knew now that this tall white man was a god greater than the shriveled vulturelike being who had ruled them from the mountain.

They fell back peacefully and let Hazzard's party pass. And Hazzard spoke a warning then: "Run! Run for your lives! *Huetenzo!* I have set my curse on Omoxotl."

The Indians shot terrified glances at the volcano. Then they turned and fled toward the jungle. Hazzard's party followed. The ground was shaking. A steady roar of rocks sounded all around them as tremors shook down the boulders. Another piece of a cliff broke away and almost blocked the trail. They climbed over it, pushed on.

They reached the last downward slant of the trail before it entered the green wall of the jungle. A sound that was greater than any explosion broke out behind them. A sound that was the living, furious symbol of all tumult lifted its gigantic voice above the mountain. The earth shook. The sky grew dark. Flame speared up from the top of the crater, flame and gas, bearing aloft with it tons of structural steel and concrete, tons of riveted steel plate.

The mountain had spat out the great valve as a monster might spit some unsavory thing from its throat. But, though the valve was gone now, the mountain wasn't done with its violence. Those tons of water had built up a pressure in the bowels of the earth that spelled a cataclysm. Lava, hot and livid, was pushing up to the top of the crater. Millions of pounds of pressure was behind it.

Hazzard led his party into the jungle. They reached it just as the first small stones the volcano had disgorged commenced hurtling down. They made their way through a green world of roaring sound and somber shadows. Monkeys fled through the trees chattering in panic. Parrots screamed past. Jaguars slunk ahead of them along the trail, for once forgetting their terror and hatred of human beings in the greater fear of the volcano. Omoxotl was on the rampage. Terror's Shadow was living up to its name.

They were five miles away when the biggest explosion of all came—a gigantic upheaval that blew off the whole top of Omoxotl.

After it had subsided, when the fires began flickering out and a slow, somber brooding peace descended on the jungle, Mary Parker said with a tinge of regret:

"Now we shall never know who the Phoenix was."

Captain Hazzard heard her, turned, and asked a question: "How well did you know your father's partner, Kurt Gordon?"

"Not very well. I've only seen him once or twice and that was a good while ago. Why?"

"Ask your father when he gets better and can speak. He will uphold me, I think, when I tell you that the Phoenix was Kurt Gordon."

"Gordon—the Phoenix?"

"Yes. Those gases changed him, shriveled his body; made him look so horrible that even his own family wouldn't recognize him. It's barely possible that even your father didn't know who he was. But it was Gordon. I came across some papers in his safe which proved it. He'd been in Central America for years.

"He must have been studying Omoxotl, dreaming secret dreams of power. He probably used money that belonged to your father's partnership with him to lay the foundation of his project. But he had to have more money than that. He got it cleverly. It necessitated a tie-up with a New York gang, however."

"Why?"

"Jewels," said Captain Hazzard. "That's what the slaves were doing. Gordon used the heat of the volcano to make synthetic gems that couldn't be told from nature's products, sapphires, emeralds, diamonds. That's why these Indians were so free with their emeralds. That's one reason they were so loyal to the Phoenix. And his New York gang was his outlet. The jewels were smuggled into the U.S., sold at a big profit, and the millions that Gordon got for them financed his mad ambitions for world dominion."

Hazzard looked back. The crater of Omoxotl—the lost city— was still smoking. It was a giant sinister torch lifting up into the dome of the sky. It was the funeral pyre of the Phoenix.